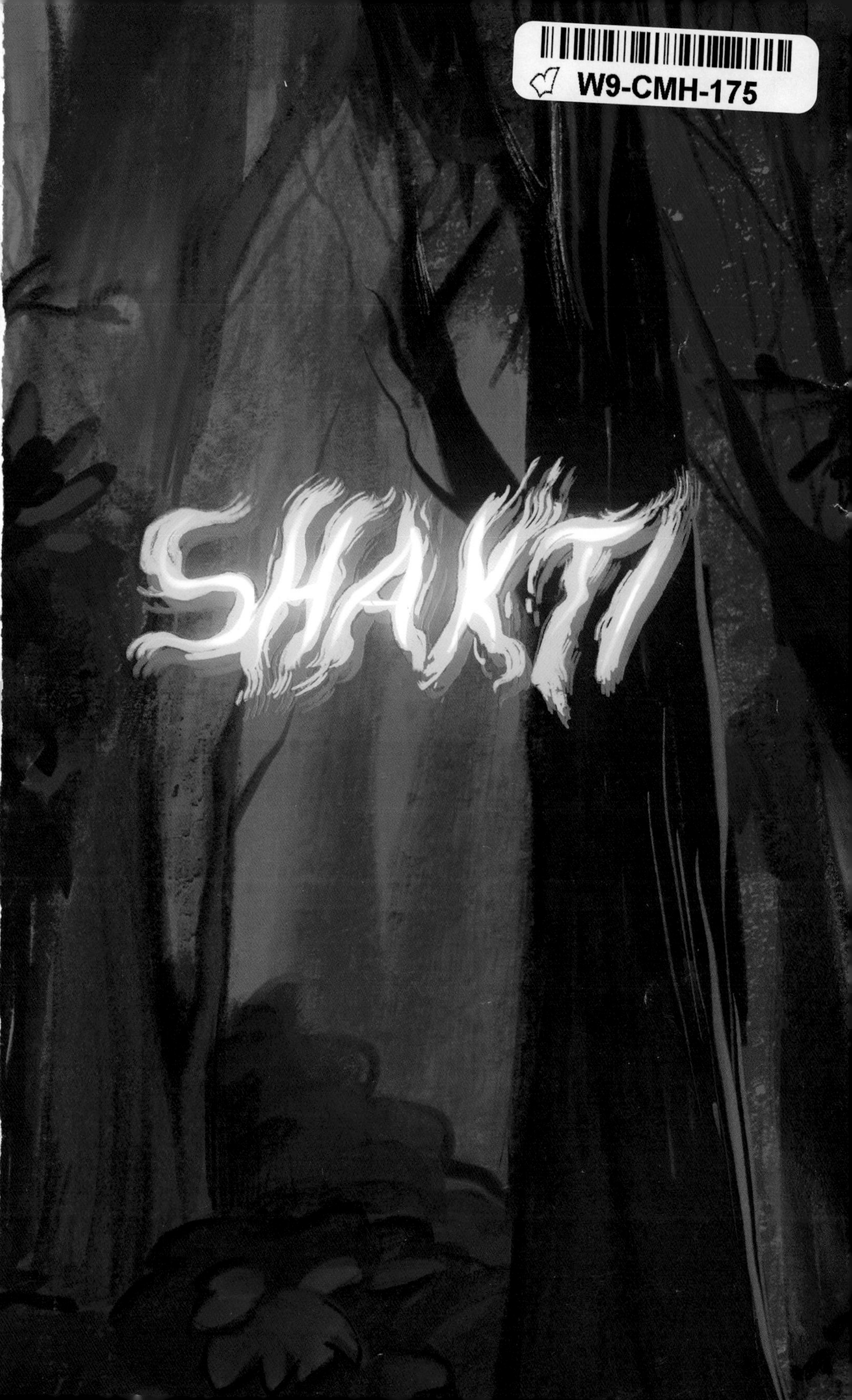
SHAKTI

*For Varun.*

*And for all the little witches
out there. May you never
forget your magic. May you
remake the world.*

—S. S.


*For Nidhi, whose friendship
gives me Shakti.*

—N. H. A.

HarperAlley is an imprint of HarperCollins Publishers.

Shakti
Text copyright © 2023 by SJ Sindu
Illustrations copyright © 2023 by Nabi H. Ali
All rights reserved. Manufactured in Bosnia and Herzegovina.
No part of this book may be used or reproduced in any manner whatsoever without written
permission except in the case of brief quotations embodied in critical articles and reviews. For
information address HarperCollins Children's Books, a division of HarperCollins Publishers,
195 Broadway, New York, NY 10007.
www.harperalley.com

Library of Congress Control Number: 2022948034
ISBN 978-0-06-309013-2 — ISBN 978-0-06-309011-8 (pbk.)

The artist used Procreate to create the illustrations for this book.
Typography by Elaine Lopez-Levine and Maddy Price
23  24  25  26  27   GPS   10  9  8  7  6  5  4  3  2  1

First Edition

# SHAKTI

## SJ SINDU

## NABI H. ALI

An Imprint of HarperCollinsPublishers

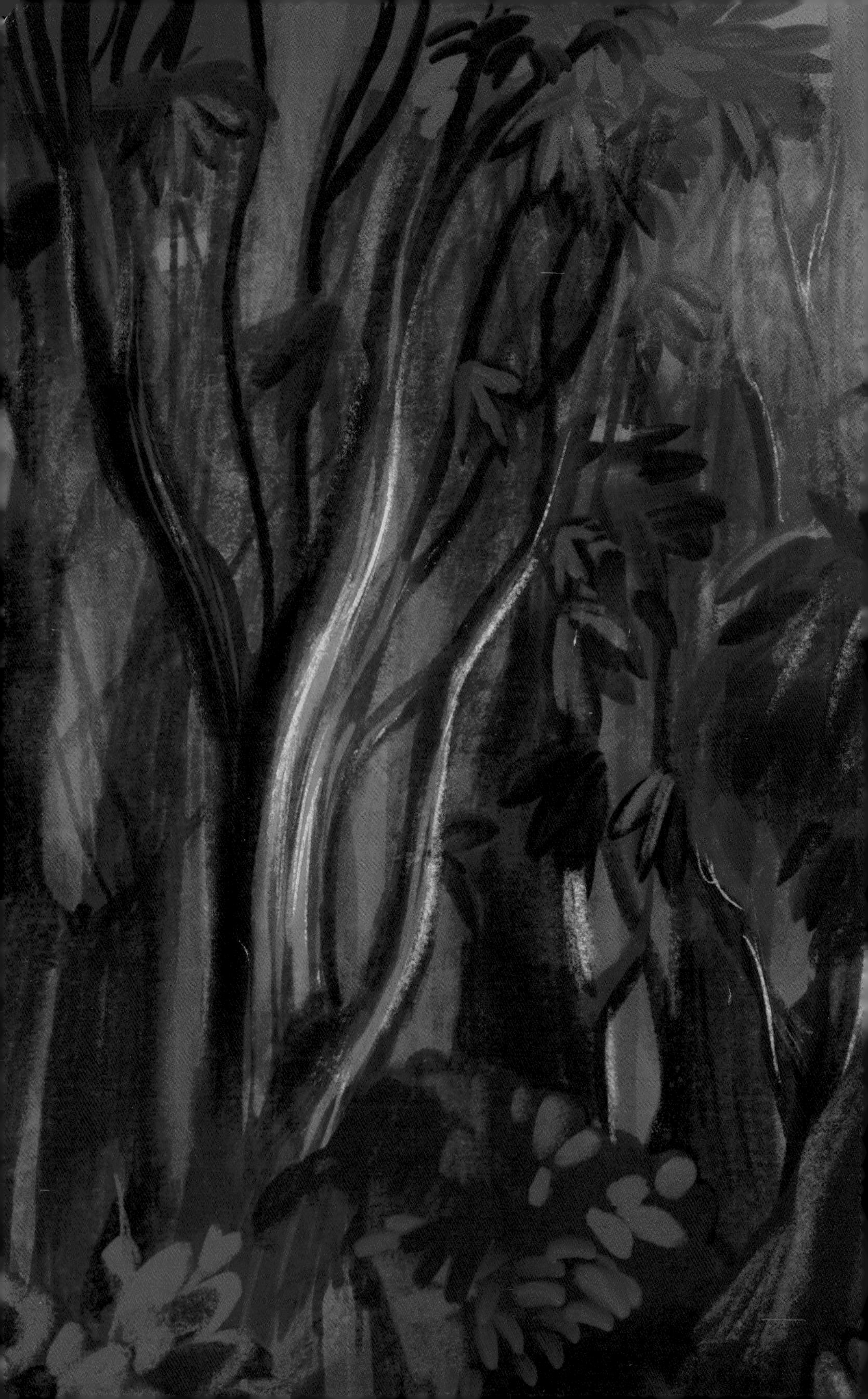

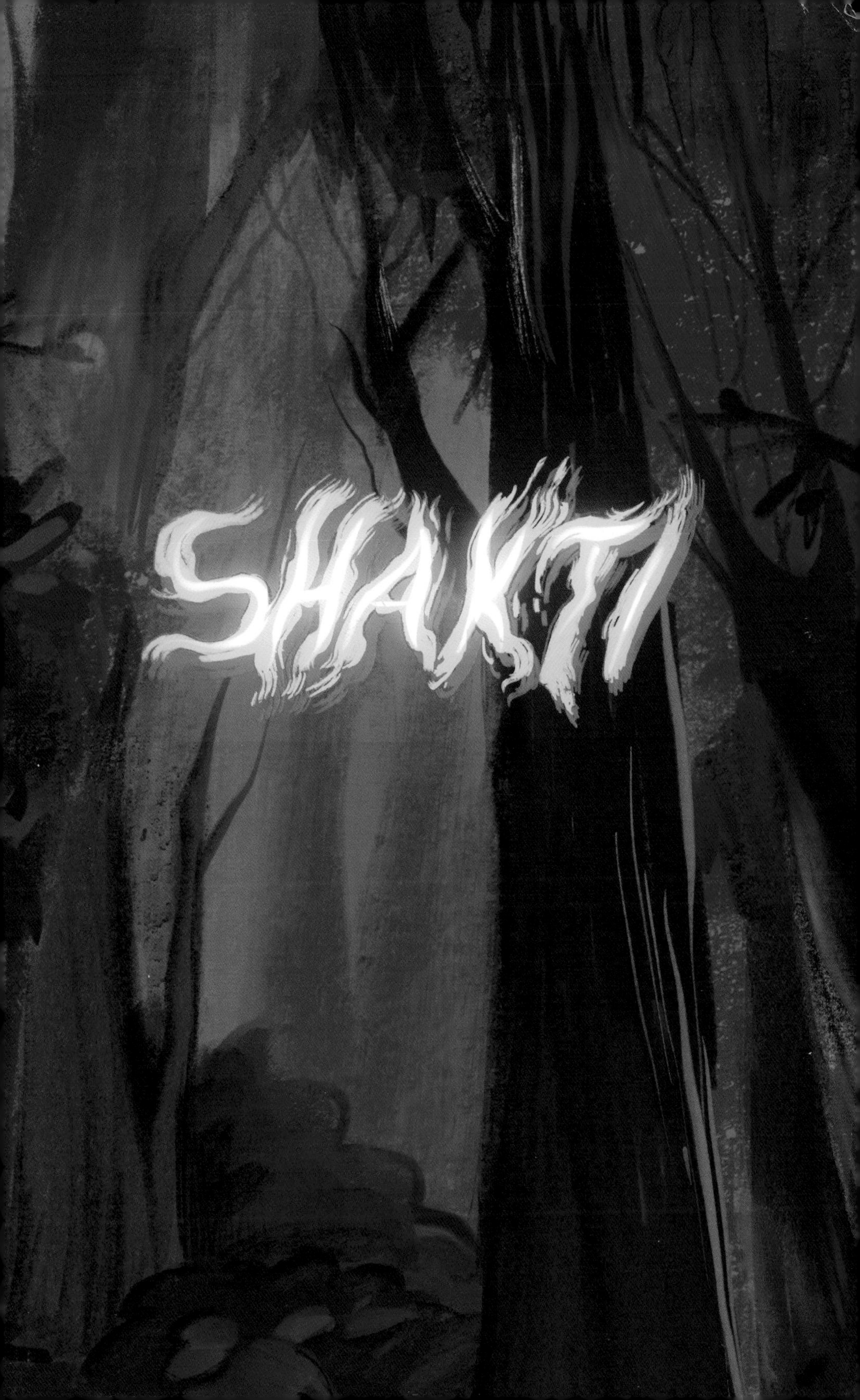
SHAKTI

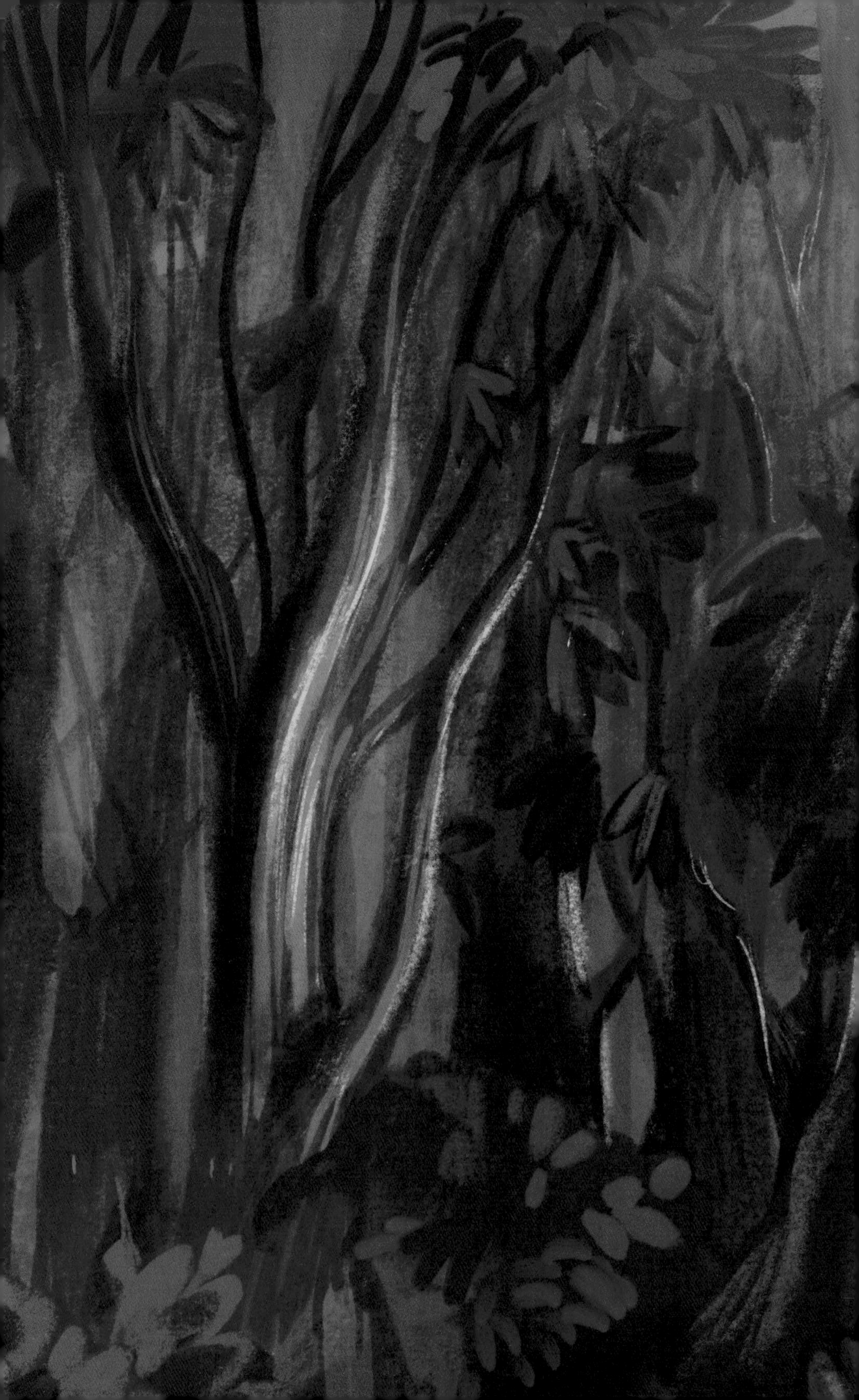

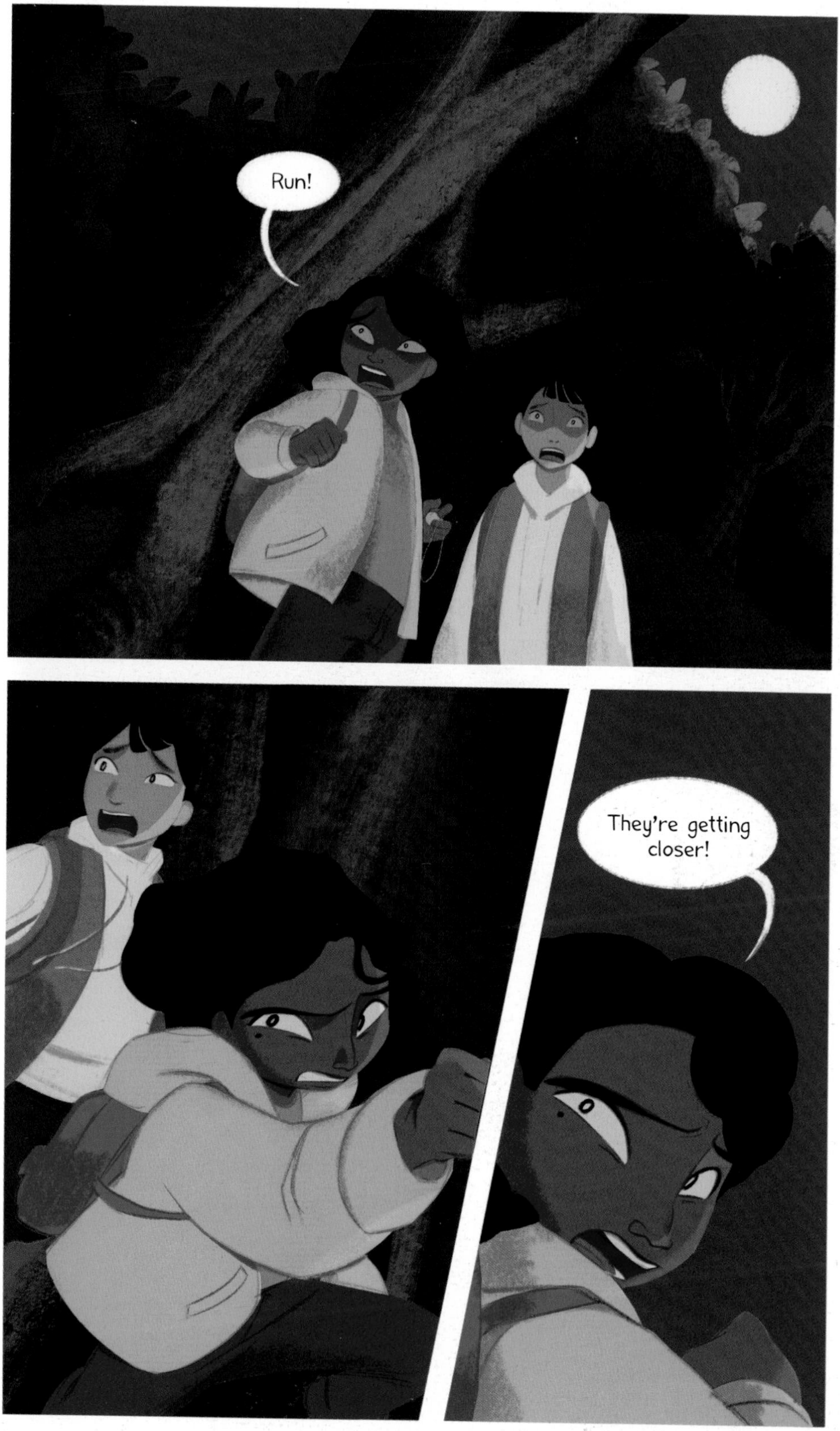
Run!
They're getting closer!

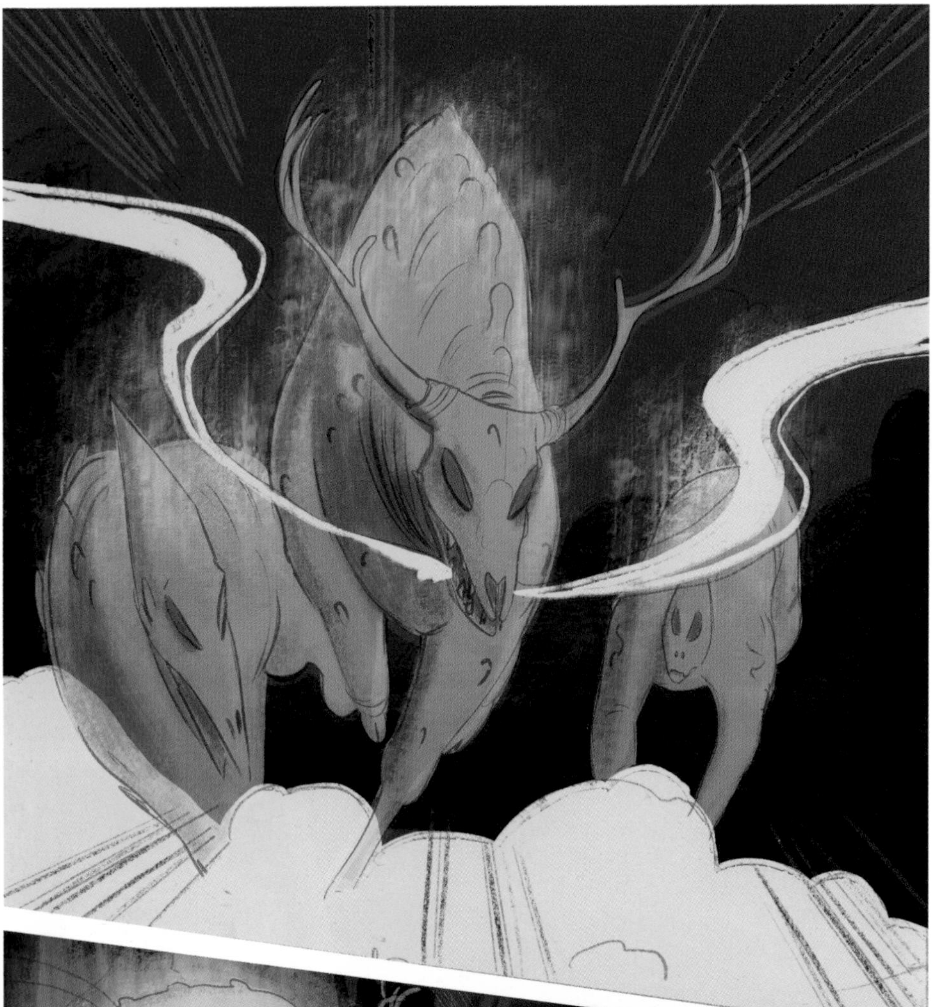

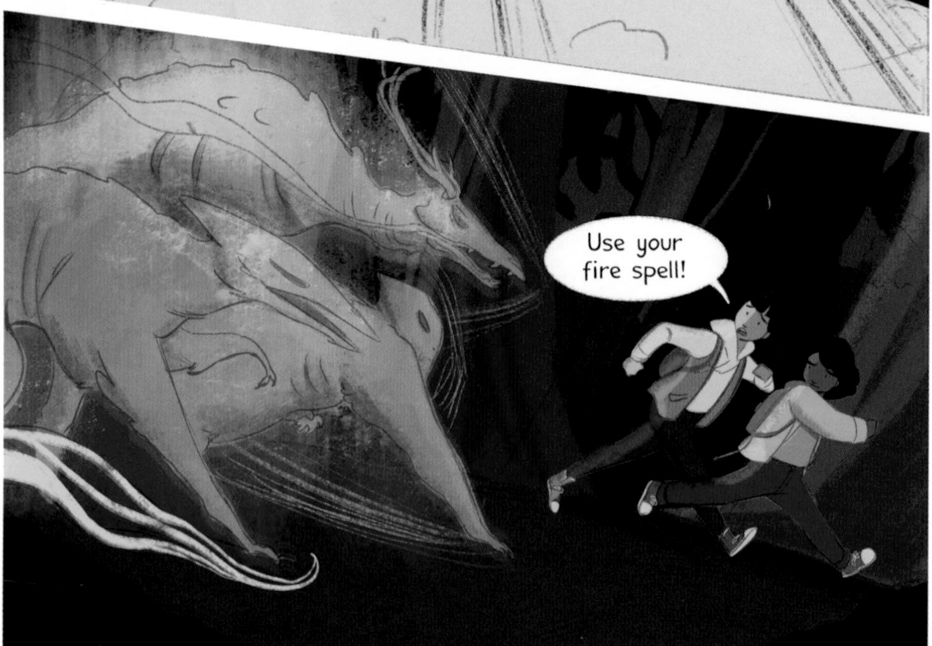
Use your fire spell!

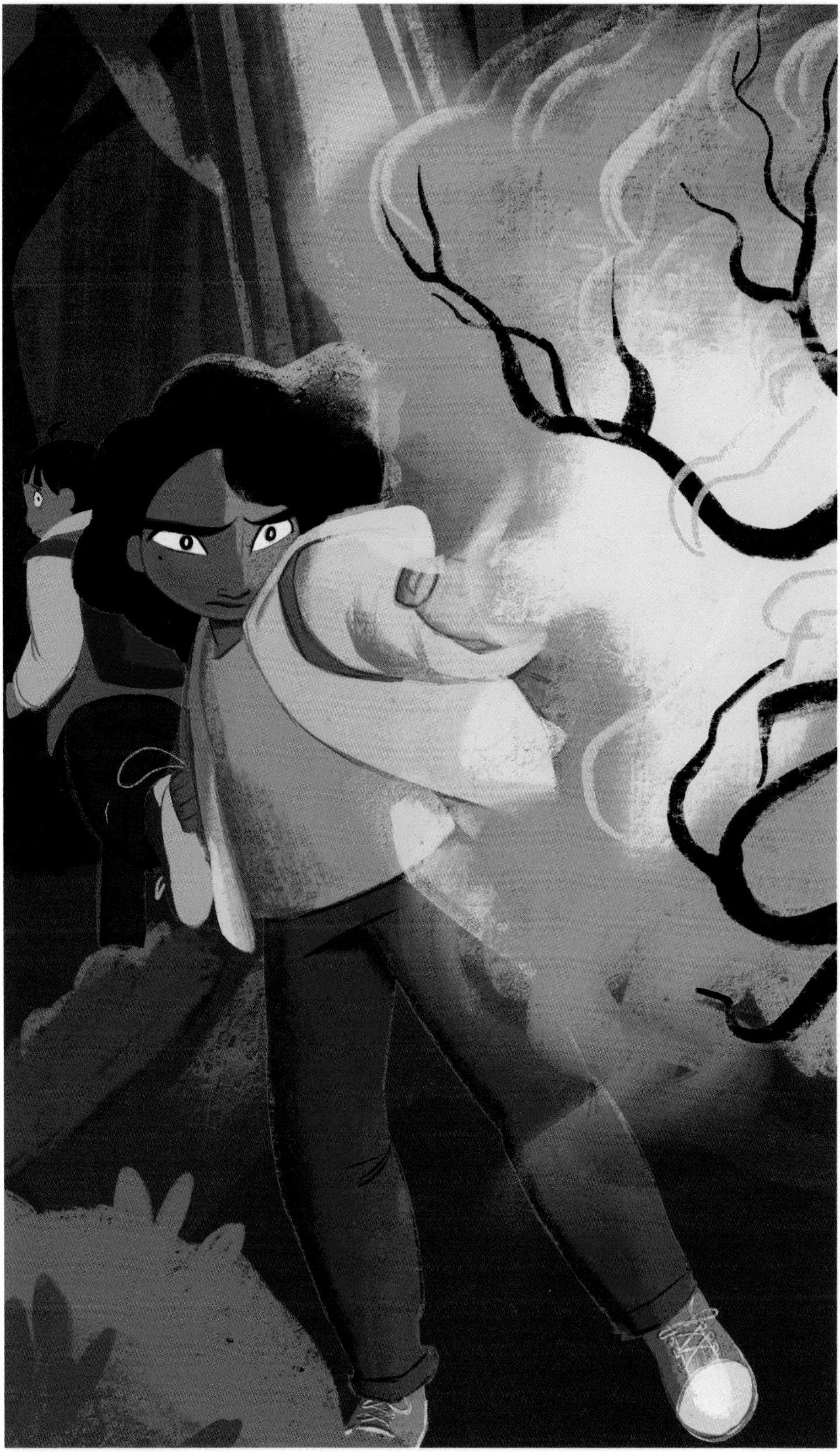

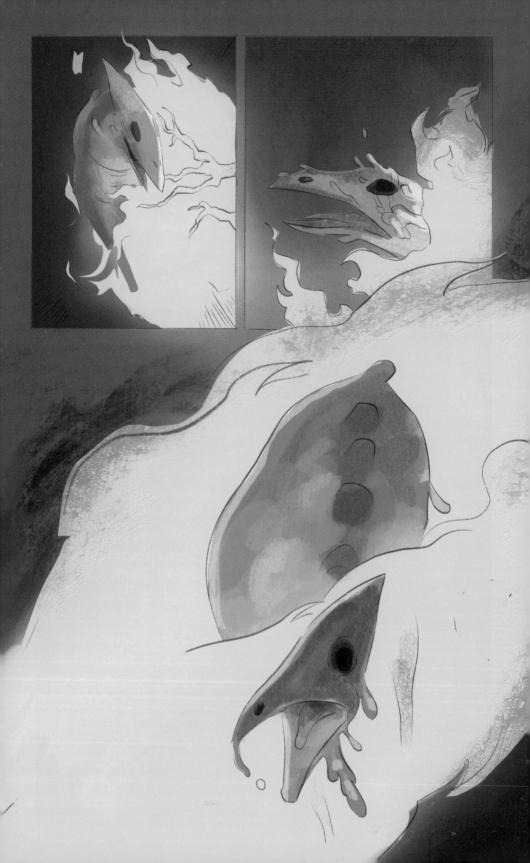

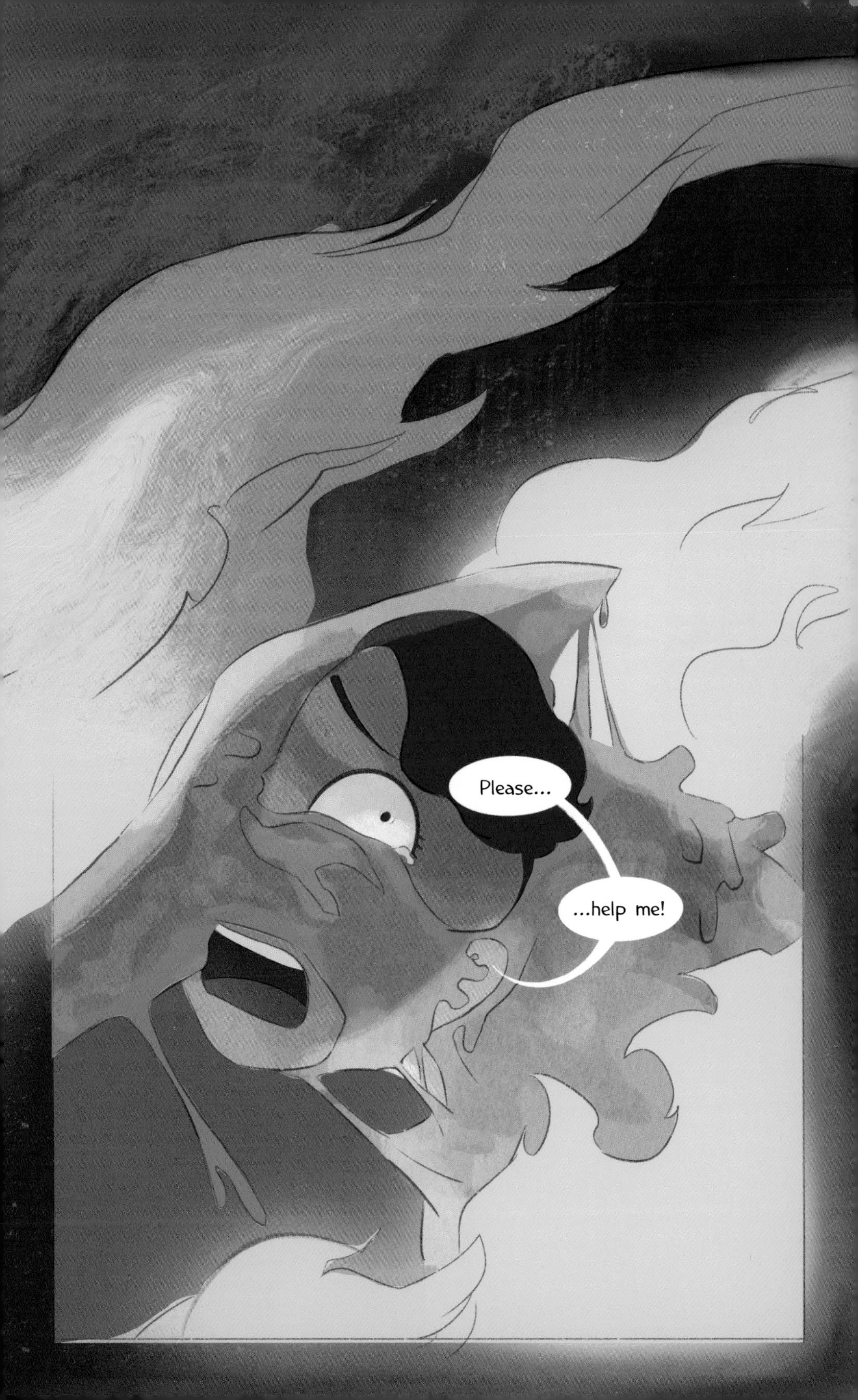
Please...
...help me!

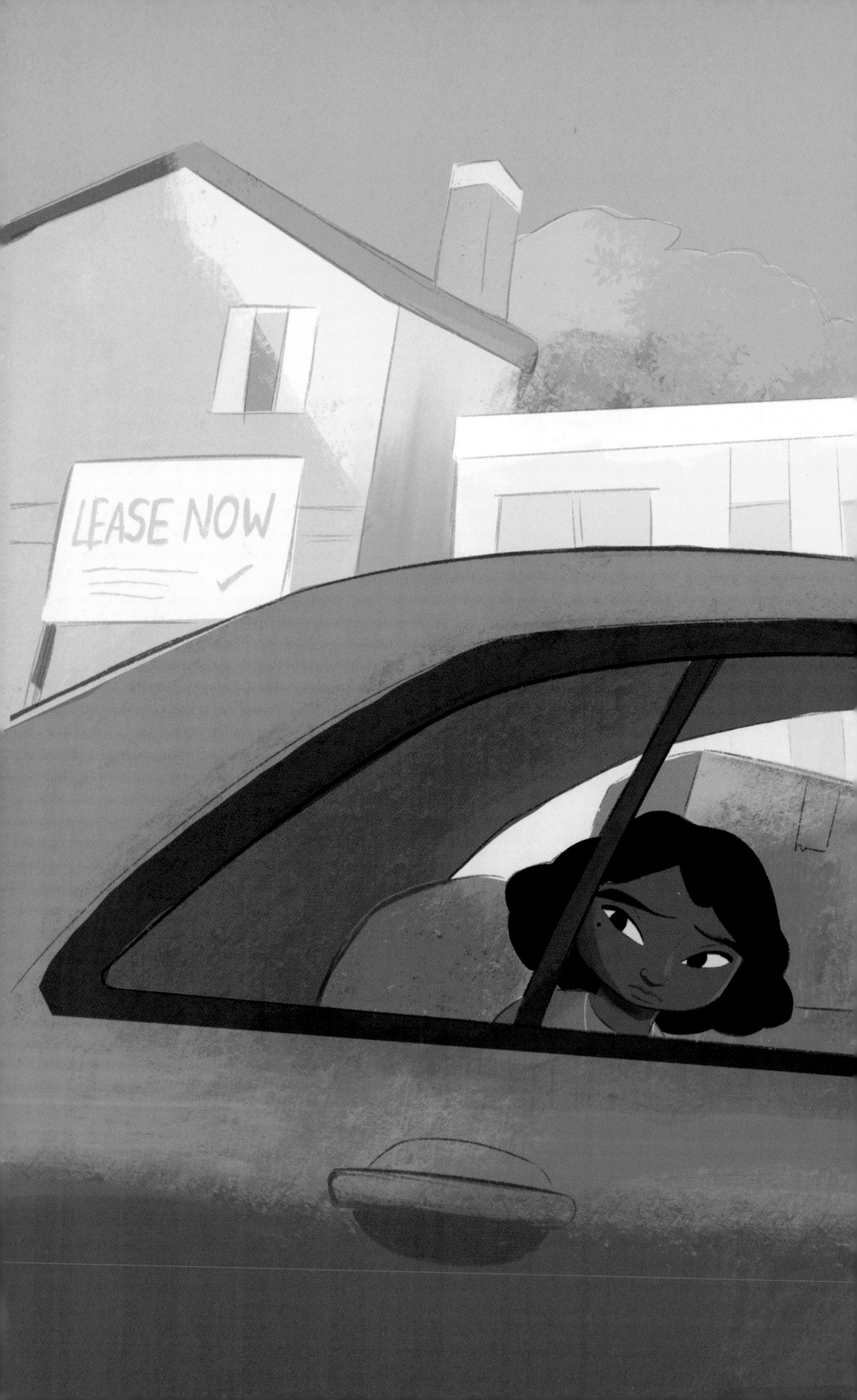
LEASE NOW

# Chapter 1

TWO MONTHS EARLIER...

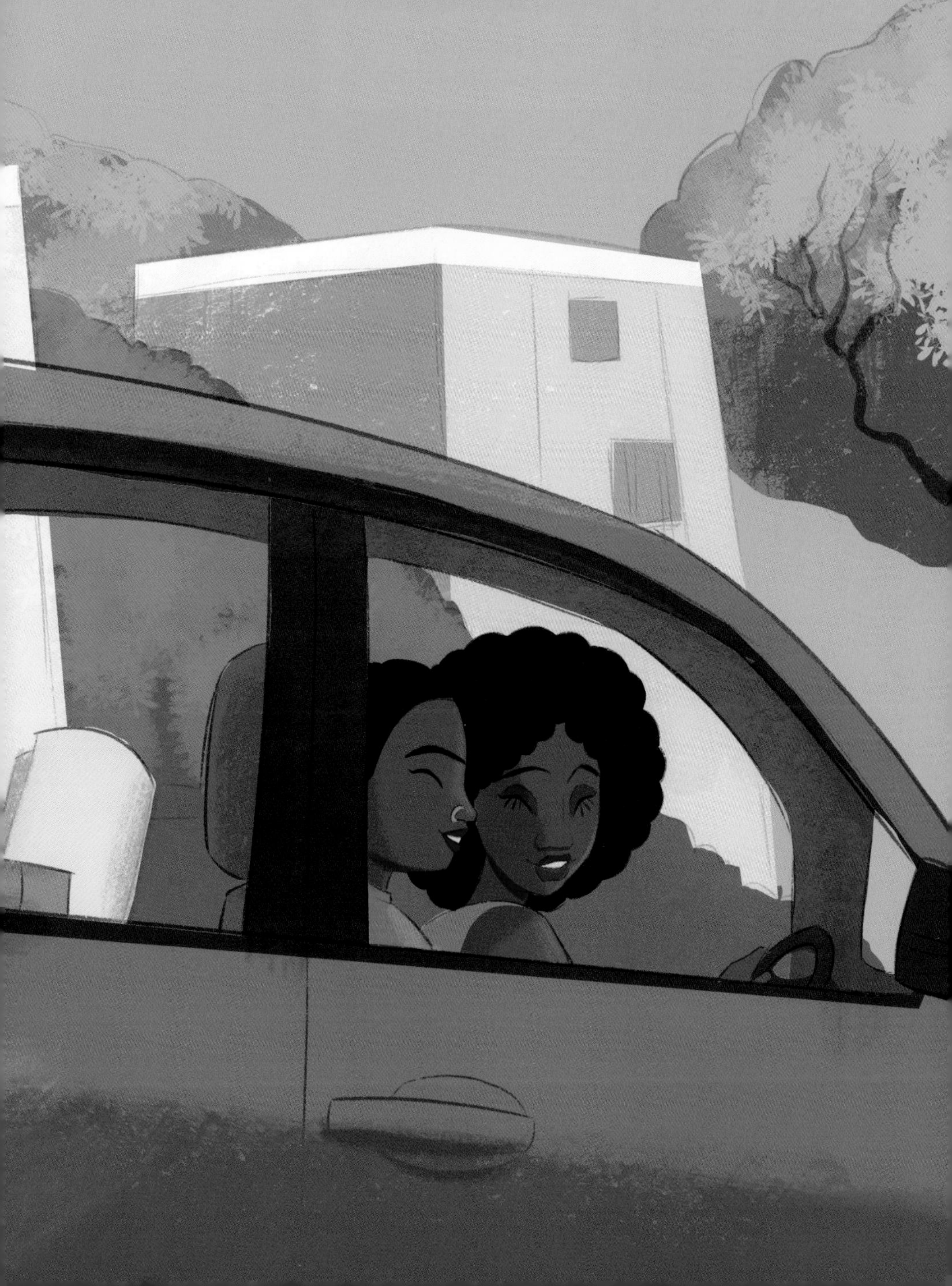

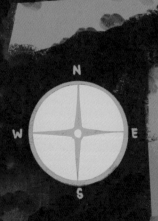

**Amherst-Pelham
Regional Middle School**

When we first moved to Amherst, I thought it was just a sleepy little town. Oh, how wrong I was.

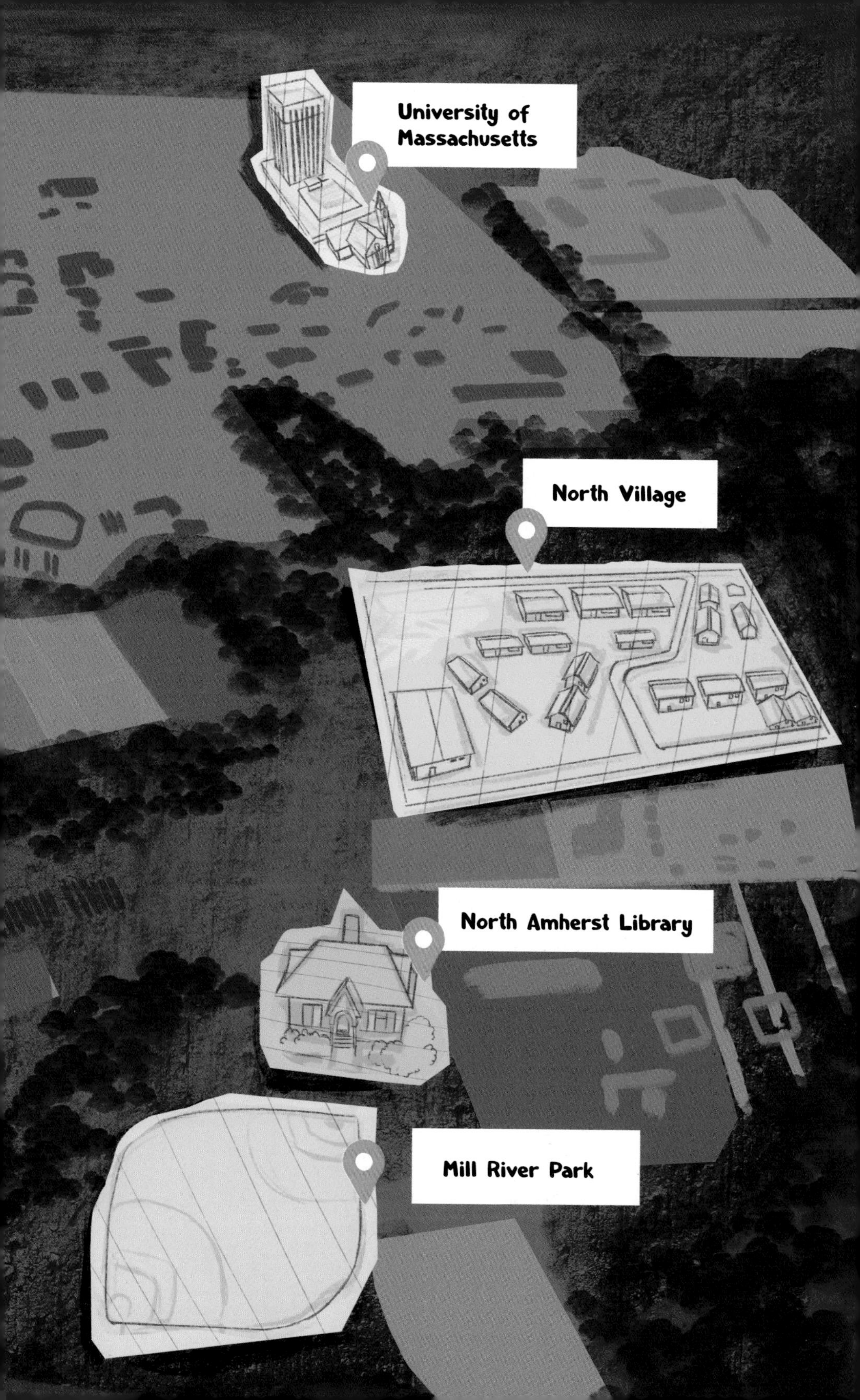
University of Massachusetts
North Village
North Amherst Library
Mill River Park

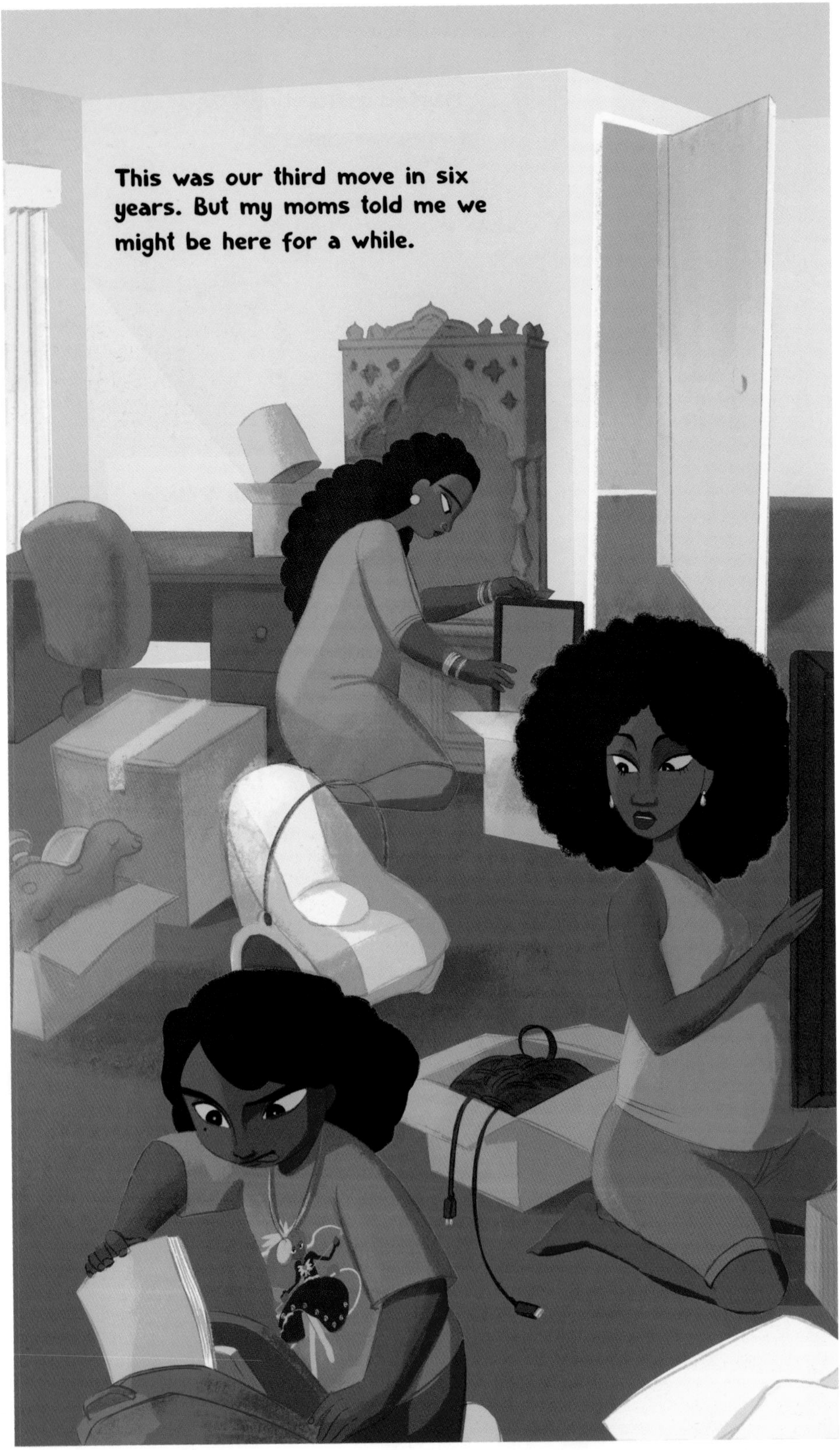
This was our third move in six years. But my moms told me we might be here for a while.

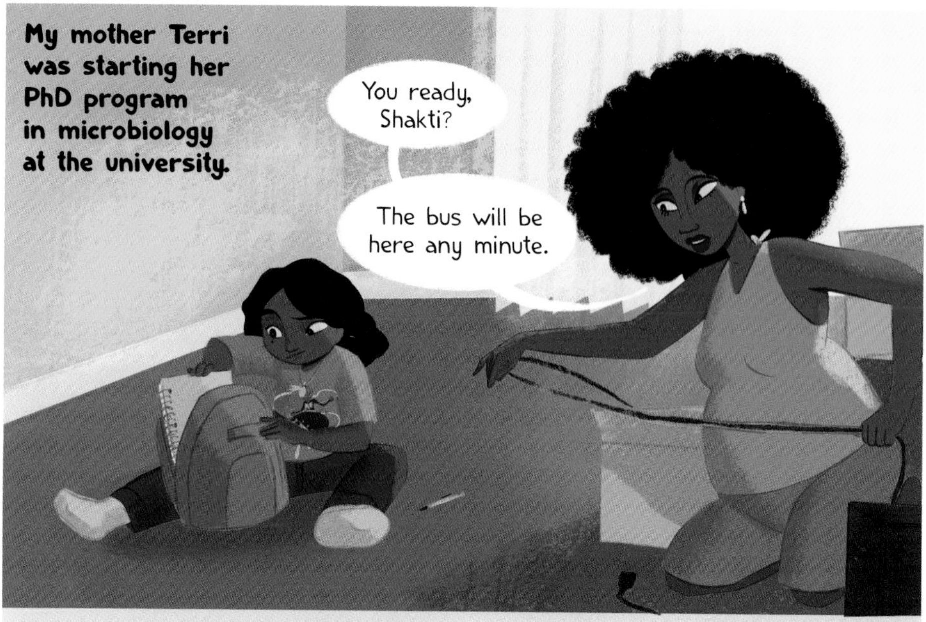
My mother Terri was starting her PhD program in microbiology at the university.
You ready, Shakti?
The bus will be here any minute.

My mother Rita is a programmer...

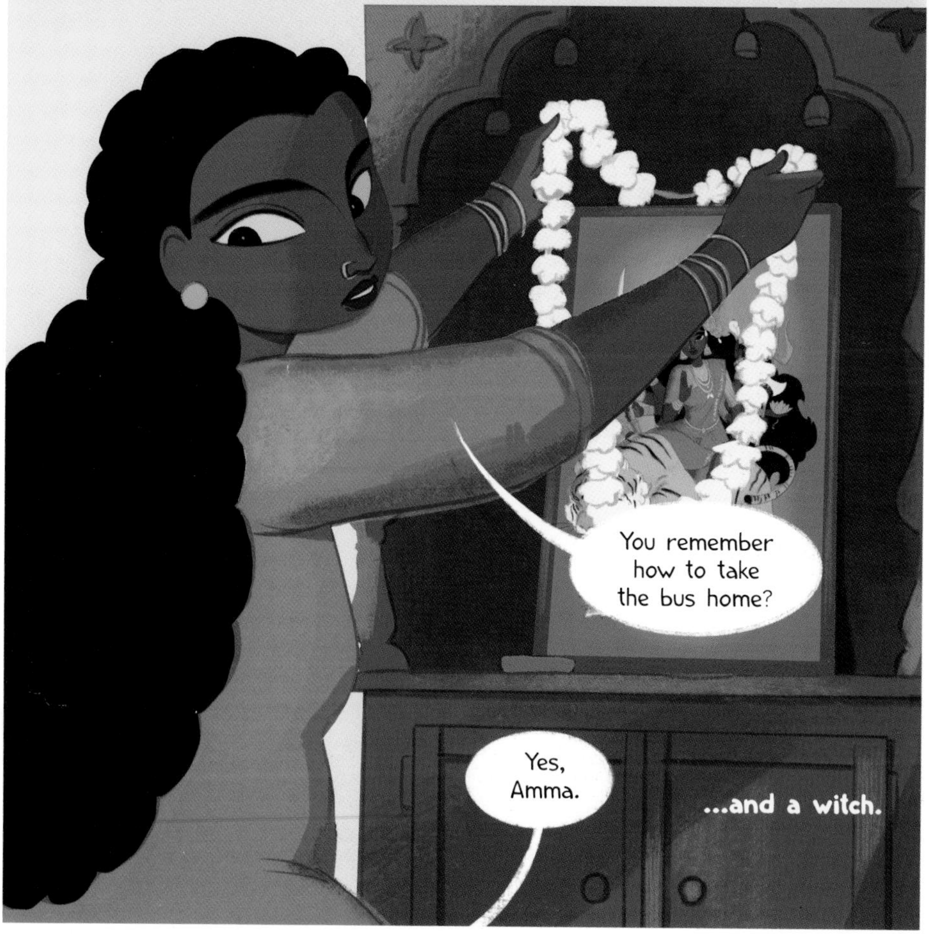
You remember how to take the bus home?
Yes, Amma.
...and a witch.

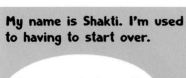

My name is Shakti. I'm used to having to start over.

Come pray to Durga Ma for a good start to the school year.

You might be wondering if she's a good witch or a bad witch, but magic doesn't really work like that. Magic is simply a tool, like a sword. It exists all around us, woven into the universe itself.

Witches like Amma are simply able to tap into the magic already there, to call it to do their bidding.

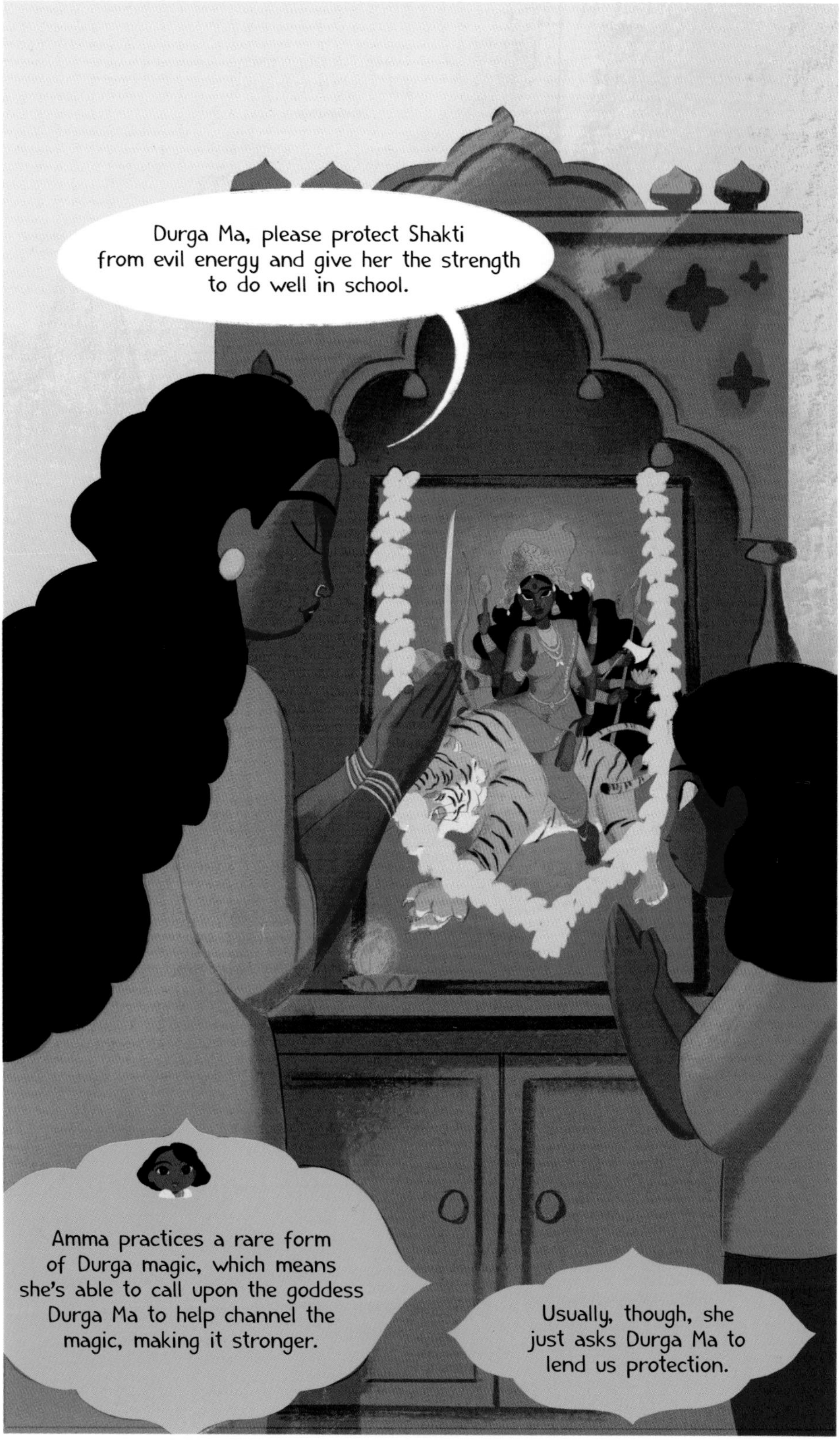
Durga Ma, please protect Shakti from evil energy and give her the strength to do well in school.
Amma practices a rare form of Durga magic, which means she's able to call upon the goddess Durga Ma to help channel the magic, making it stronger.
Usually, though, she just asks Durga Ma to lend us protection.

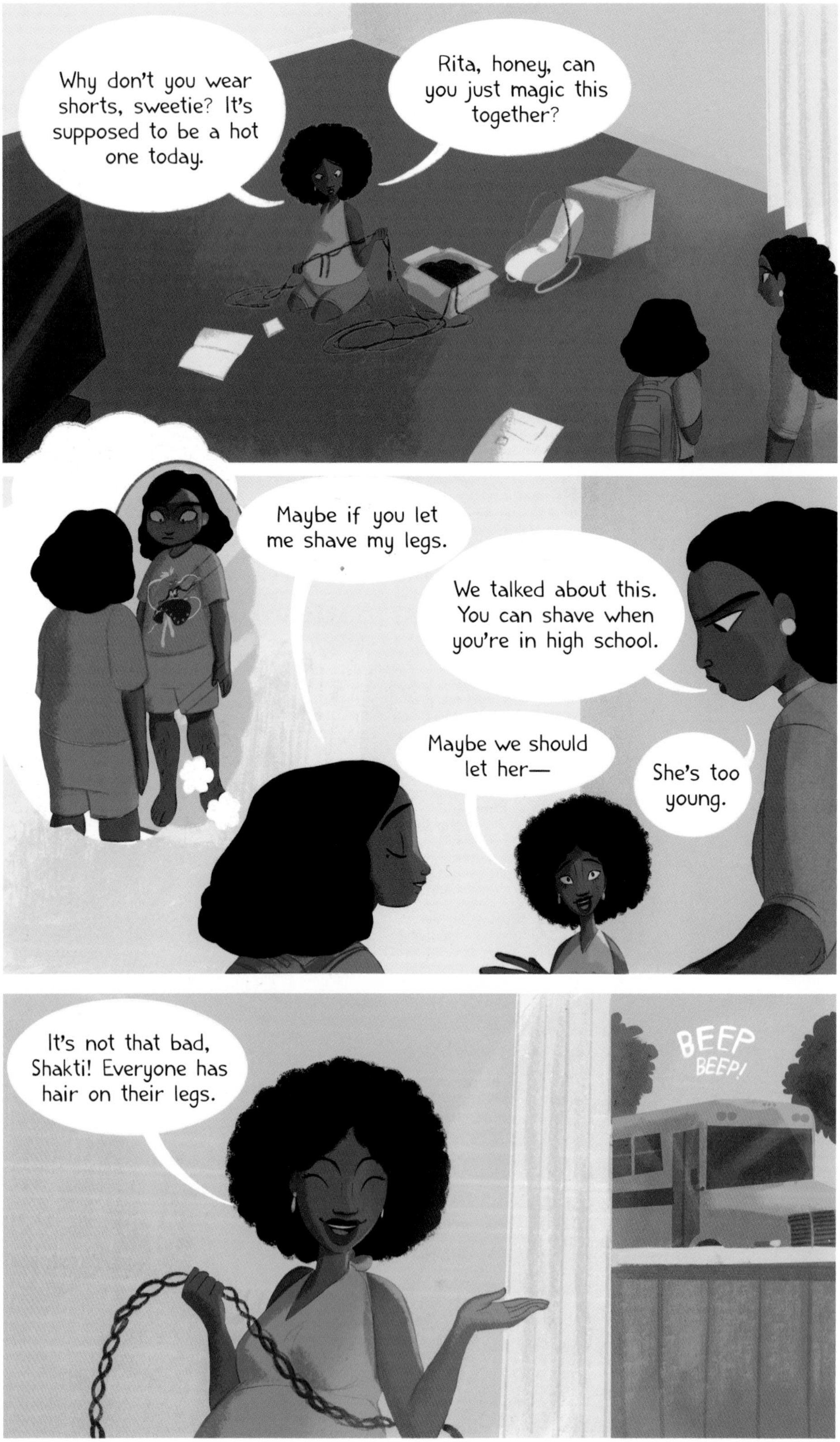
Why don't you wear shorts, sweetie? It's supposed to be a hot one today.
Rita, honey, can you just magic this together?
Maybe if you let me shave my legs.
We talked about this. You can shave when you're in high school.
Maybe we should let her—
She's too young.
It's not that bad, Shakti! Everyone has hair on their legs.
BEEP
BEEP!

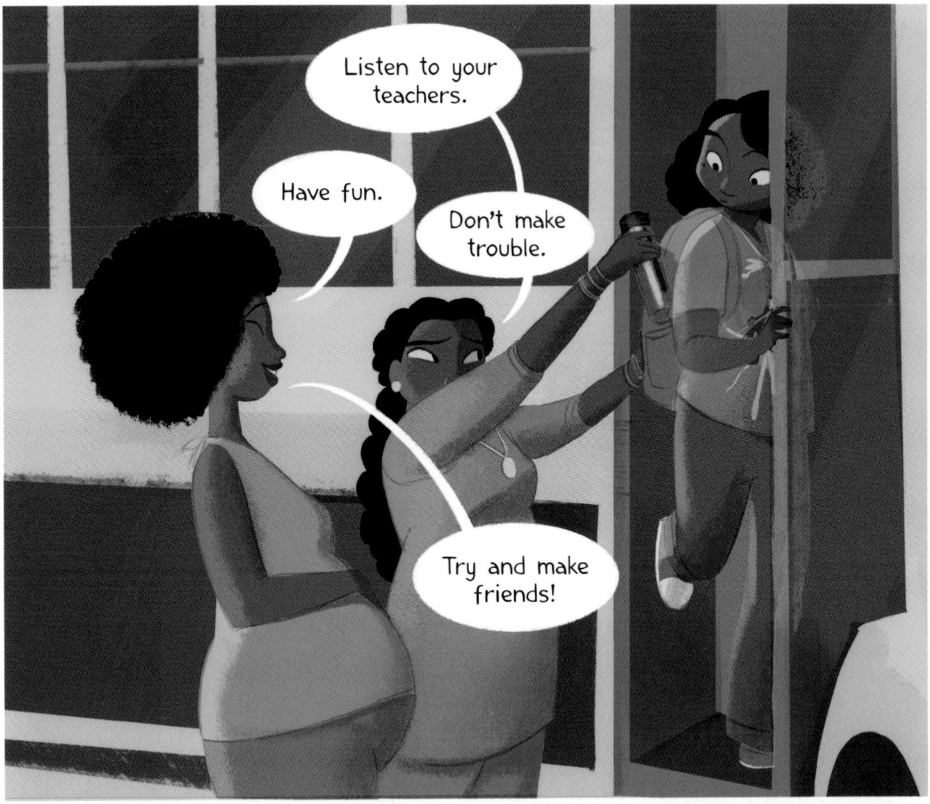
Listen to your teachers.
Have fun.
Don't make trouble.
Try and make friends!

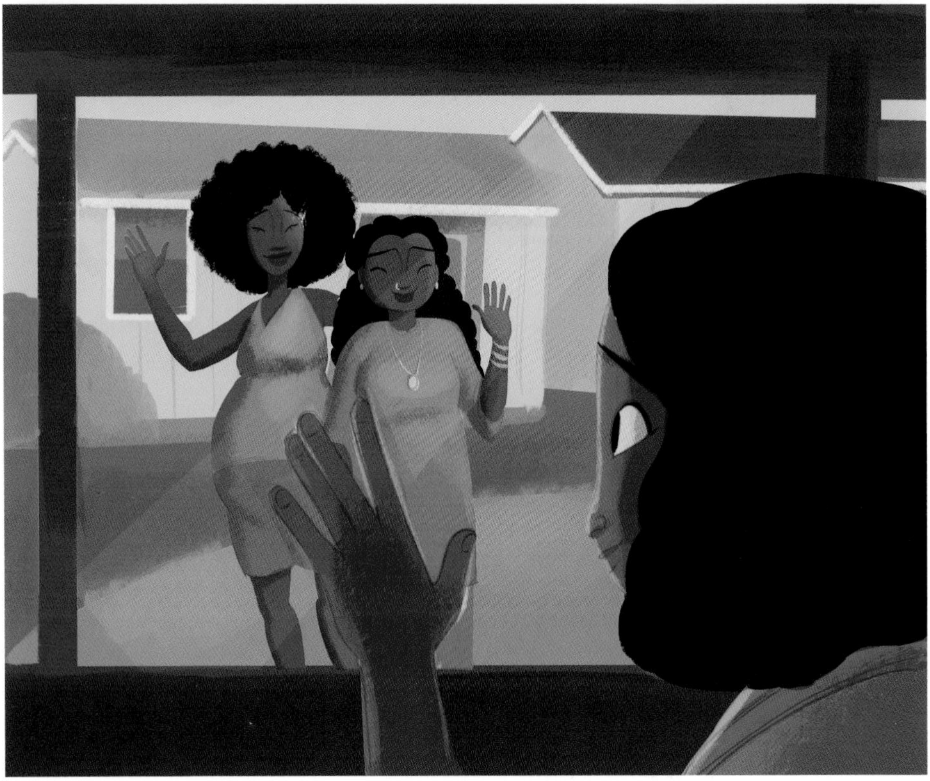

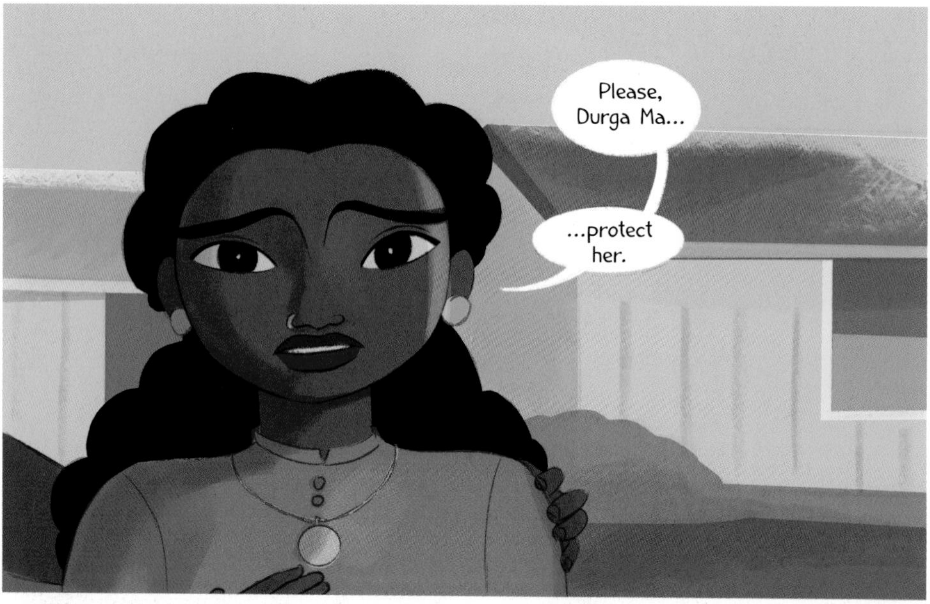
Please, Durga Ma...
...protect her.

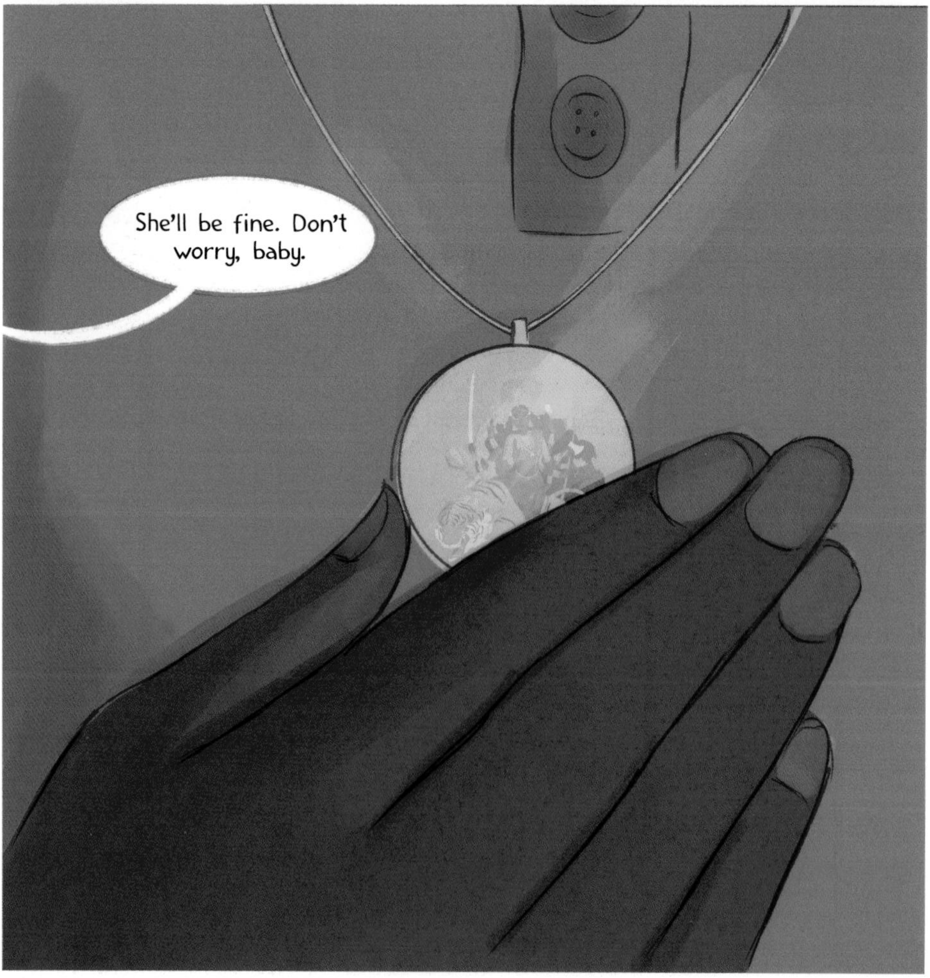
She'll be fine. Don't worry, baby.

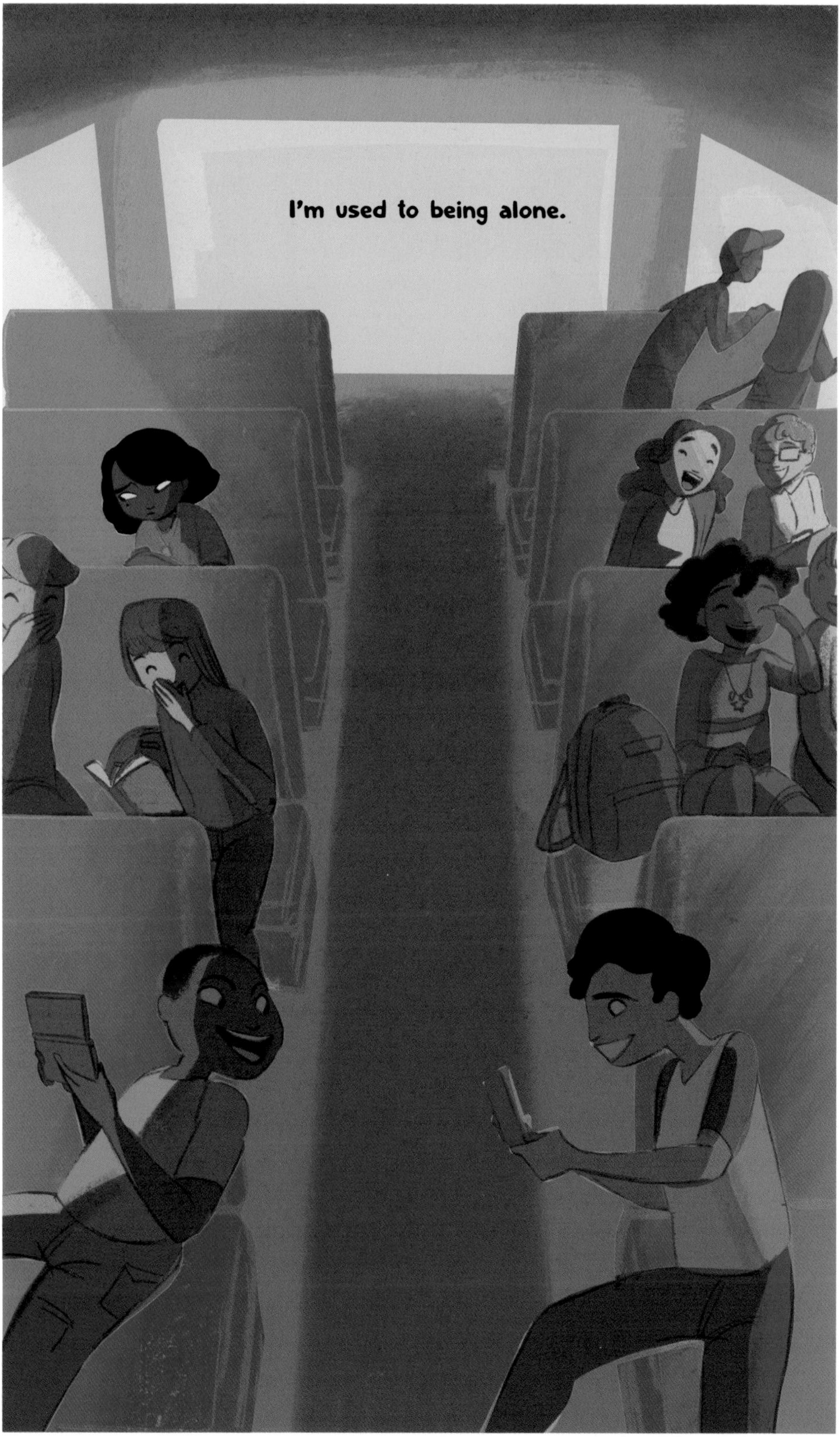
I'm used to being alone.

**Amherst-Pelham Regional Middle School (ARMS)**

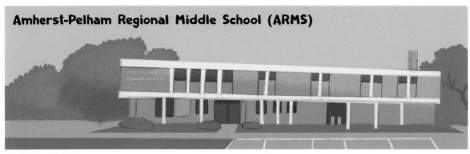

**Homeroom with Mrs. Feller**

Every first day of a new school is hard, but right from the beginning, I could tell something was off at ARMS.

It's a new shade. Sabrina wears it in the latest episode.

**Algebra with Ms. Wolpin**

No one? How about Kelly?

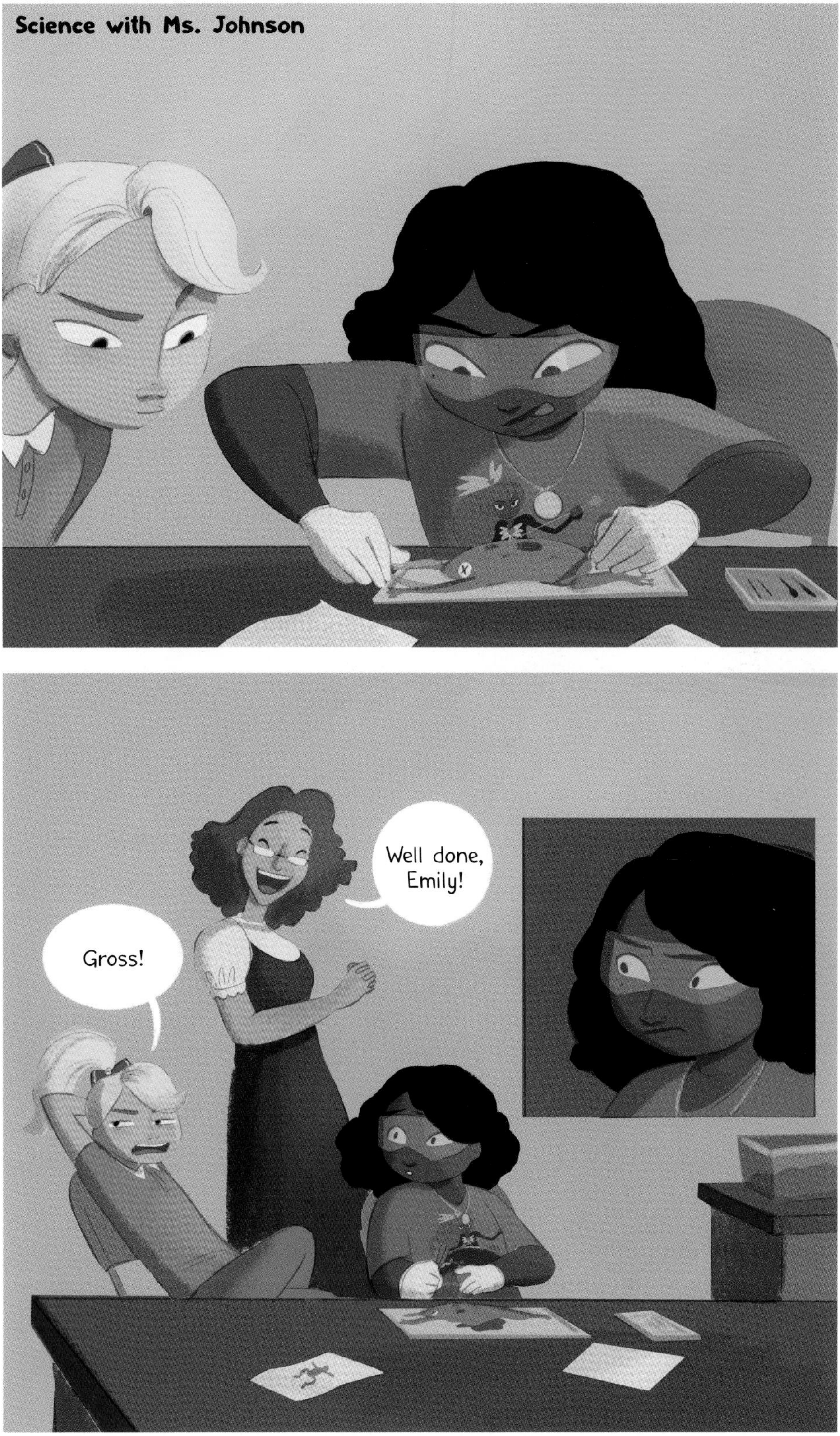
Science with Ms. Johnson
Well done, Emily!
Gross!

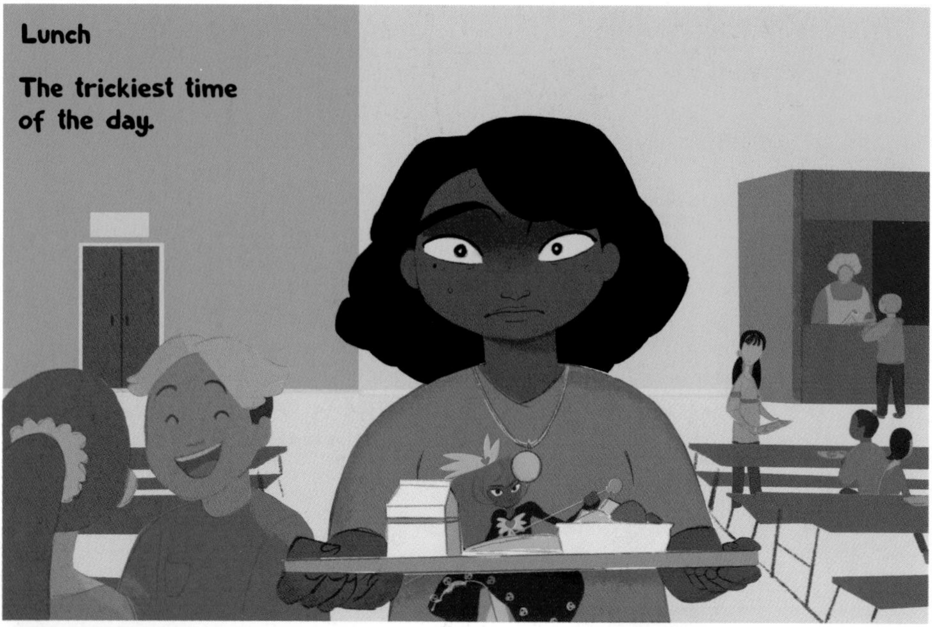
Lunch
The trickiest time of the day.

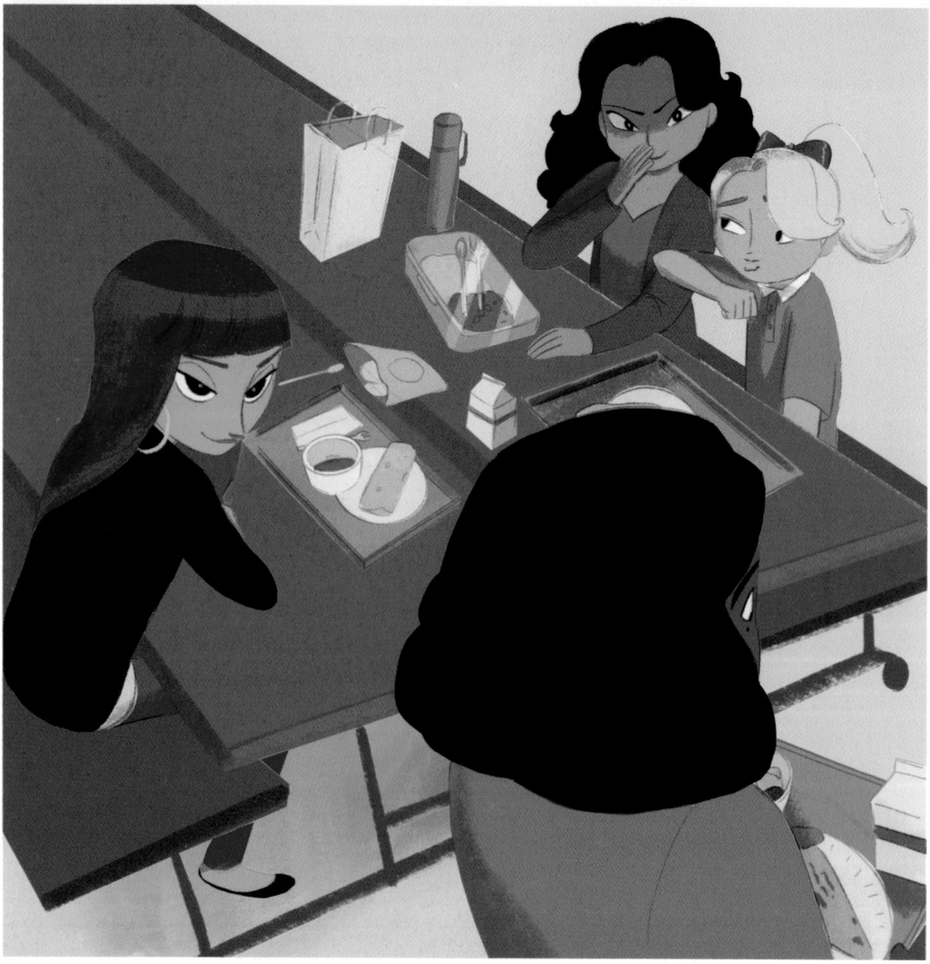

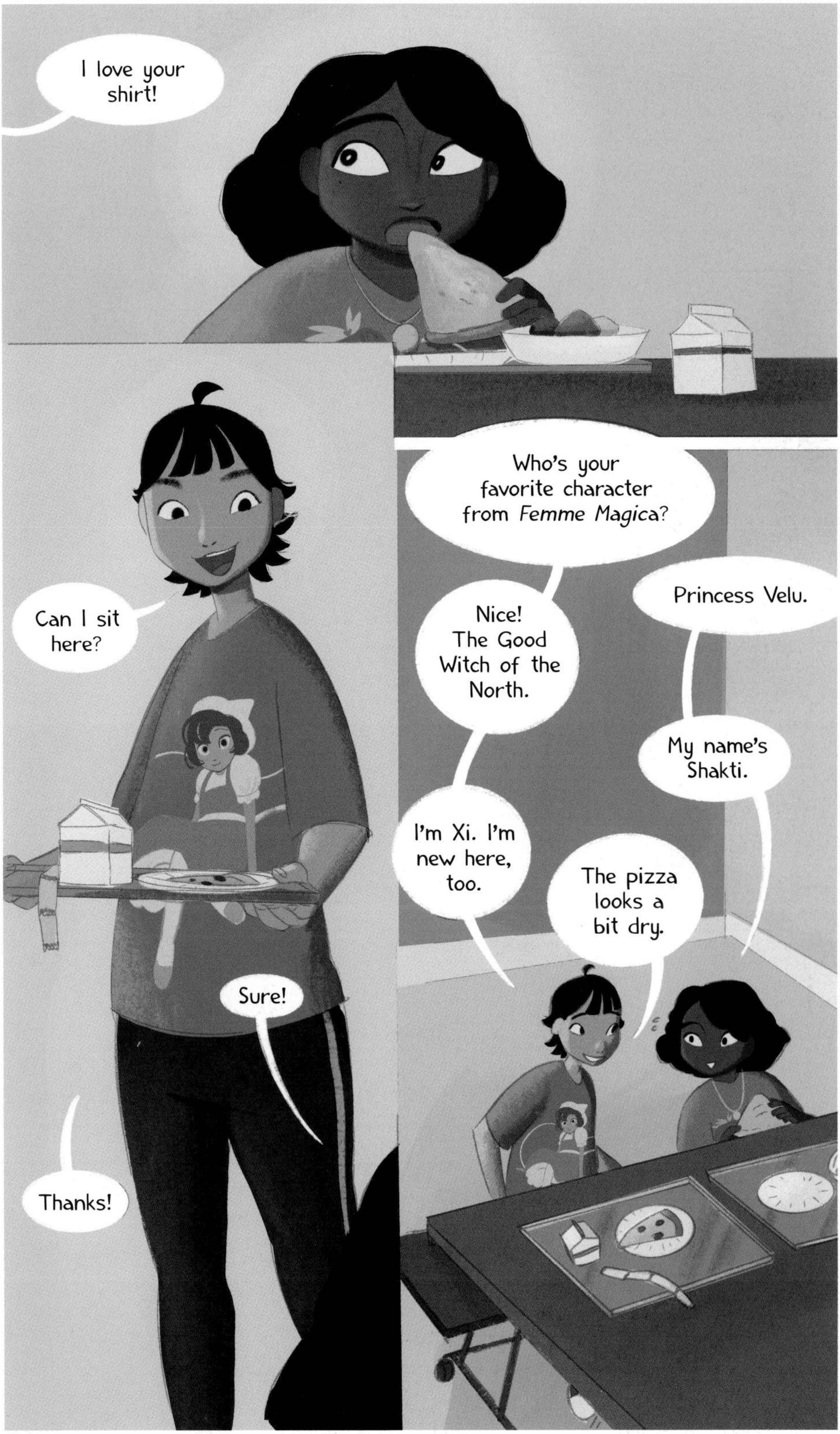
I love your shirt!
Can I sit here?
Sure!
Thanks!
Who's your favorite character from *Femme Magica*?
Princess Velu.
Nice! The Good Witch of the North.
My name's Shakti.
I'm Xi. I'm new here, too.
The pizza looks a bit dry.

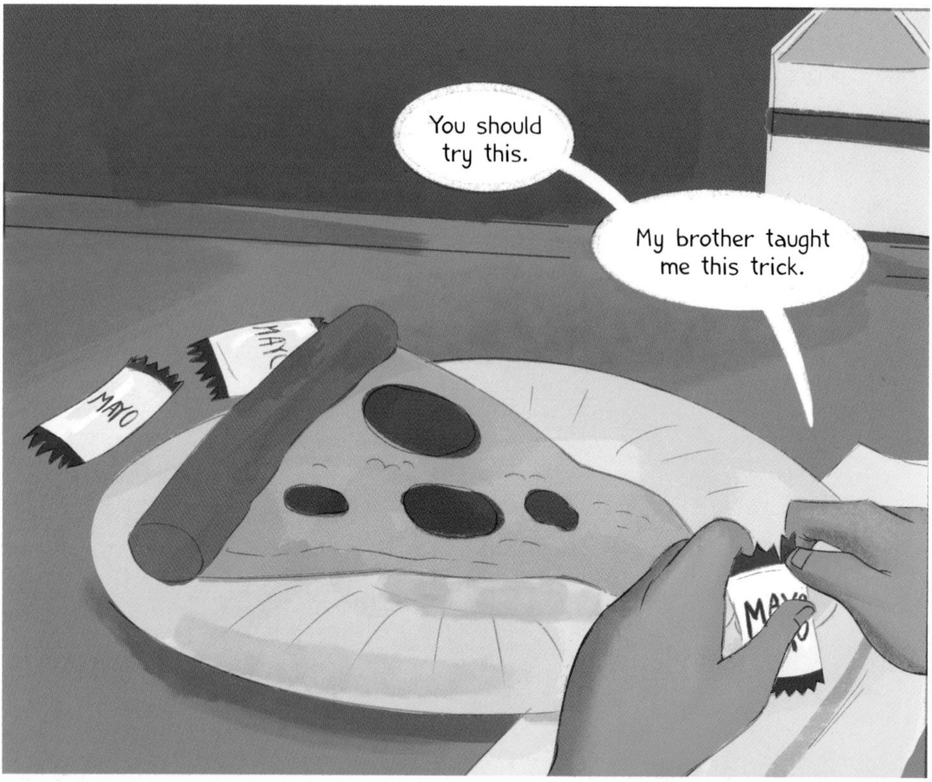
You should try this.
My brother taught me this trick.
MAYO
MAYO
MAYO

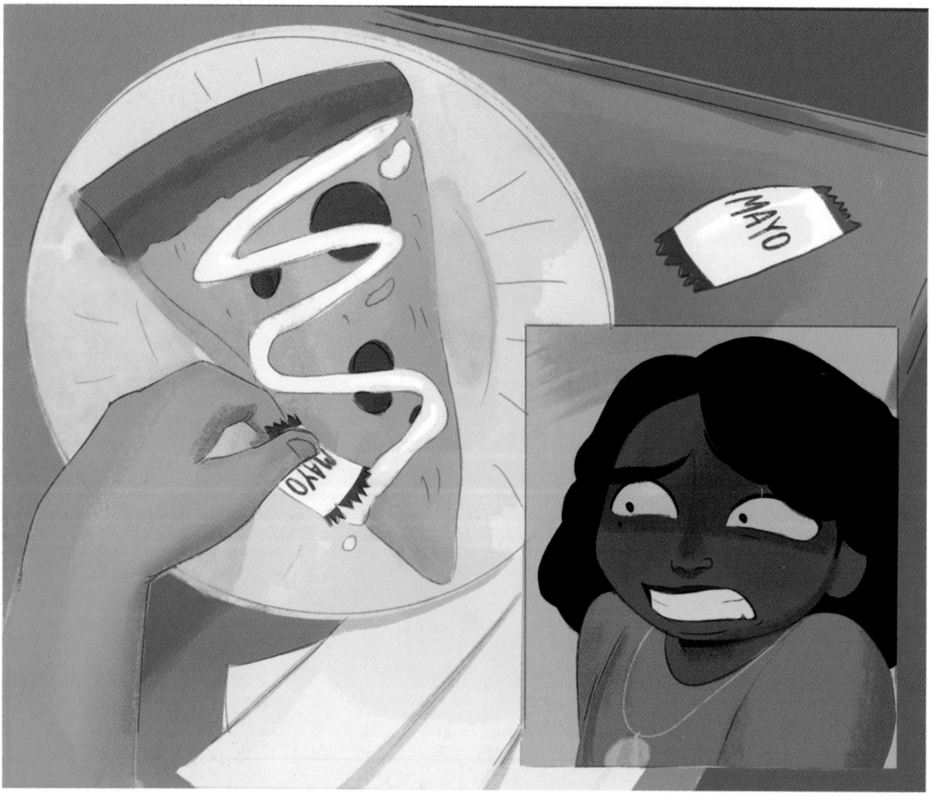
MAYO
MAYO

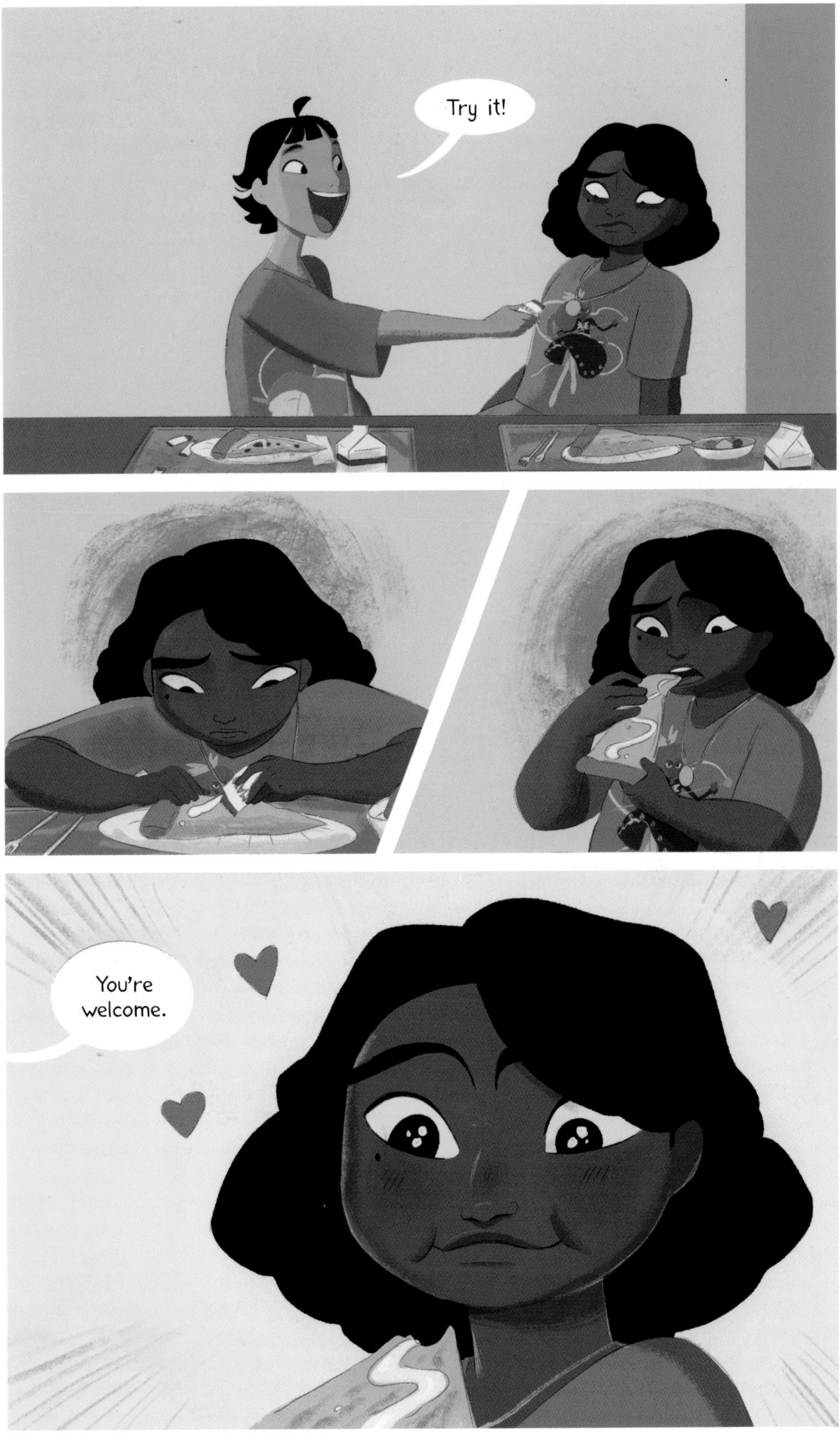
Try it!
You're welcome.

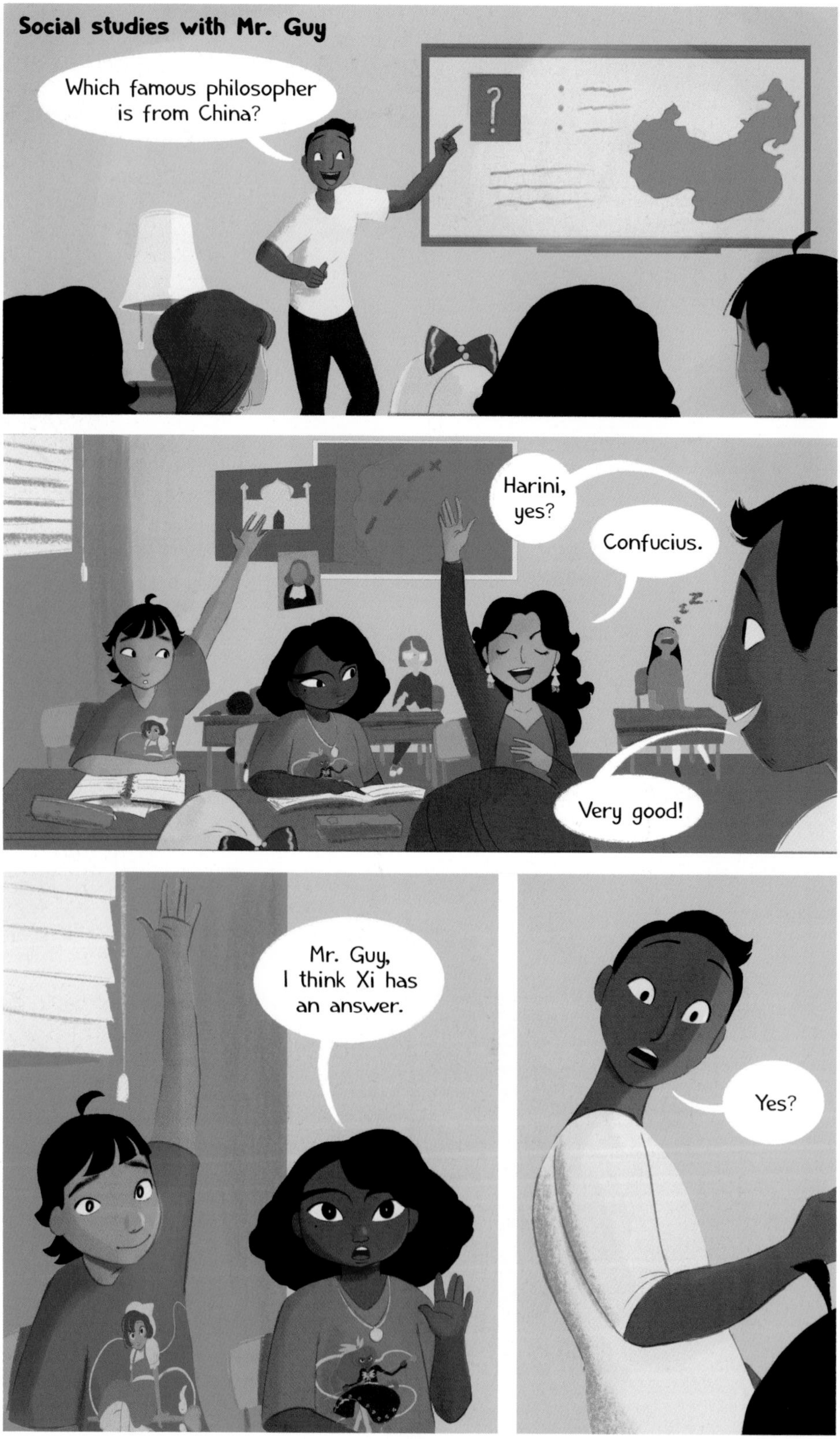
Social studies with Mr. Guy
Which famous philosopher is from China?
Harini, yes?
Confucius.
Very good!
Mr. Guy, I think Xi has an answer.
Yes?

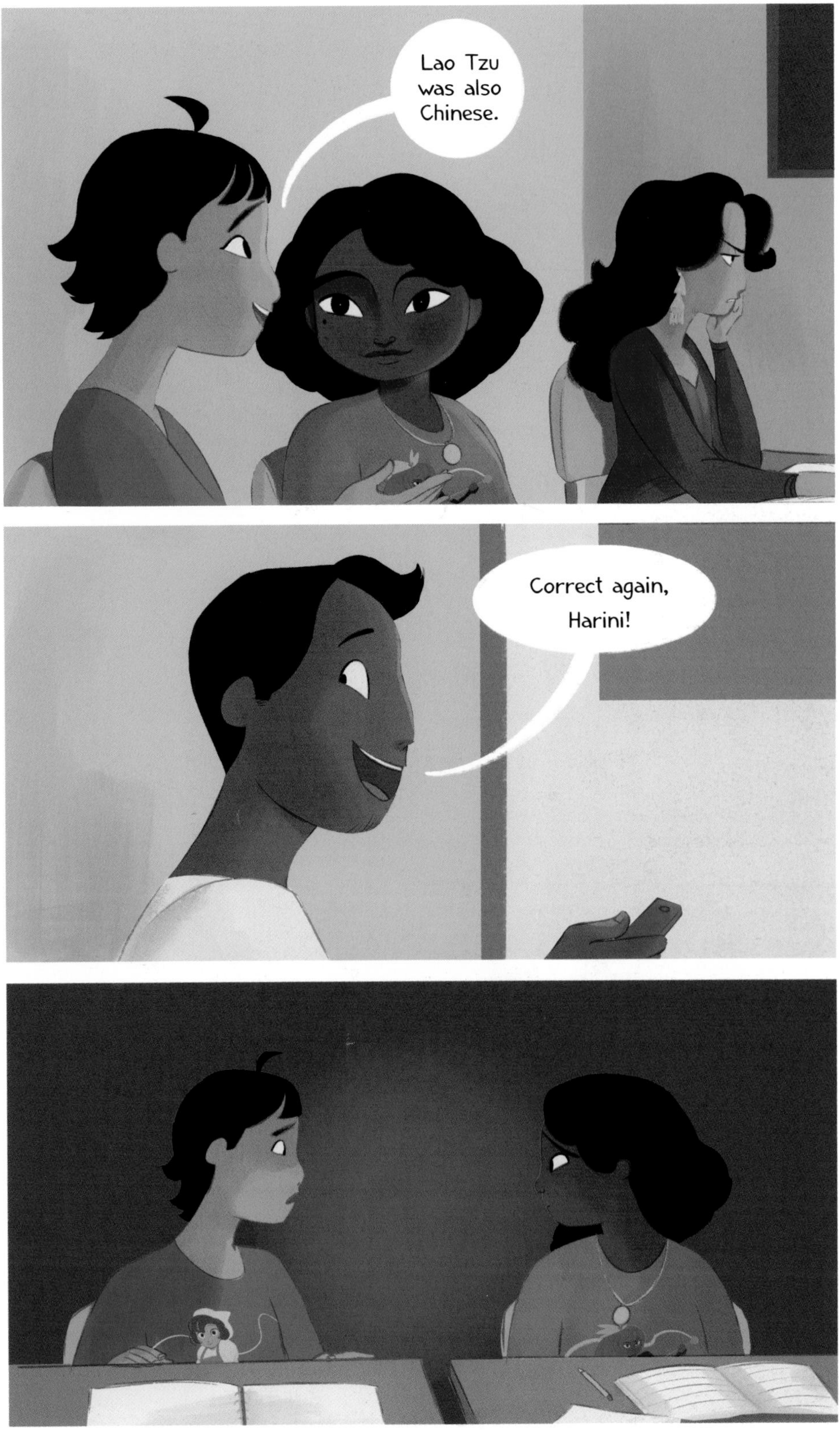
Lao Tzu was also Chinese.
Correct again, Harini!

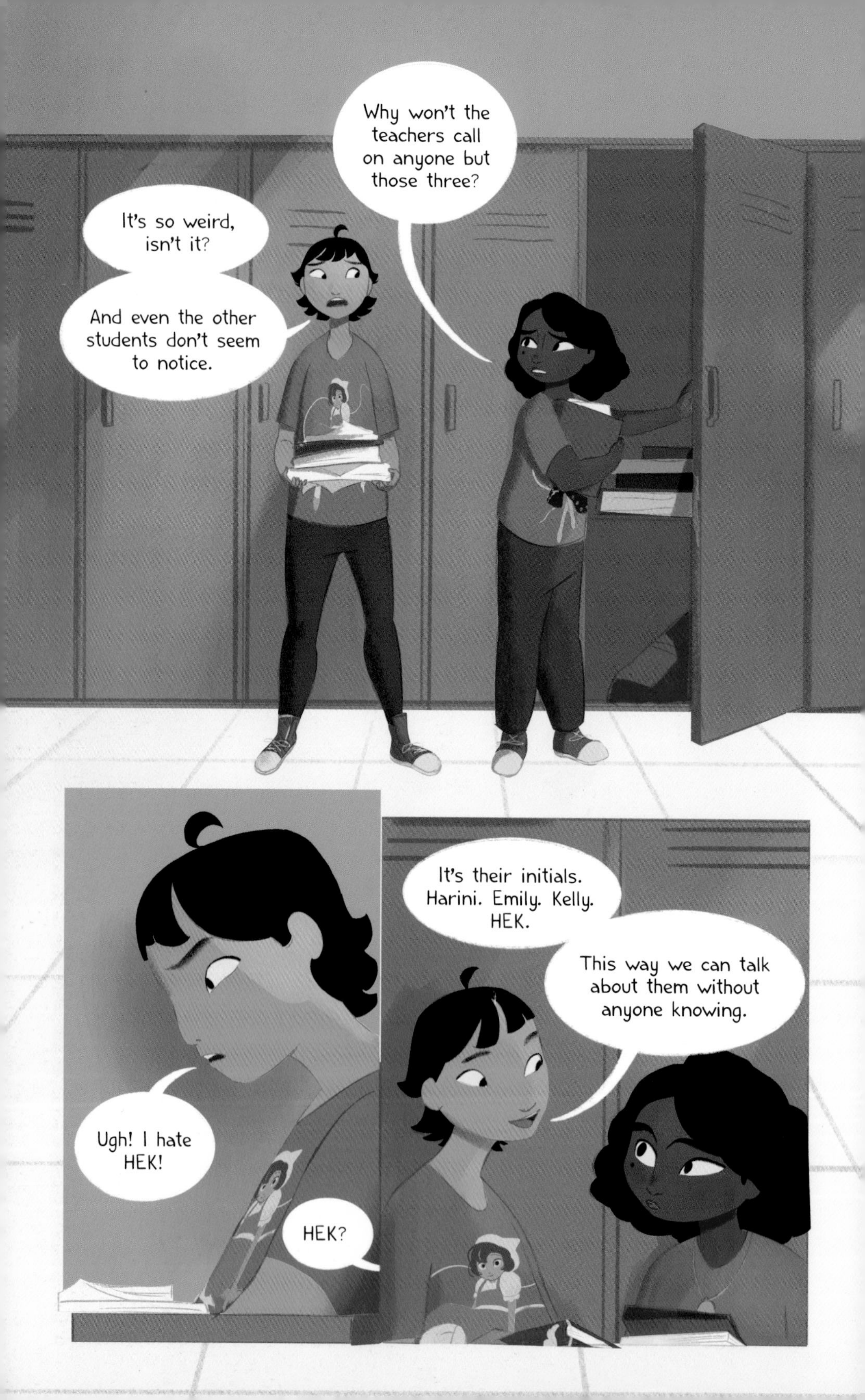

It's so weird, isn't it?
And even the other students don't seem to notice.
Why won't the teachers call on anyone but those three?
Ugh! I hate HEK!
HEK?
It's their initials. Harini. Emily. Kelly. HEK.
This way we can talk about them without anyone knowing.

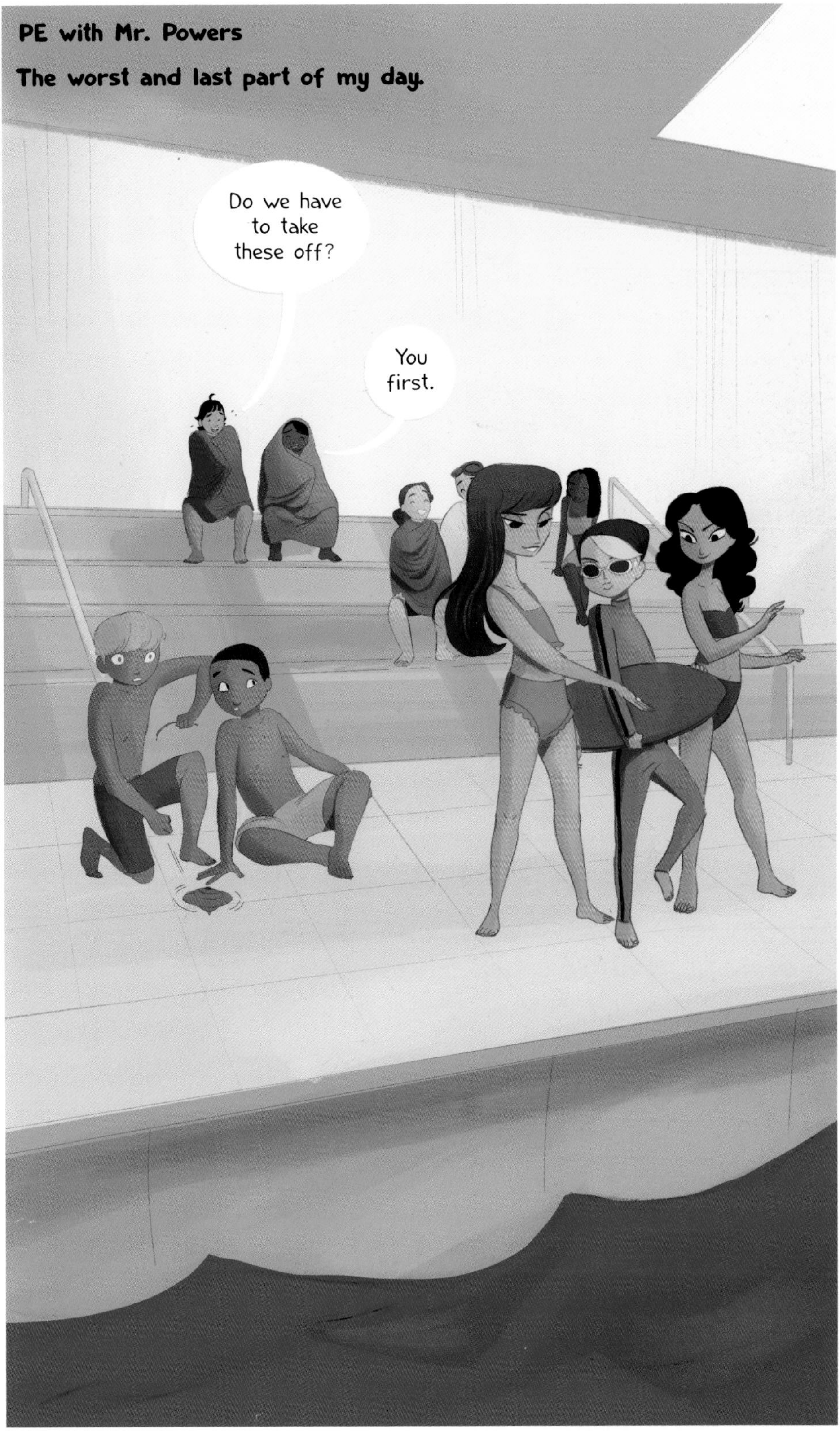
PE with Mr. Powers
The worst and last part of my day.
Do we have to take these off?
You first.

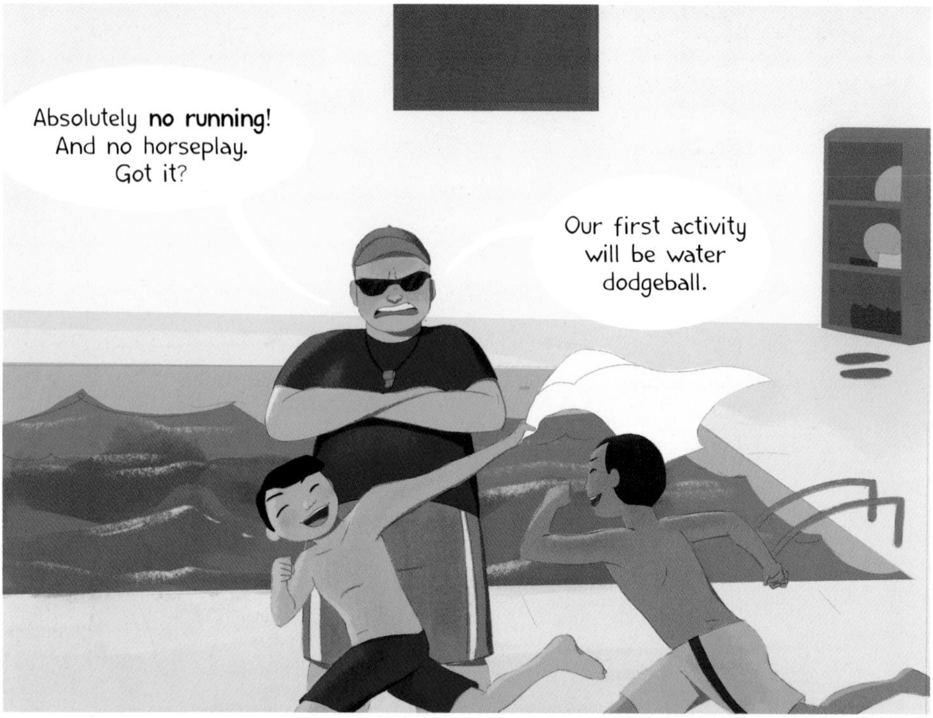
Absolutely **no running**! And no horseplay. Got it?
Our first activity will be water dodgeball.

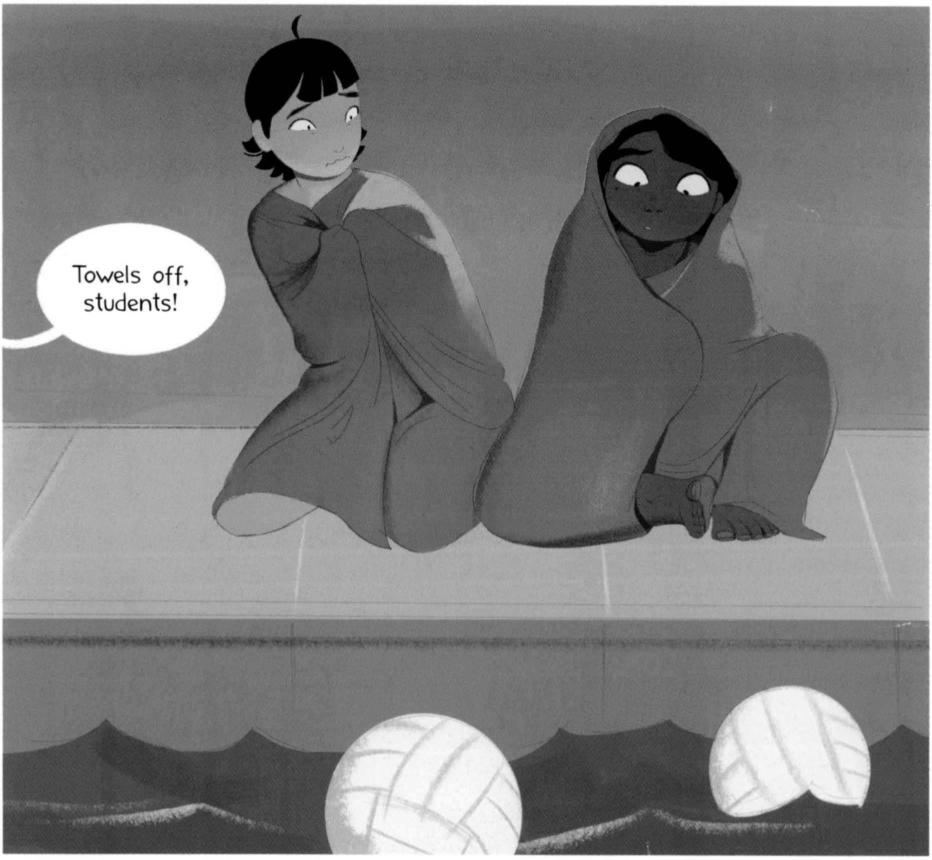
Towels off, students!

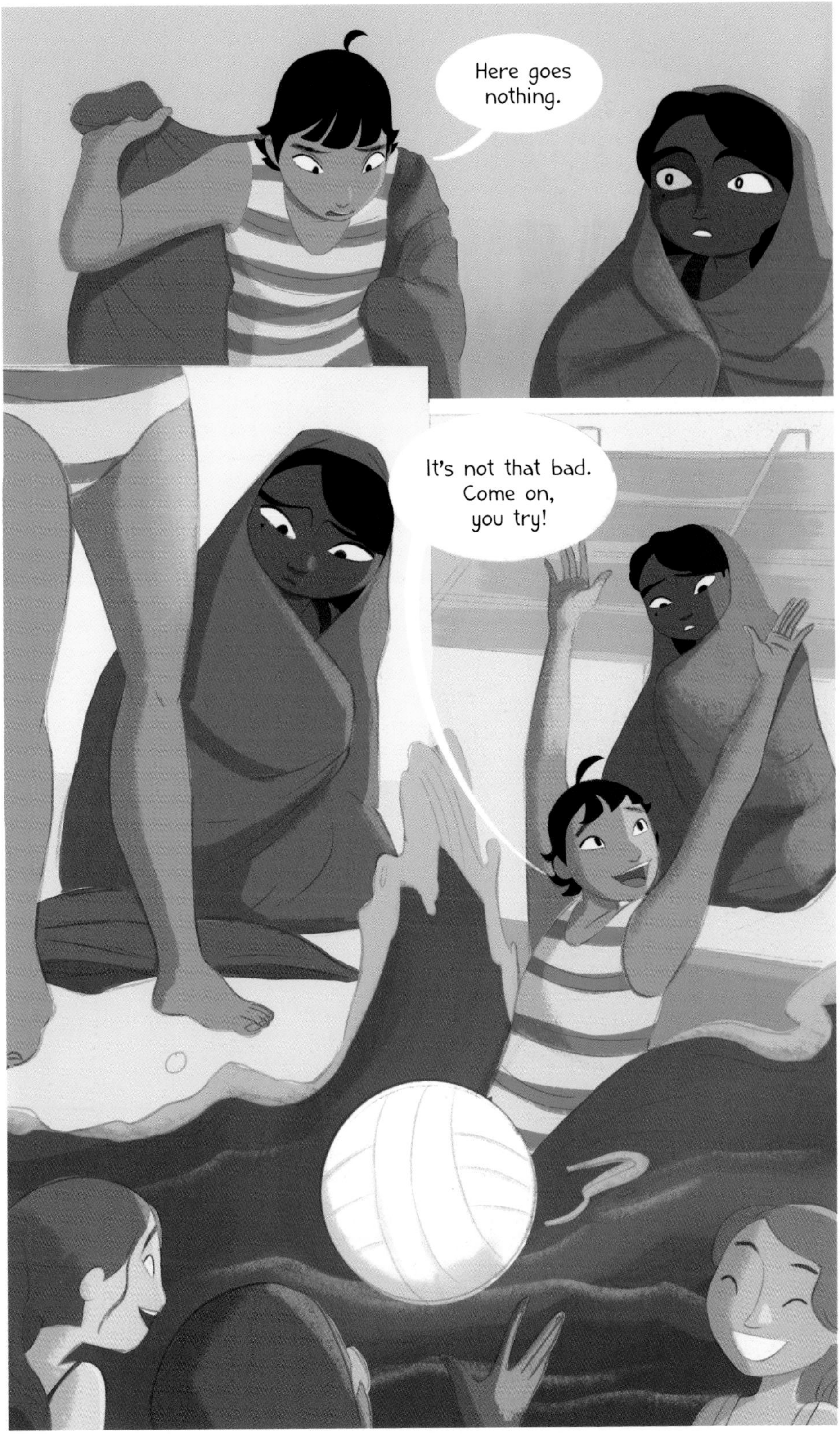
Here goes nothing.
It's not that bad. Come on, you try!

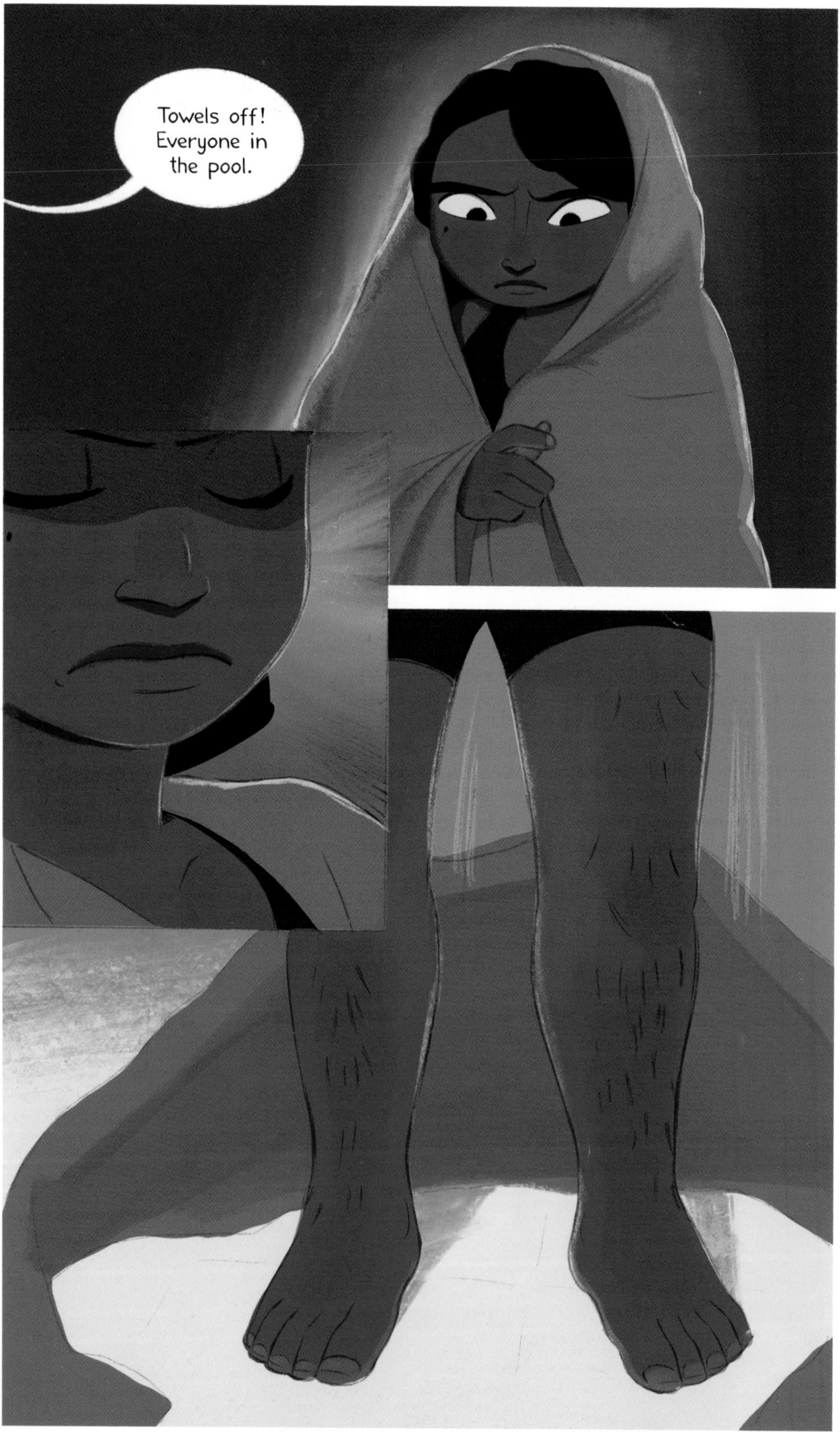
Towels off! Everyone in the pool.

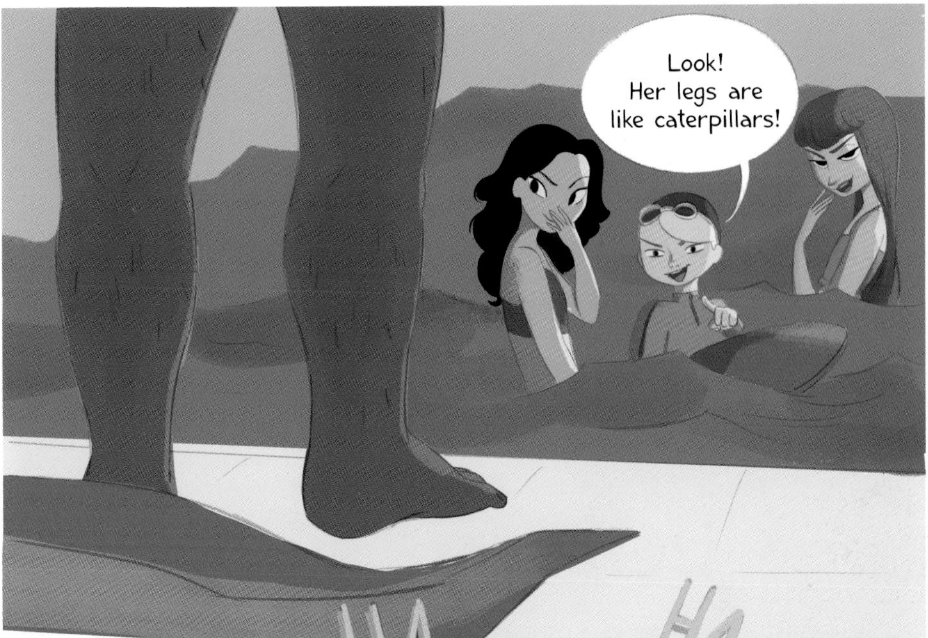
Look!
Her legs are
like caterpillars!
HA
HA

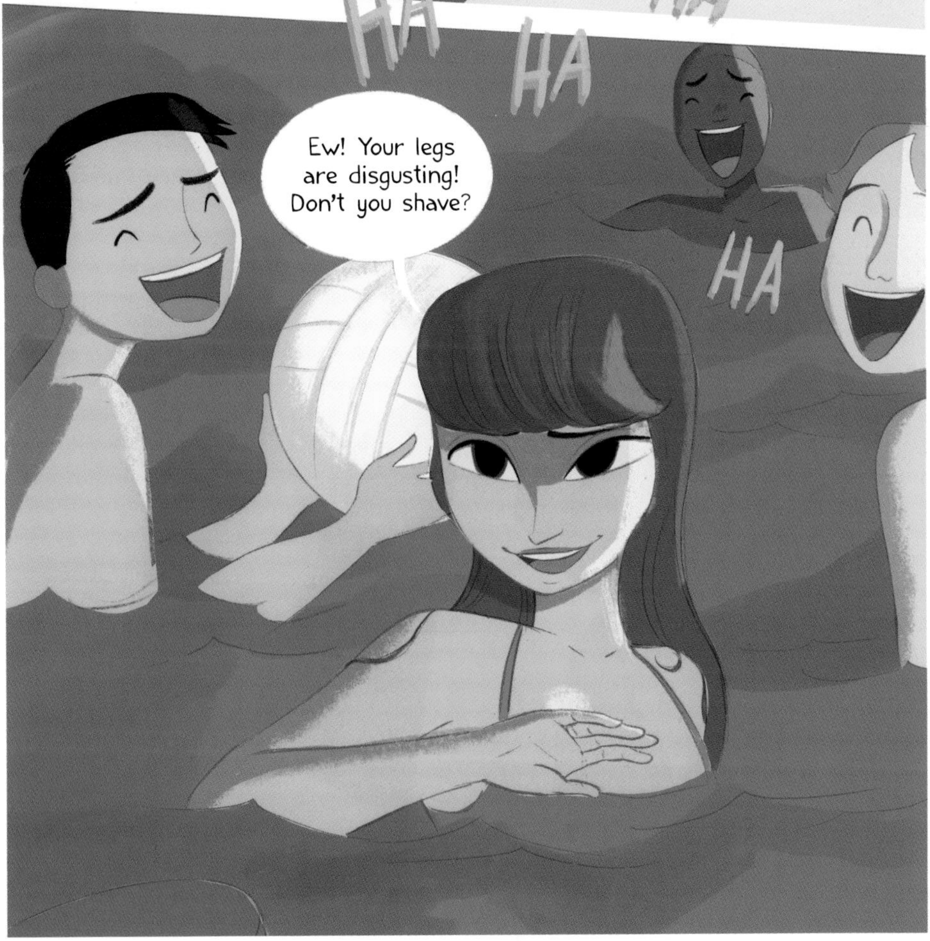
HA
Ew! Your legs
are disgusting!
Don't you shave?
HA

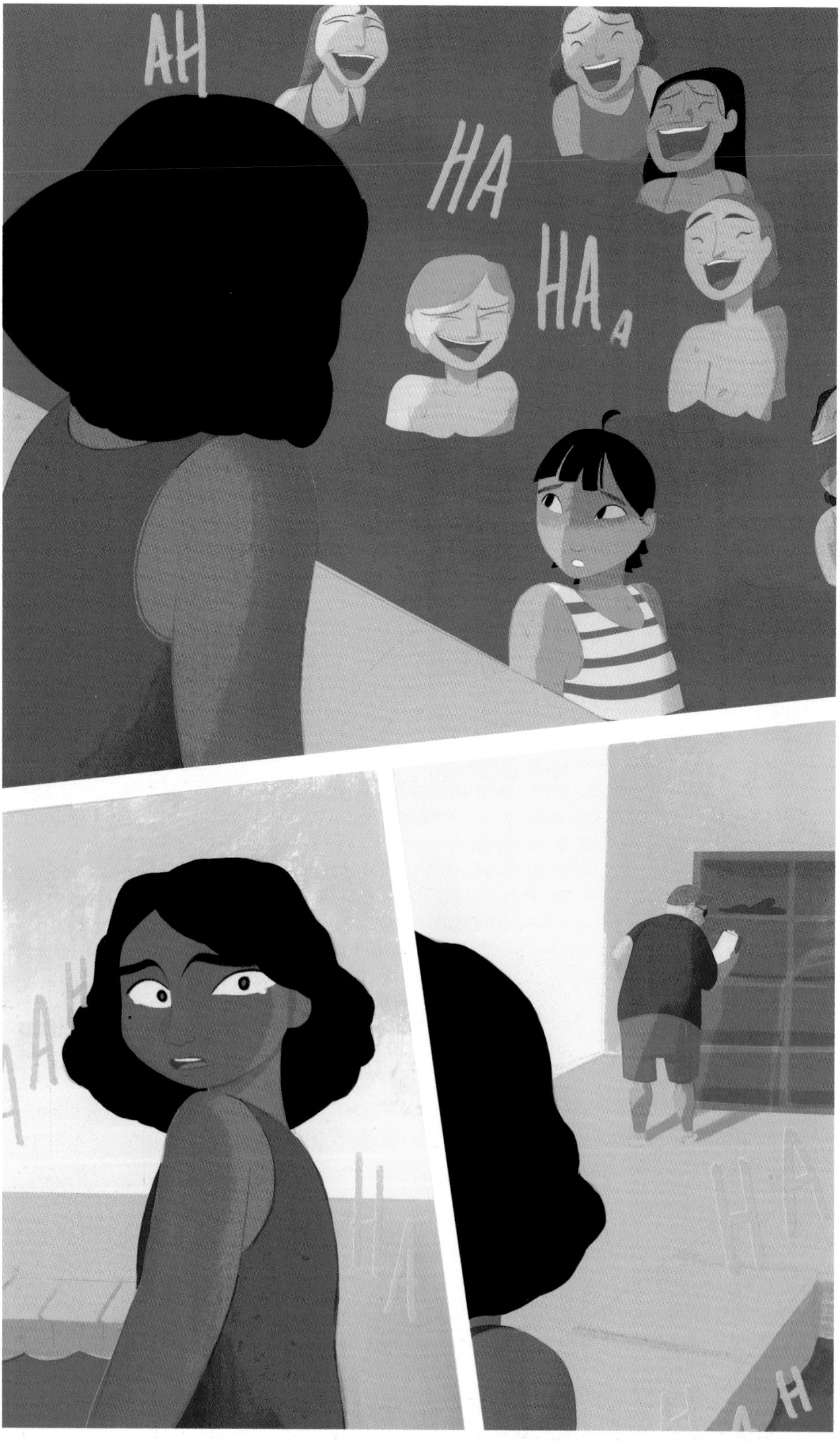
AH
HA
HA A
HA
HAH

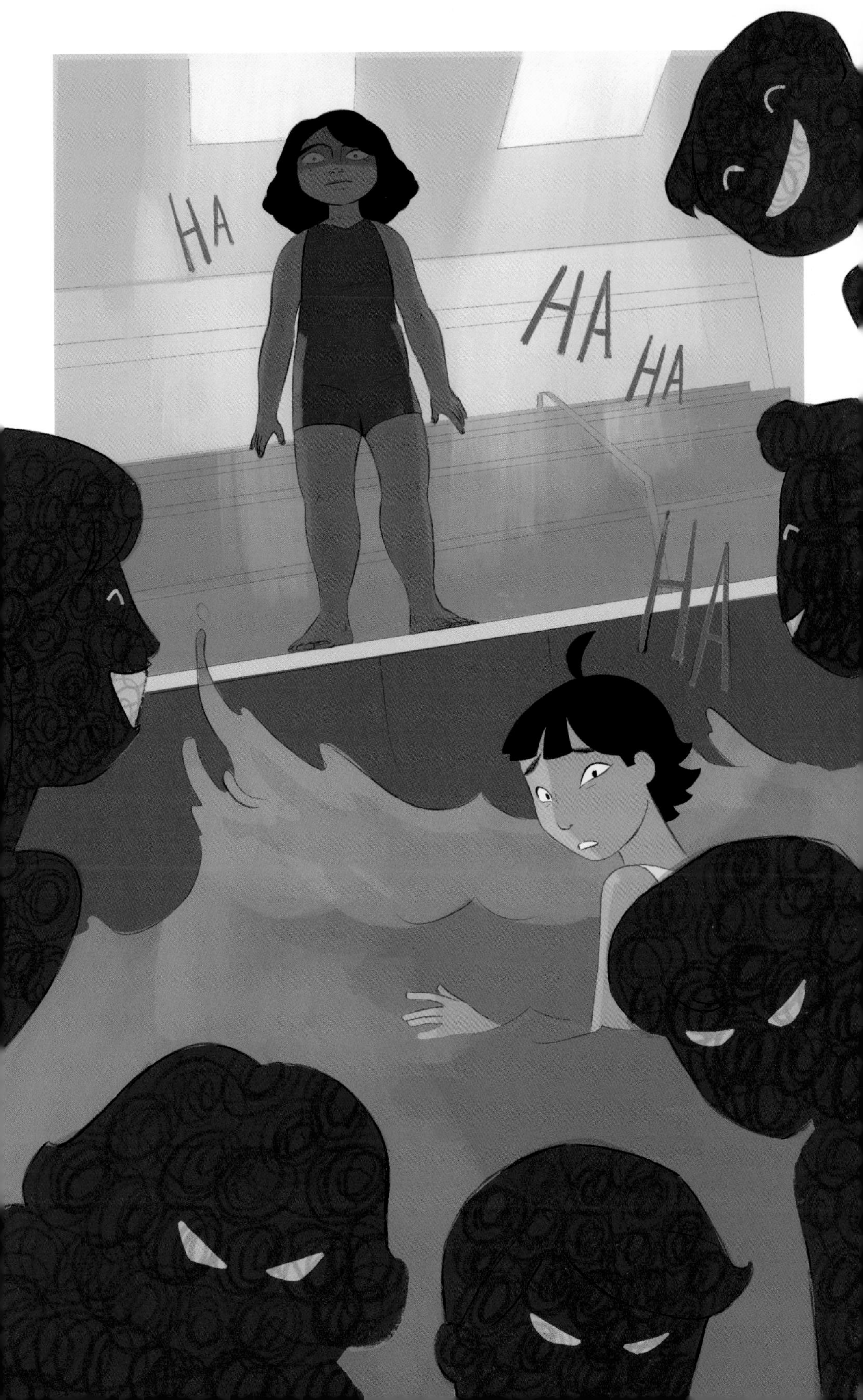
HA
HA
HA
HA

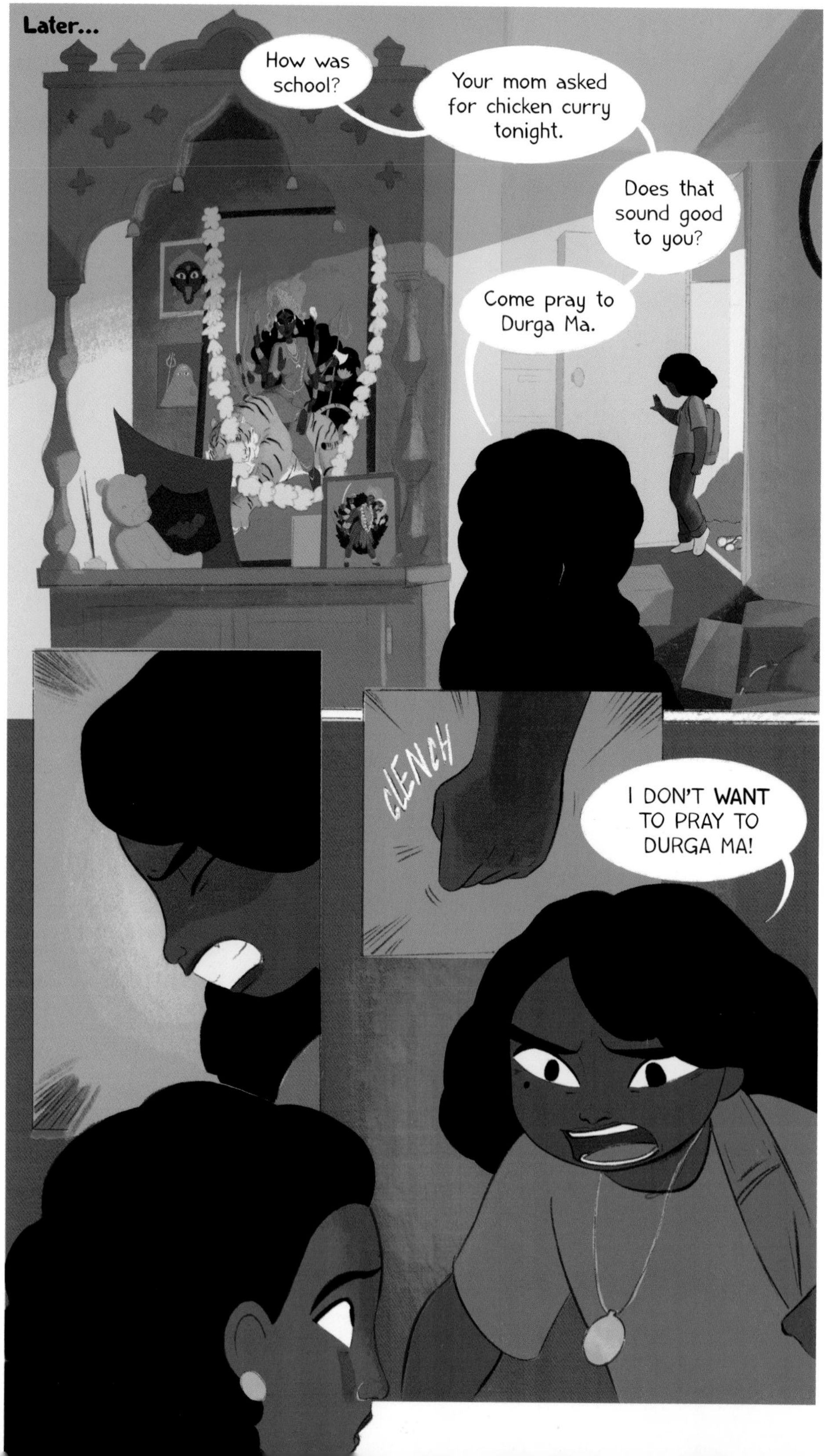
Later...
How was school?
Your mom asked for chicken curry tonight.
Does that sound good to you?
Come pray to Durga Ma.
CLENCH
I DON'T **WANT** TO PRAY TO DURGA MA!

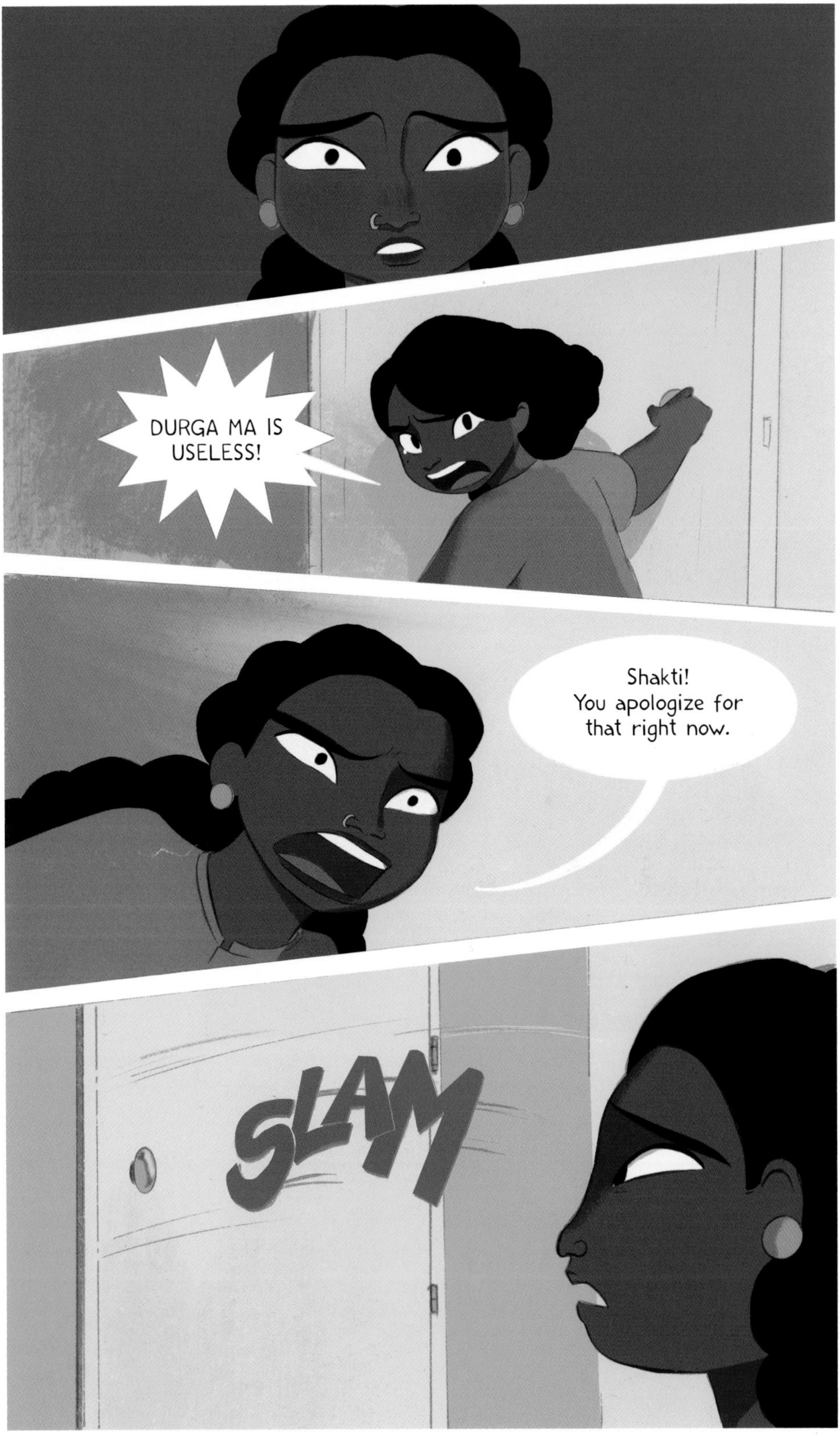
DURGA MA IS USELESS!
Shakti! You apologize for that right now.
SLAM

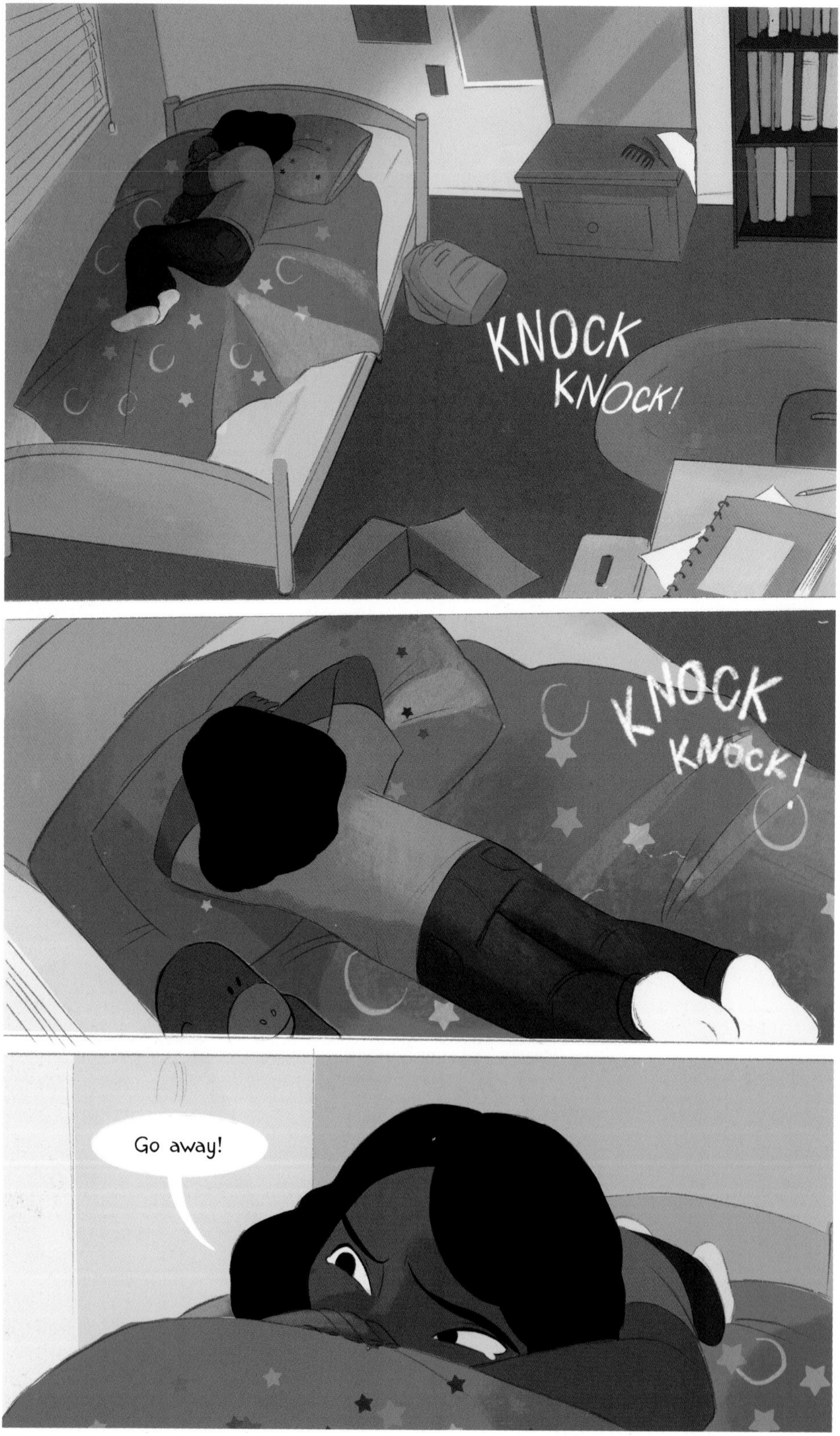
KNOCK
KNOCK!
KNOCK
KNOCK!
Go away!

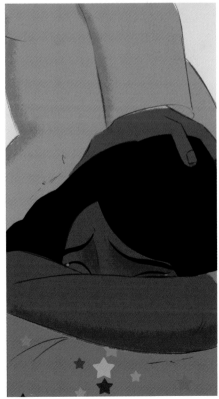

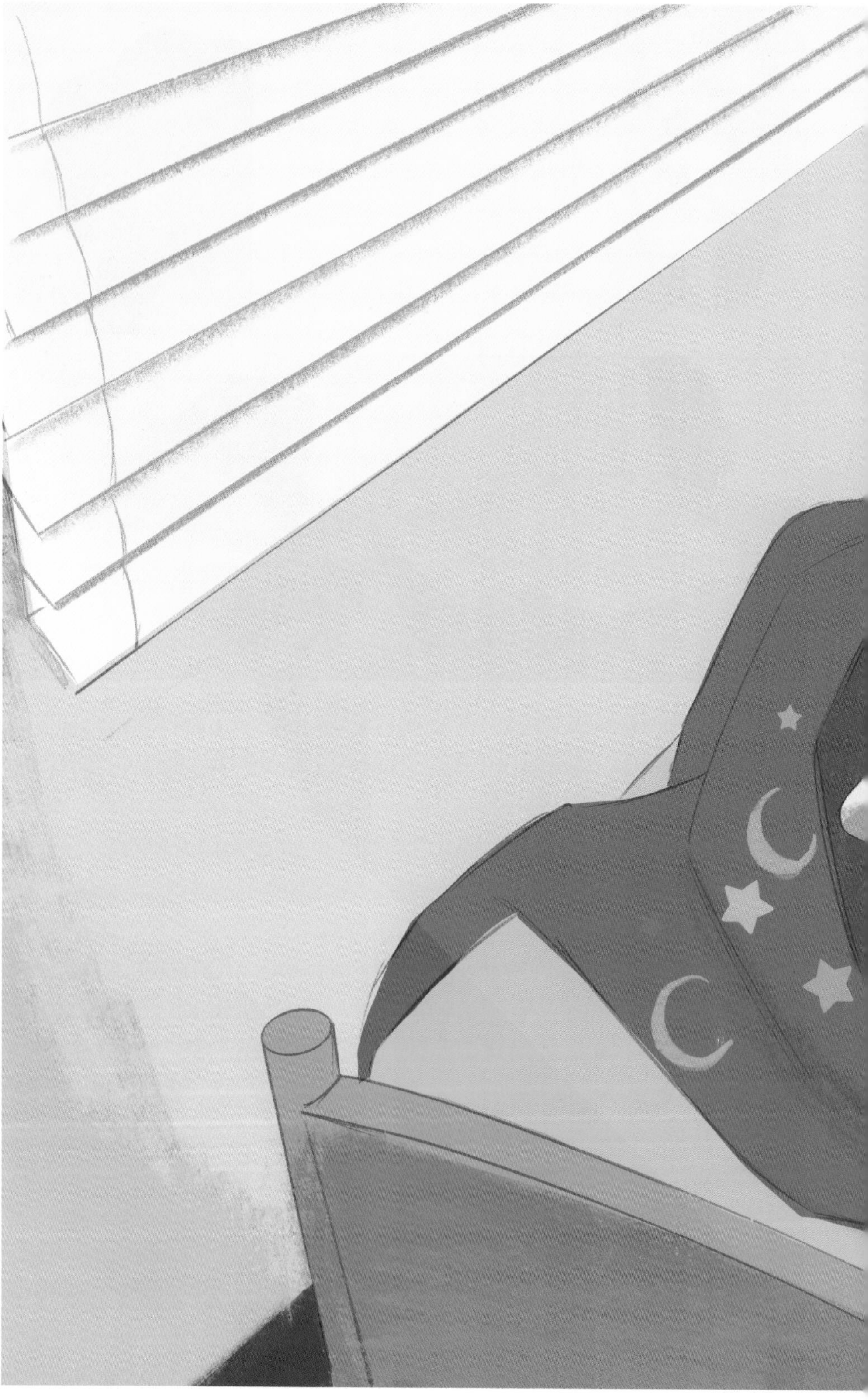

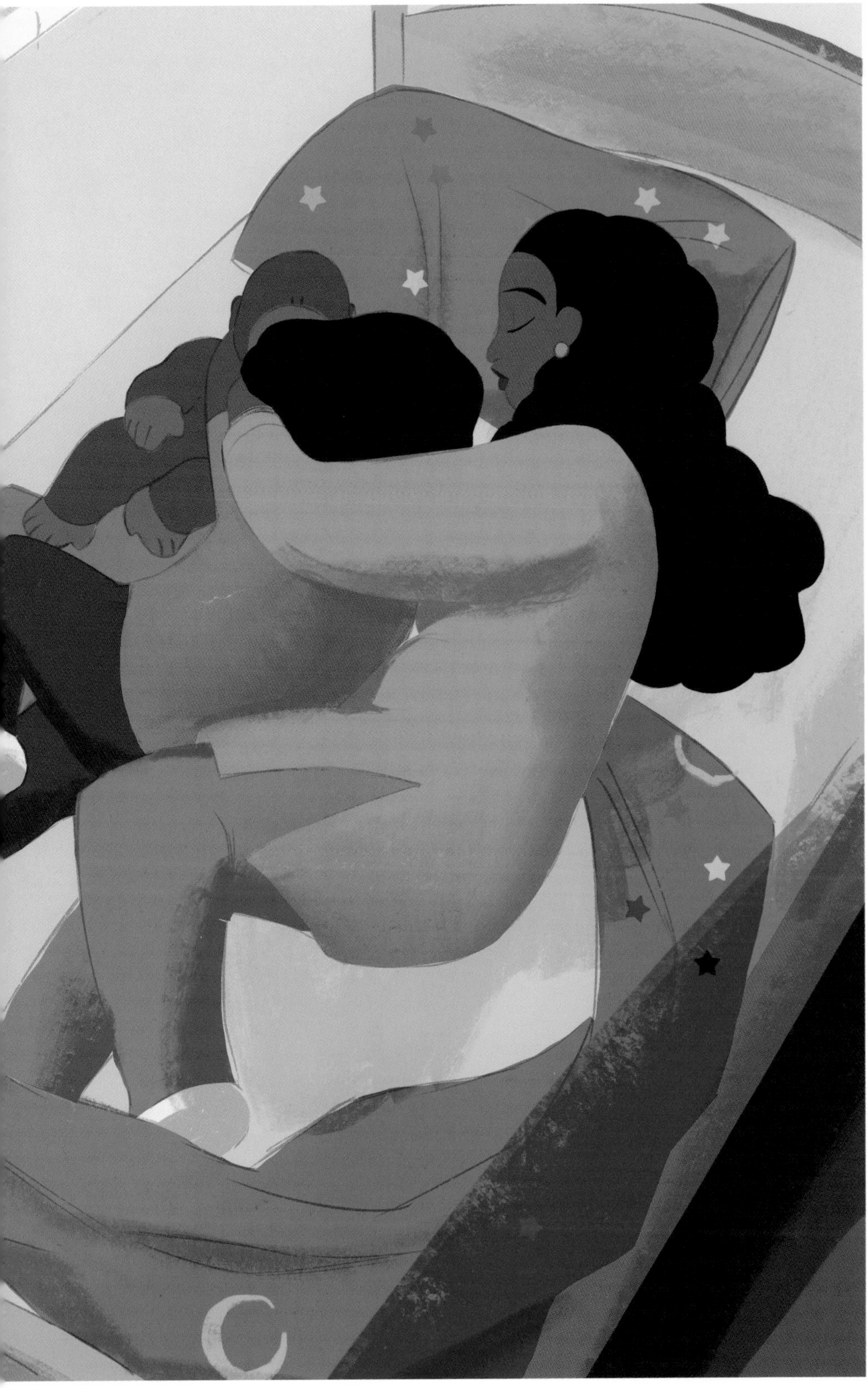

# Interlude:

## WHO IS DURGA MA, ANYWAY?

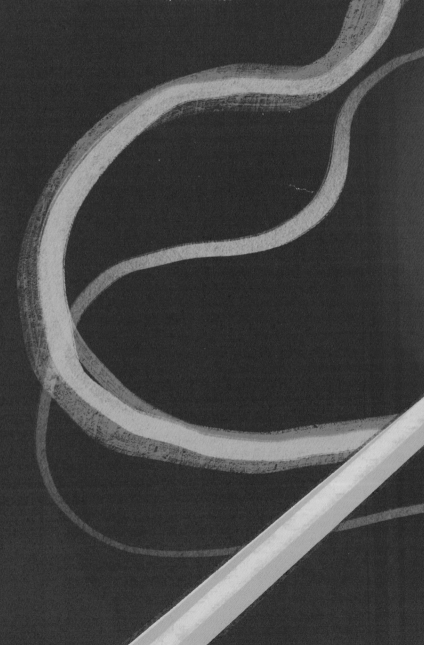

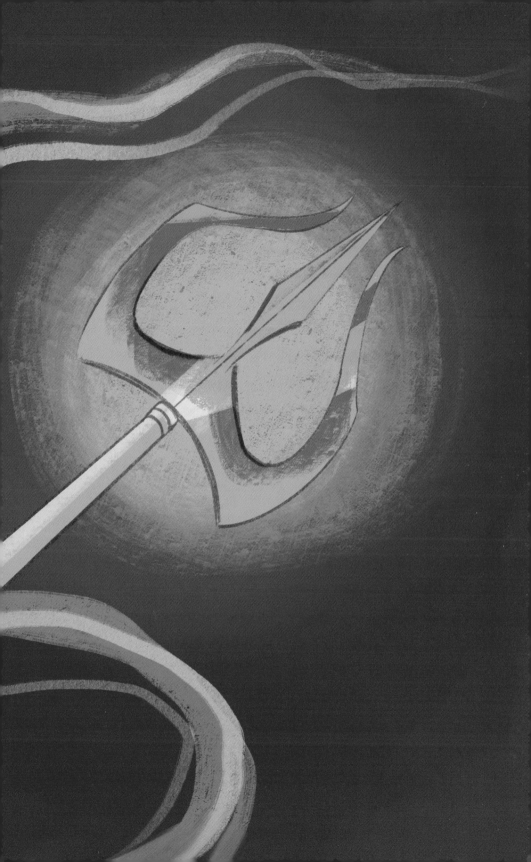

In legend, Durga is the goddess of strength. She is born whenever the universe needs her protection, and after each battle, she vanishes.

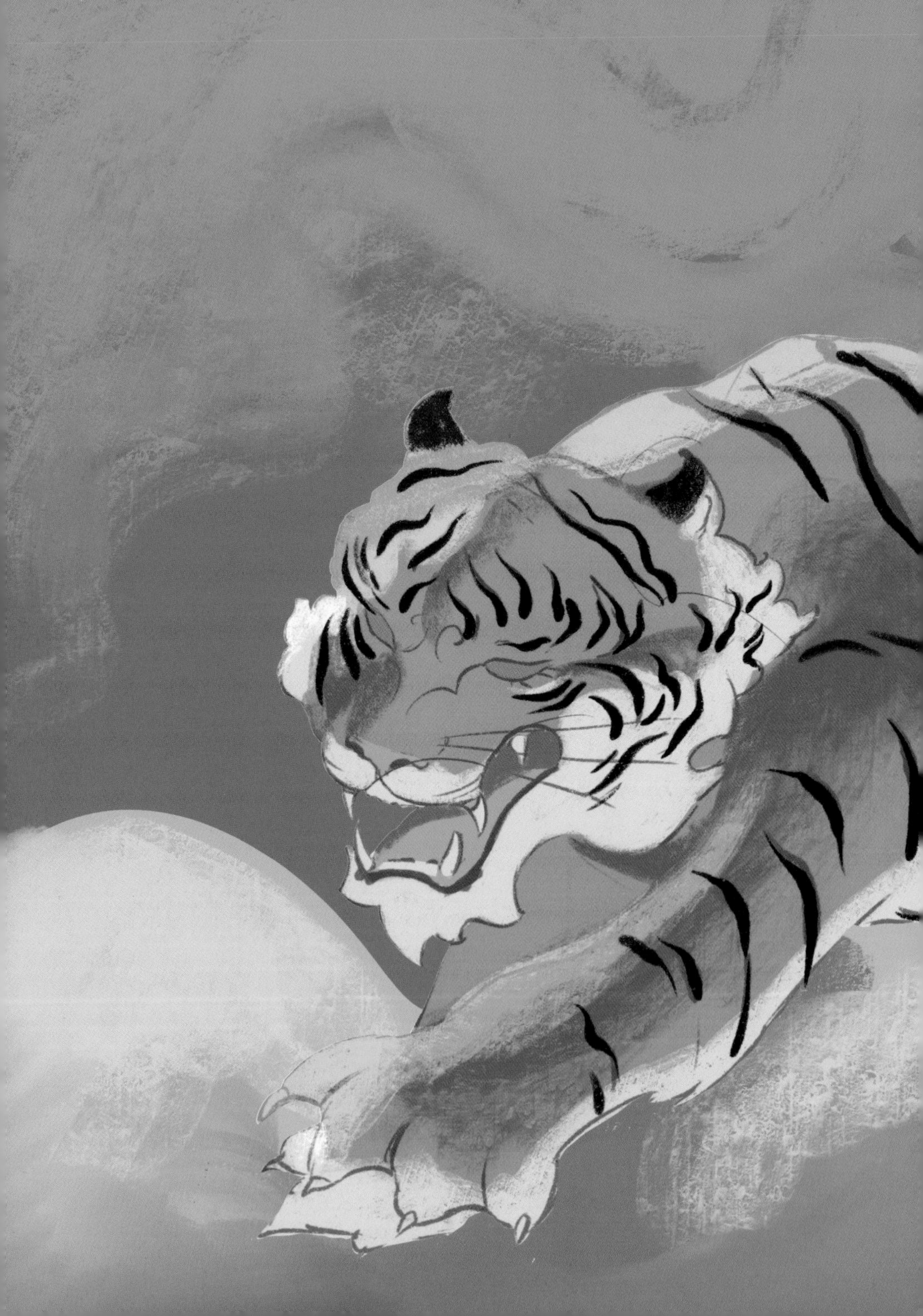

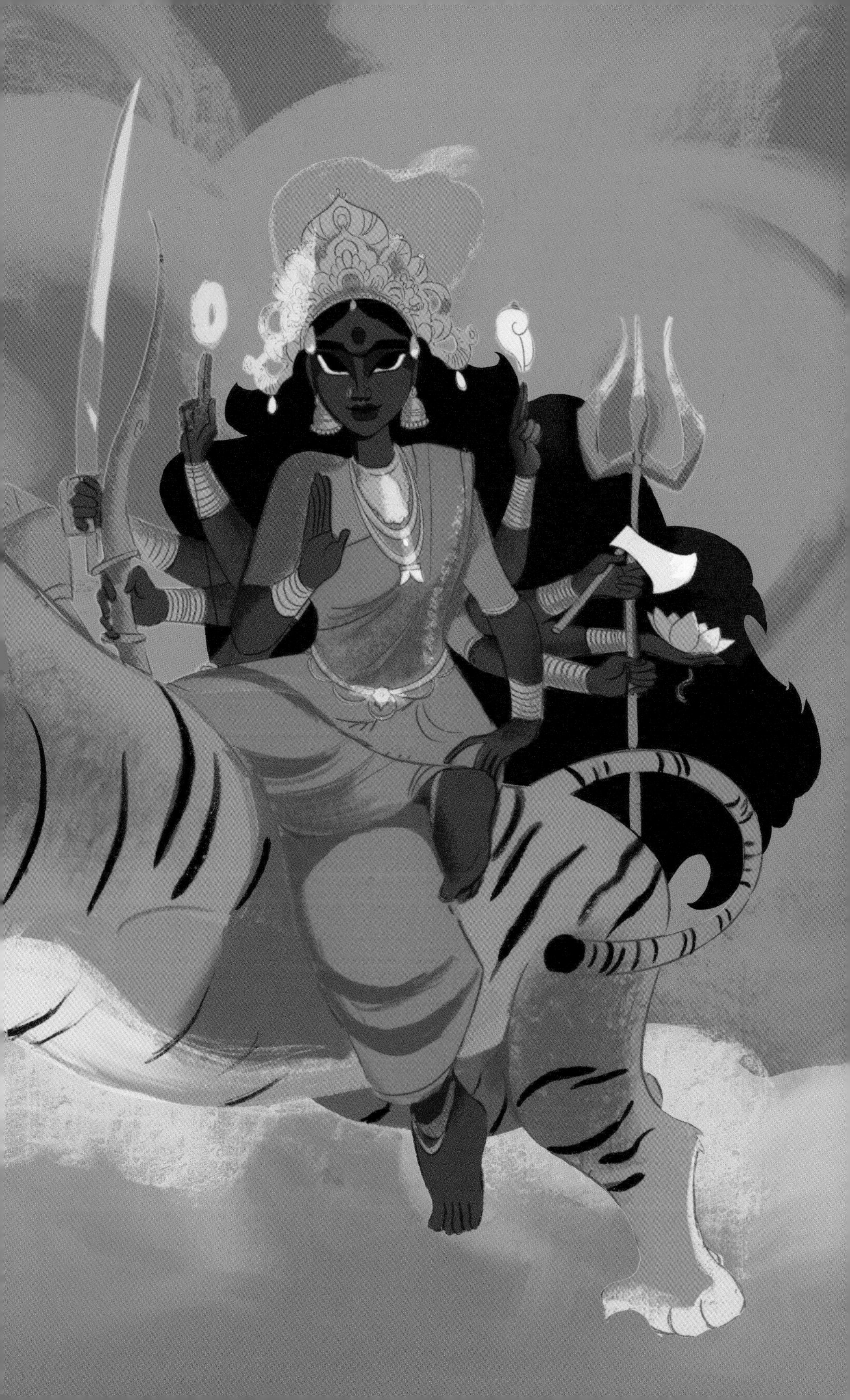

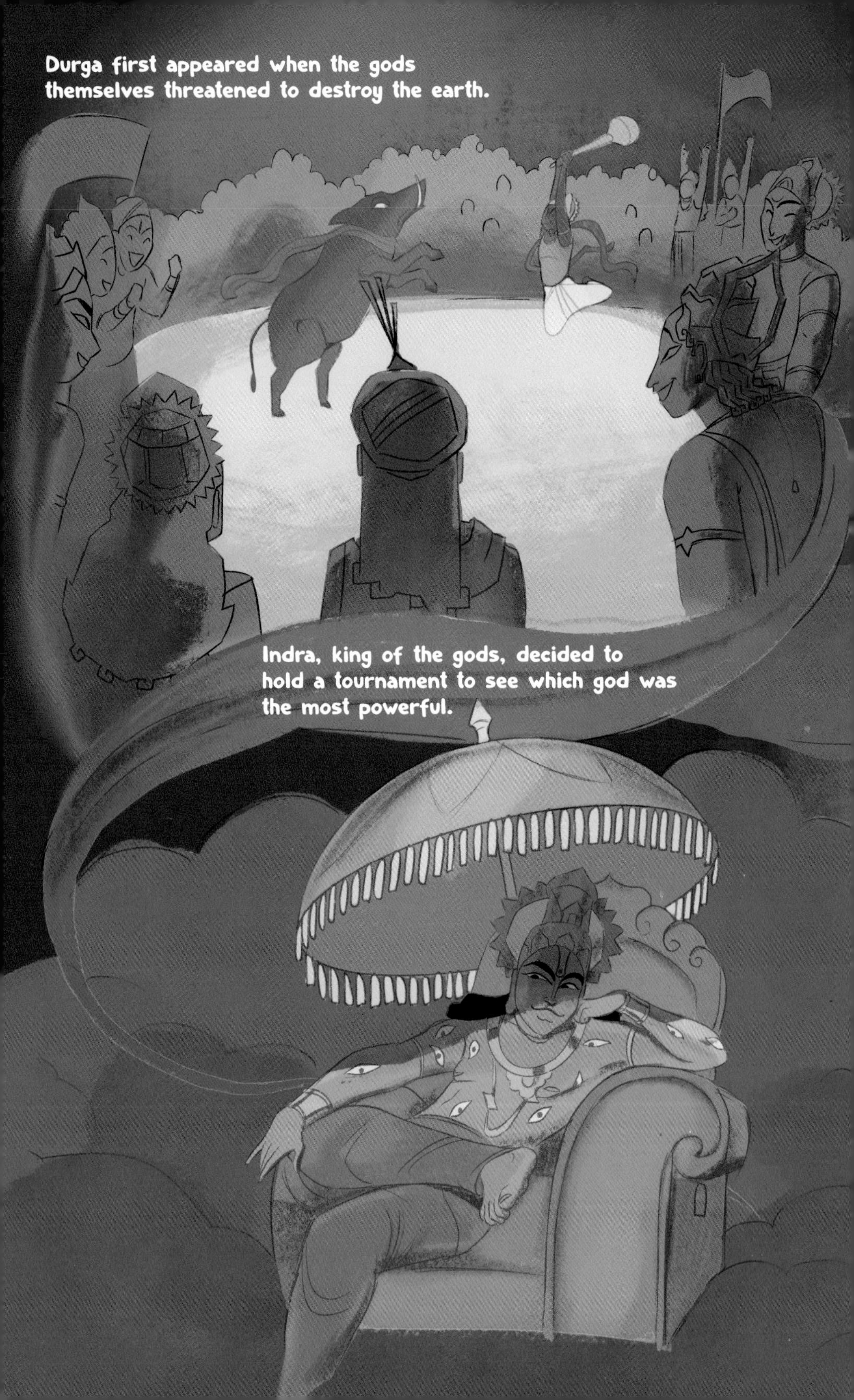
Durga first appeared when the gods themselves threatened to destroy the earth.
Indra, king of the gods, decided to hold a tournament to see which god was the most powerful.

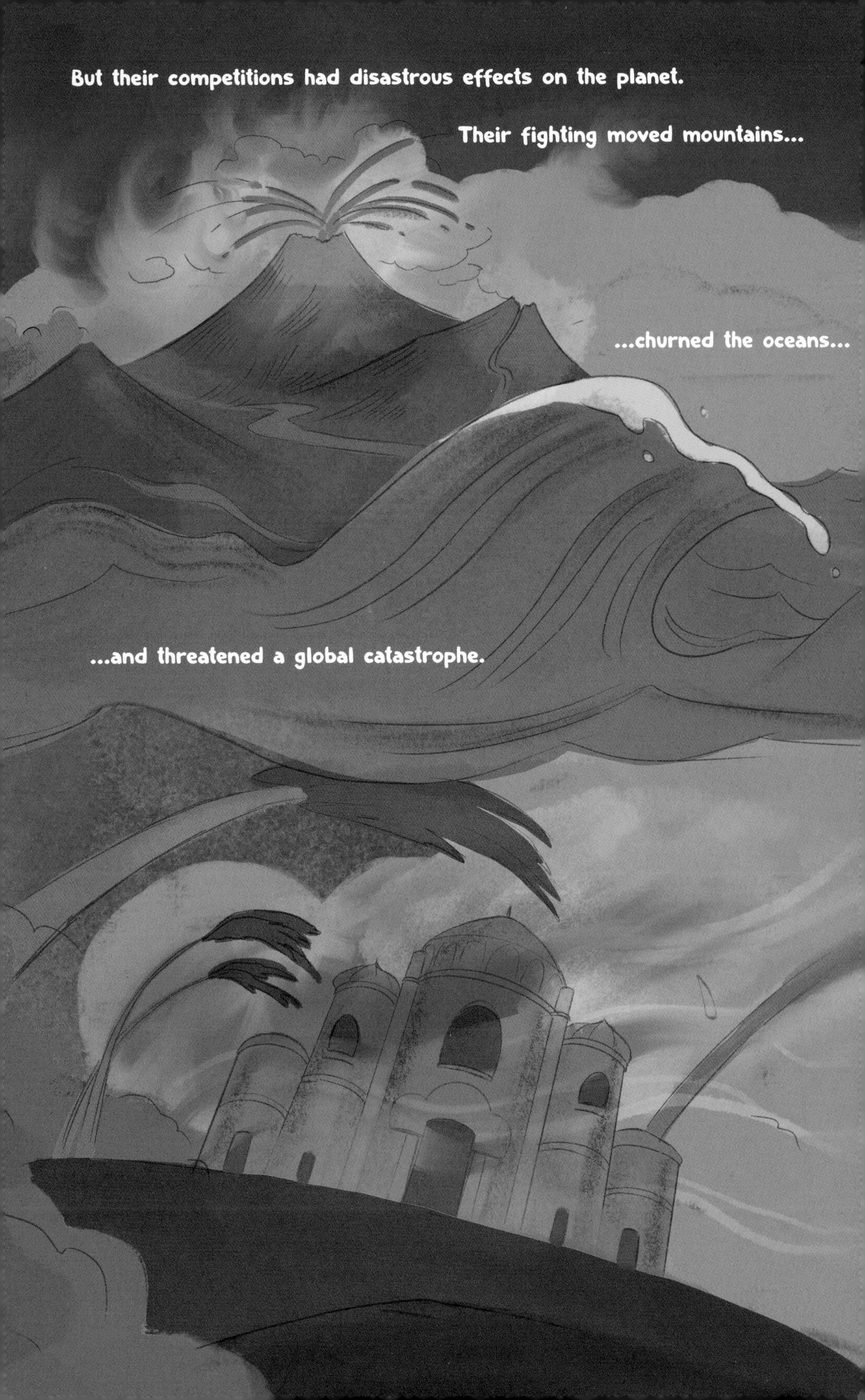
But their competitions had disastrous effects on the planet.
Their fighting moved mountains...
...churned the oceans...
...and threatened a global catastrophe.

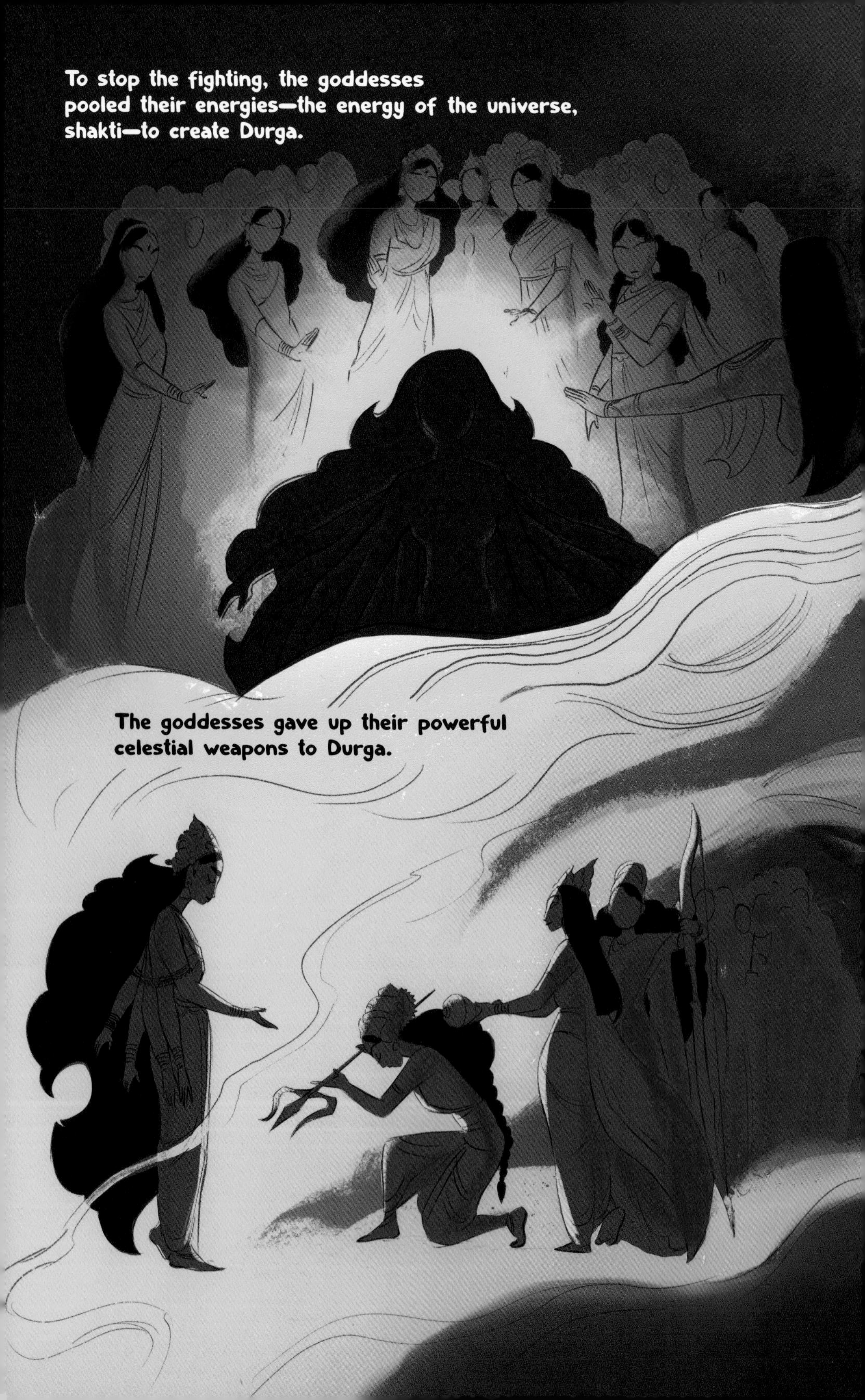
To stop the fighting, the goddesses pooled their energies—the energy of the universe, shakti—to create Durga.
The goddesses gave up their powerful celestial weapons to Durga.

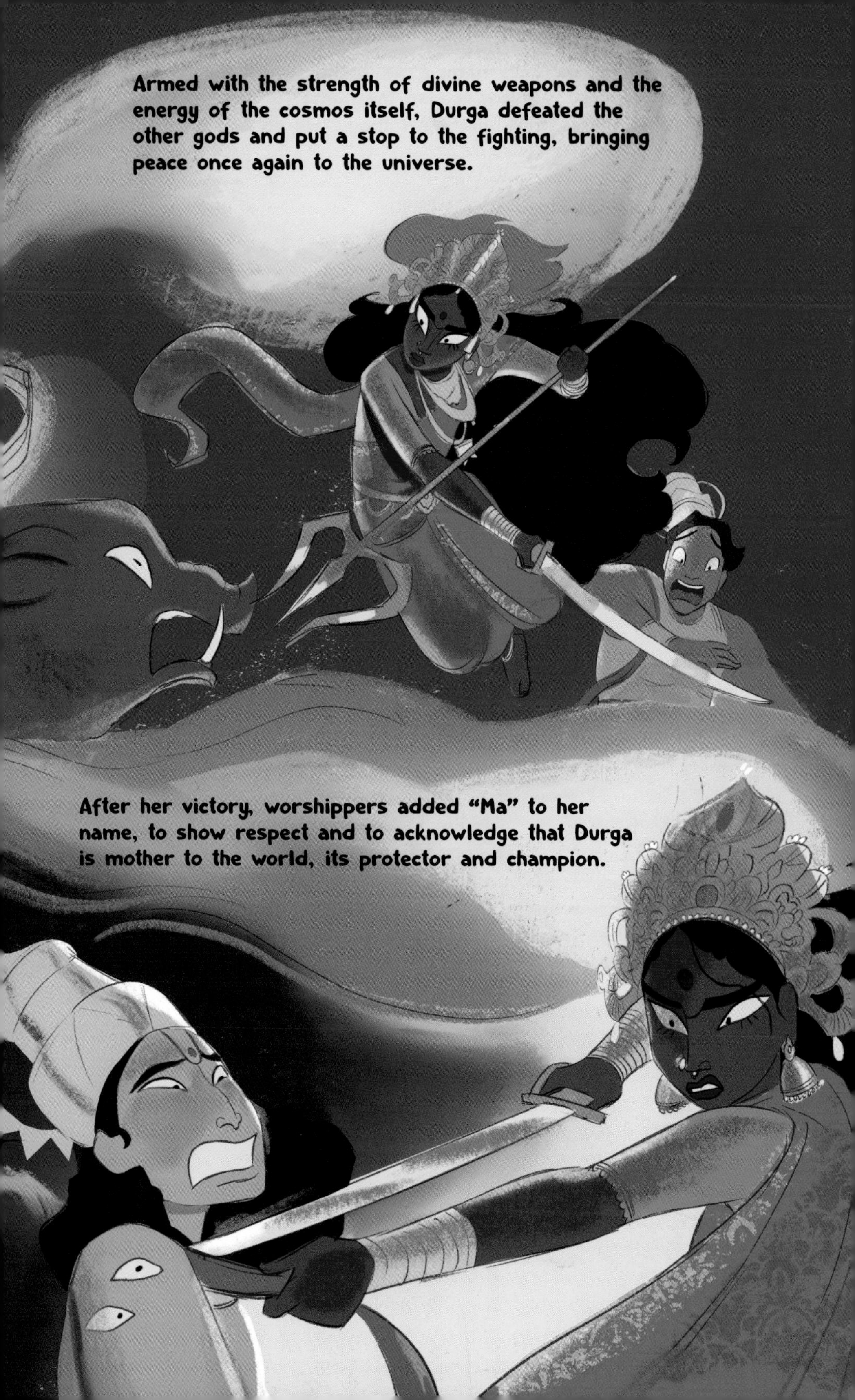
Armed with the strength of divine weapons and the energy of the cosmos itself, Durga defeated the other gods and put a stop to the fighting, bringing peace once again to the universe.
After her victory, worshippers added "Ma" to her name, to show respect and to acknowledge that Durga is mother to the world, its protector and champion.

When I was born, my mothers named me Shakti, which means "energy of the universe." Shakti is also the name for the magic that is woven into the cosmos, the same magic we all call on.

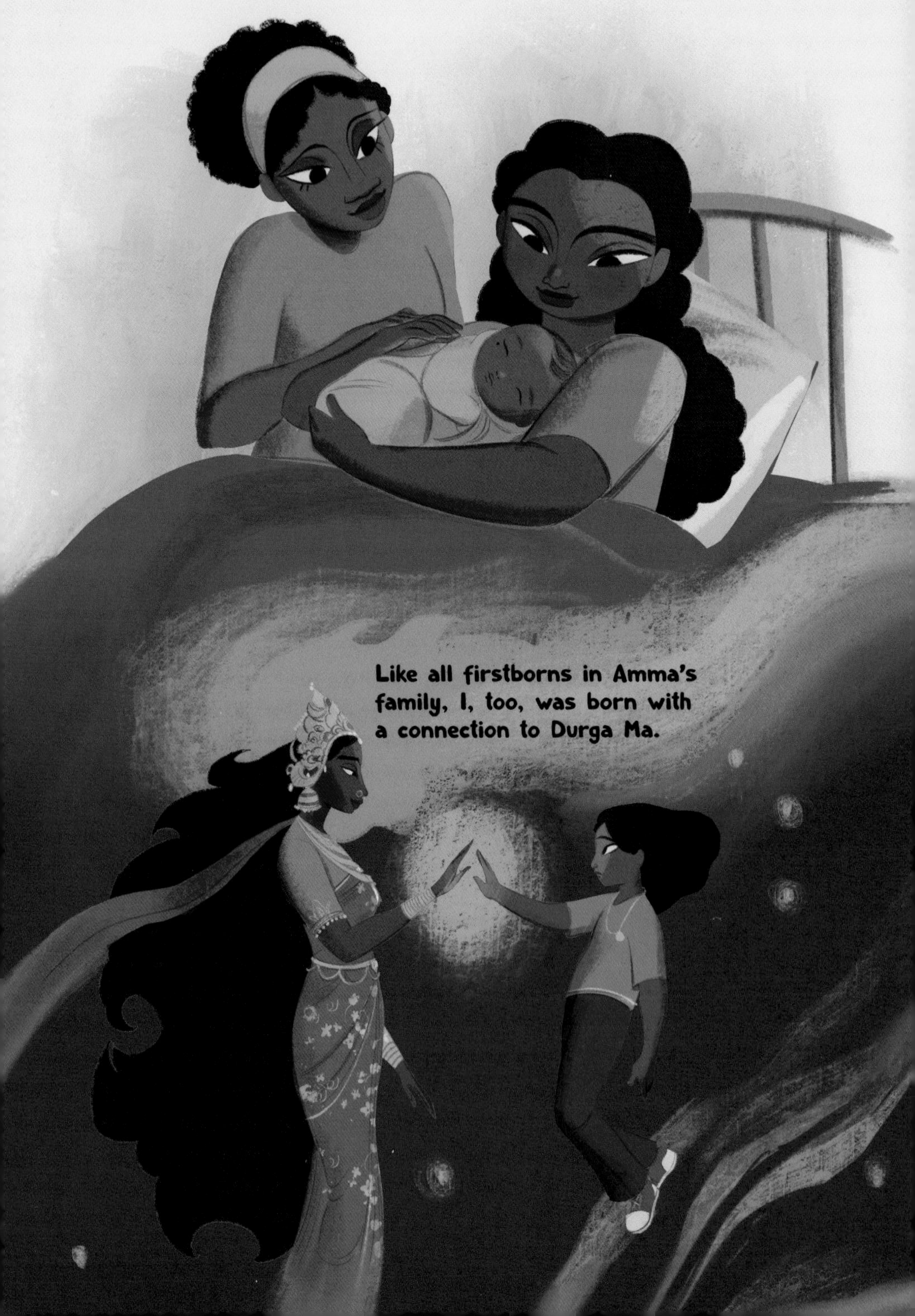
Like all firstborns in Amma's family, I, too, was born with a connection to Durga Ma.

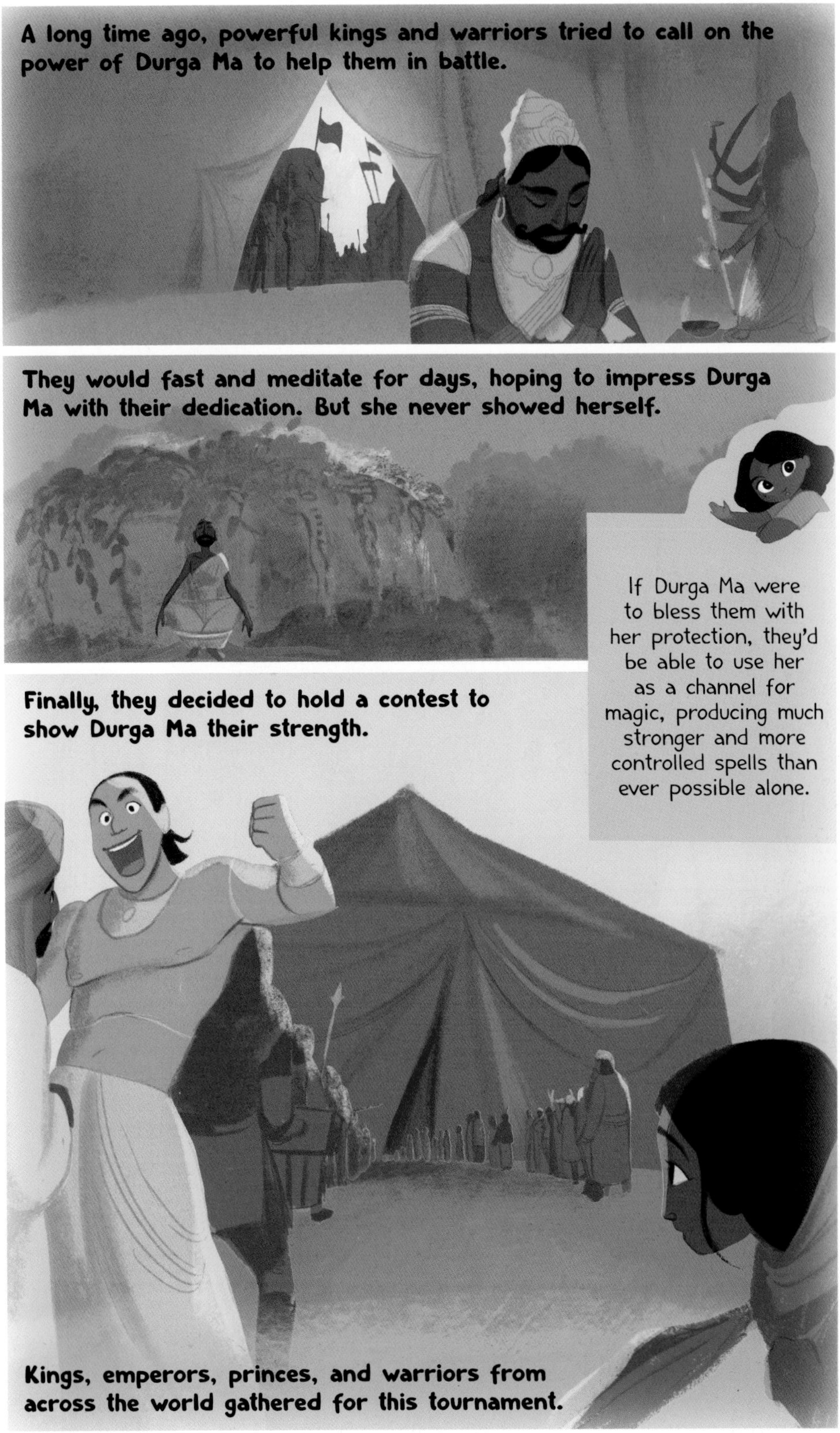
A long time ago, powerful kings and warriors tried to call on the power of Durga Ma to help them in battle.
They would fast and meditate for days, hoping to impress Durga Ma with their dedication. But she never showed herself.
If Durga Ma were to bless them with her protection, they'd be able to use her as a channel for magic, producing much stronger and more controlled spells than ever possible alone.
Finally, they decided to hold a contest to show Durga Ma their strength.
Kings, emperors, princes, and warriors from across the world gathered for this tournament.

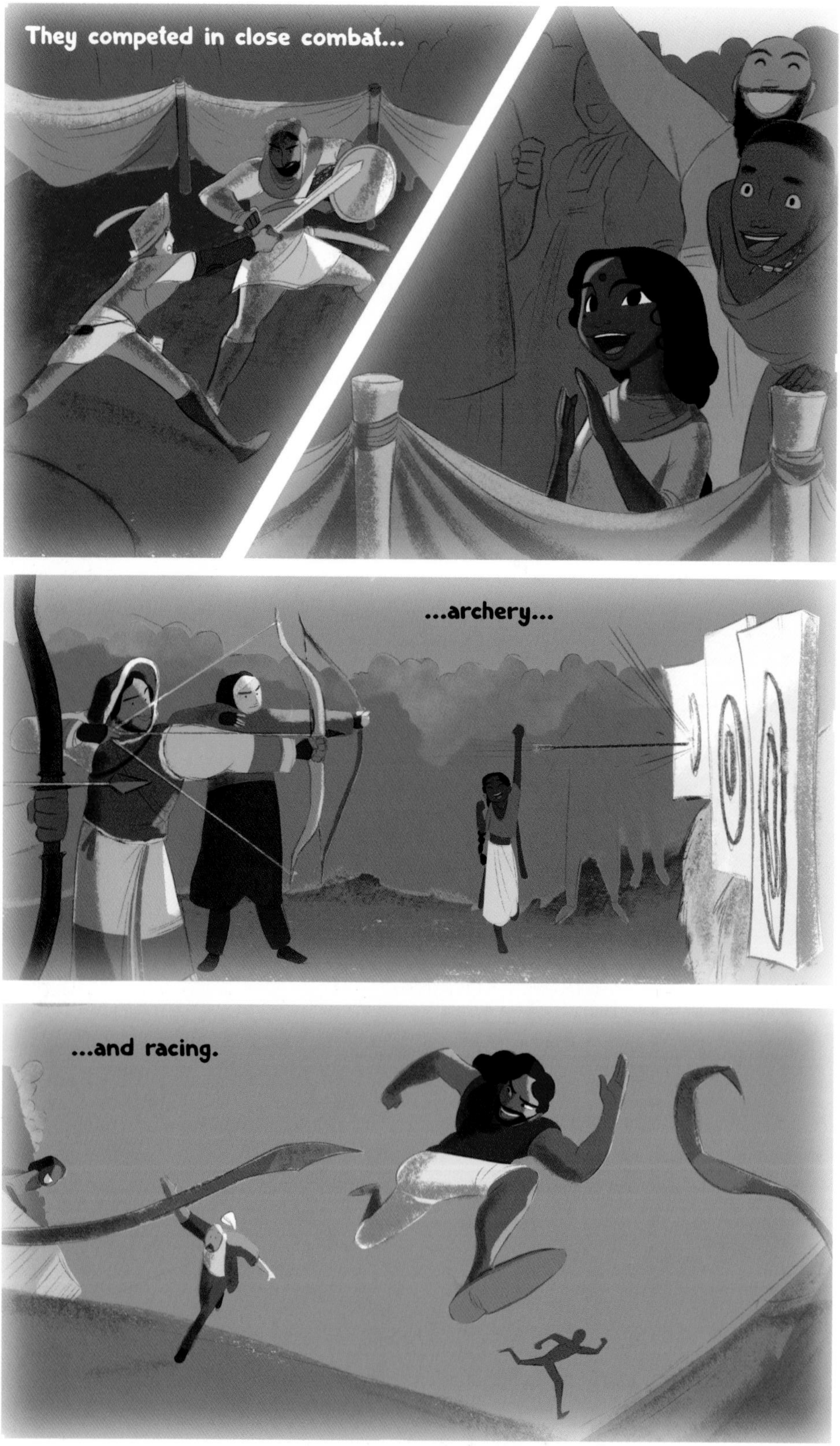
They competed in close combat...
...archery...
...and racing.

But the main event, the feat of all feats, was to be the face-off between man and tiger.

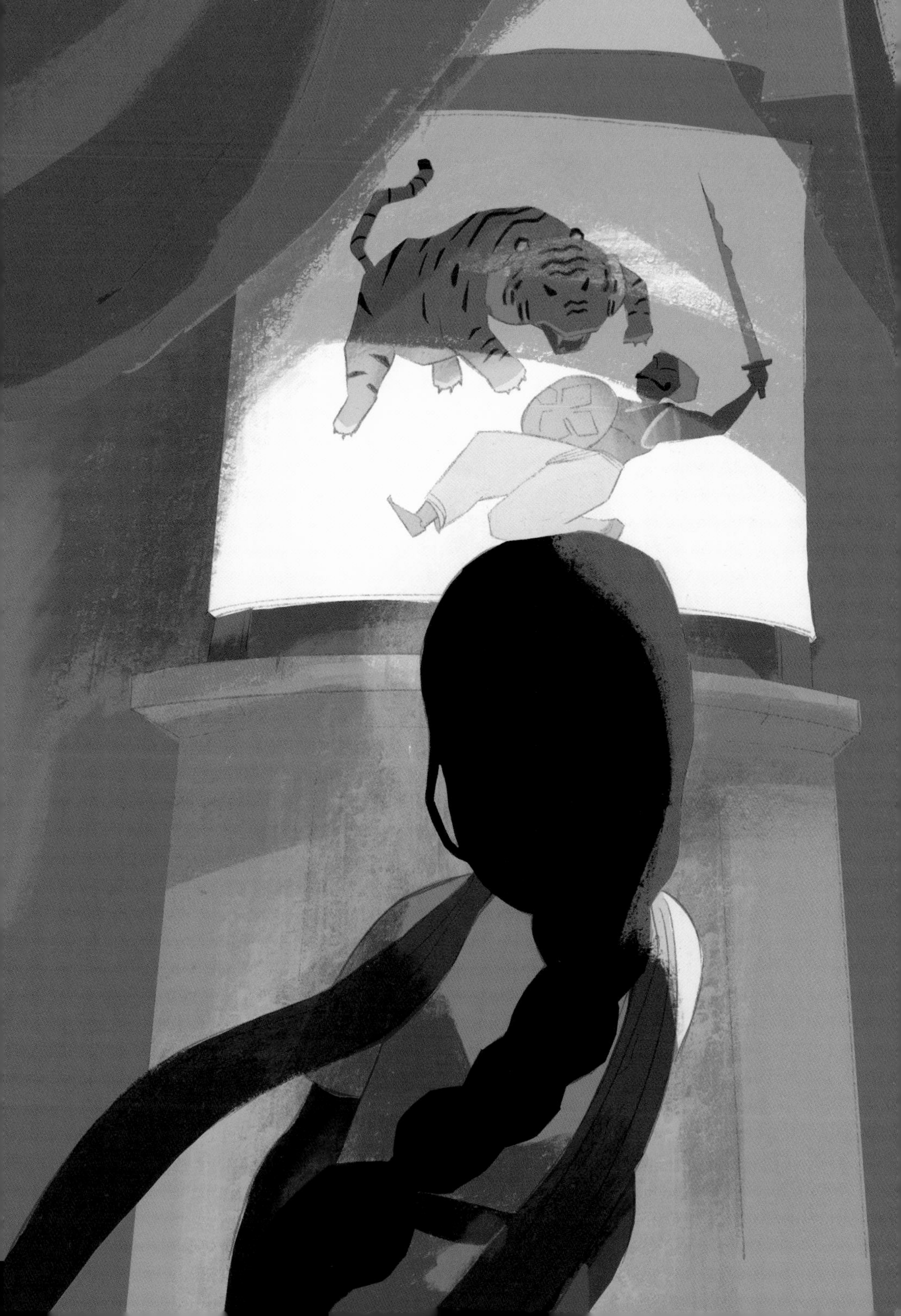

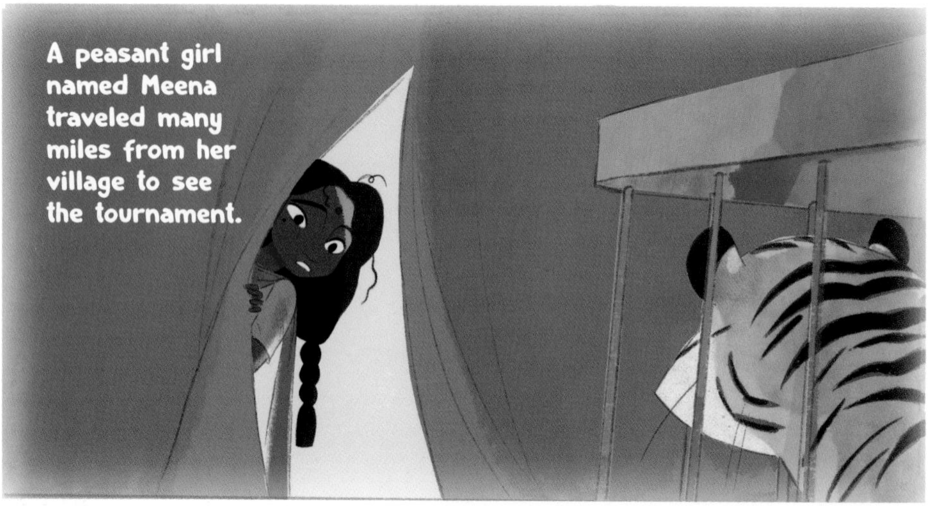
A peasant girl named Meena traveled many miles from her village to see the tournament.

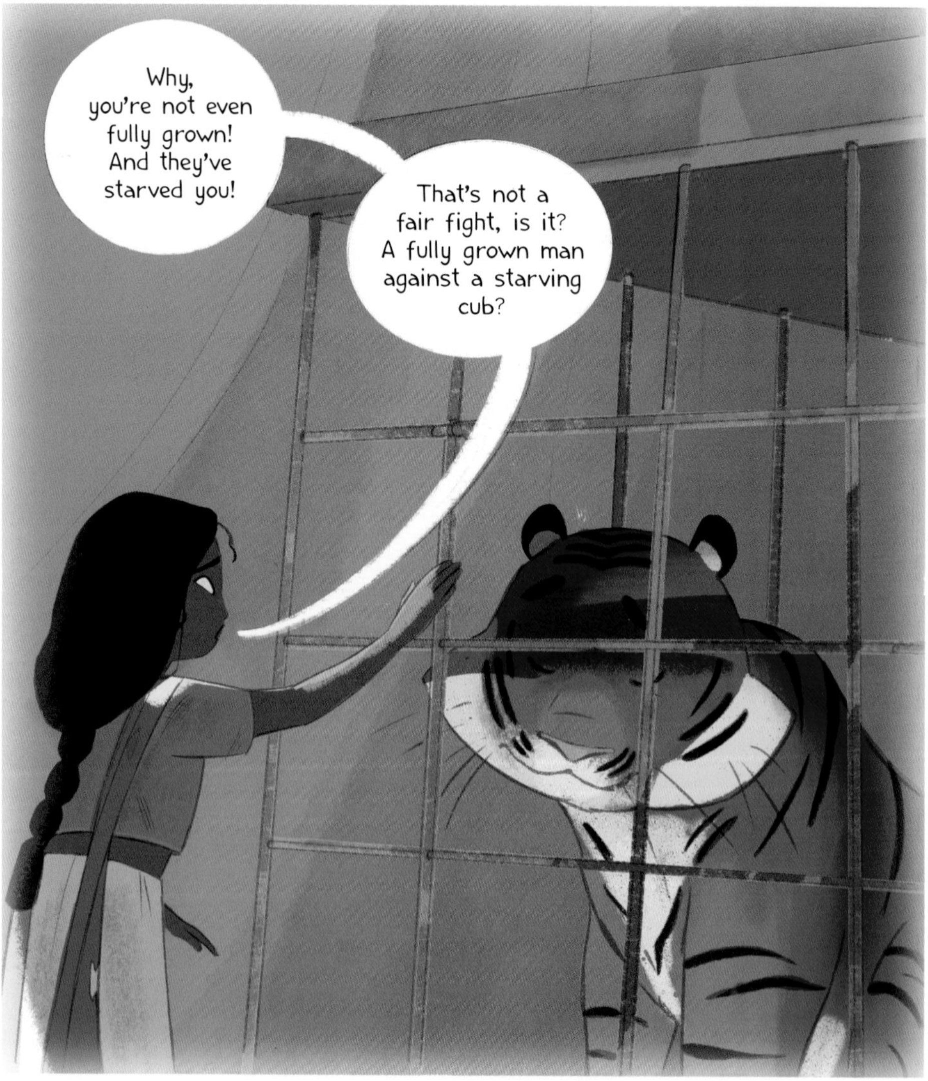
Why, you're not even fully grown! And they've starved you!
That's not a fair fight, is it? A fully grown man against a starving cub?

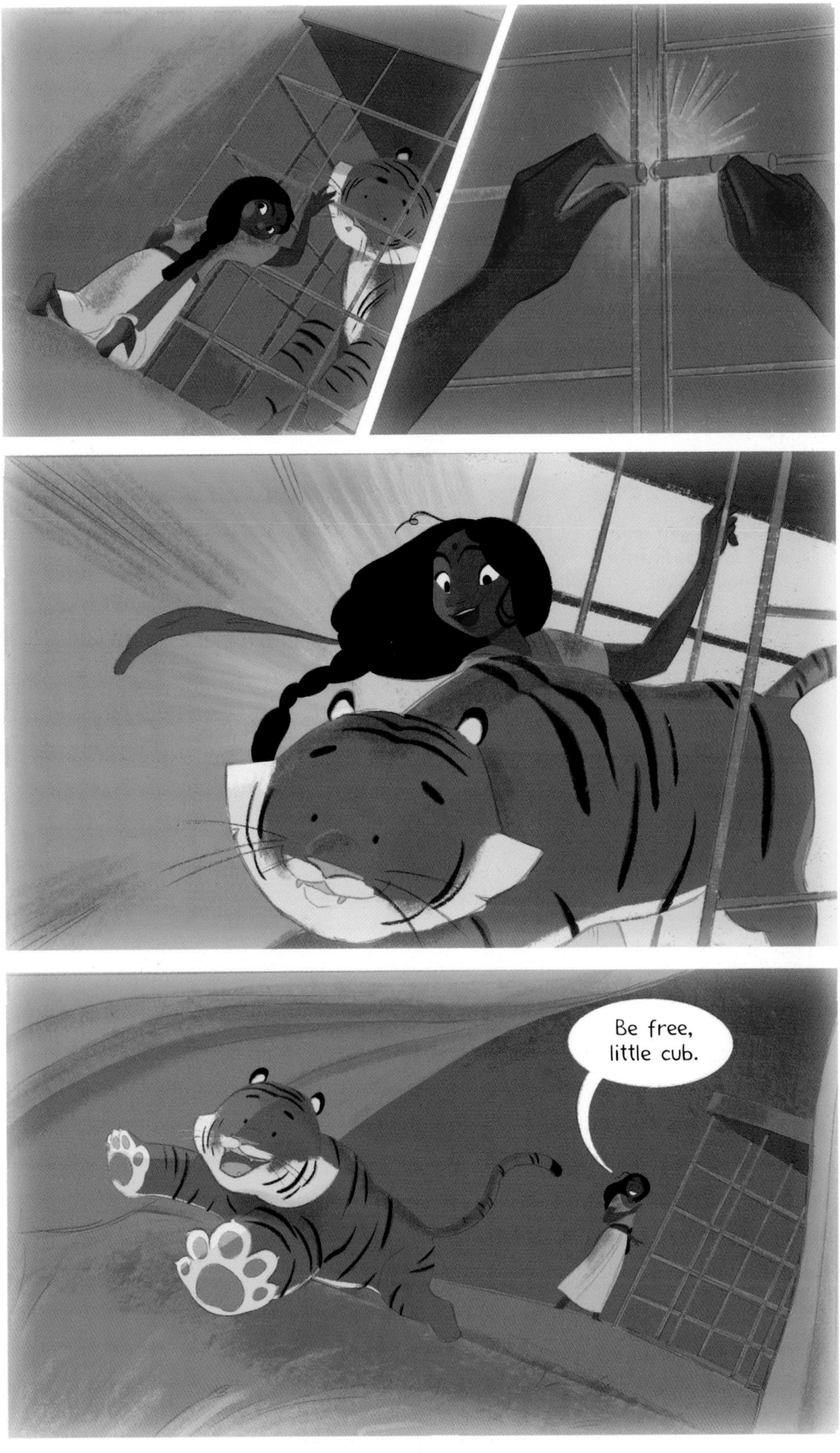
Be free,
little cub.

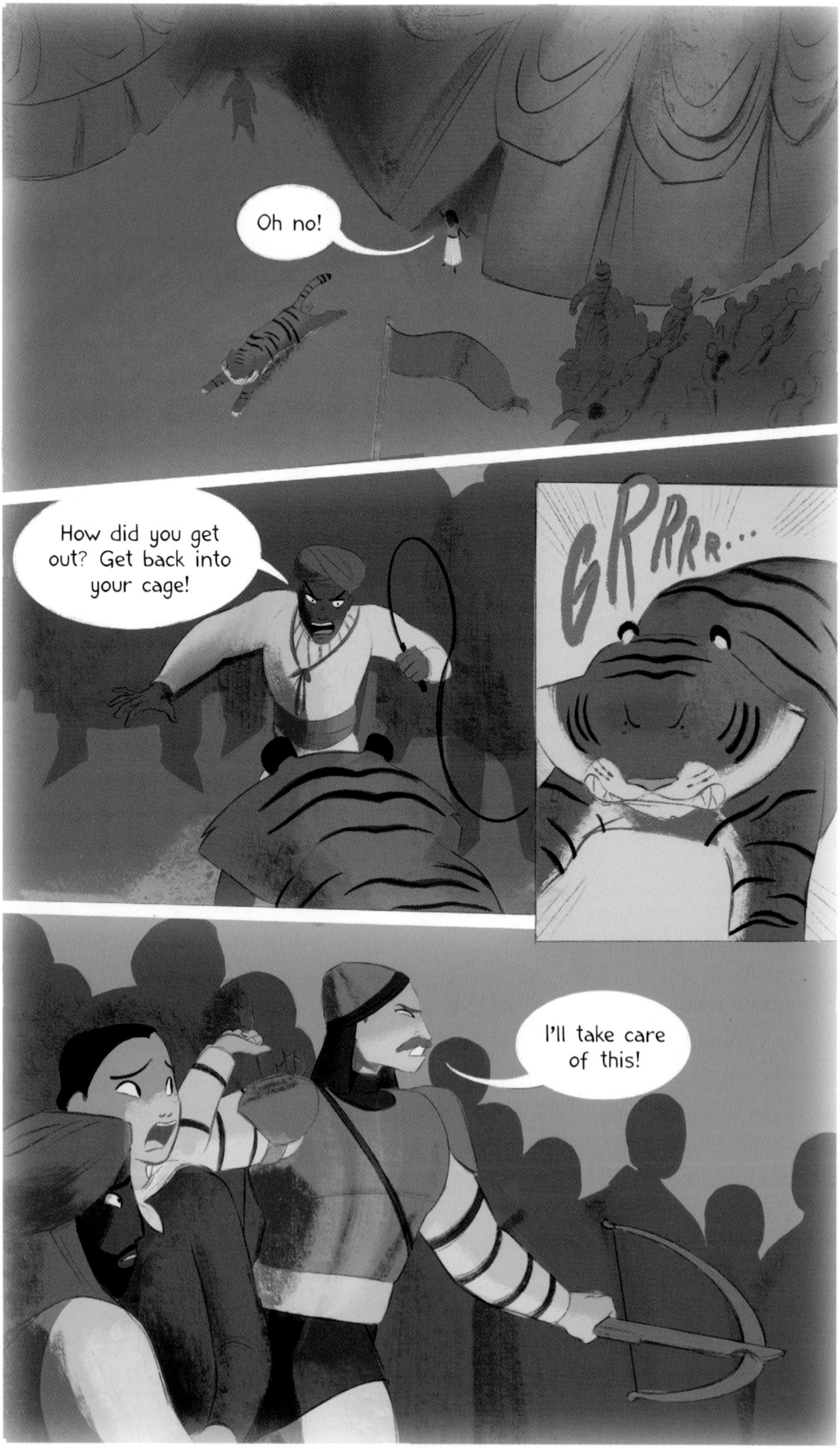
Oh no!
How did you get out? Get back into your cage!
GRRRR...
I'll take care of this!

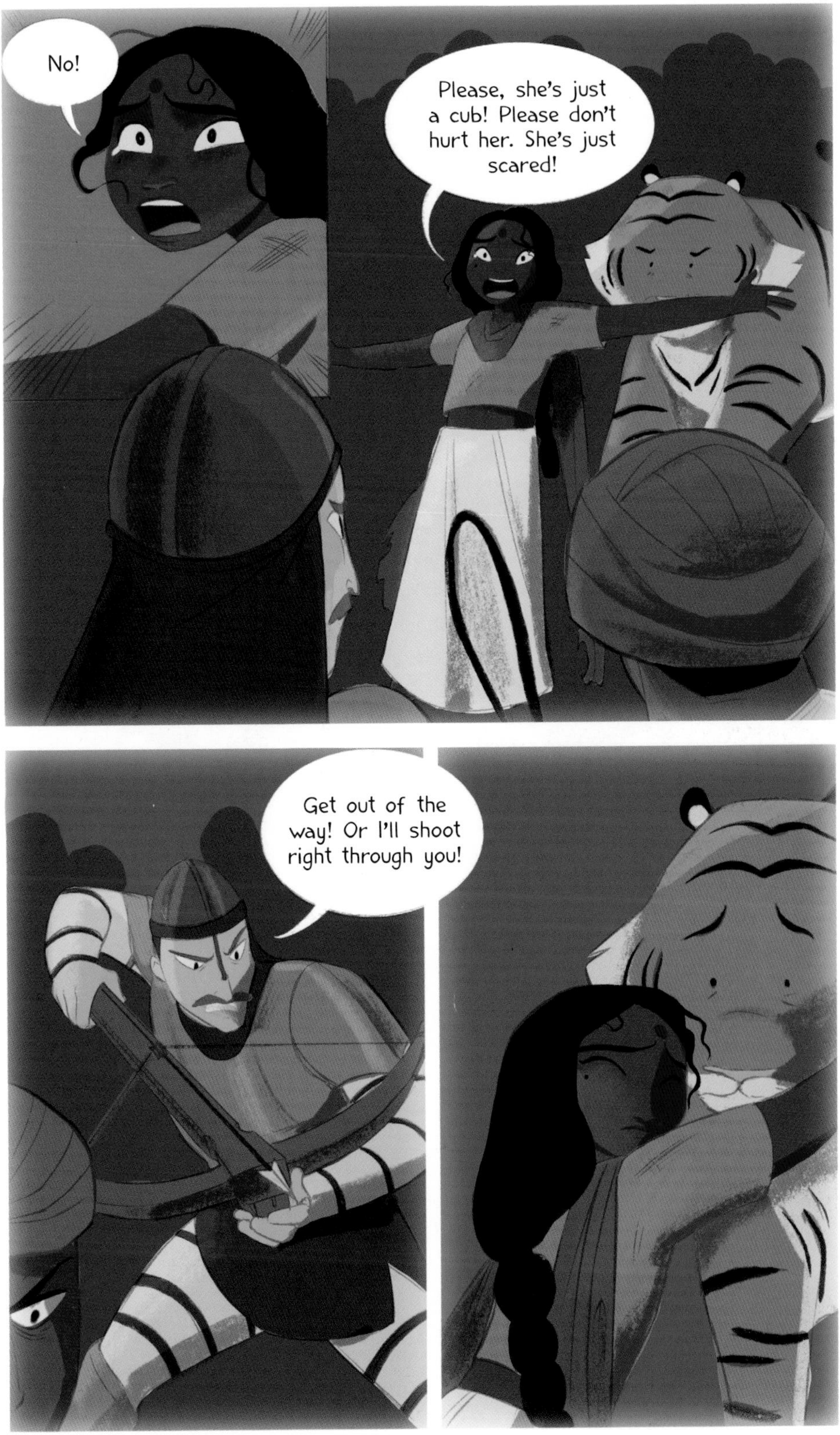
No!
Please, she's just a cub! Please don't hurt her. She's just scared!
Get out of the way! Or I'll shoot right through you!

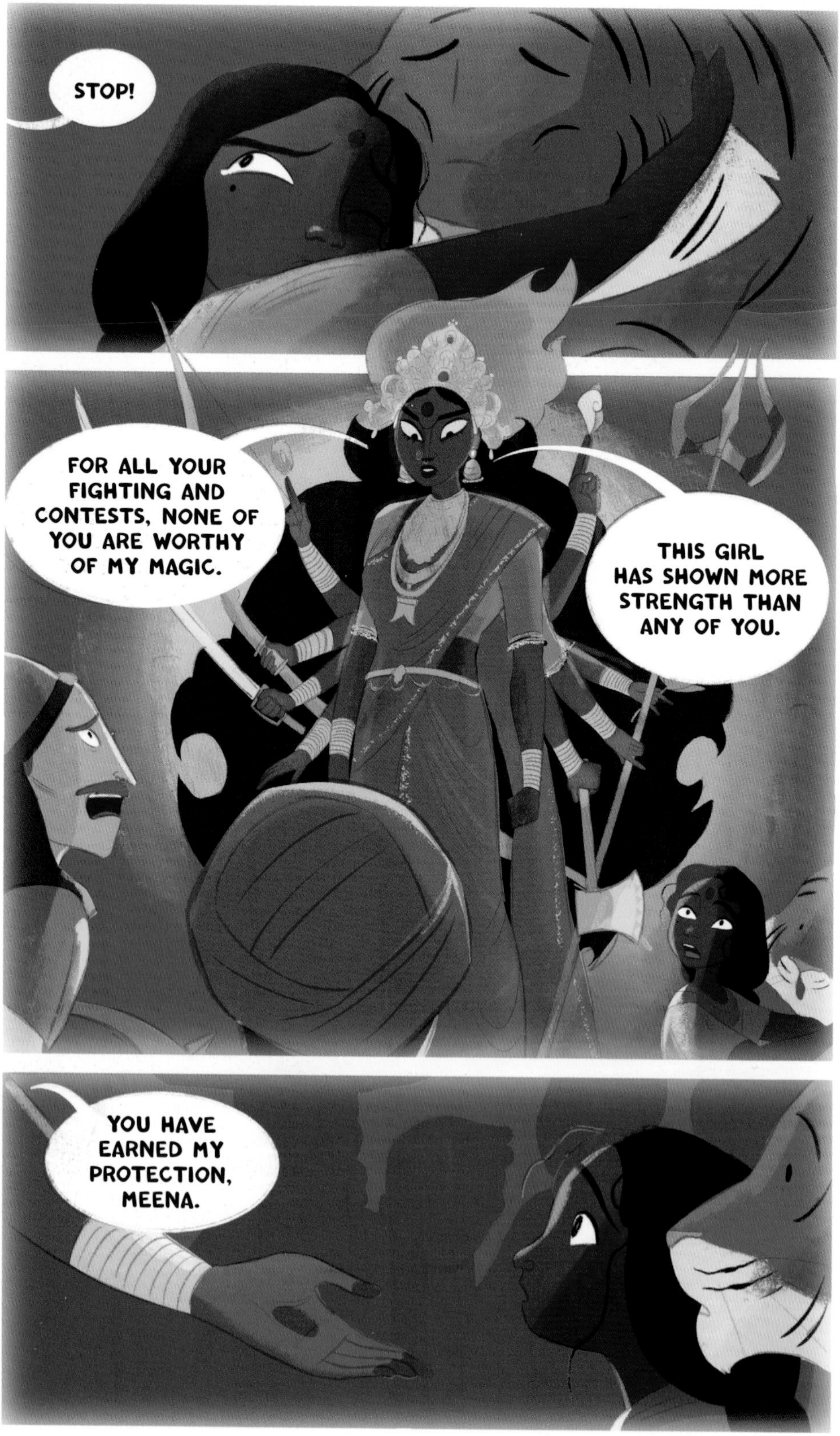
STOP!
FOR ALL YOUR FIGHTING AND CONTESTS, NONE OF YOU ARE WORTHY OF MY MAGIC.
THIS GIRL HAS SHOWN MORE STRENGTH THAN ANY OF YOU.
YOU HAVE EARNED MY PROTECTION, MEENA.

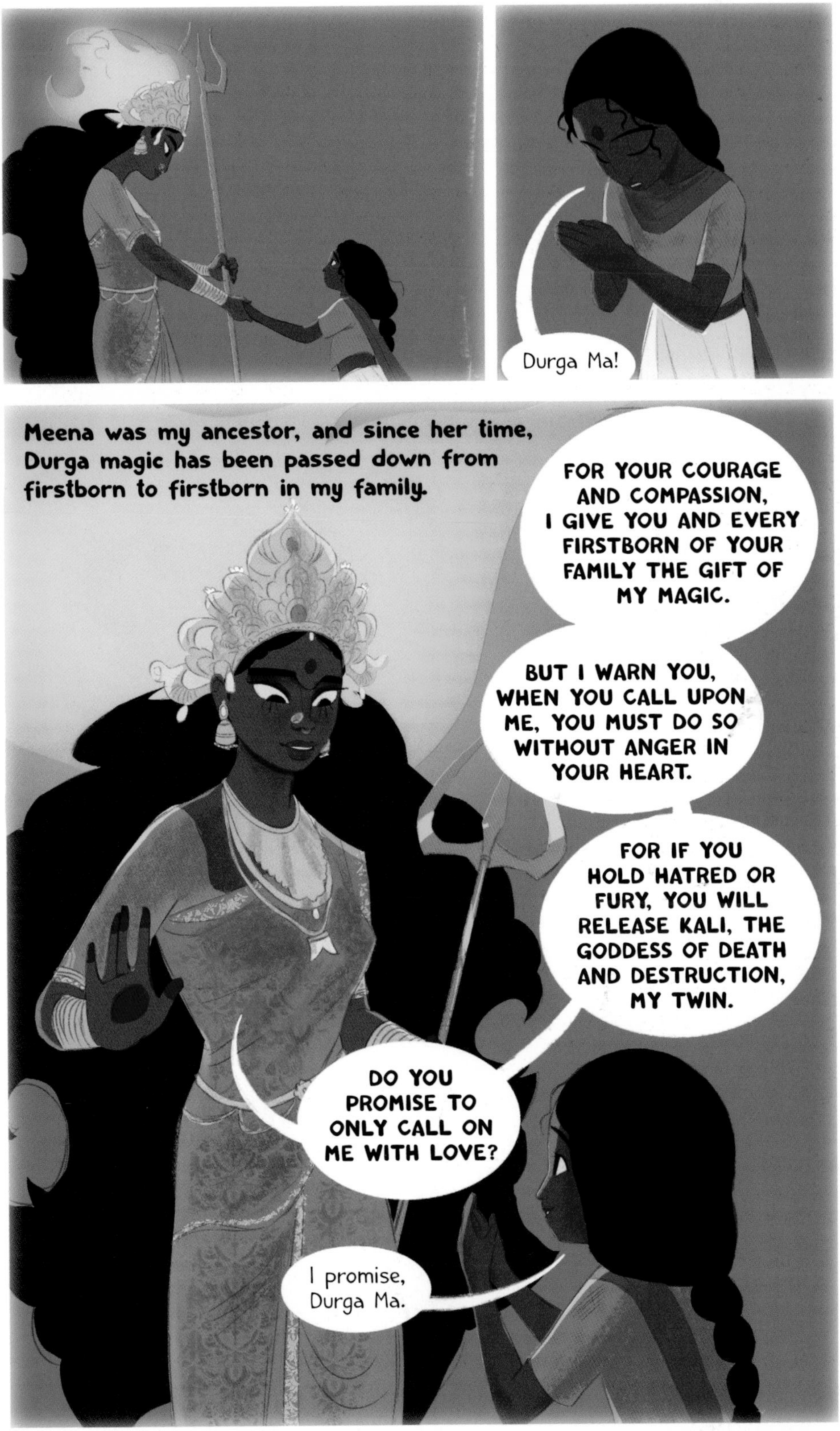
Durga Ma!
Meena was my ancestor, and since her time, Durga magic has been passed down from firstborn to firstborn in my family.
FOR YOUR COURAGE AND COMPASSION, I GIVE YOU AND EVERY FIRSTBORN OF YOUR FAMILY THE GIFT OF MY MAGIC.
BUT I WARN YOU, WHEN YOU CALL UPON ME, YOU MUST DO SO WITHOUT ANGER IN YOUR HEART.
FOR IF YOU HOLD HATRED OR FURY, YOU WILL RELEASE KALI, THE GODDESS OF DEATH AND DESTRUCTION, MY TWIN.
DO YOU PROMISE TO ONLY CALL ON ME WITH LOVE?
I promise, Durga Ma.

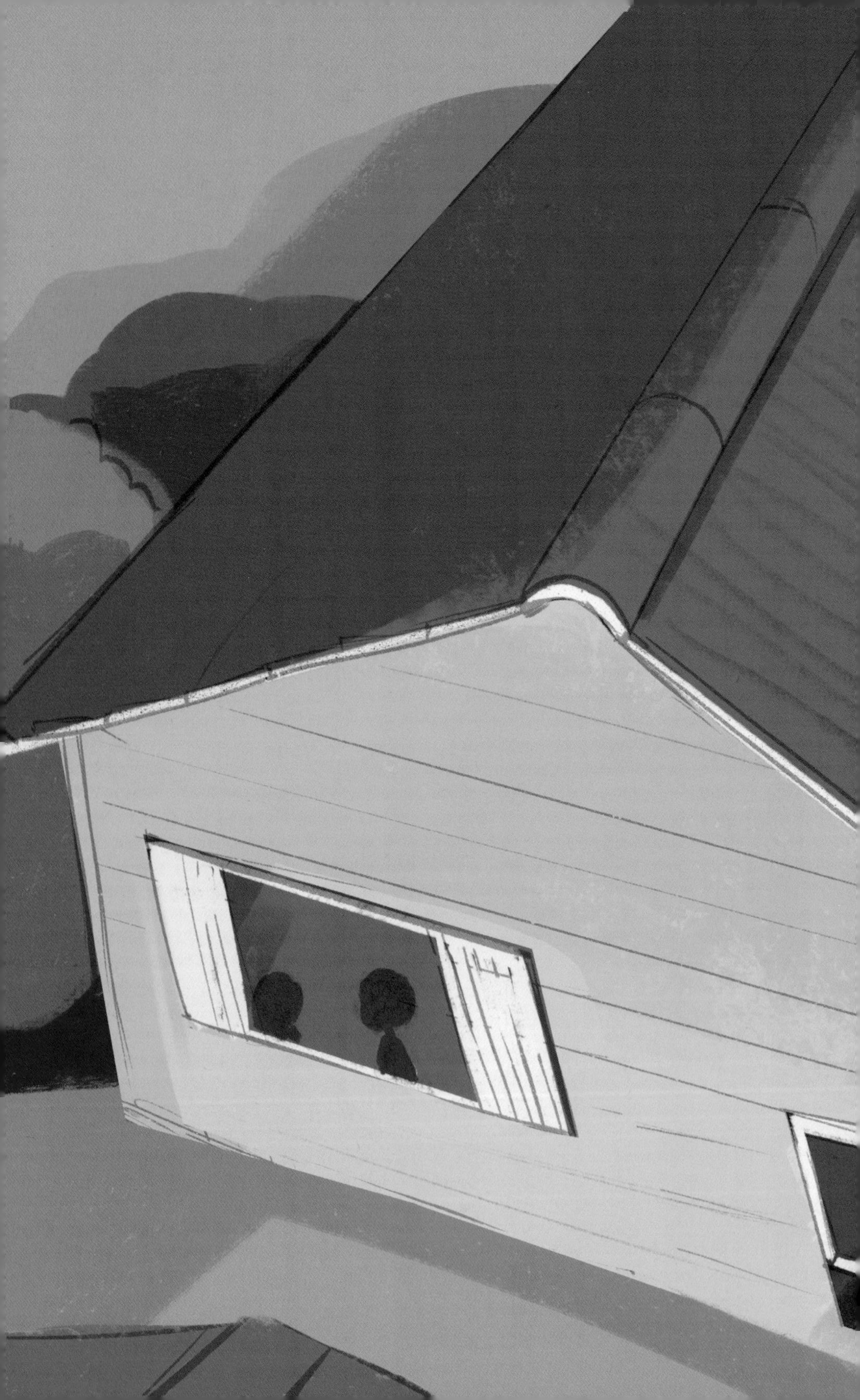

# Chapter 2

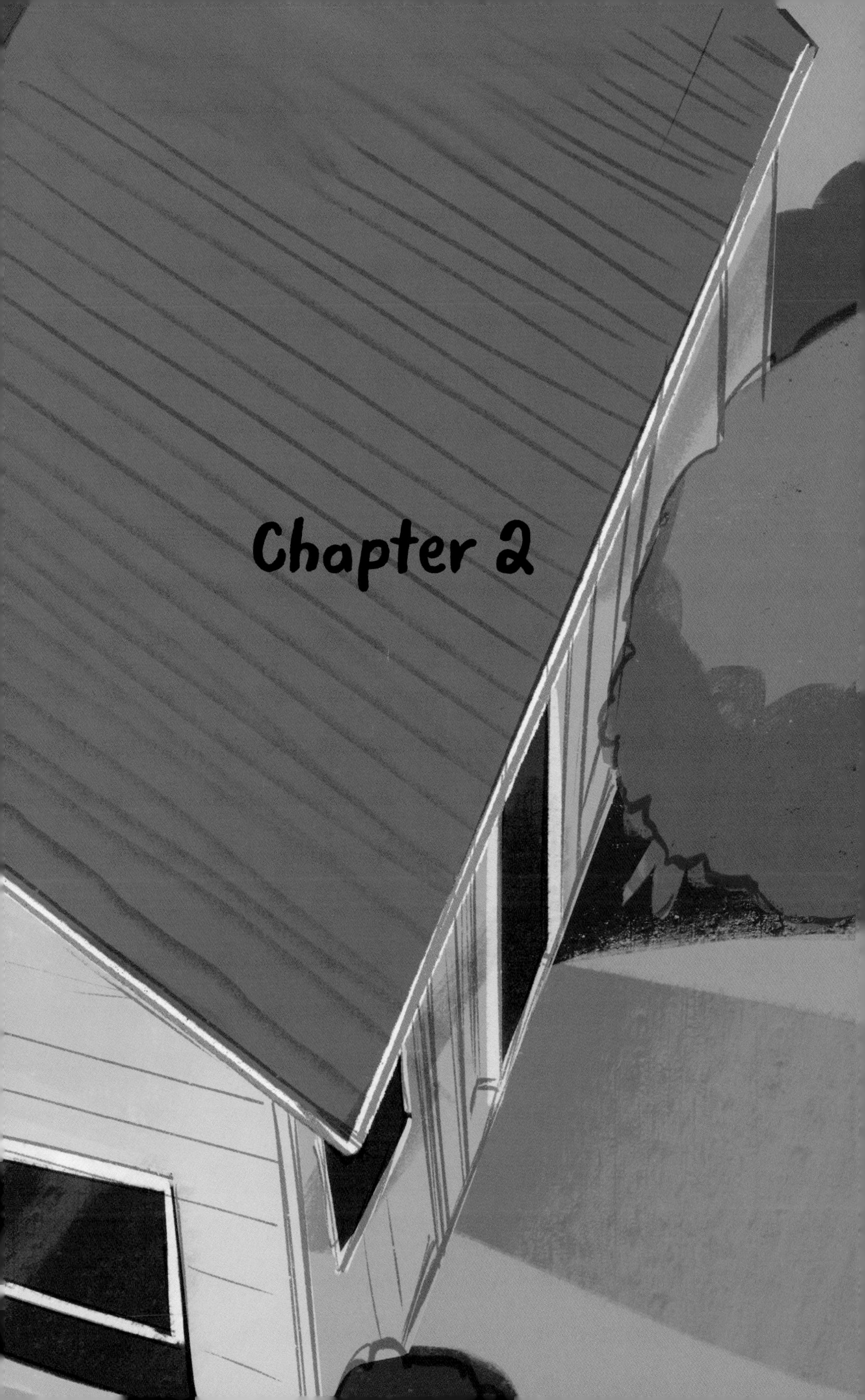

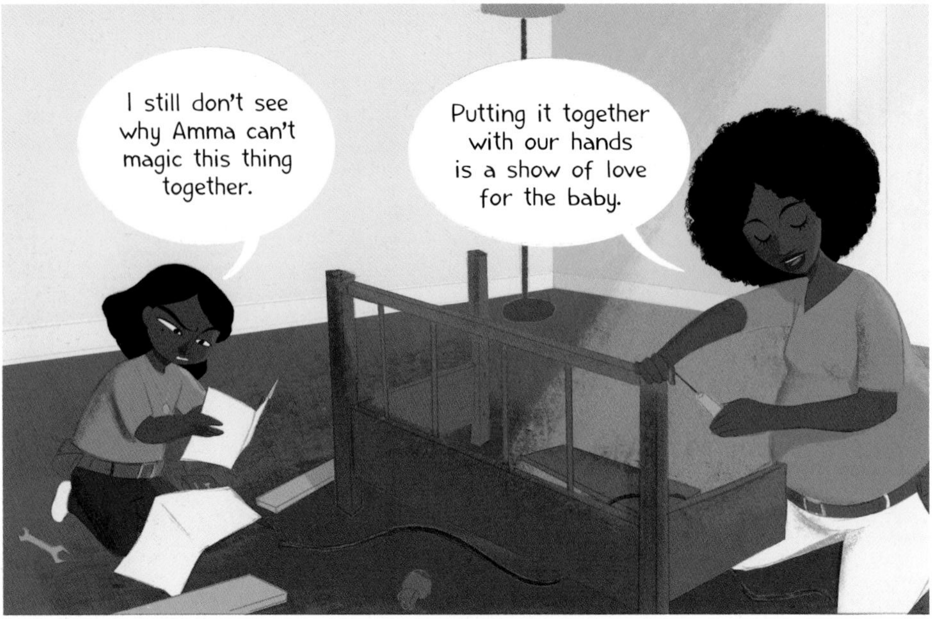
I still don't see why Amma can't magic this thing together.
Putting it together with our hands is a show of love for the baby.

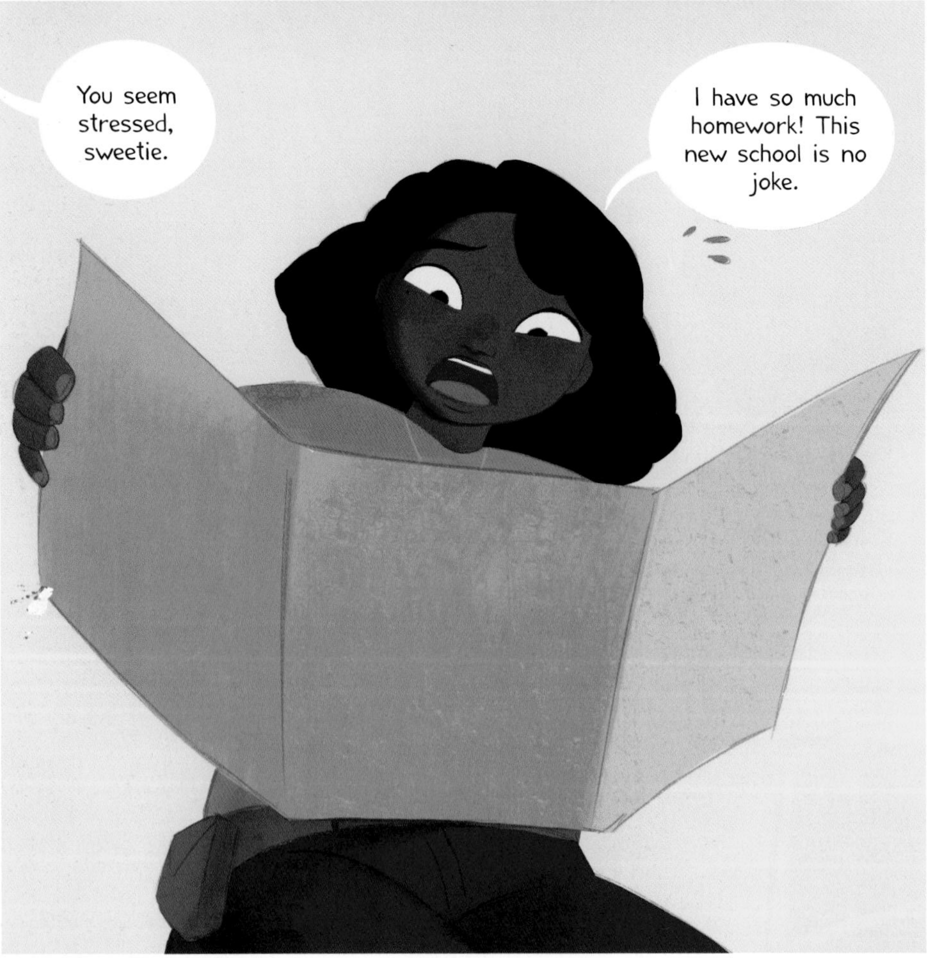
You seem stressed, sweetie.
I have so much homework! This new school is no joke.

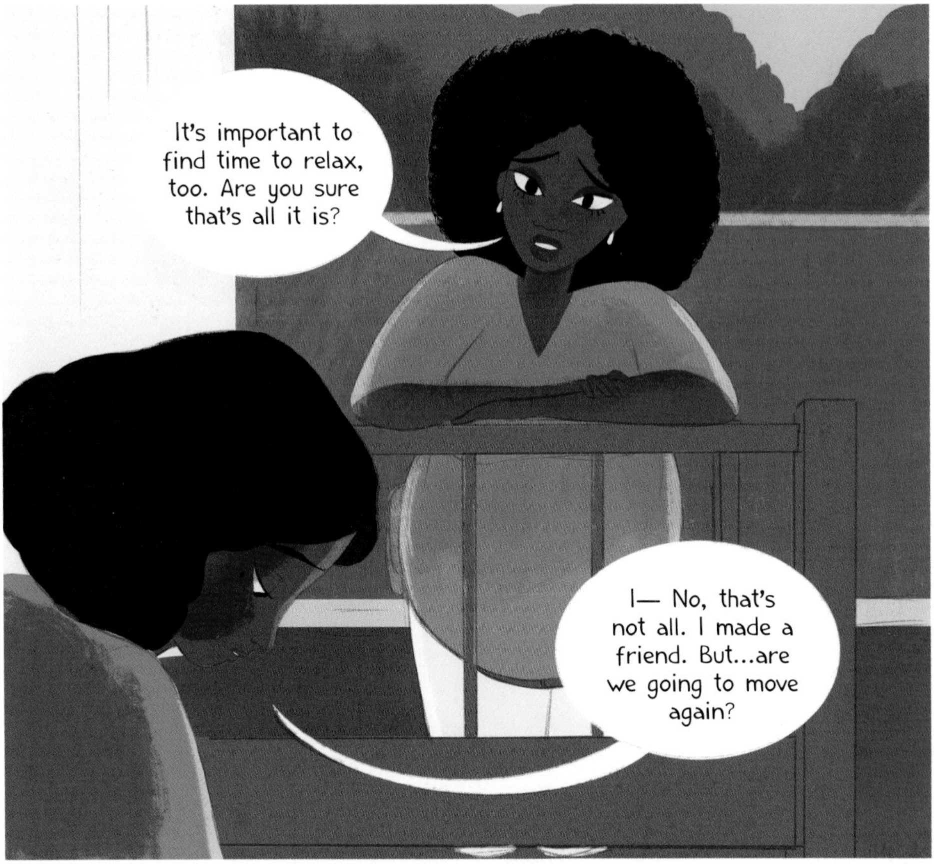
It's important to find time to relax, too. Are you sure that's all it is?
I— No, that's not all. I made a friend. But...are we going to move again?

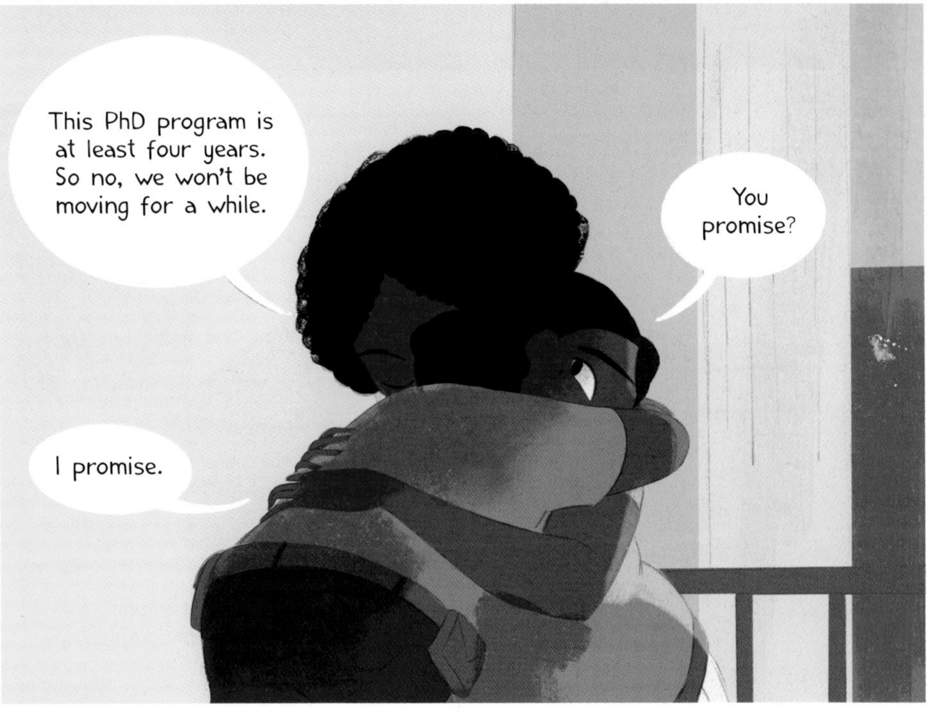
This PhD program is at least four years. So no, we won't be moving for a while.
You promise?
I promise.

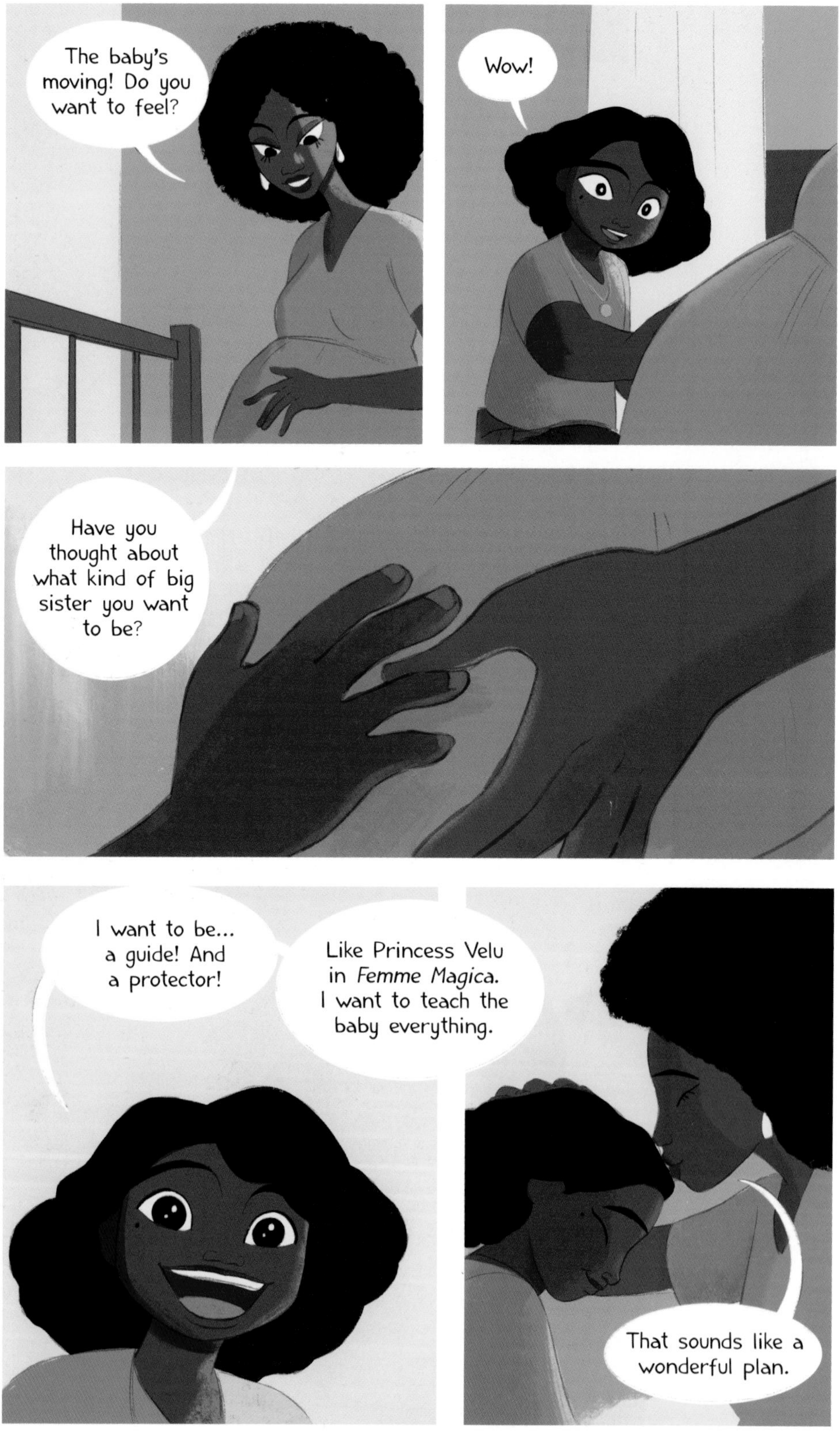

The baby's moving! Do you want to feel?
Wow!
Have you thought about what kind of big sister you want to be?
I want to be... a guide! And a protector!
Like Princess Velu in *Femme Magica*. I want to teach the baby everything.
That sounds like a wonderful plan.

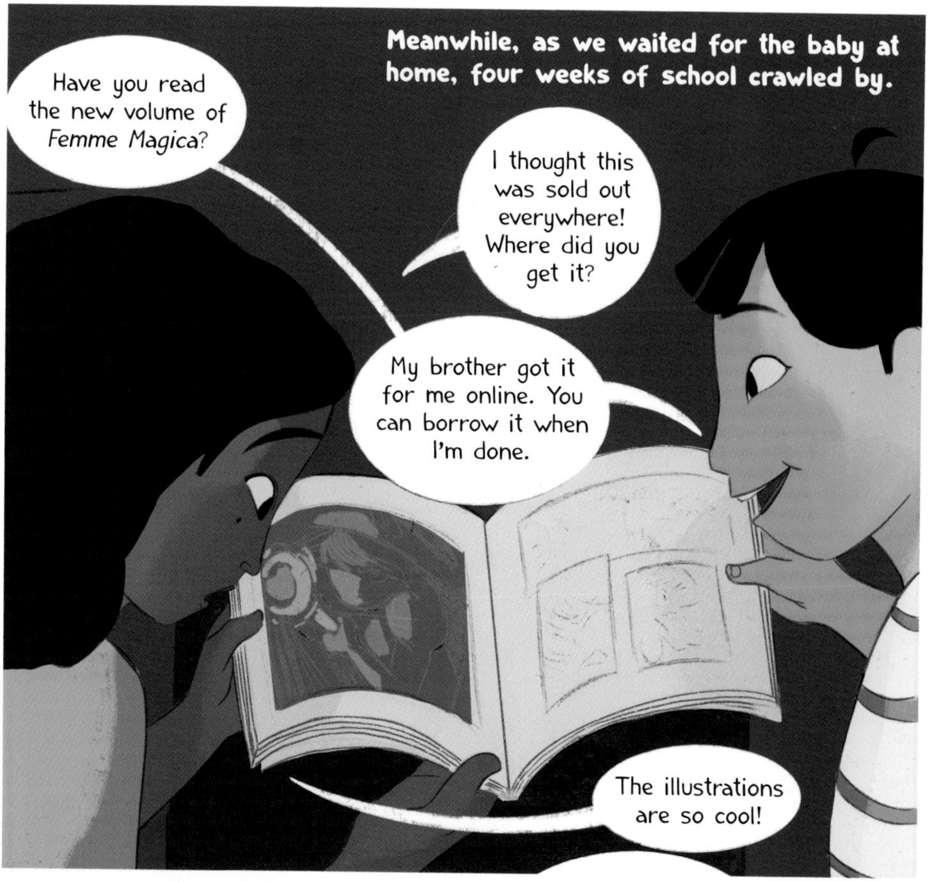
Meanwhile, as we waited for the baby at home, four weeks of school crawled by.
Have you read the new volume of Femme Magica?
I thought this was sold out everywhere! Where did you get it?
My brother got it for me online. You can borrow it when I'm done.
The illustrations are so cool!

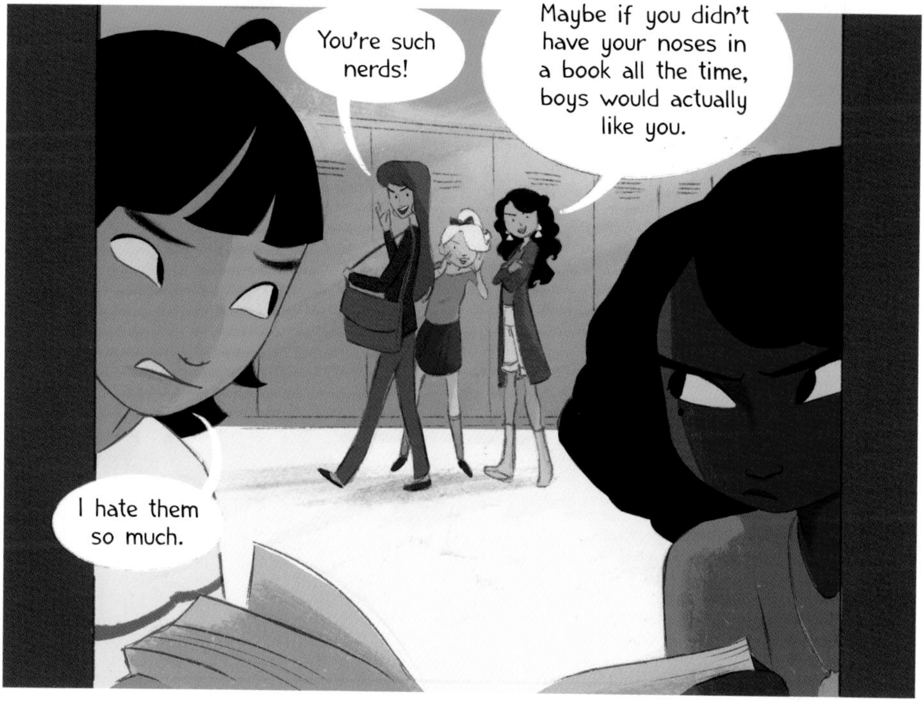
You're such nerds!
Maybe if you didn't have your noses in a book all the time, boys would actually like you.
I hate them so much.

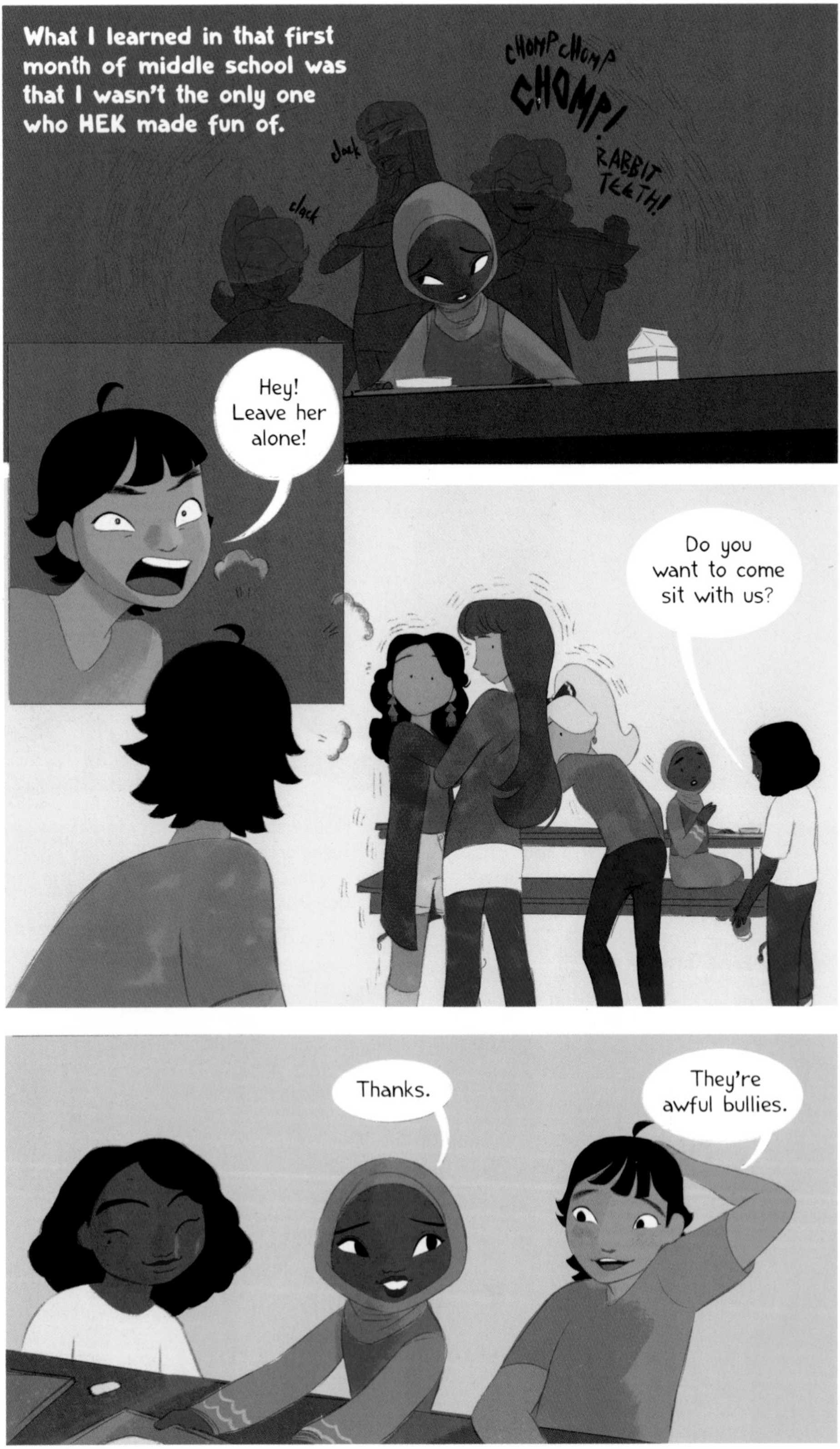
What I learned in that first month of middle school was that I wasn't the only one who HEK made fun of.
CHOMP CHOMP
CHOMP!
RABBIT TEETH!
clack
clack
Hey! Leave her alone!
Do you want to come sit with us?
Thanks.
They're awful bullies.

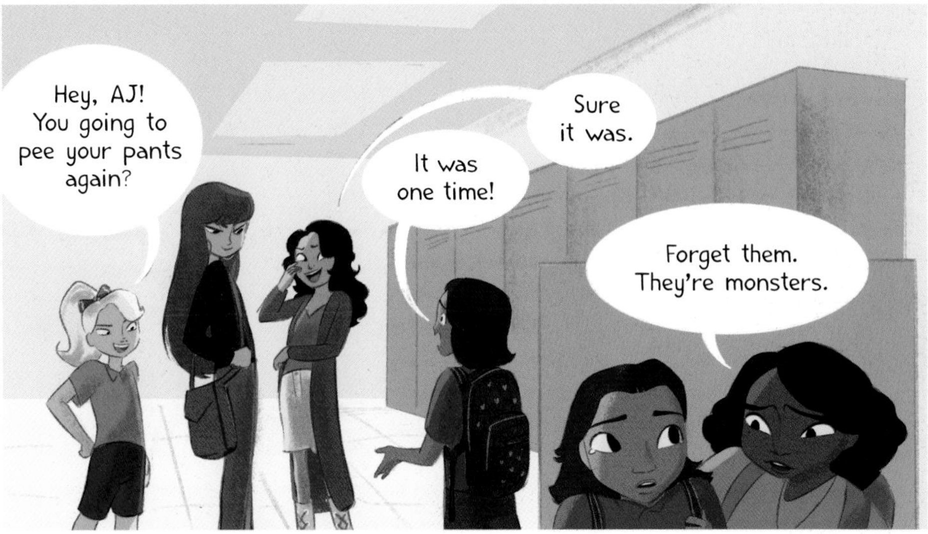
Hey, AJ! You going to pee your pants again?
It was one time!
Sure it was.
Forget them. They're monsters.

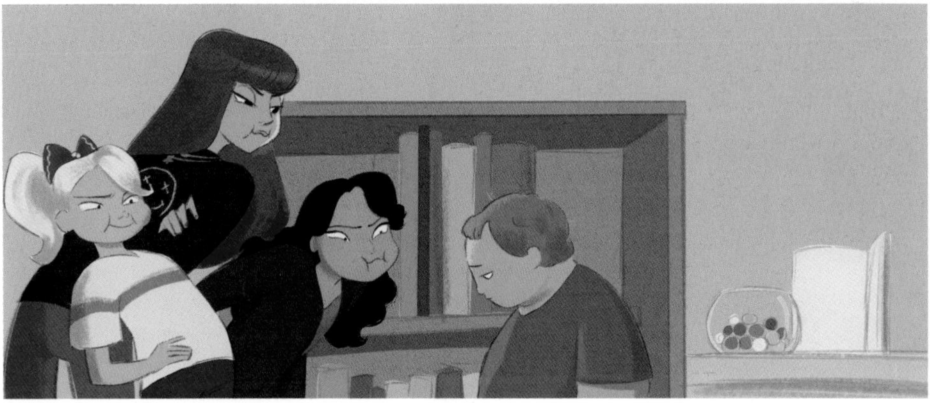

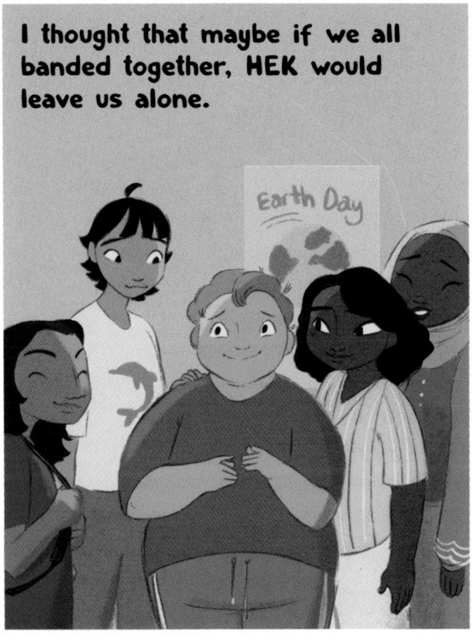
I thought that maybe if we all banded together, HEK would leave us alone.
Earth Day

**That didn't happen, but we did all become friends.**

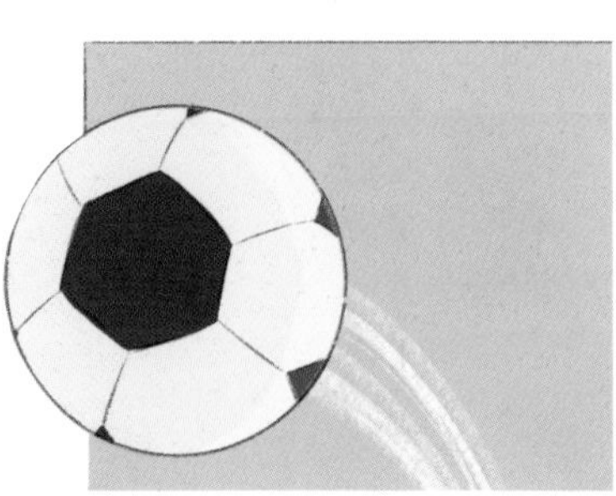

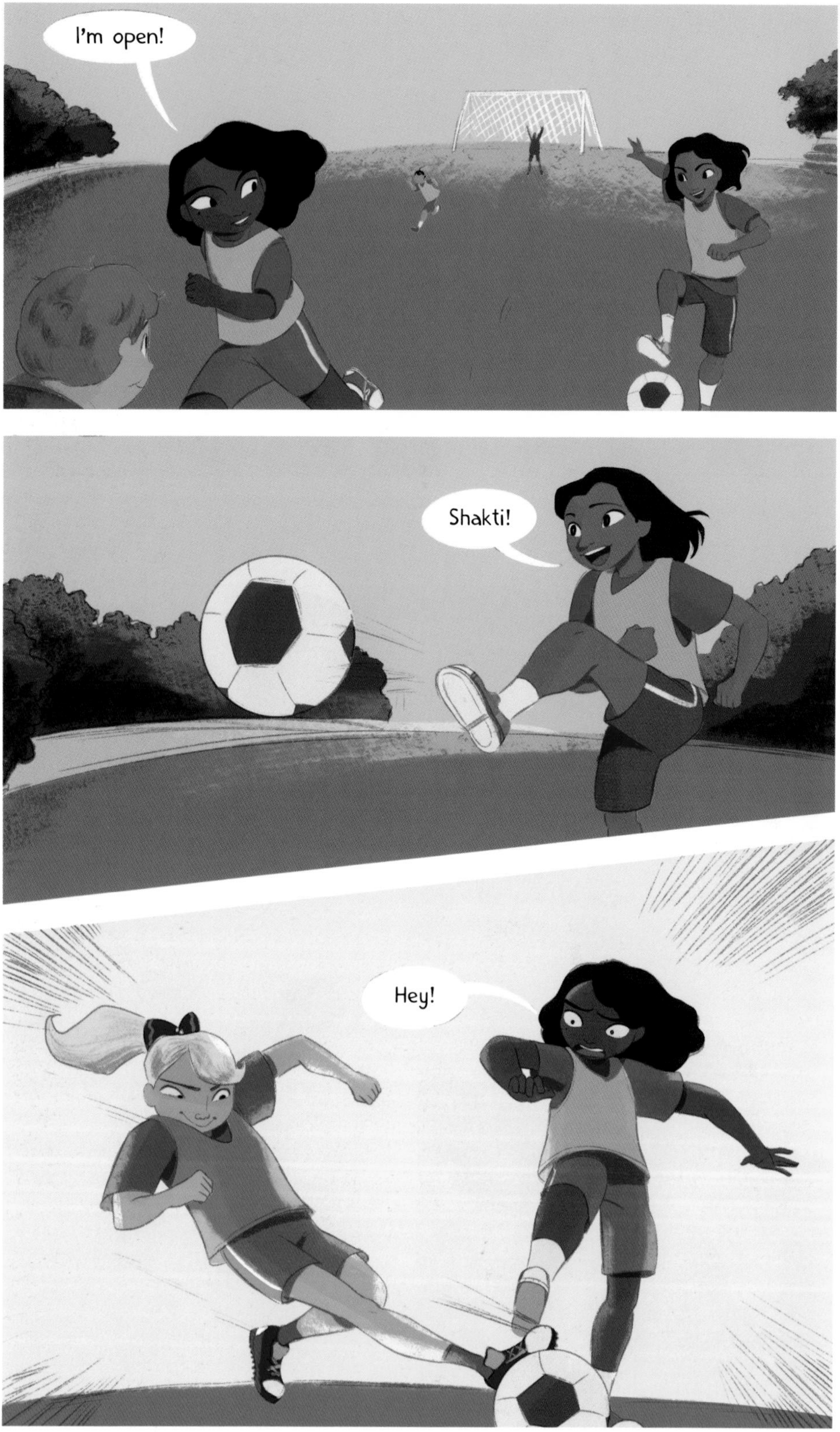
I'm open!
Shakti!
Hey!

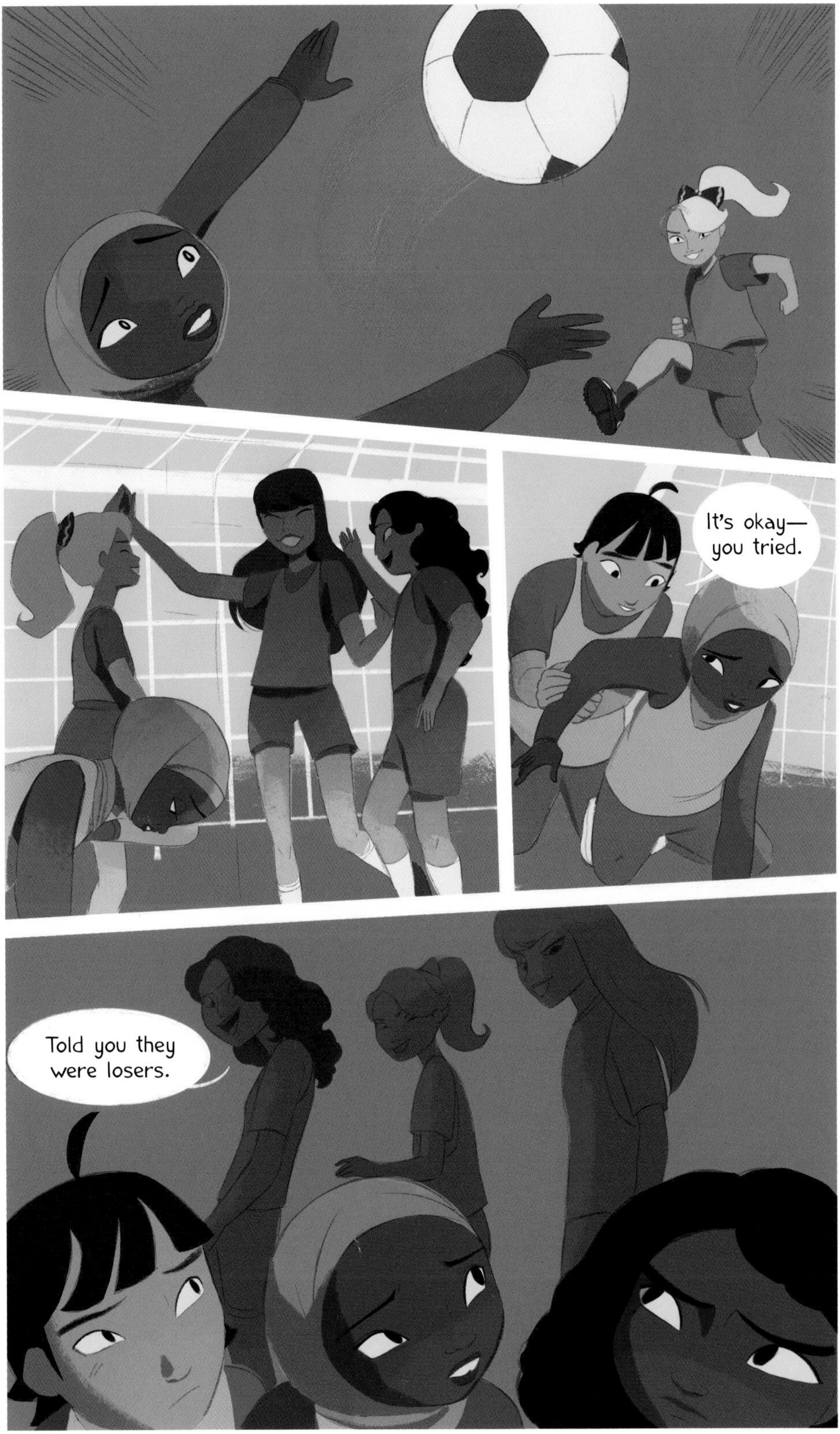
It's okay—
you tried.
Told you they
were losers.

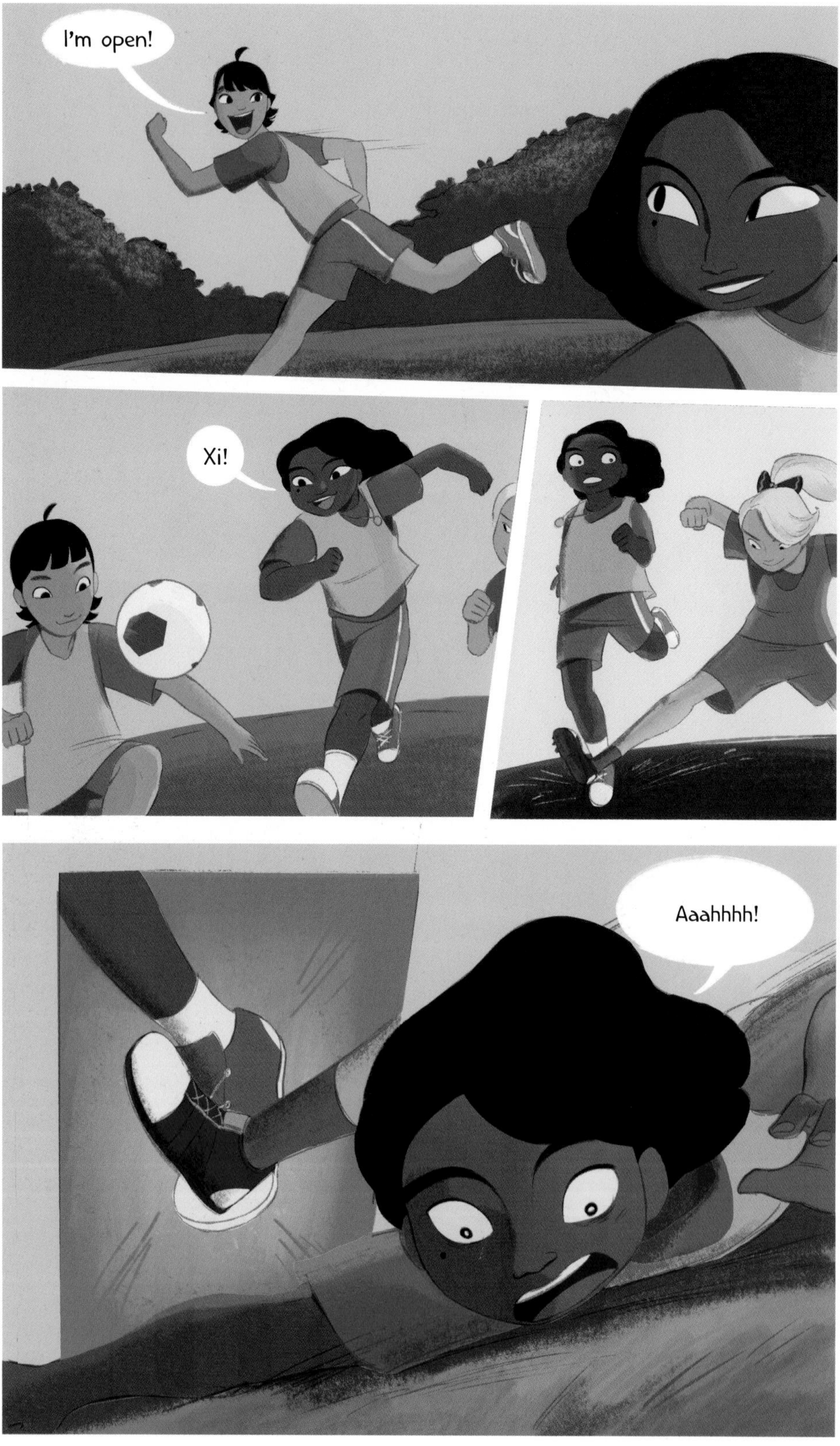
I'm open!
Xi!
Aaahhhh!

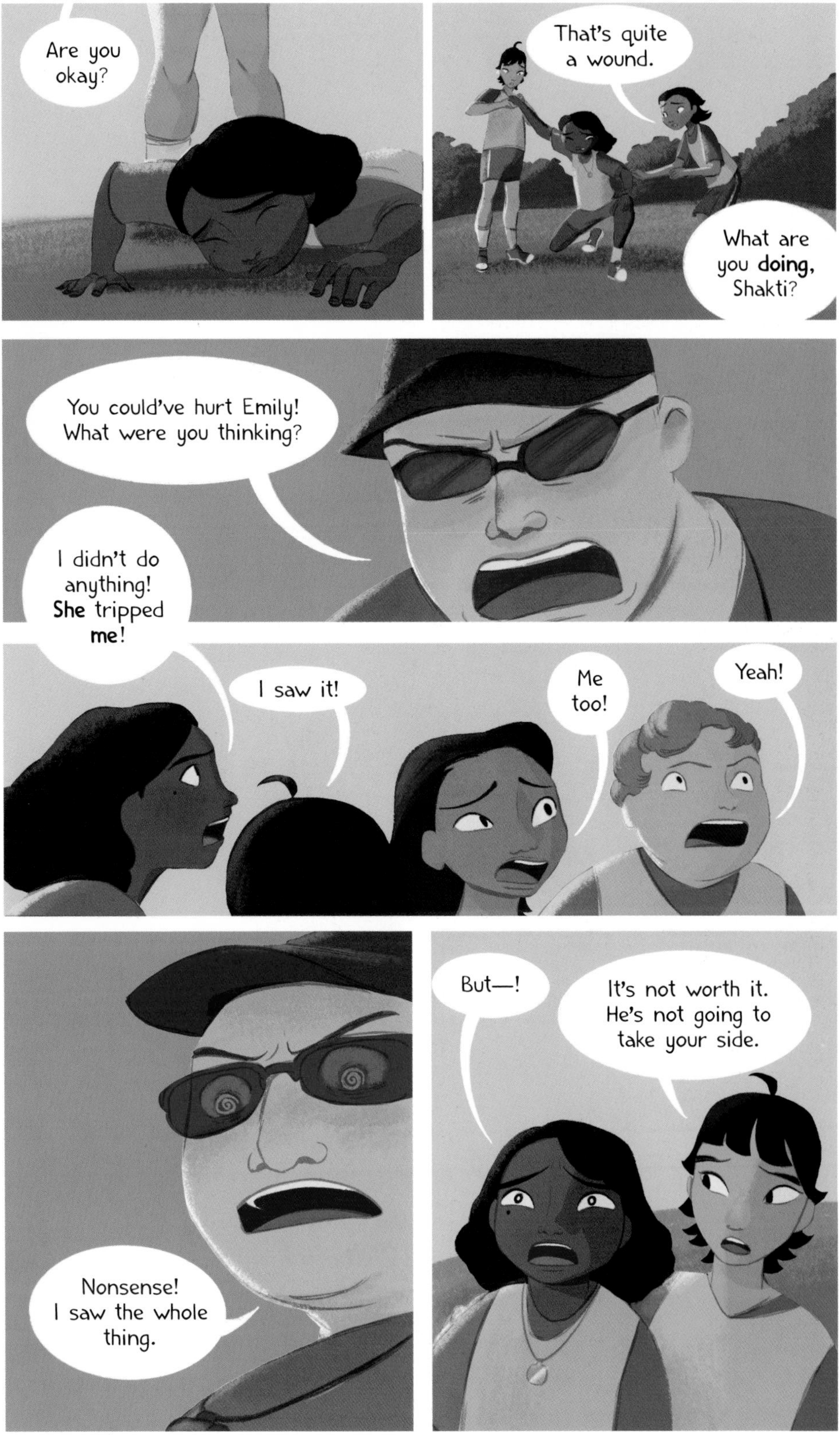
Are you okay?
That's quite a wound.
What are you **doing,** Shakti?
You could've hurt Emily! What were you thinking?
I didn't do anything! **She** tripped **me**!
I saw it!
Me too!
Yeah!
Nonsense! I saw the whole thing.
But—!
It's not worth it. He's not going to take your side.

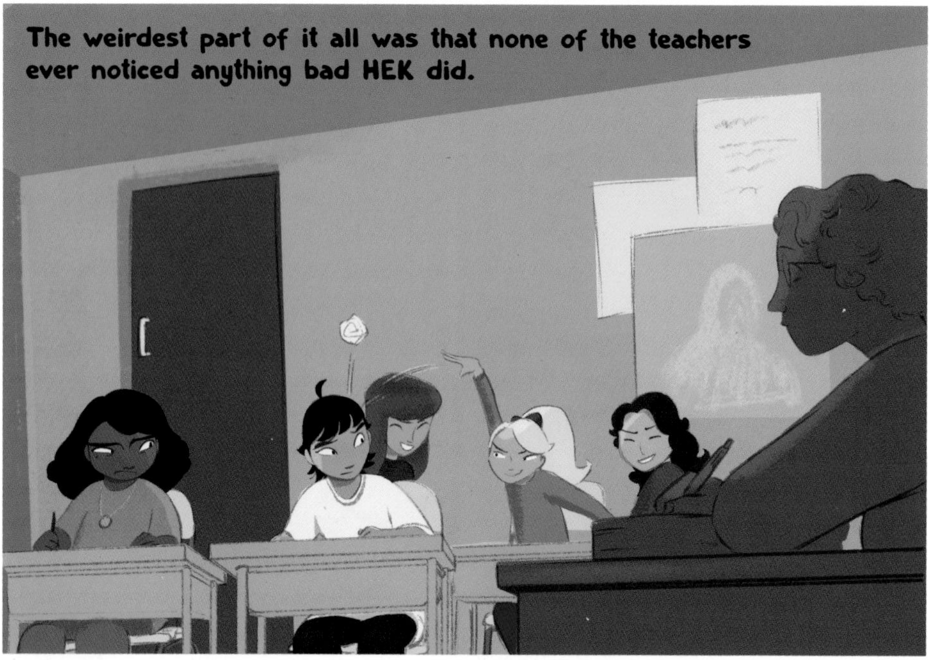
The weirdest part of it all was that none of the teachers ever noticed anything bad HEK did.

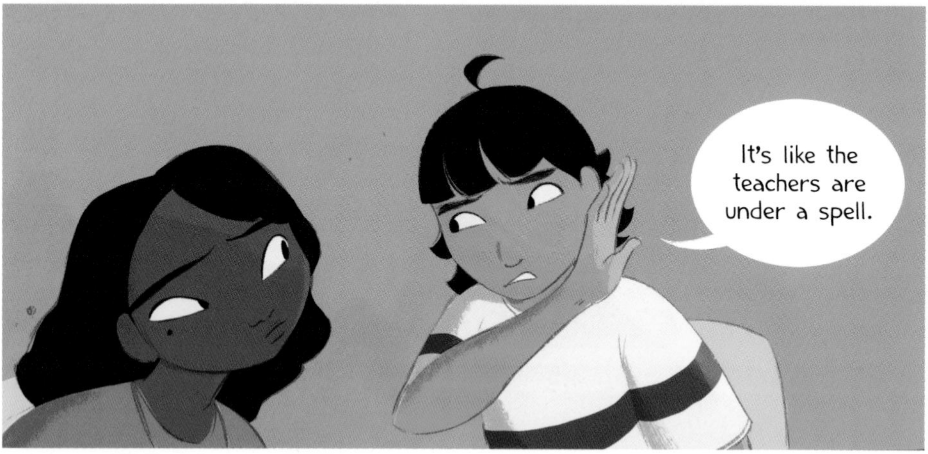
It's like the teachers are under a spell.

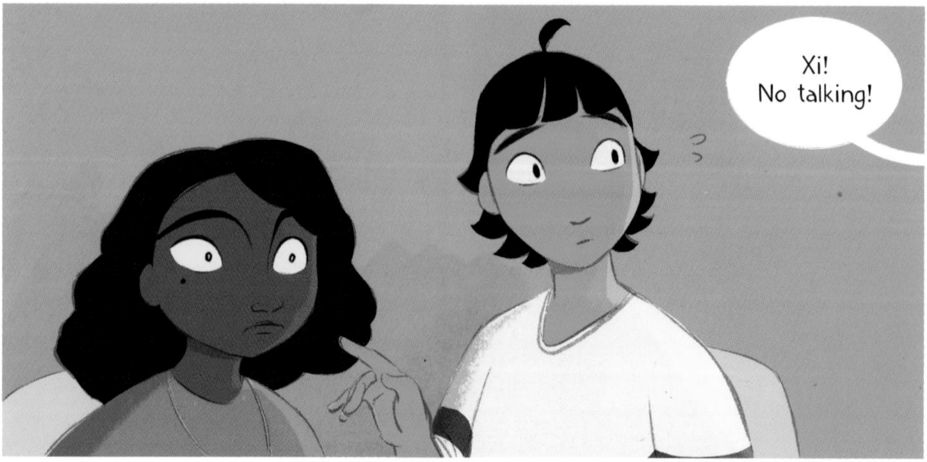
Xi!
No talking!

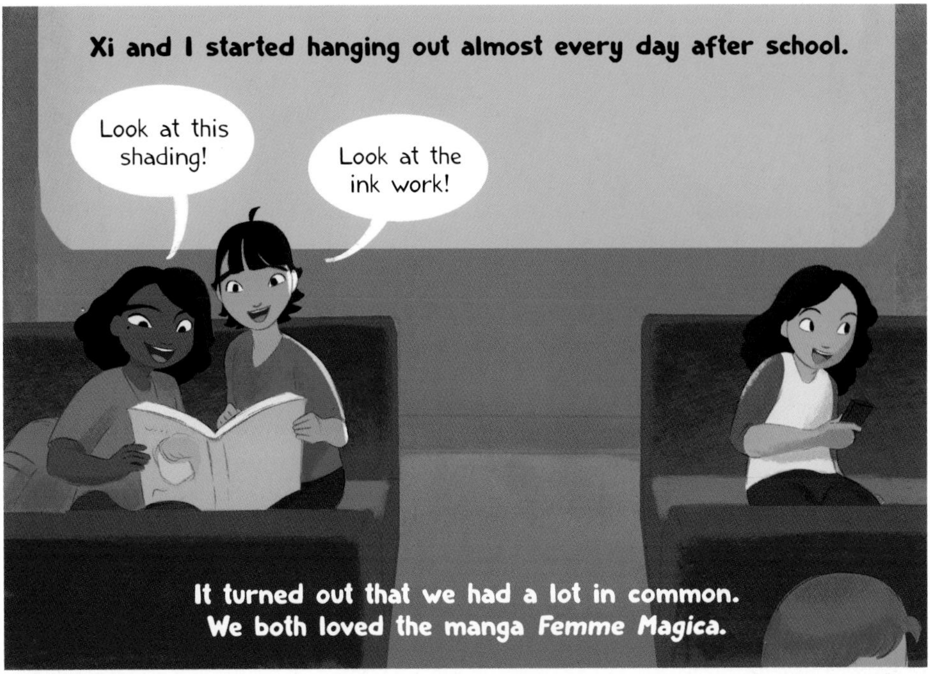
Xi and I started hanging out almost every day after school.
Look at this shading!
Look at the ink work!
It turned out that we had a lot in common.
We both loved the manga *Femme Magica*.

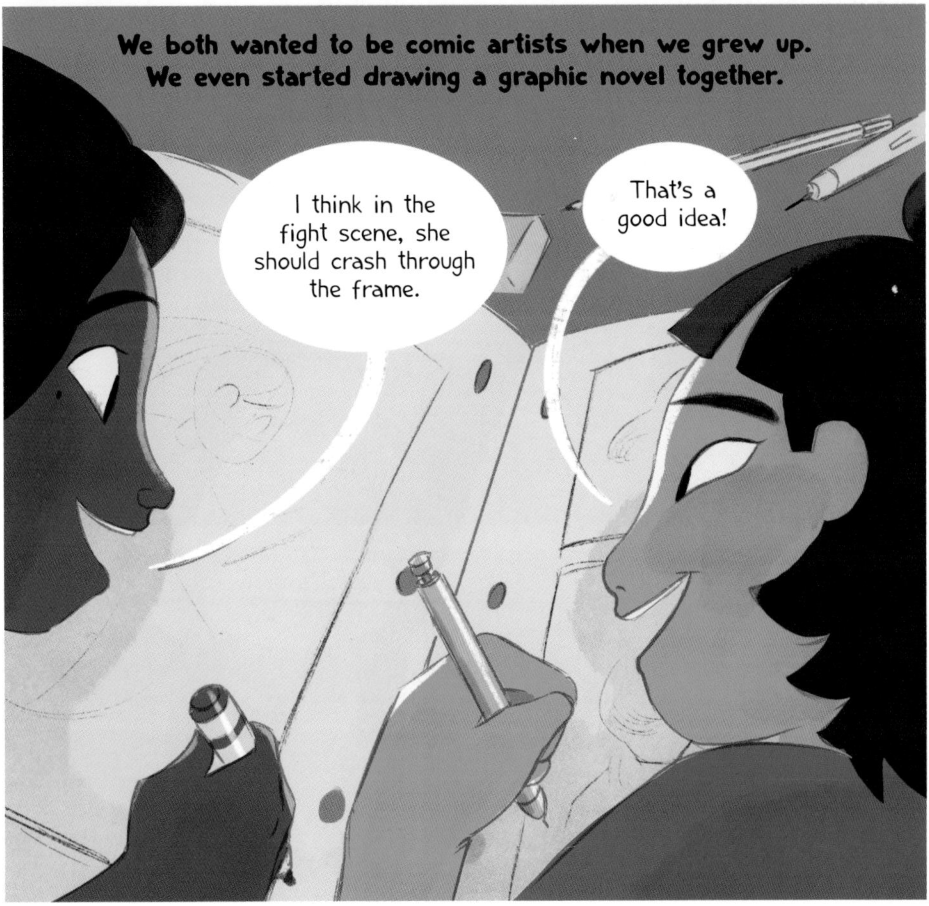
We both wanted to be comic artists when we grew up.
We even started drawing a graphic novel together.
I think in the fight scene, she should crash through the frame.
That's a good idea!

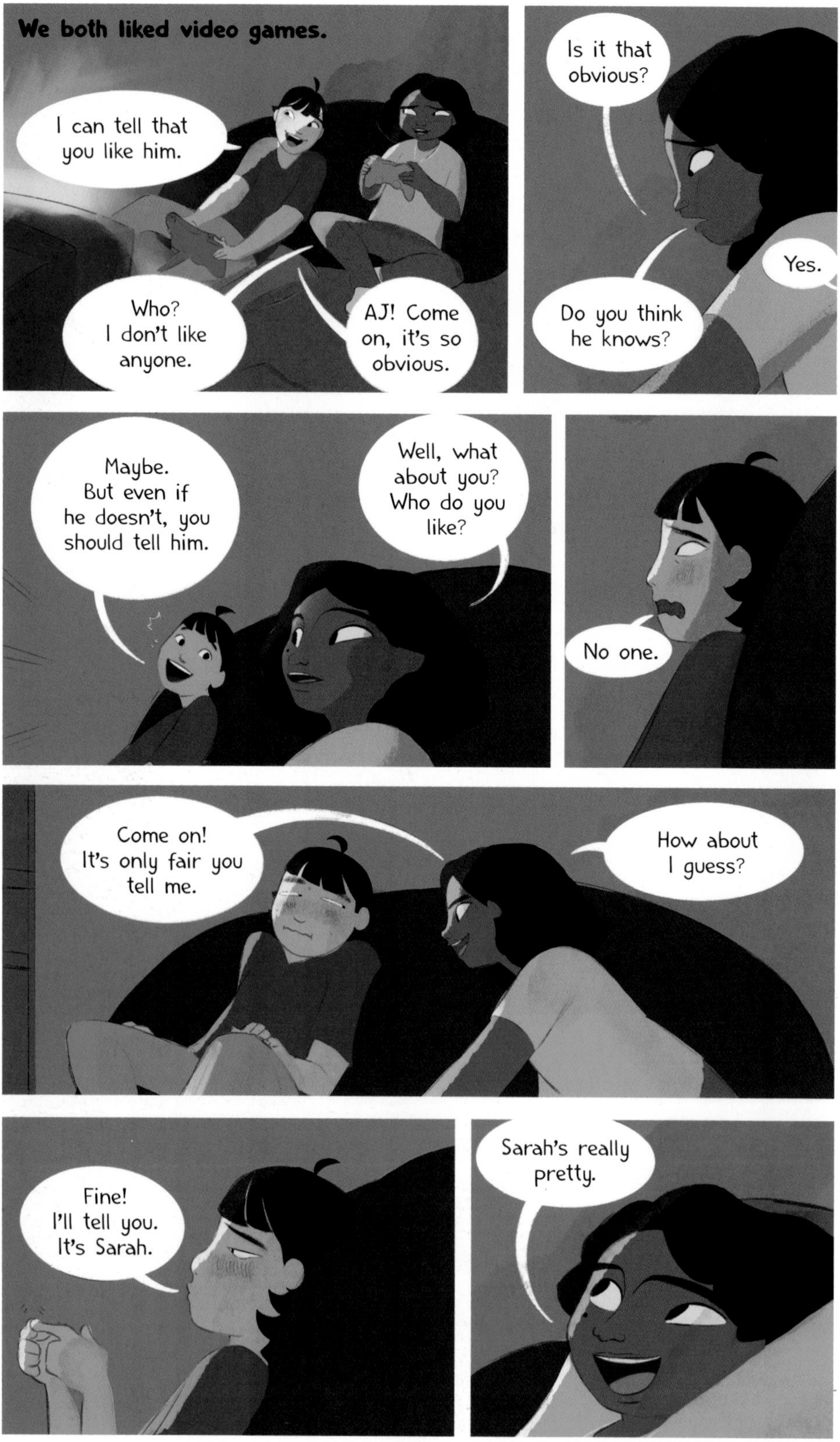
We both liked video games.
I can tell that you like him.
Who? I don't like anyone.
AJ! Come on, it's so obvious.
Is it that obvious?
Do you think he knows?
Yes.
Maybe. But even if he doesn't, you should tell him.
Well, what about you? Who do you like?
No one.
Come on! It's only fair you tell me.
How about I guess?
Fine! I'll tell you. It's Sarah.
Sarah's really pretty.

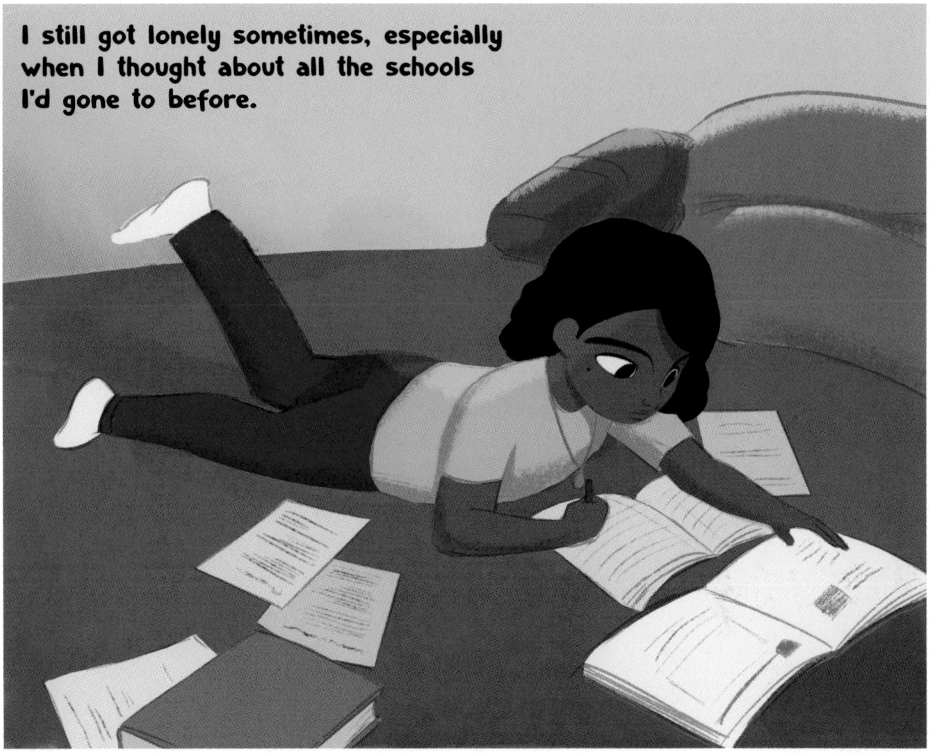
I still got lonely sometimes, especially when I thought about all the schools I'd gone to before.

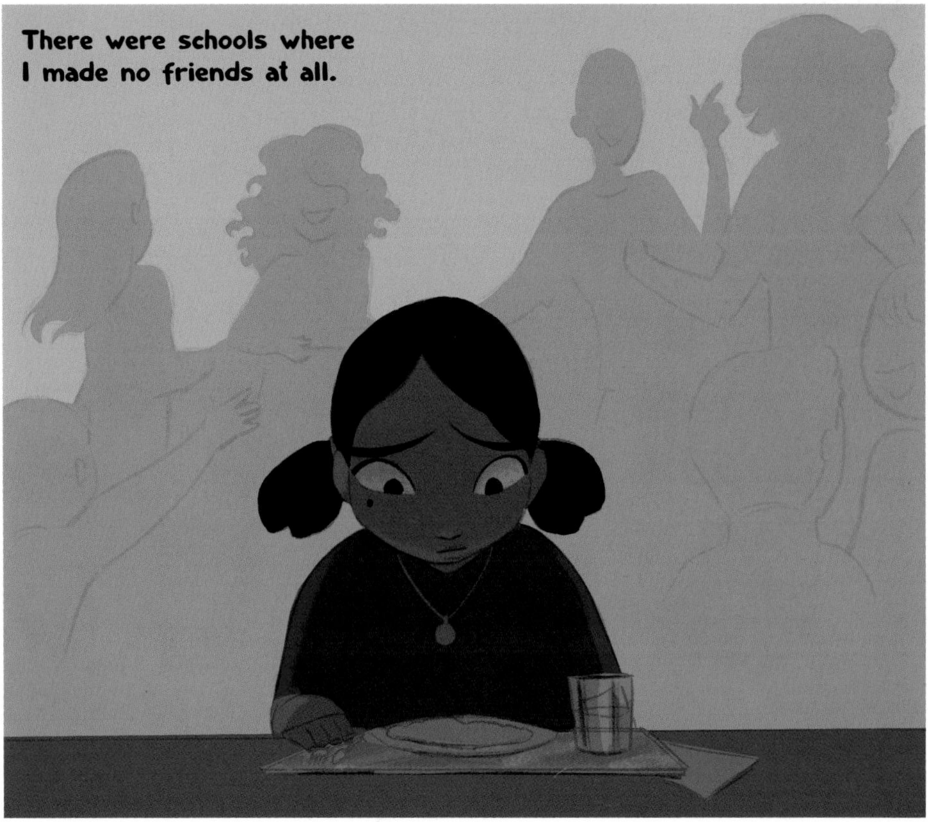
There were schools where I made no friends at all.

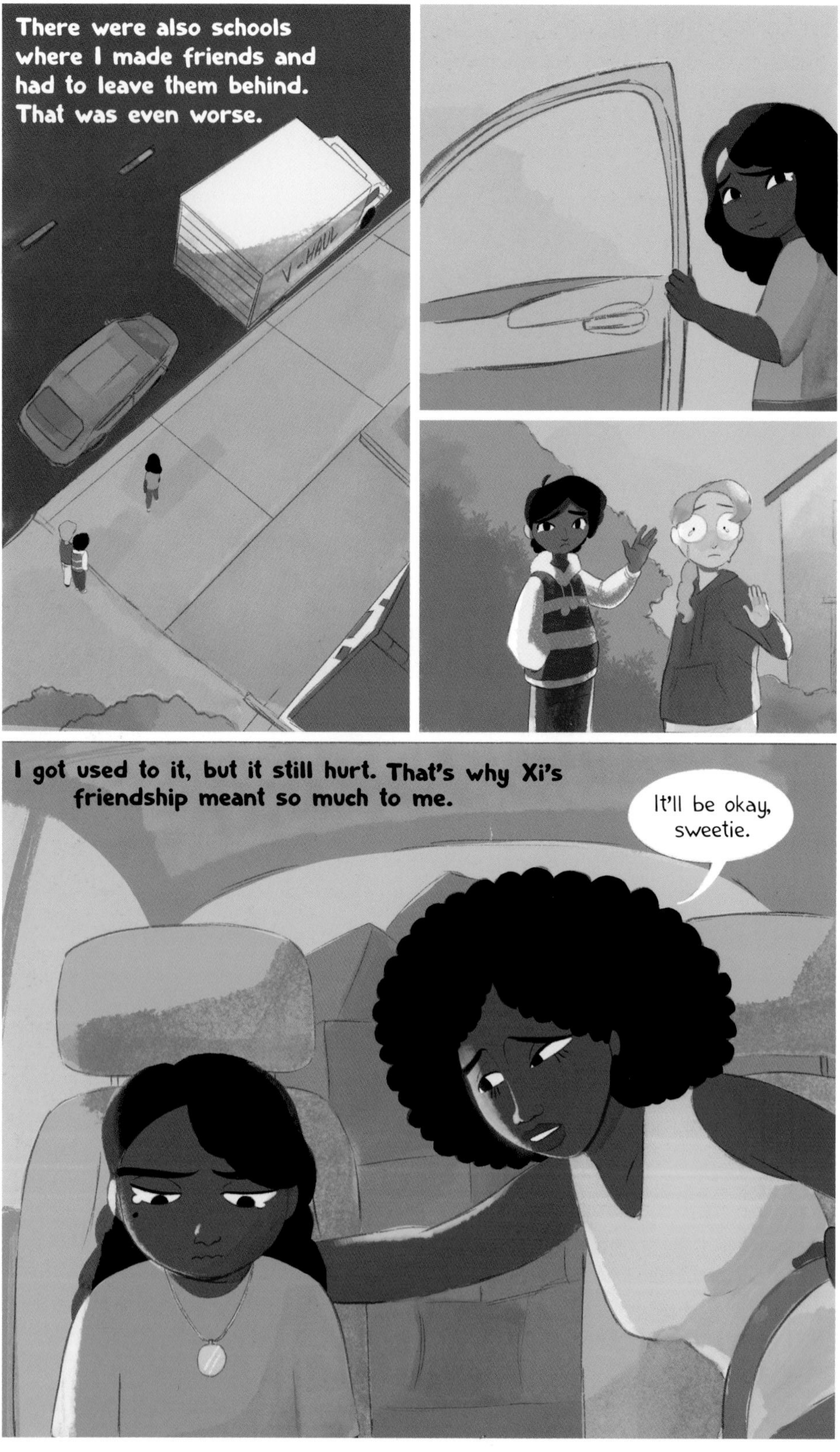
There were also schools where I made friends and had to leave them behind. That was even worse.
I got used to it, but it still hurt. That's why Xi's friendship meant so much to me.
It'll be okay, sweetie.

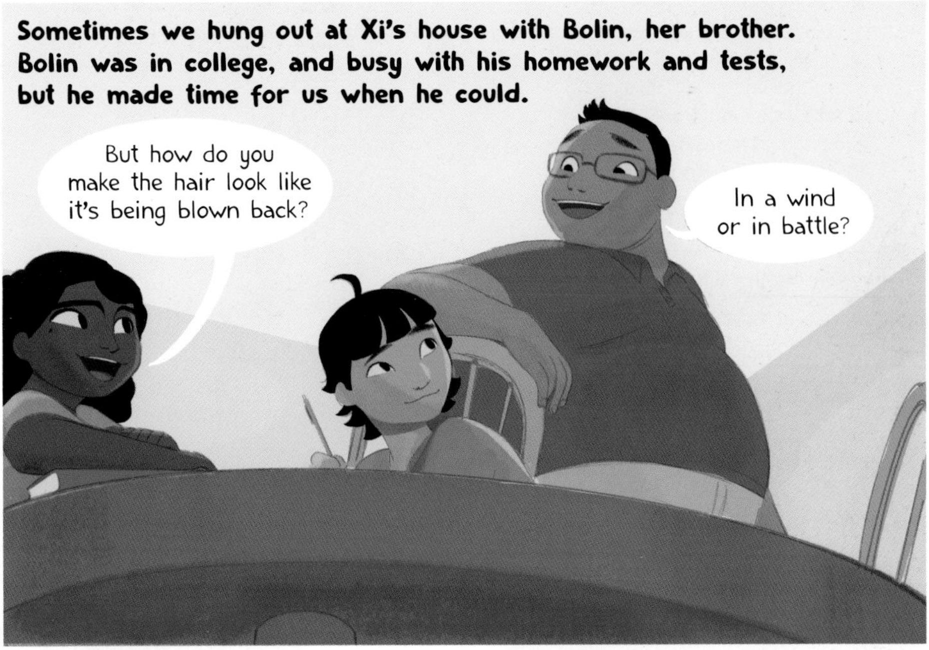
Sometimes we hung out at Xi's house with Bolin, her brother. Bolin was in college, and busy with his homework and tests, but he made time for us when he could.
But how do you make the hair look like it's being blown back?
In a wind or in battle?

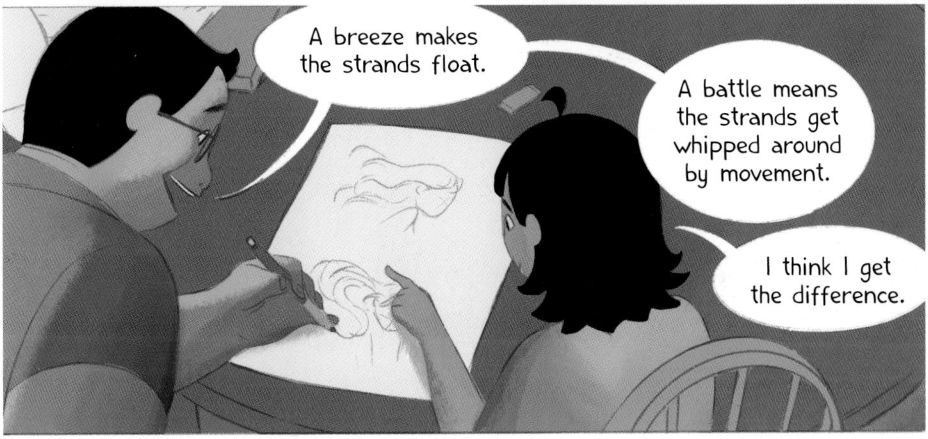
A breeze makes the strands float.
A battle means the strands get whipped around by movement.
I think I get the difference.

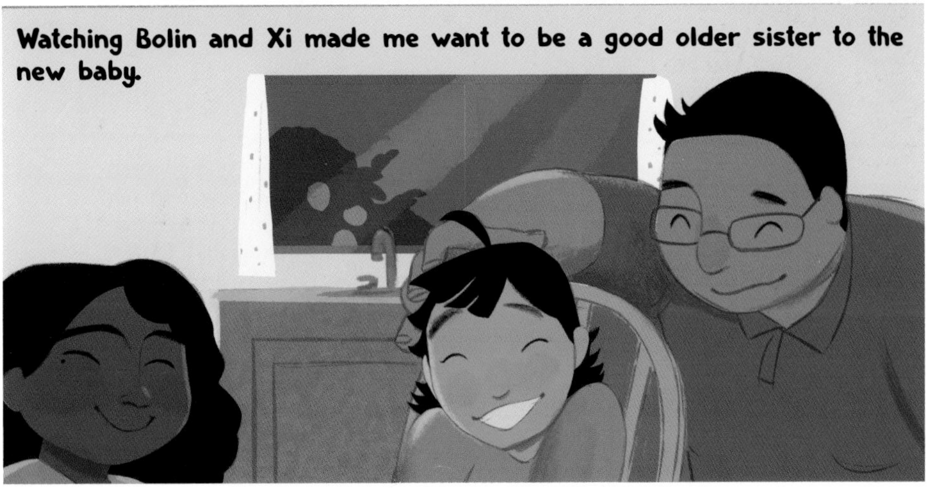
Watching Bolin and Xi made me want to be a good older sister to the new baby.

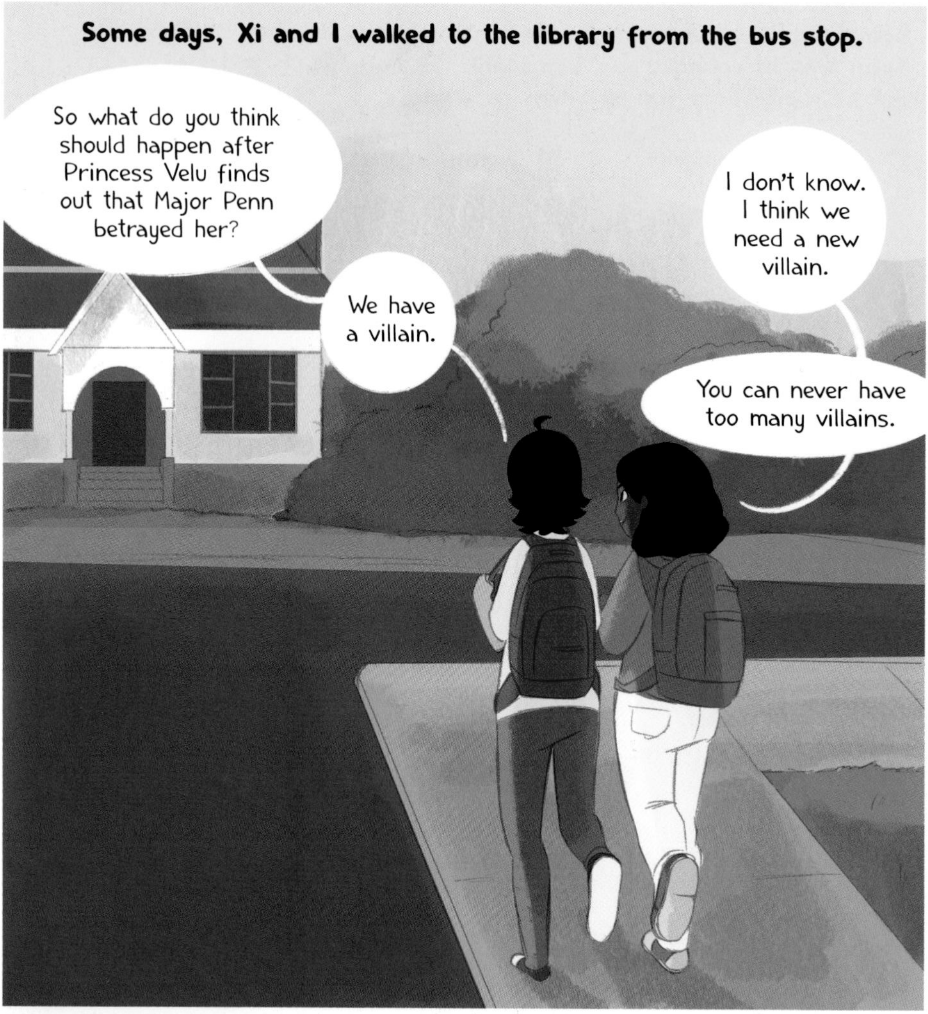
Some days, Xi and I walked to the library from the bus stop.
So what do you think should happen after Princess Velu finds out that Major Penn betrayed her?
We have a villain.
I don't know. I think we need a new villain.
You can never have too many villains.

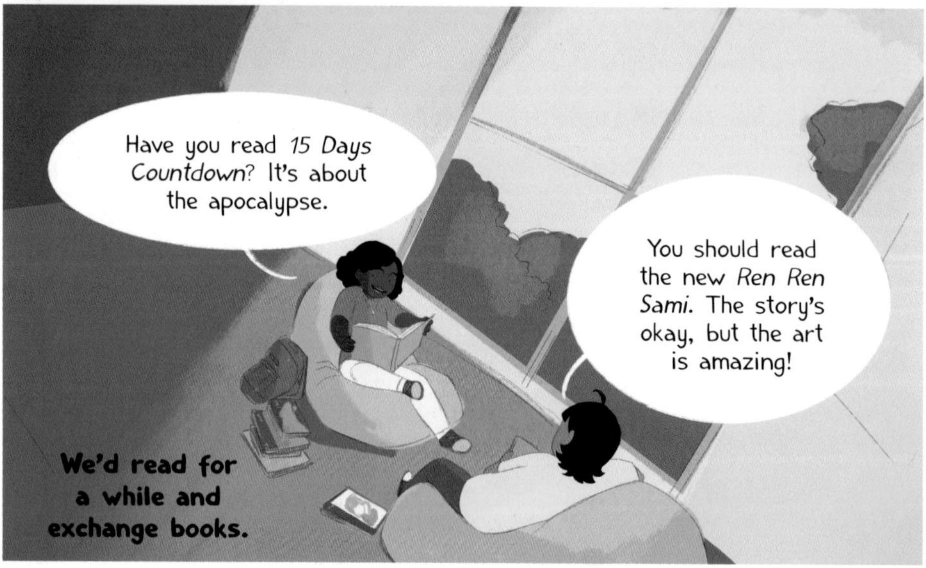
Have you read *15 Days Countdown*? It's about the apocalypse.
You should read the new *Ren Ren Sami*. The story's okay, but the art is amazing!
We'd read for a while and exchange books.

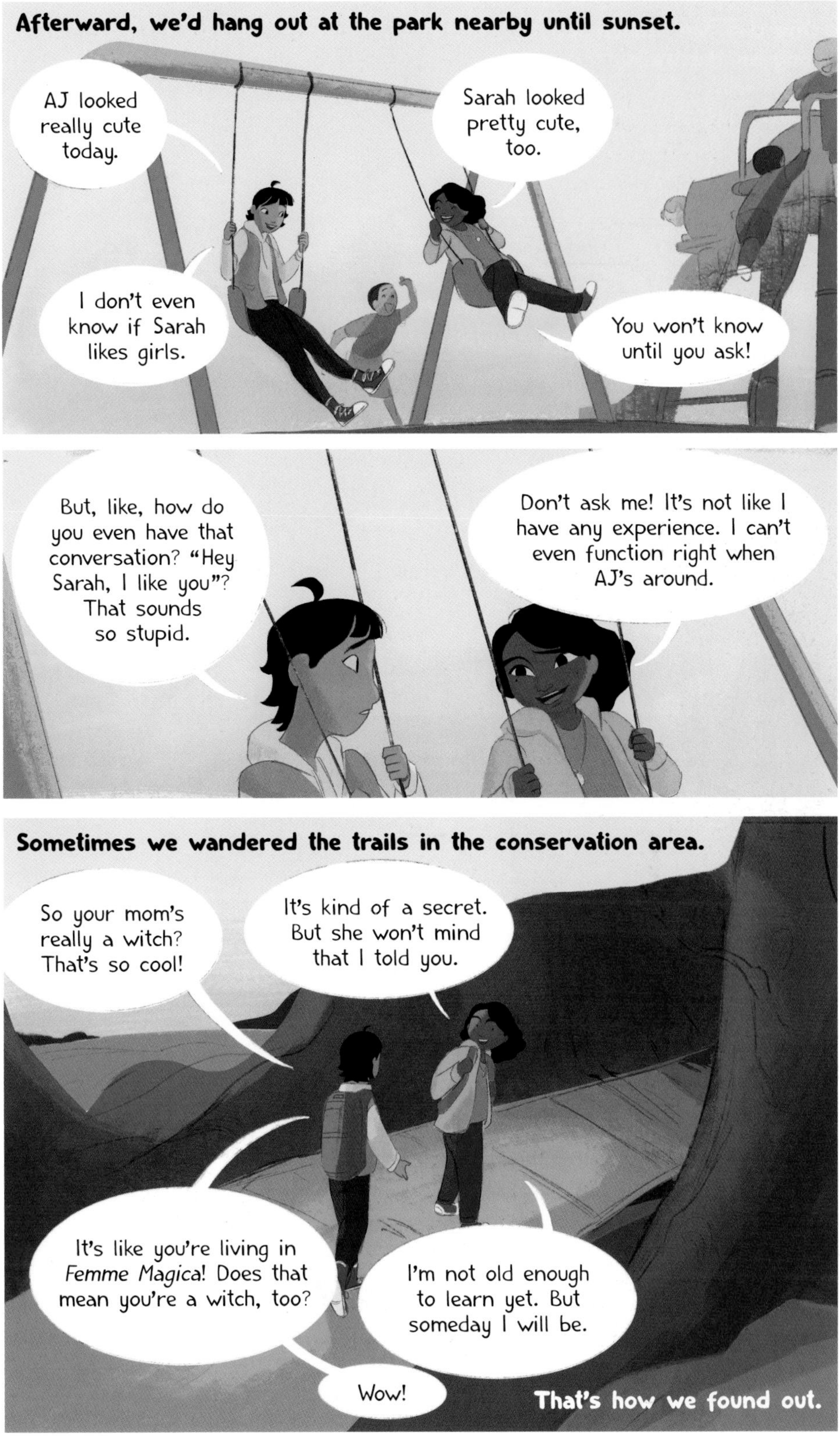
Afterward, we'd hang out at the park nearby until sunset.
AJ looked really cute today.
Sarah looked pretty cute, too.
I don't even know if Sarah likes girls.
You won't know until you ask!
But, like, how do you even have that conversation? "Hey Sarah, I like you"? That sounds so stupid.
Don't ask me! It's not like I have any experience. I can't even function right when AJ's around.
Sometimes we wandered the trails in the conservation area.
So your mom's really a witch? That's so cool!
It's kind of a secret. But she won't mind that I told you.
It's like you're living in *Femme Magica*! Does that mean you're a witch, too?
I'm not old enough to learn yet. But someday I will be.
Wow!
That's how we found out.

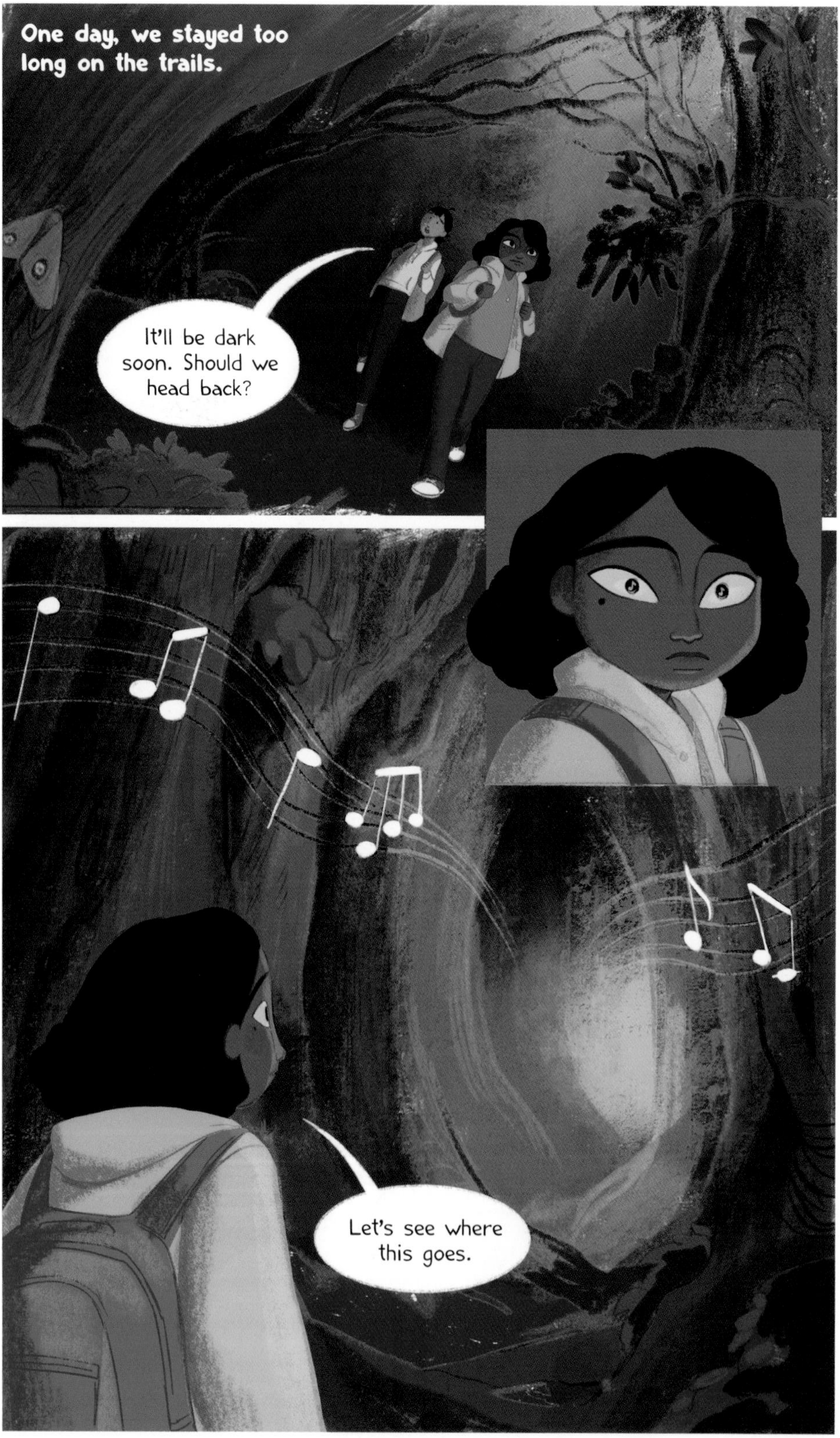
One day, we stayed too long on the trails.
It'll be dark soon. Should we head back?
Let's see where this goes.

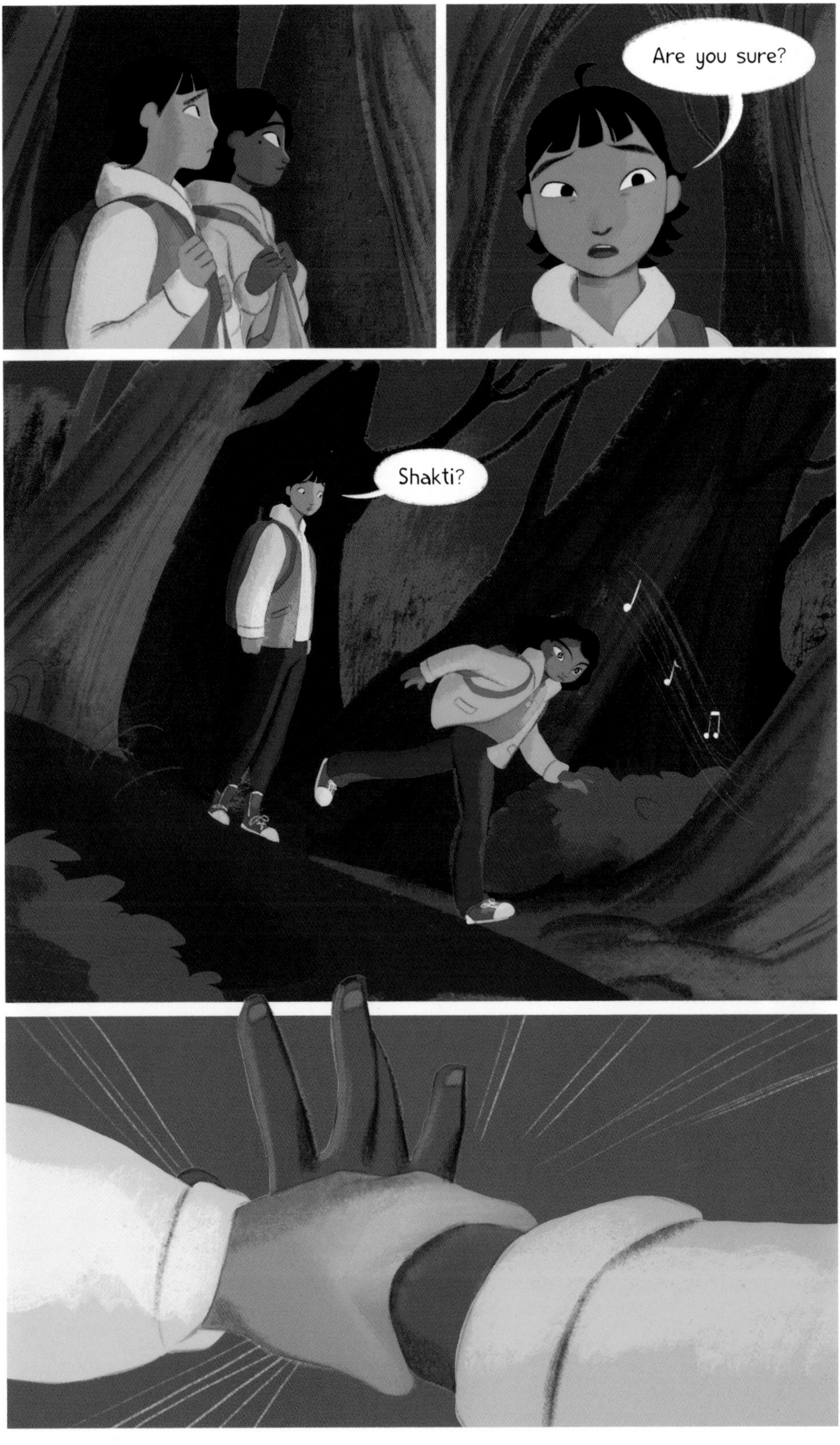
Are you sure?
Shakti?

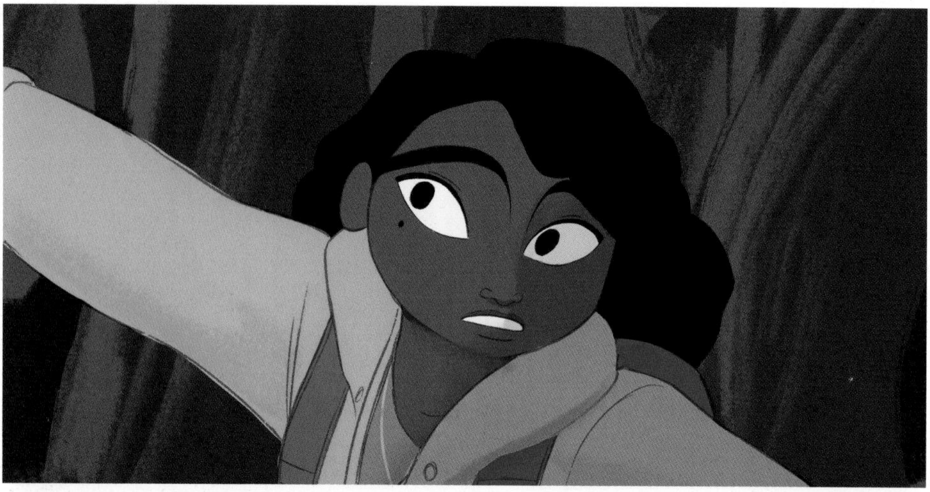

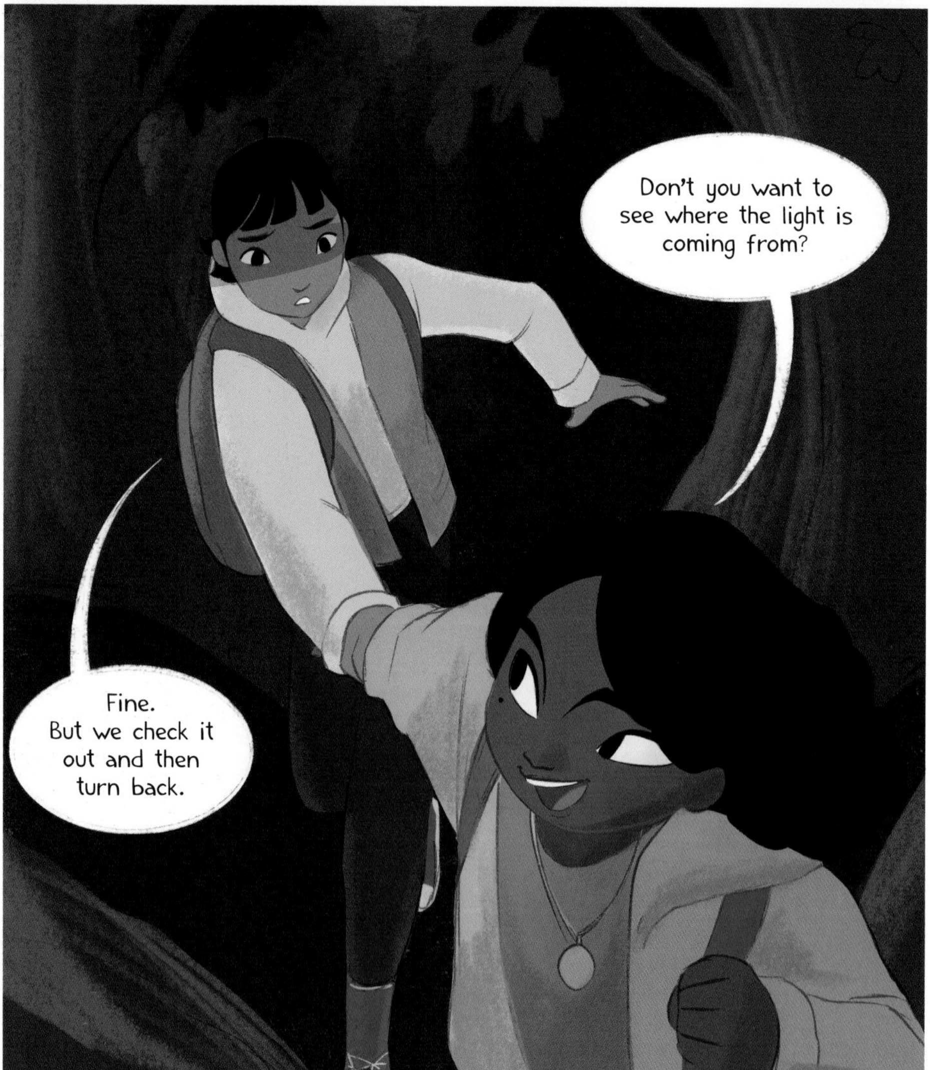
Don't you want to see where the light is coming from?
Fine. But we check it out and then turn back.

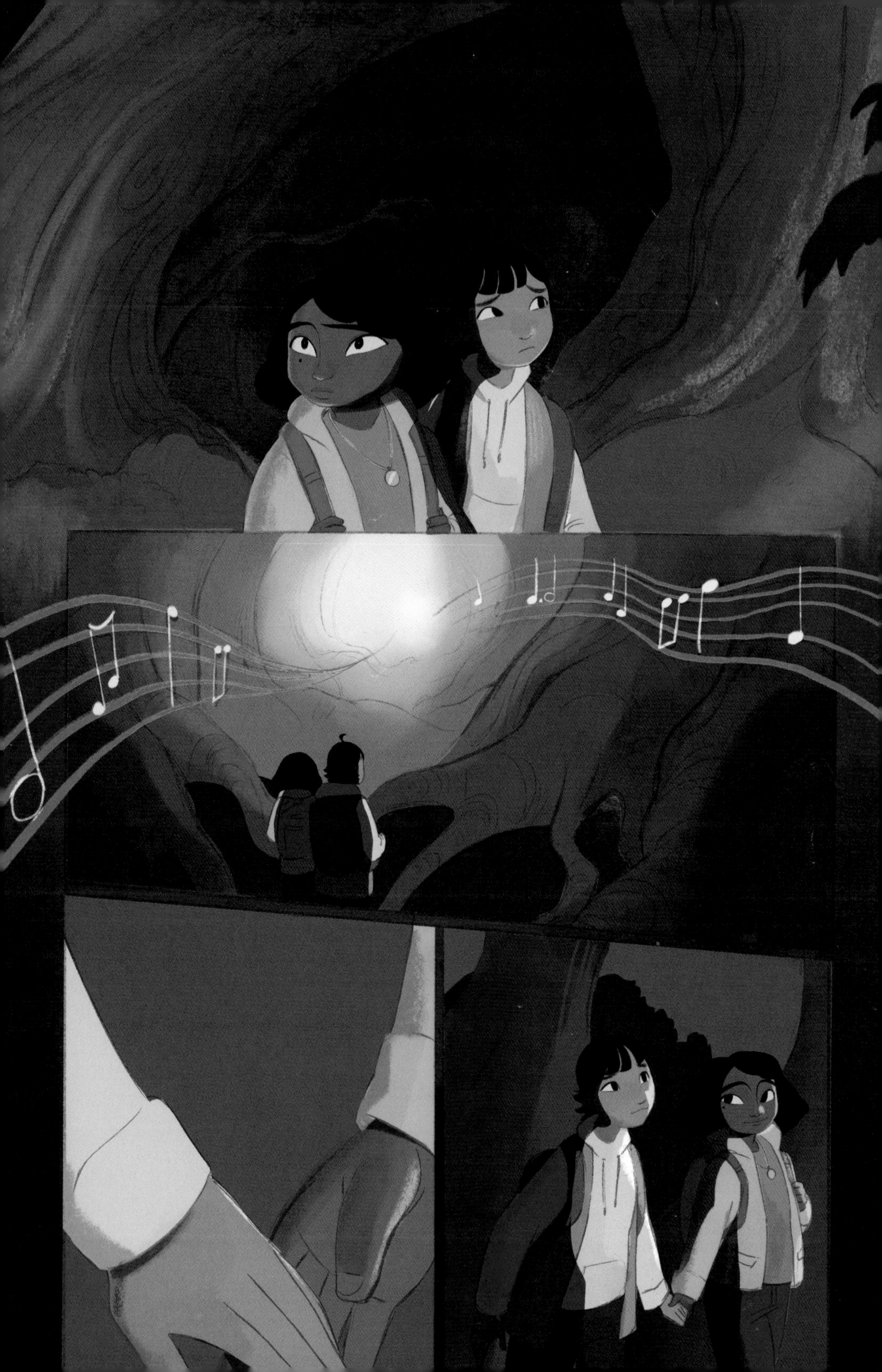

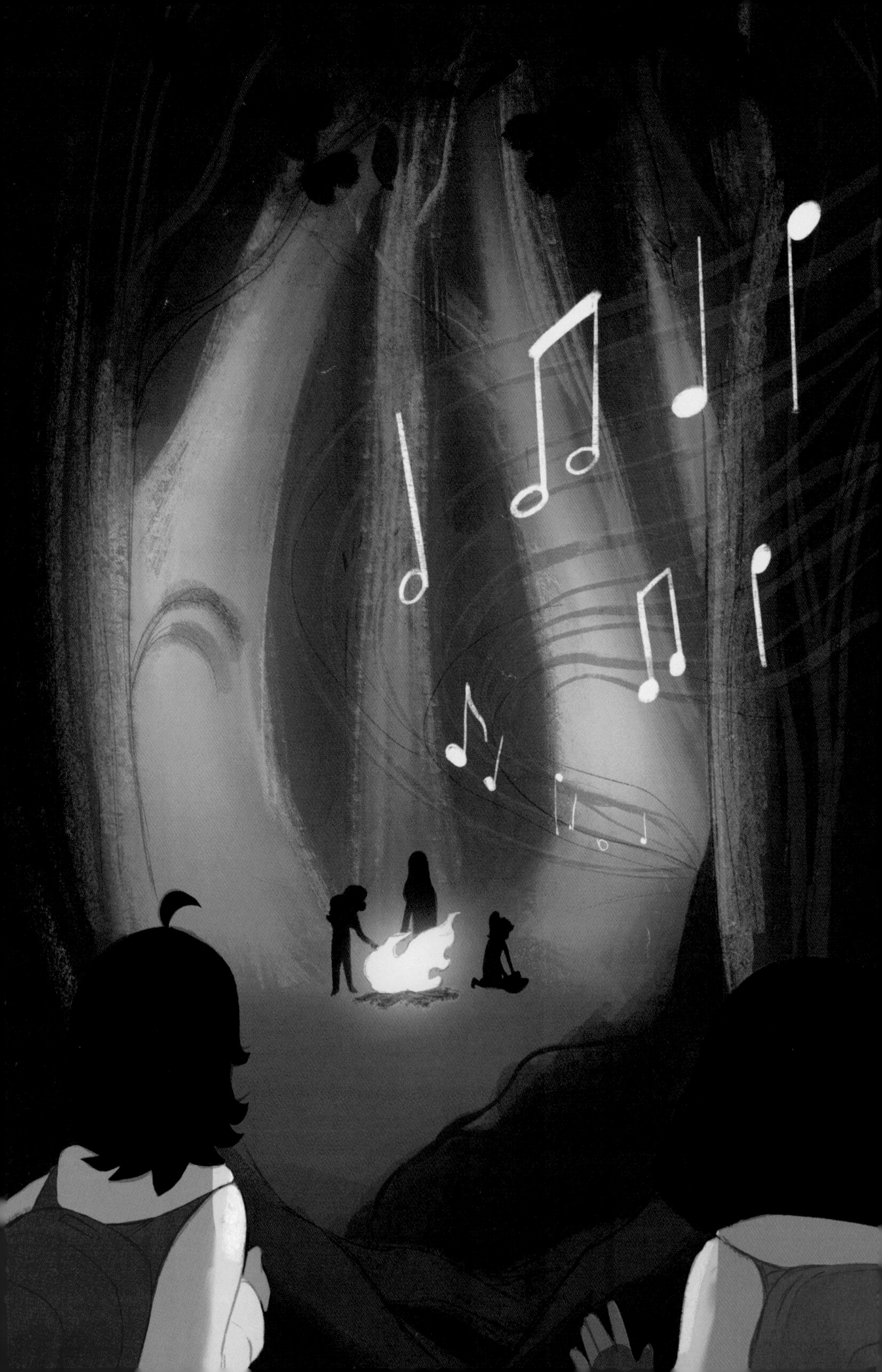

Look!

It's playing by itself!

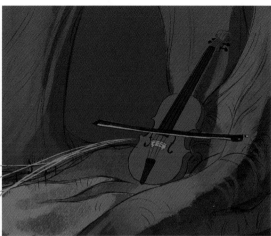

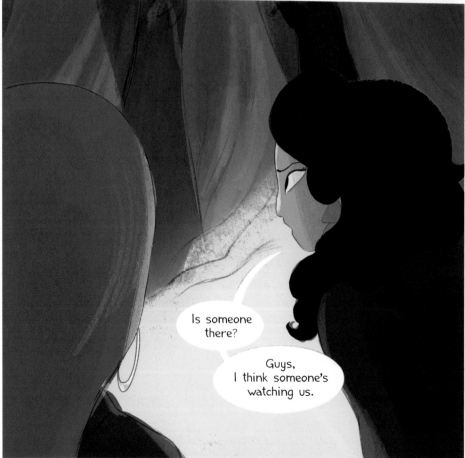

Is someone there?

Guys, I think someone's watching us.

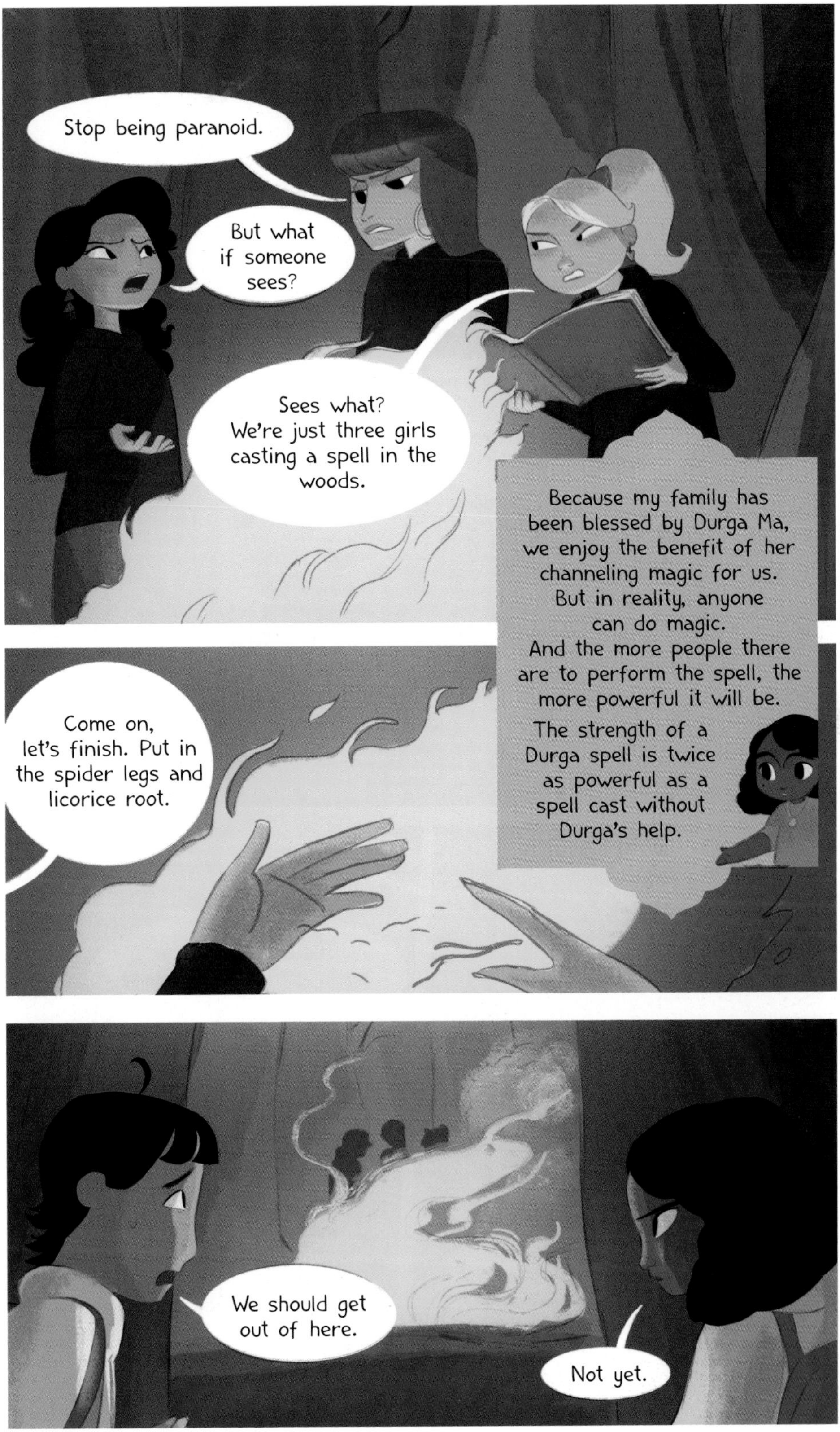
Stop being paranoid.
But what if someone sees?
Sees what? We're just three girls casting a spell in the woods.
Because my family has been blessed by Durga Ma, we enjoy the benefit of her channeling magic for us. But in reality, anyone can do magic. And the more people there are to perform the spell, the more powerful it will be.
The strength of a Durga spell is twice as powerful as a spell cast without Durga's help.
Come on, let's finish. Put in the spider legs and licorice root.
We should get out of here.
Not yet.

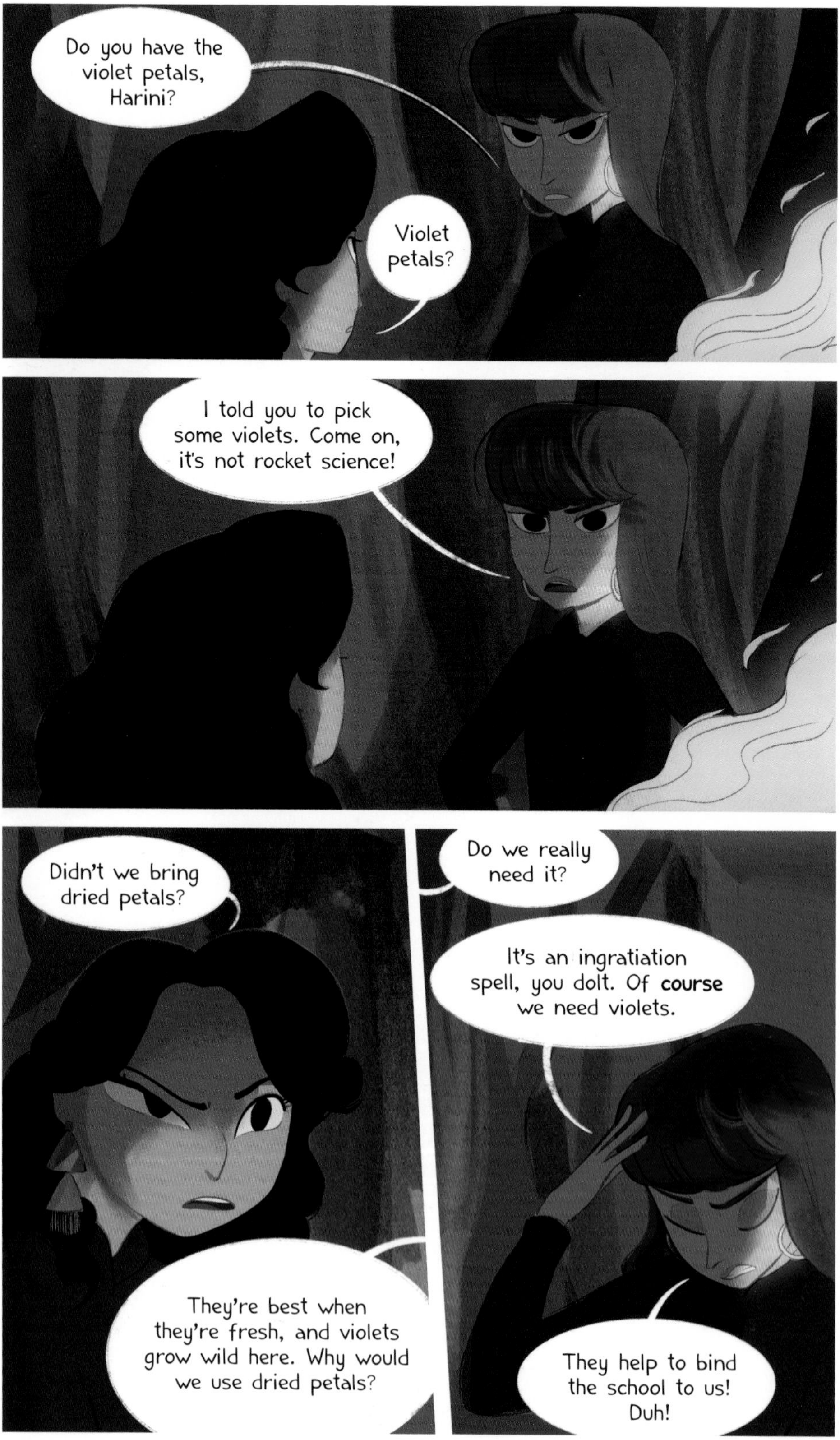
Do you have the violet petals, Harini?
Violet petals?
I told you to pick some violets. Come on, it's not rocket science!
Didn't we bring dried petals?
They're best when they're fresh, and violets grow wild here. Why would we use dried petals?
Do we really need it?
It's an ingratiation spell, you dolt. Of **course** we need violets.
They help to bind the school to us! Duh!

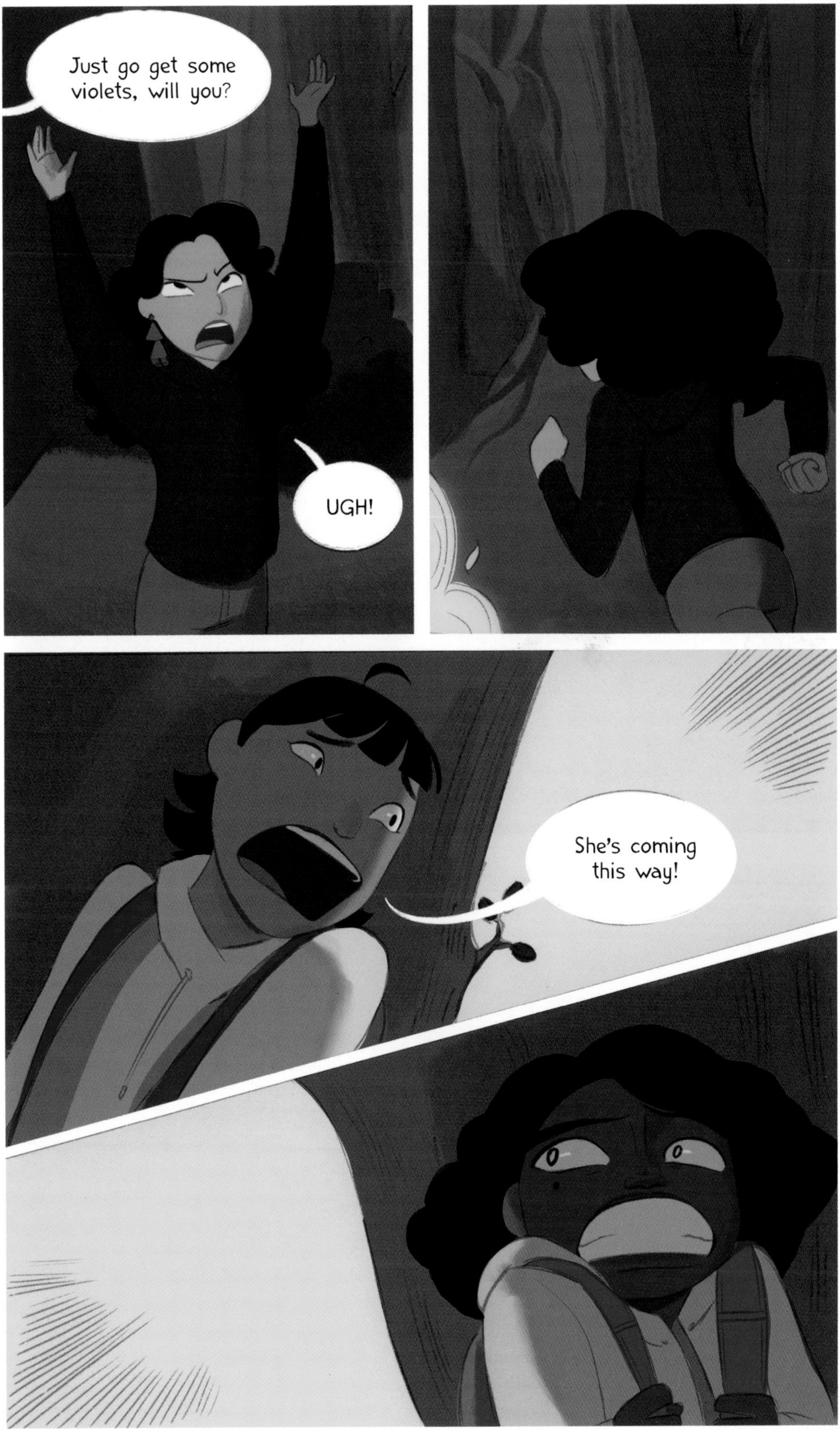
Just go get some violets, will you?
UGH!
She's coming this way!

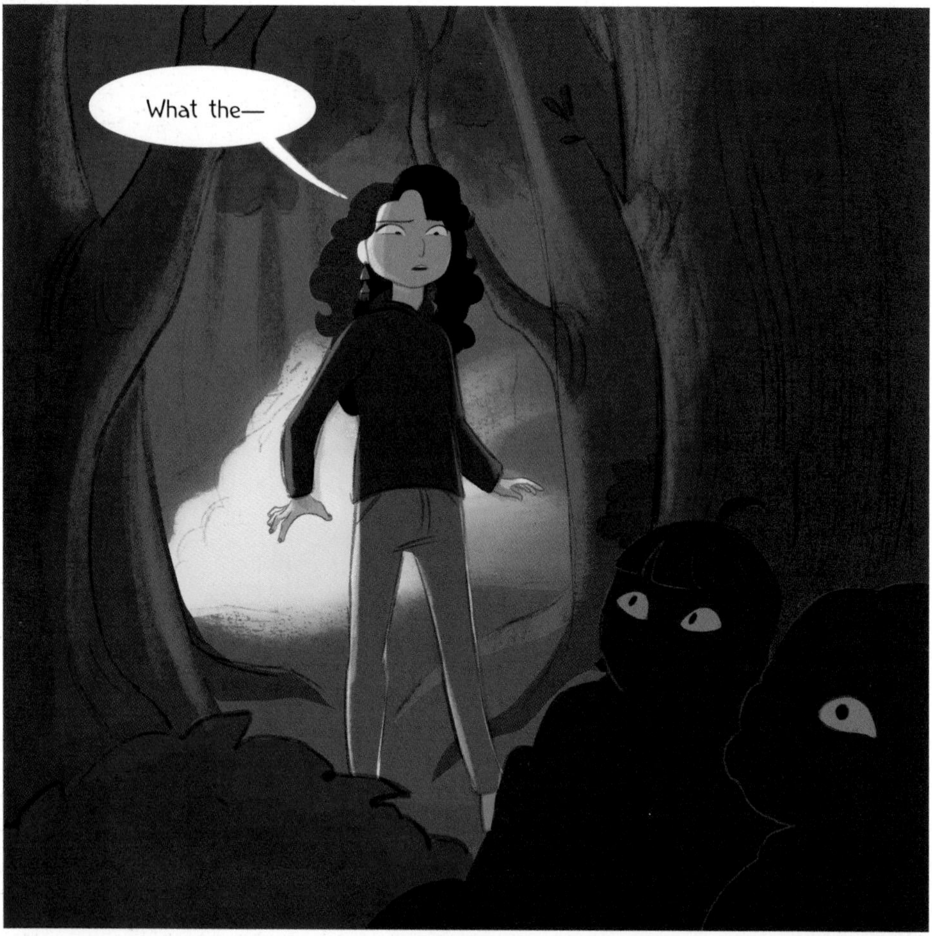
What the—

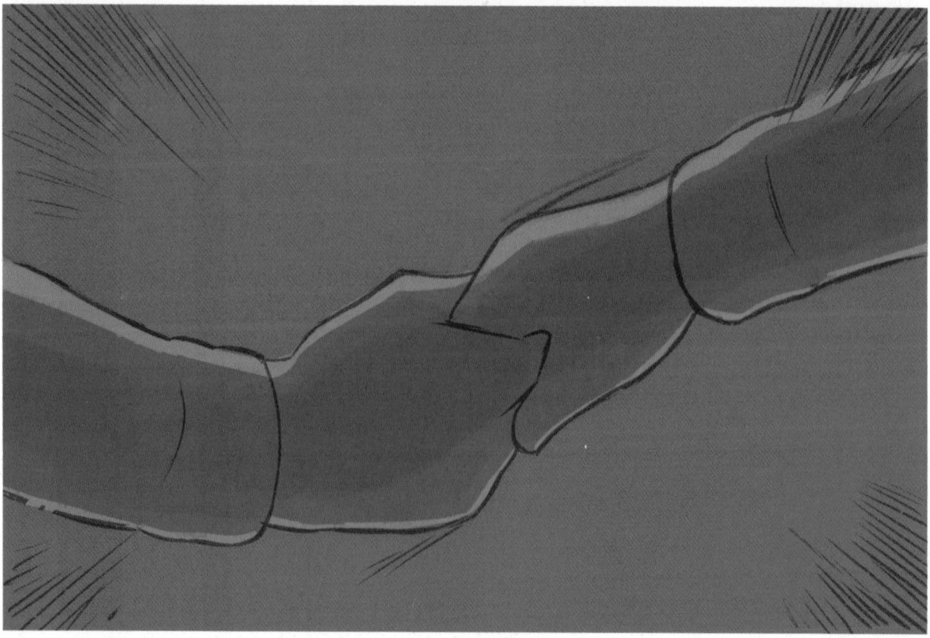

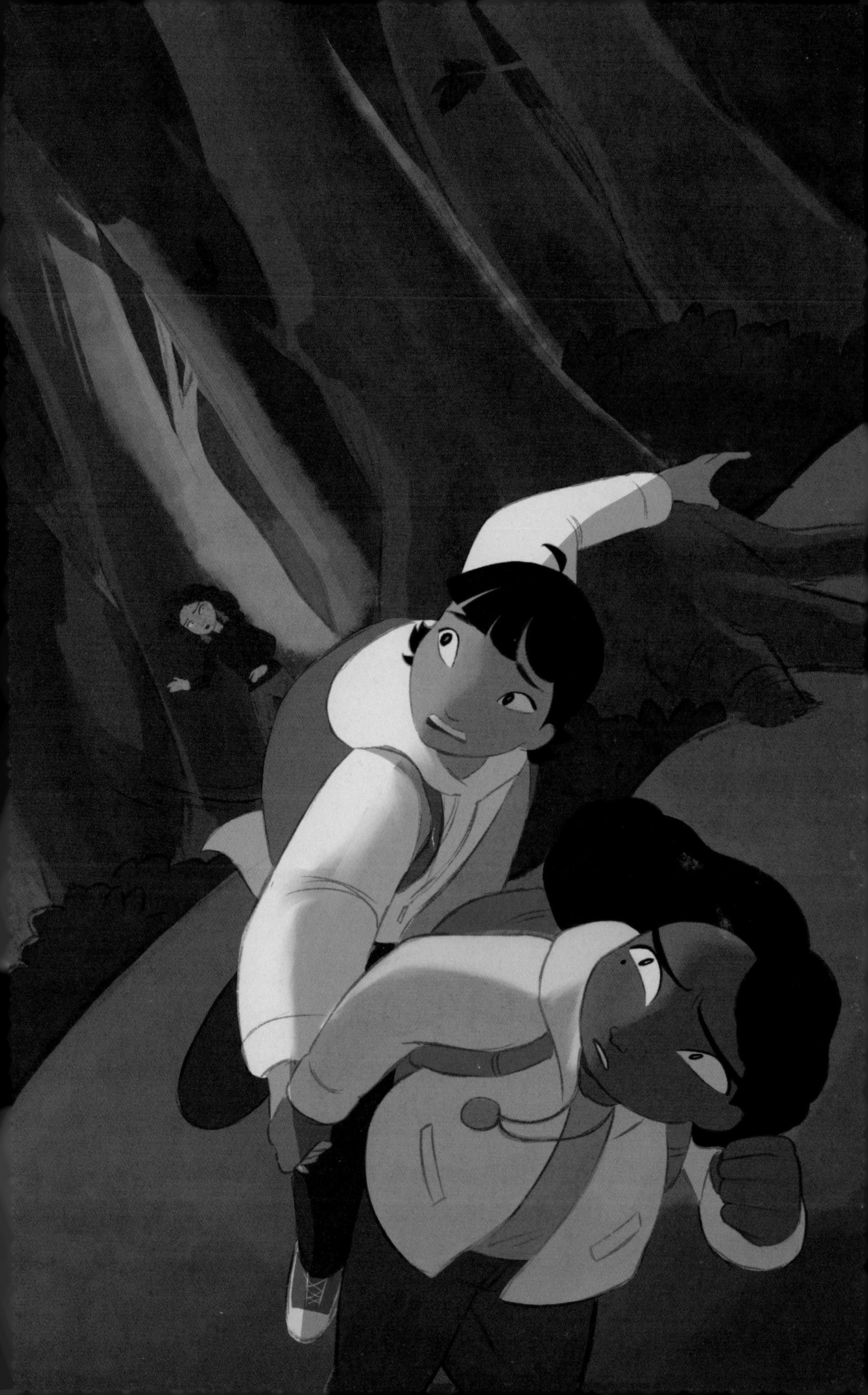

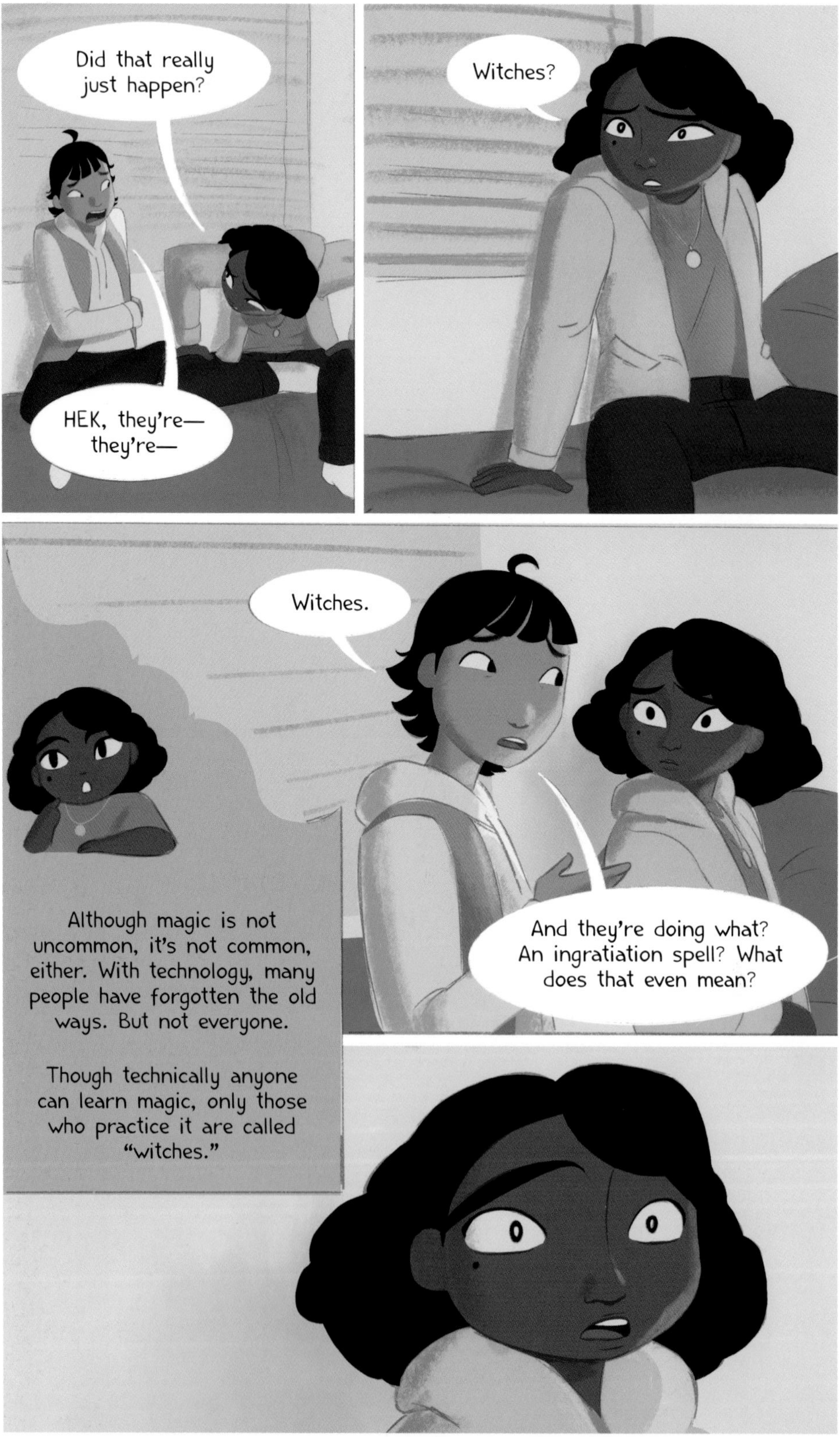
Did that really just happen?
HEK, they're—they're—
Witches?
Witches.
Although magic is not uncommon, it's not common, either. With technology, many people have forgotten the old ways. But not everyone.
Though technically anyone can learn magic, only those who practice it are called "witches."
And they're doing what? An ingratiation spell? What does that even mean?

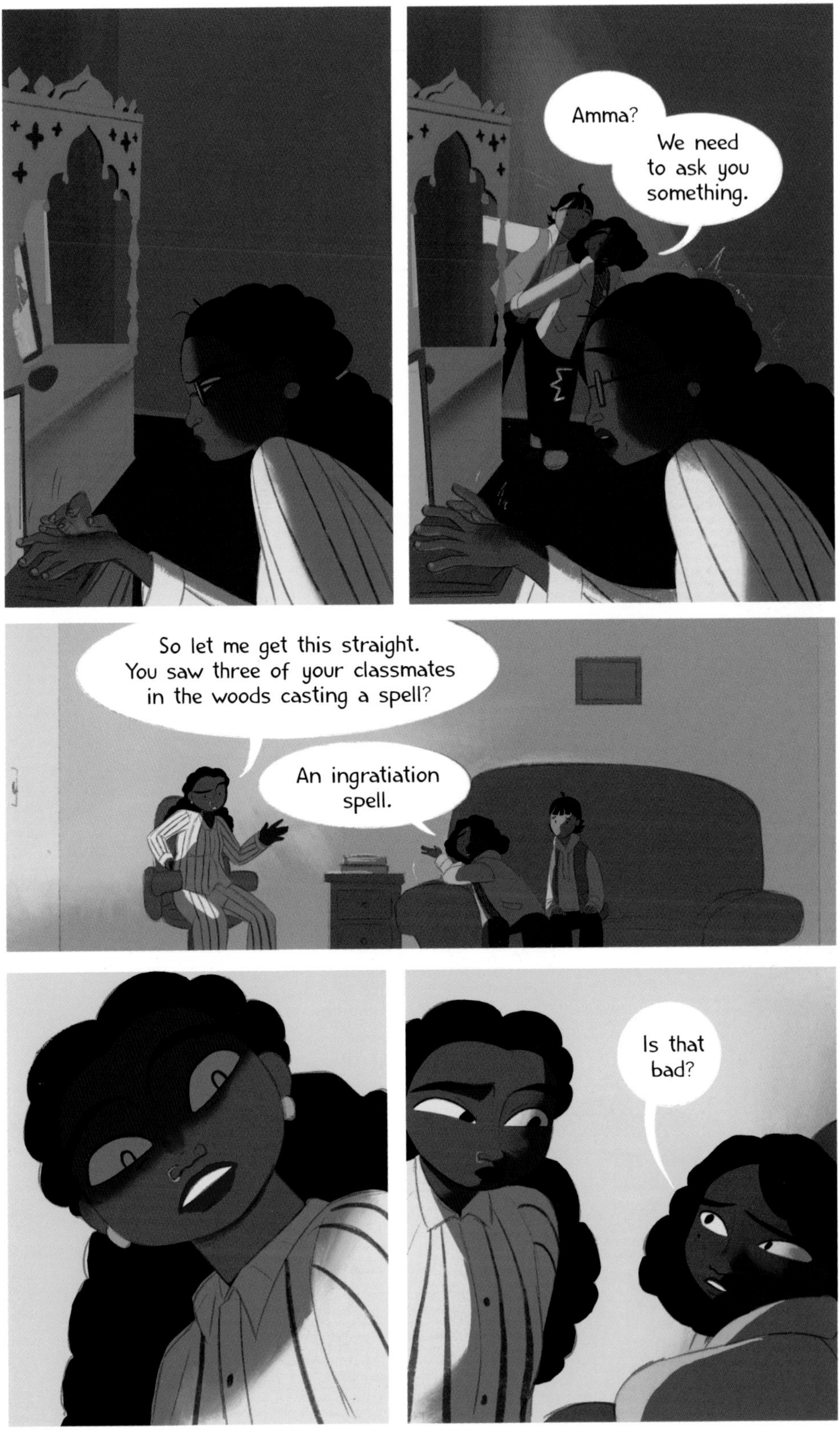
Amma?
We need to ask you something.
So let me get this straight. You saw three of your classmates in the woods casting a spell?
An ingratiation spell.
Is that bad?

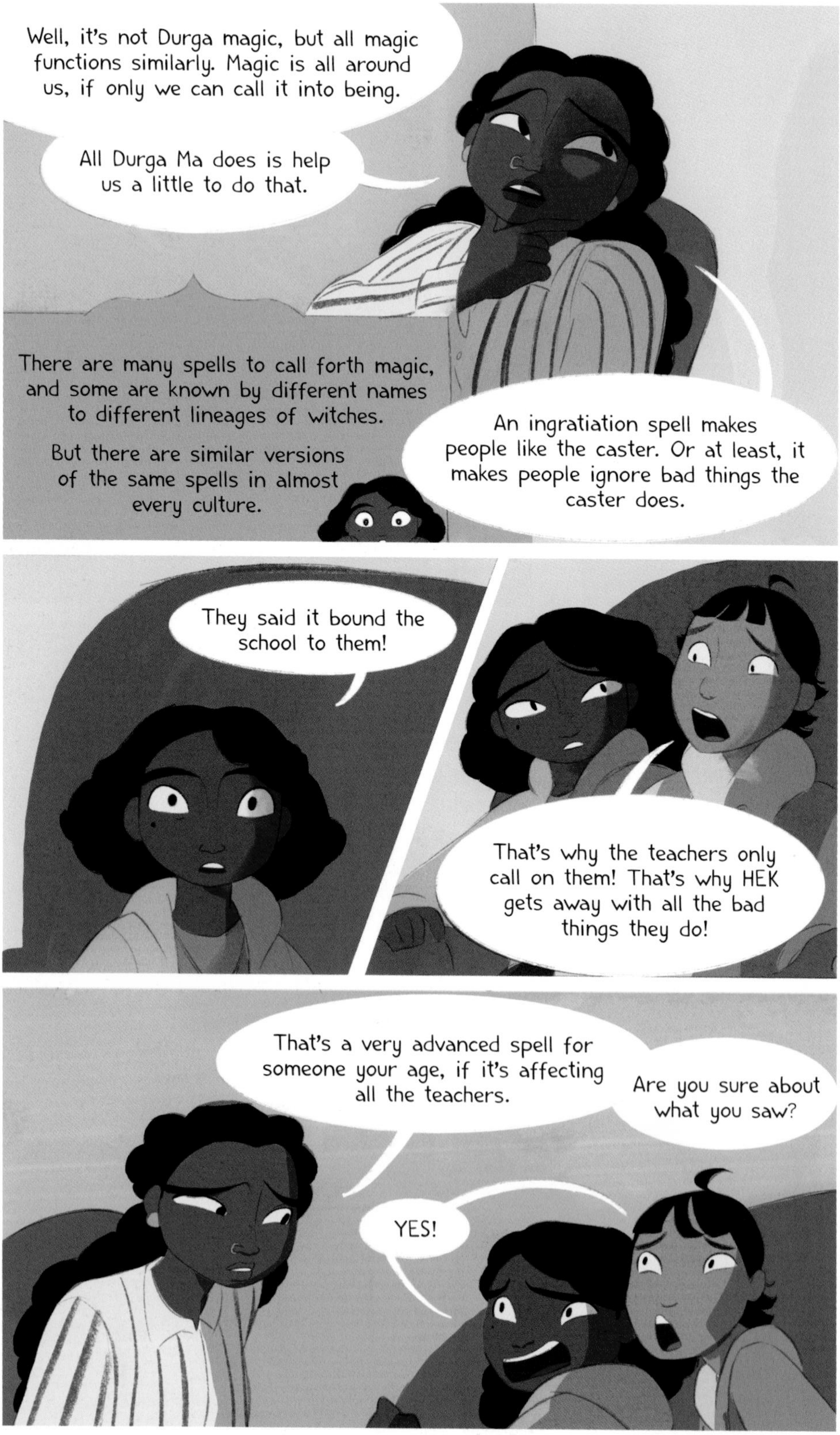
Well, it's not Durga magic, but all magic functions similarly. Magic is all around us, if only we can call it into being.
All Durga Ma does is help us a little to do that.
There are many spells to call forth magic, and some are known by different names to different lineages of witches.
But there are similar versions of the same spells in almost every culture.
An ingratiation spell makes people like the caster. Or at least, it makes people ignore bad things the caster does.
They said it bound the school to them!
That's why the teachers only call on them! That's why HEK gets away with all the bad things they do!
That's a very advanced spell for someone your age, if it's affecting all the teachers.
Are you sure about what you saw?
YES!

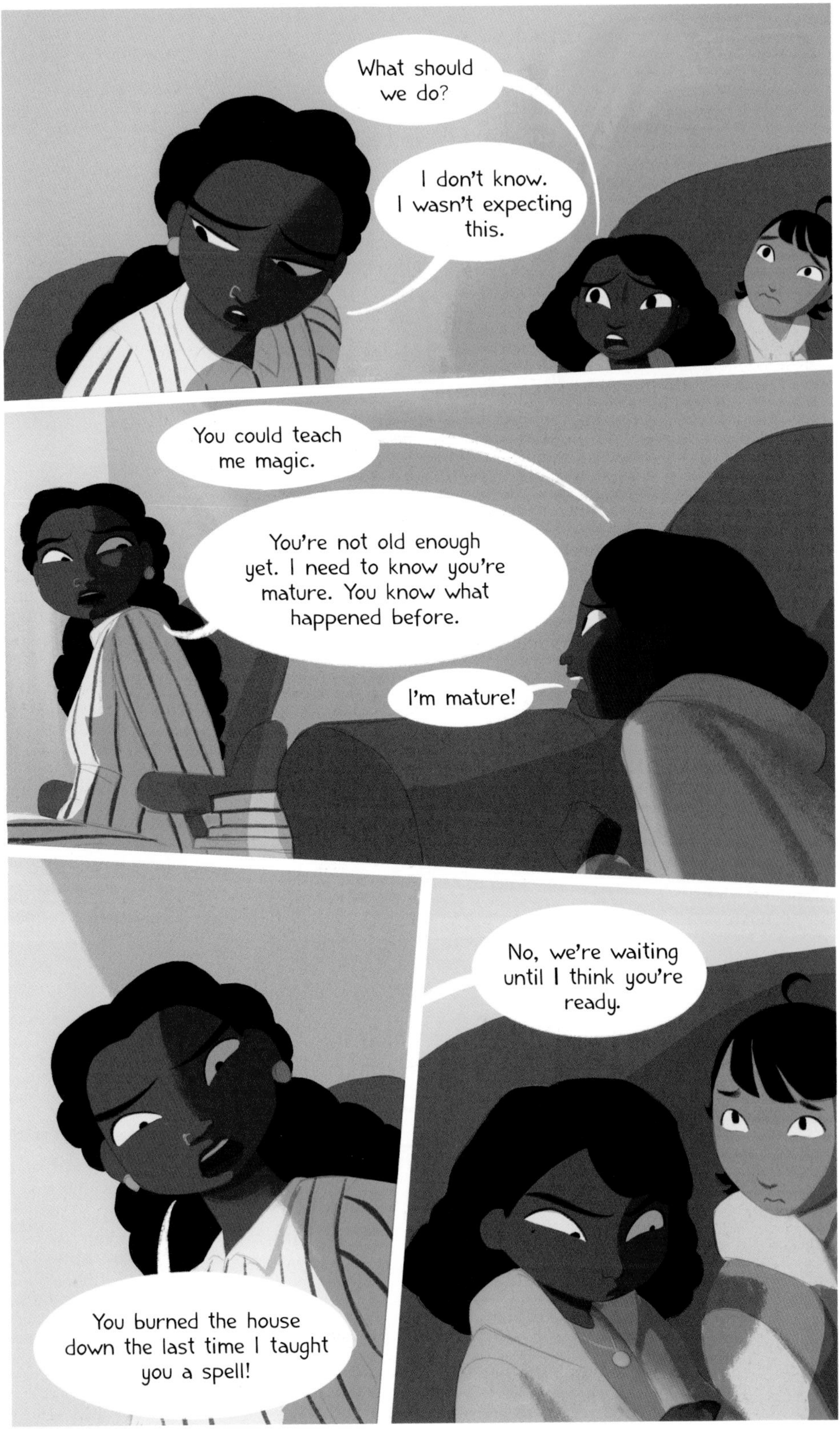
What should we do?
I don't know. I wasn't expecting this.
You could teach me magic.
You're not old enough yet. I need to know you're mature. You know what happened before.
I'm mature!
You burned the house down the last time I taught you a spell!
No, we're waiting until I think you're ready.

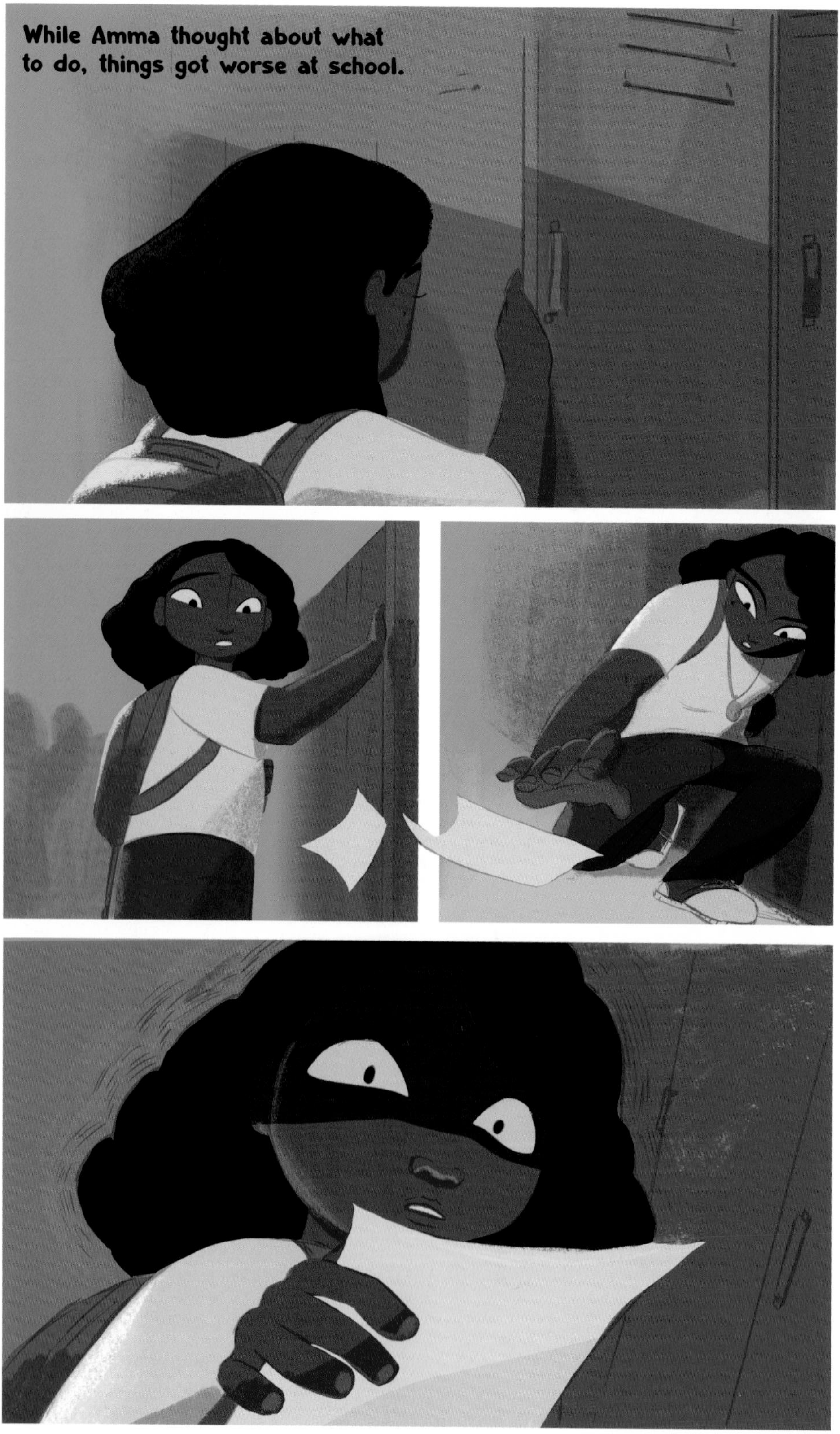
While Amma thought about what
to do, things got worse at school.

You're an ugly, hairy b
and NO ONE will
ever like you ♡

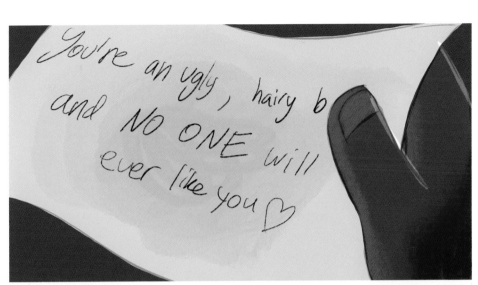

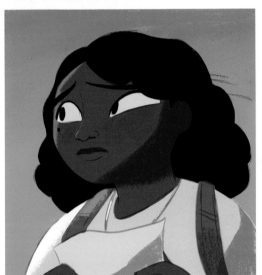

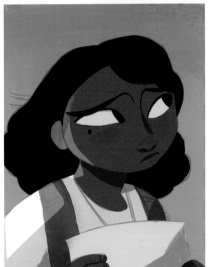

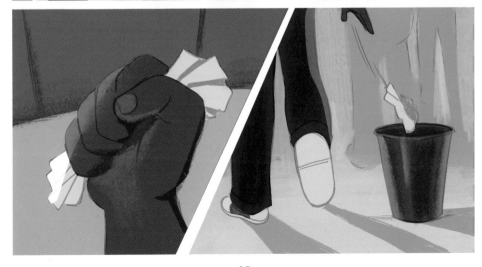

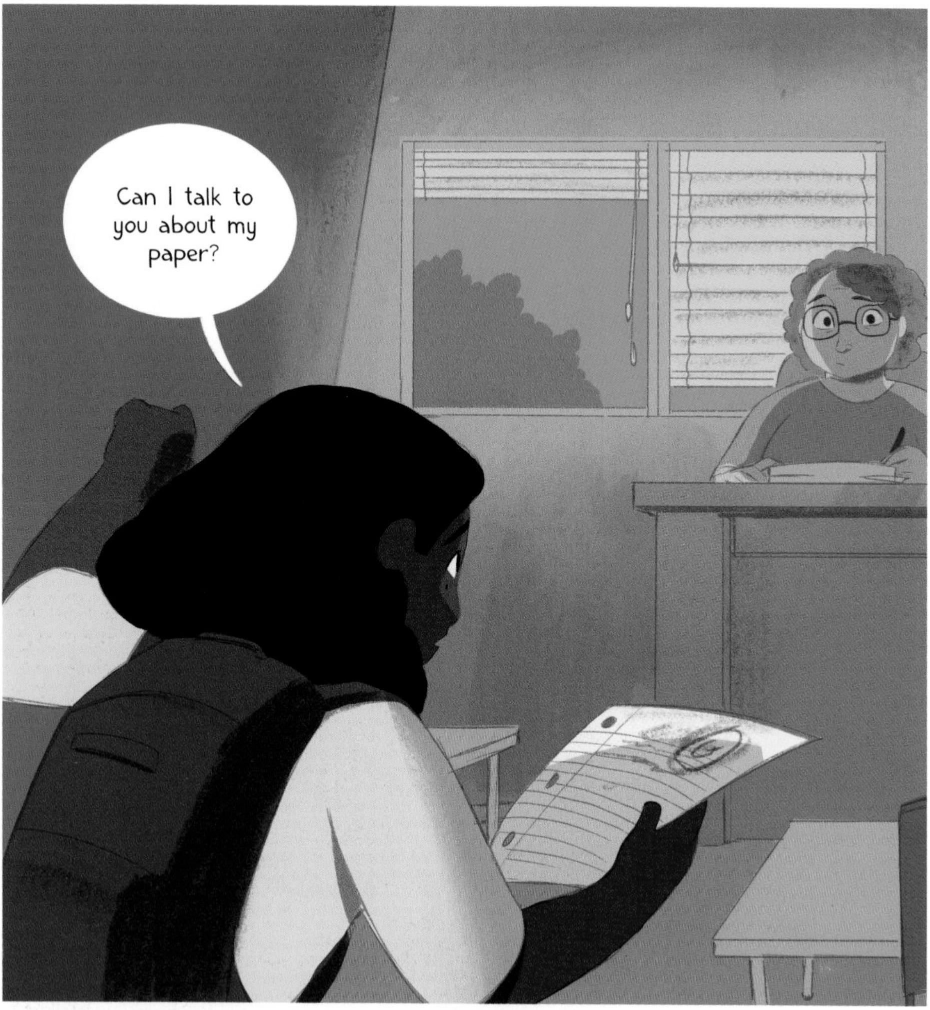
Can I talk to you about my paper?

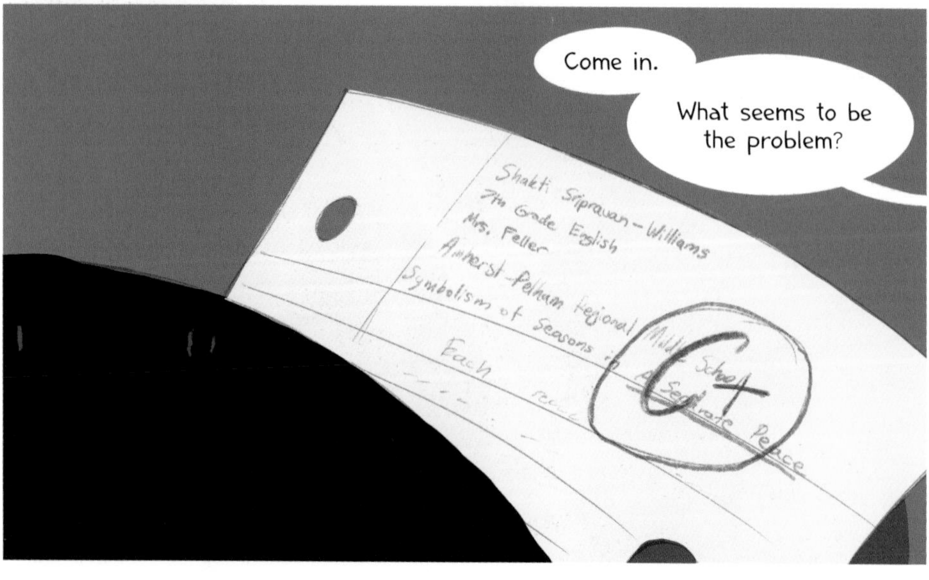
Come in.
What seems to be the problem?
Shakti Sripravan-Williams
7th Grade English
Mrs. Feller
C+

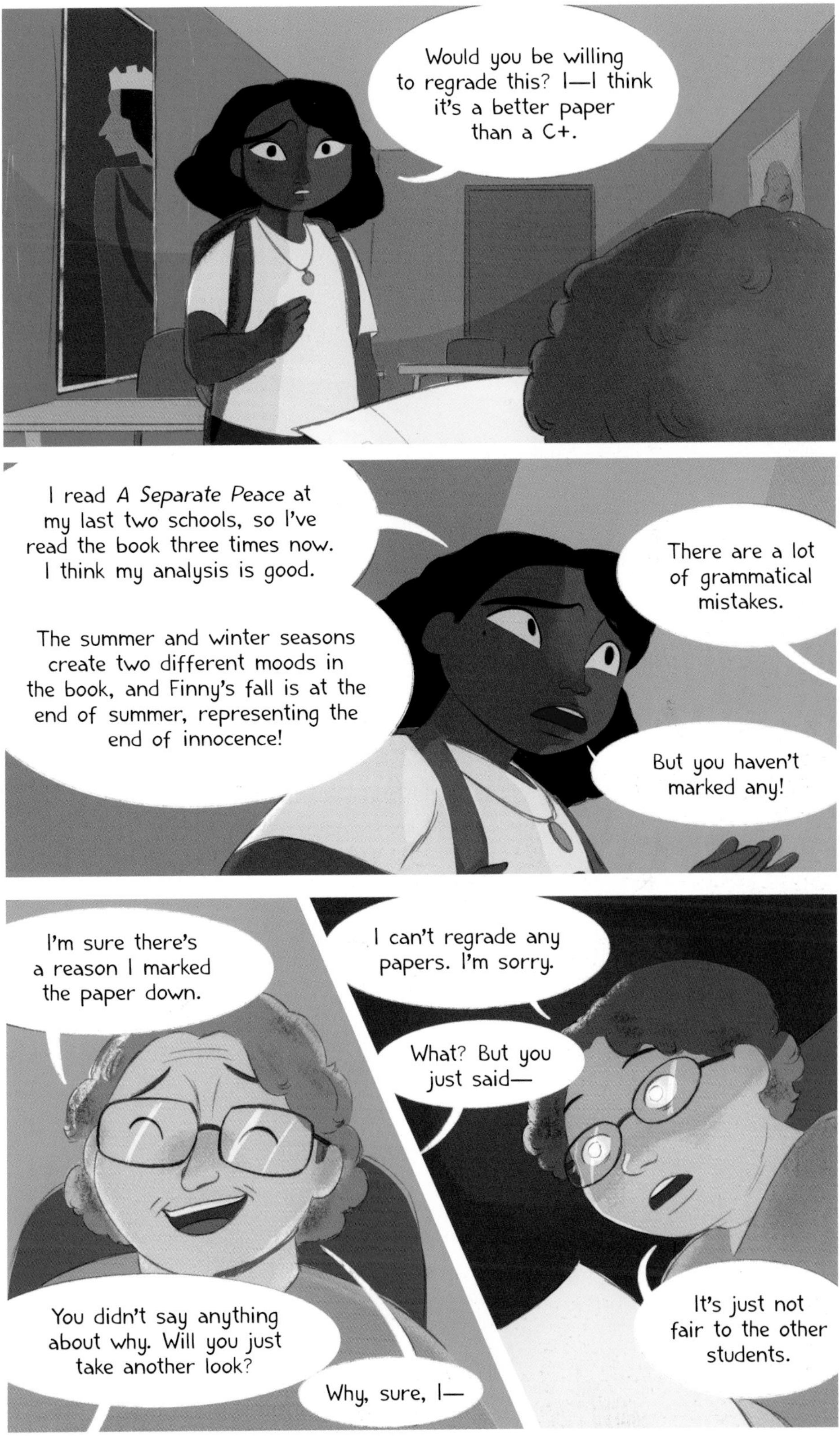
Would you be willing to regrade this? I—I think it's a better paper than a C+.
I read *A Separate Peace* at my last two schools, so I've read the book three times now. I think my analysis is good.
The summer and winter seasons create two different moods in the book, and Finny's fall is at the end of summer, representing the end of innocence!
There are a lot of grammatical mistakes.
But you haven't marked any!
I'm sure there's a reason I marked the paper down.
You didn't say anything about why. Will you just take another look?
Why, sure, I—
I can't regrade any papers. I'm sorry.
What? But you just said—
It's just not fair to the other students.

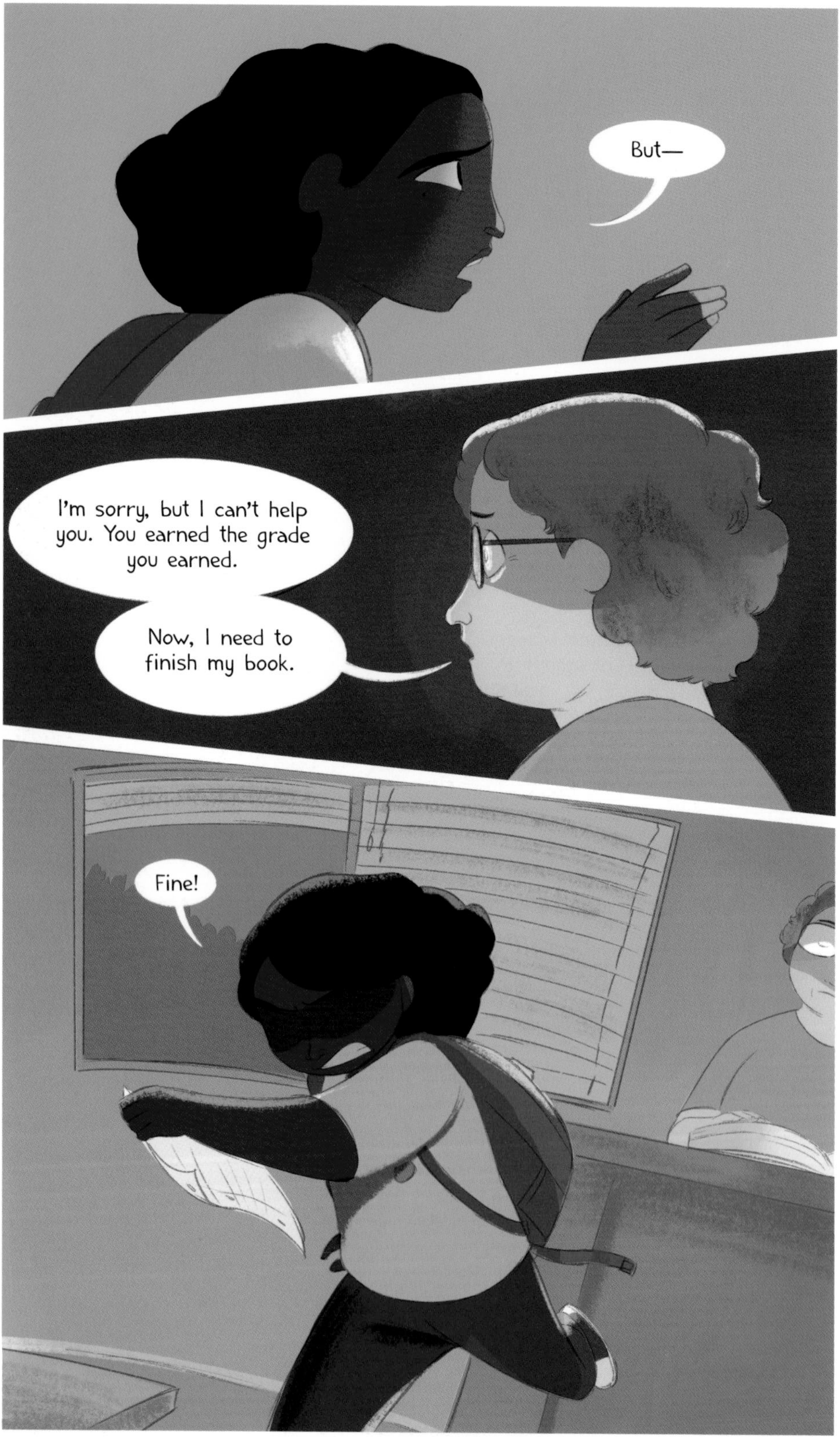
But—
I'm sorry, but I can't help you. You earned the grade you earned.
Now, I need to finish my book.
Fine!

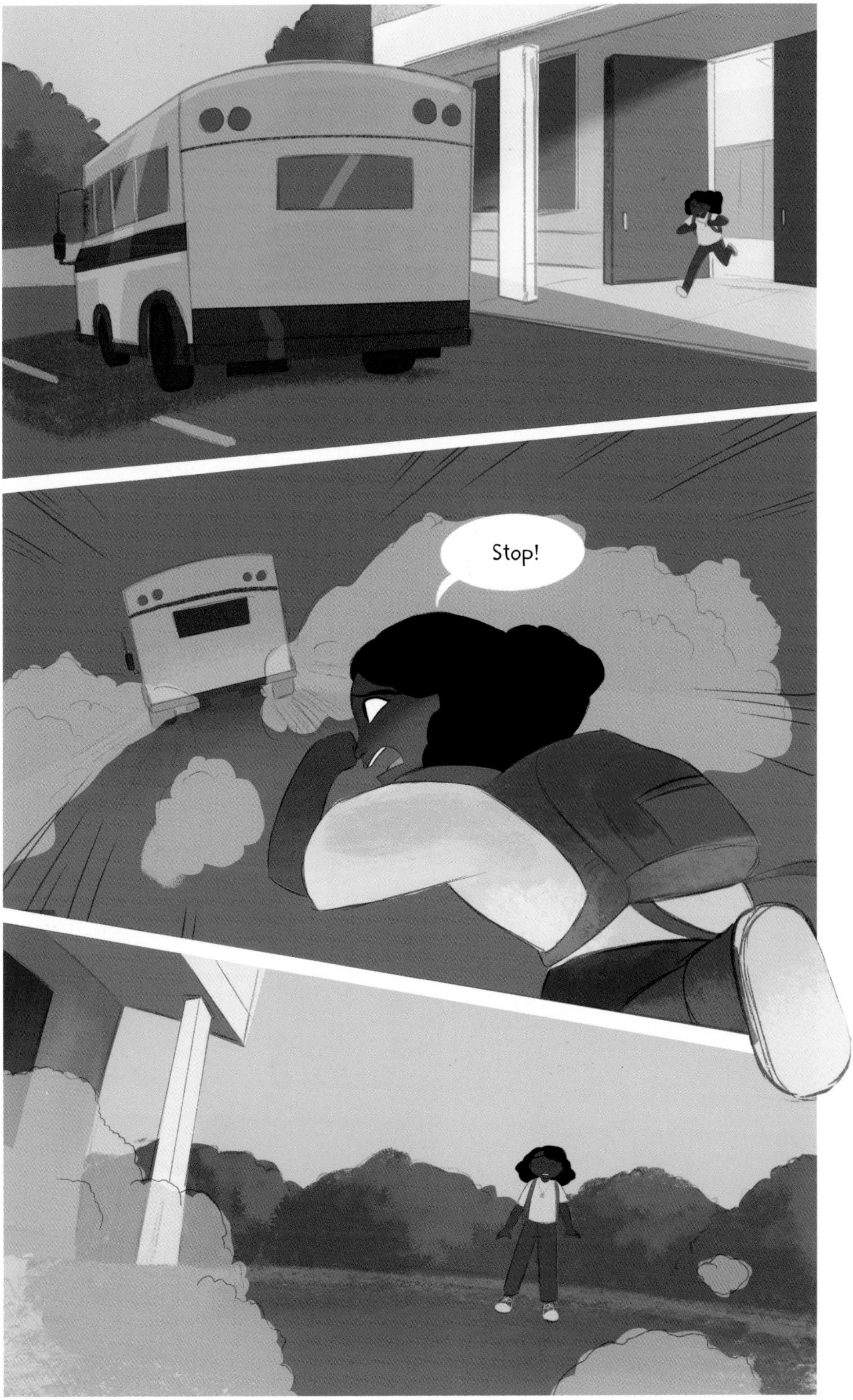
Stop!

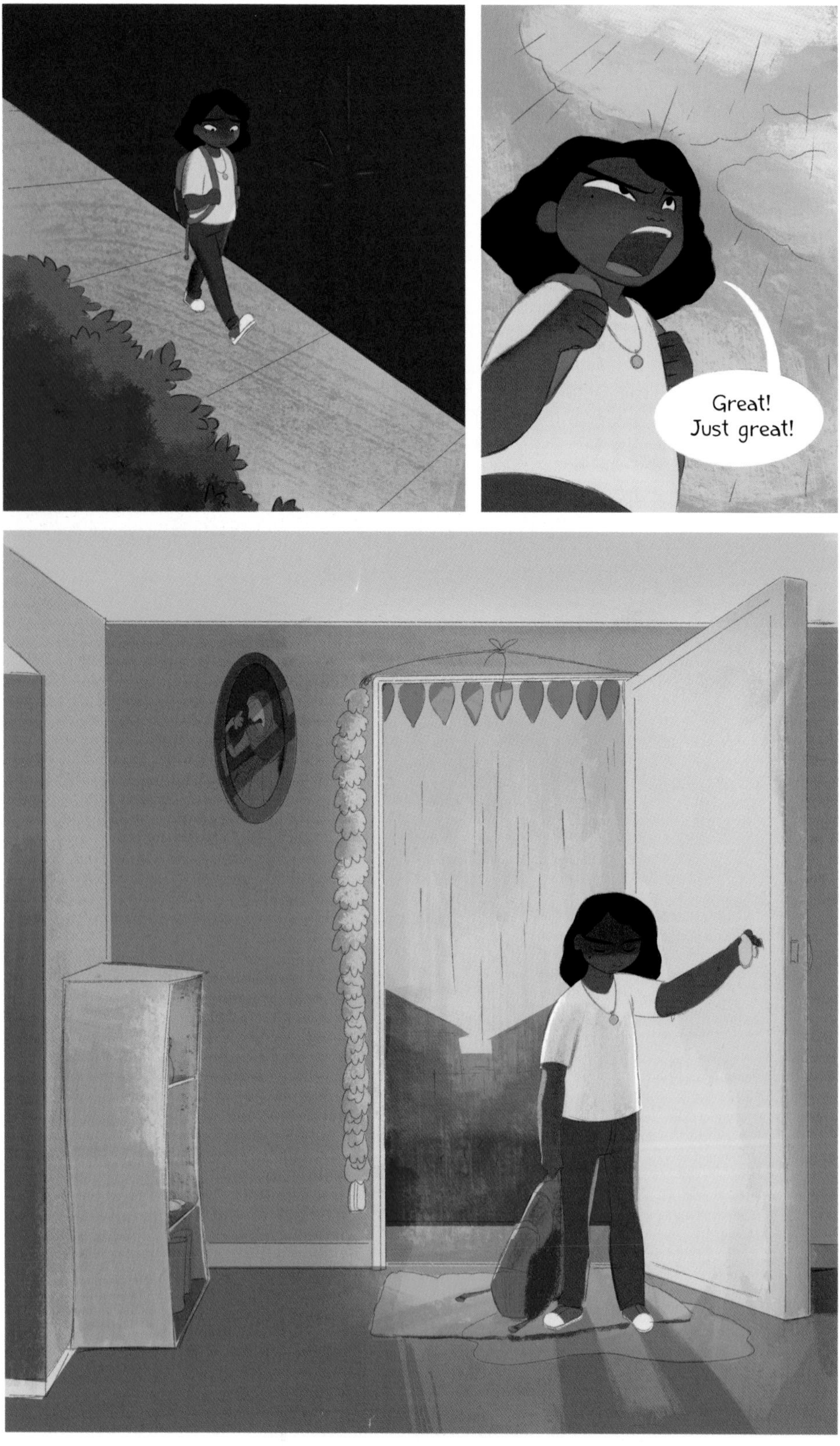
Great!
Just great!

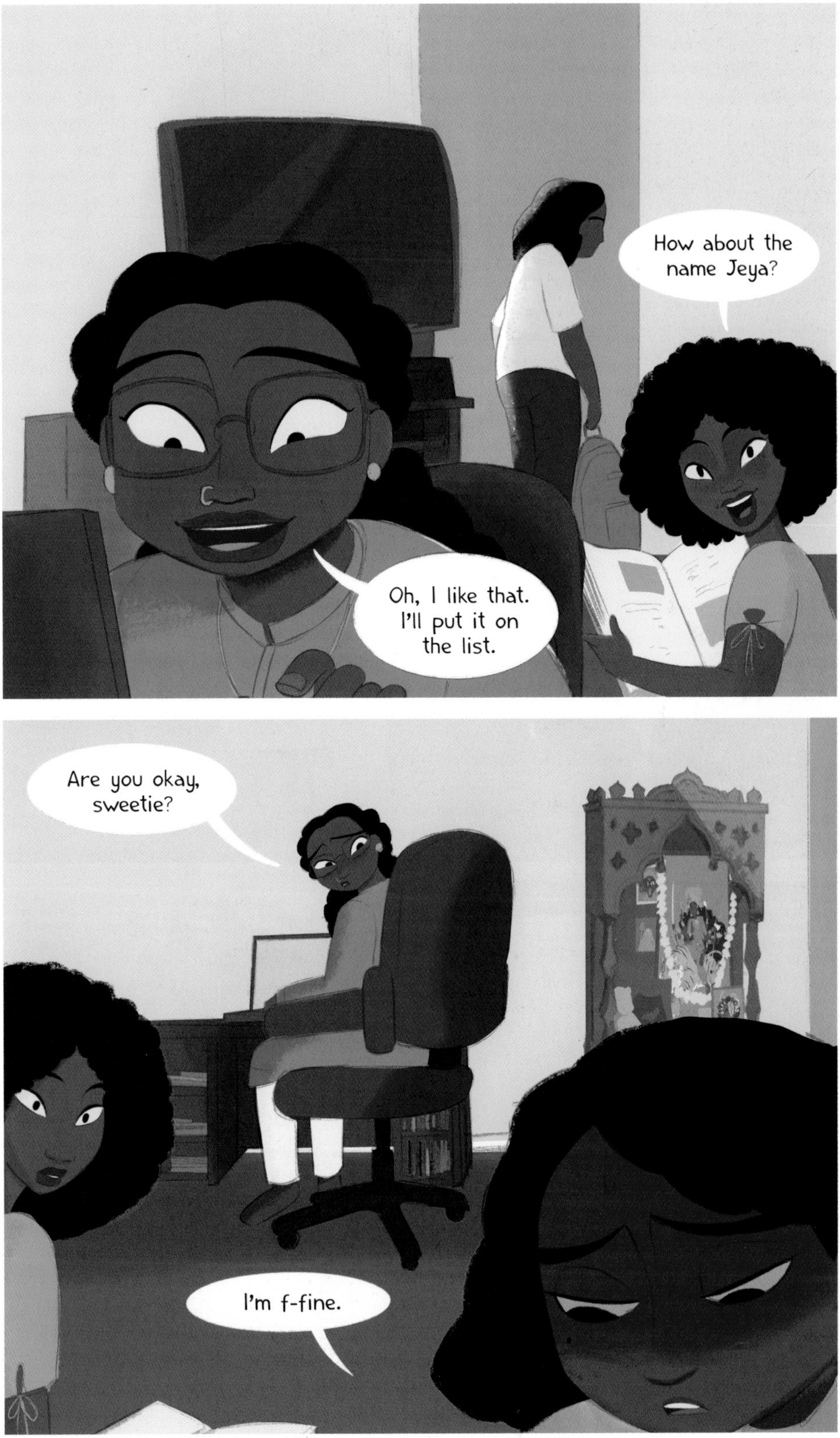
How about the name Jeya?
Oh, I like that. I'll put it on the list.
Are you okay, sweetie?
I'm f-fine.

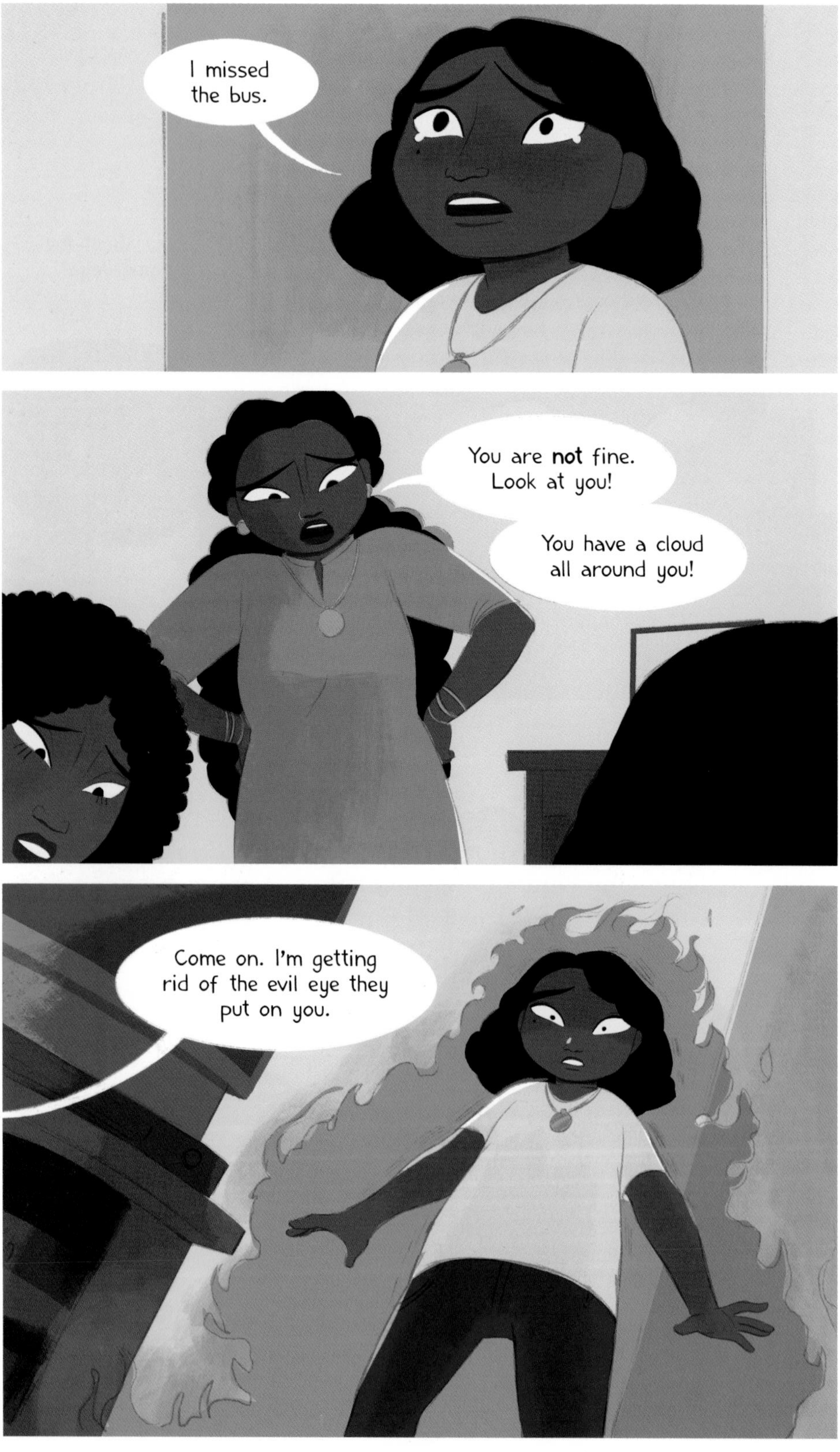
I missed the bus.
You are **not** fine. Look at you!
You have a cloud all around you!
Come on. I'm getting rid of the evil eye they put on you.

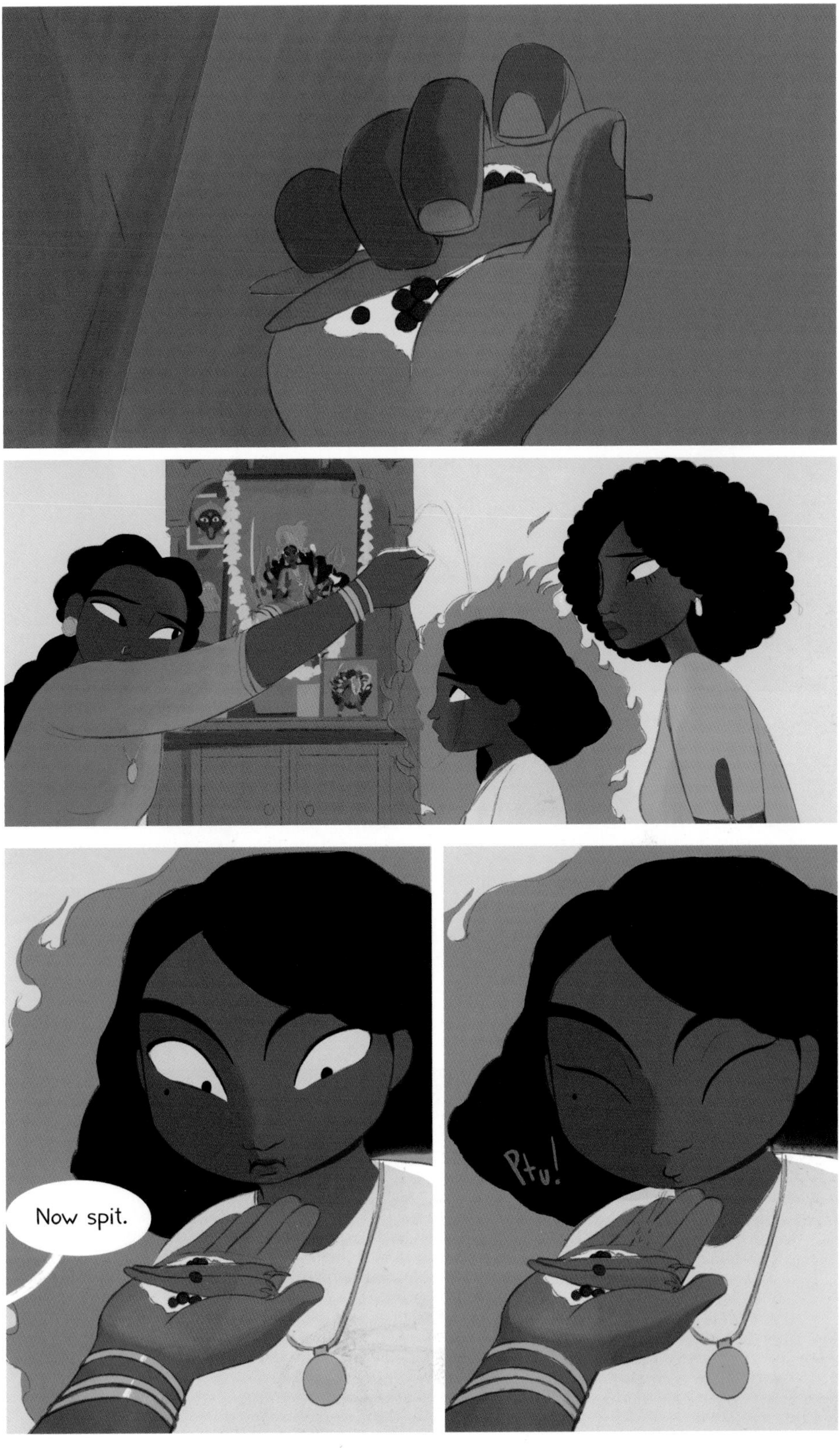
Now spit.
Ptu!

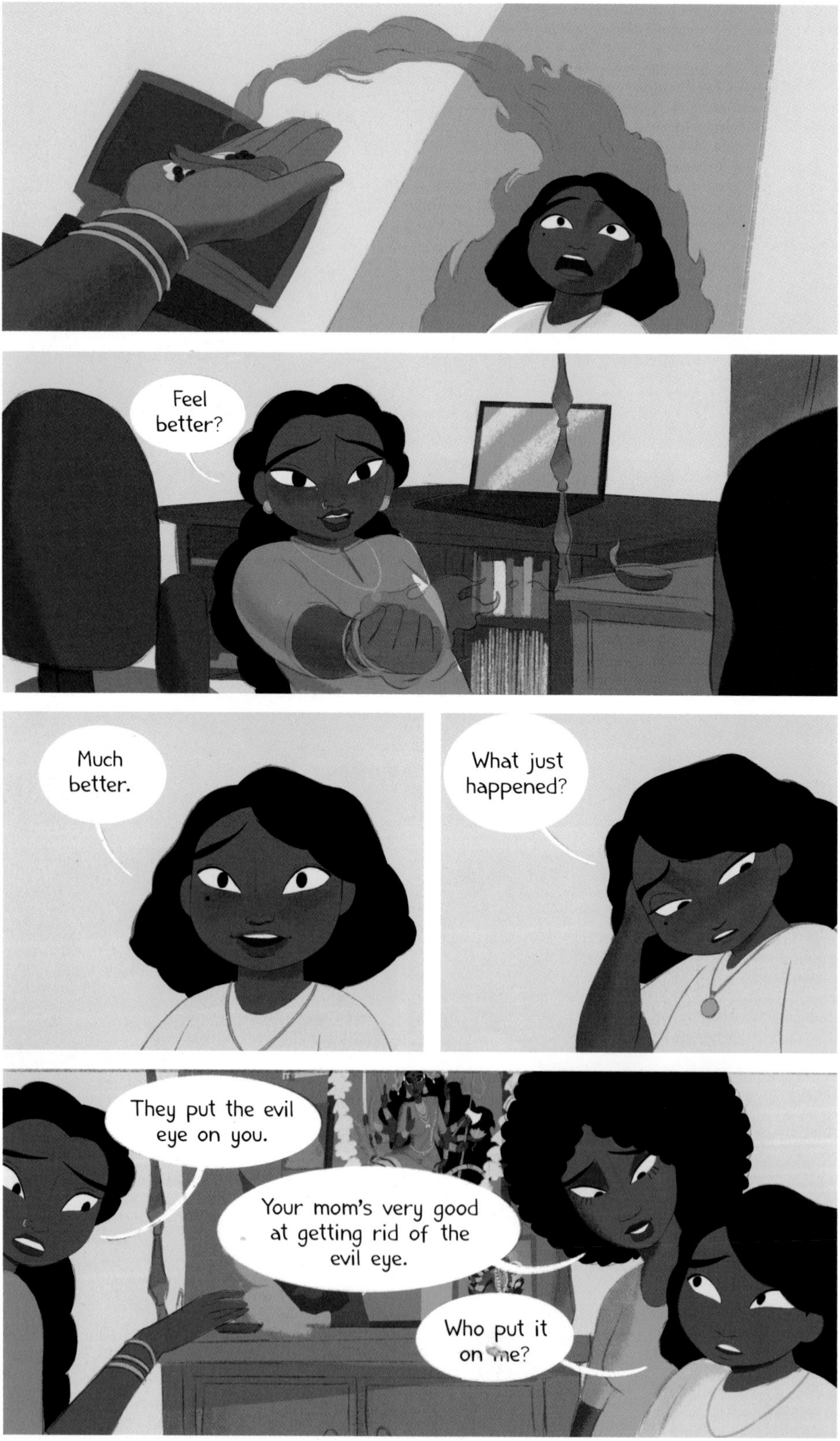
Feel better?
Much better.
What just happened?
They put the evil eye on you.
Your mom's very good at getting rid of the evil eye.
Who put it on me?

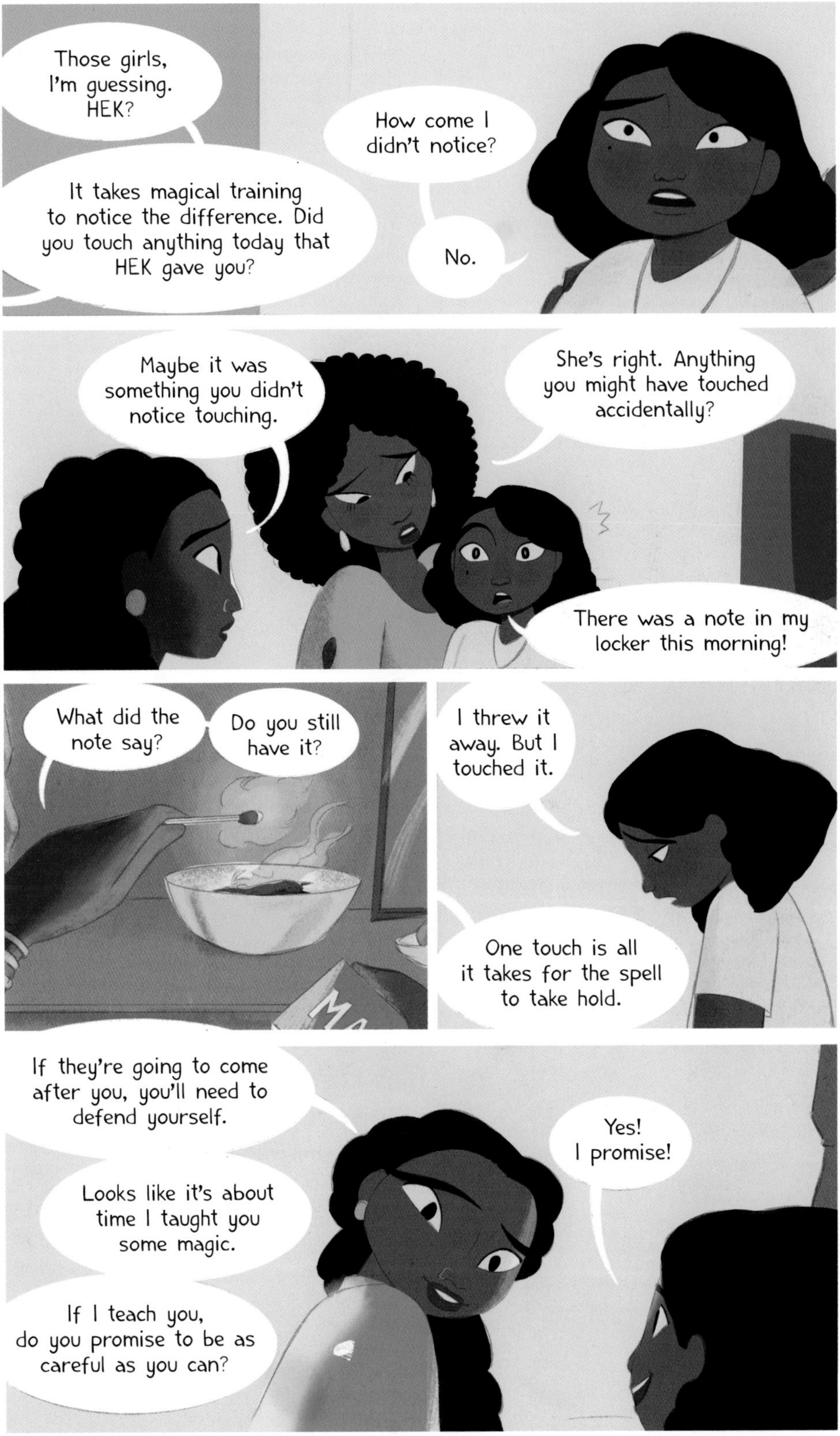
Those girls, I'm guessing. HEK?
It takes magical training to notice the difference. Did you touch anything today that HEK gave you?
How come I didn't notice?
No.
Maybe it was something you didn't notice touching.
She's right. Anything you might have touched accidentally?
There was a note in my locker this morning!
What did the note say?
Do you still have it?
I threw it away. But I touched it.
One touch is all it takes for the spell to take hold.
If they're going to come after you, you'll need to defend yourself.
Looks like it's about time I taught you some magic.
If I teach you, do you promise to be as careful as you can?
Yes! I promise!

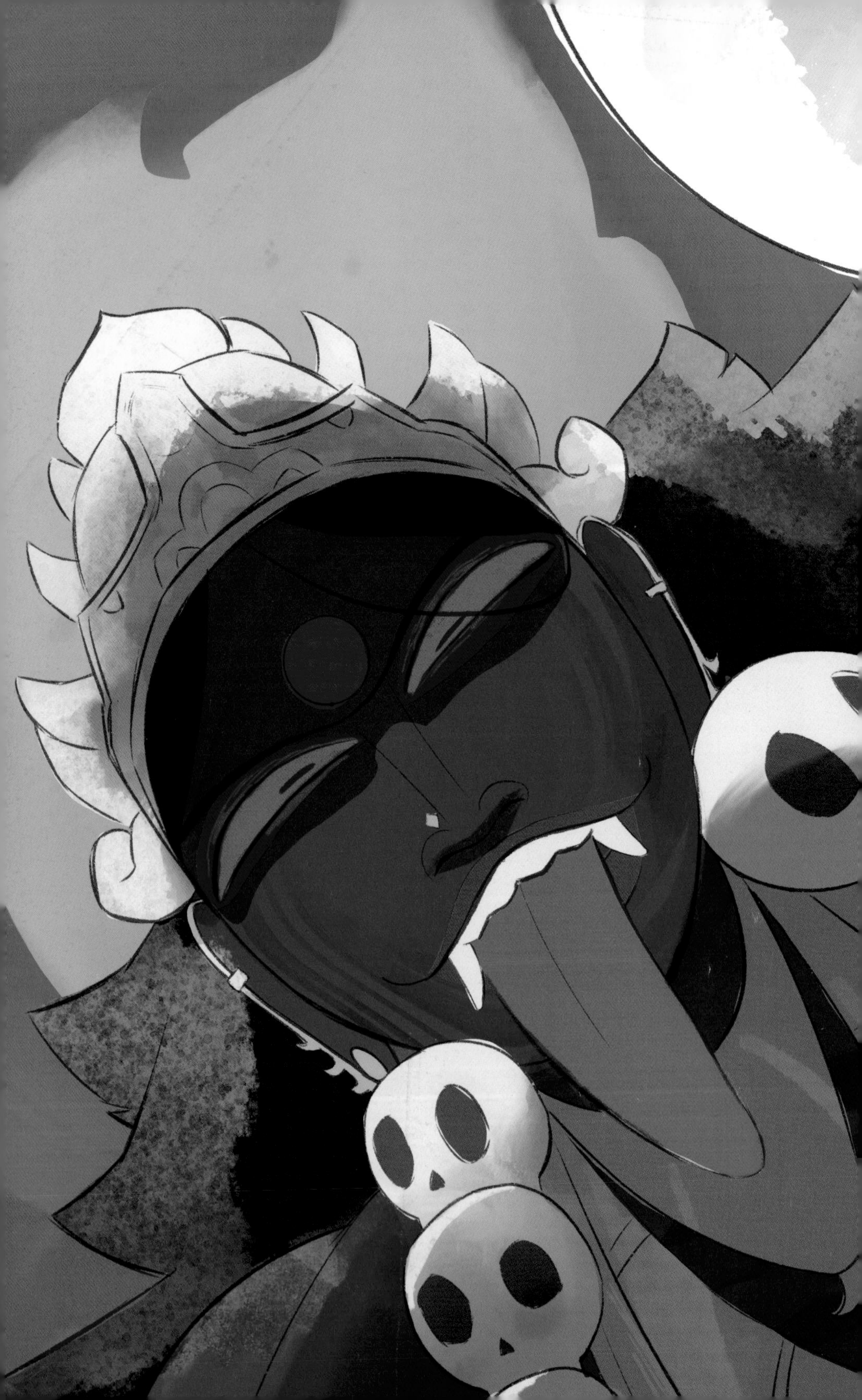

# Interlude:
## THE PROBLEM OF KALI MA

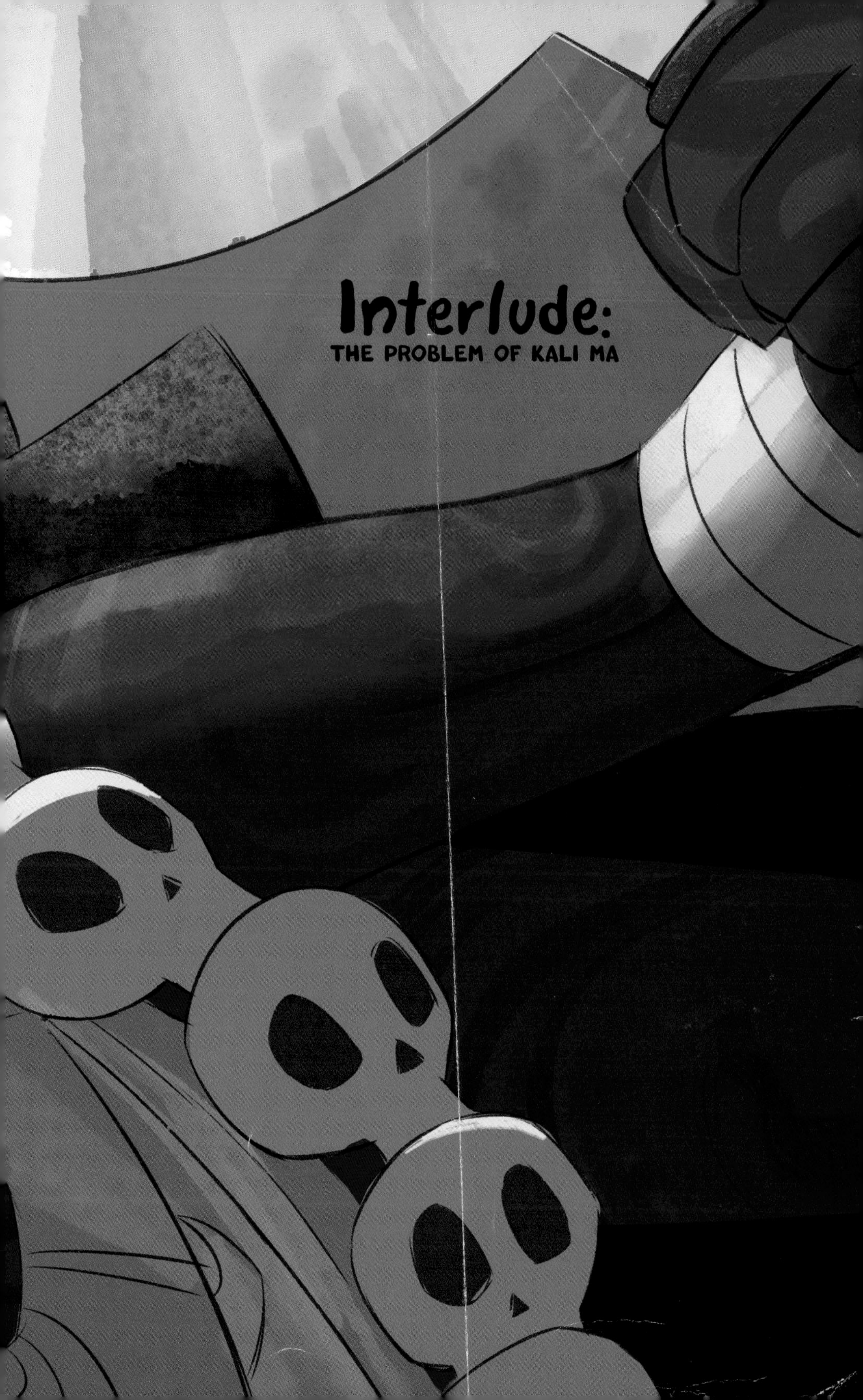

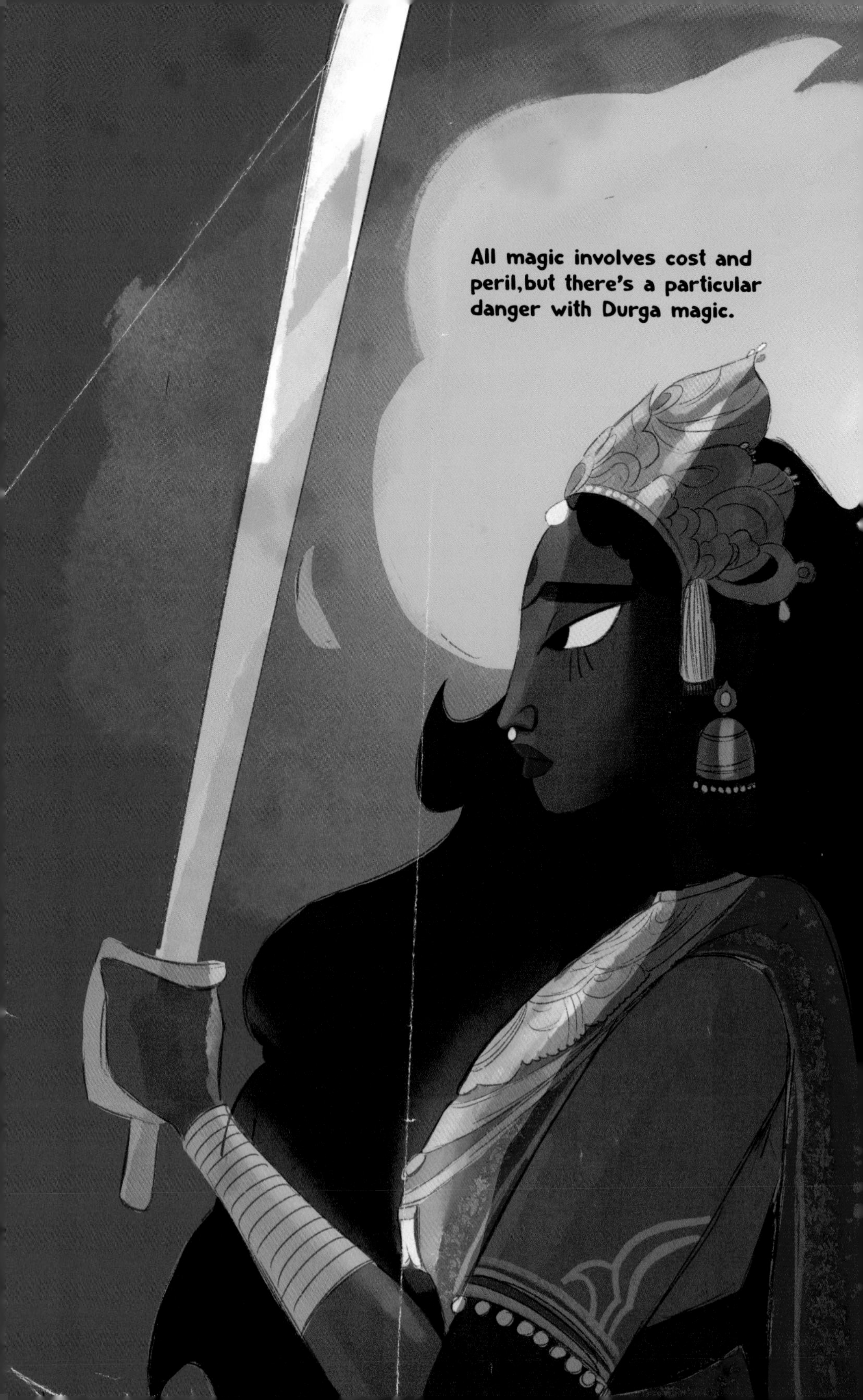
All magic involves cost and peril, but there's a particular danger with Durga magic.

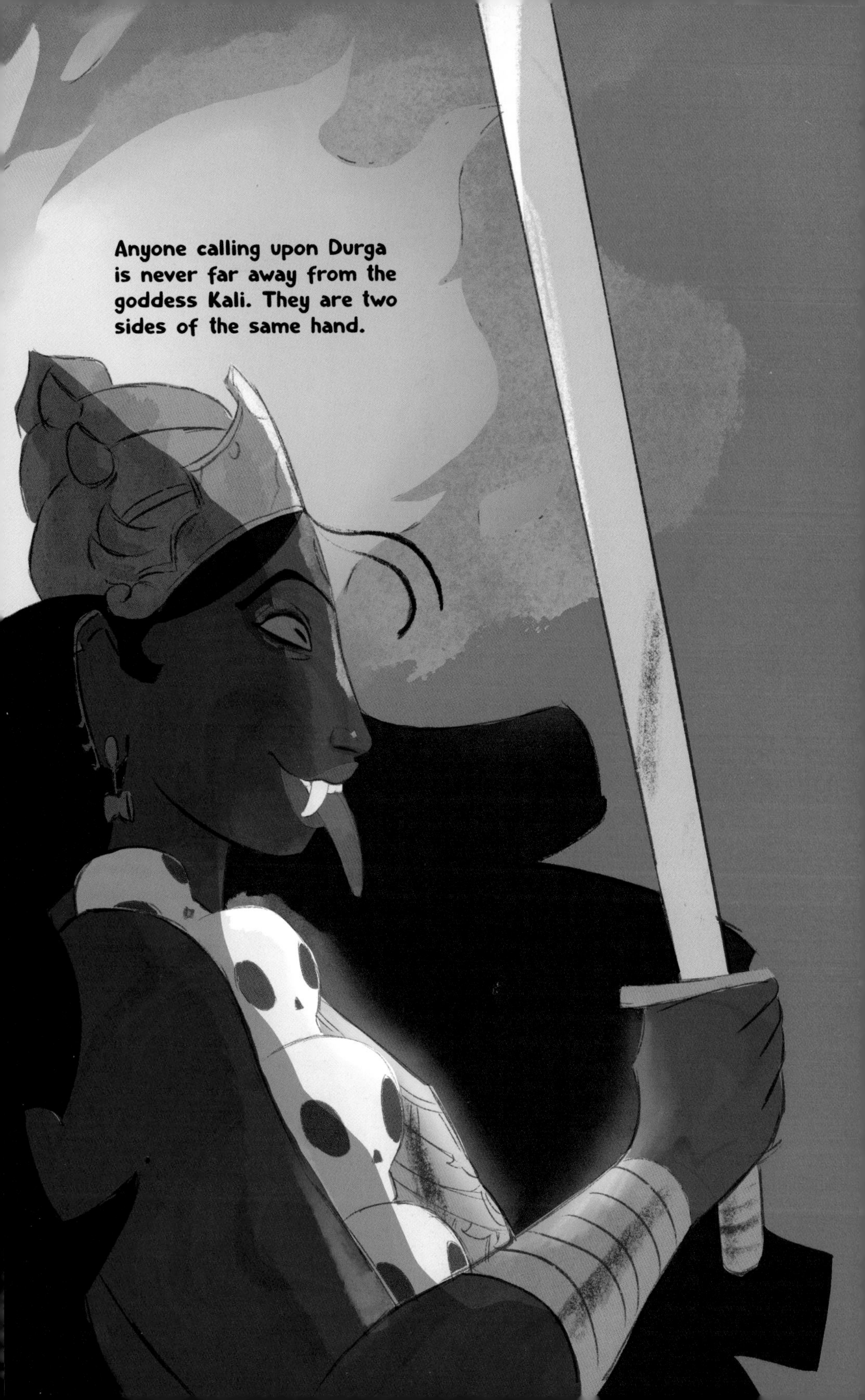
Anyone calling upon Durga is never far away from the goddess Kali. They are two sides of the same hand.

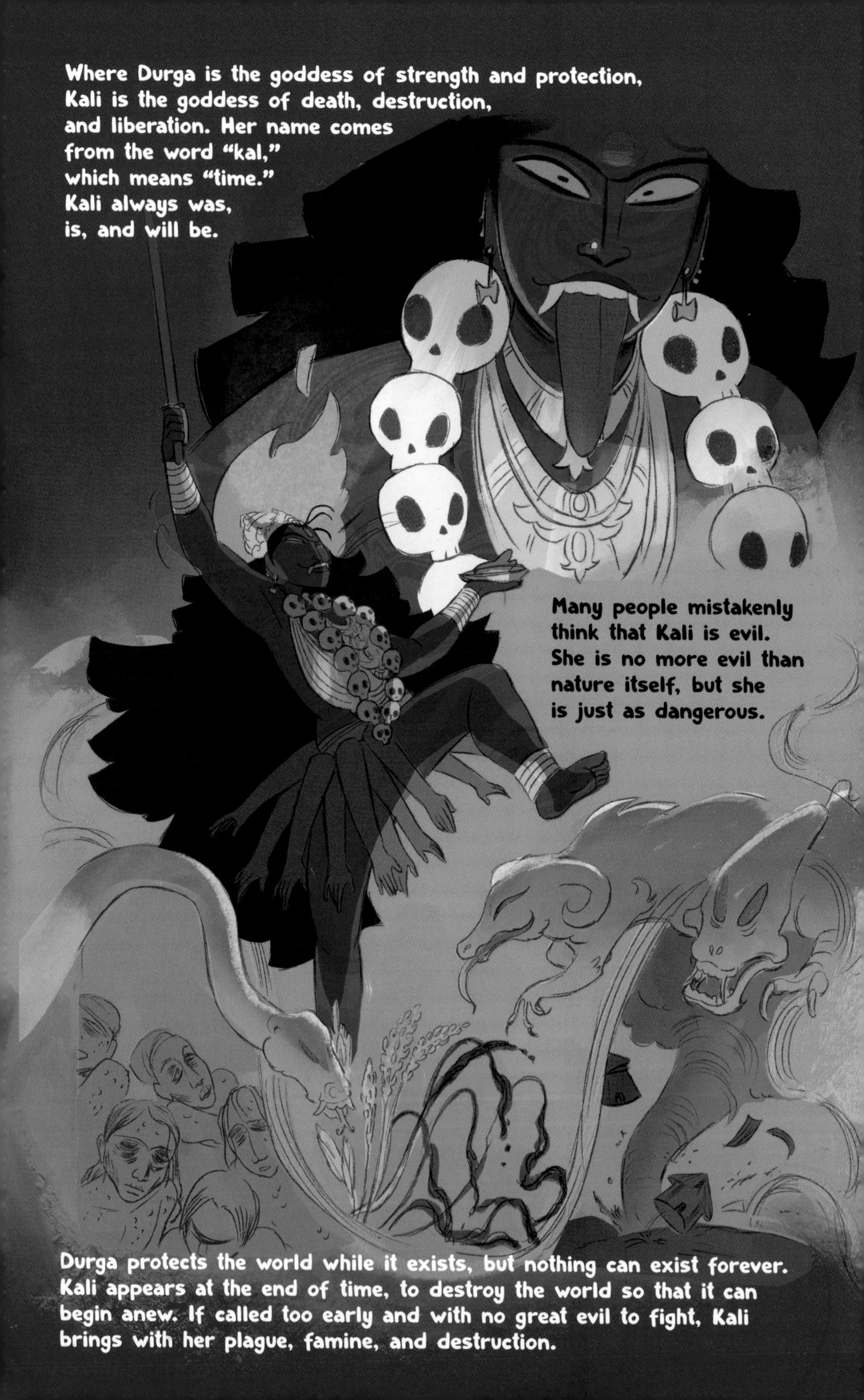
Where Durga is the goddess of strength and protection, Kali is the goddess of death, destruction, and liberation. Her name comes from the word "kal," which means "time." Kali always was, is, and will be.
Many people mistakenly think that Kali is evil. She is no more evil than nature itself, but she is just as dangerous.
Durga protects the world while it exists, but nothing can exist forever. Kali appears at the end of time, to destroy the world so that it can begin anew. If called too early and with no great evil to fight, Kali brings with her plague, famine, and destruction.

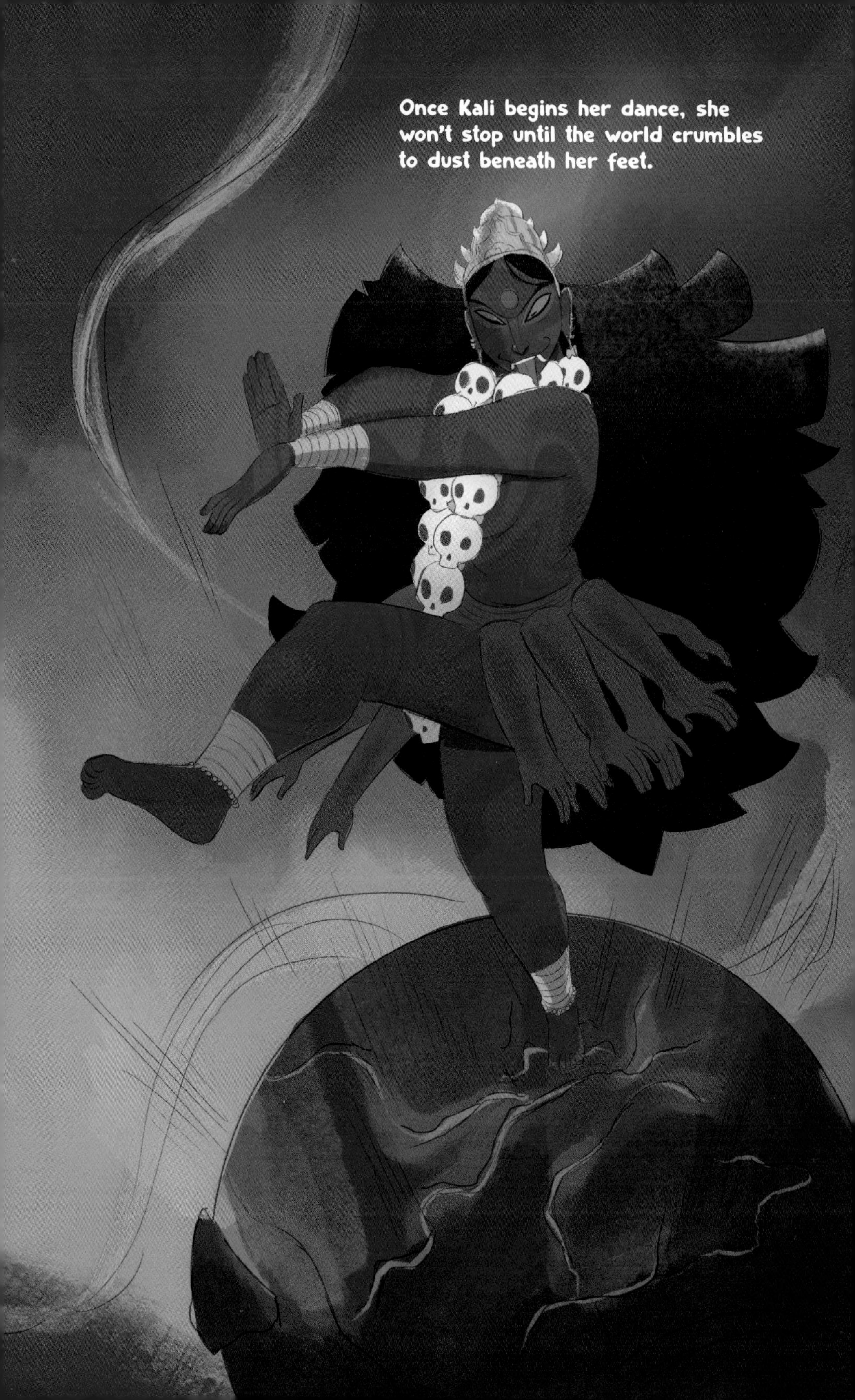
Once Kali begins her dance, she won't stop until the world crumbles to dust beneath her feet.

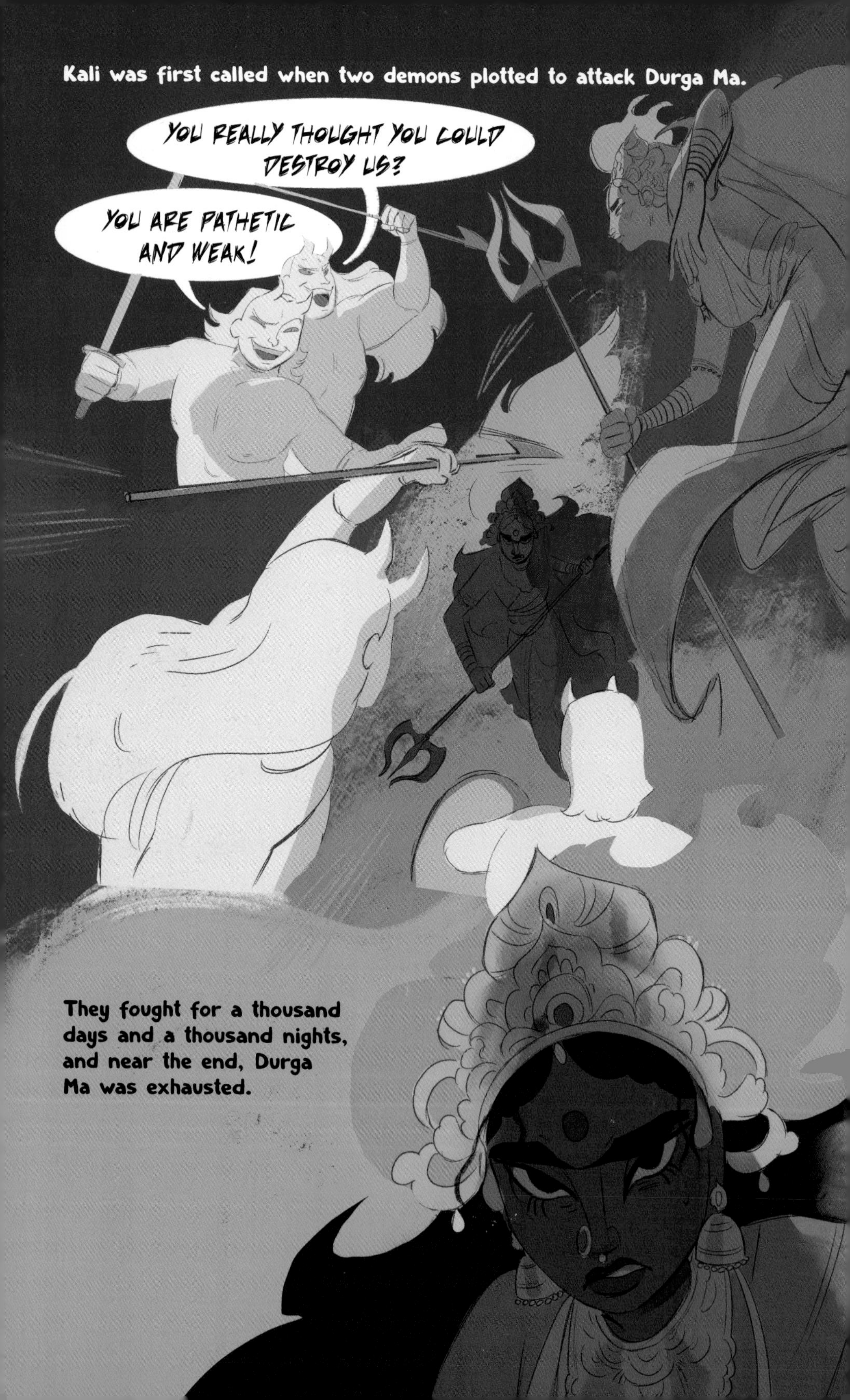
Kali was first called when two demons plotted to attack Durga Ma.
YOU REALLY THOUGHT YOU COULD DESTROY US?
YOU ARE PATHETIC AND WEAK!
They fought for a thousand days and a thousand nights, and near the end, Durga Ma was exhausted.

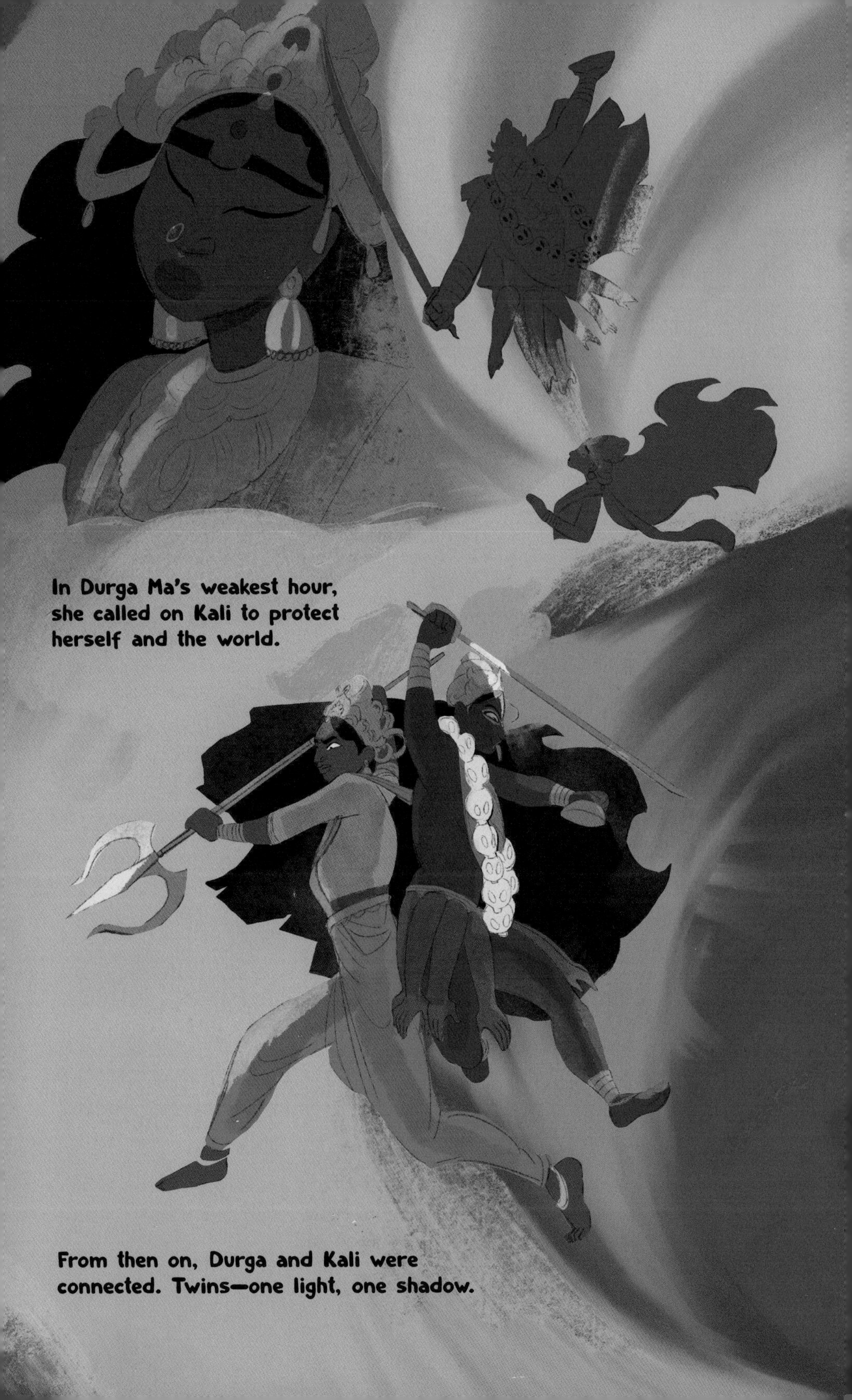

In Durga Ma's weakest hour, she called on Kali to protect herself and the world.

From then on, Durga and Kali were connected. Twins—one light, one shadow.

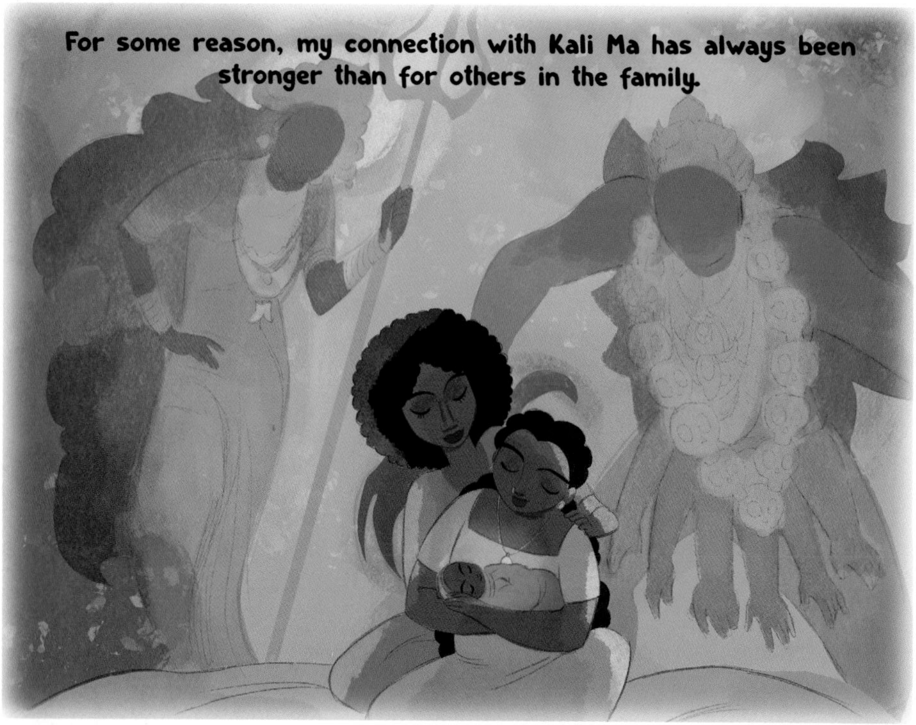
For some reason, my connection with Kali Ma has always been stronger than for others in the family.

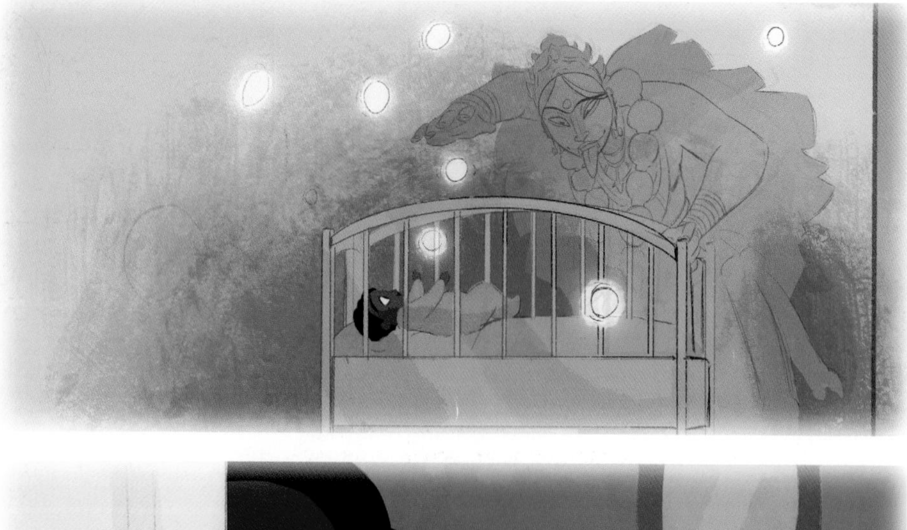

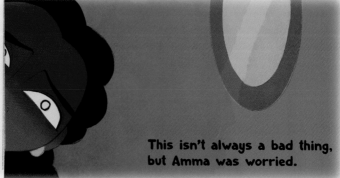

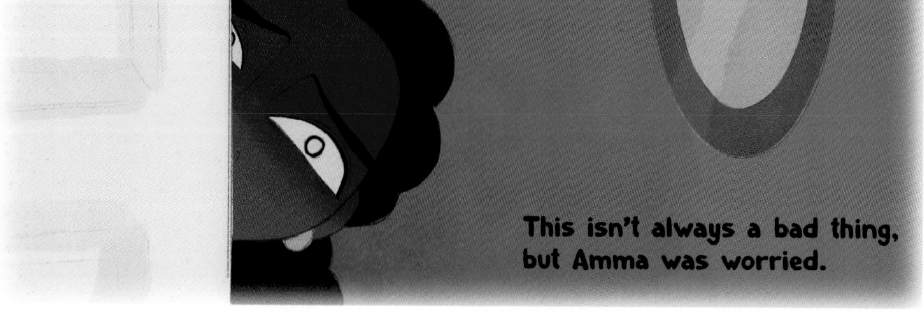
This isn't always a bad thing, but Amma was worried.

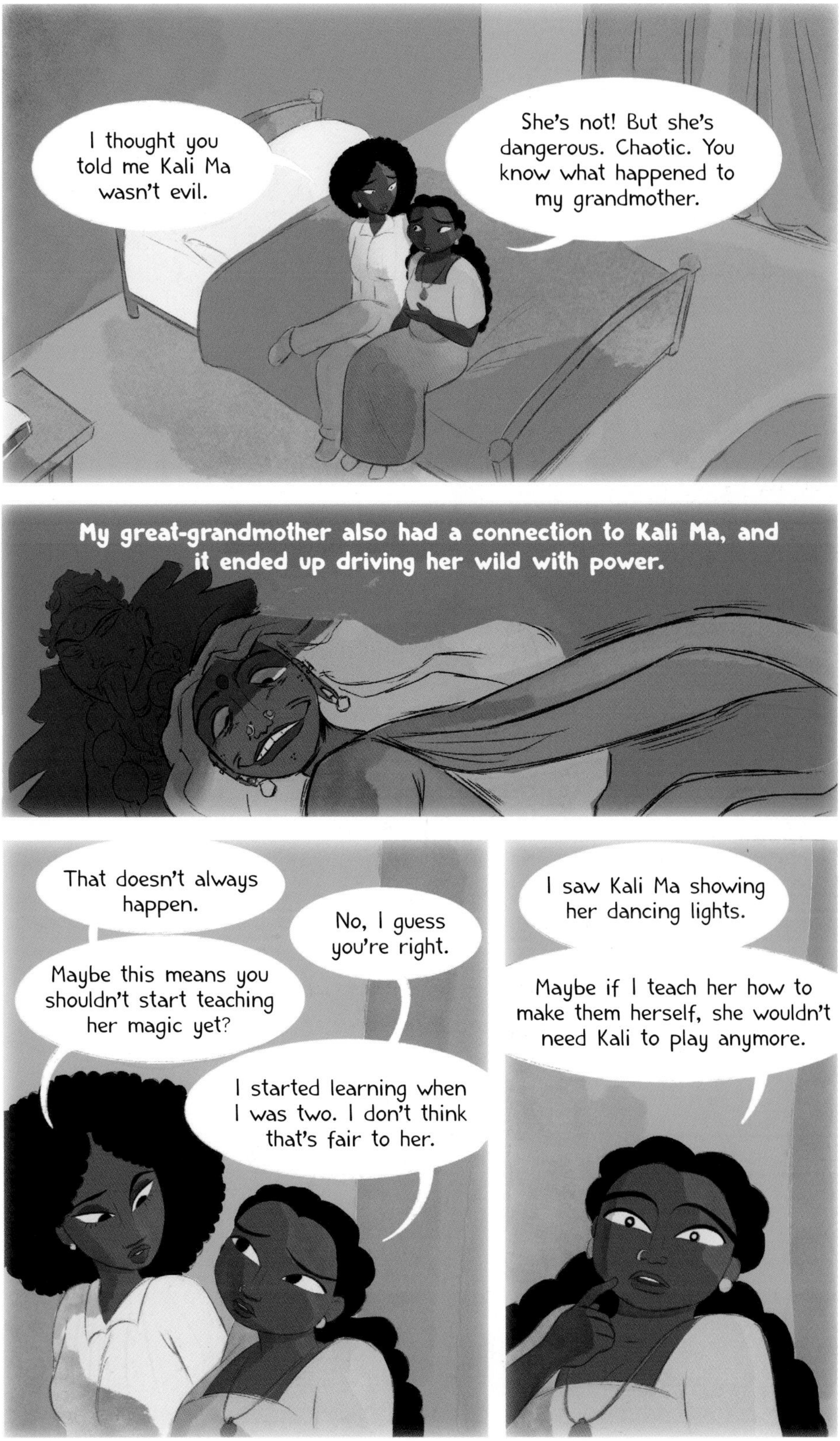
I thought you told me Kali Ma wasn't evil.
She's not! But she's dangerous. Chaotic. You know what happened to my grandmother.
My great-grandmother also had a connection to Kali Ma, and it ended up driving her wild with power.
That doesn't always happen.
Maybe this means you shouldn't start teaching her magic yet?
No, I guess you're right.
I started learning when I was two. I don't think that's fair to her.
I saw Kali Ma showing her dancing lights.
Maybe if I teach her how to make them herself, she wouldn't need Kali to play anymore.

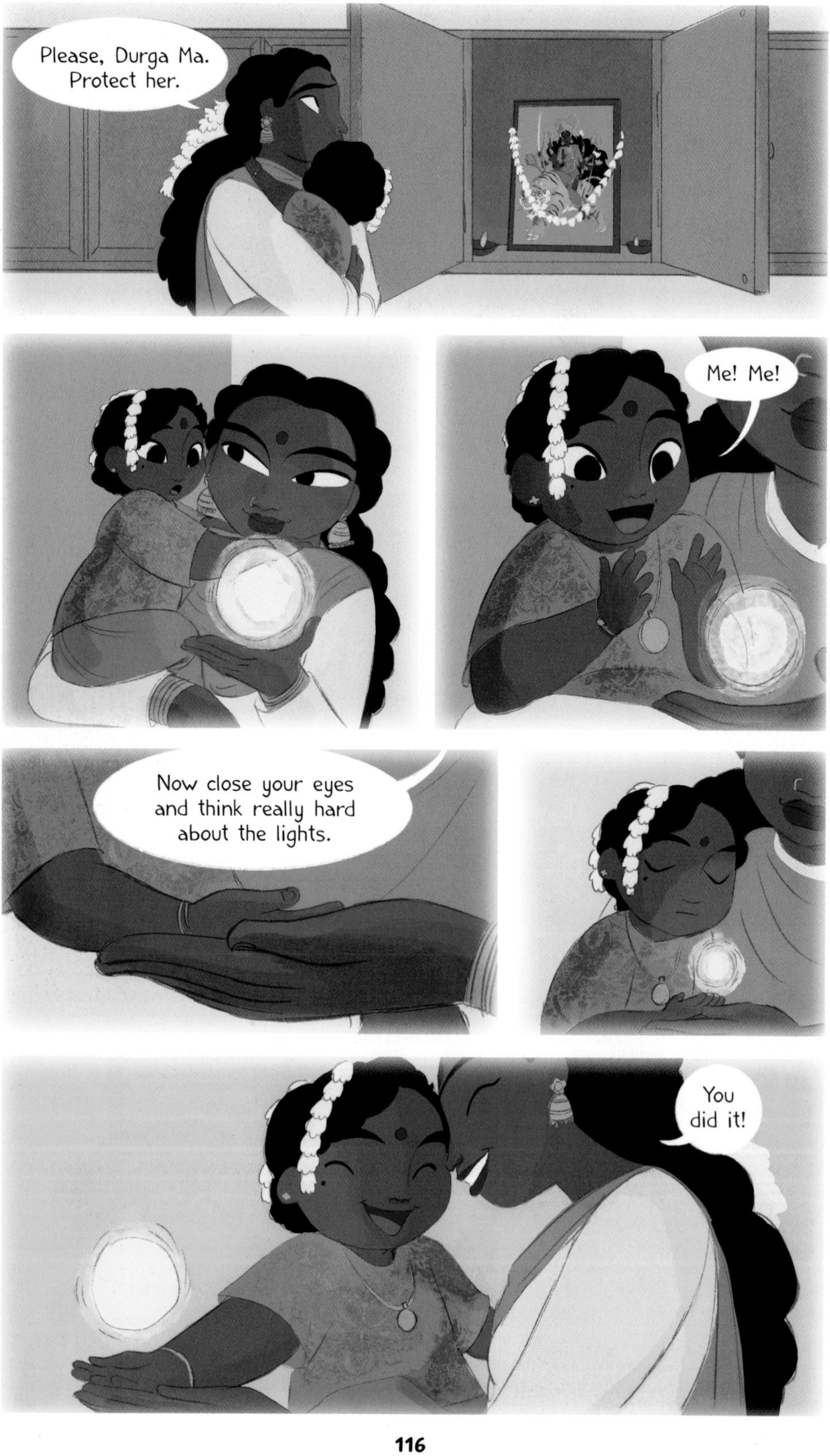
Please, Durga Ma. Protect her.
Me! Me!
Now close your eyes and think really hard about the lights.
You did it!

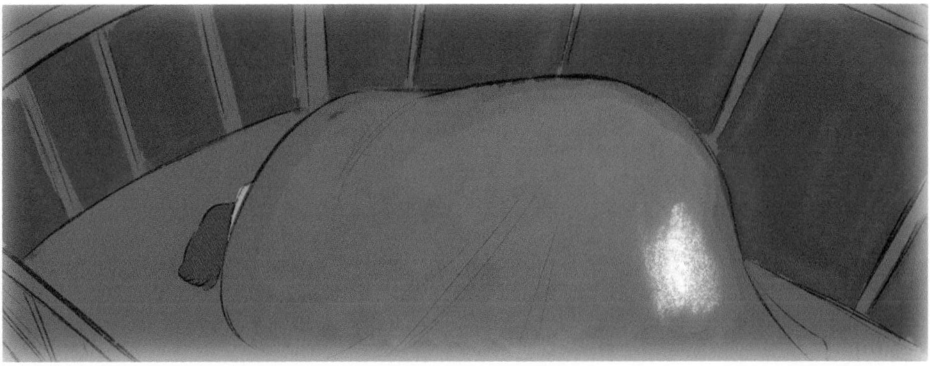

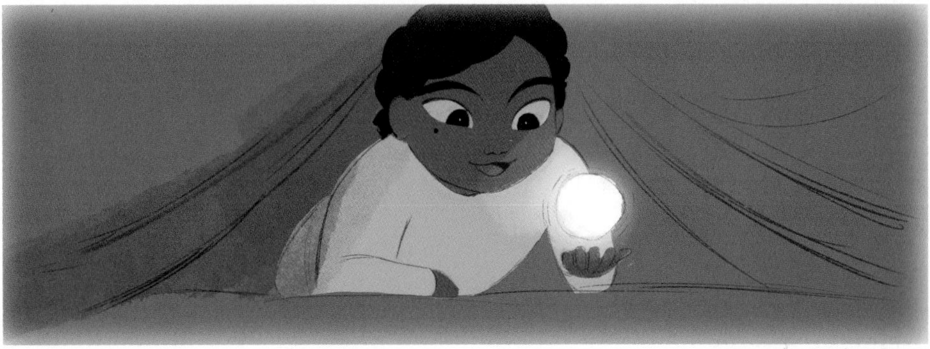

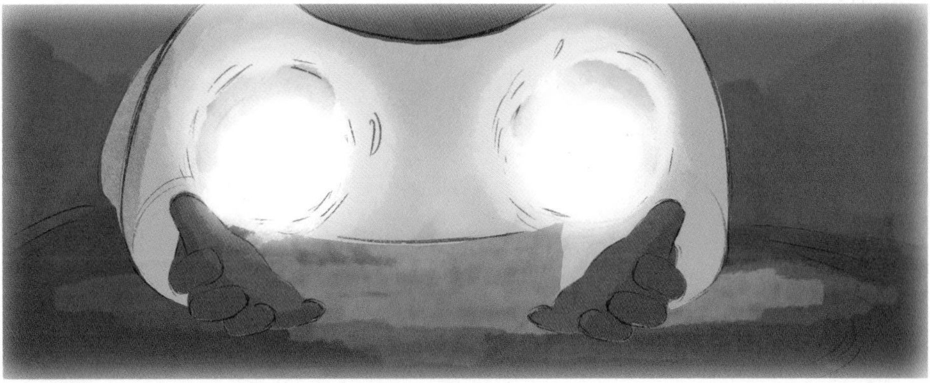

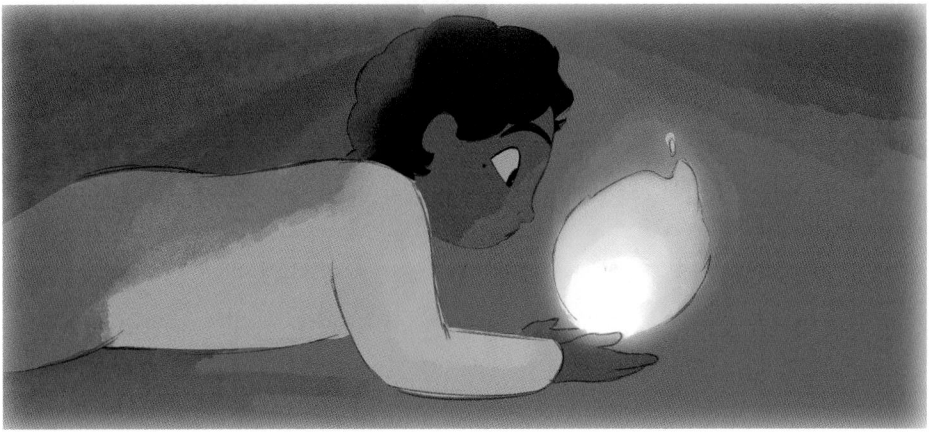

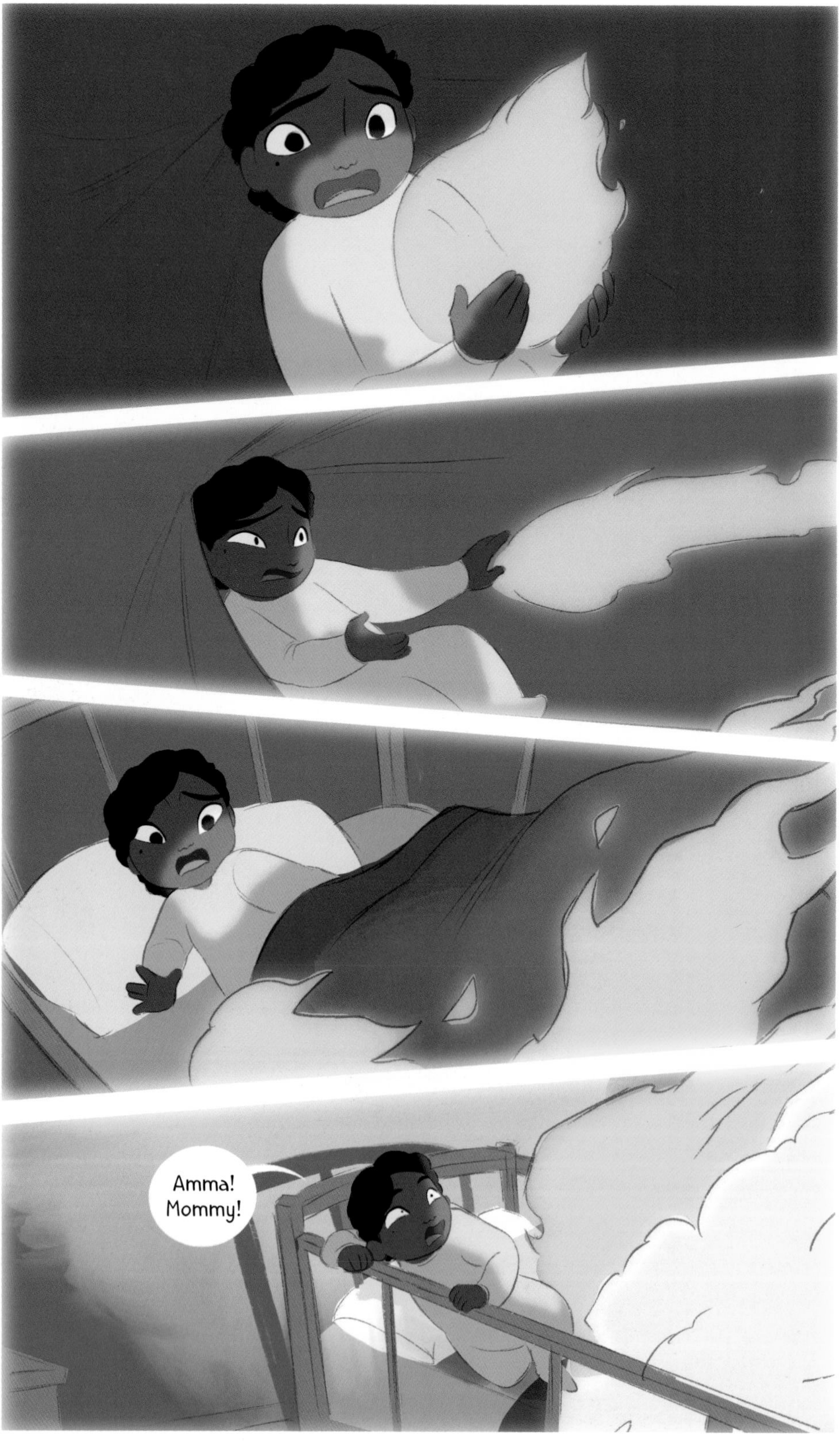
Amma!
Mommy!

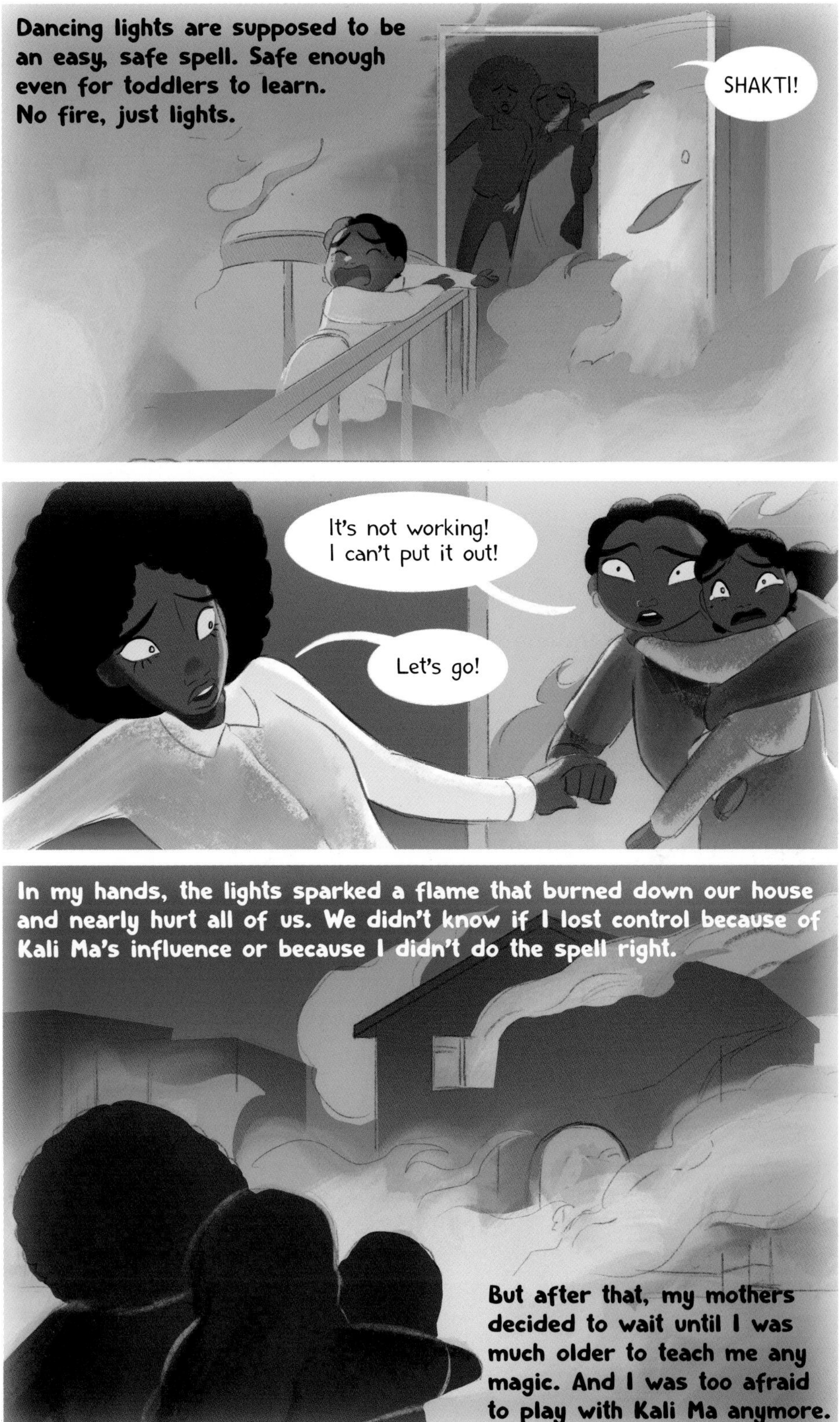
Dancing lights are supposed to be an easy, safe spell. Safe enough even for toddlers to learn. No fire, just lights.
SHAKTI!
It's not working! I can't put it out!
Let's go!
In my hands, the lights sparked a flame that burned down our house and nearly hurt all of us. We didn't know if I lost control because of Kali Ma's influence or because I didn't do the spell right.
But after that, my mothers decided to wait until I was much older to teach me any magic. And I was too afraid to play with Kali Ma anymore.

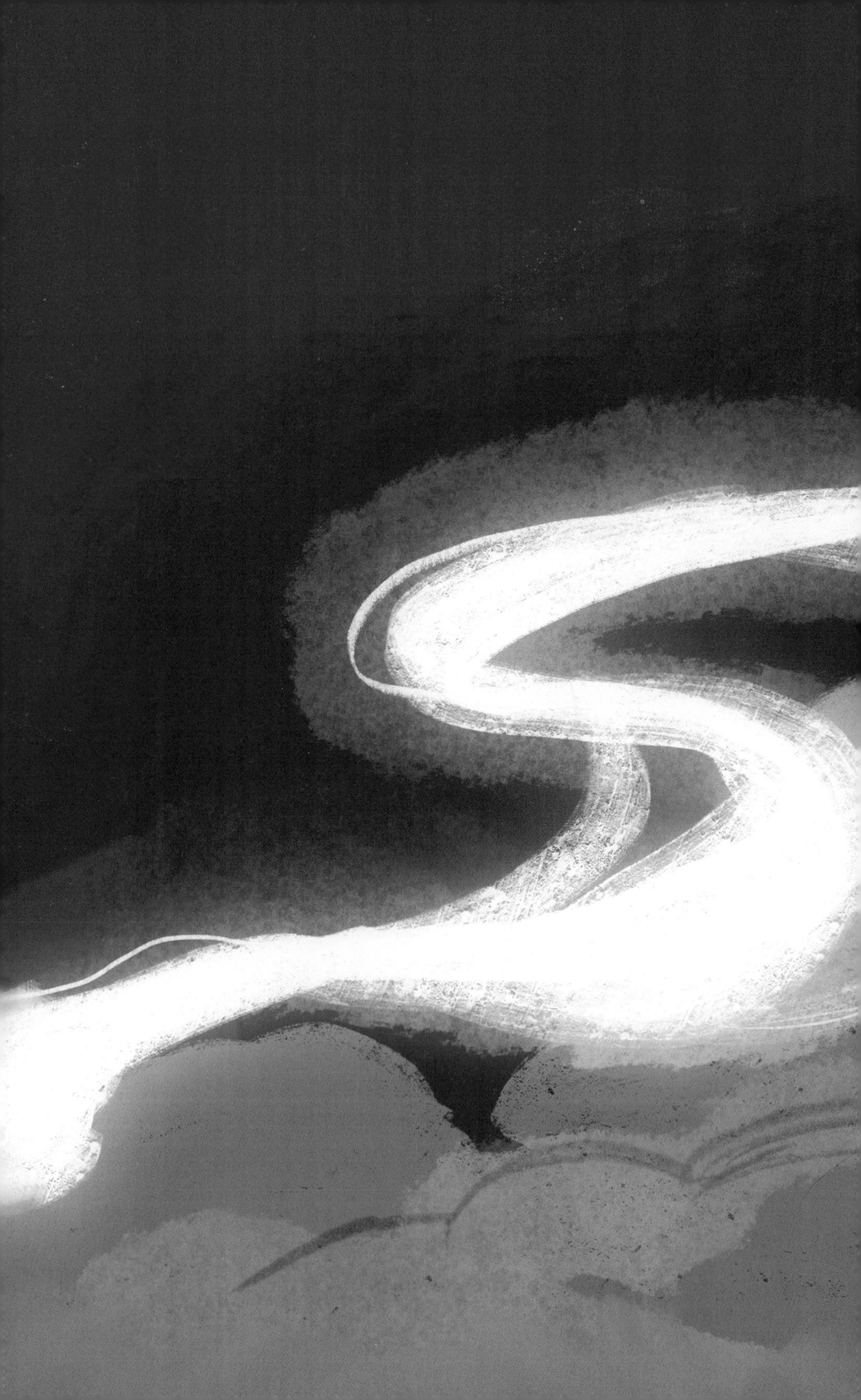

# Chapter 3

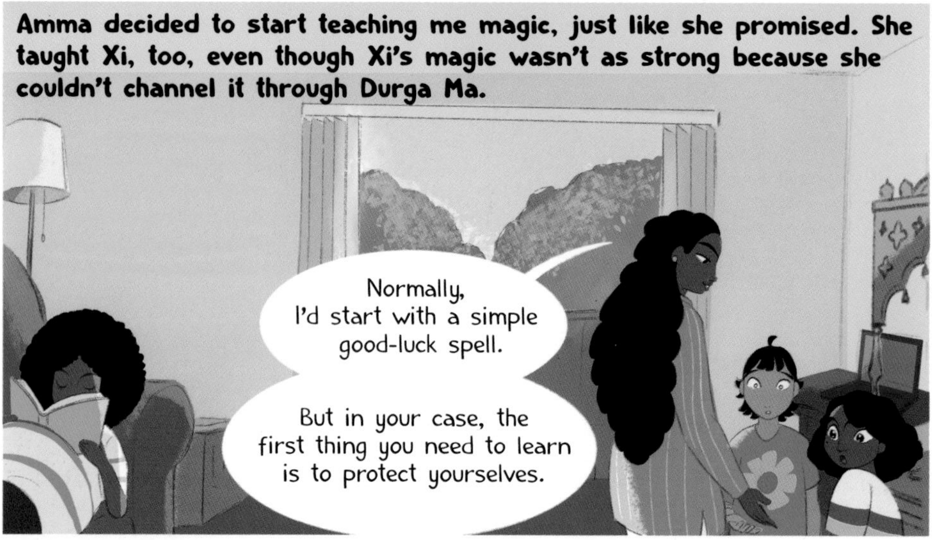
Amma decided to start teaching me magic, just like she promised. She taught Xi, too, even though Xi's magic wasn't as strong because she couldn't channel it through Durga Ma.
Normally, I'd start with a simple good-luck spell.
But in your case, the first thing you need to learn is to protect yourselves.

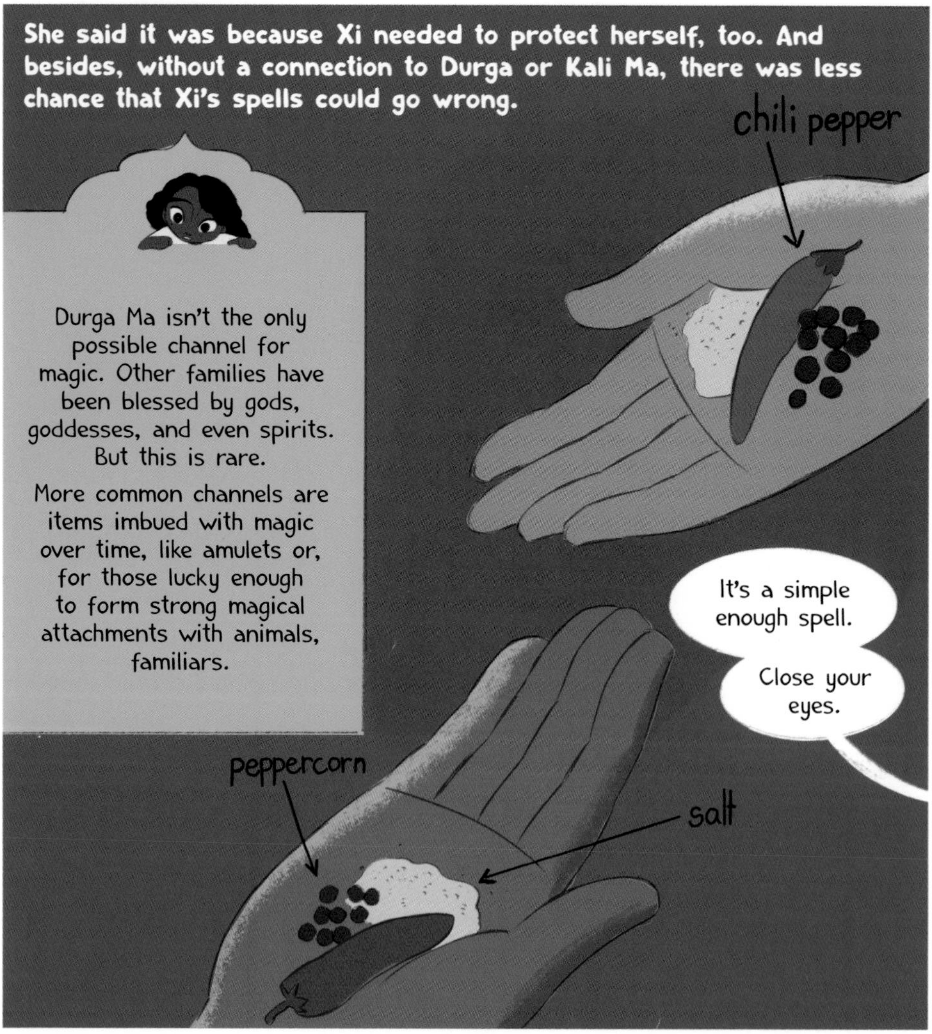
She said it was because Xi needed to protect herself, too. And besides, without a connection to Durga or Kali Ma, there was less chance that Xi's spells could go wrong.
Durga Ma isn't the only possible channel for magic. Other families have been blessed by gods, goddesses, and even spirits. But this is rare.
More common channels are items imbued with magic over time, like amulets or, for those lucky enough to form strong magical attachments with animals, familiars.
chili pepper
It's a simple enough spell.
Close your eyes.
peppercorn
salt

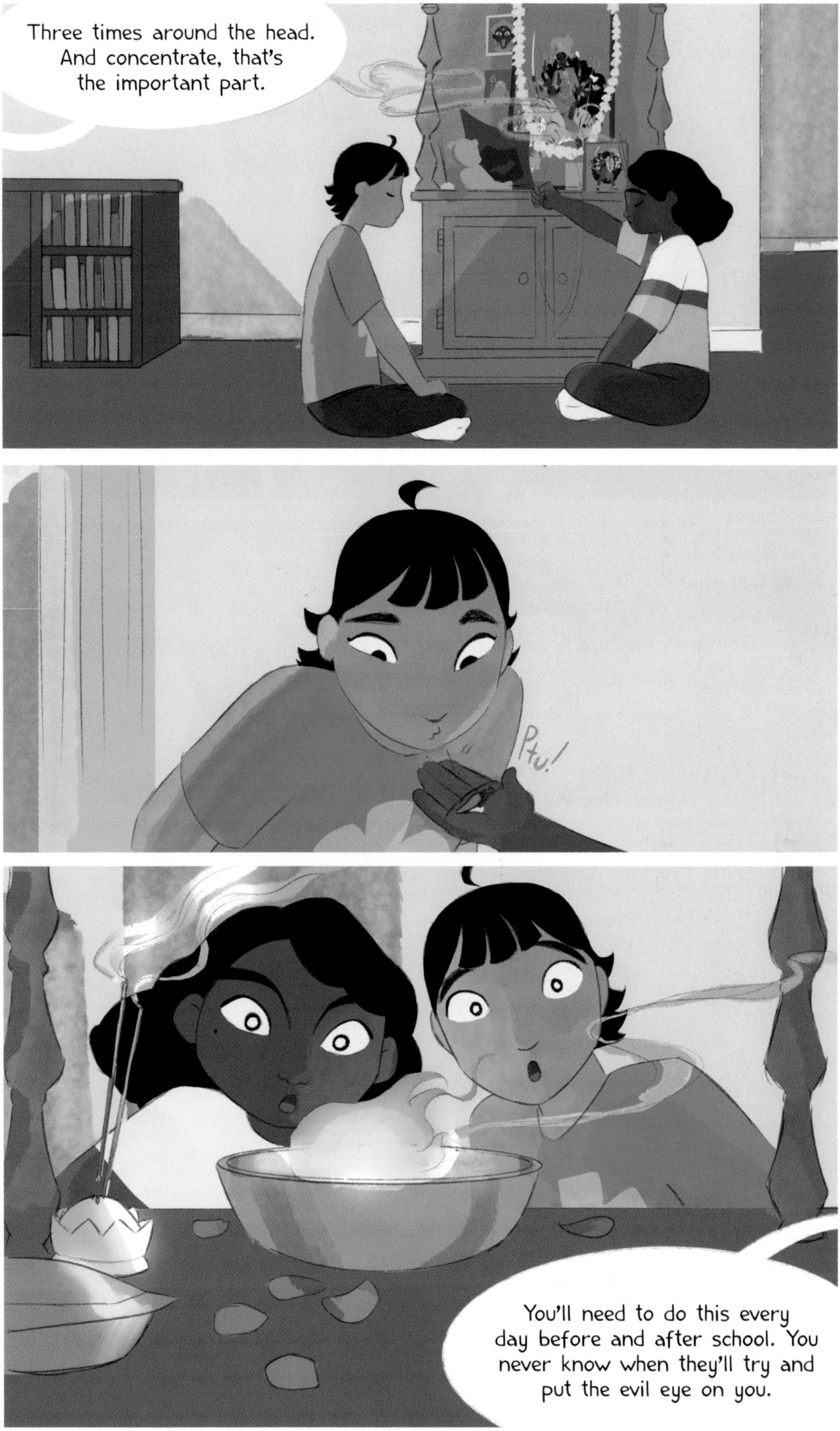
Three times around the head. And concentrate, that's the important part.
Ptu!
You'll need to do this every day before and after school. You never know when they'll try and put the evil eye on you.

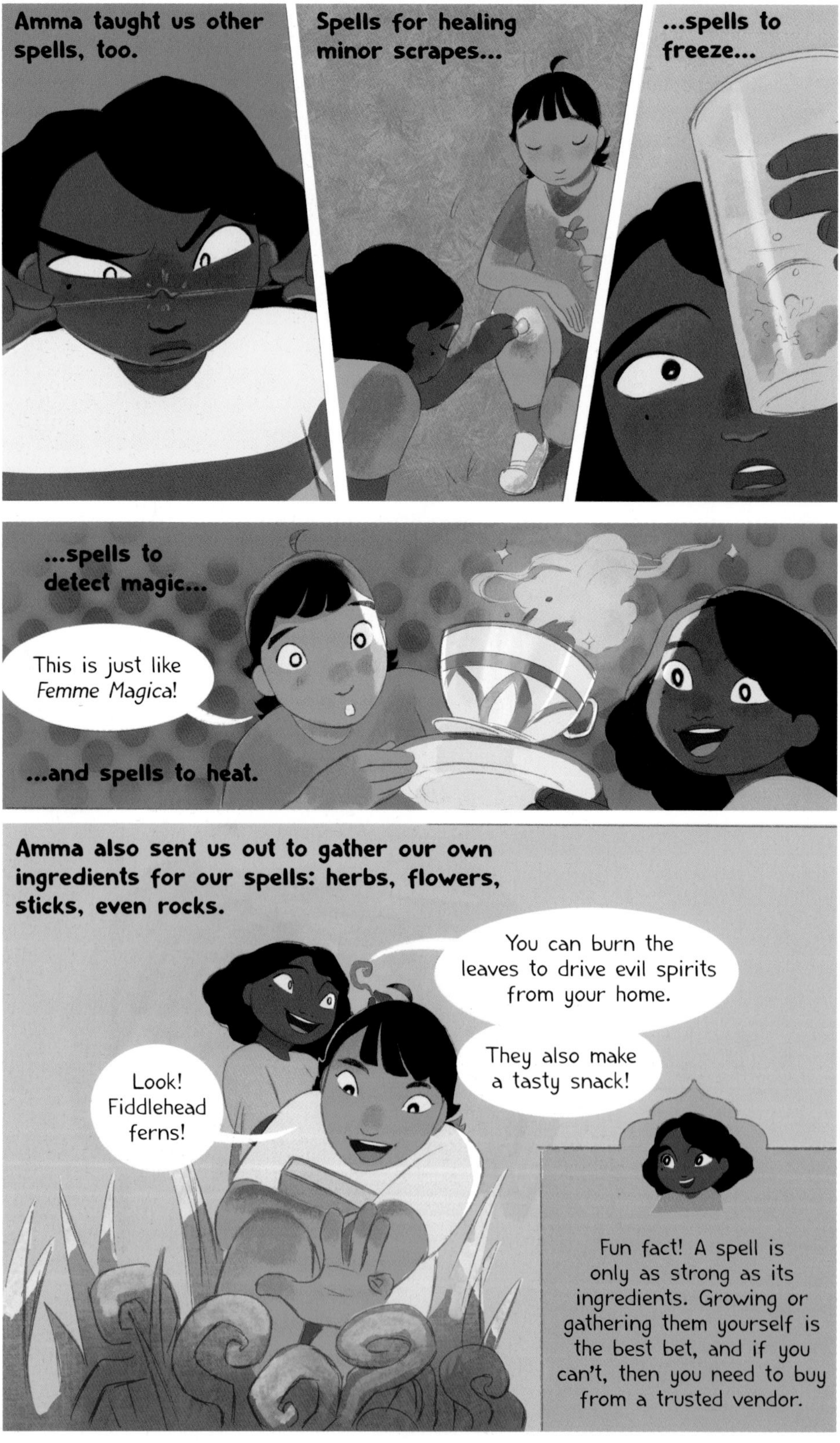
Amma taught us other spells, too.
Spells for healing minor scrapes...
...spells to freeze...
...spells to detect magic...
This is just like *Femme Magica*!
...and spells to heat.
Amma also sent us out to gather our own ingredients for our spells: herbs, flowers, sticks, even rocks.
You can burn the leaves to drive evil spirits from your home.
They also make a tasty snack!
Look! Fiddlehead ferns!
Fun fact! A spell is only as strong as its ingredients. Growing or gathering them yourself is the best bet, and if you can't, then you need to buy from a trusted vendor.

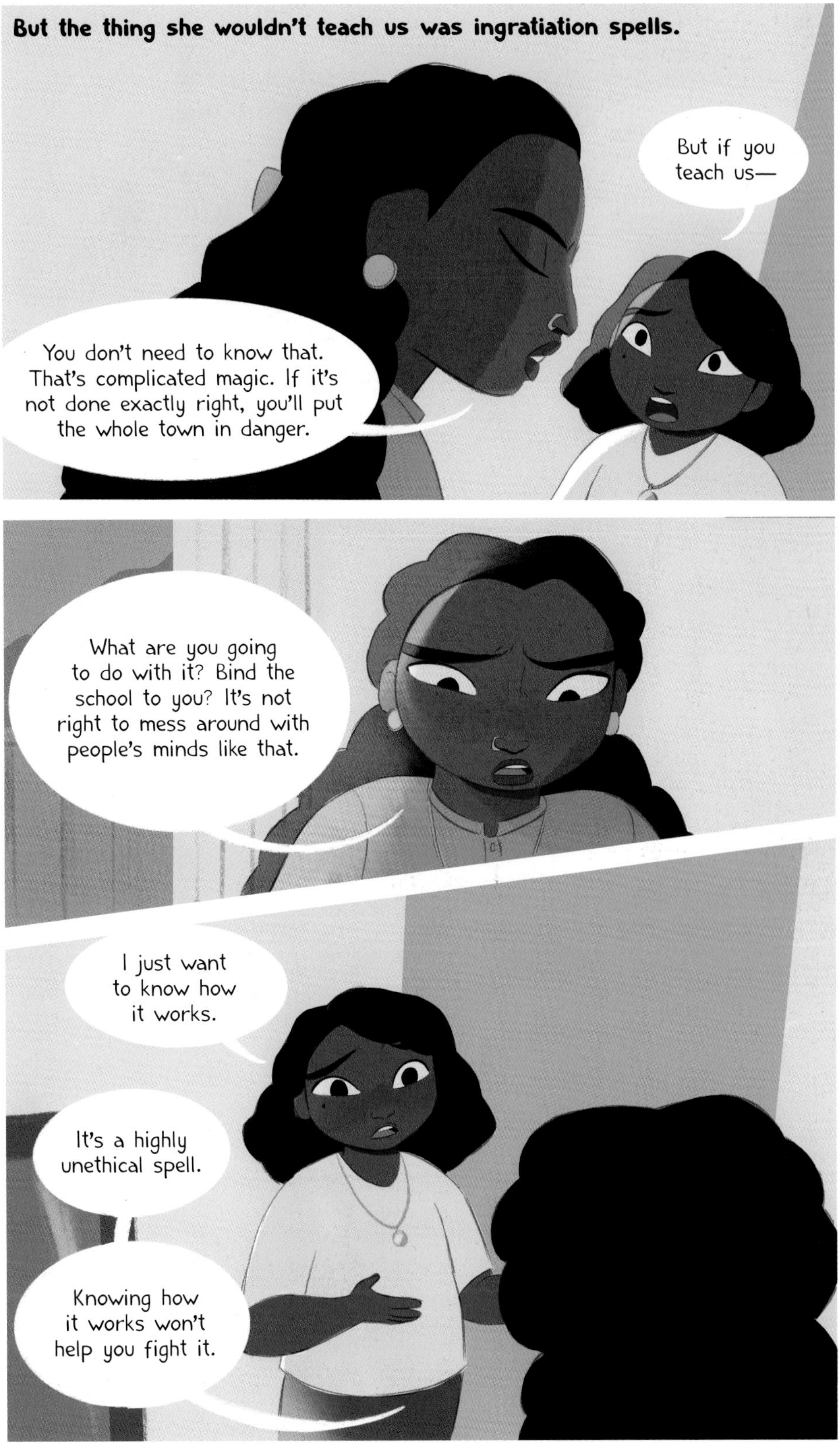
But the thing she wouldn't teach us was ingratiation spells.
But if you teach us—
You don't need to know that. That's complicated magic. If it's not done exactly right, you'll put the whole town in danger.
What are you going to do with it? Bind the school to you? It's not right to mess around with people's minds like that.
I just want to know how it works.
It's a highly unethical spell.
Knowing how it works won't help you fight it.

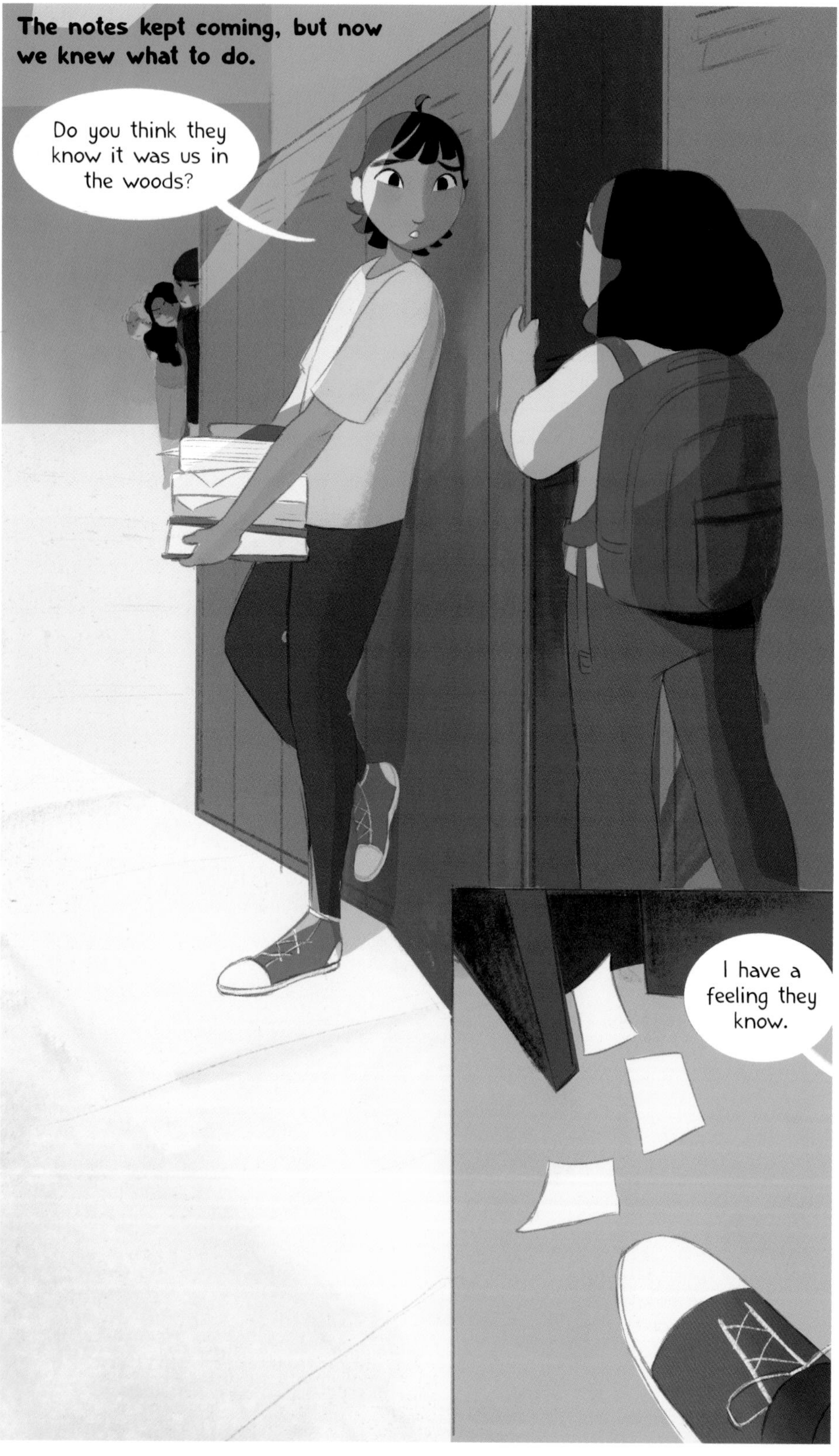
The notes kept coming, but now we knew what to do.
Do you think they know it was us in the woods?
I have a feeling they know.

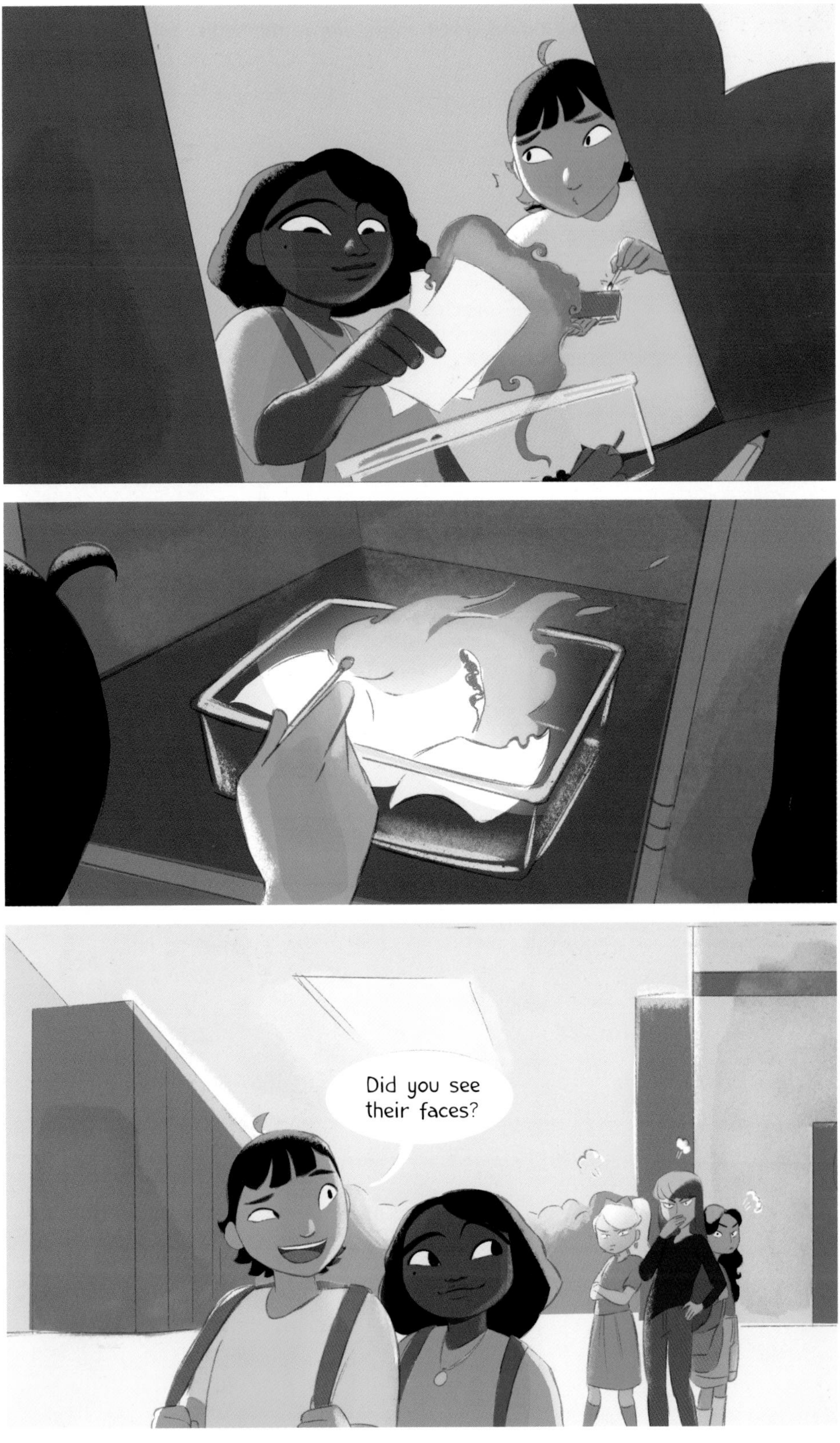
Did you see their faces?

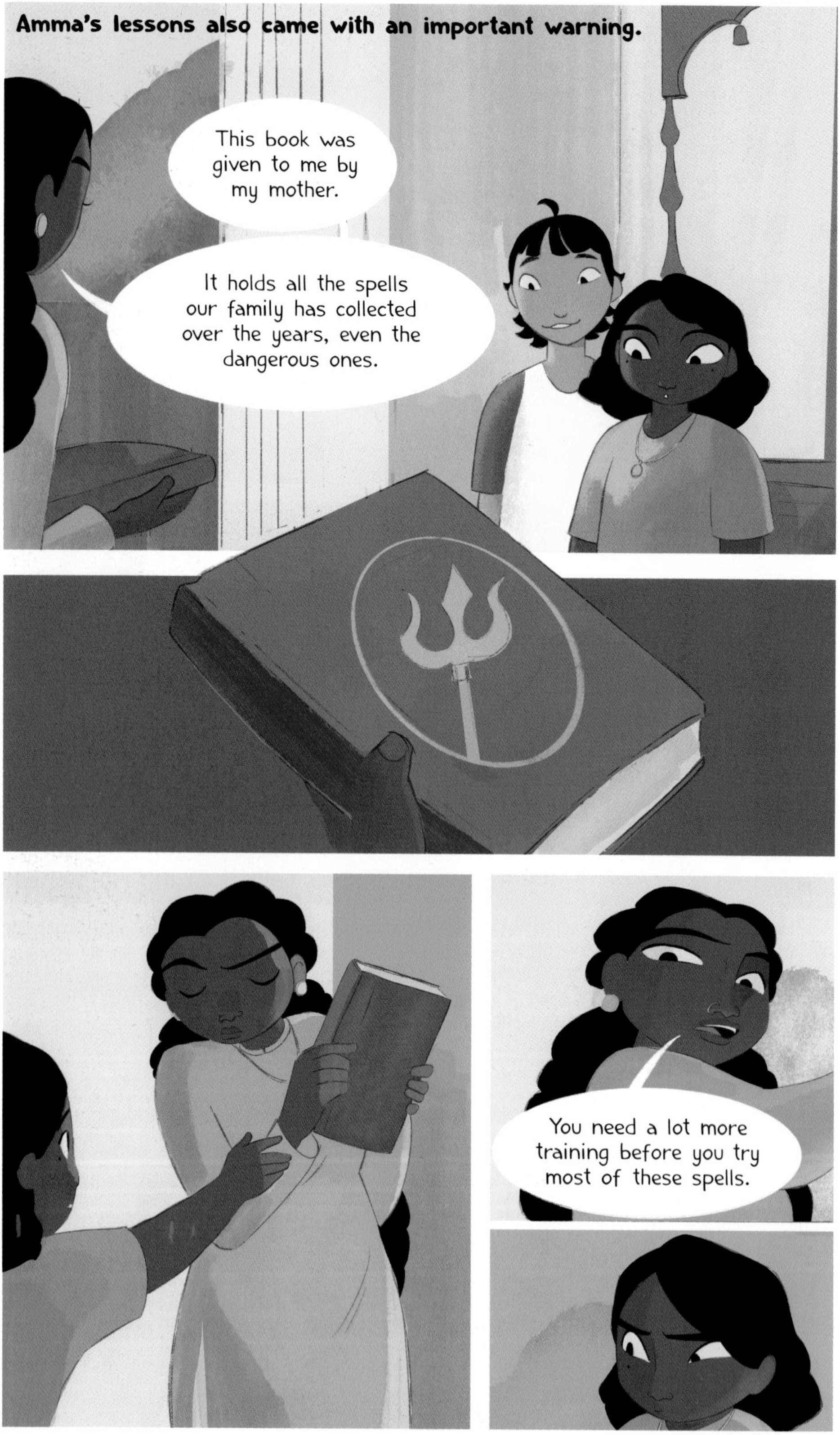
Amma's lessons also came with an important warning.
This book was given to me by my mother.
It holds all the spells our family has collected over the years, even the dangerous ones.
You need a lot more training before you try most of these spells.

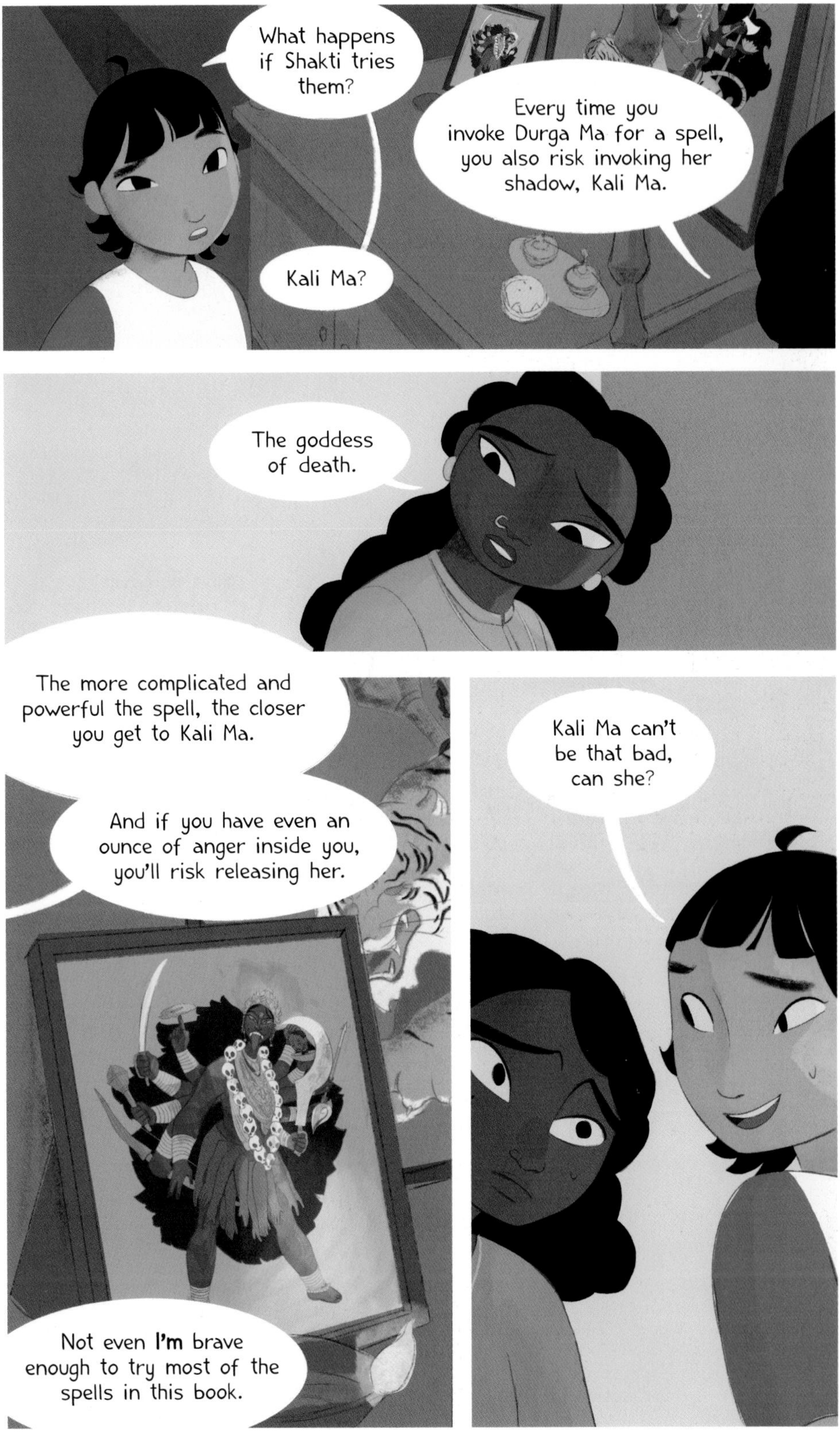

What happens if Shakti tries them?
Every time you invoke Durga Ma for a spell, you also risk invoking her shadow, Kali Ma.
Kali Ma?
The goddess of death.
The more complicated and powerful the spell, the closer you get to Kali Ma.
And if you have even an ounce of anger inside you, you'll risk releasing her.
Not even **I'm** brave enough to try most of the spells in this book.
Kali Ma can't be that bad, can she?

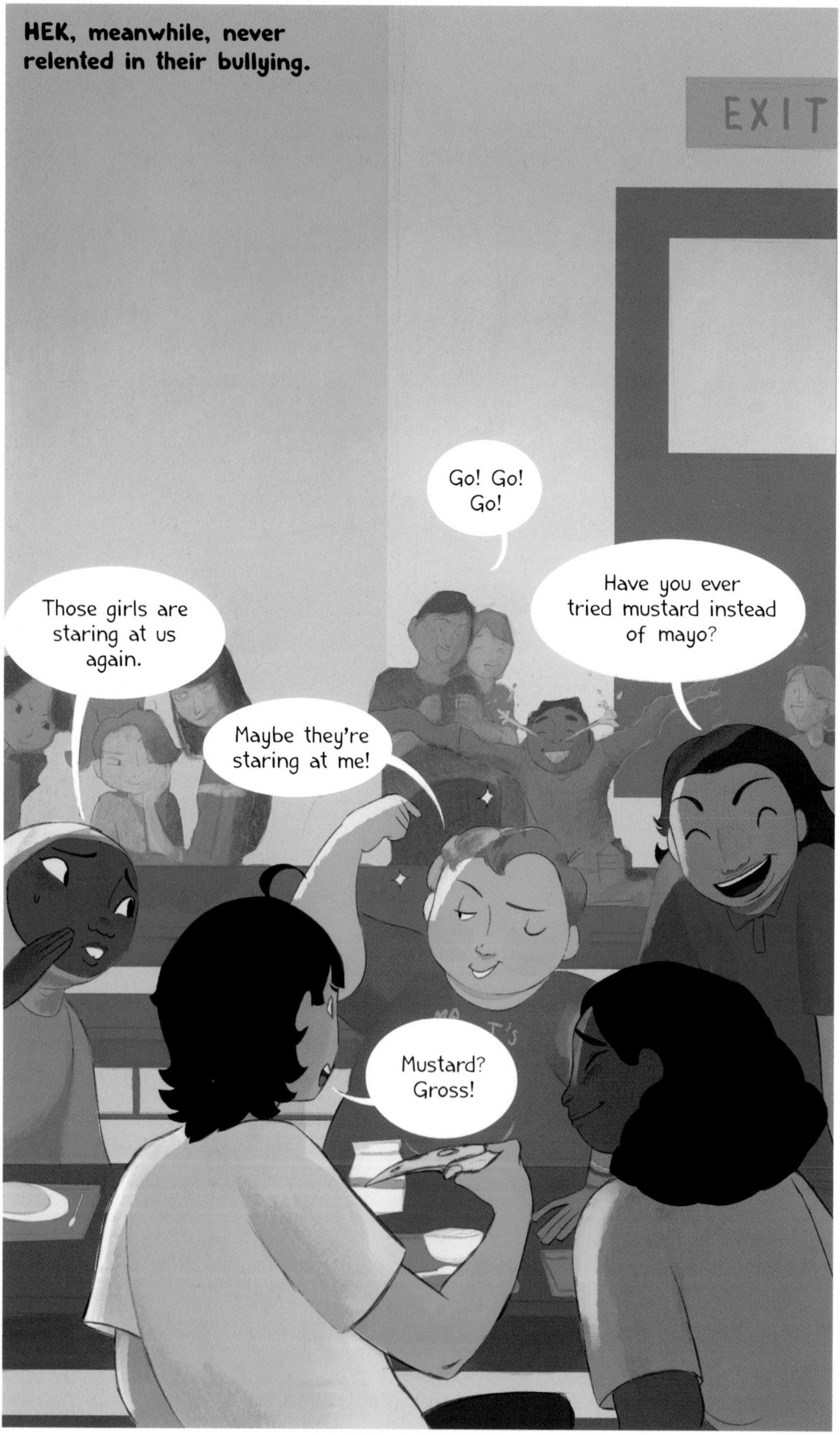
HEK, meanwhile, never relented in their bullying.
Go! Go! Go!
Those girls are staring at us again.
Have you ever tried mustard instead of mayo?
Maybe they're staring at me!
Mustard? Gross!
EXIT

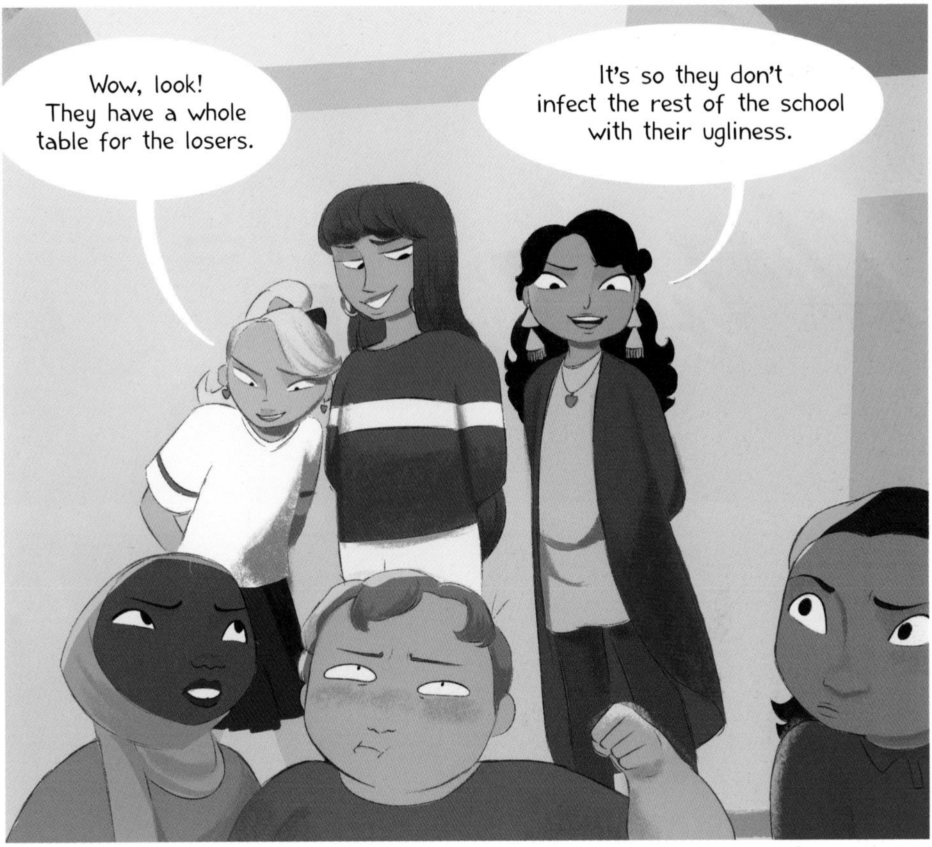
Wow, look!
They have a whole
table for the losers.
It's so they don't
infect the rest of the school
with their ugliness.

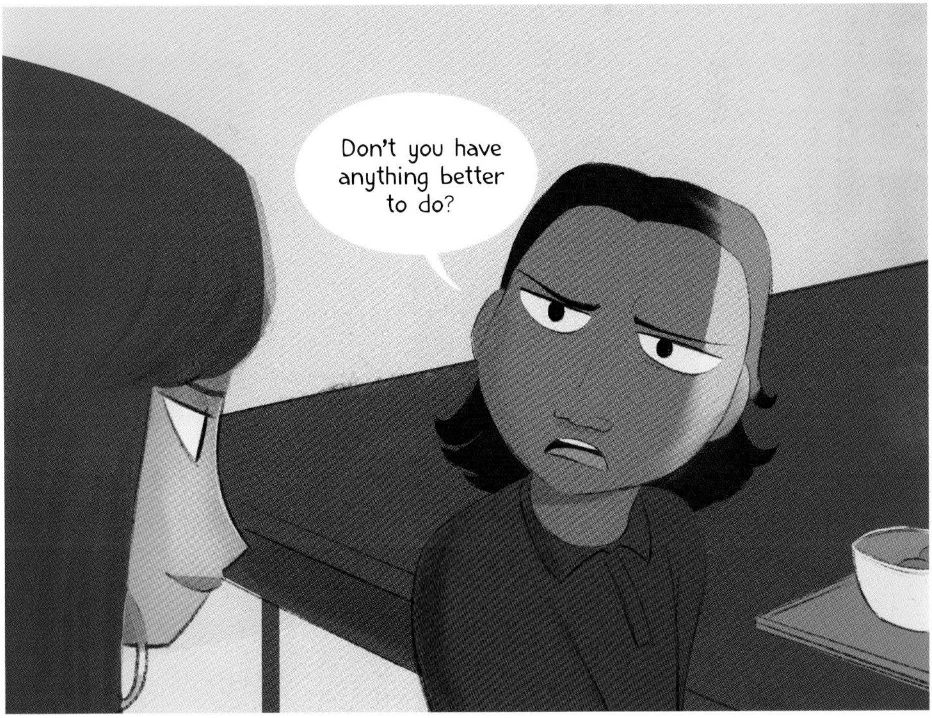
Don't you have
anything better
to do?

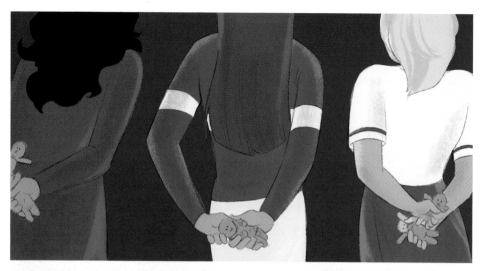

You're useless, ugly **losers**.

Come on, let's go.

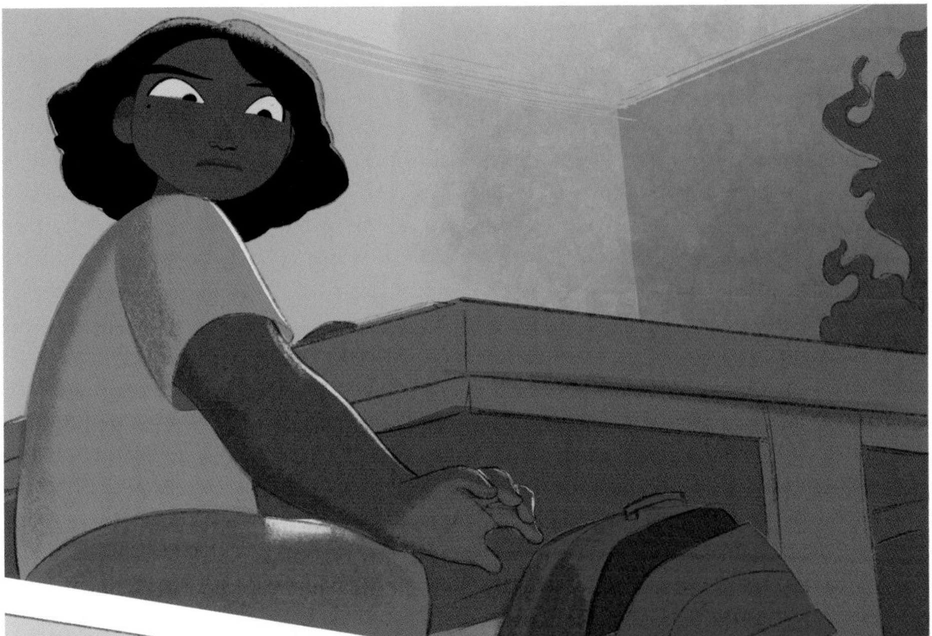

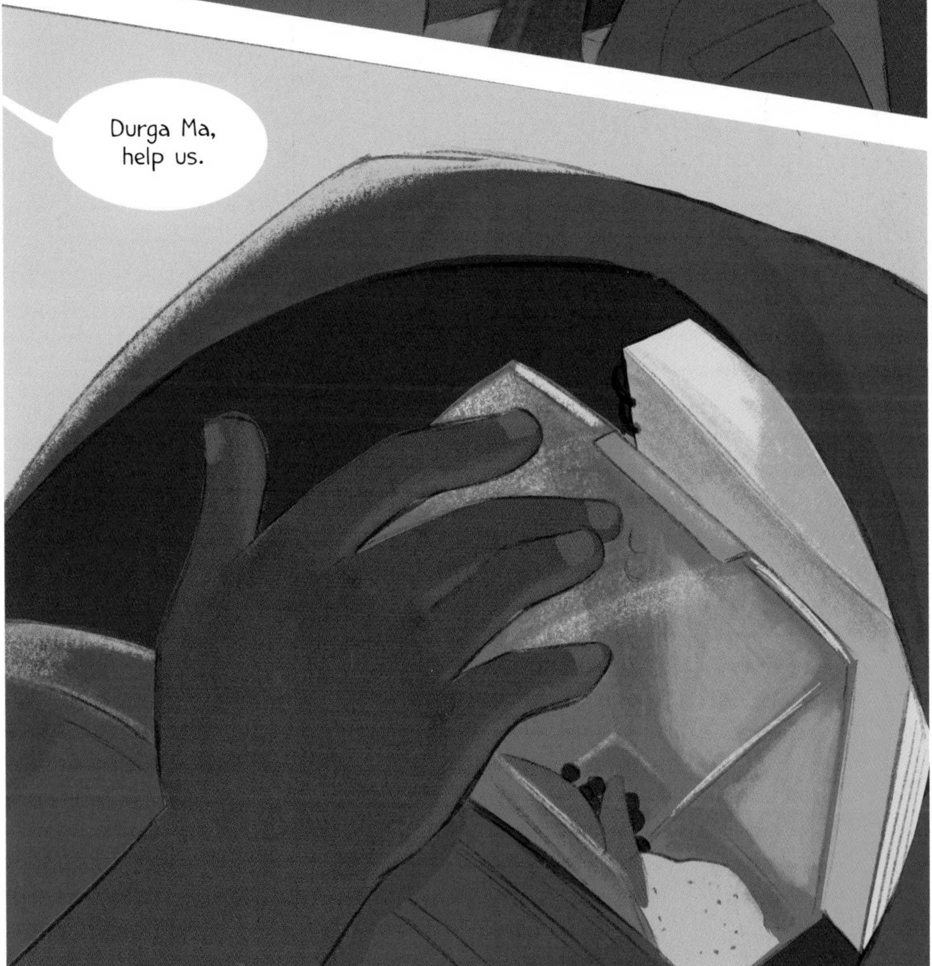

Durga Ma, help us.

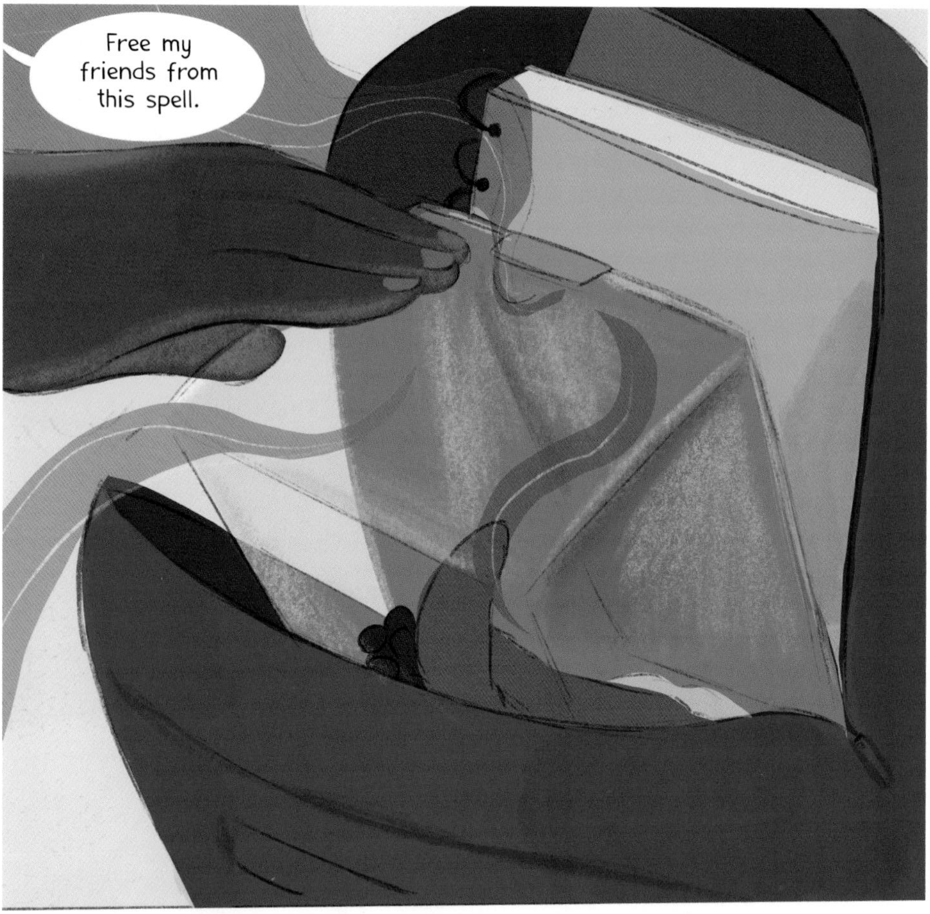
Free my friends from this spell.
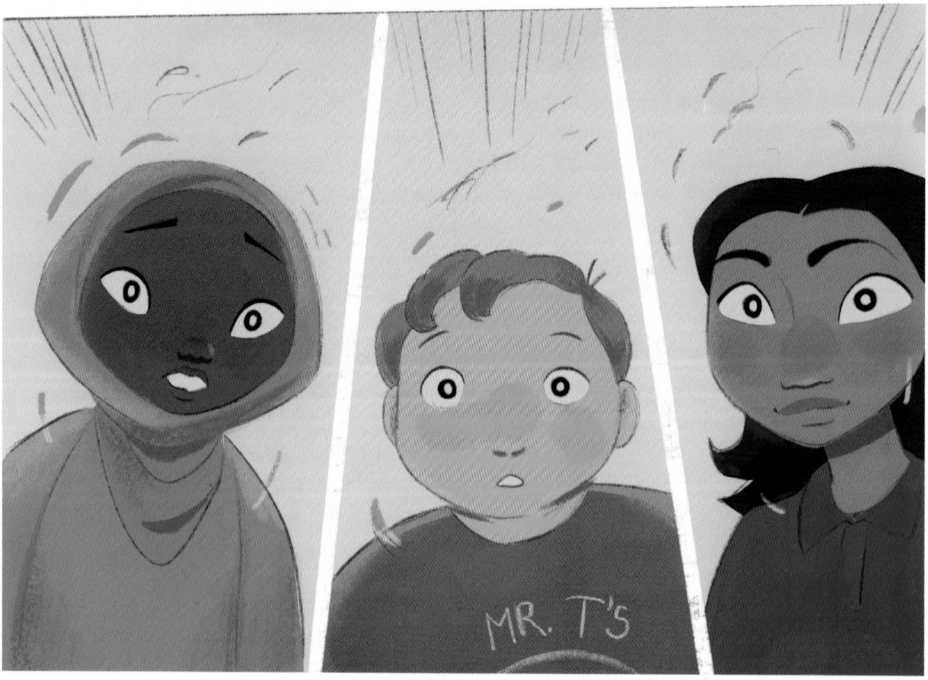
MR. T'S

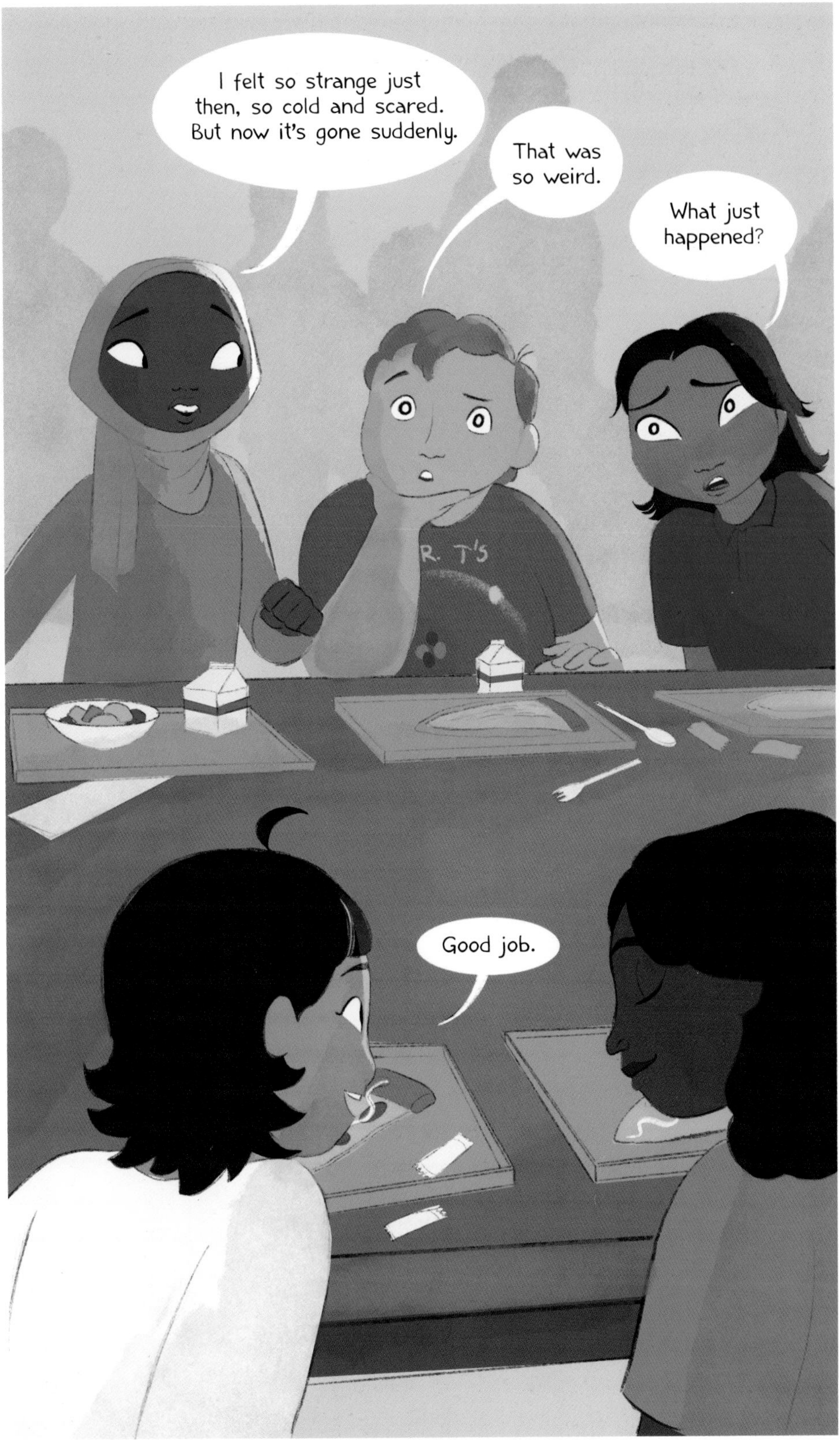
I felt so strange just then, so cold and scared. But now it's gone suddenly.
That was so weird.
What just happened?
Good job.

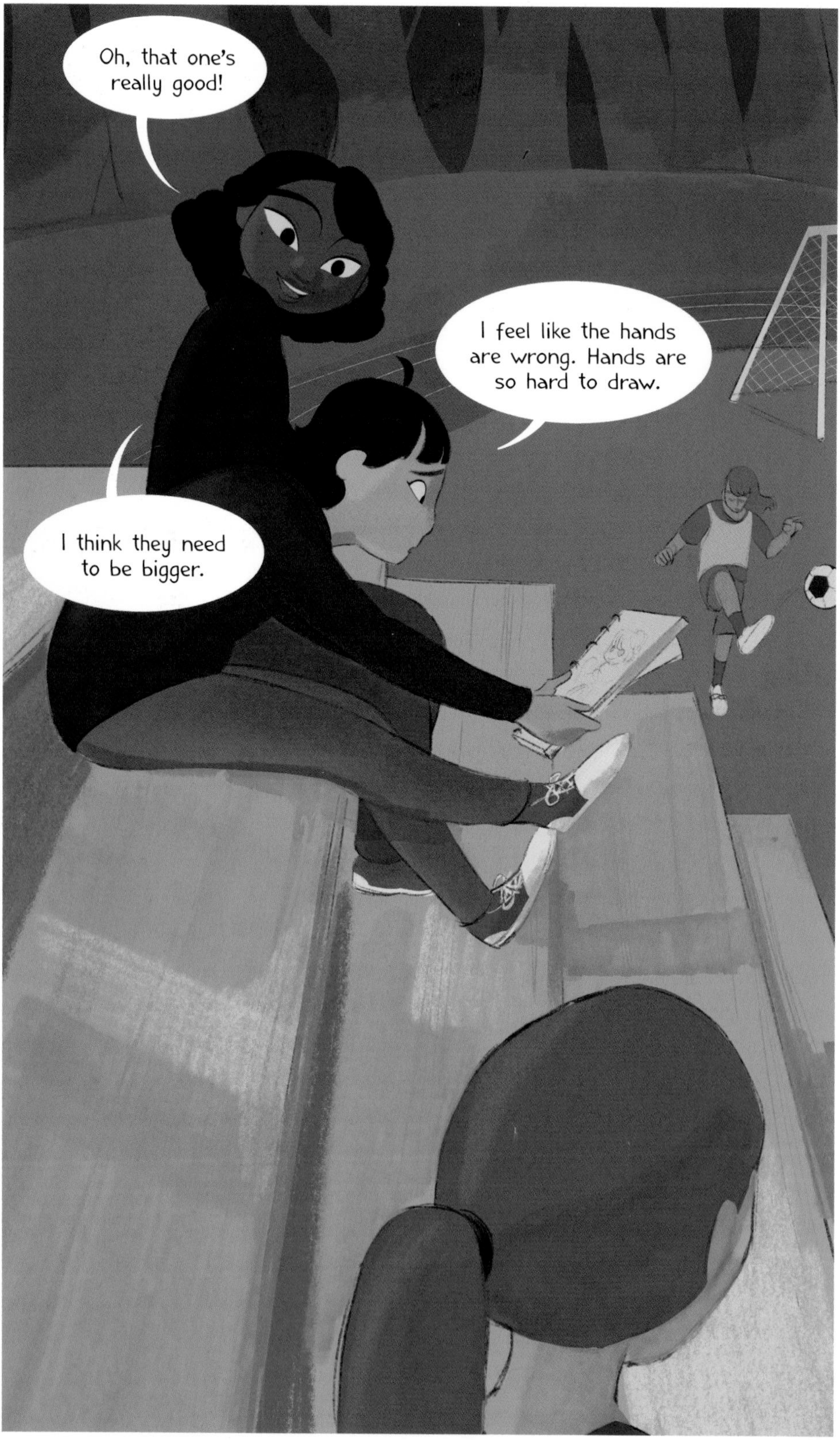
Oh, that one's really good!
I feel like the hands are wrong. Hands are so hard to draw.
I think they need to be bigger.

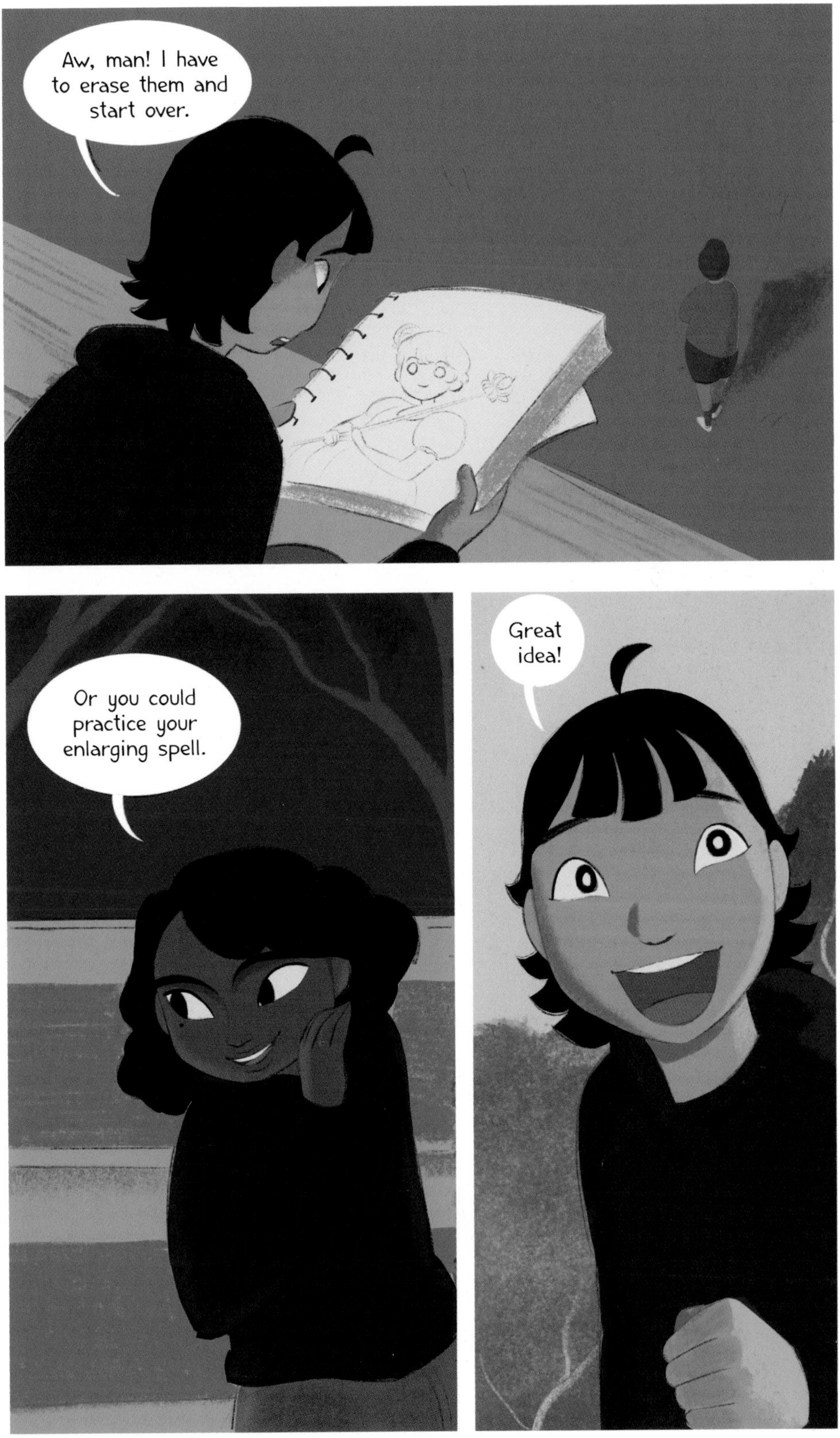
Aw, man! I have to erase them and start over.
Or you could practice your enlarging spell.
Great idea!

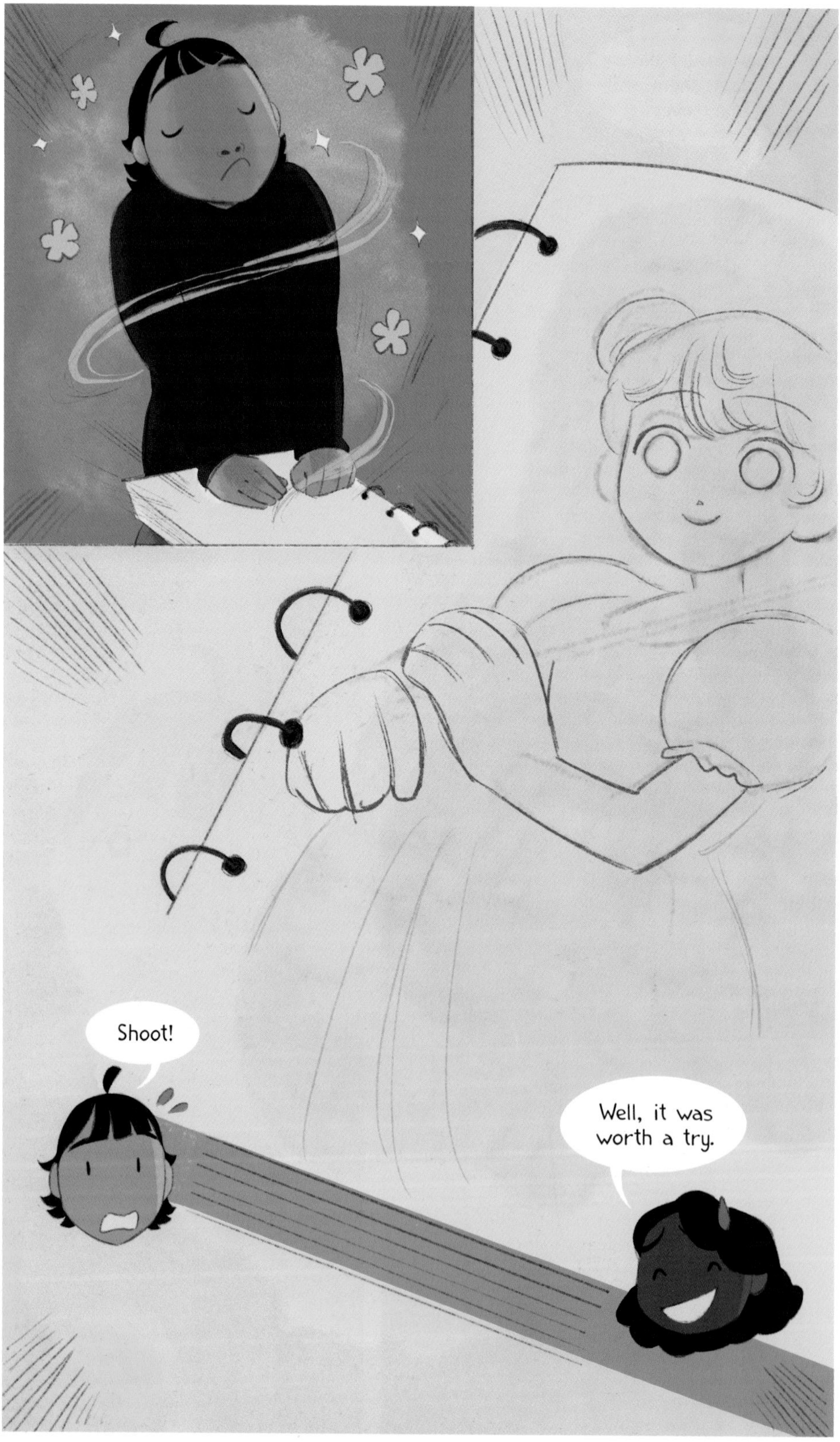
Shoot!
Well, it was worth a try.

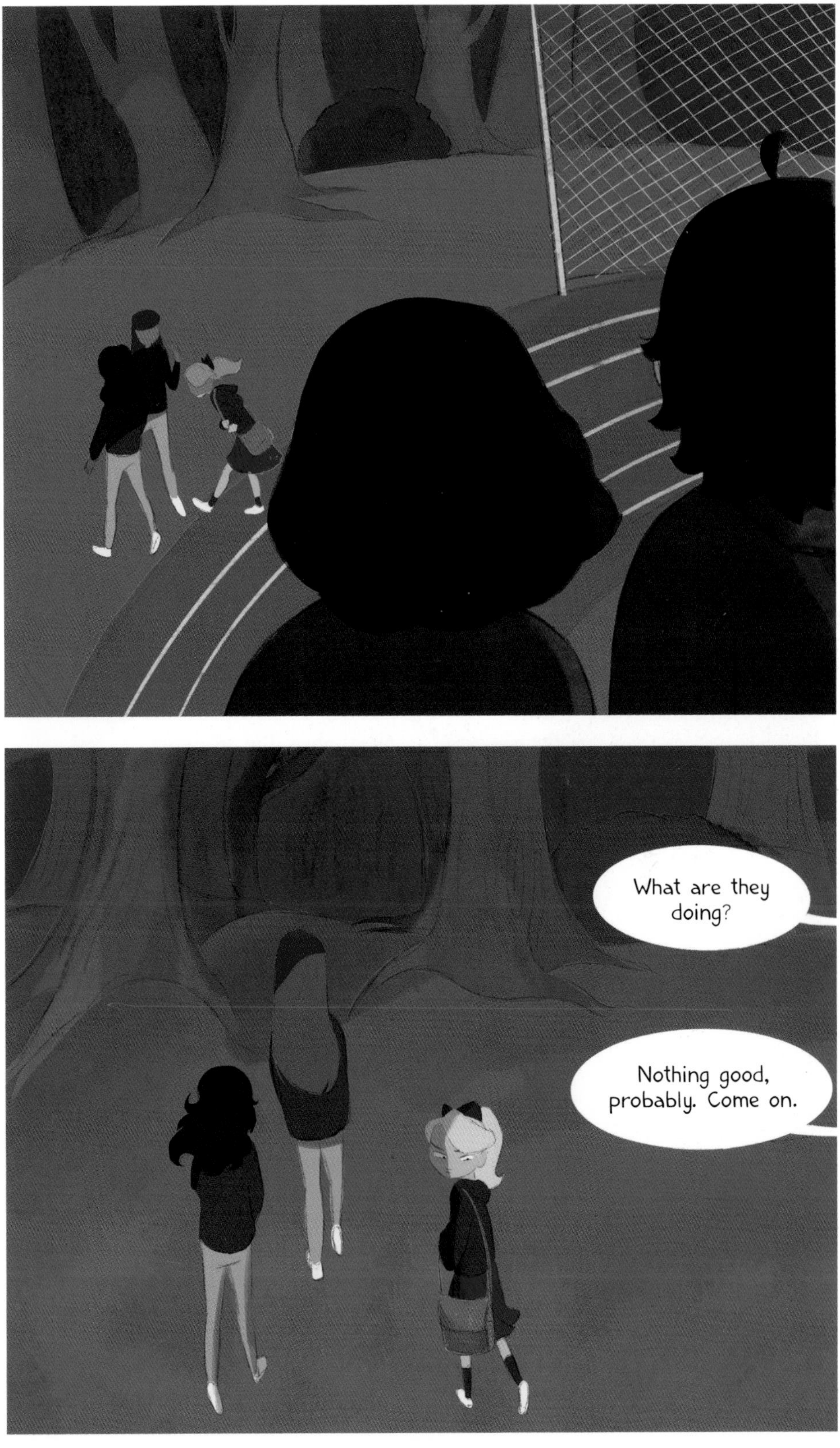
What are they doing?
Nothing good, probably. Come on.

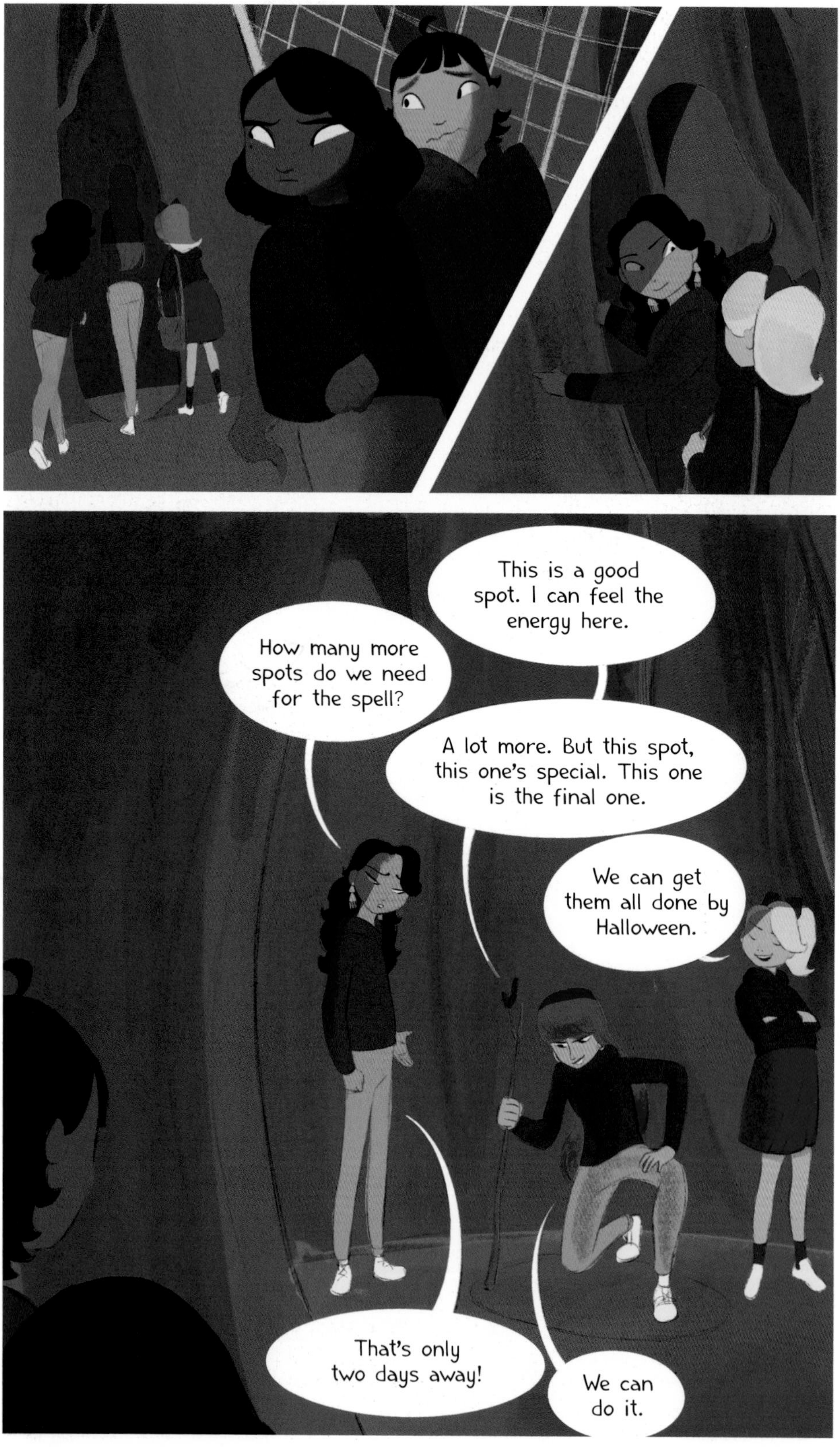
This is a good spot. I can feel the energy here.
How many more spots do we need for the spell?
A lot more. But this spot, this one's special. This one is the final one.
We can get them all done by Halloween.
That's only two days away!
We can do it.

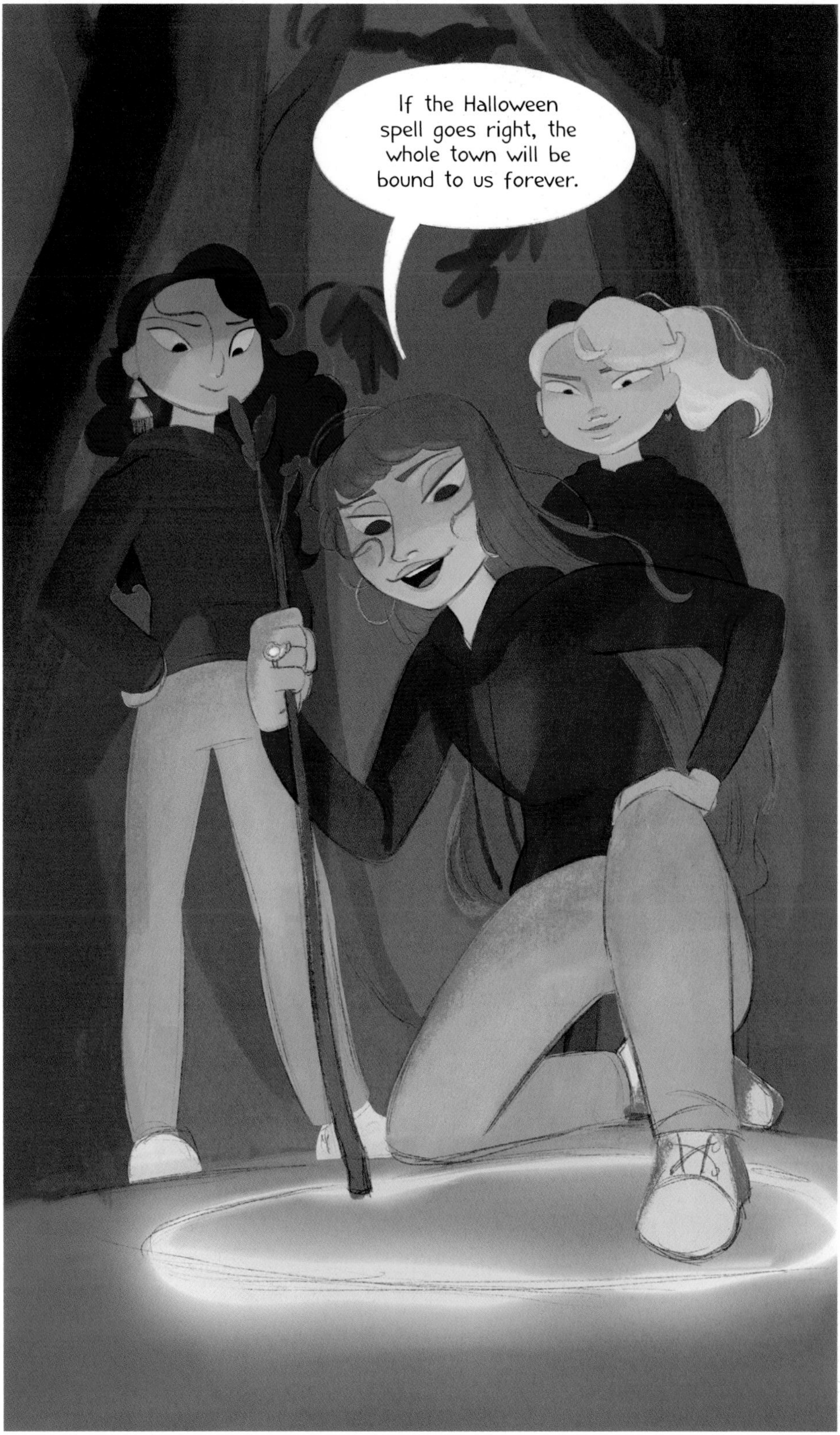
If the Halloween spell goes right, the whole town will be bound to us forever.

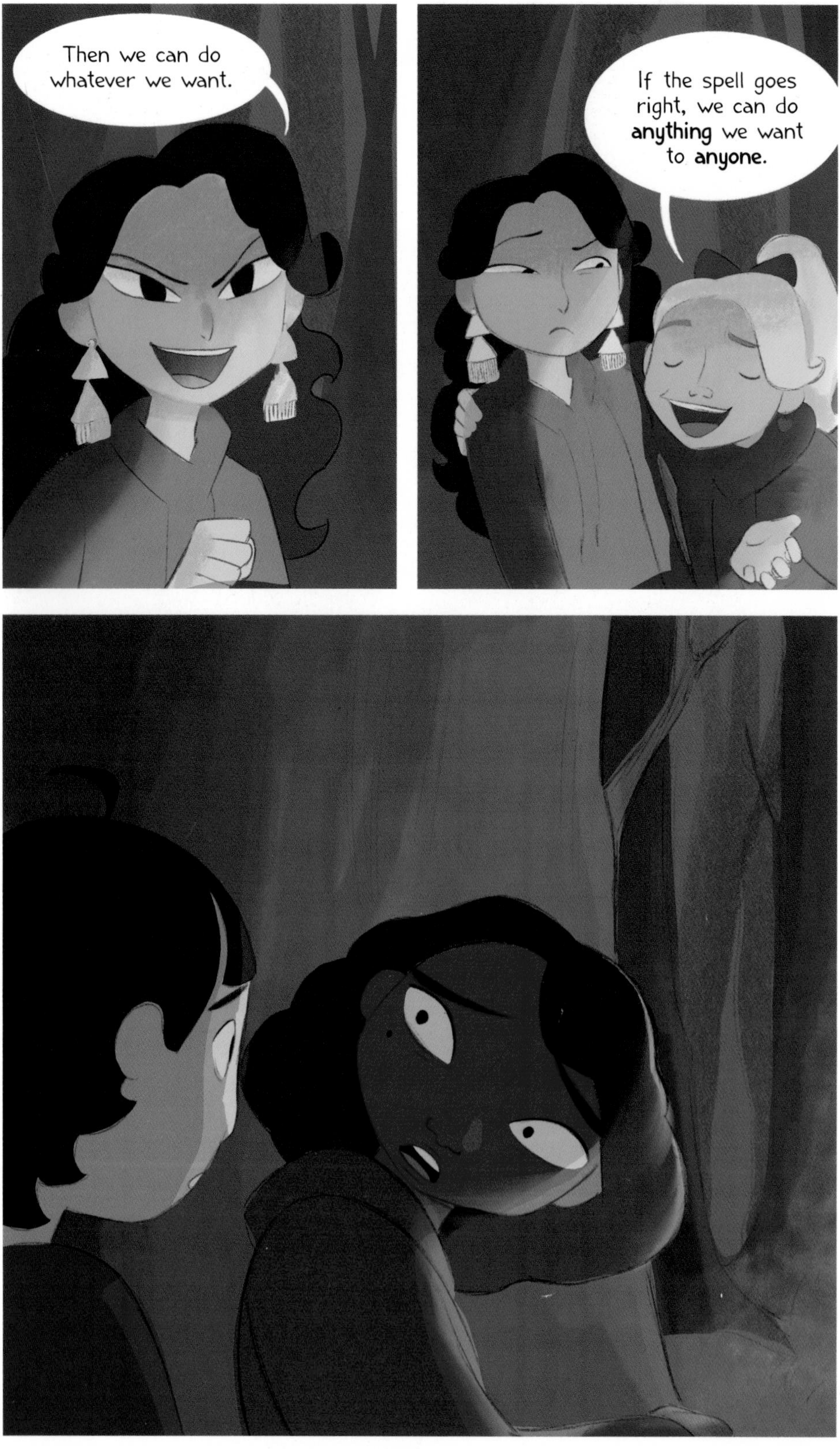
Then we can do whatever we want.
If the spell goes right, we can do **anything** we want to **anyone**.

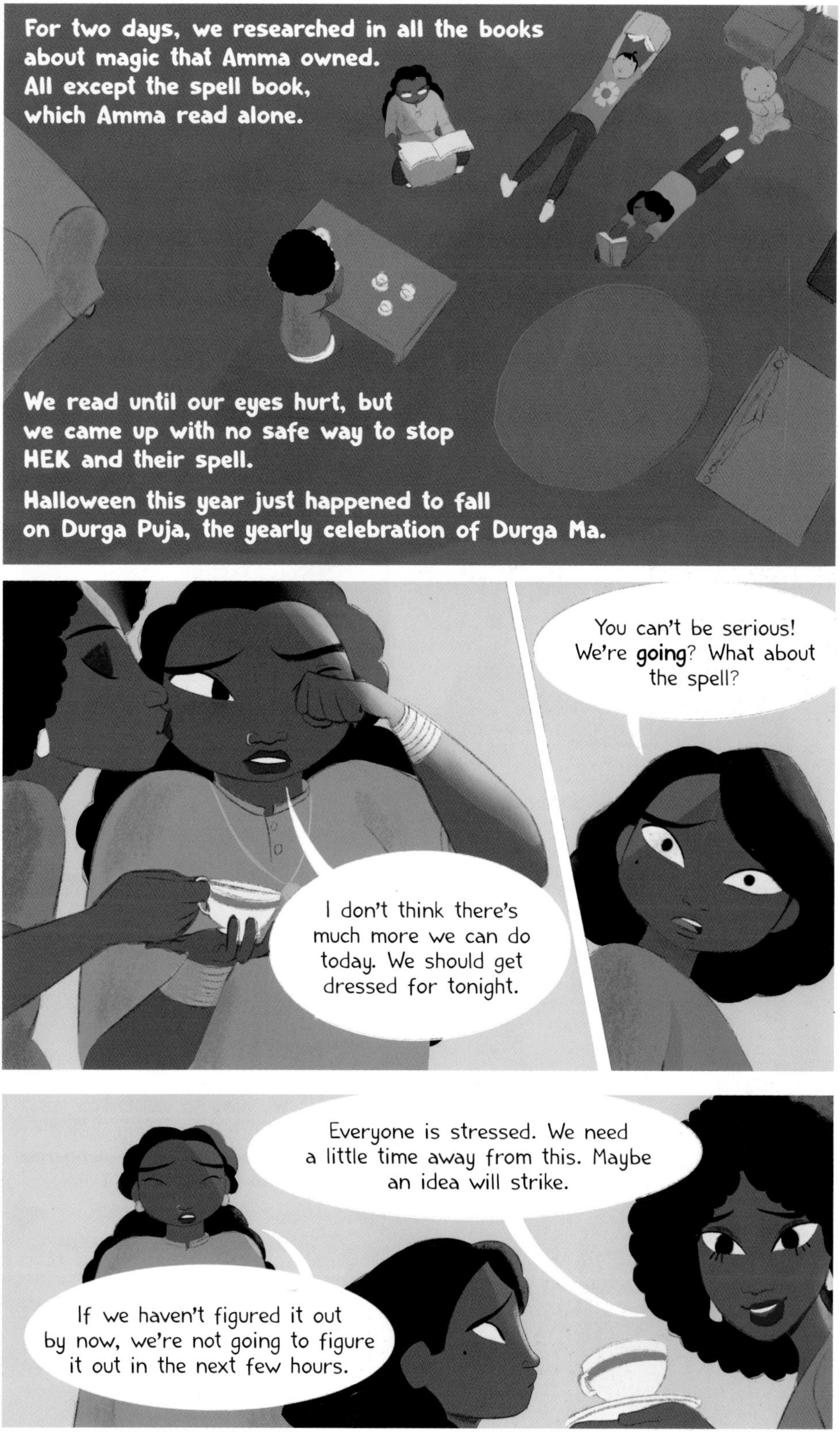
For two days, we researched in all the books about magic that Amma owned. All except the spell book, which Amma read alone.
We read until our eyes hurt, but we came up with no safe way to stop HEK and their spell.
Halloween this year just happened to fall on Durga Puja, the yearly celebration of Durga Ma.
I don't think there's much more we can do today. We should get dressed for tonight.
You can't be serious! We're **going**? What about the spell?
Everyone is stressed. We need a little time away from this. Maybe an idea will strike.
If we haven't figured it out by now, we're not going to figure it out in the next few hours.

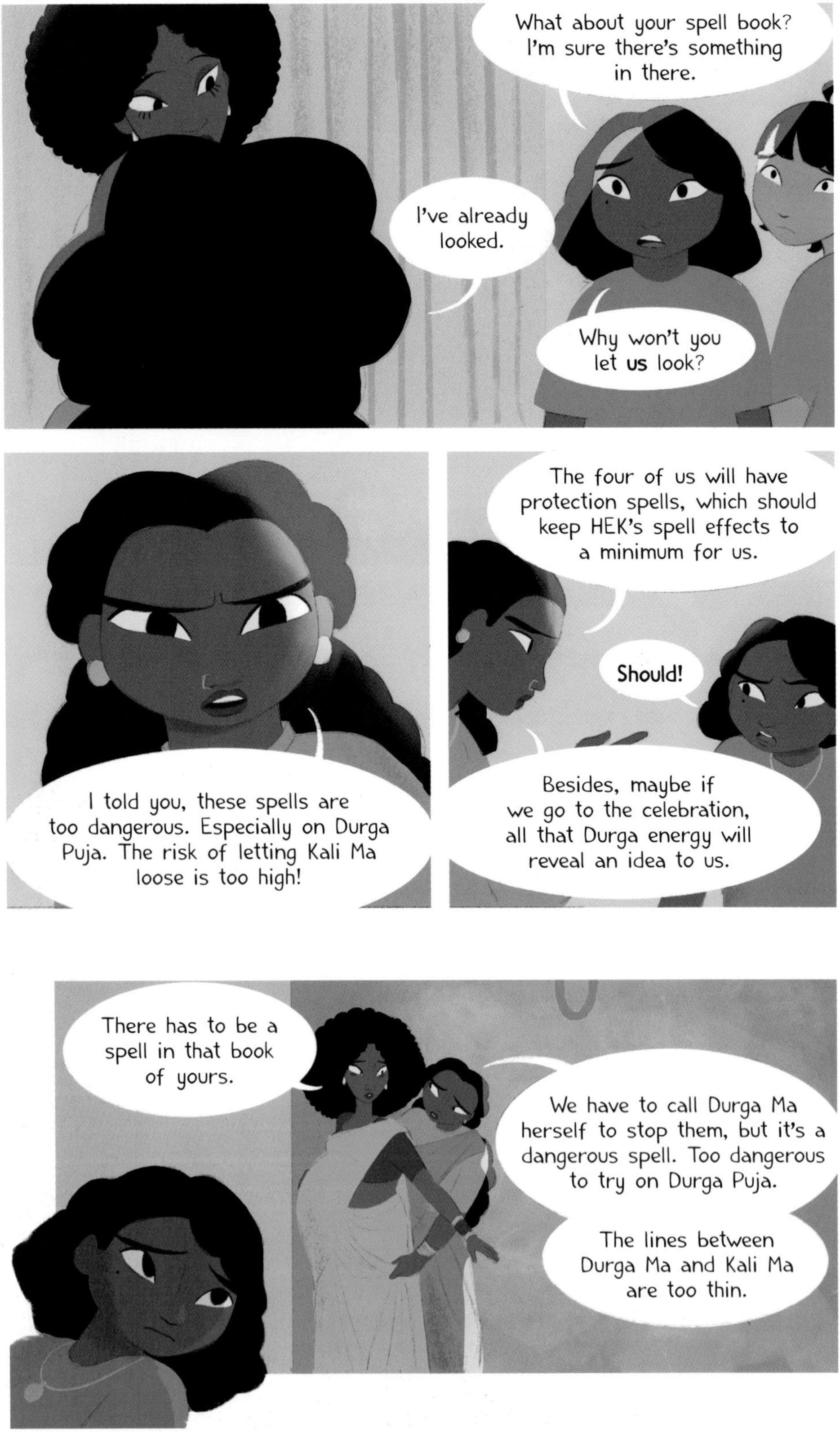
What about your spell book? I'm sure there's something in there.
I've already looked.
Why won't you let **us** look?
I told you, these spells are too dangerous. Especially on Durga Puja. The risk of letting Kali Ma loose is too high!
The four of us will have protection spells, which should keep HEK's spell effects to a minimum for us.
**Should!**
Besides, maybe if we go to the celebration, all that Durga energy will reveal an idea to us.
There has to be a spell in that book of yours.
We have to call Durga Ma herself to stop them, but it's a dangerous spell. Too dangerous to try on Durga Puja.
The lines between Durga Ma and Kali Ma are too thin.

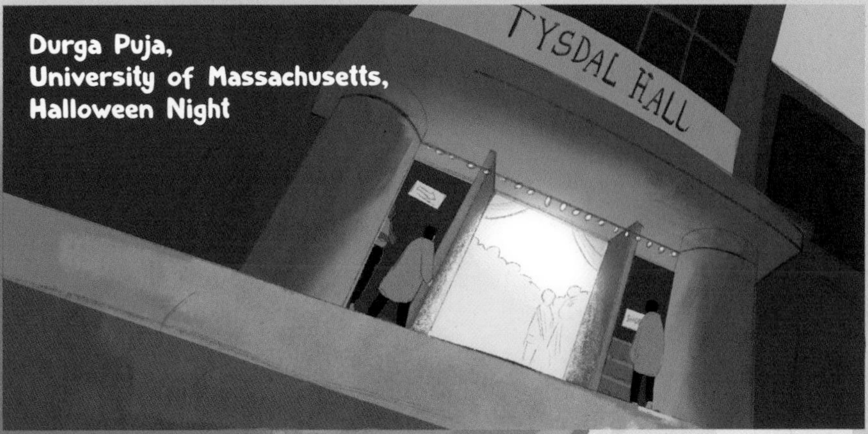
Durga Puja,
University of Massachusetts,
Halloween Night
TYSDAL HALL

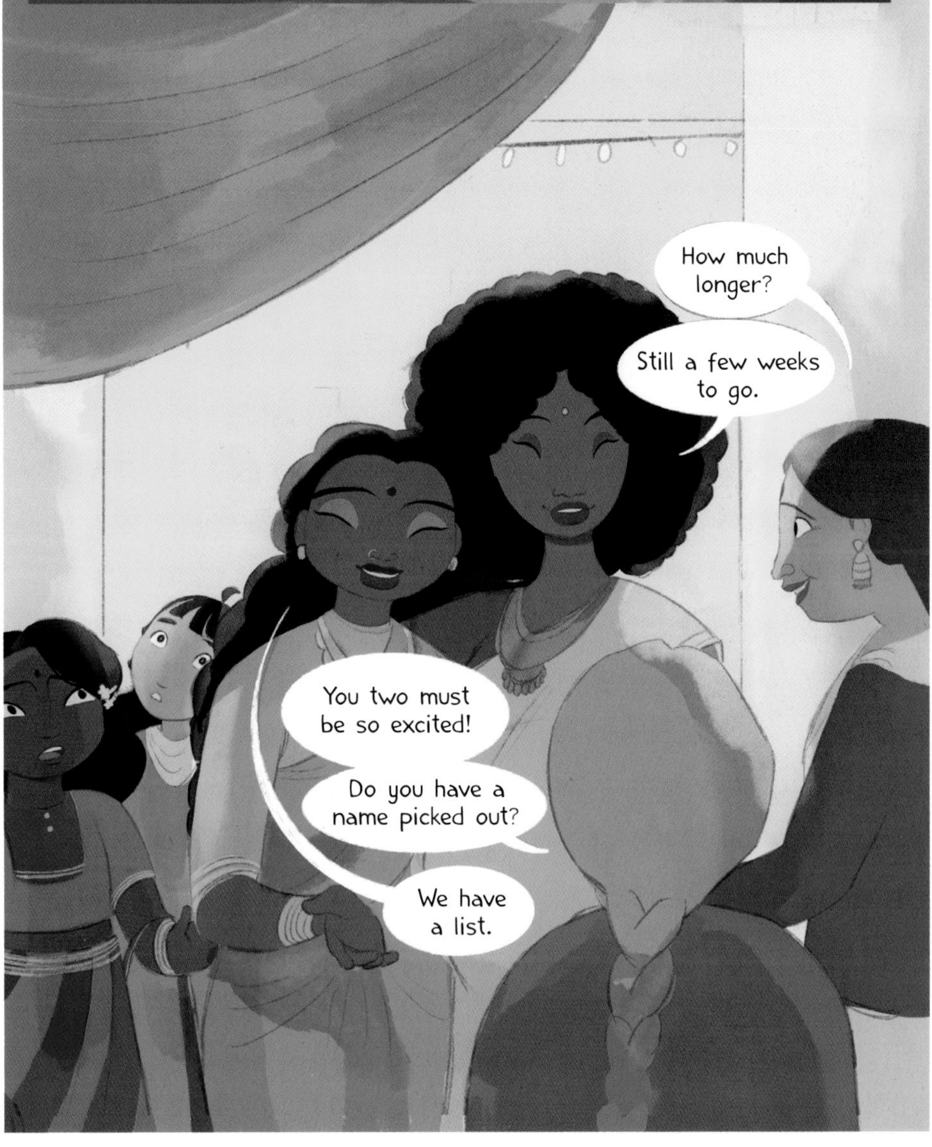
How much longer?
Still a few weeks to go.
You two must be so excited!
Do you have a name picked out?
We have a list.

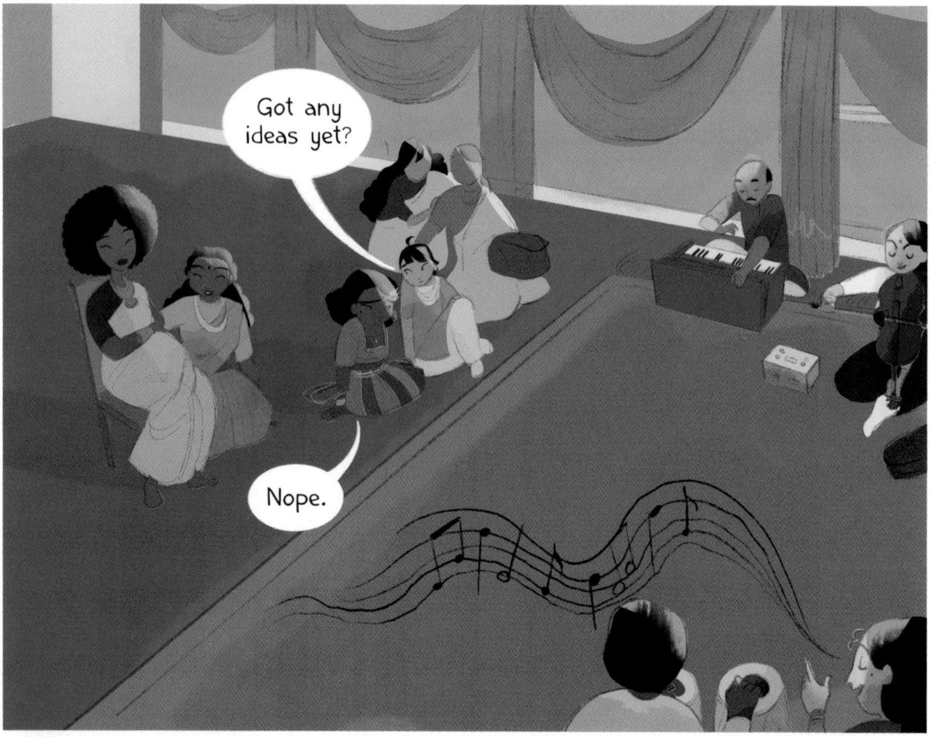
Got any ideas yet?
Nope.

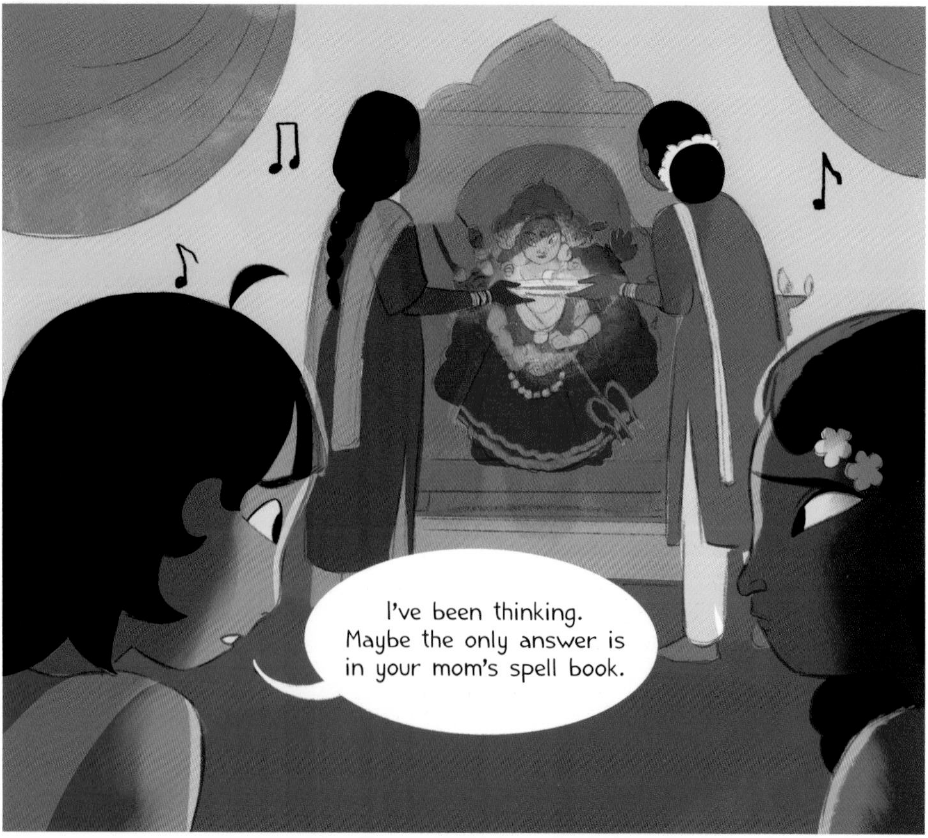
I've been thinking. Maybe the only answer is in your mom's spell book.

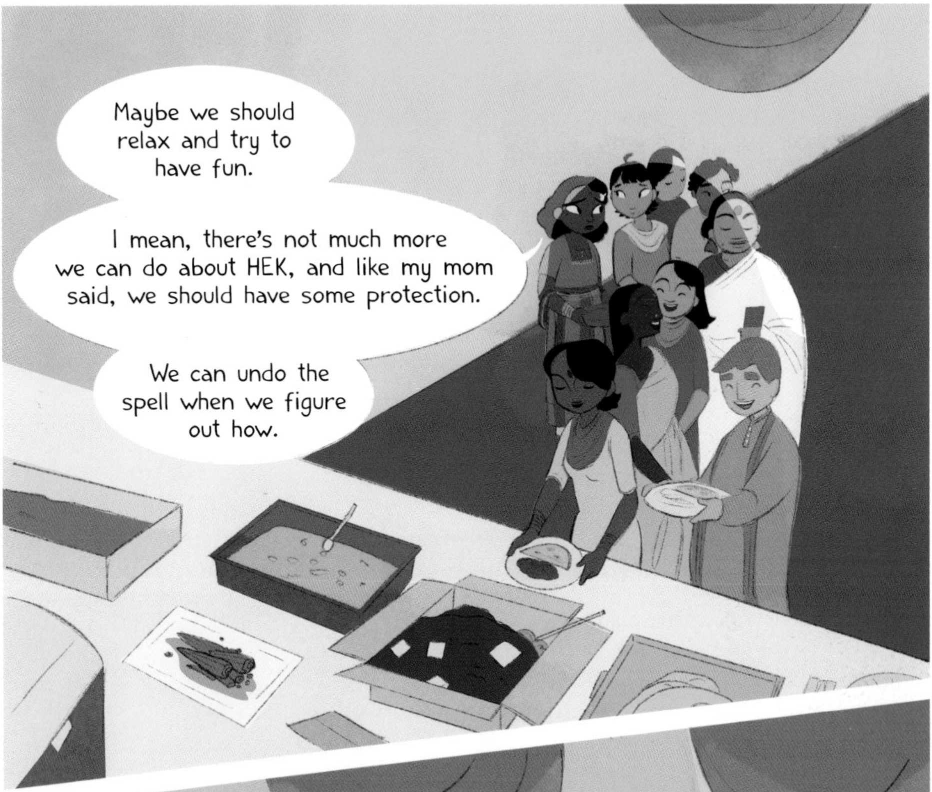
Maybe we should relax and try to have fun.
I mean, there's not much more we can do about HEK, and like my mom said, we should have some protection.
We can undo the spell when we figure out how.

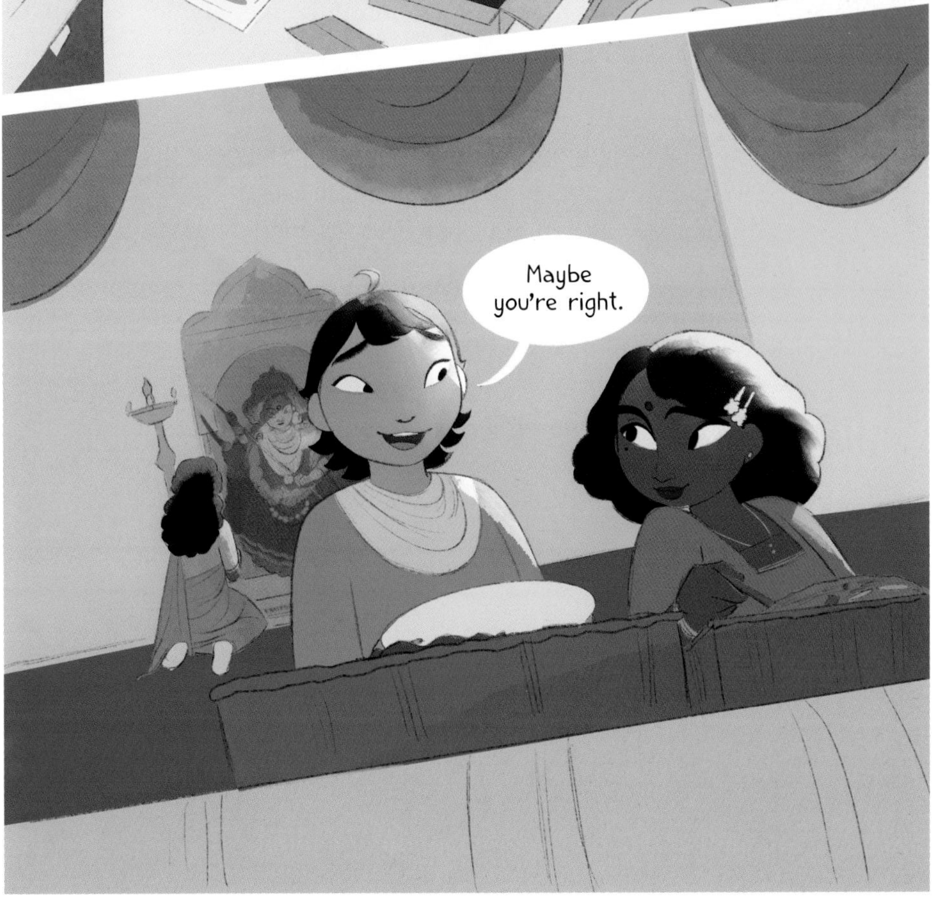
Maybe you're right.

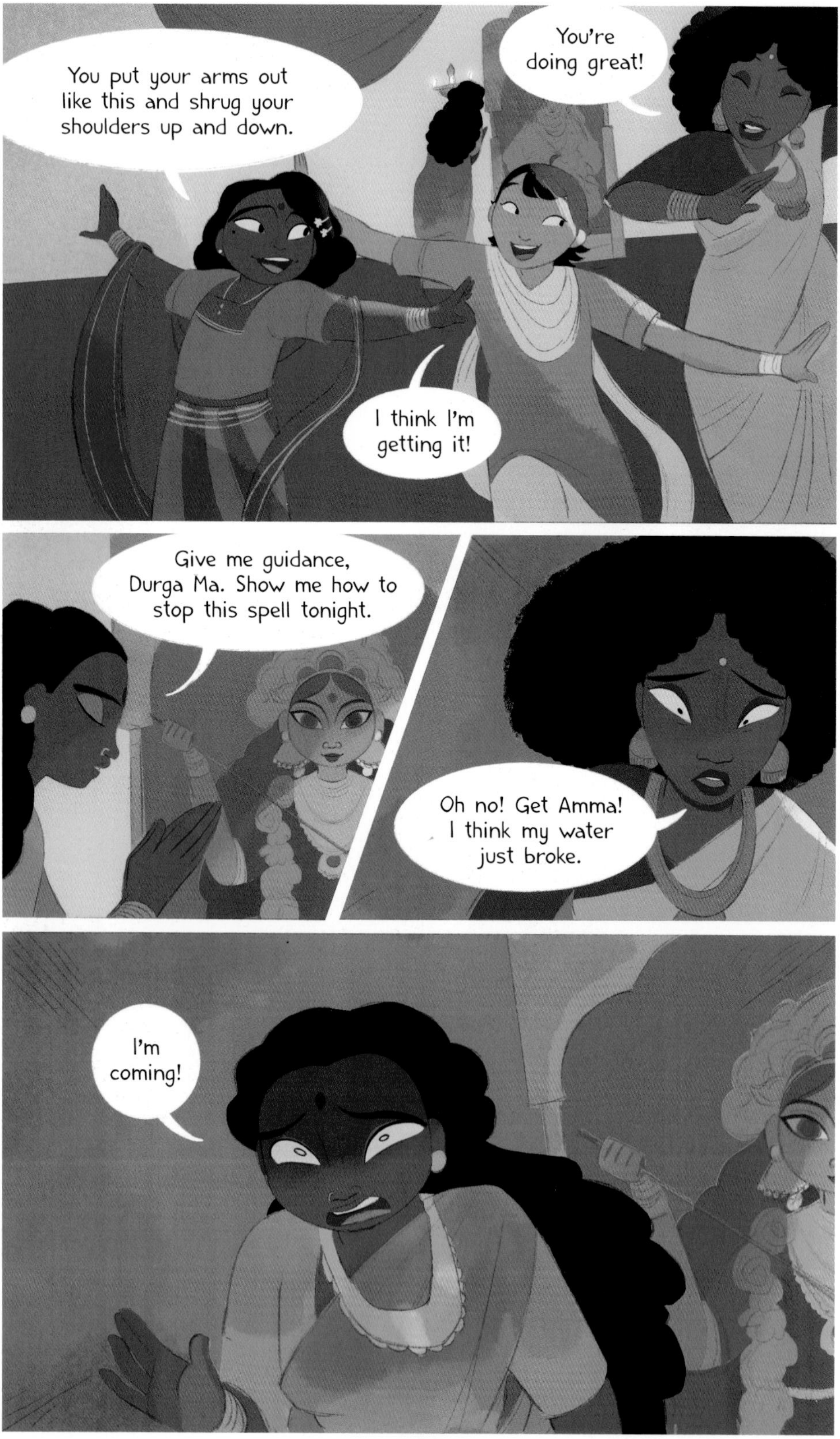
You put your arms out like this and shrug your shoulders up and down.
You're doing great!
I think I'm getting it!
Give me guidance, Durga Ma. Show me how to stop this spell tonight.
Oh no! Get Amma! I think my water just broke.
I'm coming!

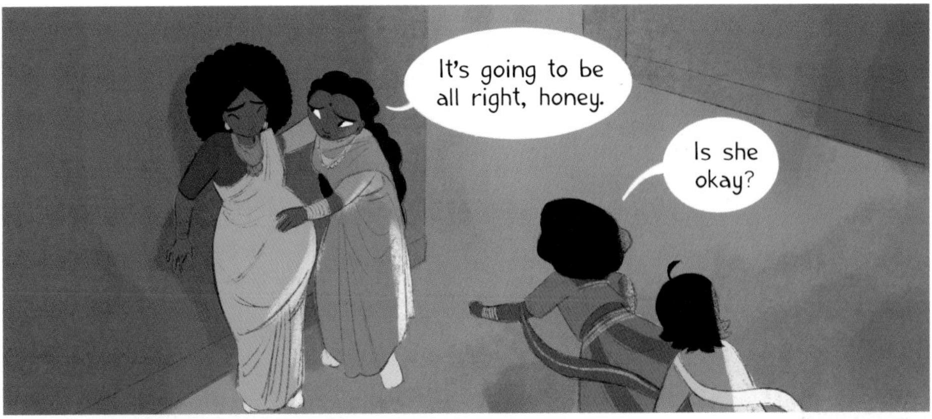
It's going to be all right, honey.
Is she okay?

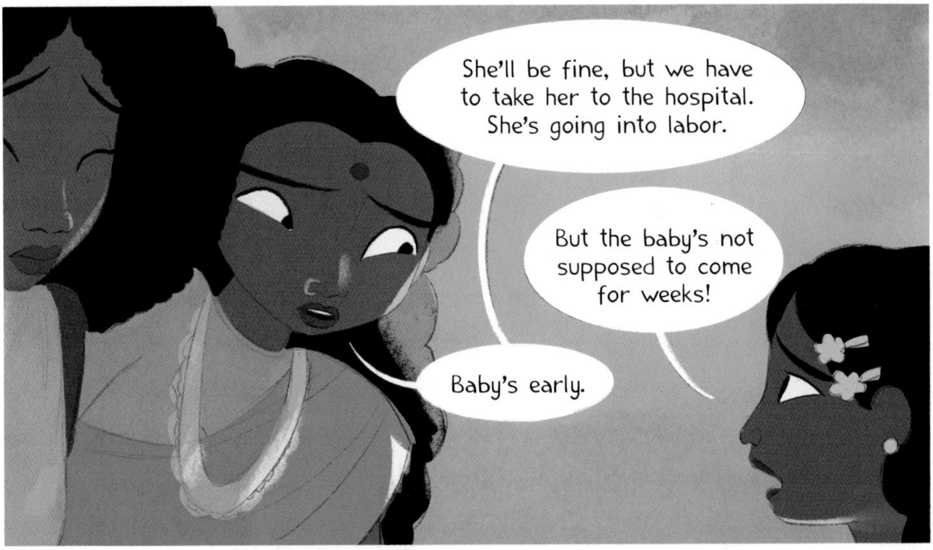
She'll be fine, but we have to take her to the hospital. She's going into labor.
But the baby's not supposed to come for weeks!
Baby's early.

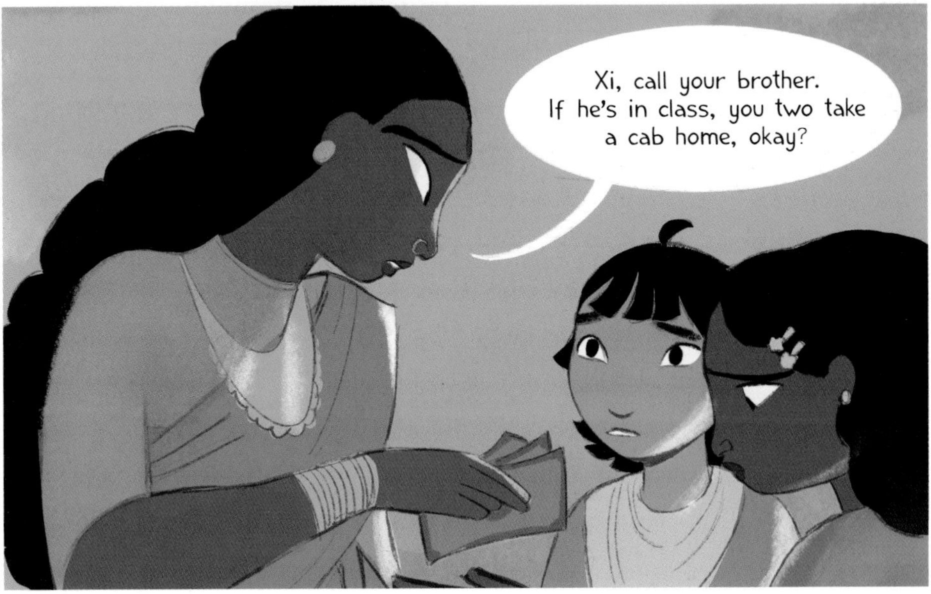
Xi, call your brother. If he's in class, you two take a cab home, okay?

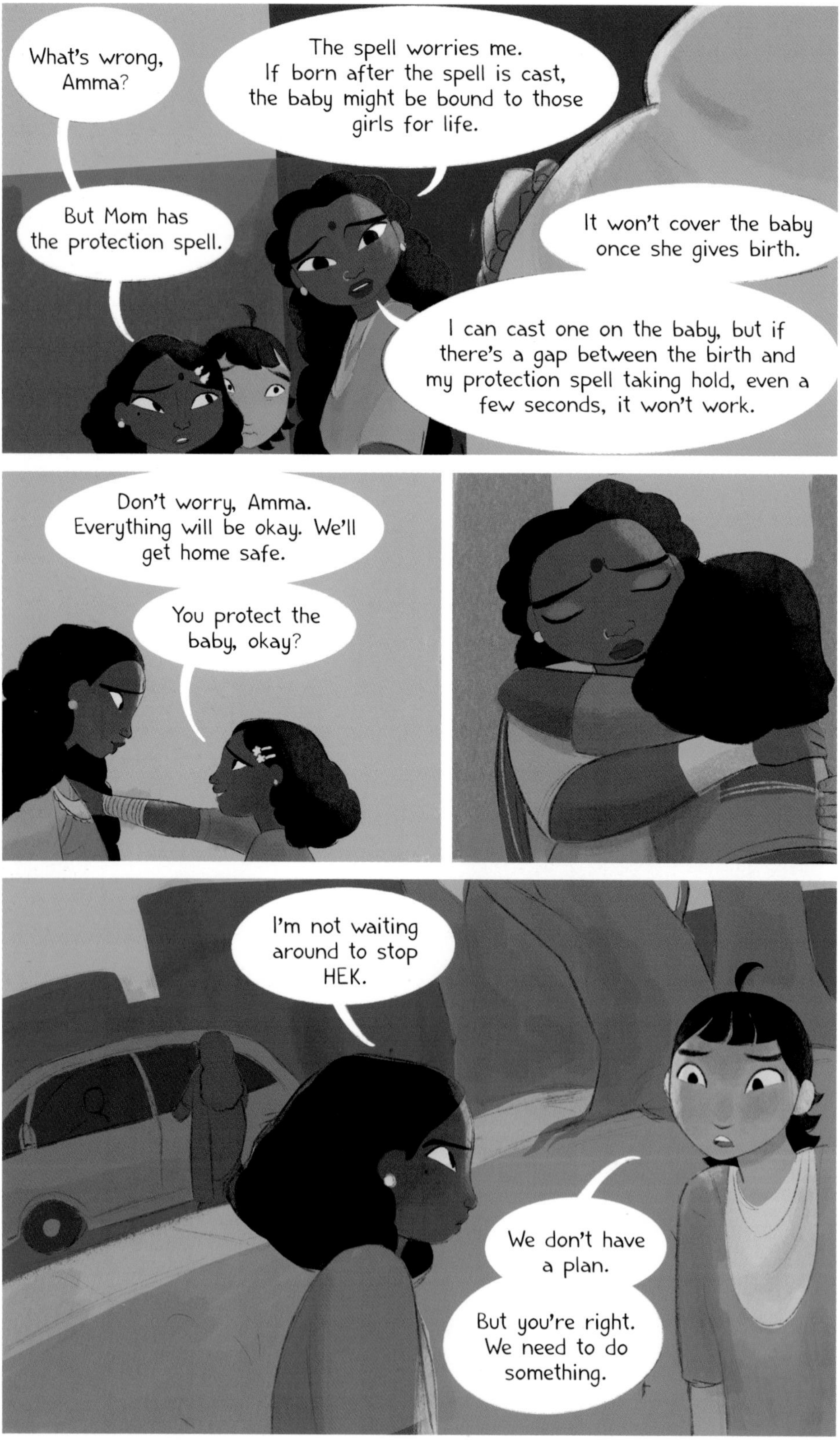
What's wrong, Amma?
The spell worries me. If born after the spell is cast, the baby might be bound to those girls for life.
But Mom has the protection spell.
It won't cover the baby once she gives birth.
I can cast one on the baby, but if there's a gap between the birth and my protection spell taking hold, even a few seconds, it won't work.
Don't worry, Amma. Everything will be okay. We'll get home safe.
You protect the baby, okay?
I'm not waiting around to stop HEK.
We don't have a plan.
But you're right. We need to do something.

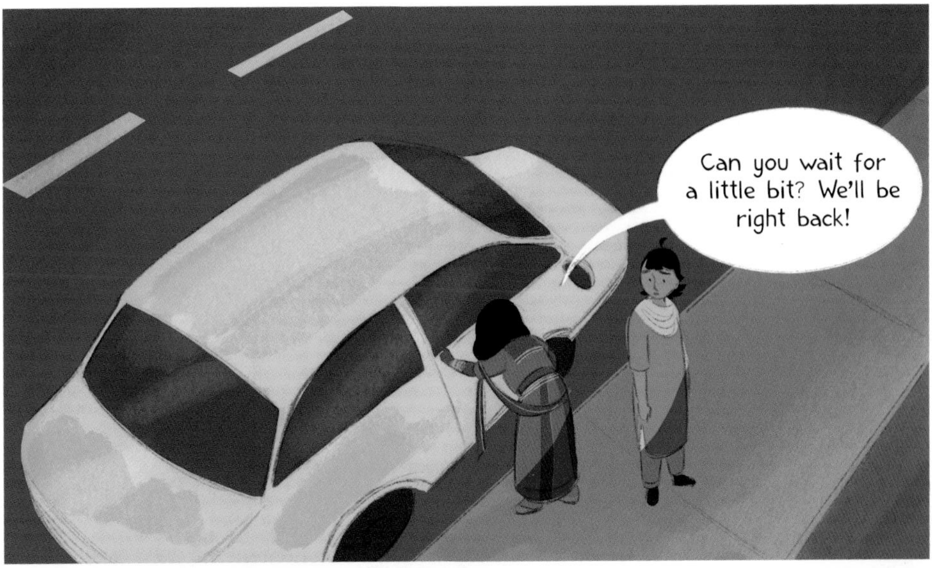
Can you wait for a little bit? We'll be right back!

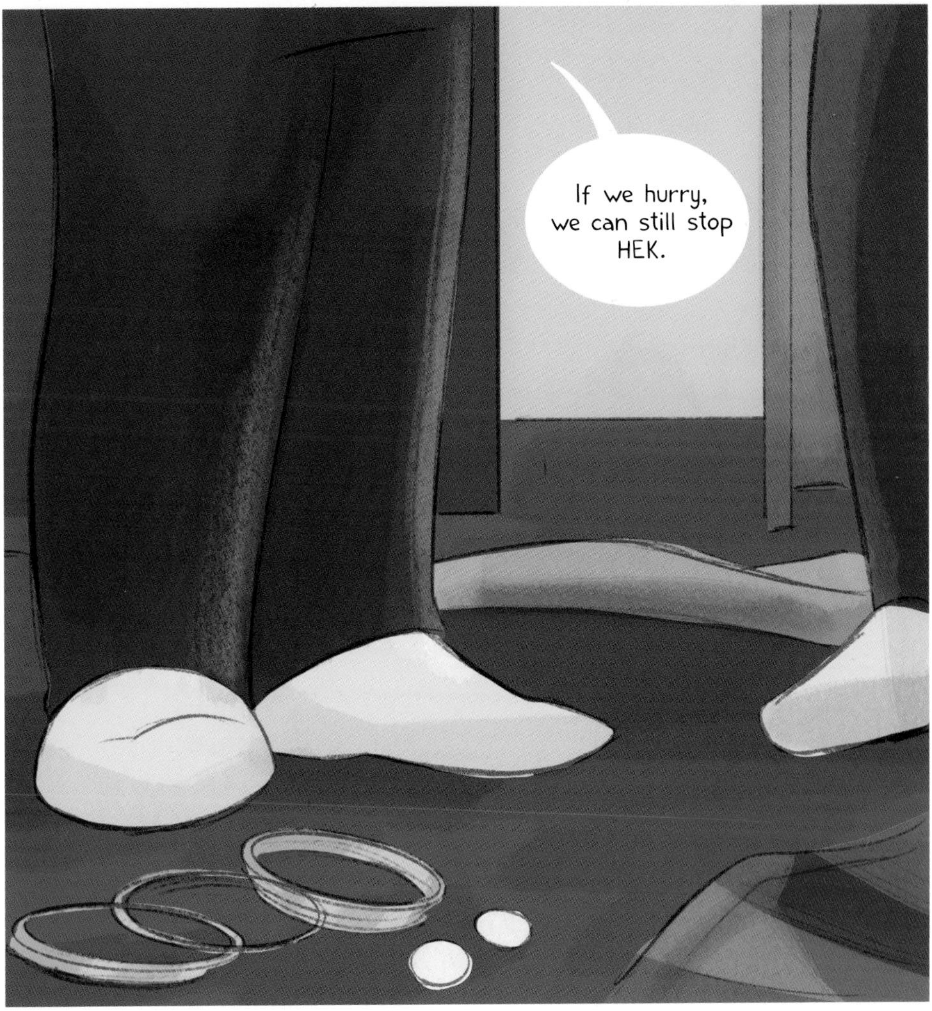
If we hurry, we can still stop HEK.

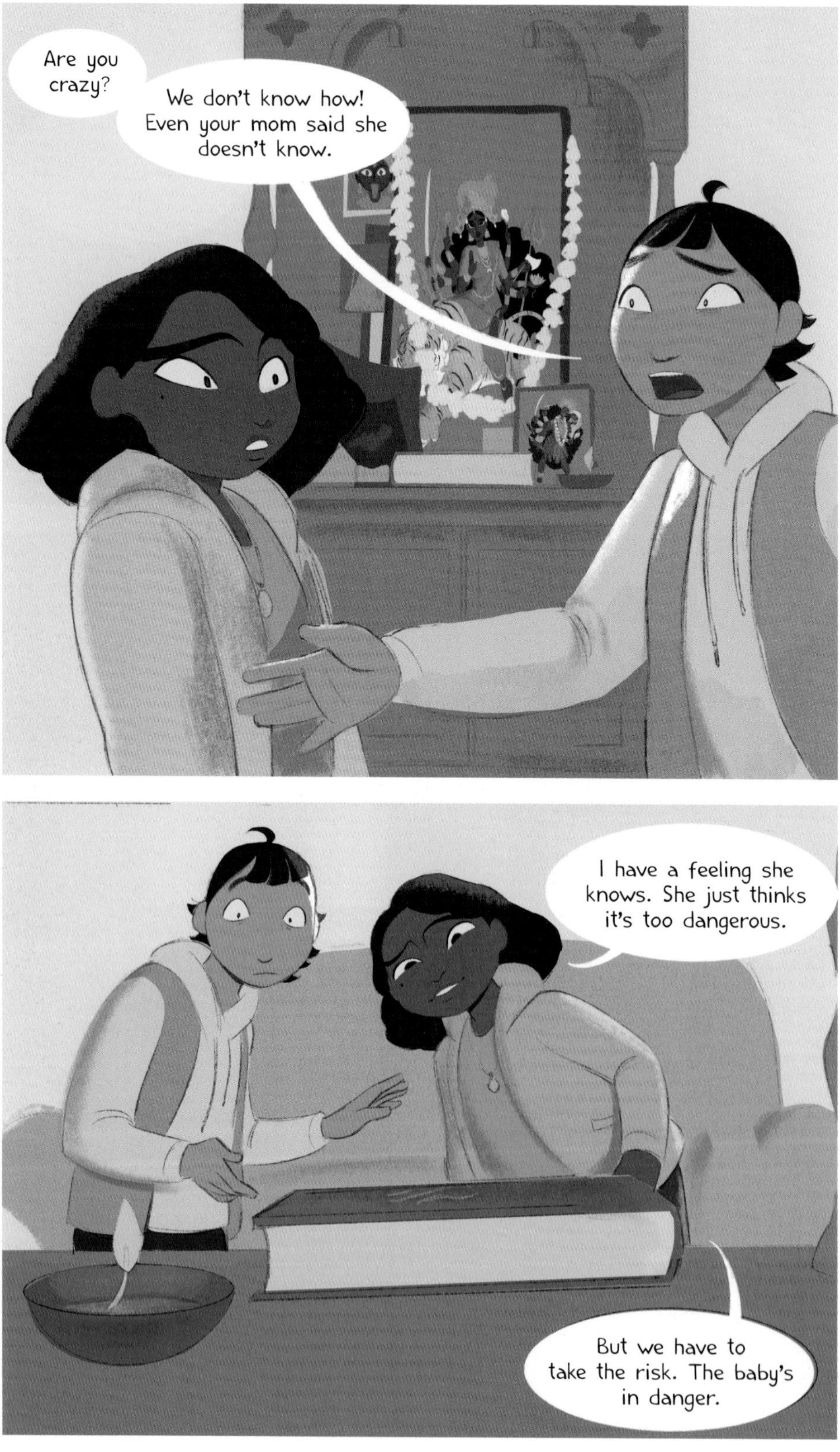
Are you crazy?
We don't know how! Even your mom said she doesn't know.
I have a feeling she knows. She just thinks it's too dangerous.
But we have to take the risk. The baby's in danger.

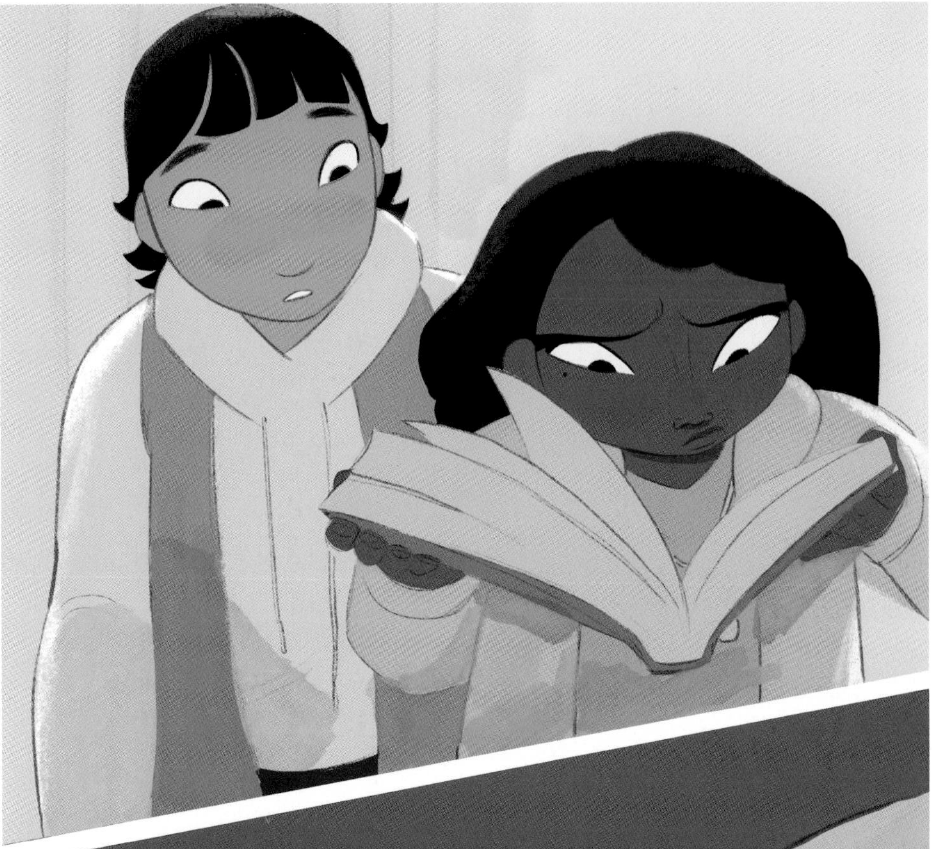

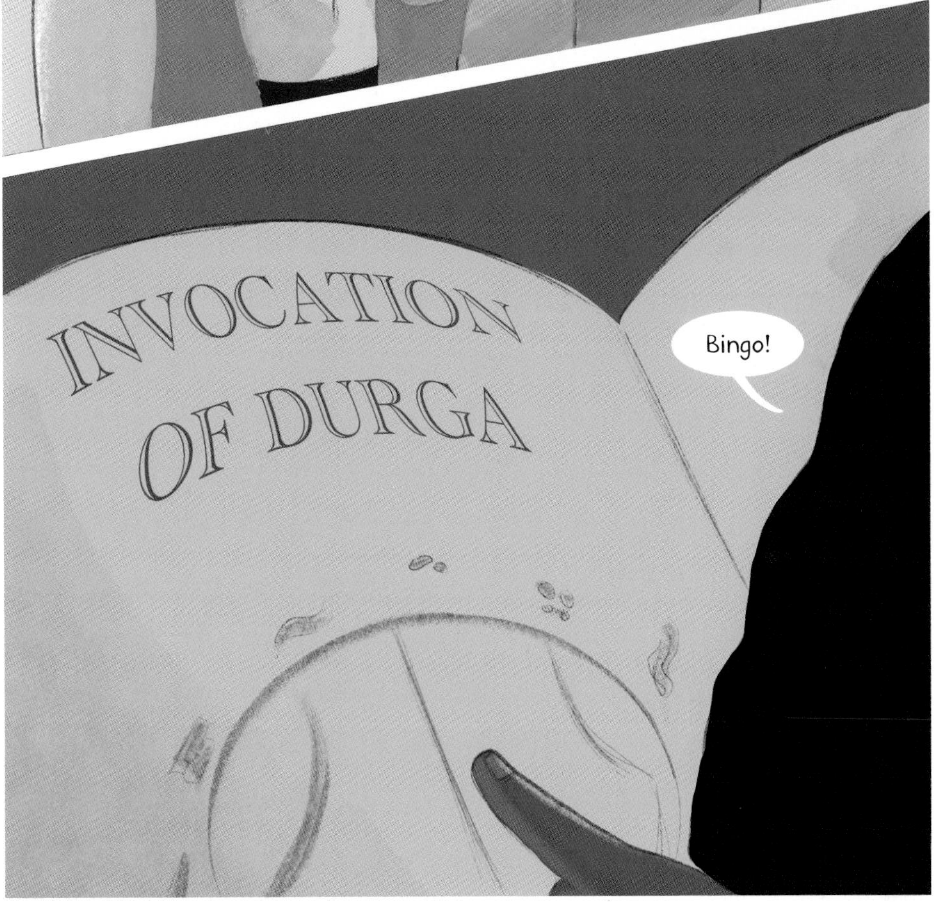
INVOCATION
OF DURGA
Bingo!

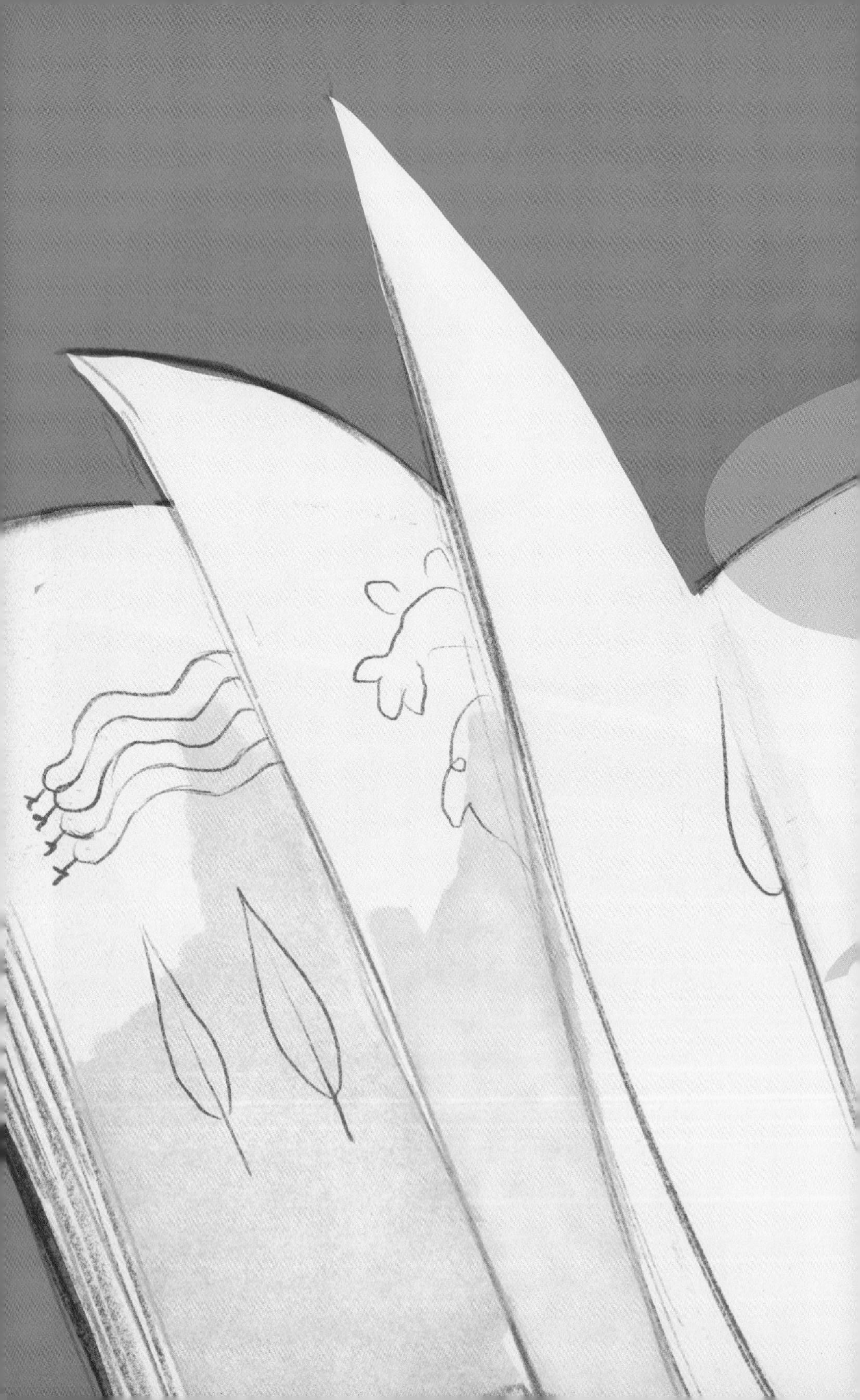

# Chapter 4

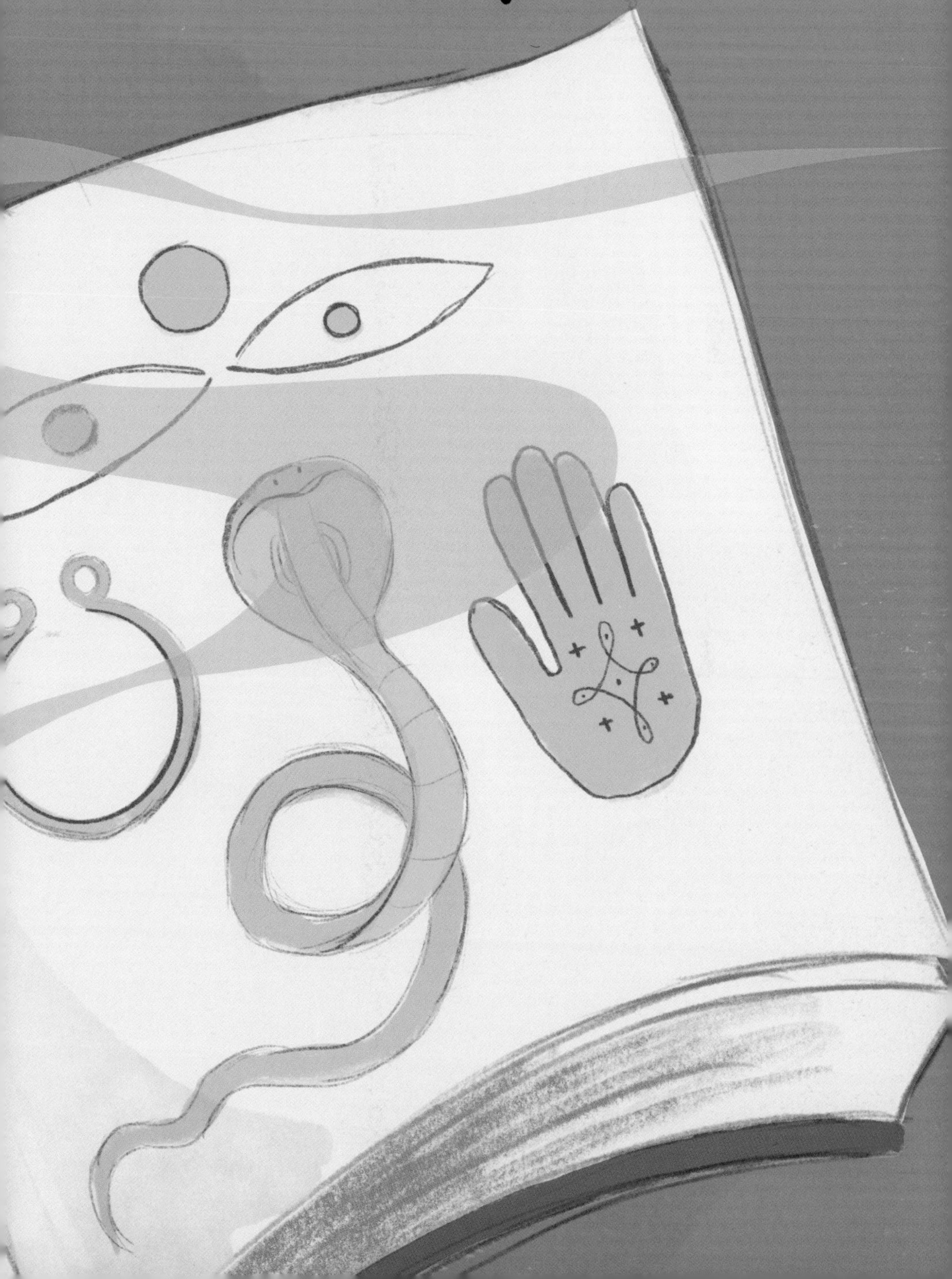

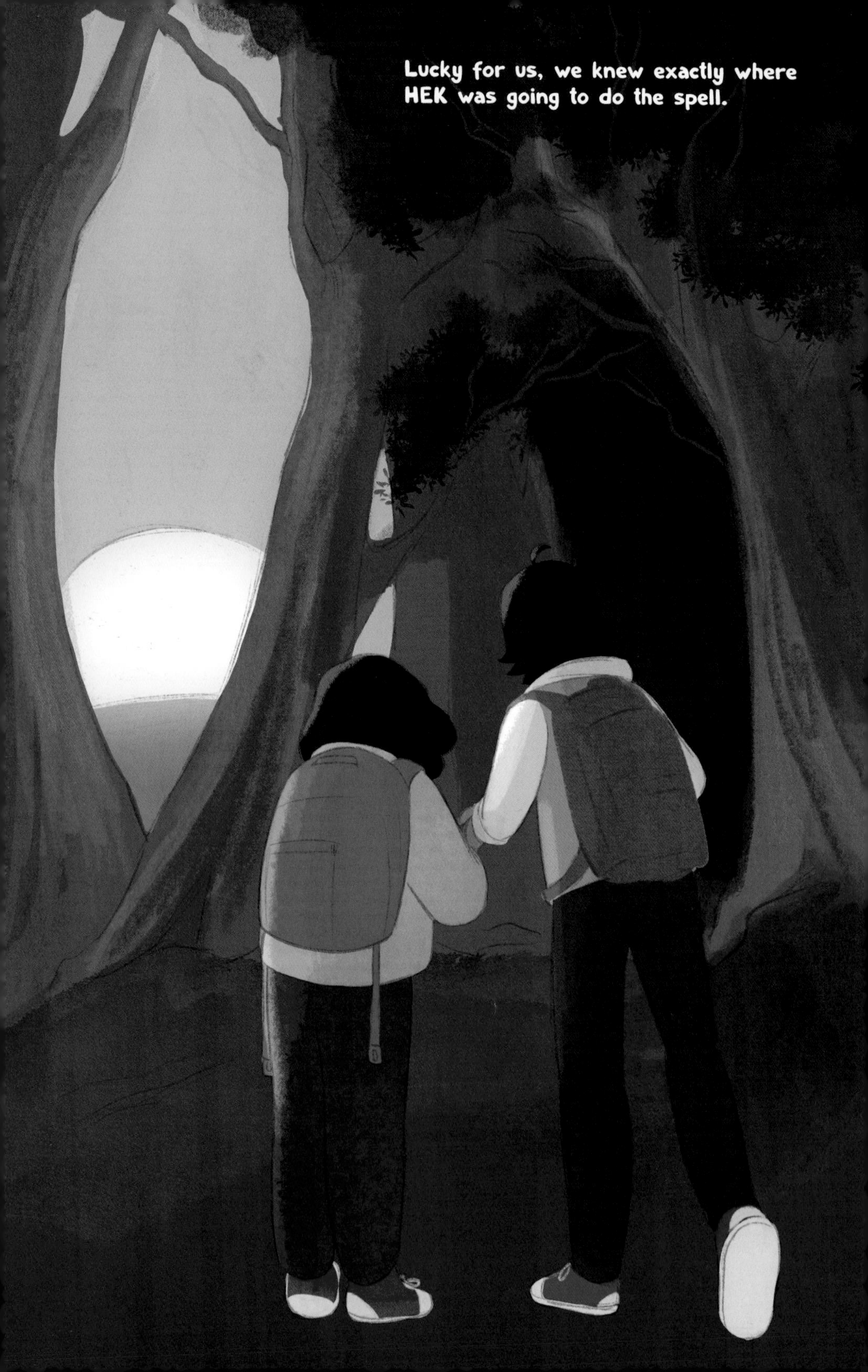
Lucky for us, we knew exactly where HEK was going to do the spell.

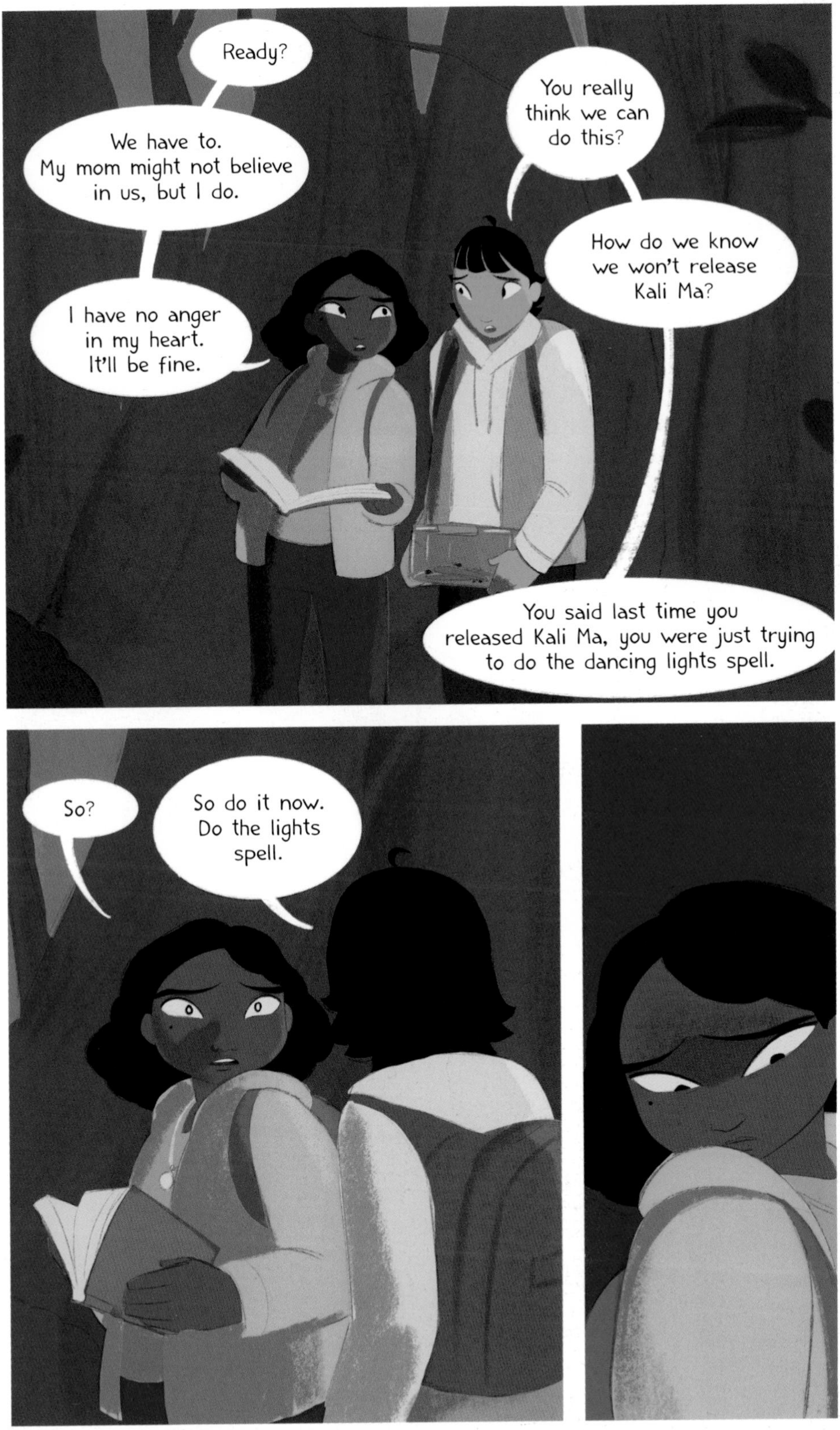
Ready?
We have to.
My mom might not believe in us, but I do.
I have no anger in my heart. It'll be fine.
You really think we can do this?
How do we know we won't release Kali Ma?
You said last time you released Kali Ma, you were just trying to do the dancing lights spell.
So?
So do it now. Do the lights spell.

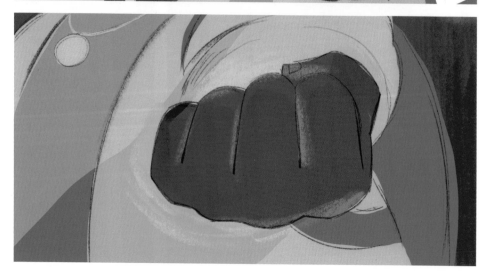

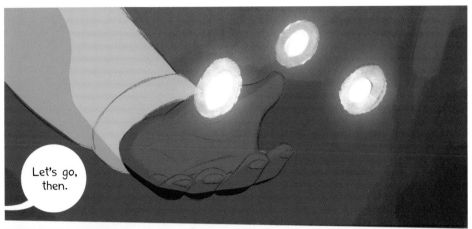

Let's go, then.

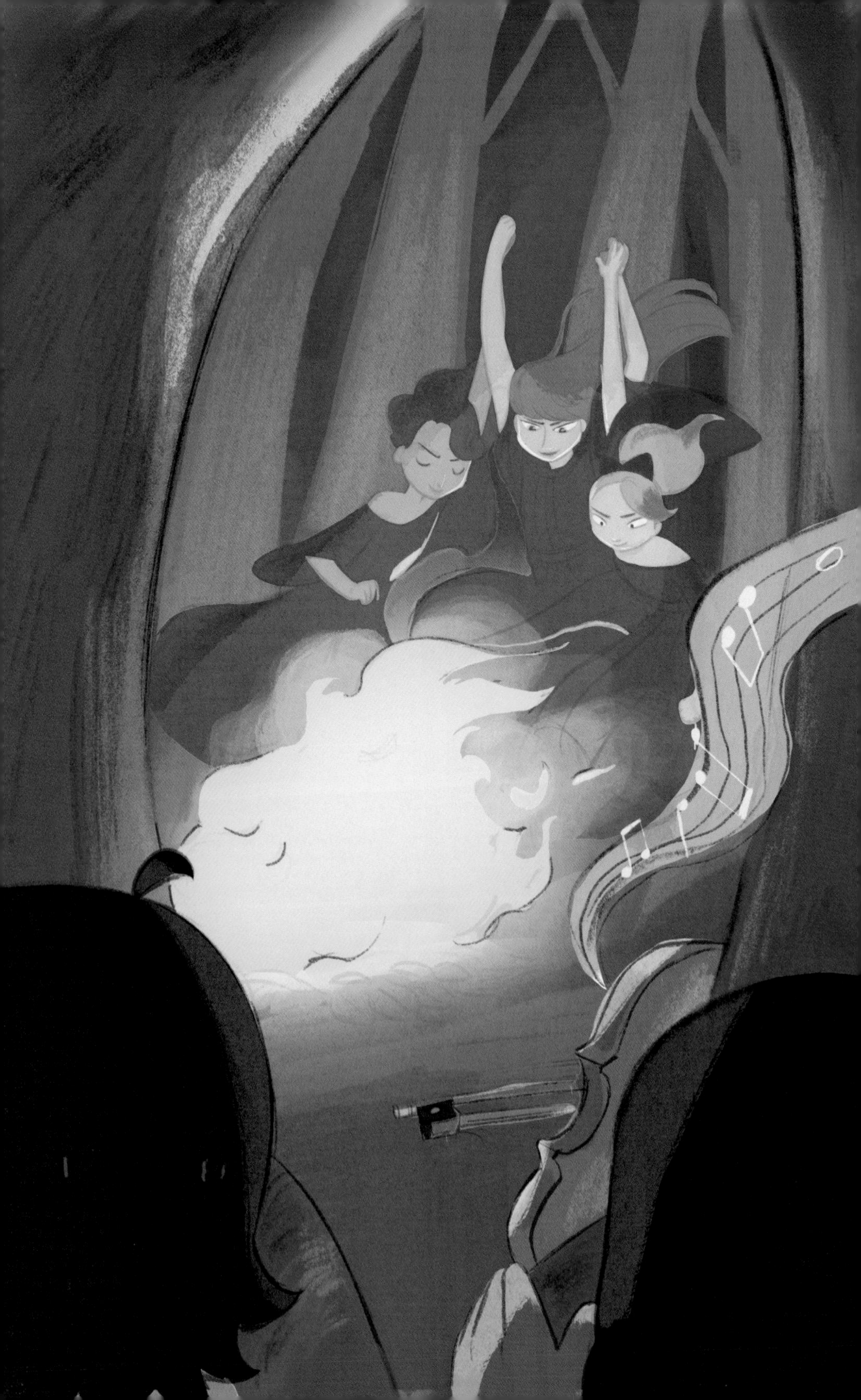

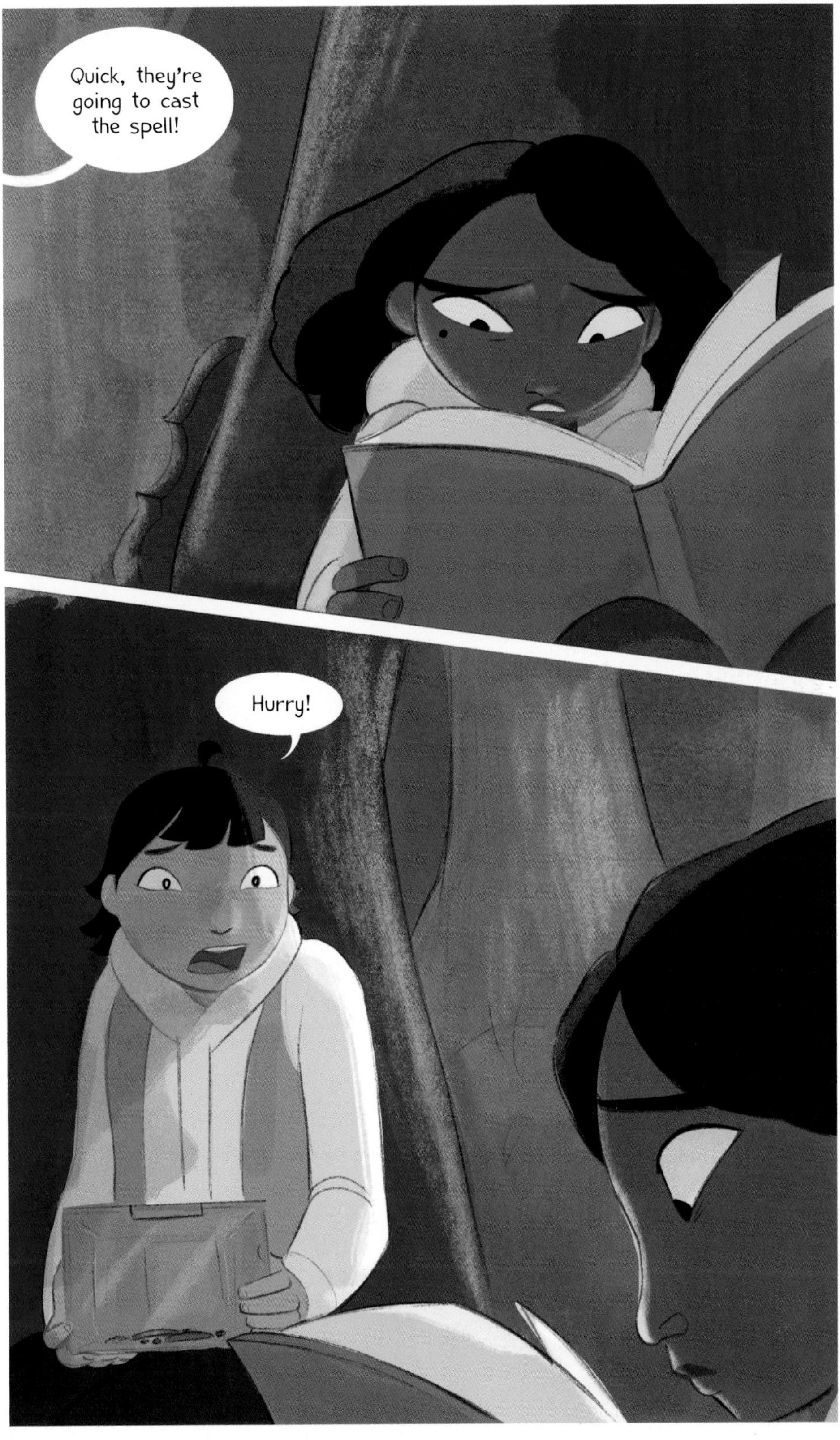
Quick, they're going to cast the spell!
Hurry!

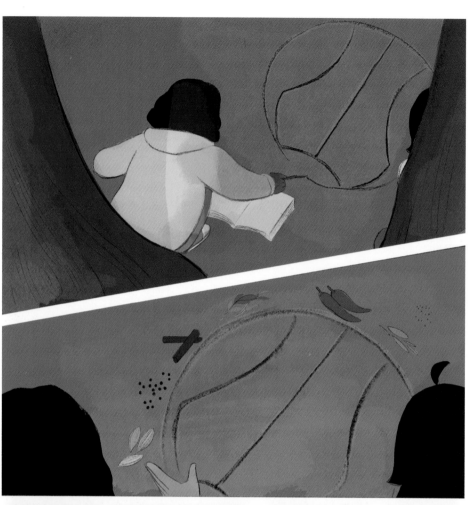

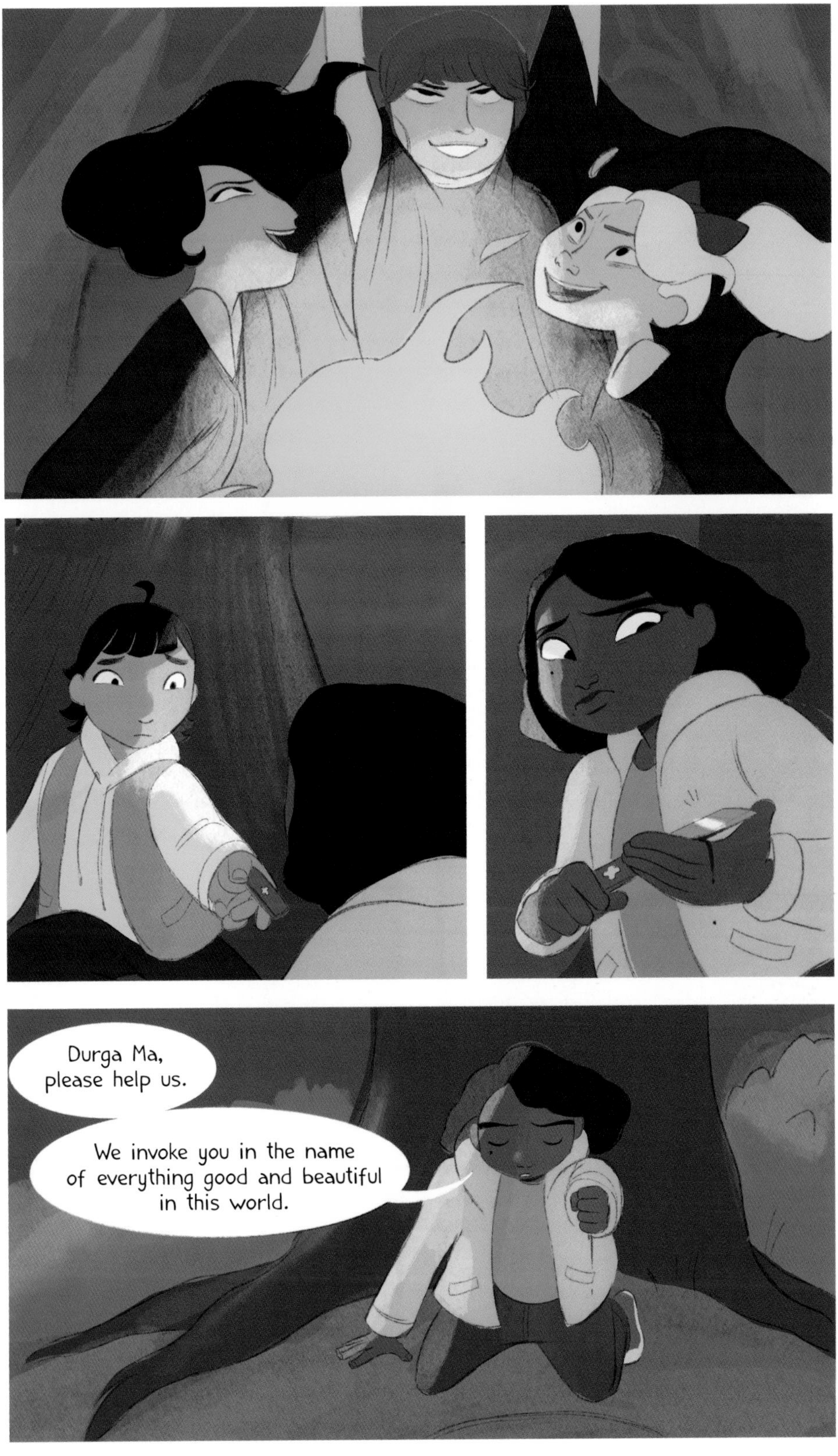
Durga Ma, please help us.
We invoke you in the name of everything good and beautiful in this world.

Durga Ma, help us save Mom and the baby.

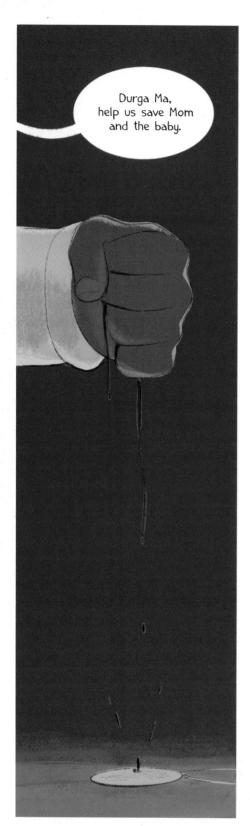

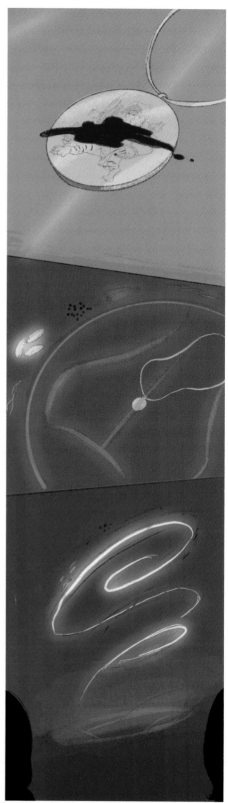

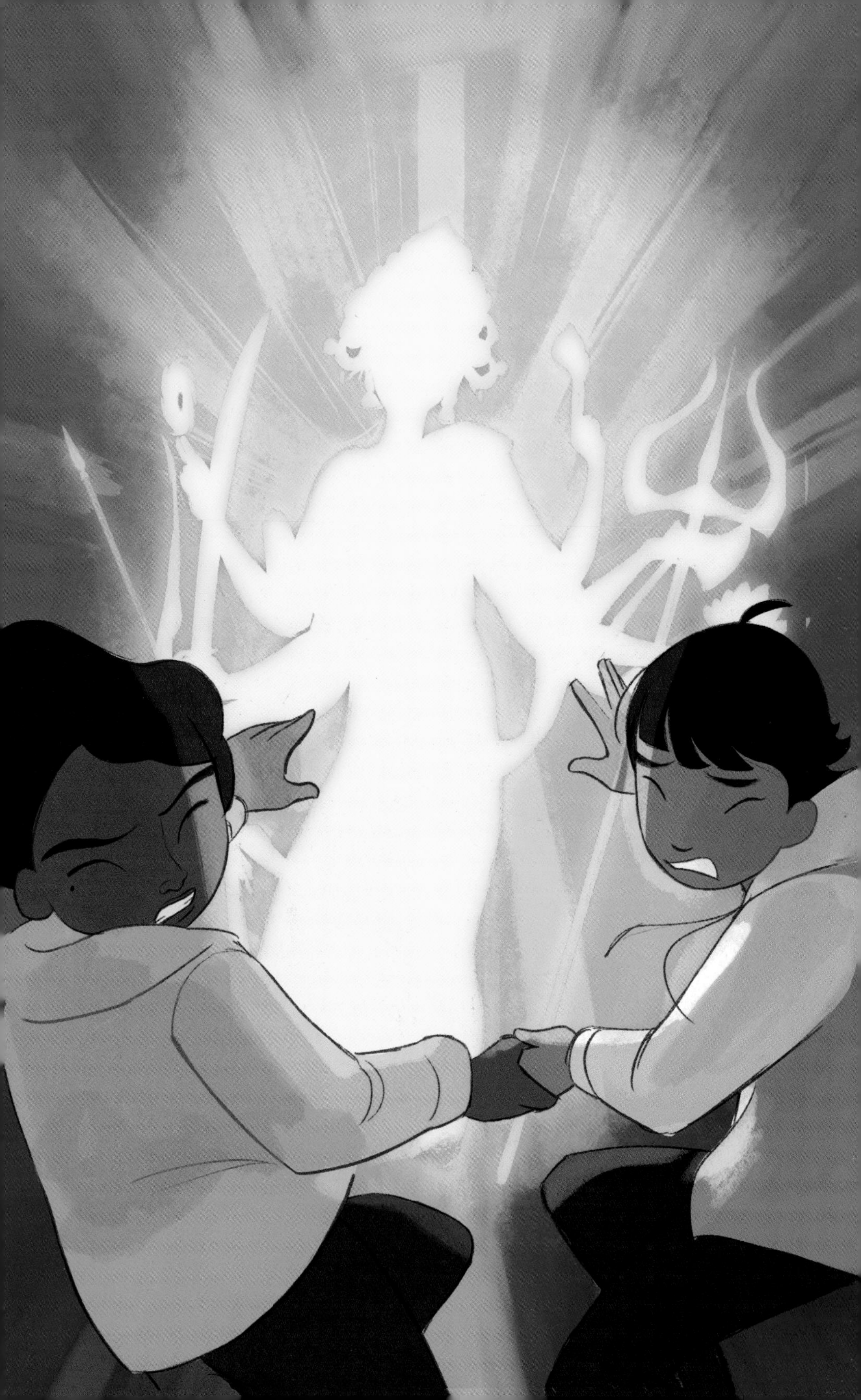

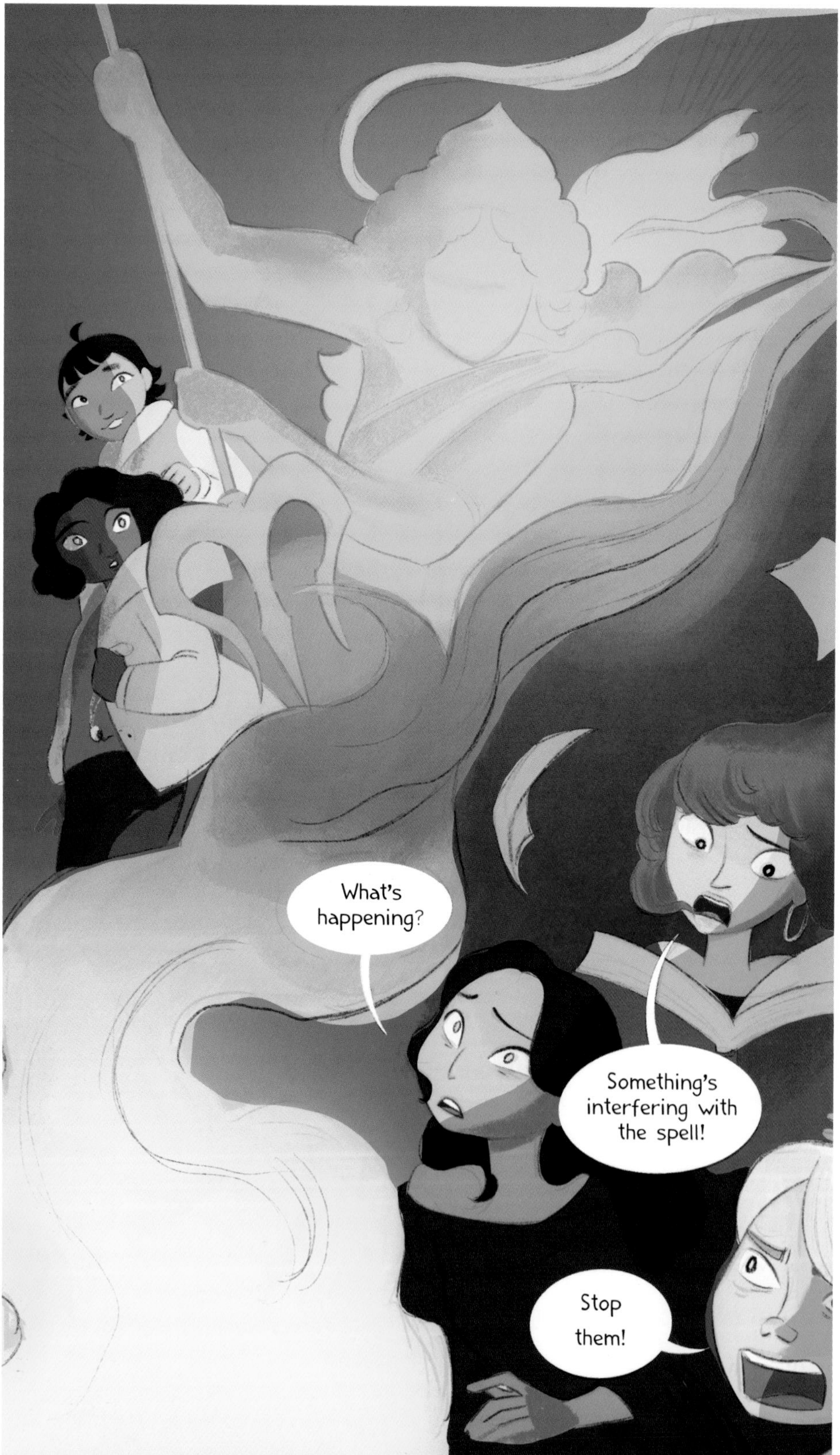
What's happening?
Something's interfering with the spell!
Stop them!

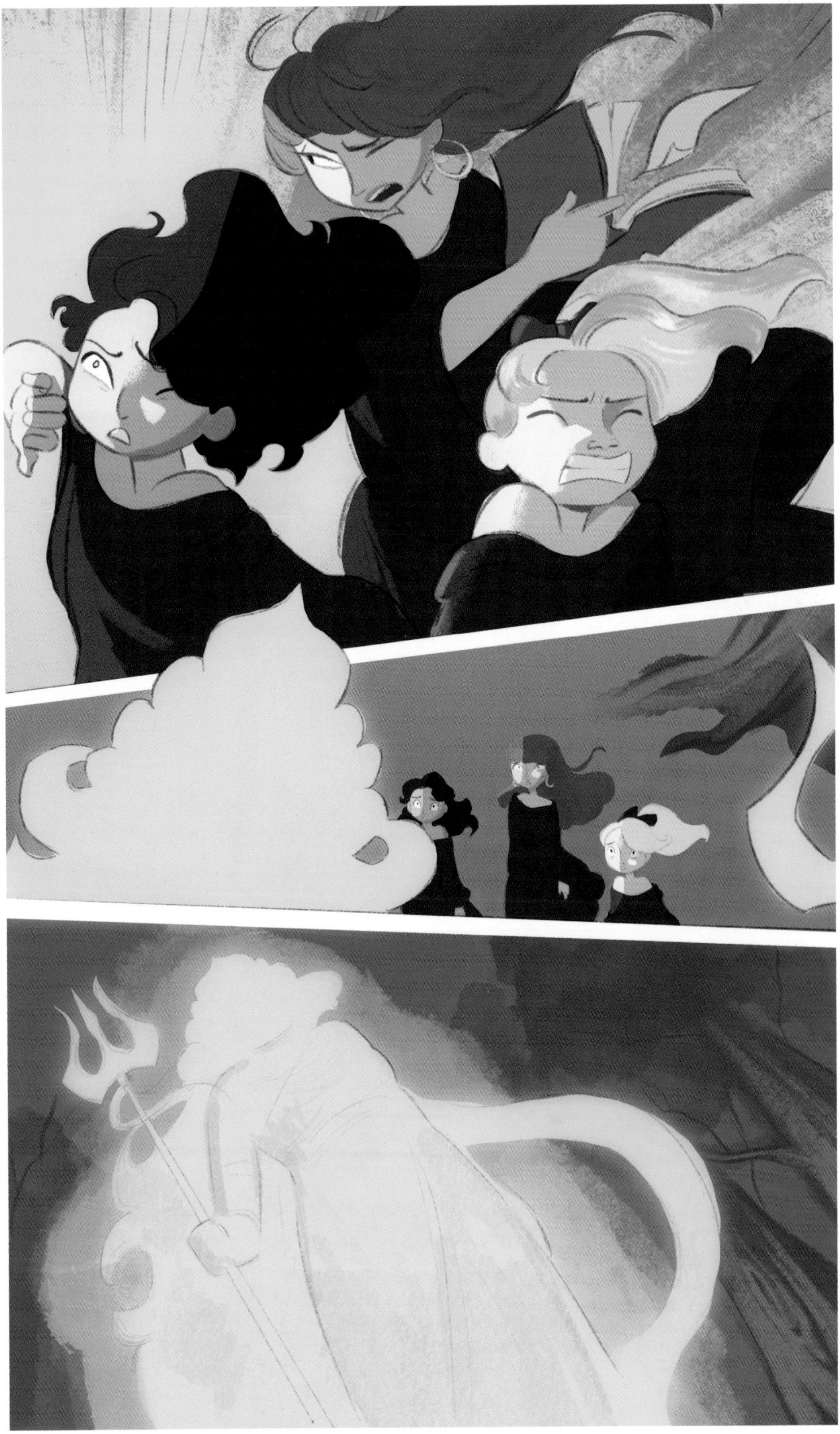

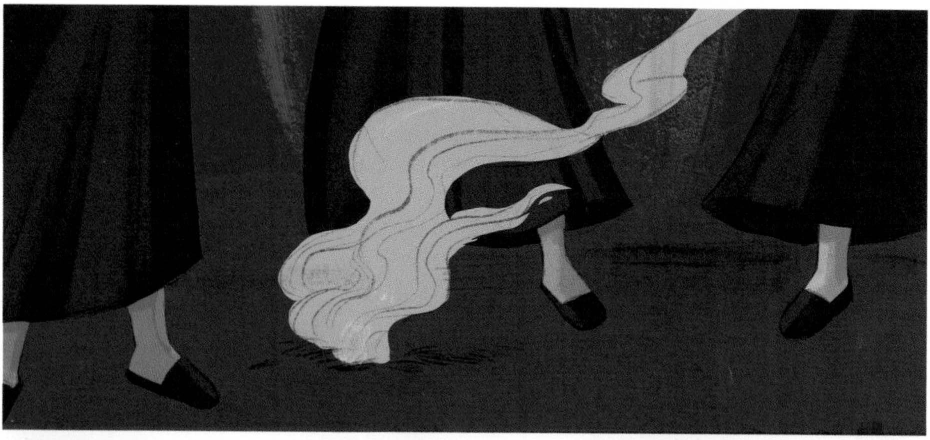

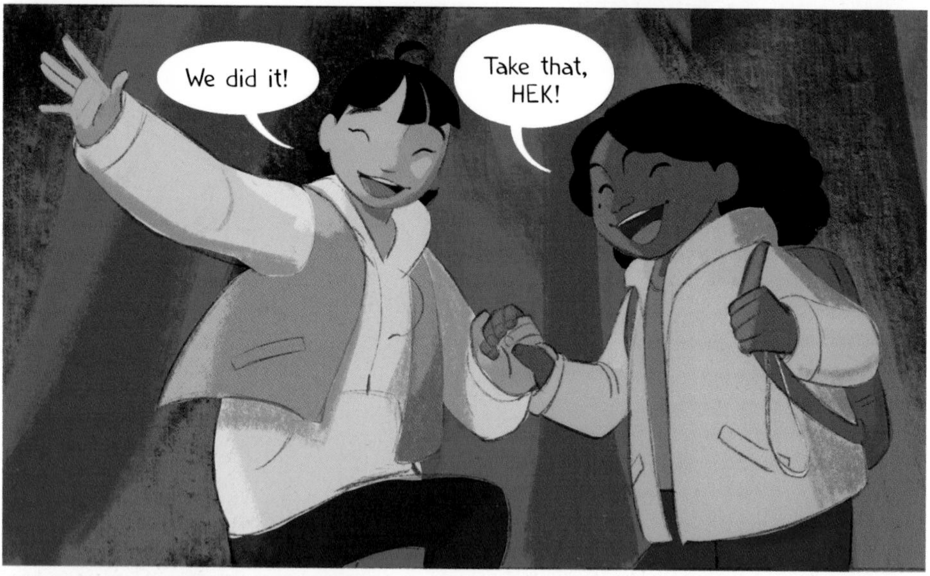
We did it!
Take that, HEK!

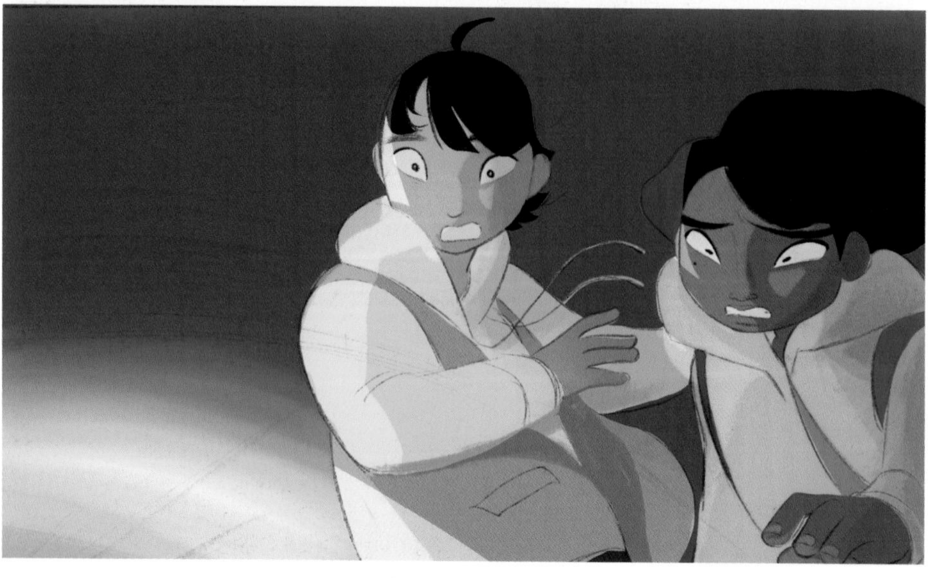

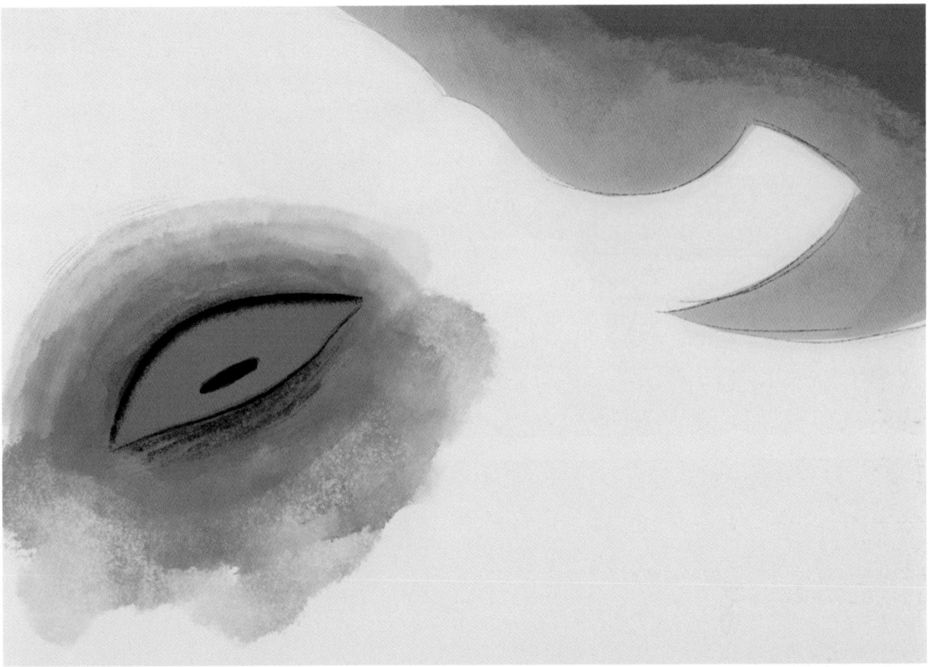

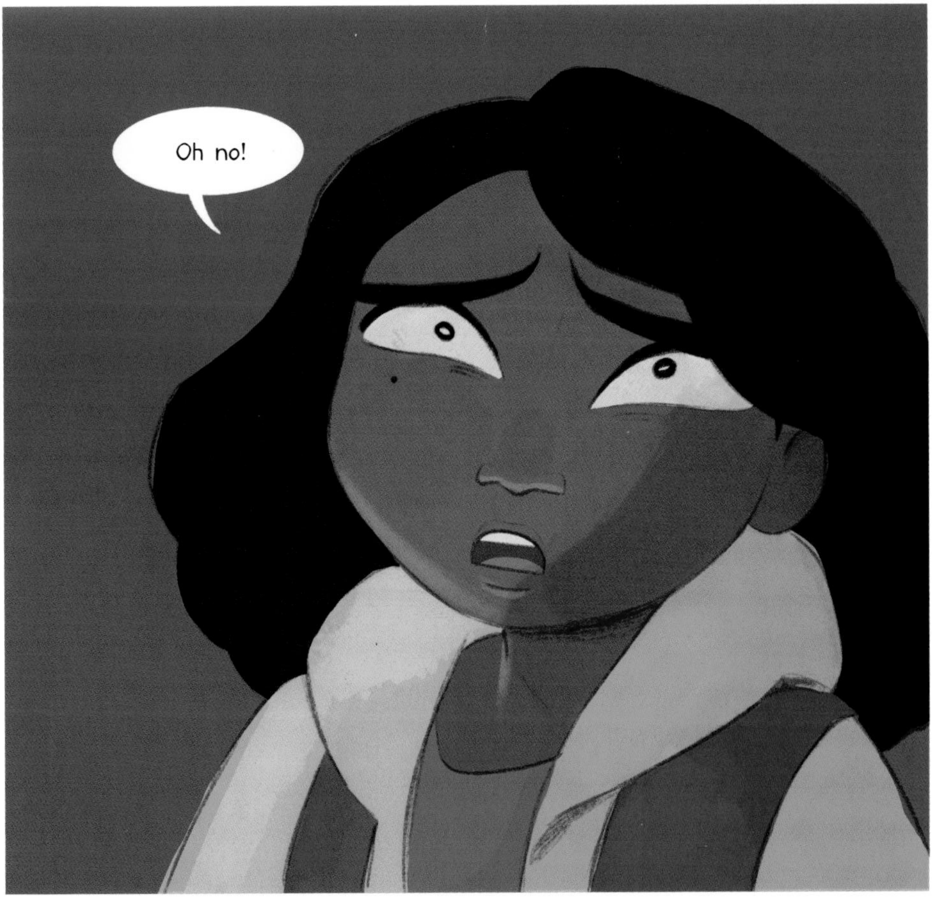
Oh no!

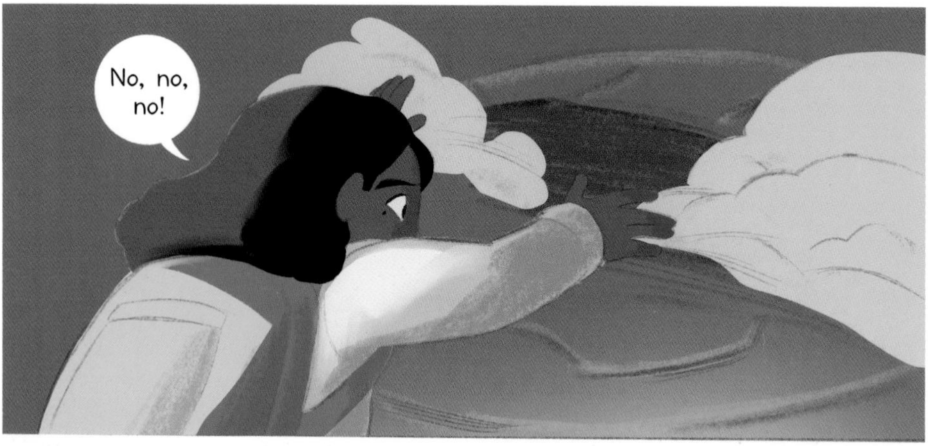
No, no, no!

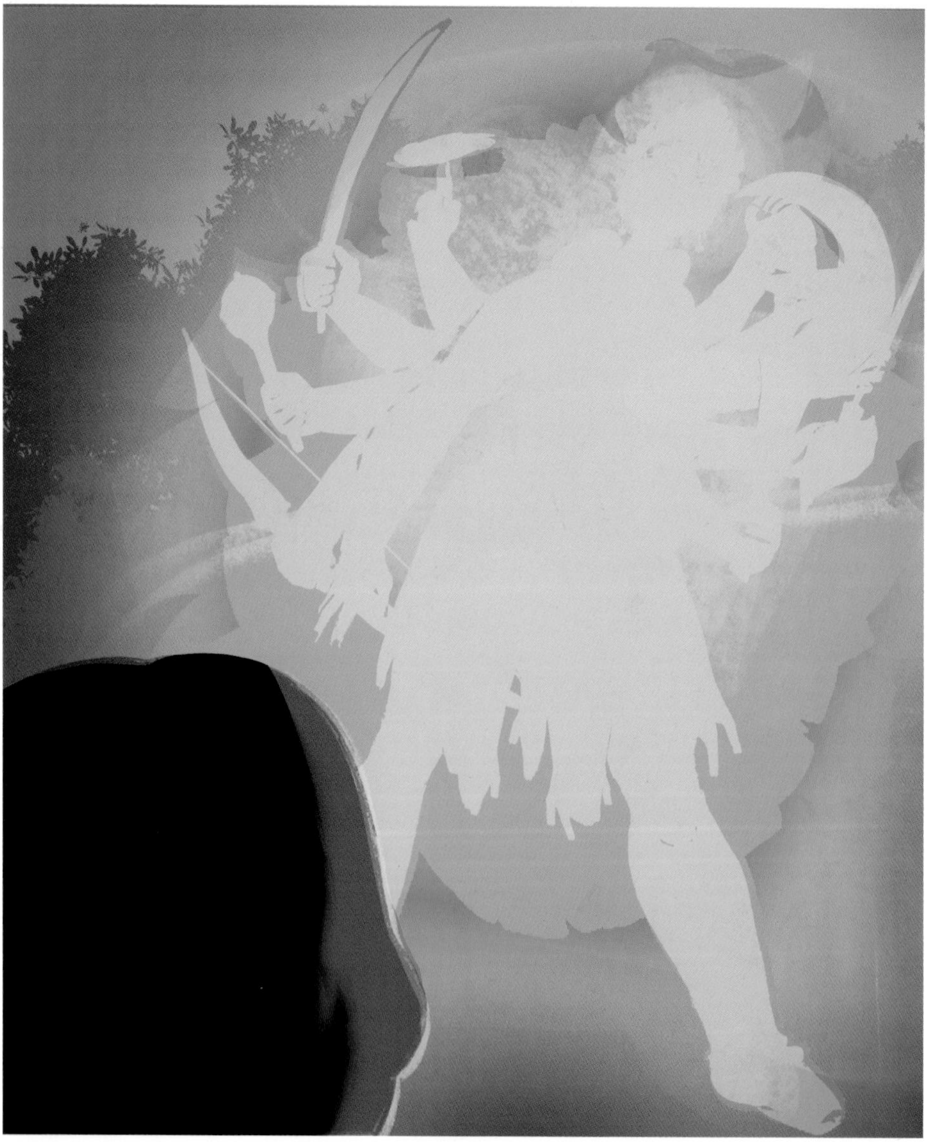

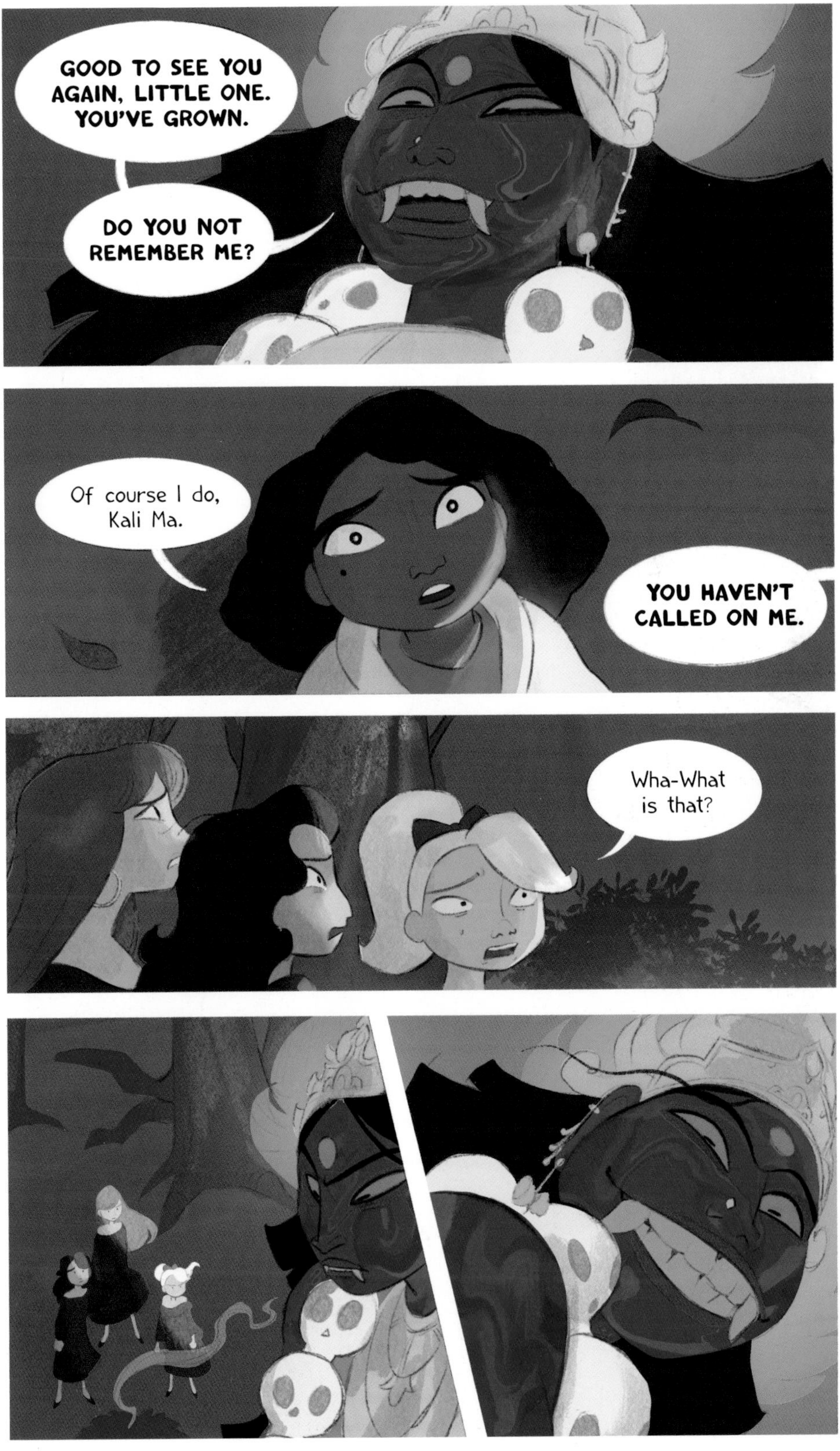
GOOD TO SEE YOU AGAIN, LITTLE ONE. YOU'VE GROWN.
DO YOU NOT REMEMBER ME?
Of course I do, Kali Ma.
YOU HAVEN'T CALLED ON ME.
Wha-What is that?

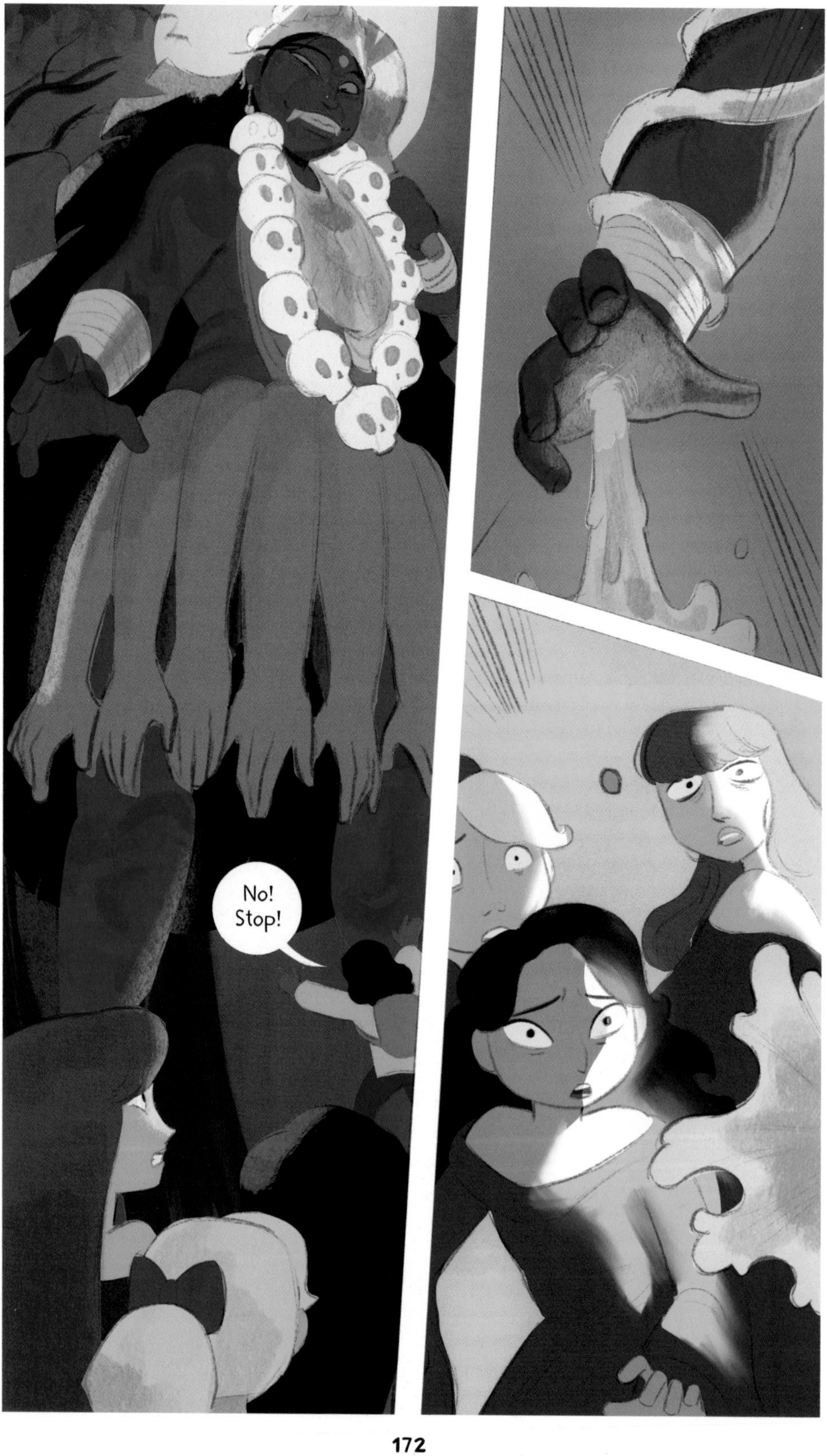
No! Stop!

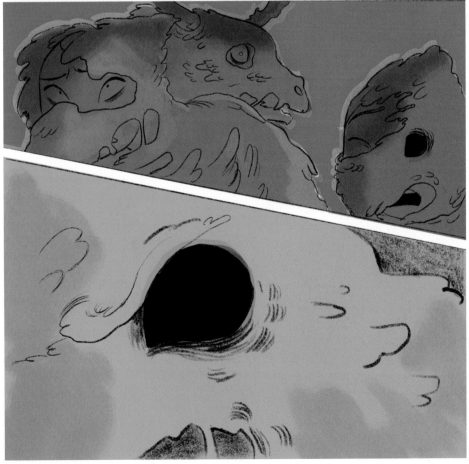

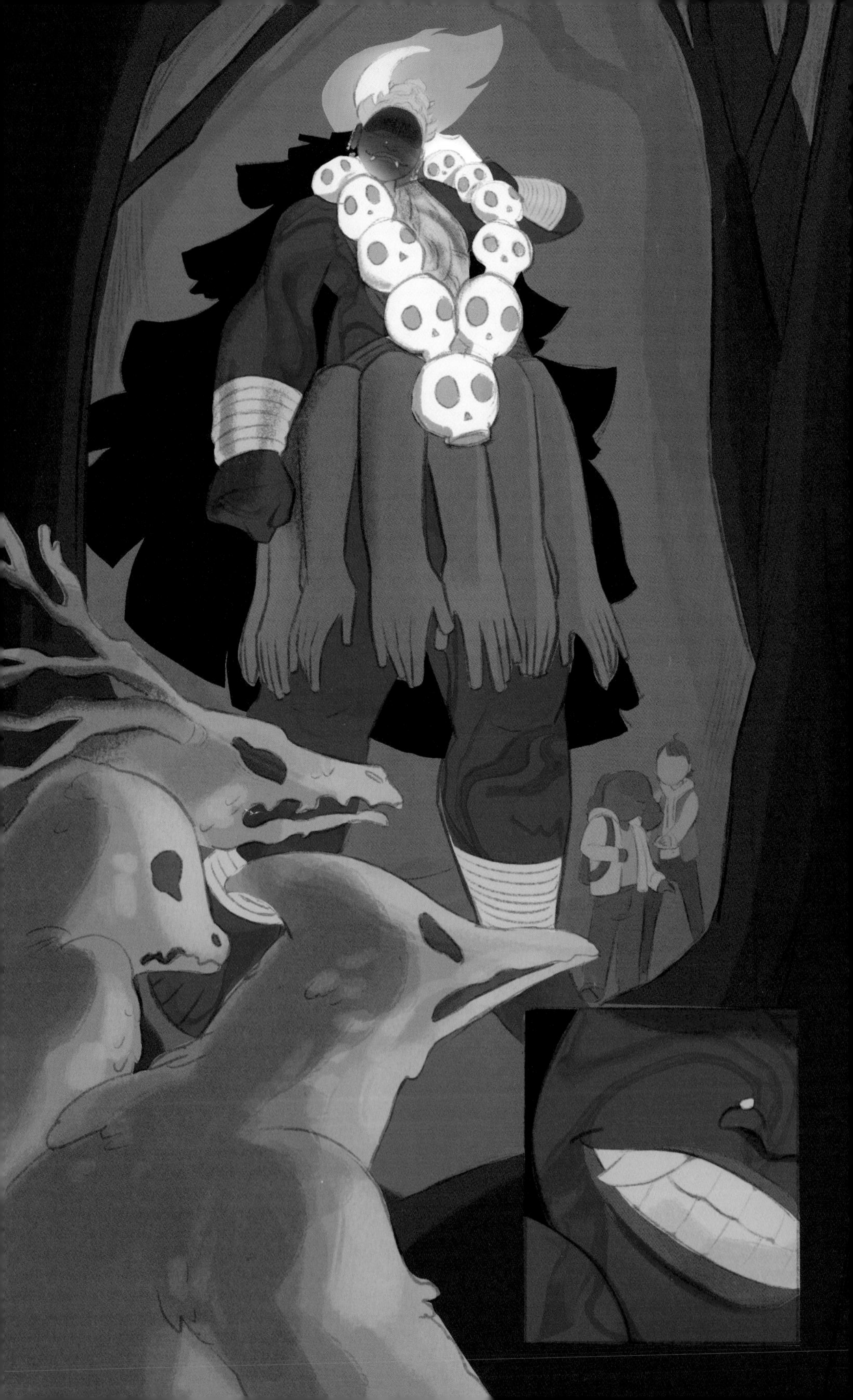

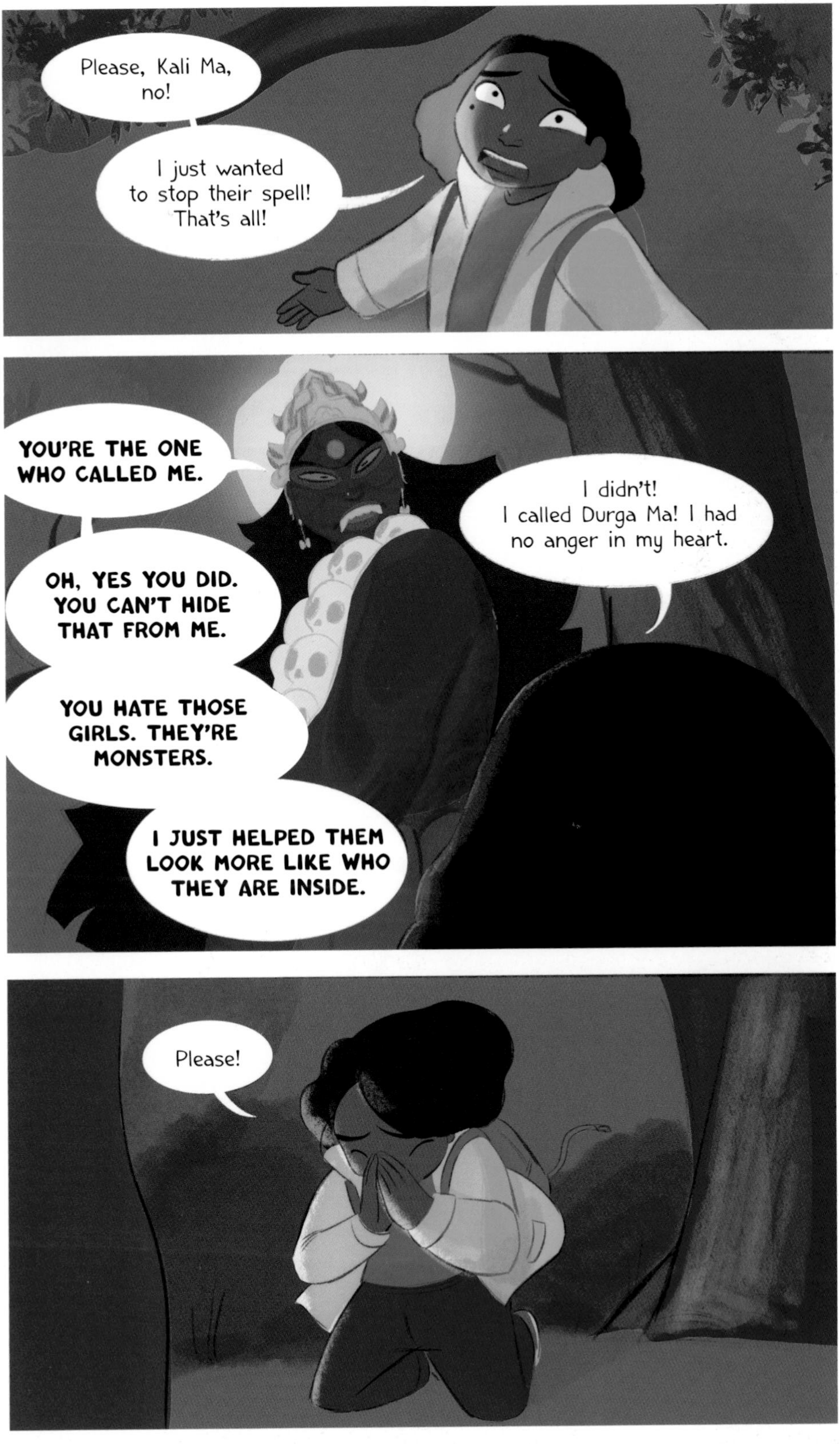
Please, Kali Ma, no!
I just wanted to stop their spell! That's all!
YOU'RE THE ONE WHO CALLED ME.
I didn't! I called Durga Ma! I had no anger in my heart.
OH, YES YOU DID. YOU CAN'T HIDE THAT FROM ME.
YOU HATE THOSE GIRLS. THEY'RE MONSTERS.
I JUST HELPED THEM LOOK MORE LIKE WHO THEY ARE INSIDE.
Please!

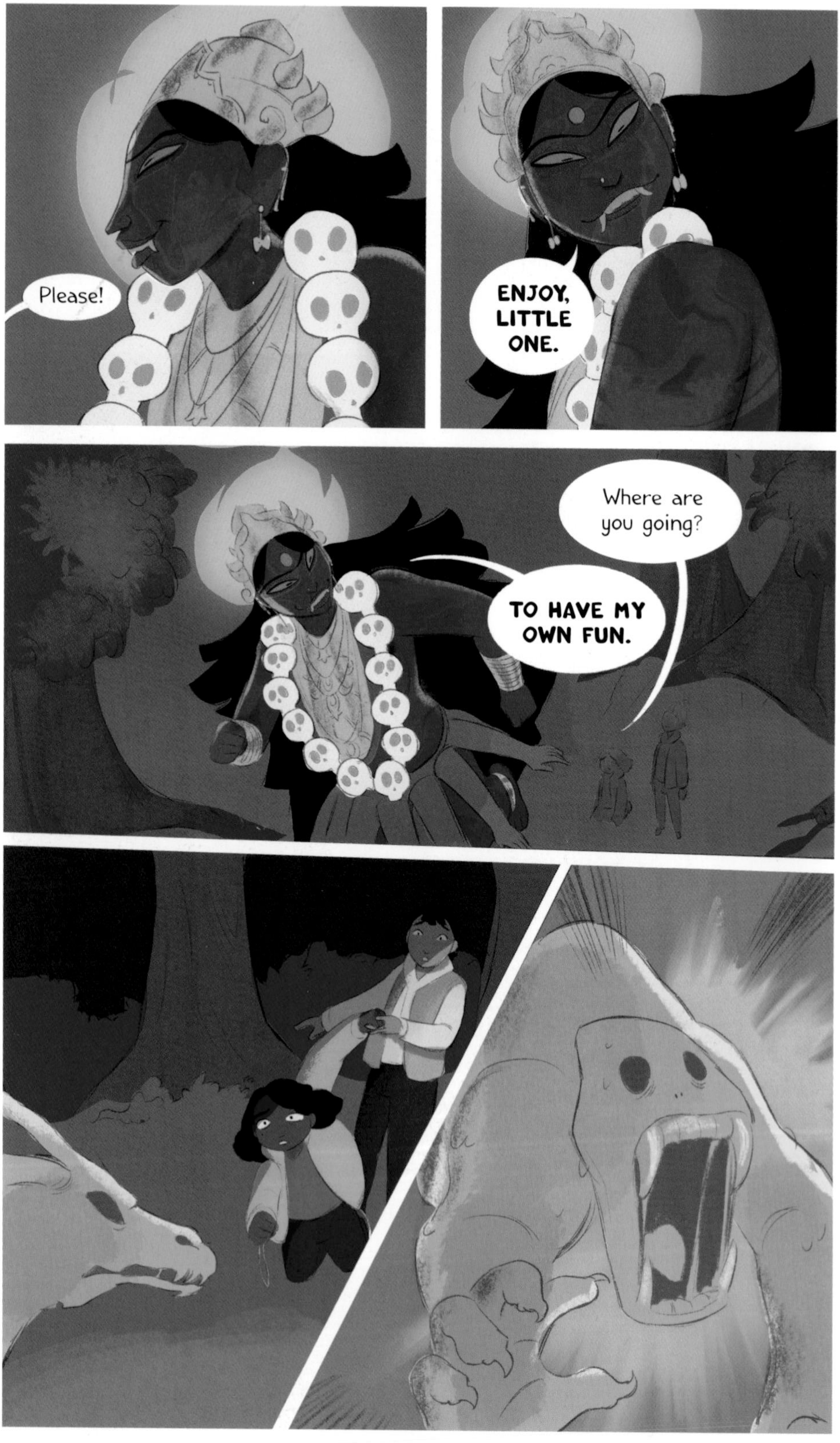
Please!
ENJOY, LITTLE ONE.
Where are you going?
TO HAVE MY OWN FUN.

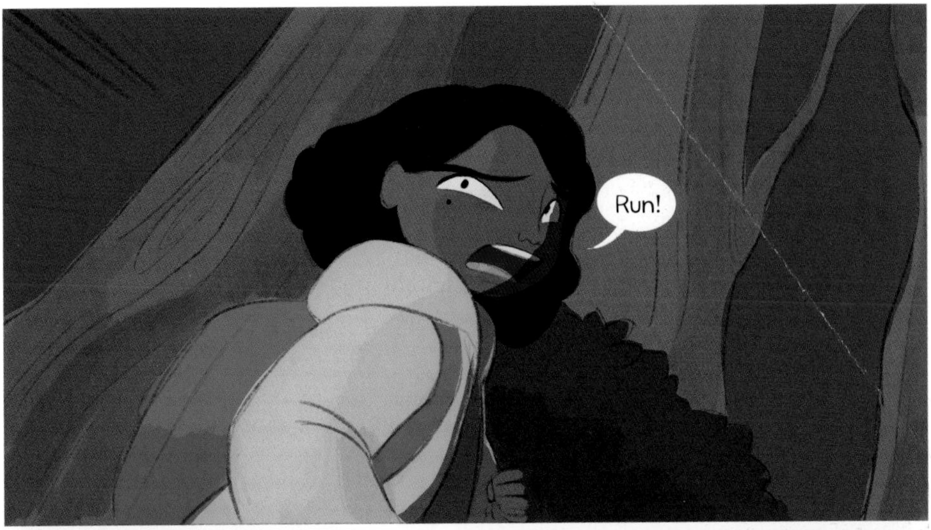
Run!

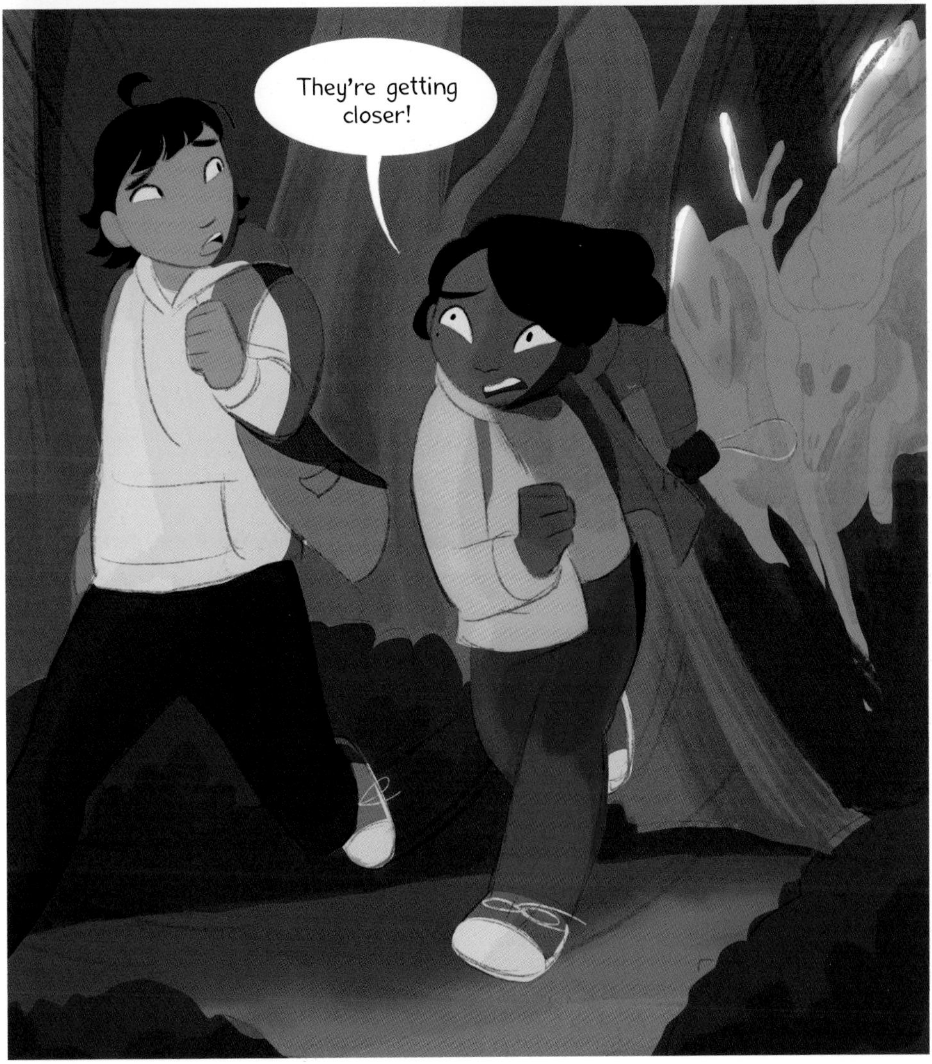
They're getting closer!

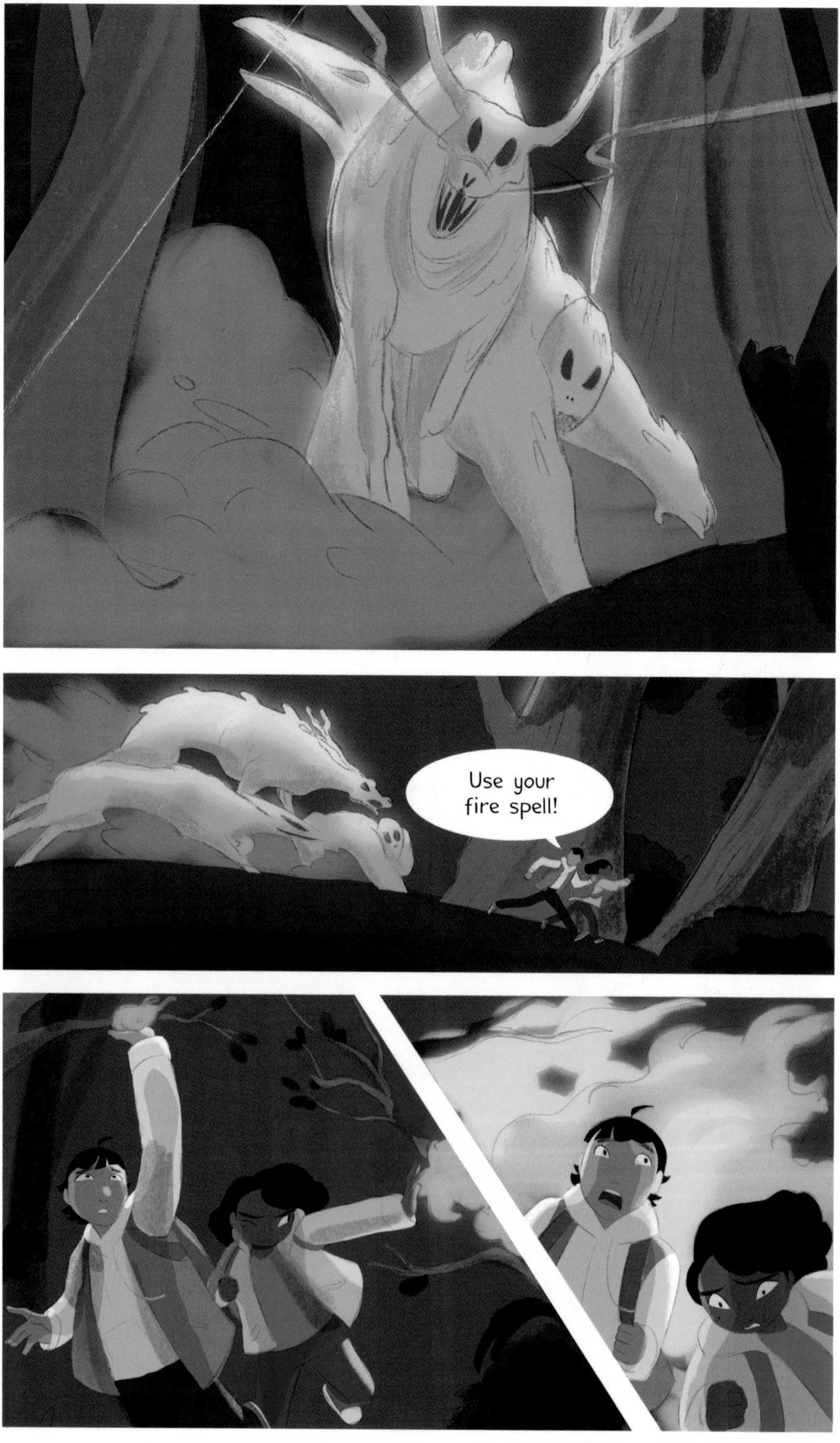
Use your
fire spell!

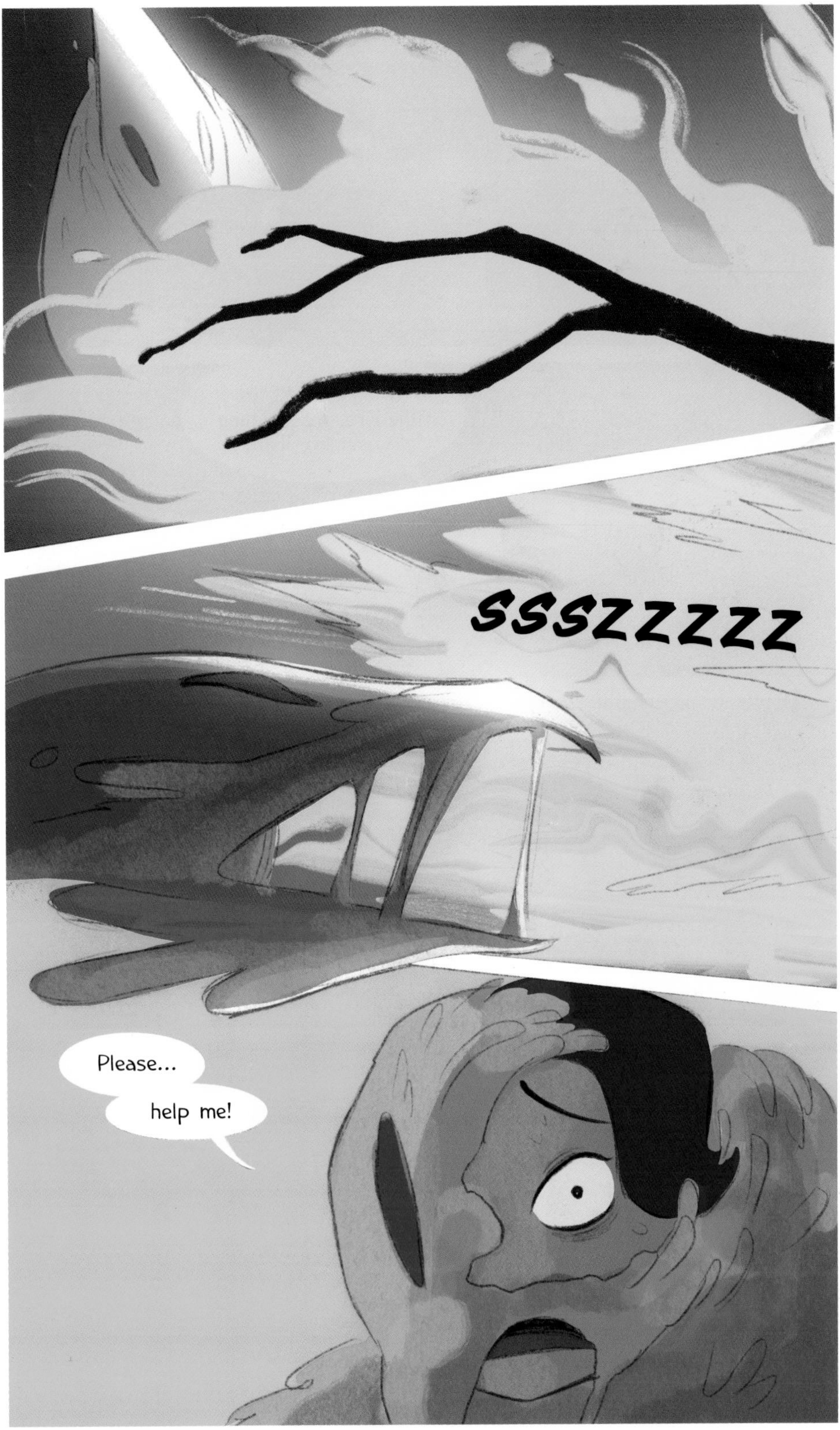
SSSZZZZZ
Please...
help me!

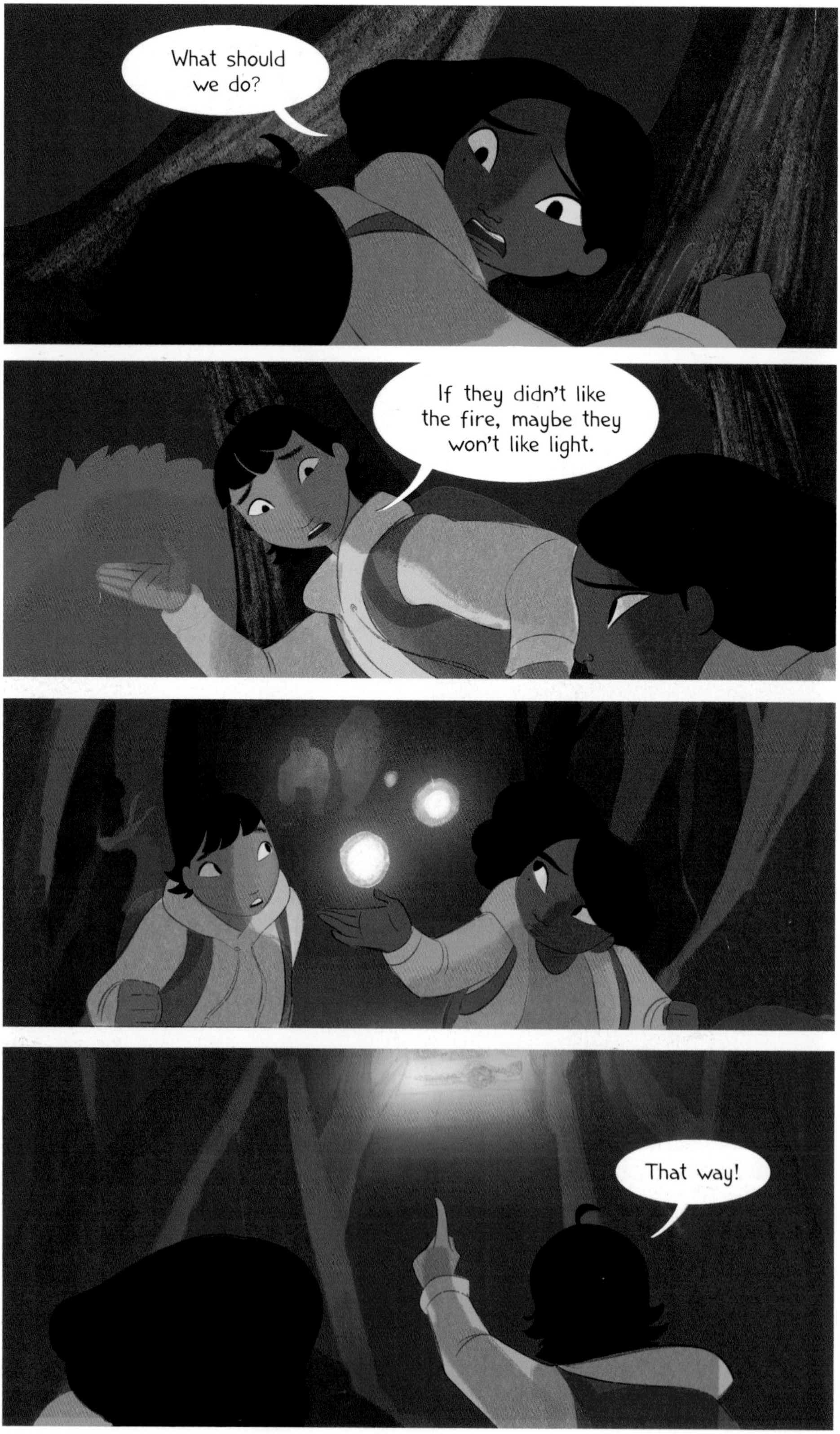
What should we do?
If they didn't like the fire, maybe they won't like light.
That way!

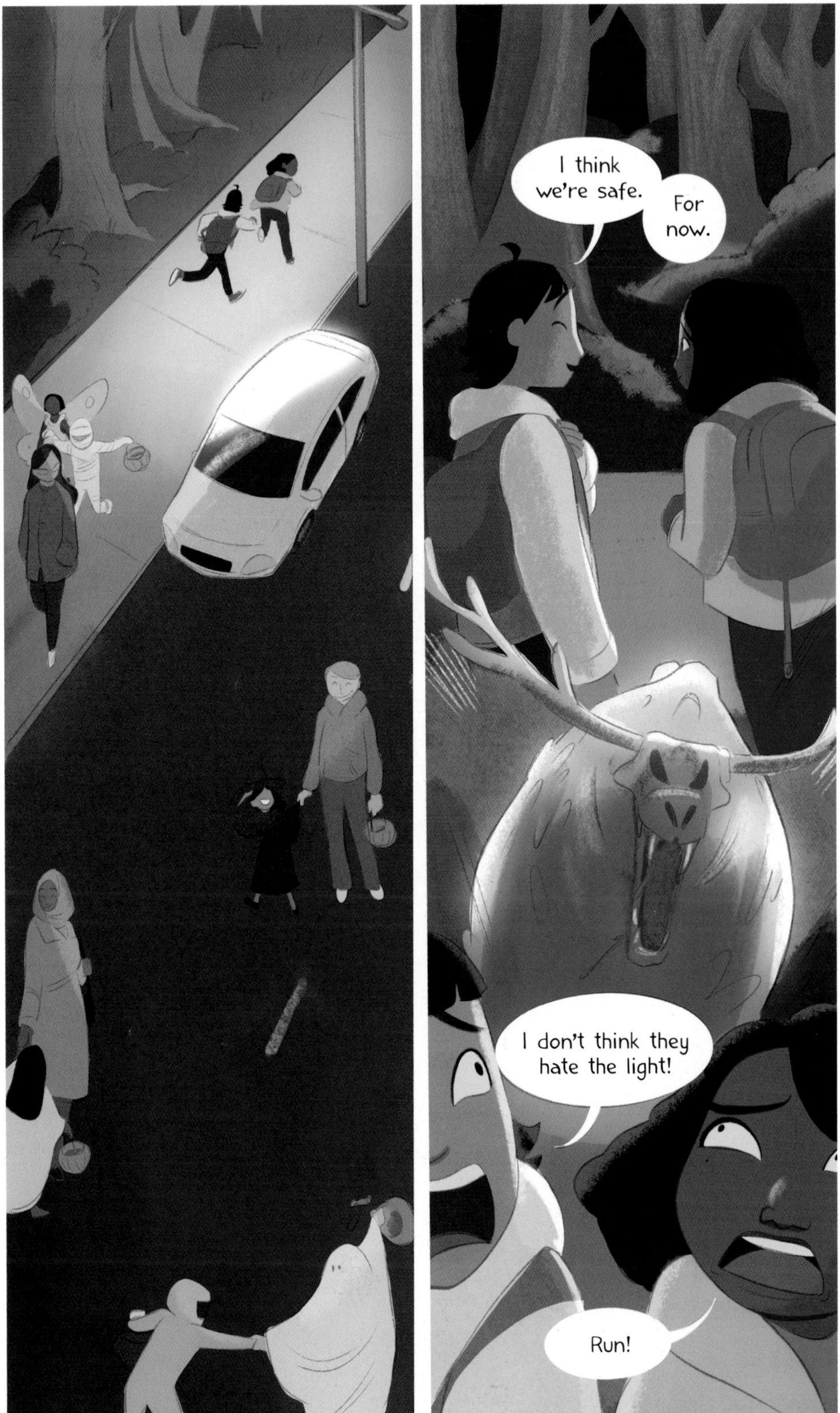
I think we're safe.
For now.
I don't think they hate the light!
Run!

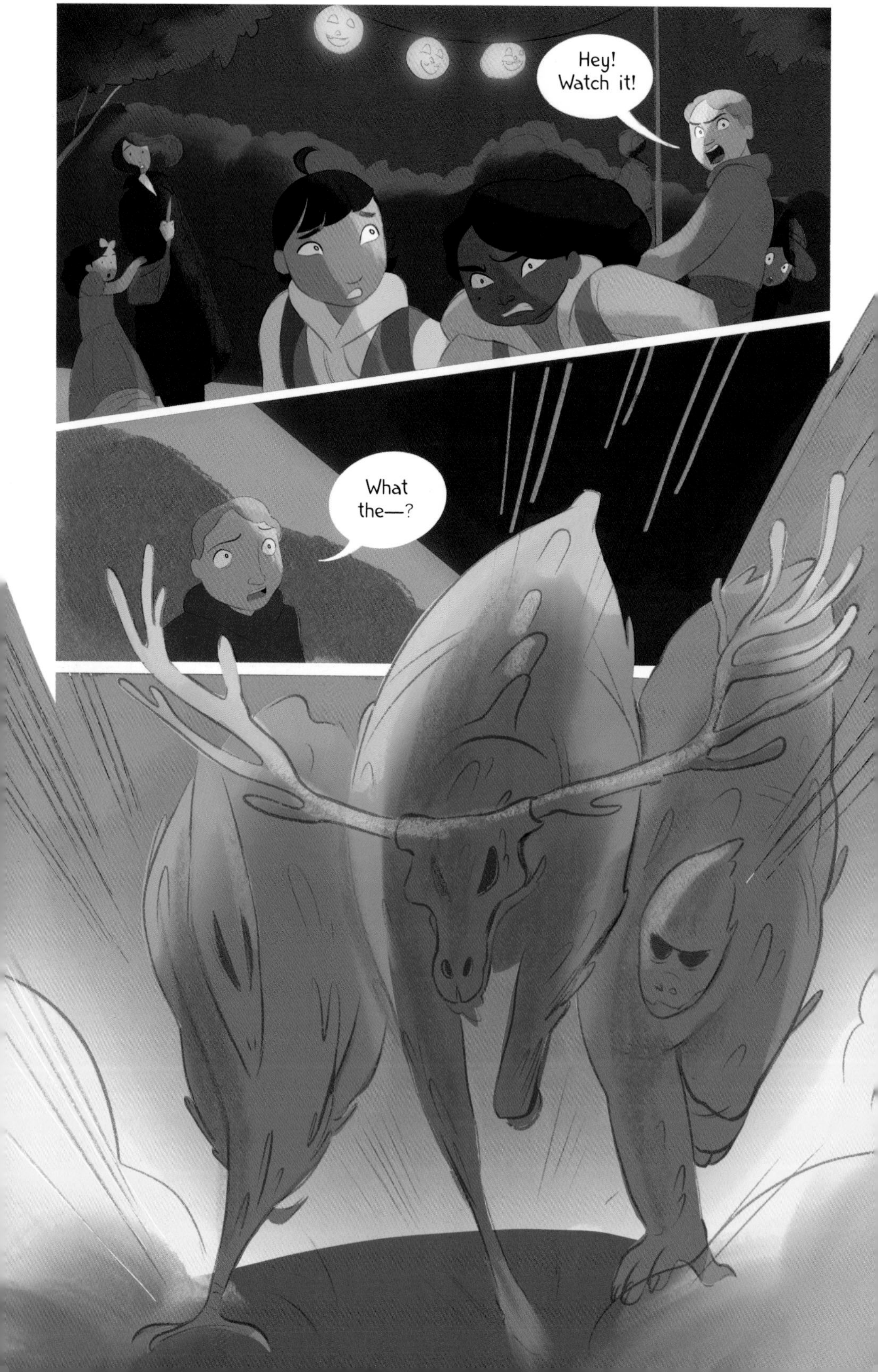
Hey! Watch it!
What the—?

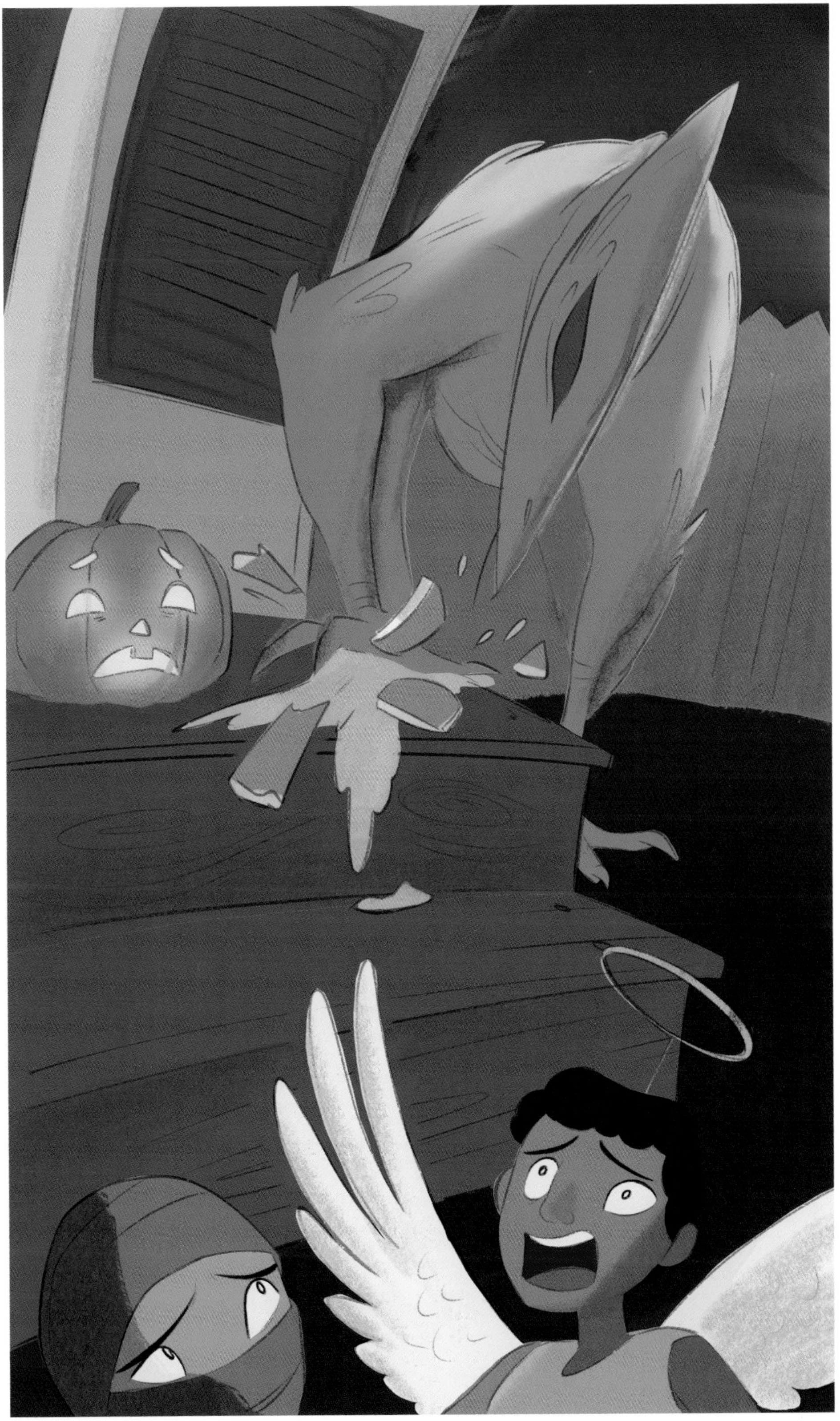

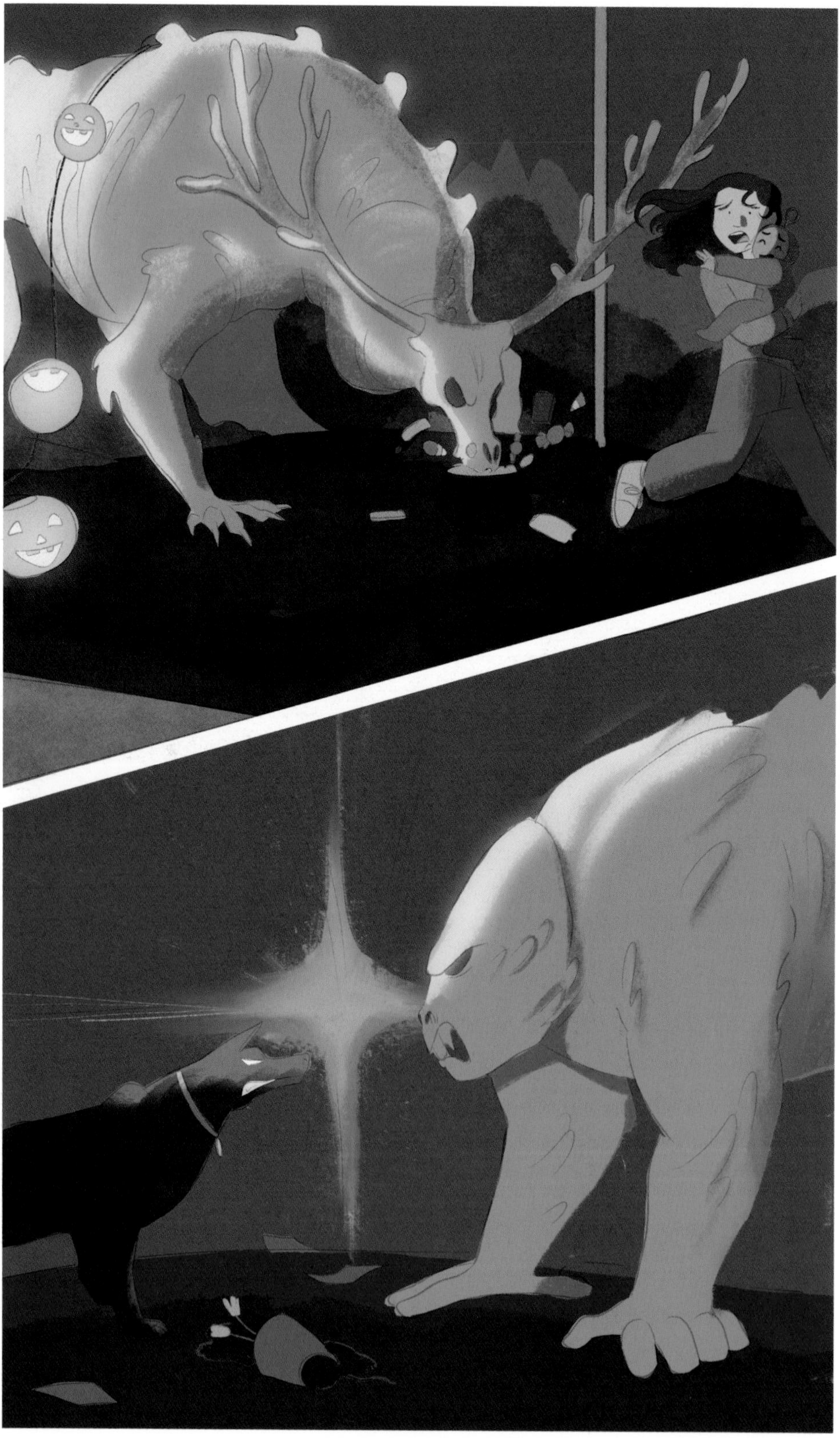

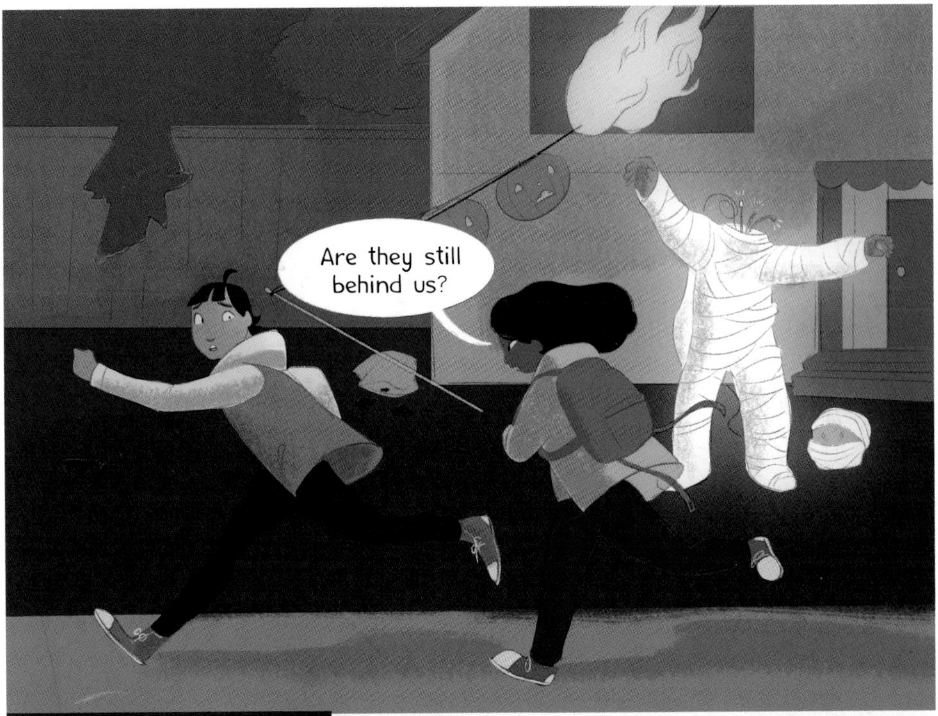
Are they still behind us?

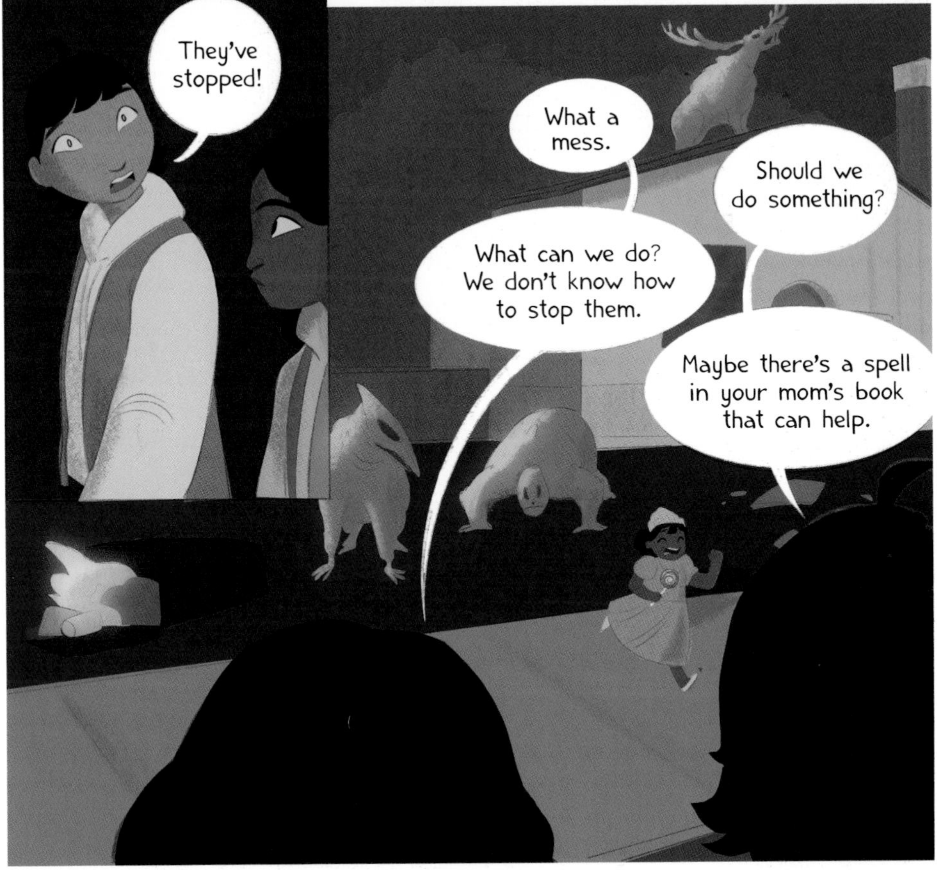
They've stopped!
What a mess.
Should we do something?
What can we do? We don't know how to stop them.
Maybe there's a spell in your mom's book that can help.

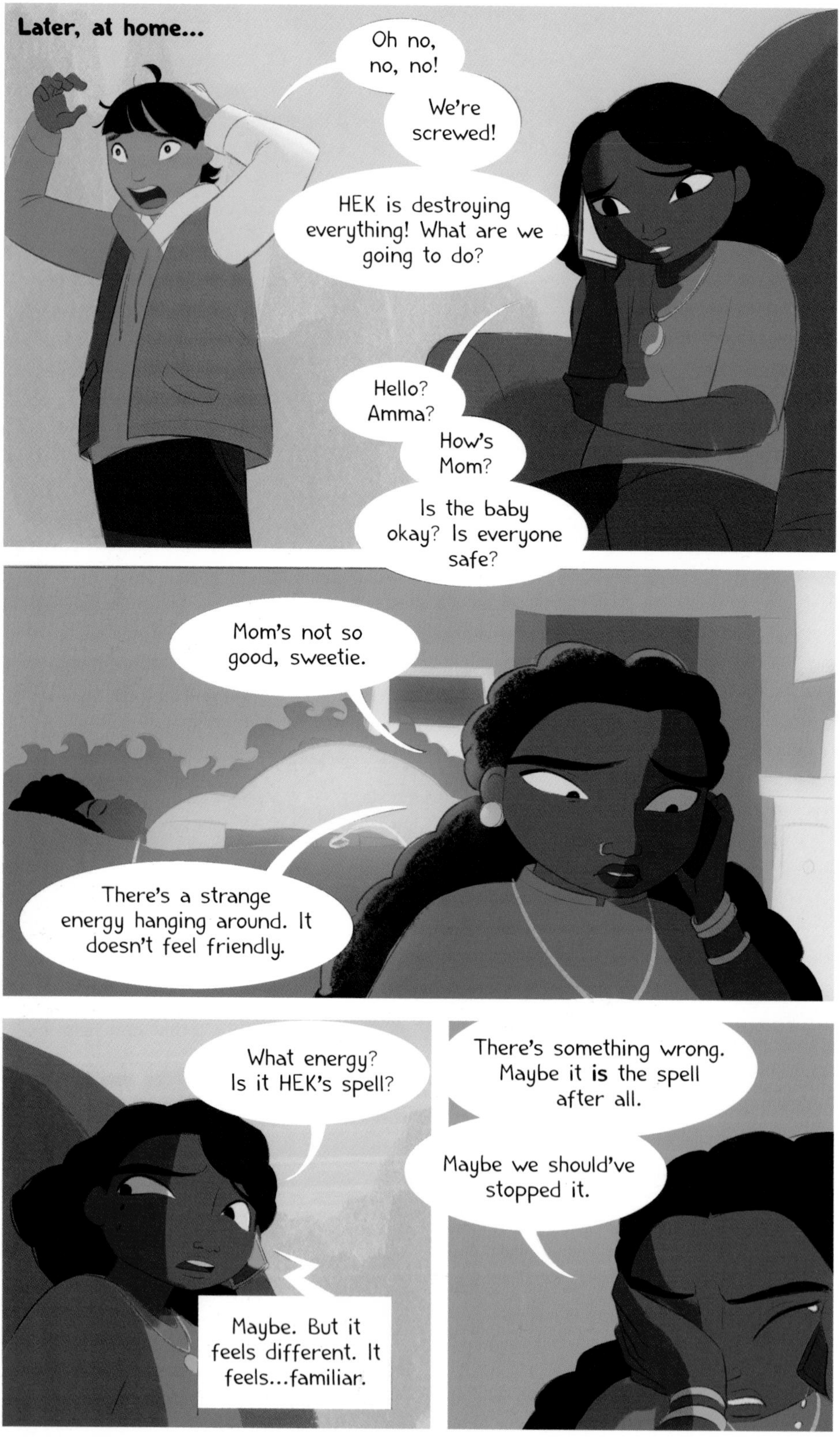
Later, at home...
Oh no, no, no!
We're screwed!
HEK is destroying everything! What are we going to do?
Hello? Amma?
How's Mom?
Is the baby okay? Is everyone safe?
Mom's not so good, sweetie.
There's a strange energy hanging around. It doesn't feel friendly.
What energy? Is it HEK's spell?
Maybe. But it feels different. It feels...familiar.
There's something wrong. Maybe it **is** the spell after all.
Maybe we should've stopped it.

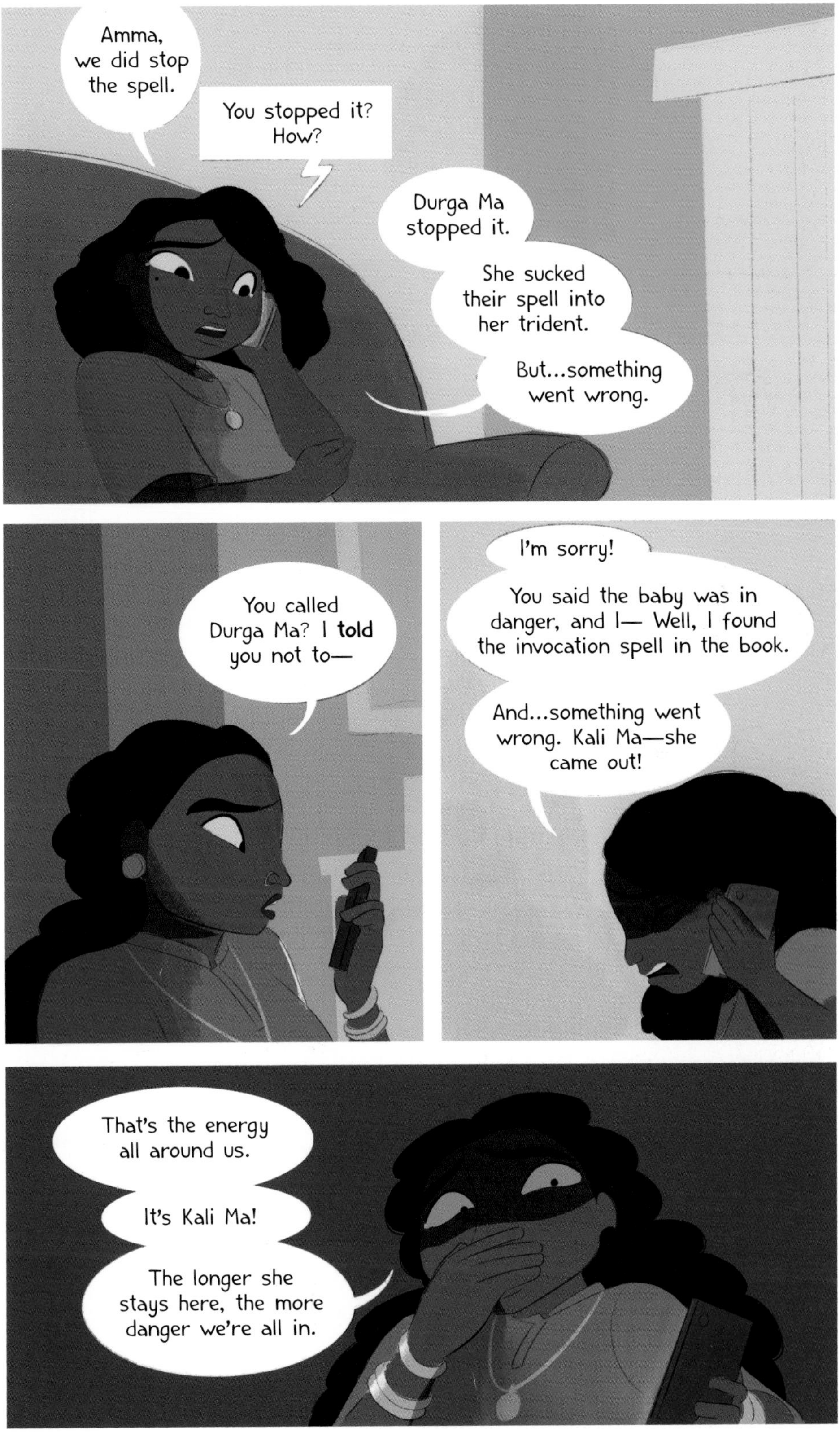
Amma, we did stop the spell.
You stopped it? How?
Durga Ma stopped it.
She sucked their spell into her trident.
But...something went wrong.
You called Durga Ma? I **told** you not to—
I'm sorry!
You said the baby was in danger, and I— Well, I found the invocation spell in the book.
And...something went wrong. Kali Ma—she came out!
That's the energy all around us.
It's Kali Ma!
The longer she stays here, the more danger we're all in.

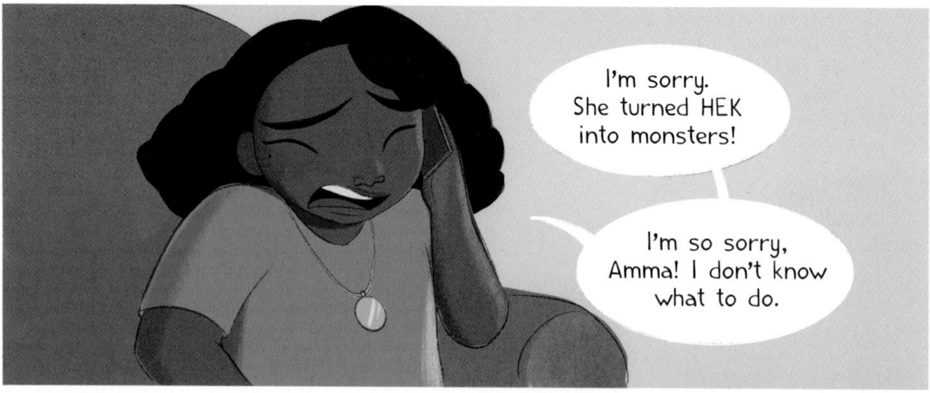
I'm sorry.
She turned HEK
into monsters!
I'm so sorry,
Amma! I don't know
what to do.

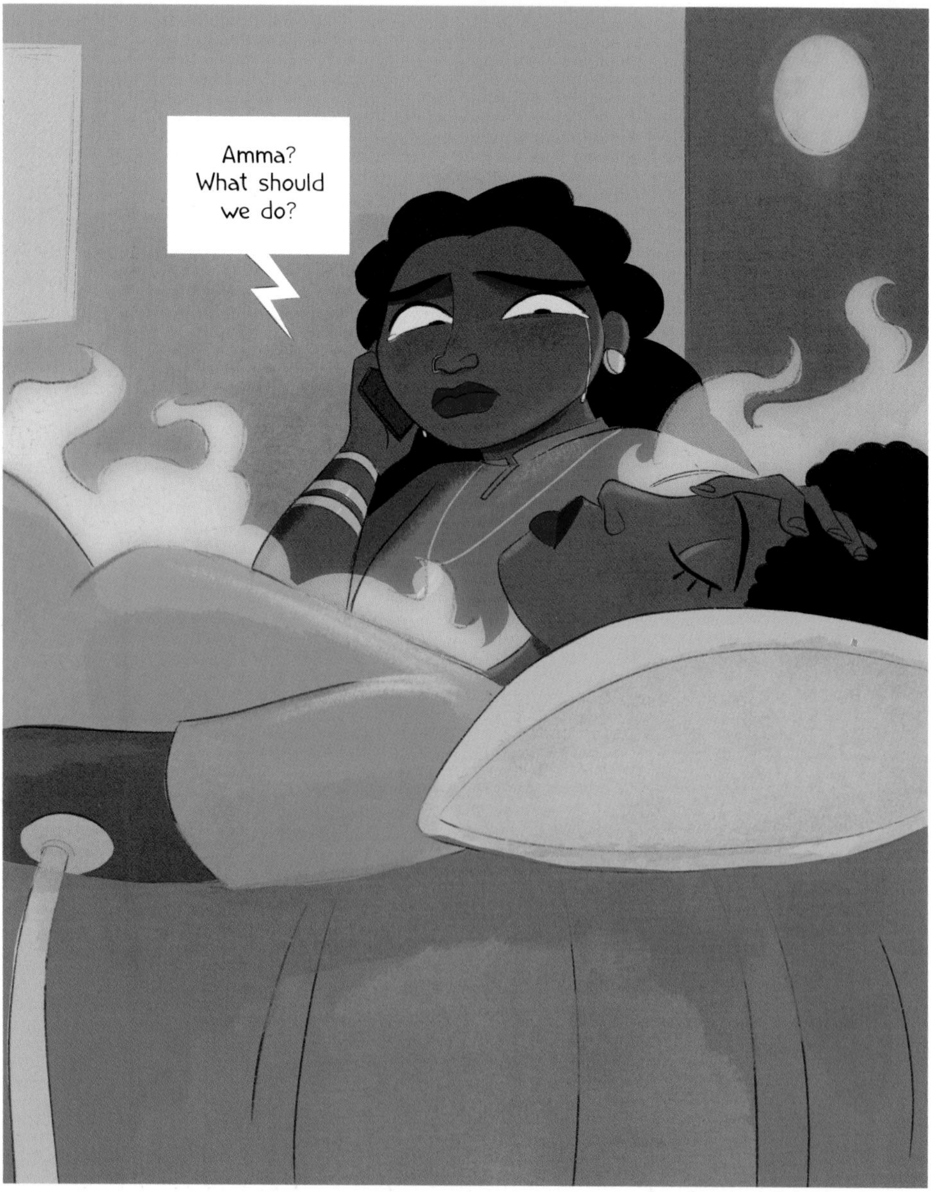
Amma?
What should
we do?

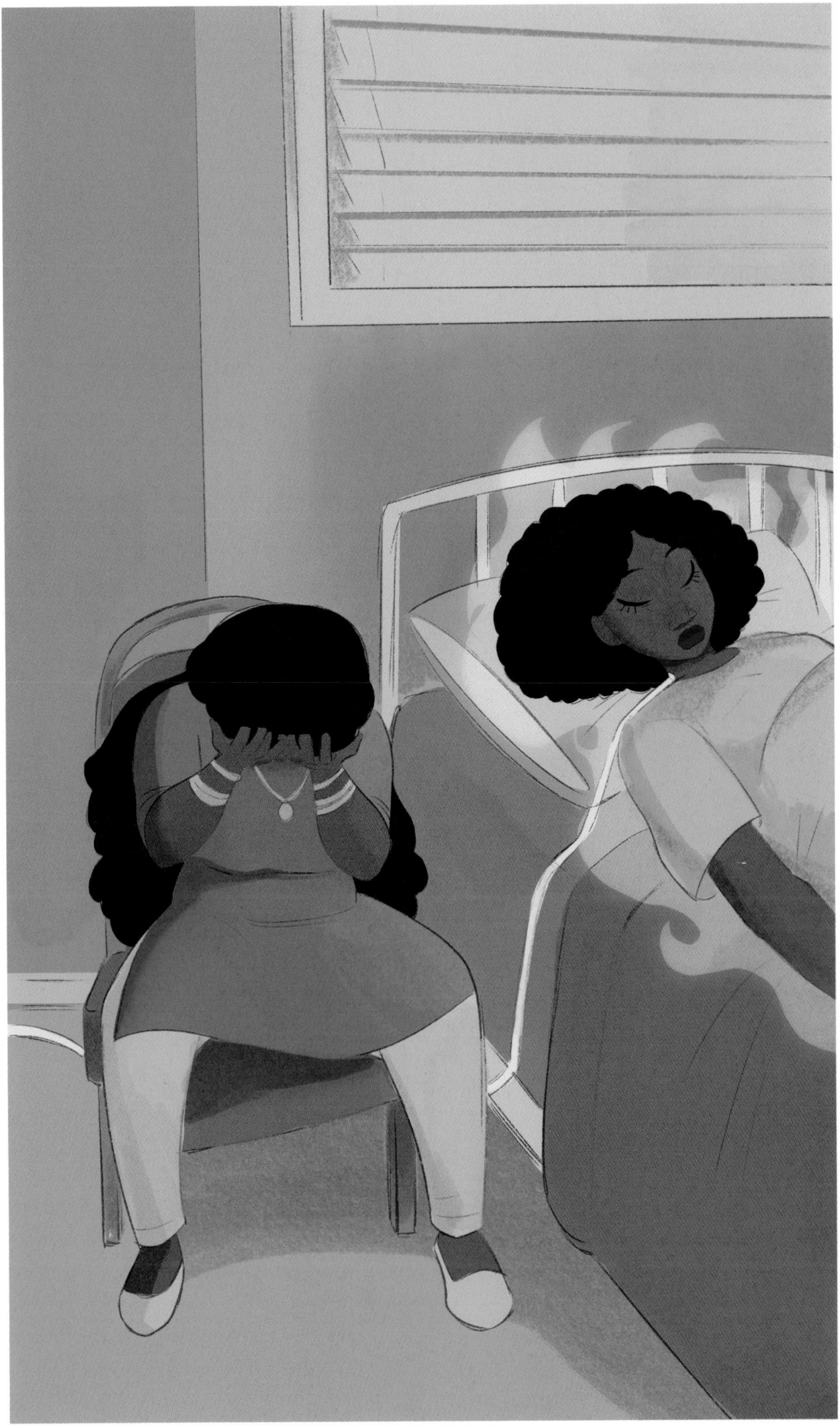

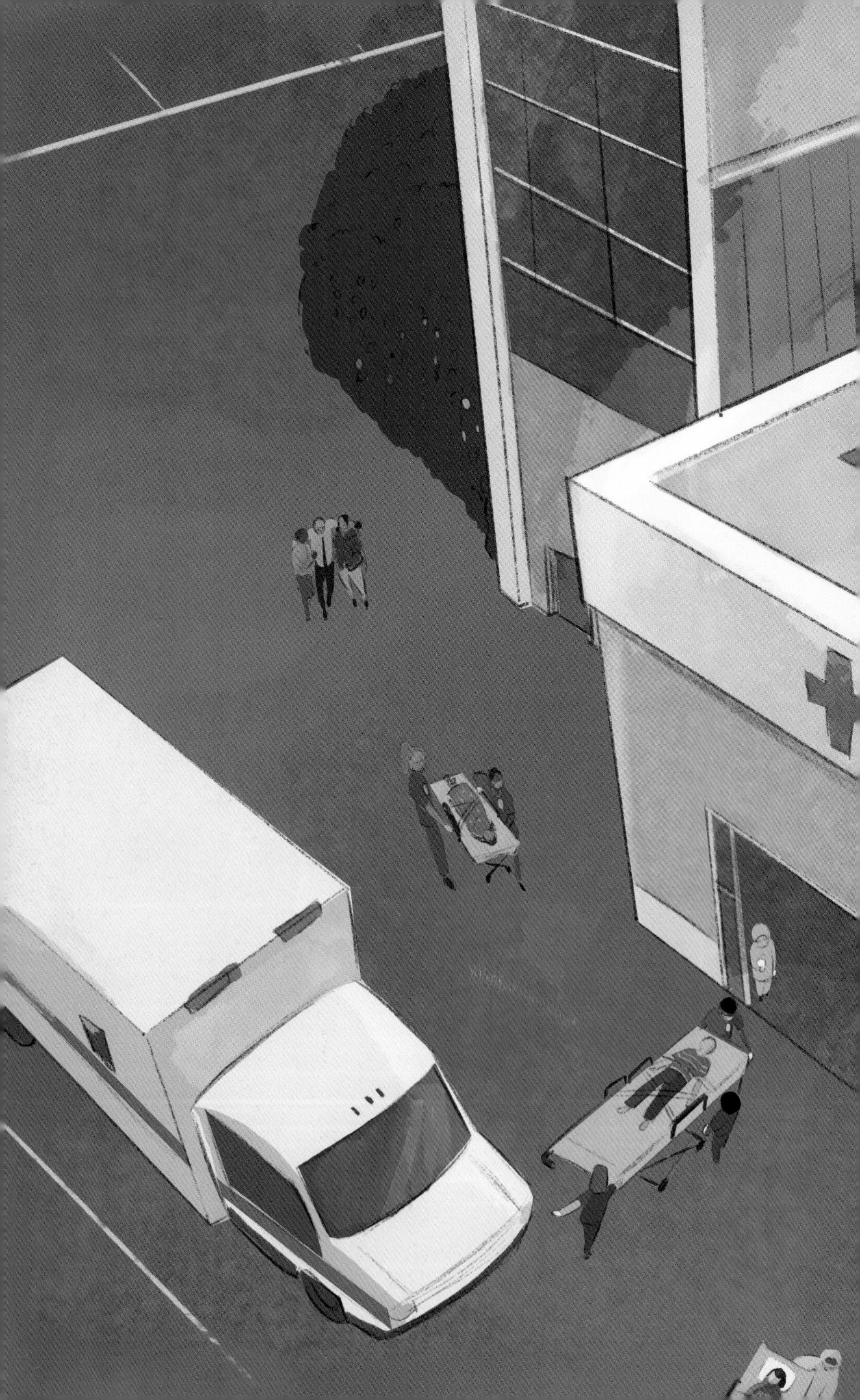

# Chapter 5

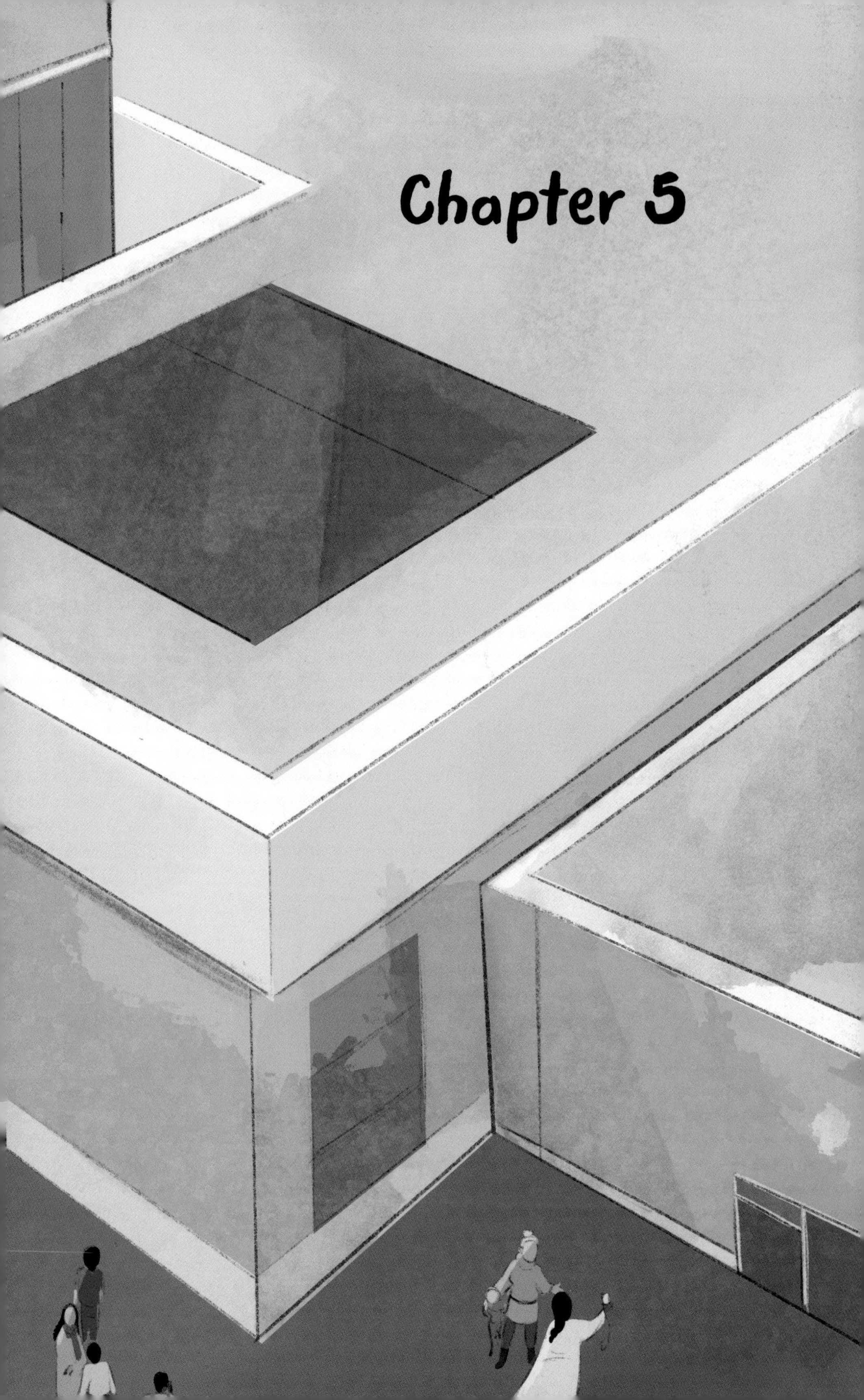

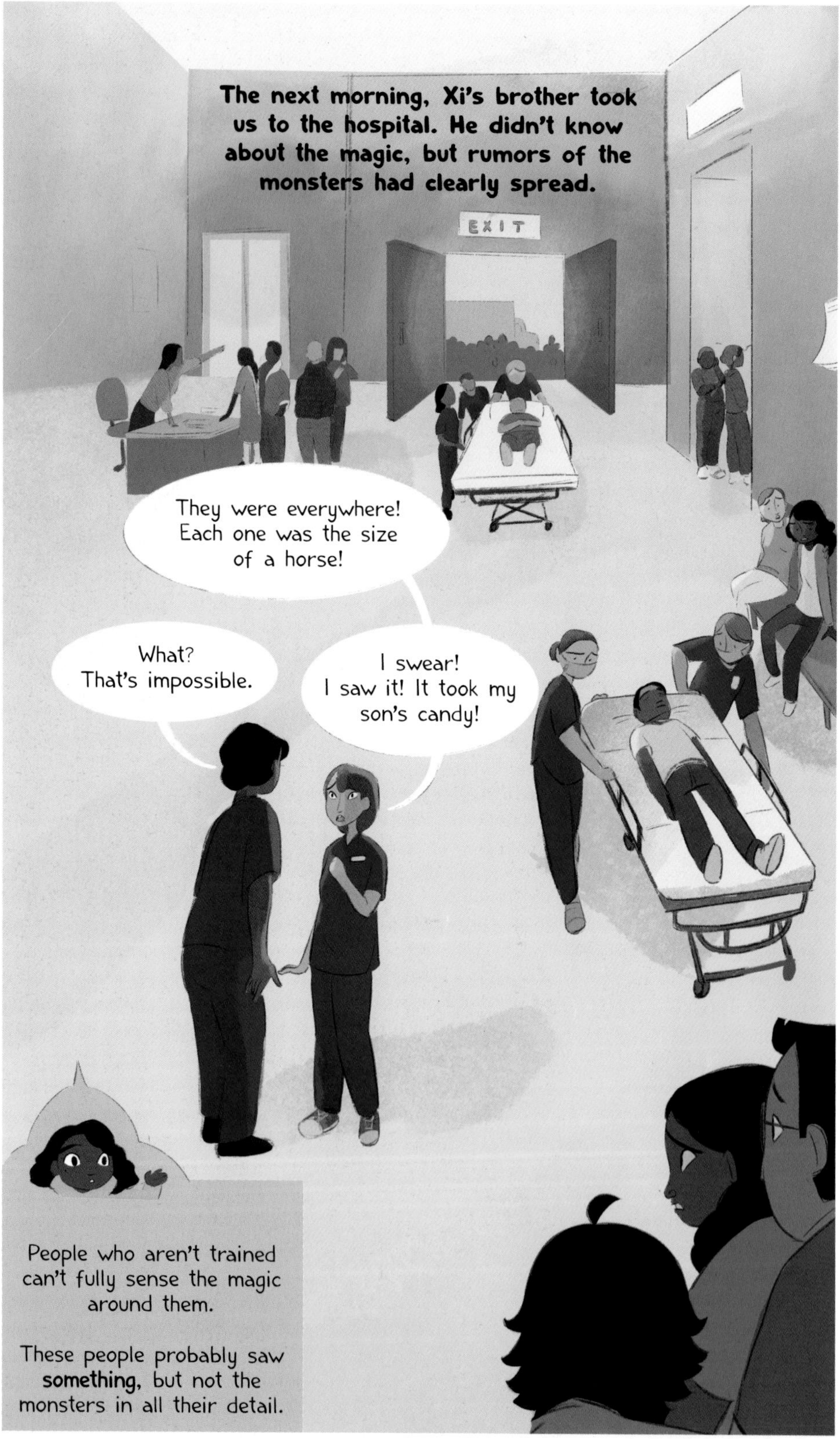
The next morning, Xi's brother took us to the hospital. He didn't know about the magic, but rumors of the monsters had clearly spread.
EXIT
They were everywhere! Each one was the size of a horse!
What? That's impossible.
I swear! I saw it! It took my son's candy!
People who aren't trained can't fully sense the magic around them.
These people probably saw **something**, but not the monsters in all their detail.

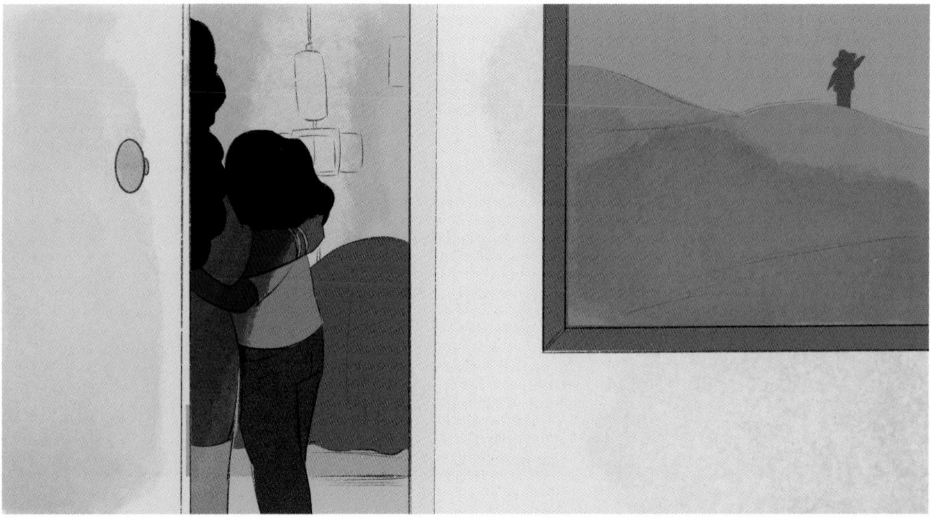

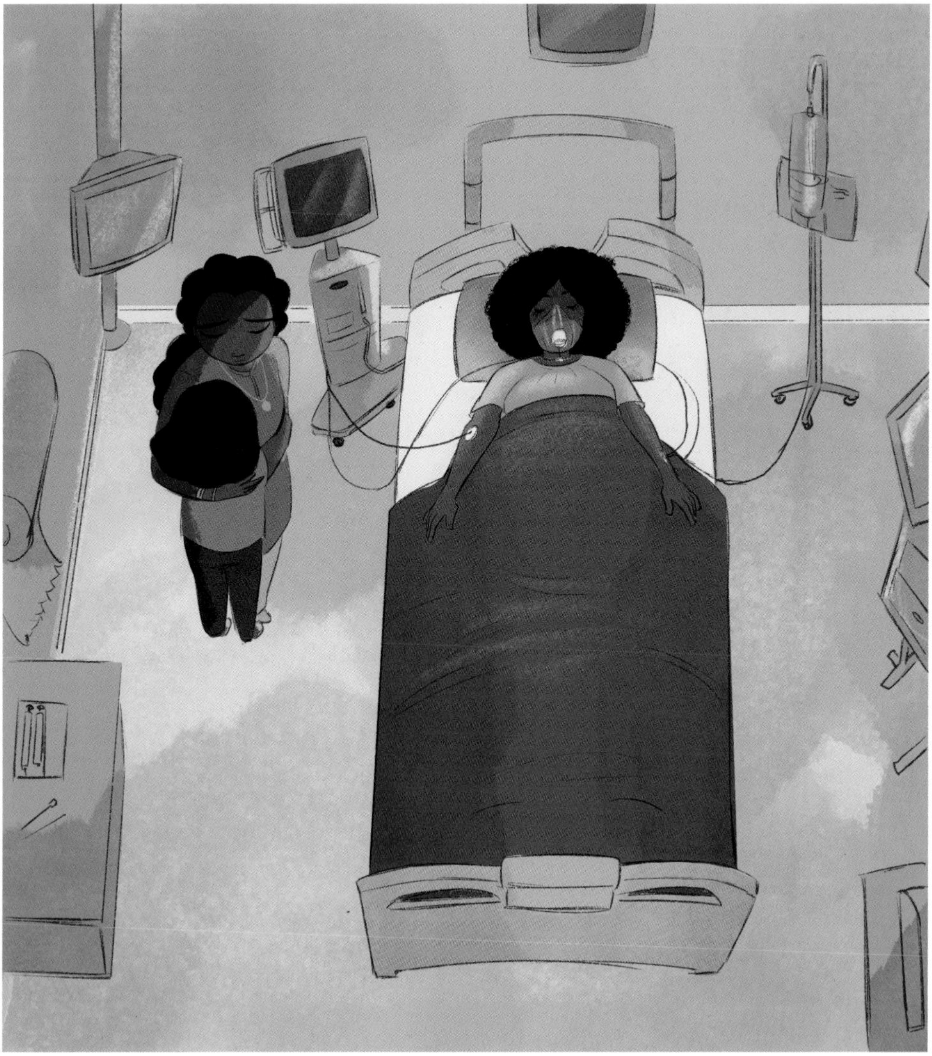

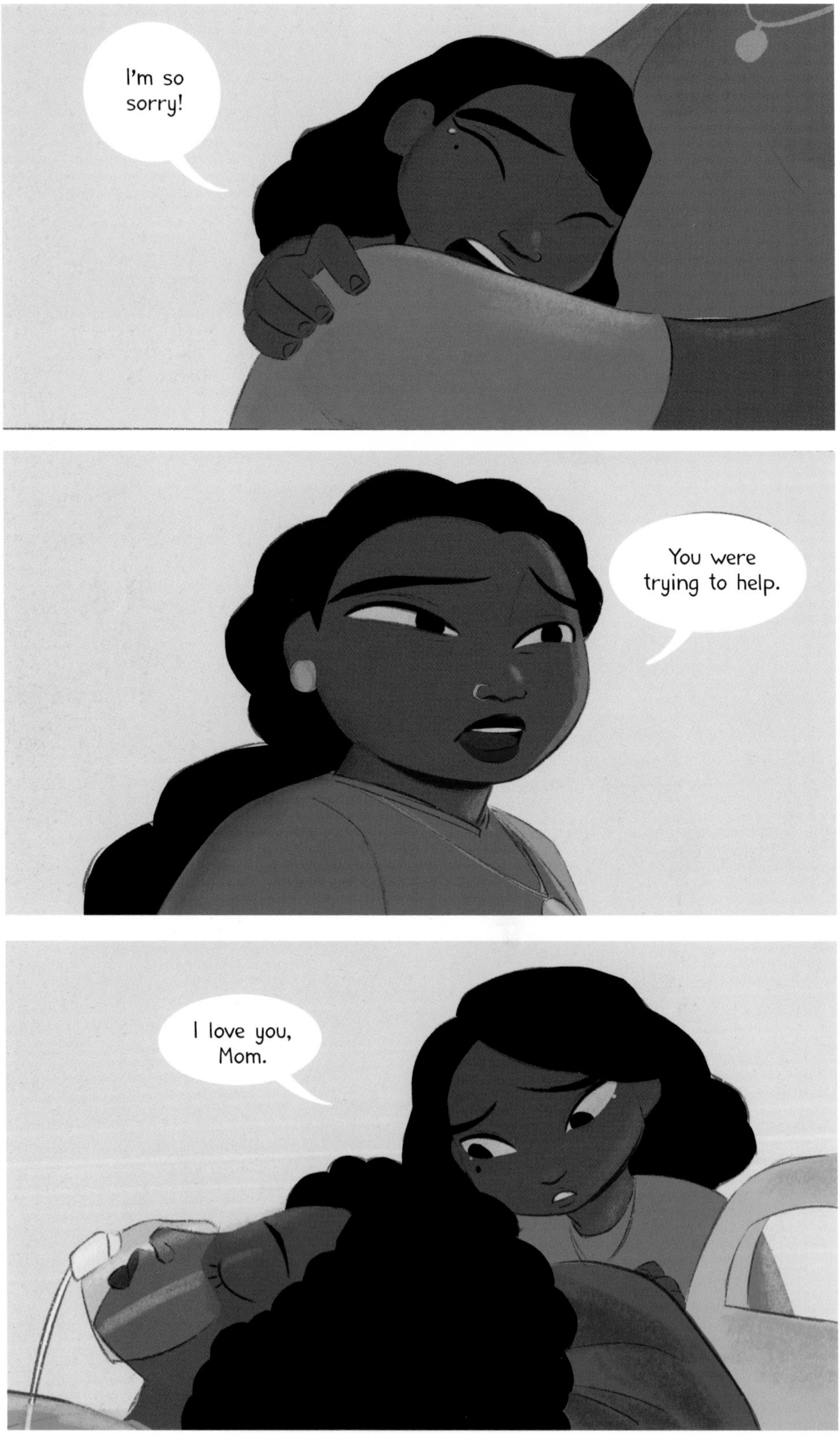
I'm so sorry!
You were trying to help.
I love you, Mom.

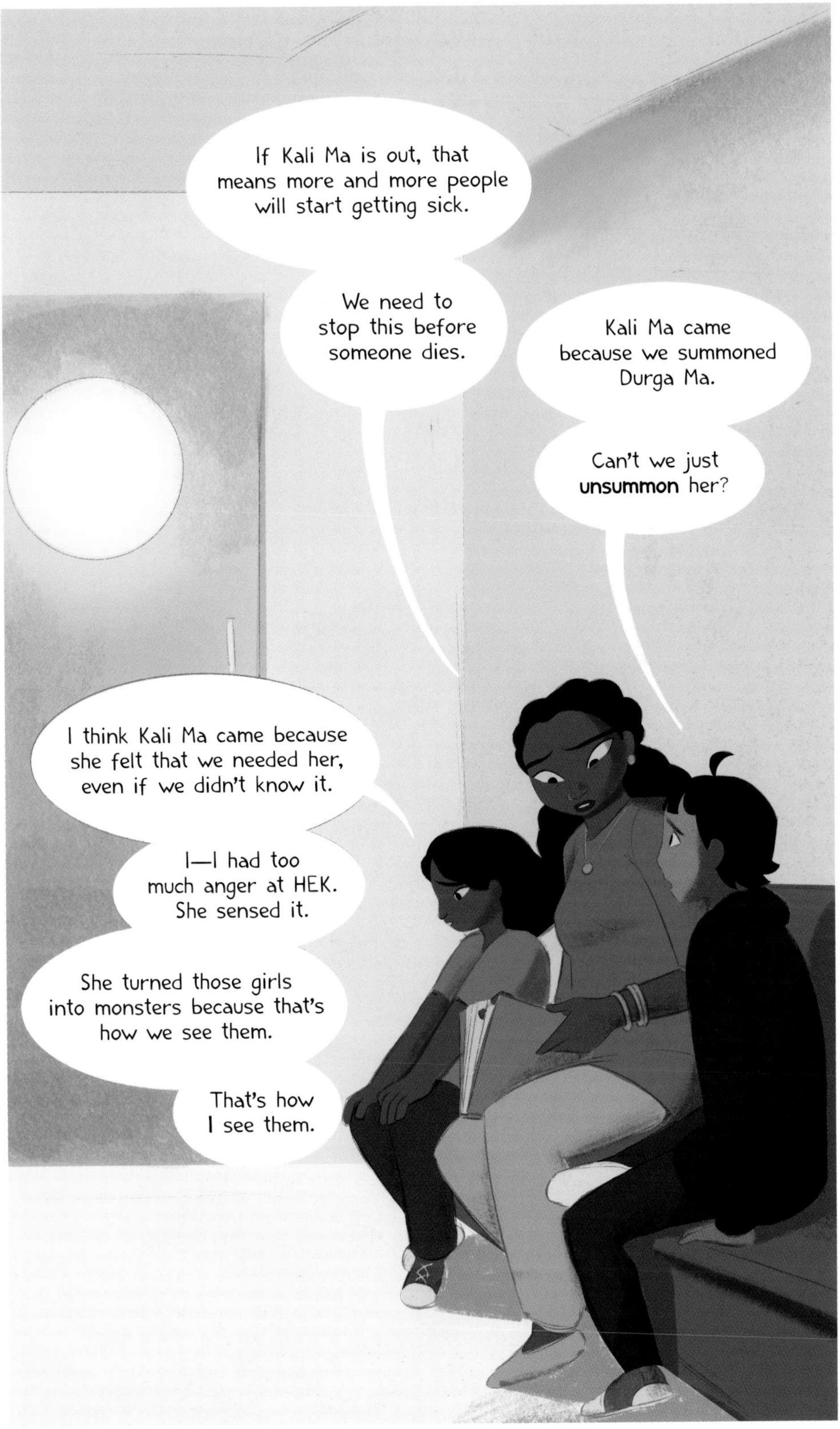
If Kali Ma is out, that means more and more people will start getting sick.
We need to stop this before someone dies.
Kali Ma came because we summoned Durga Ma.
Can't we just **unsummon** her?
I think Kali Ma came because she felt that we needed her, even if we didn't know it.
I—I had too much anger at HEK. She sensed it.
She turned those girls into monsters because that's how we see them.
That's how I see them.

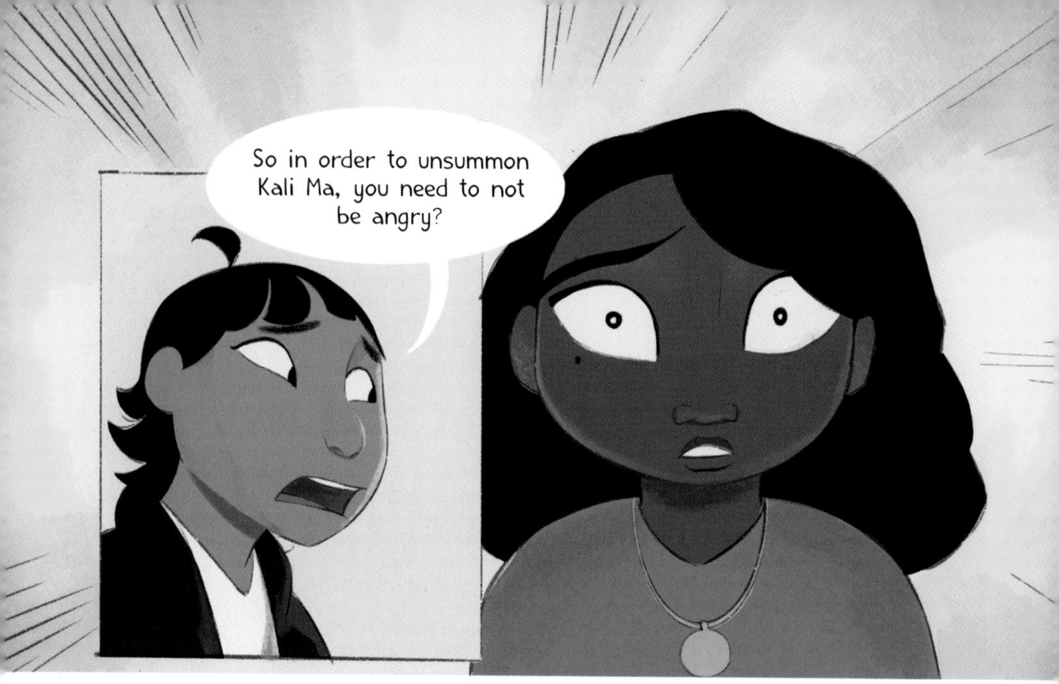
So in order to unsummon Kali Ma, you need to not be angry?

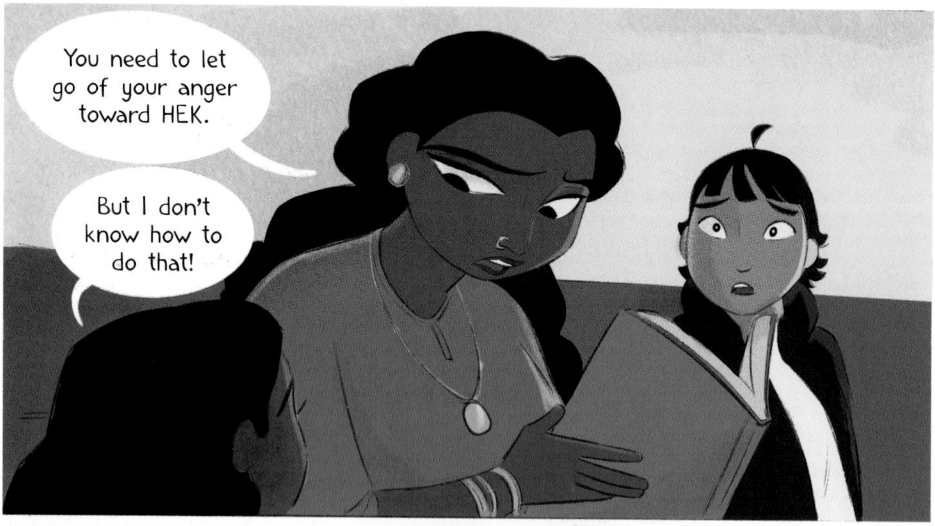
You need to let go of your anger toward HEK.
But I don't know how to do that!

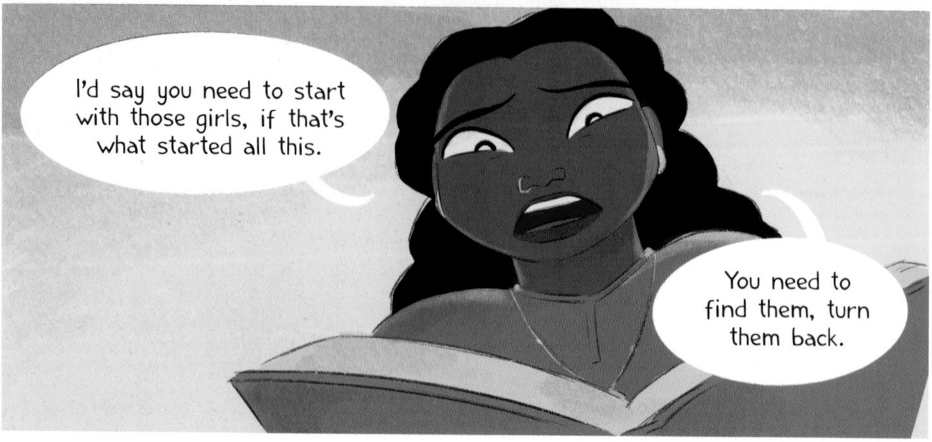
I'd say you need to start with those girls, if that's what started all this.
You need to find them, turn them back.

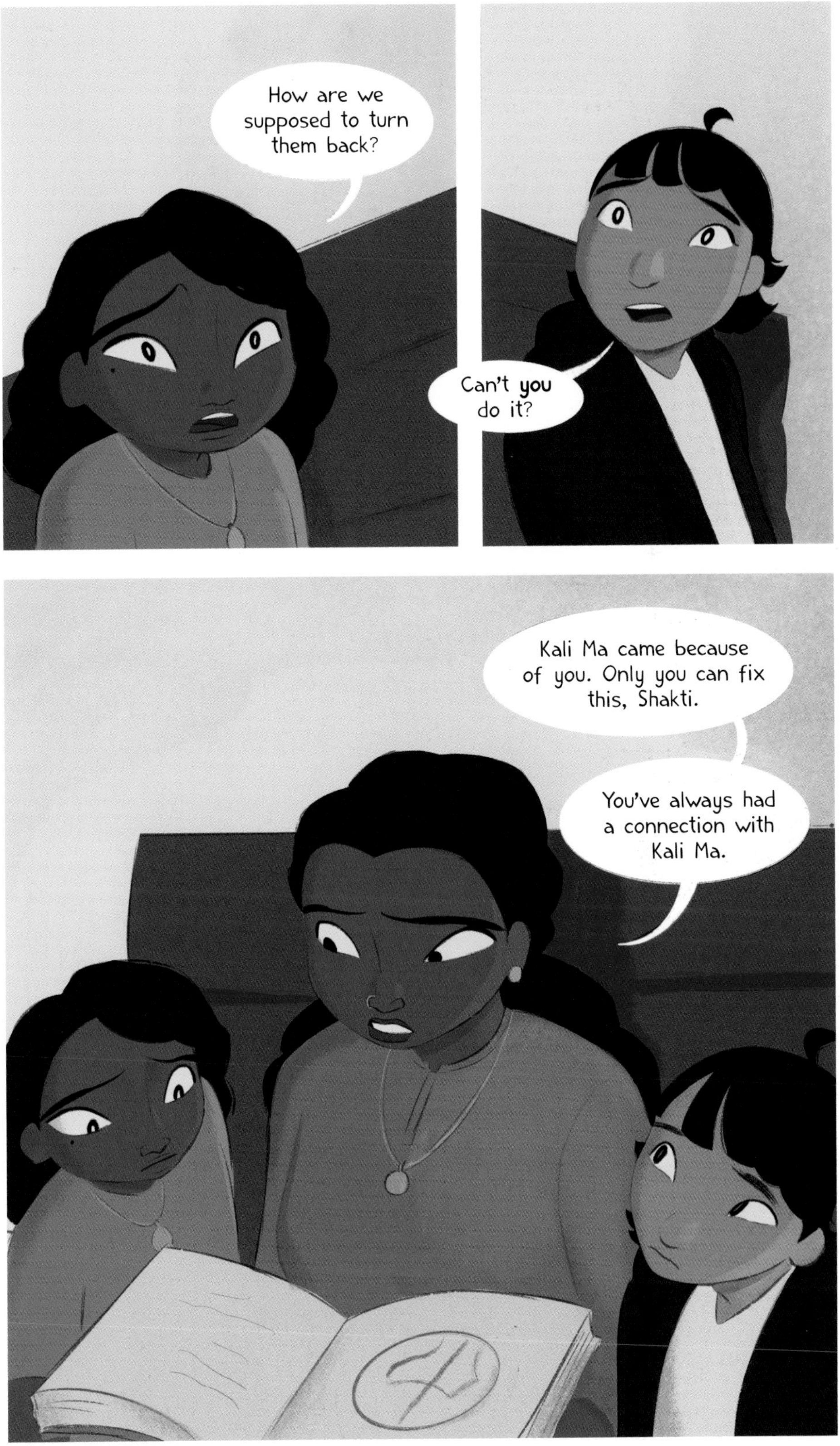
How are we supposed to turn them back?
Can't **you** do it?
Kali Ma came because of you. Only you can fix this, Shakti.
You've always had a connection with Kali Ma.

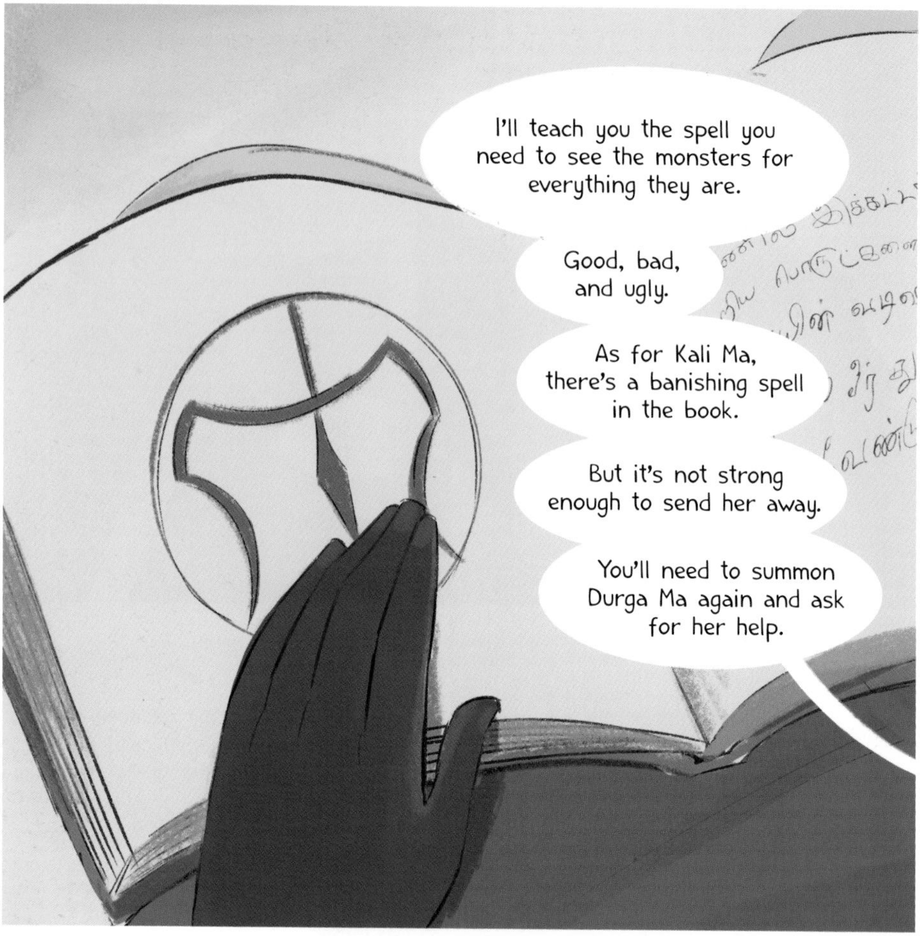
I'll teach you the spell you need to see the monsters for everything they are.
Good, bad, and ugly.
As for Kali Ma, there's a banishing spell in the book.
But it's not strong enough to send her away.
You'll need to summon Durga Ma again and ask for her help.

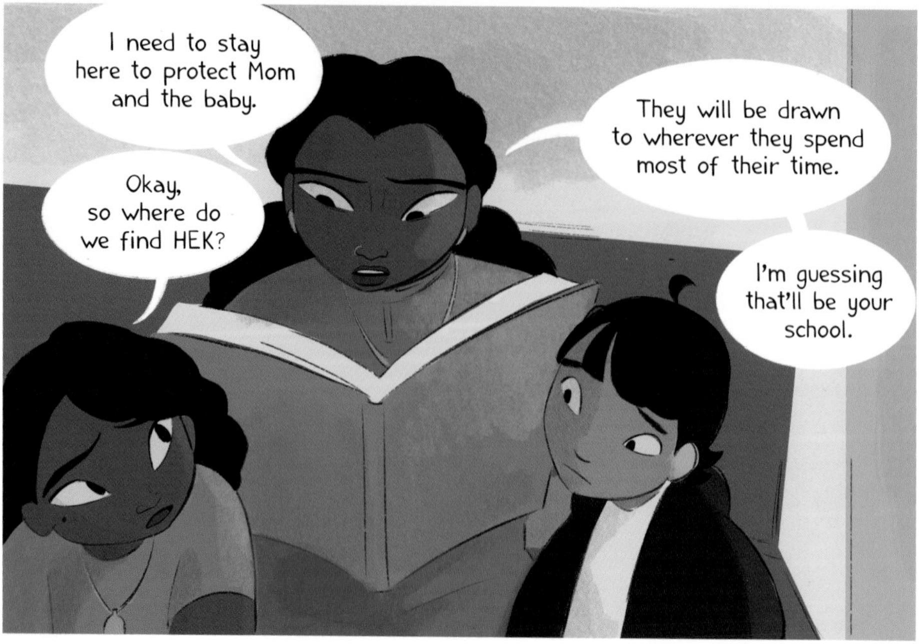
I need to stay here to protect Mom and the baby.
Okay, so where do we find HEK?
They will be drawn to wherever they spend most of their time.
I'm guessing that'll be your school.

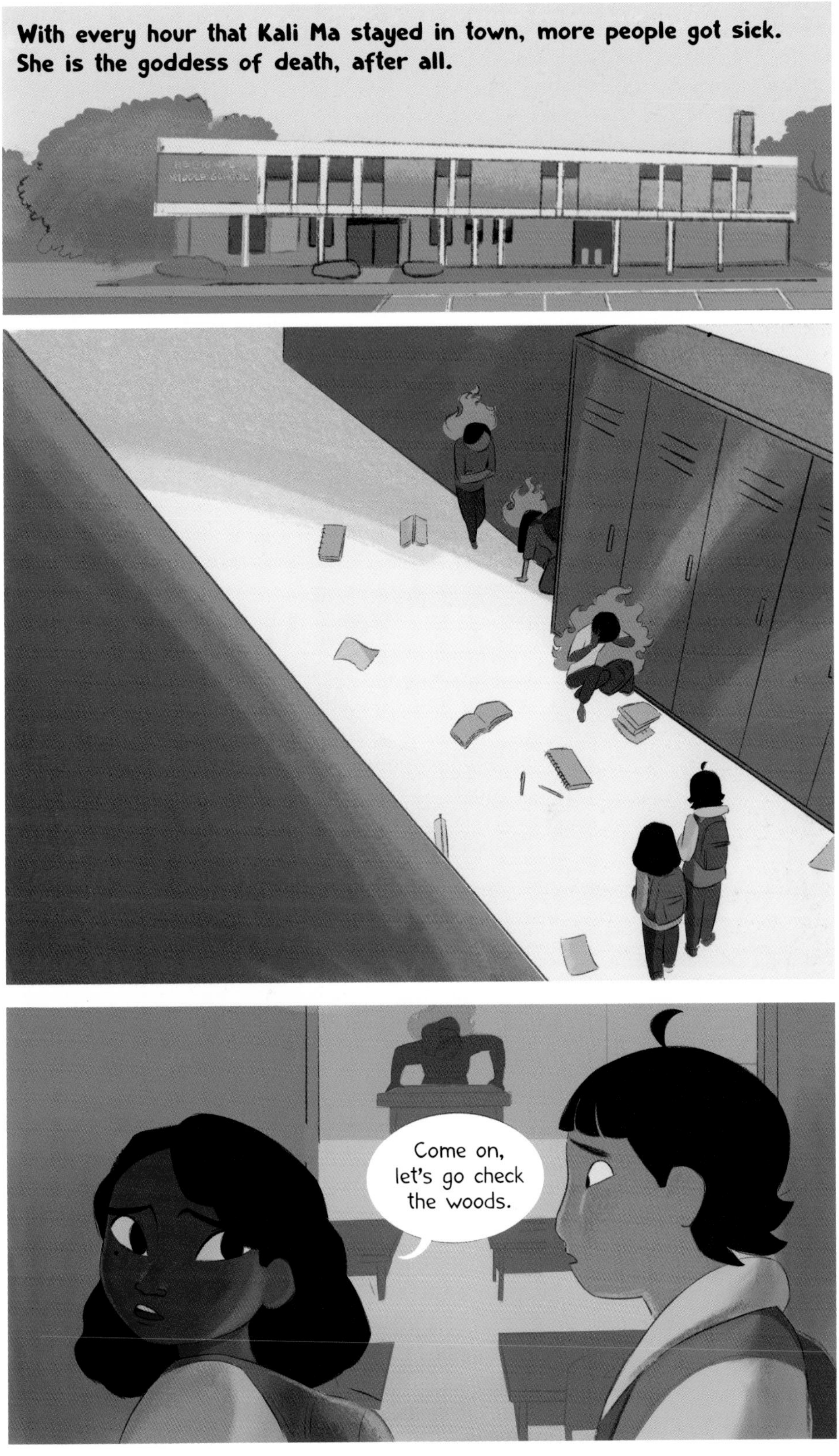
With every hour that Kali Ma stayed in town, more people got sick. She is the goddess of death, after all.
Come on, let's go check the woods.

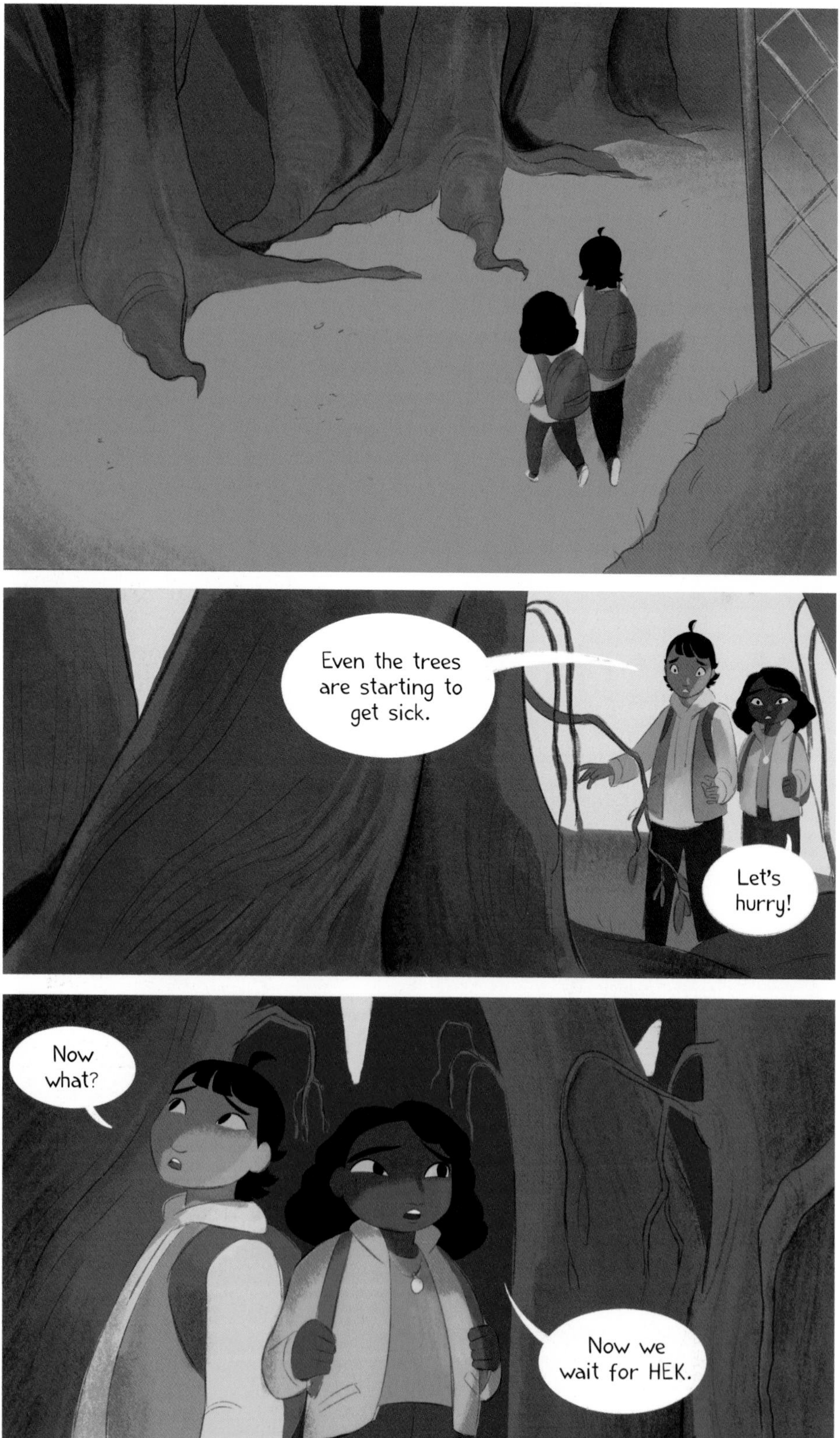
Even the trees are starting to get sick.
Let's hurry!
Now what?
Now we wait for HEK.

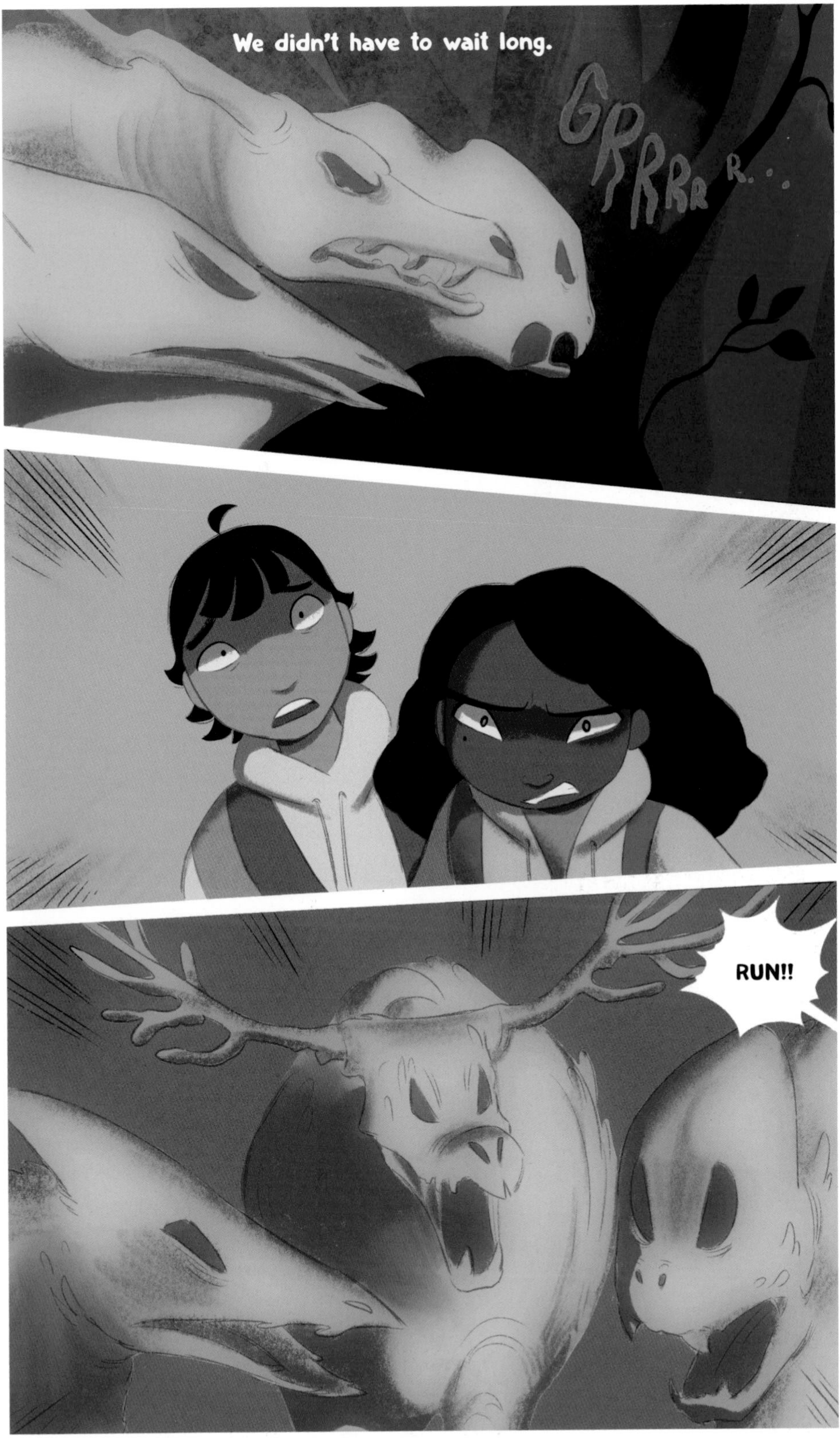
We didn't have to wait long.
GRRRRR...
RUN!!

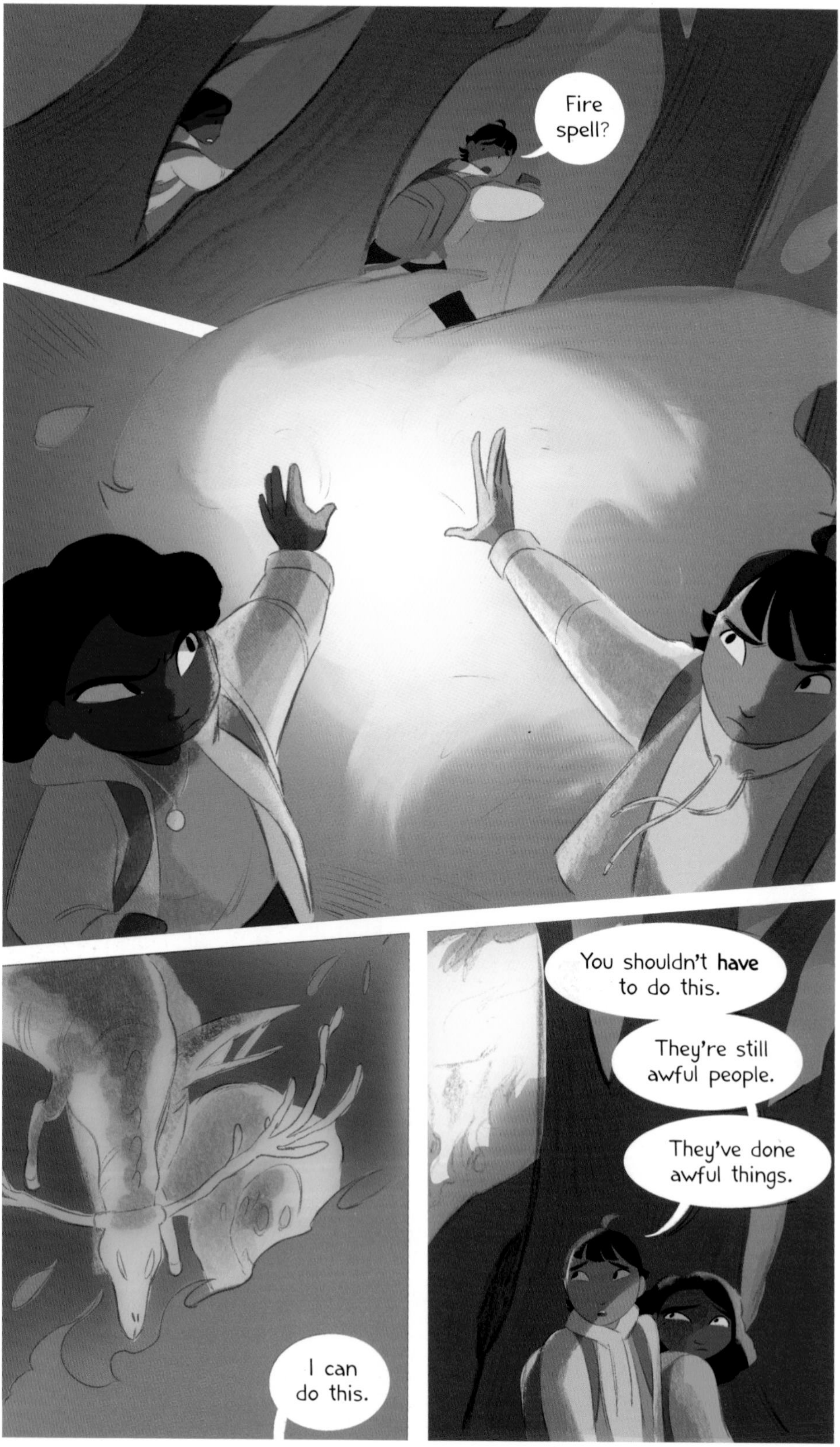
Fire spell?
I can do this.
You shouldn't **have** to do this.
They're still awful people.
They've done awful things.

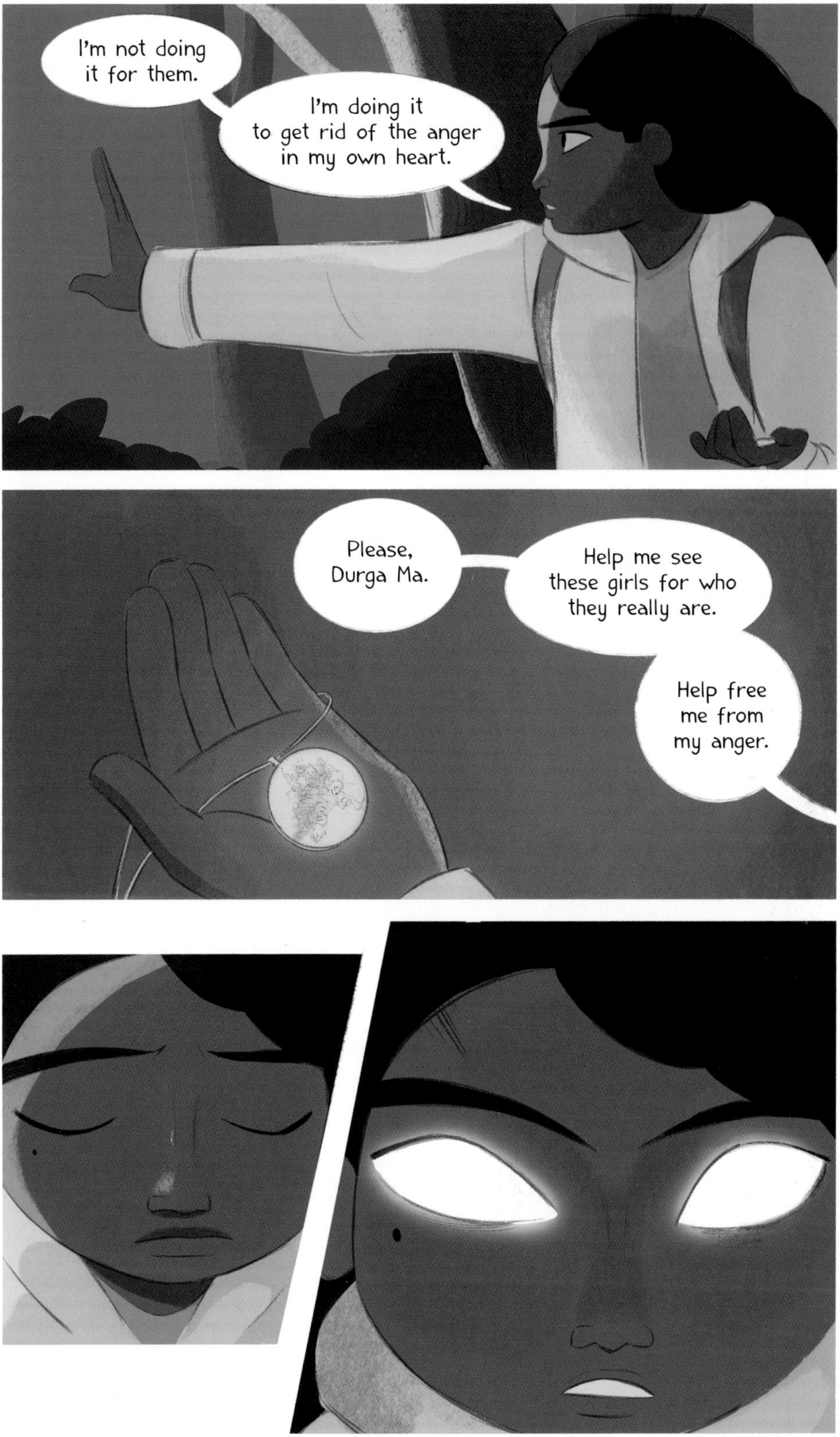
I'm not doing it for them.
I'm doing it to get rid of the anger in my own heart.
Please, Durga Ma.
Help me see these girls for who they really are.
Help free me from my anger.

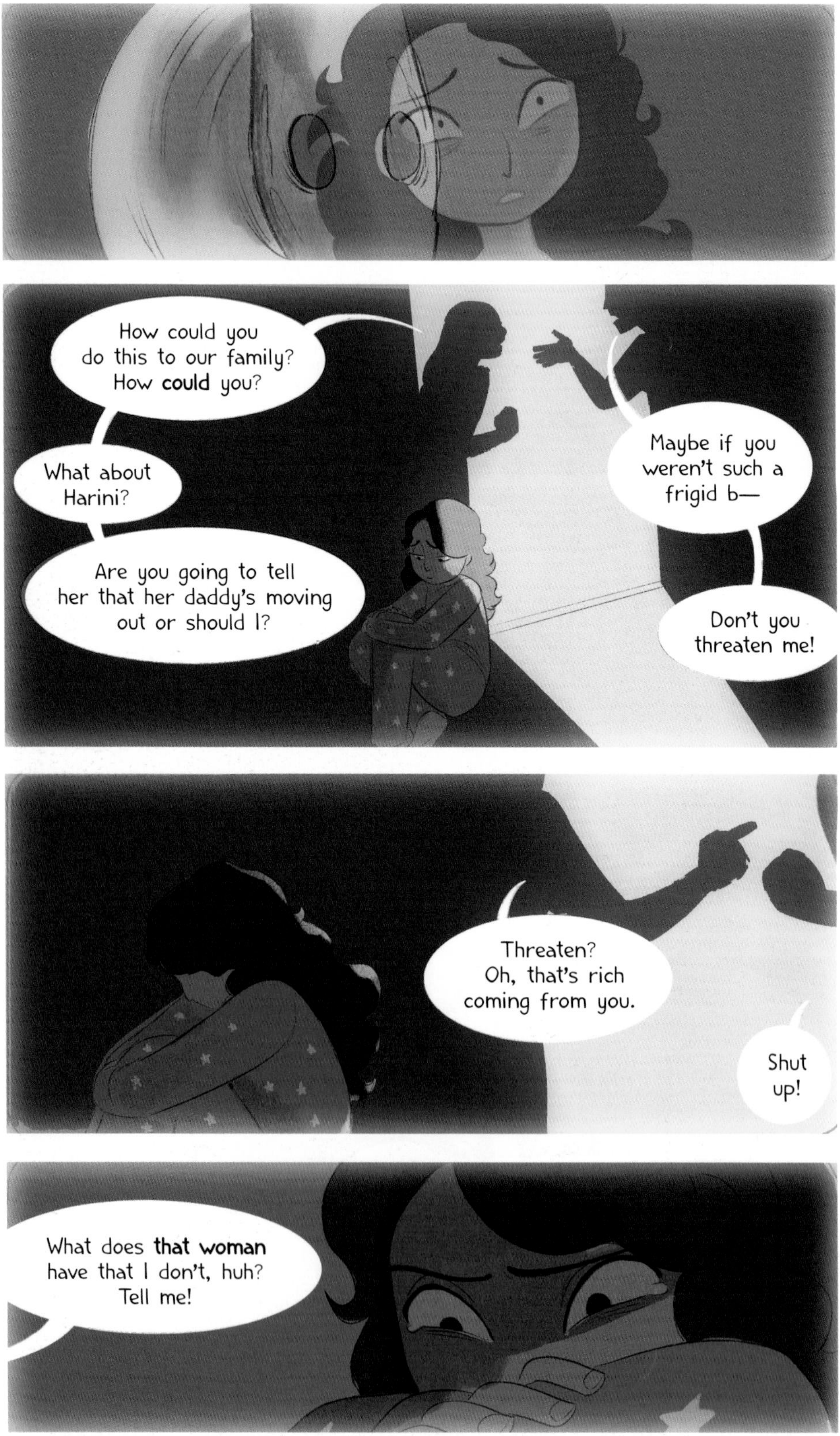
How could you do this to our family? How **could** you?
What about Harini?
Are you going to tell her that her daddy's moving out or should I?
Maybe if you weren't such a frigid b—
Don't you threaten me!
Threaten? Oh, that's rich coming from you.
Shut up!
What does **that woman** have that I don't, huh? Tell me!

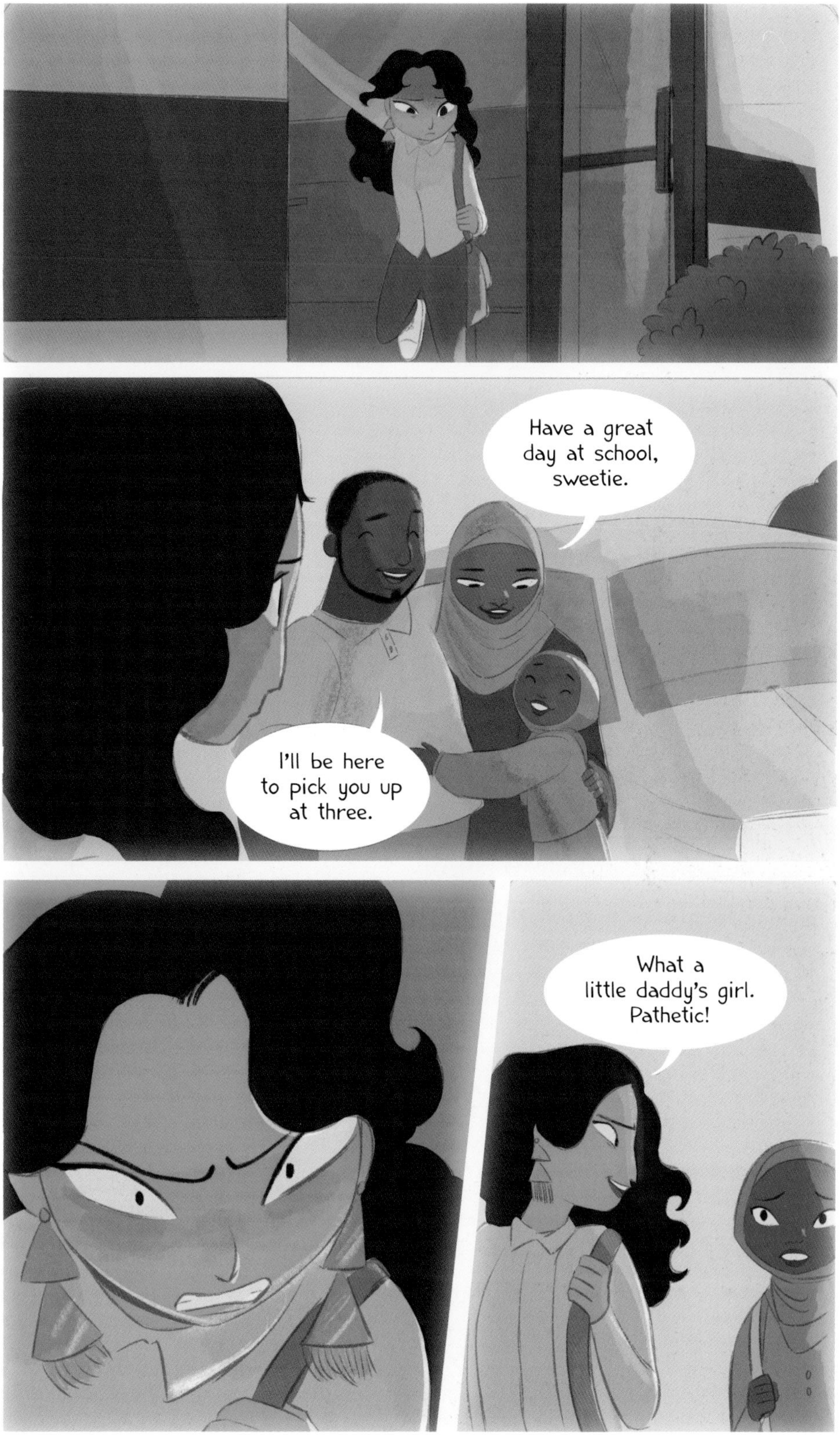
Have a great day at school, sweetie.
I'll be here to pick you up at three.
What a little daddy's girl. Pathetic!

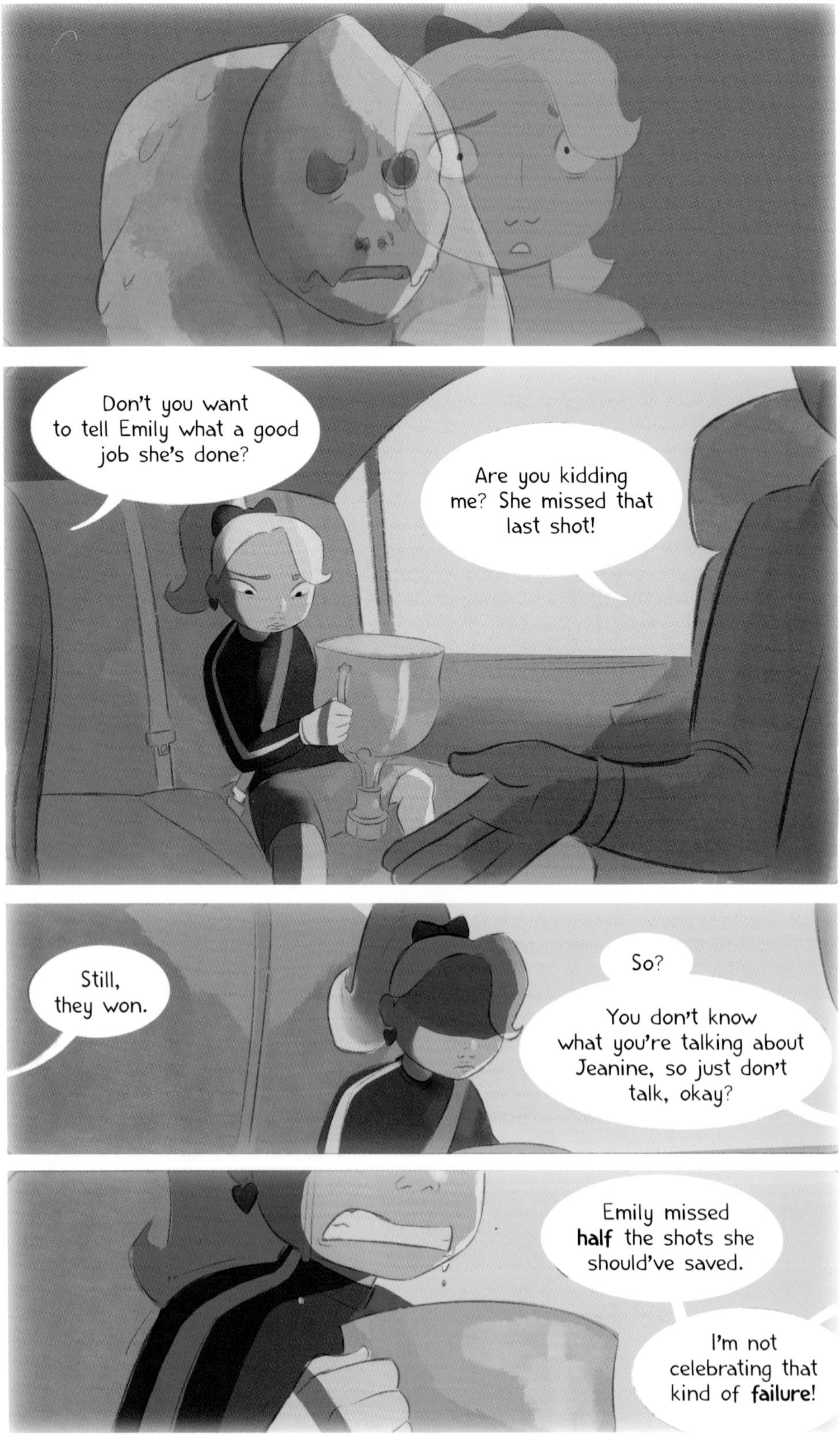
Don't you want to tell Emily what a good job she's done?
Are you kidding me? She missed that last shot!
Still, they won.
So?
You don't know what you're talking about Jeanine, so just don't talk, okay?
Emily missed **half** the shots she should've saved.
I'm not celebrating that kind of **failure**!

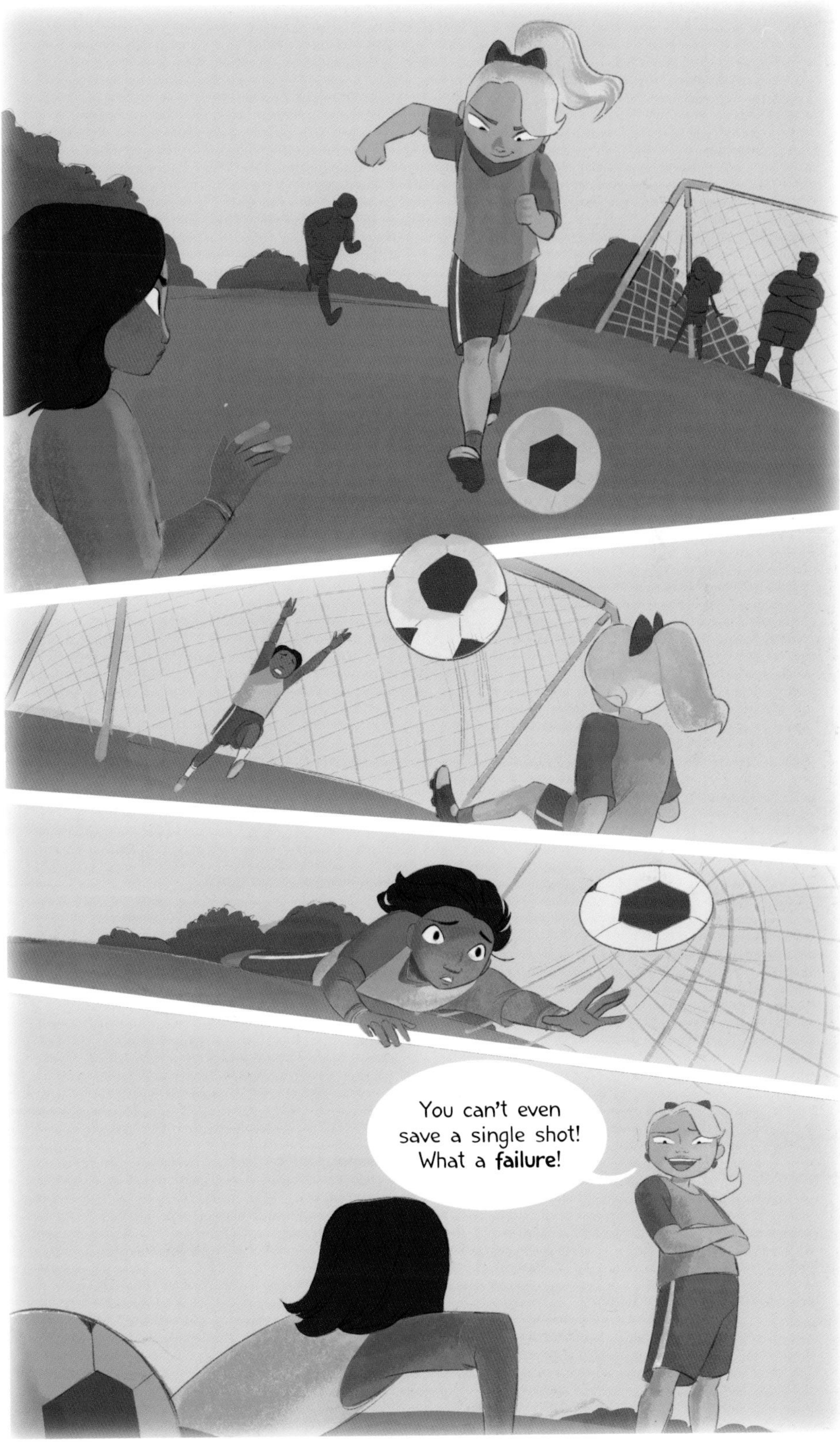
You can't even save a single shot! What a **failure**!

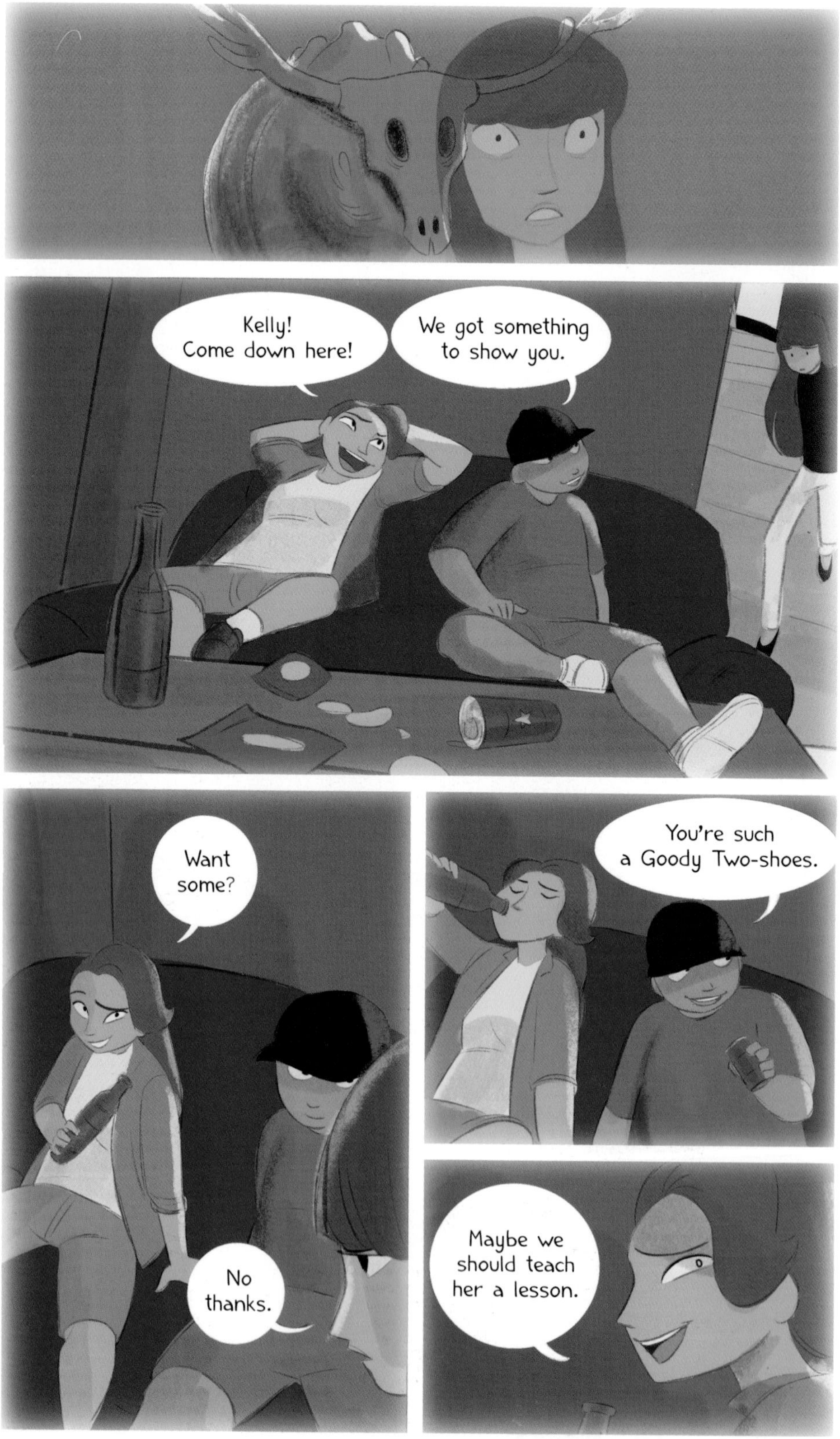
Kelly! Come down here!
We got something to show you.
Want some?
No thanks.
You're such a Goody Two-shoes.
Maybe we should teach her a lesson.

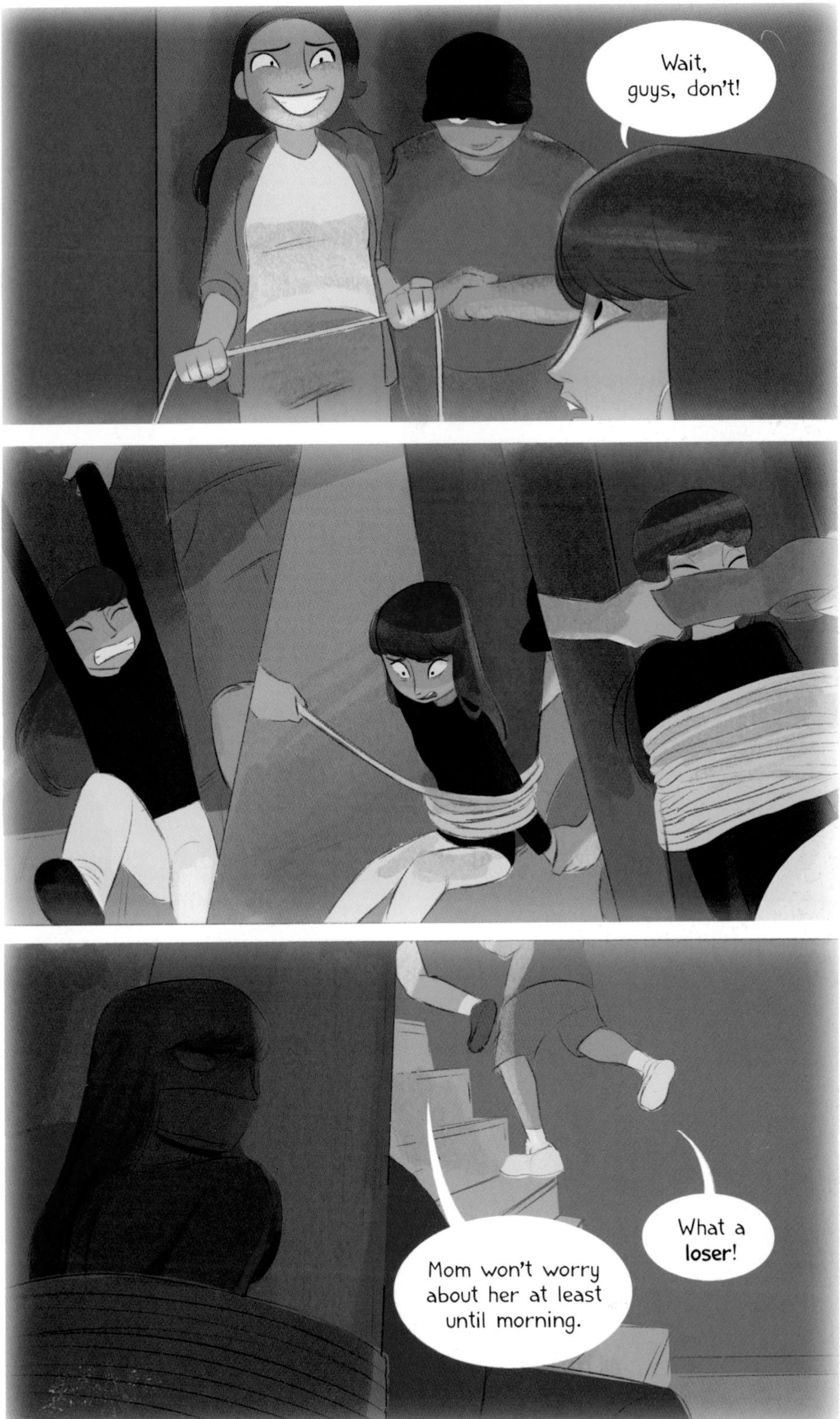
Wait, guys, don't!
What a loser!
Mom won't worry about her at least until morning.

My grandmother left this when she died. I found it in the basement.

**This** is the answer!

We can bind the town to us!

I don't know. Witchcraft?

That sounds sketchy. And hard.

Don't be such a Goody Two-shoes.

Only losers are scared. You're not a loser, are you?

This amulet belonged to my grandmother, too. It'll help us.

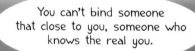

And we can always practice.

I'm not a loser.

Why can't we just bind our families?

You can't bind someone that close to you, someone who knows the real you.

Their memories of you are too strong for the spell to counteract.

But if we bind the town, at least our lives outside our homes will be great!

I say we do it!

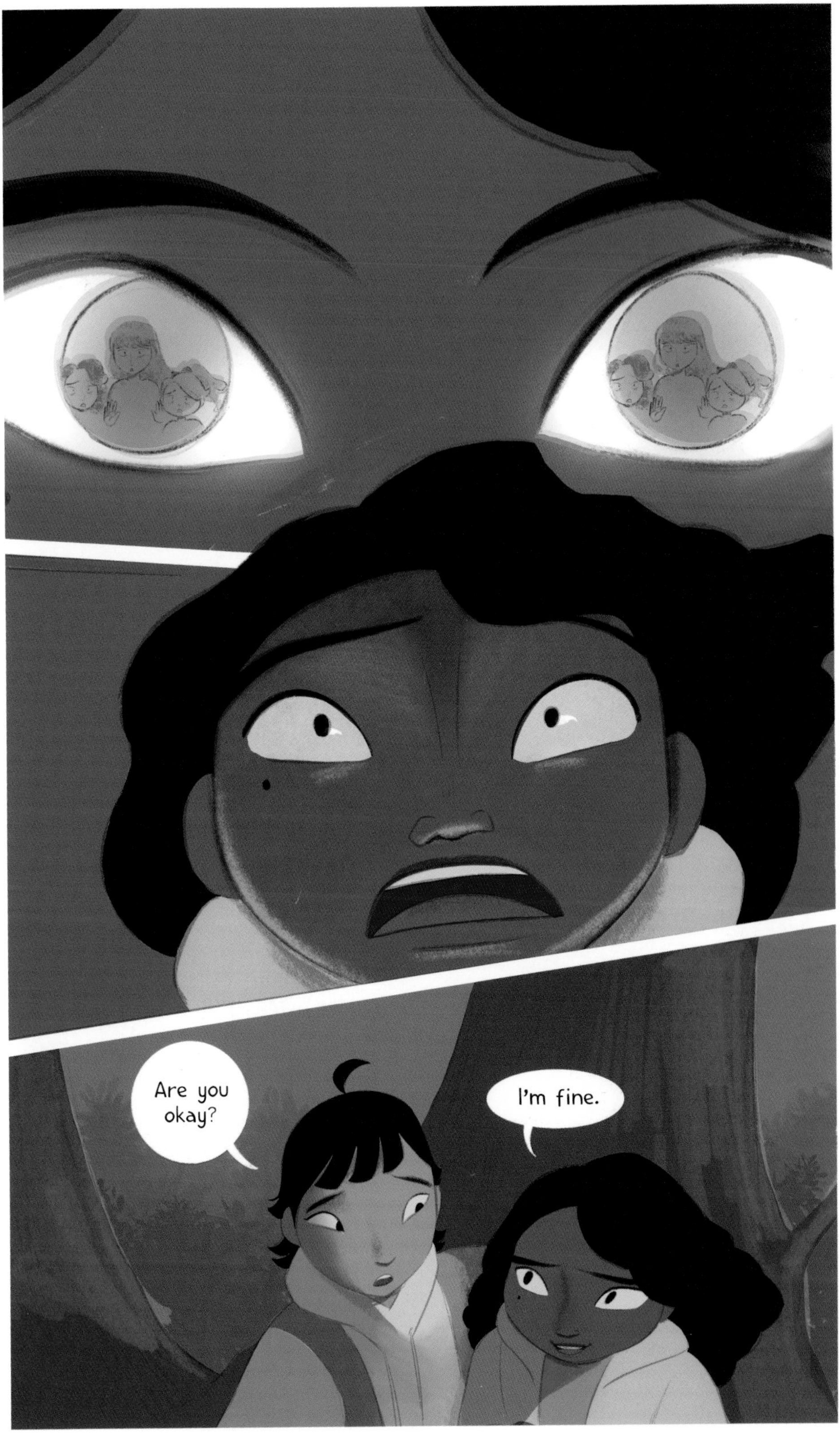
Are you okay?
I'm fine.

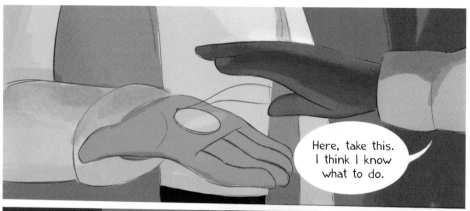

Here, take this. I think I know what to do.

I **see** you.

Nothing excuses the awful things you've done.

But you're still people, and I see your pain.

Come into the light.

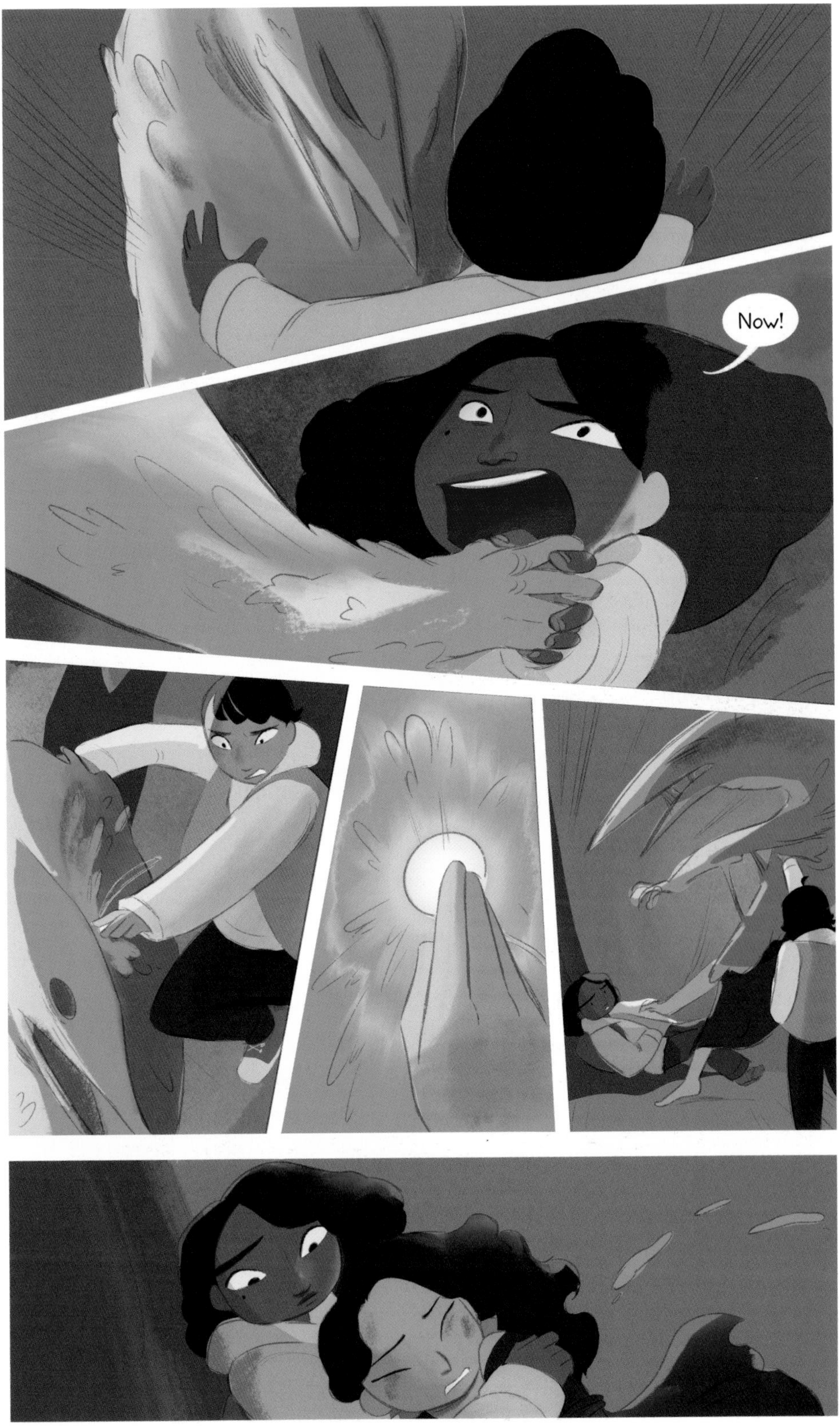
Now!

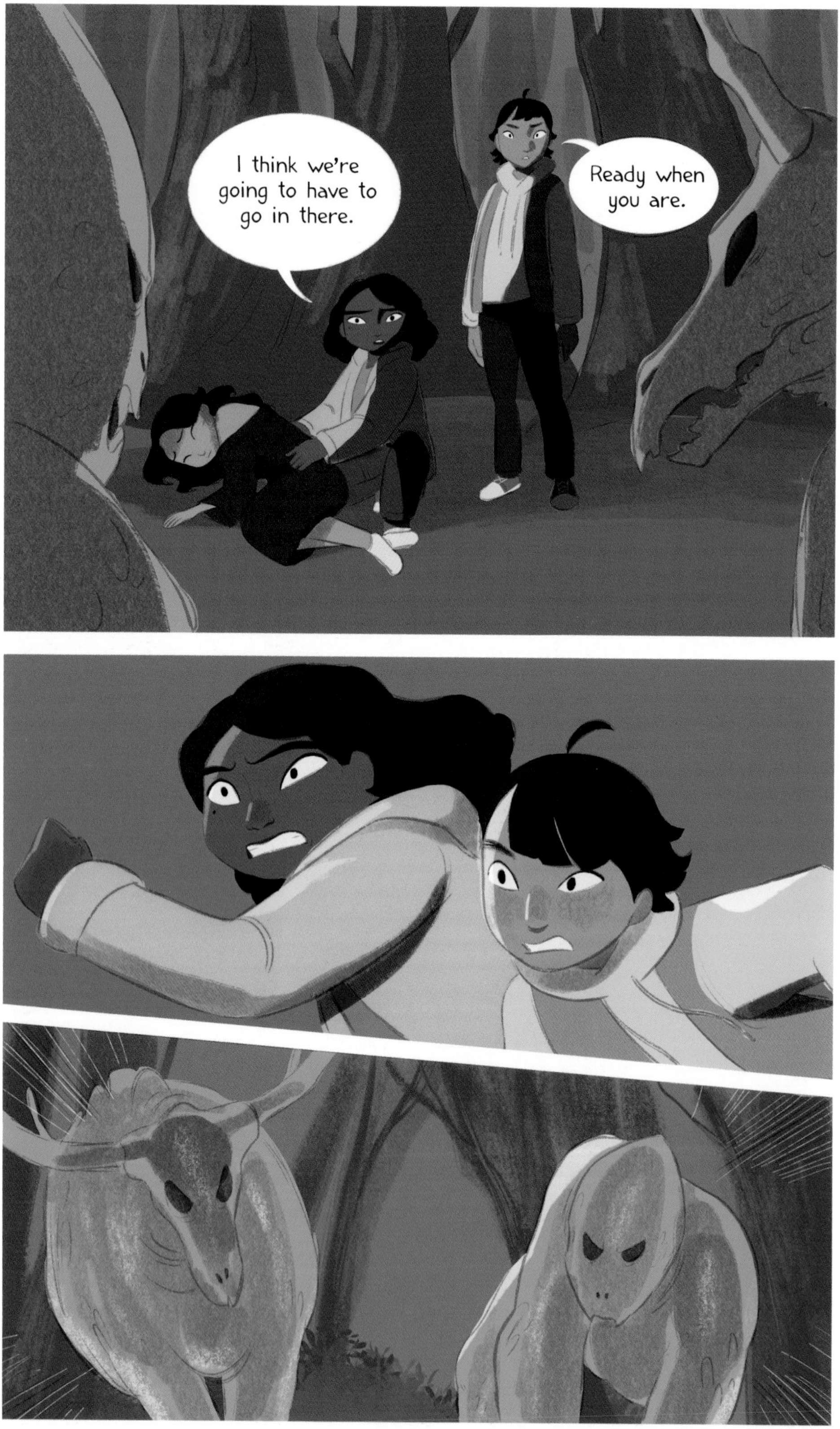
I think we're going to have to go in there.
Ready when you are.

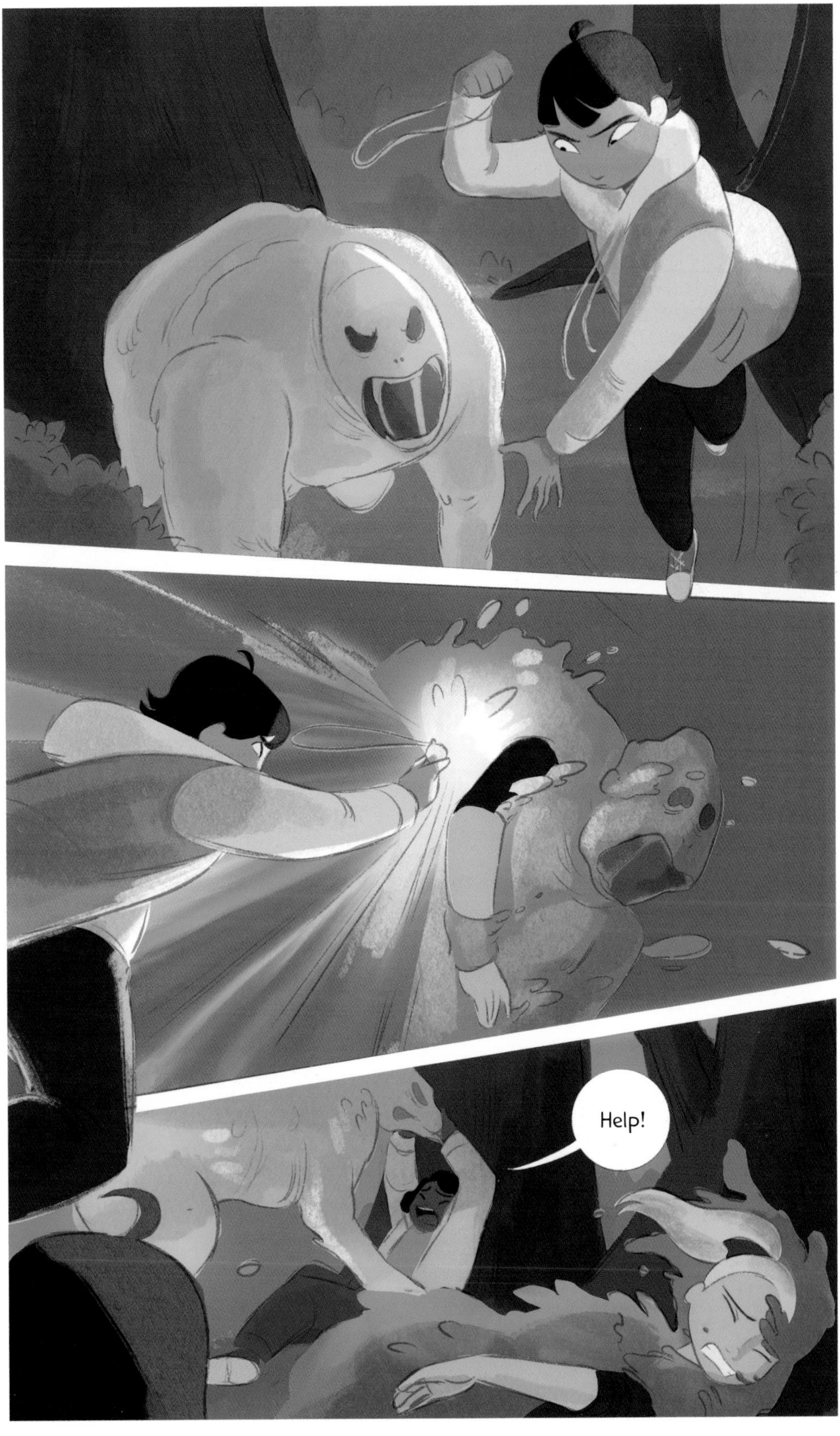
Help!

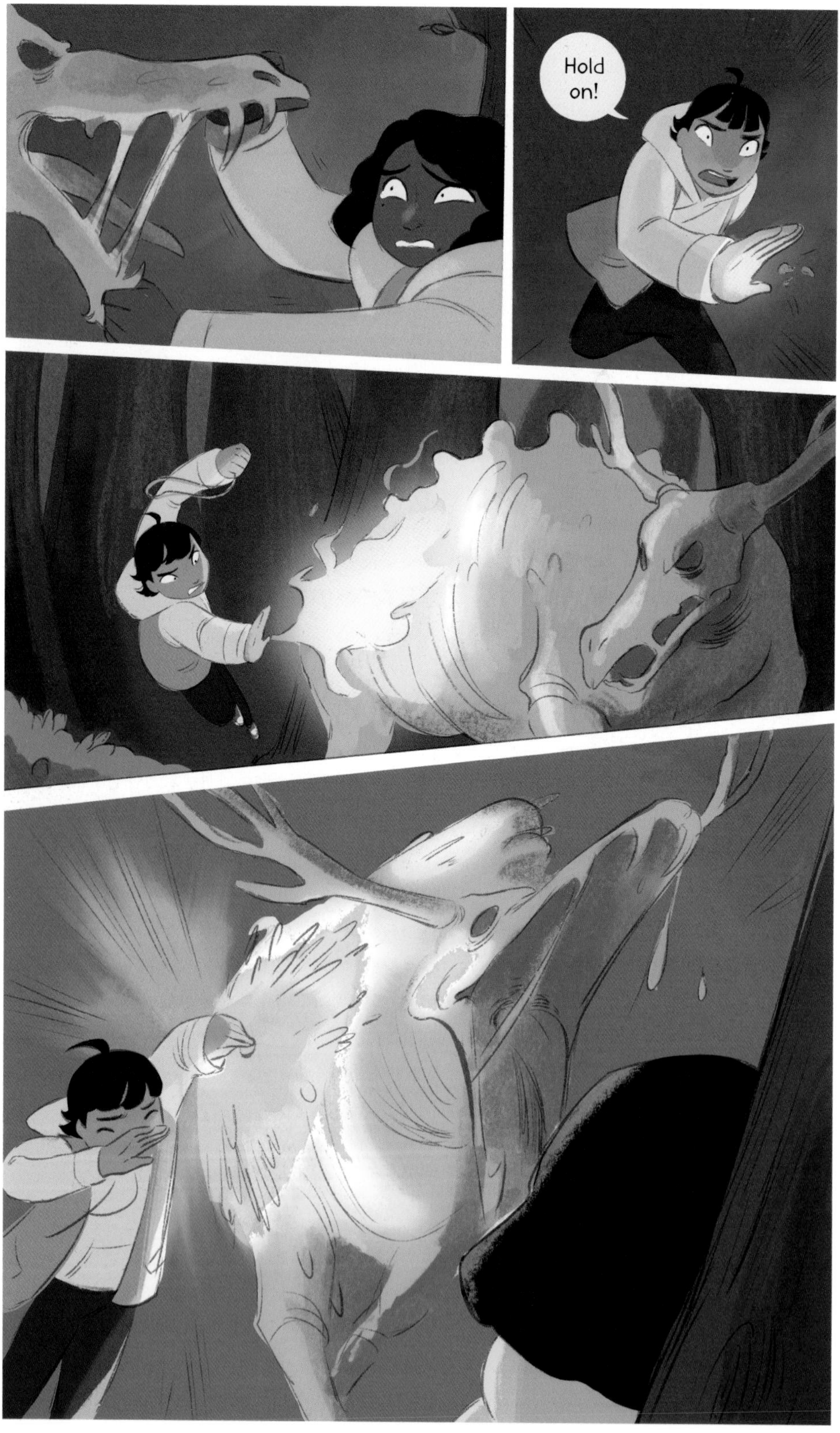
Hold on!

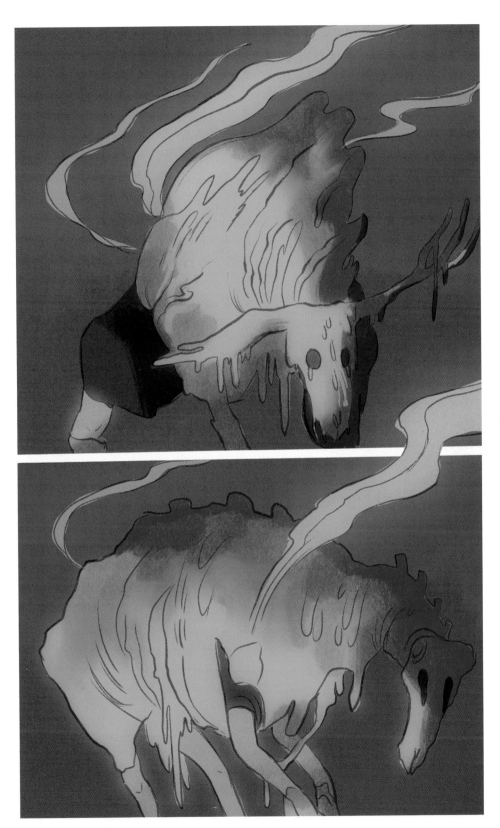

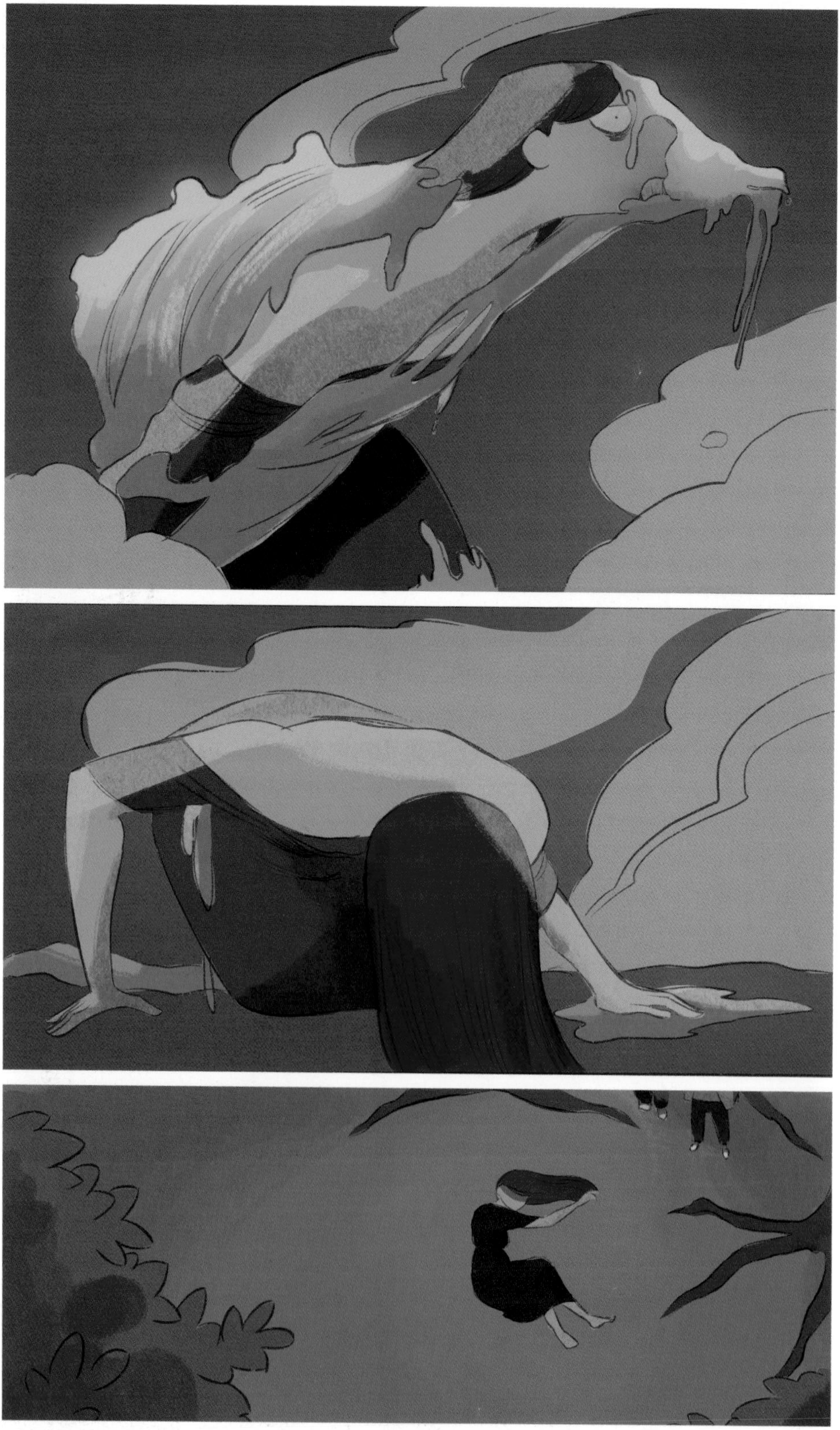

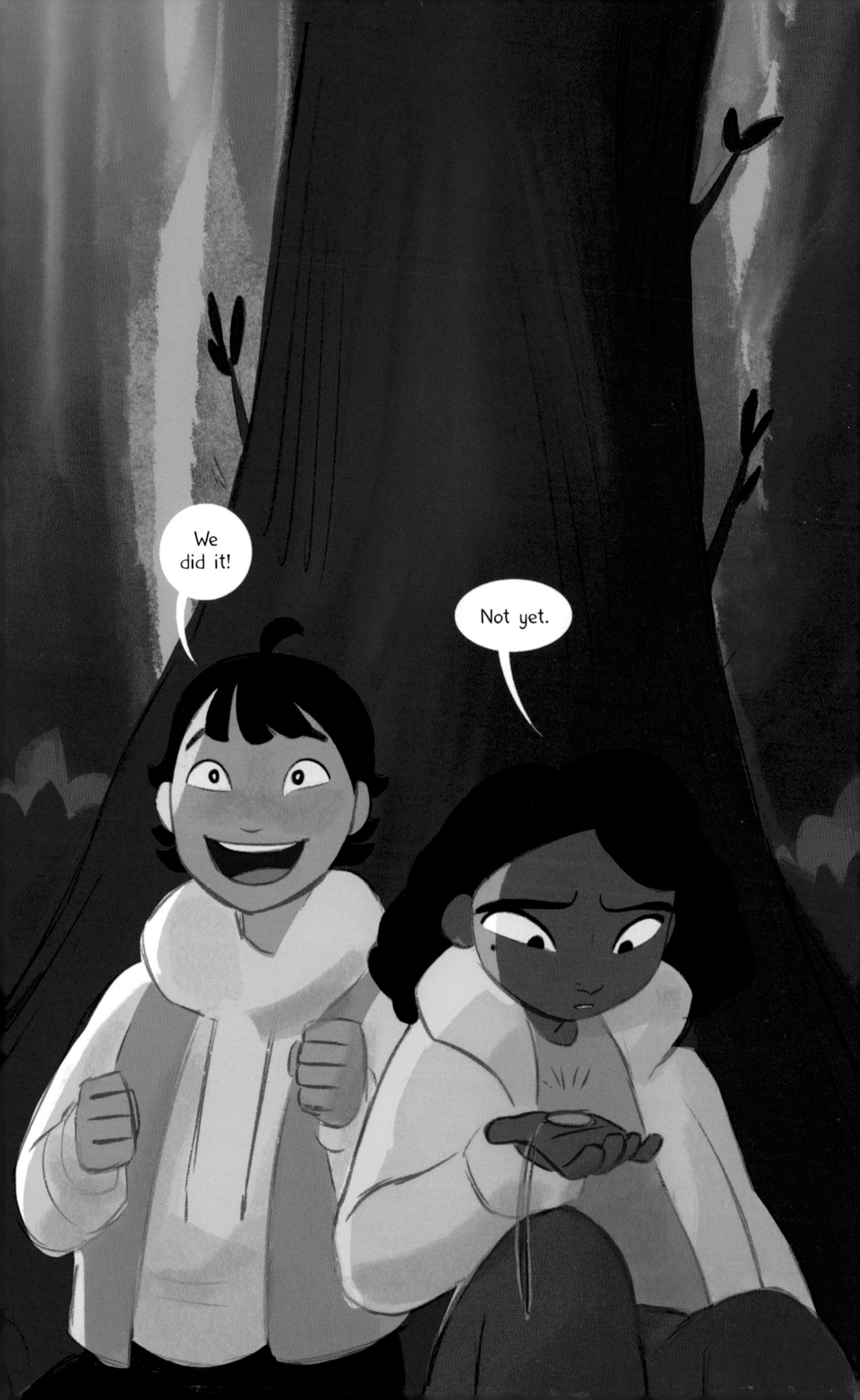
We did it!
Not yet.

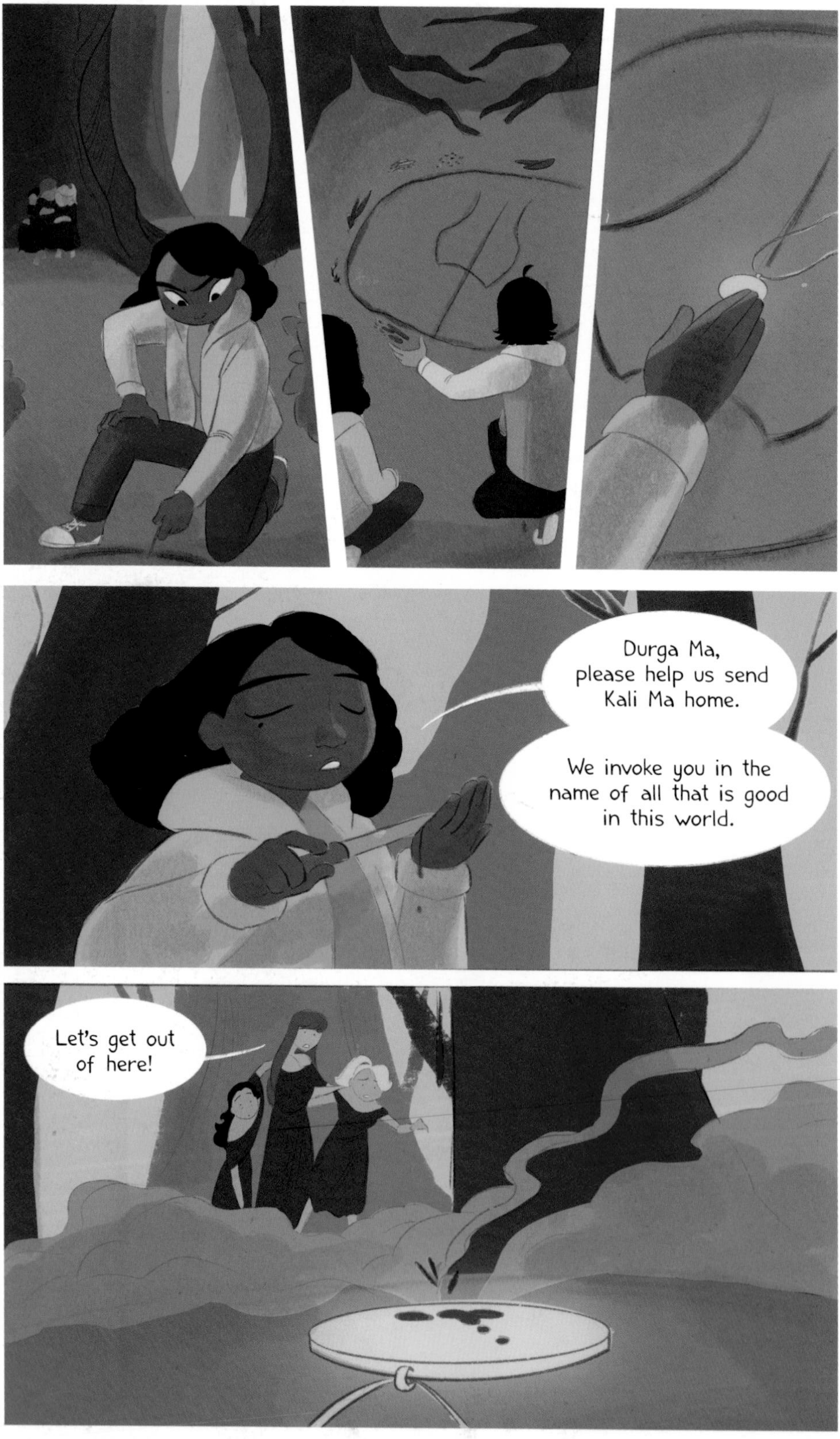
Durga Ma, please help us send Kali Ma home.
We invoke you in the name of all that is good in this world.
Let's get out of here!

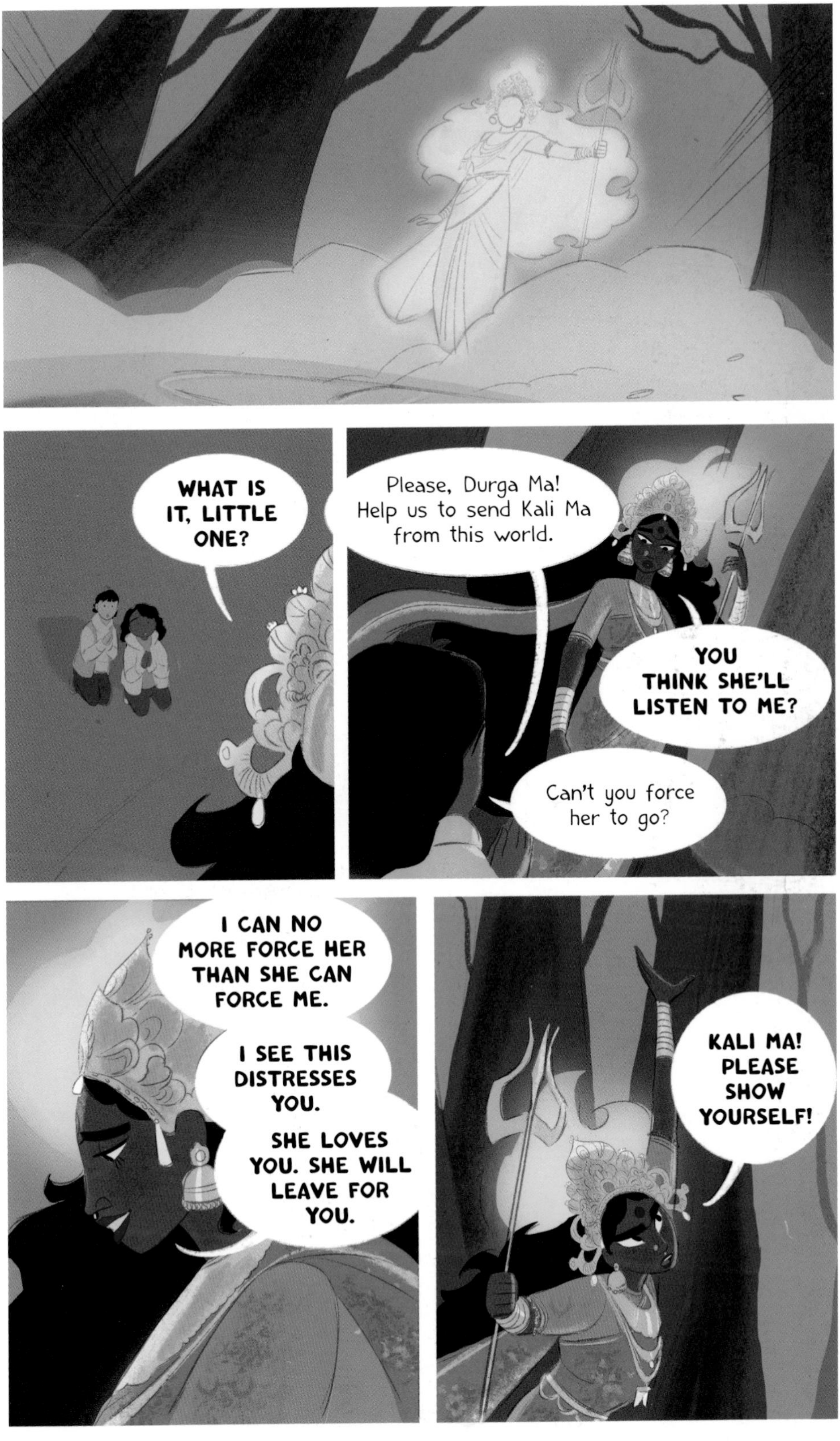
WHAT IS IT, LITTLE ONE?
Please, Durga Ma! Help us to send Kali Ma from this world.
YOU THINK SHE'LL LISTEN TO ME?
Can't you force her to go?
I CAN NO MORE FORCE HER THAN SHE CAN FORCE ME.
I SEE THIS DISTRESSES YOU.
SHE LOVES YOU. SHE WILL LEAVE FOR YOU.
KALI MA! PLEASE SHOW YOURSELF!

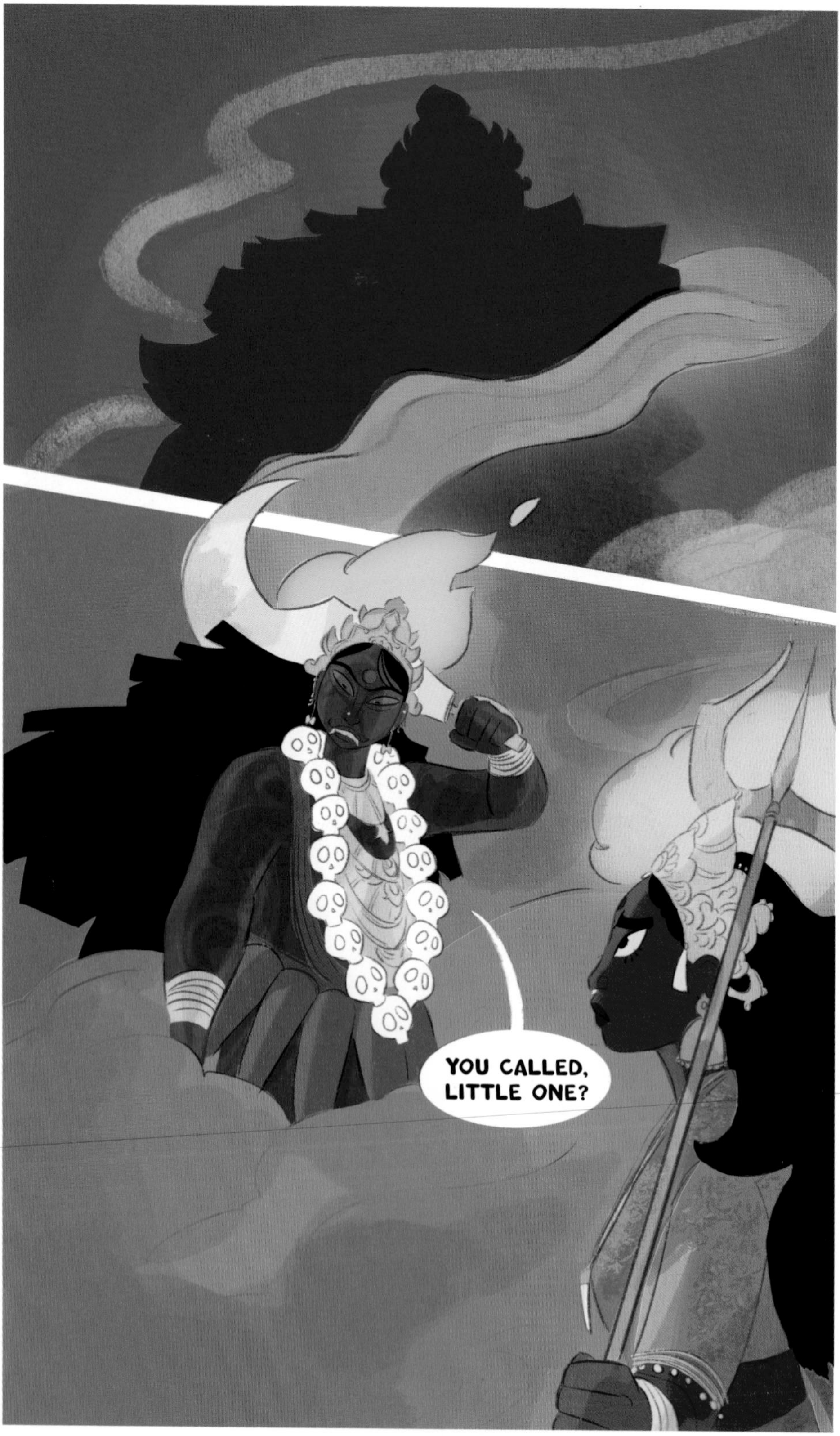
YOU CALLED, LITTLE ONE?

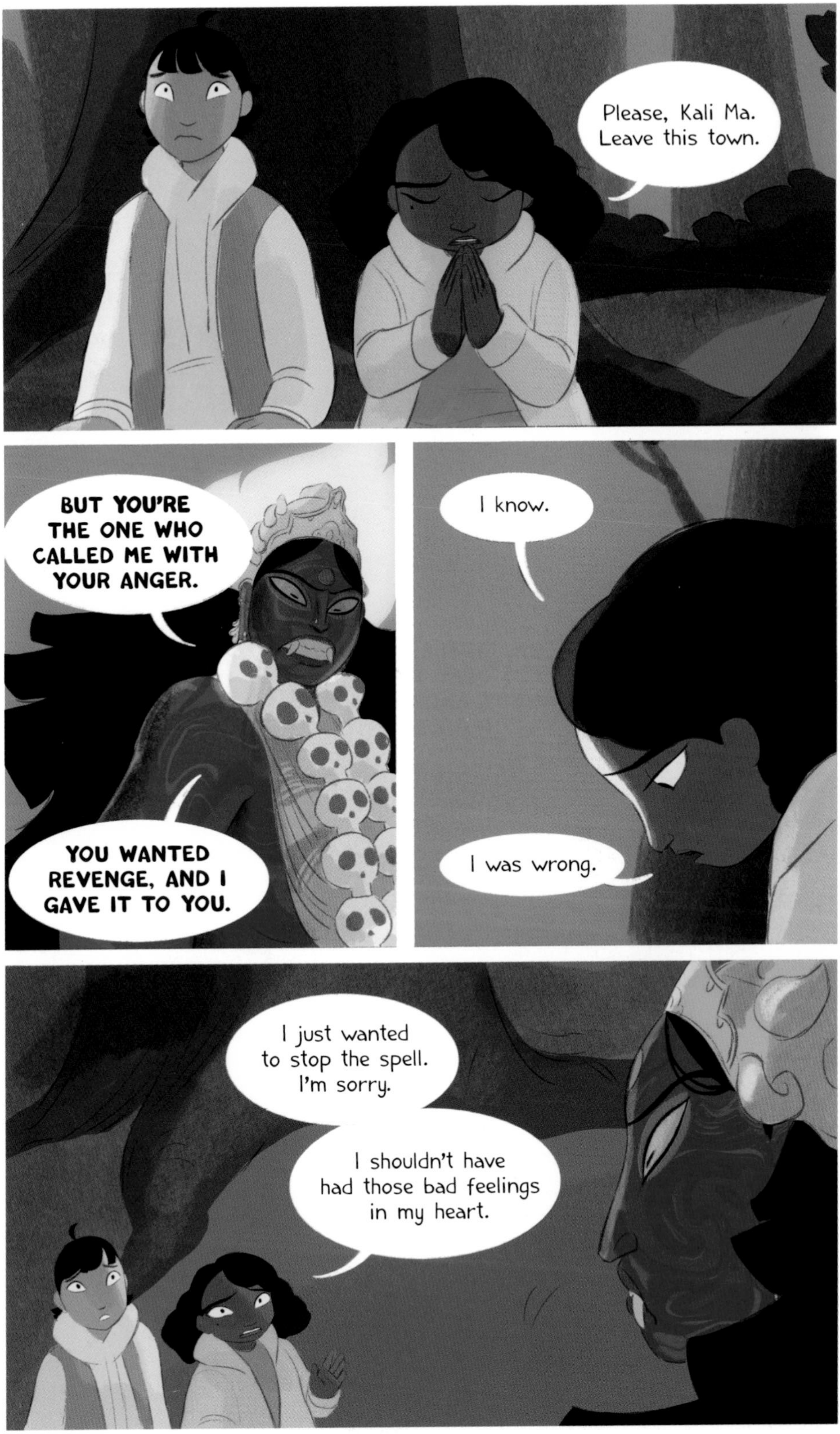
Please, Kali Ma. Leave this town.
BUT YOU'RE THE ONE WHO CALLED ME WITH YOUR ANGER.
YOU WANTED REVENGE, AND I GAVE IT TO YOU.
I know.
I was wrong.
I just wanted to stop the spell. I'm sorry.
I shouldn't have had those bad feelings in my heart.

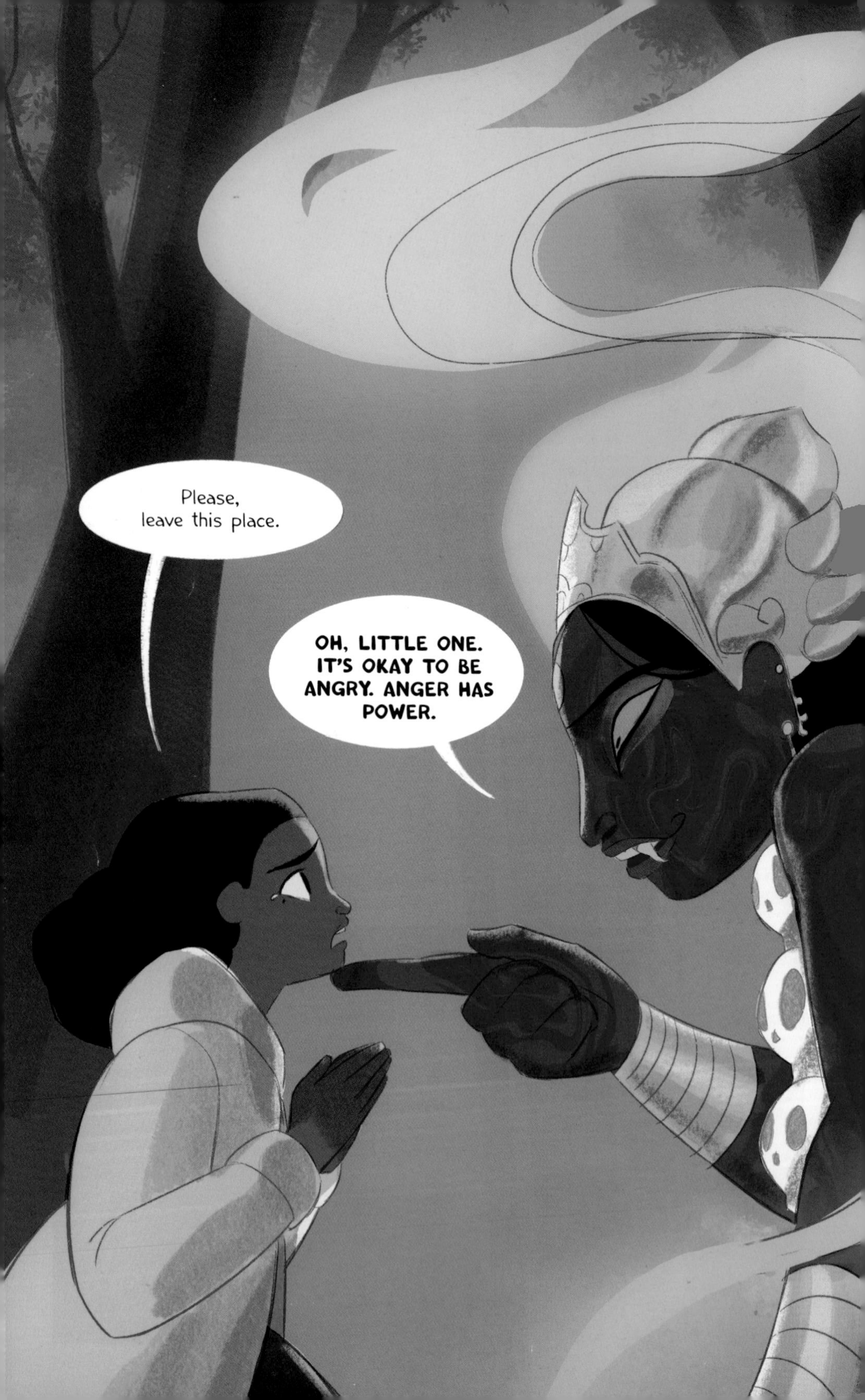
Please, leave this place.
OH, LITTLE ONE. IT'S OKAY TO BE ANGRY. ANGER HAS POWER.

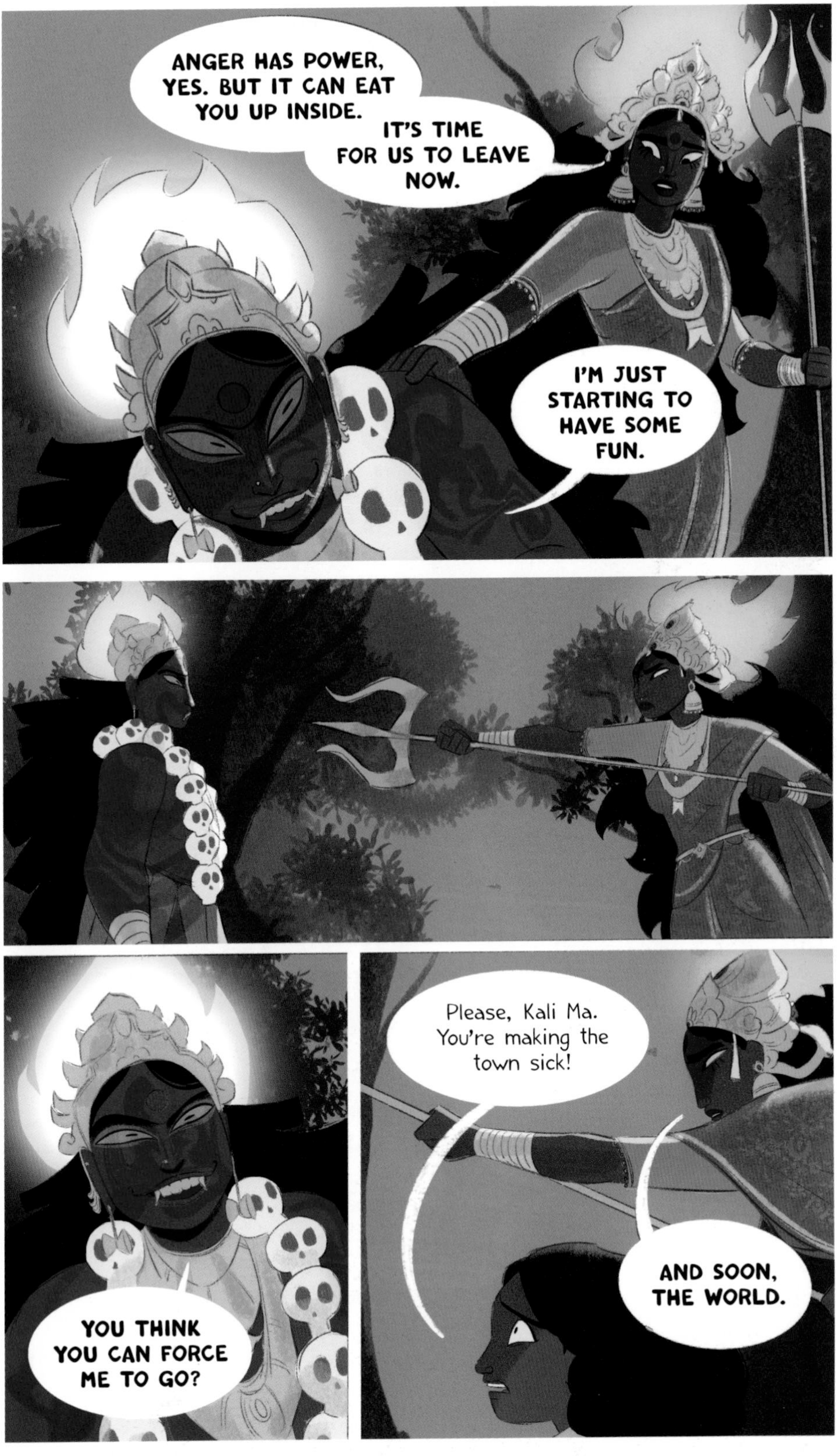
ANGER HAS POWER, YES. BUT IT CAN EAT YOU UP INSIDE.
IT'S TIME FOR US TO LEAVE NOW.
I'M JUST STARTING TO HAVE SOME FUN.
YOU THINK YOU CAN FORCE ME TO GO?
Please, Kali Ma. You're making the town sick!
AND SOON, THE WORLD.

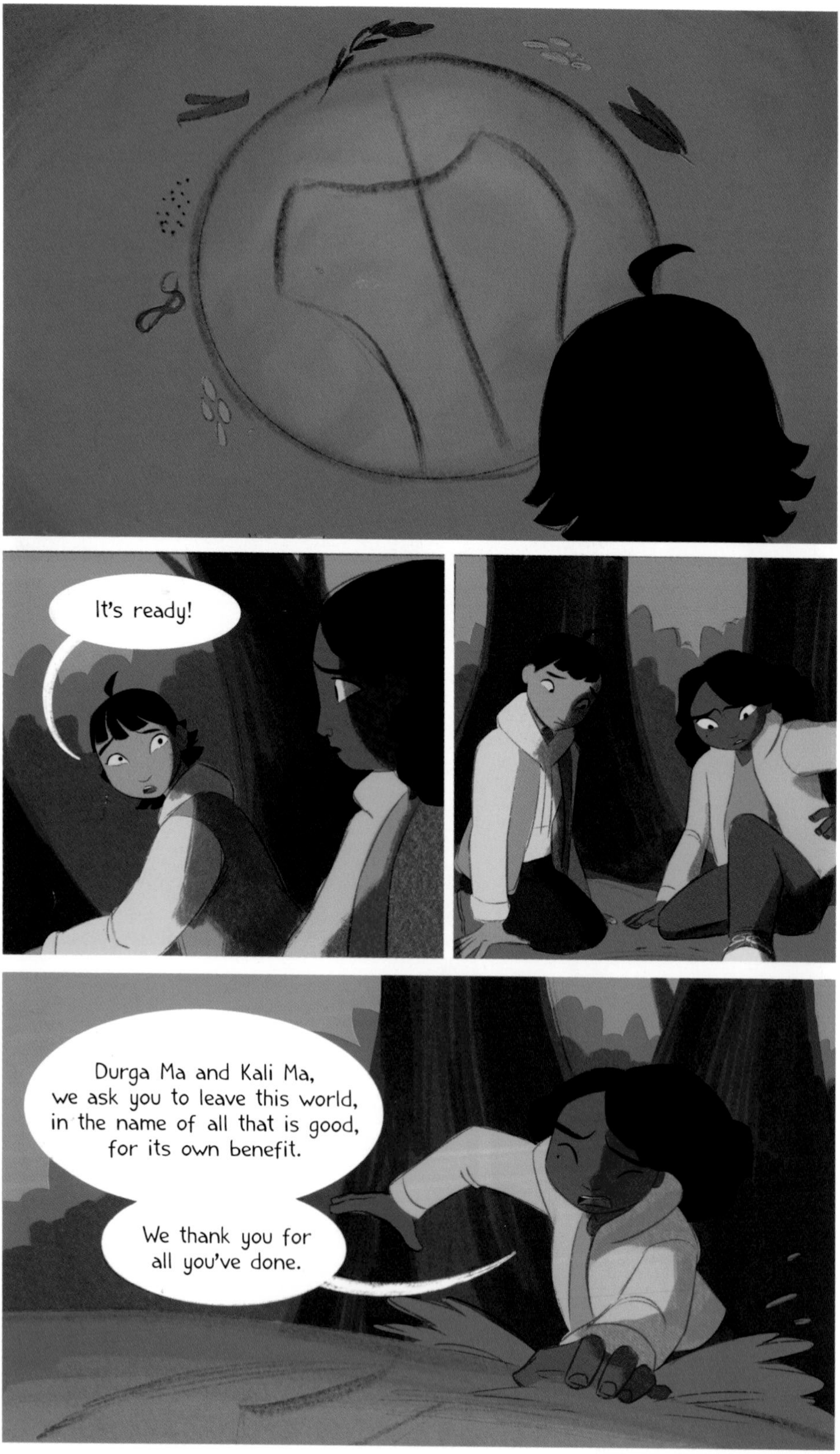
It's ready!
Durga Ma and Kali Ma, we ask you to leave this world, in the name of all that is good, for its own benefit.
We thank you for all you've done.

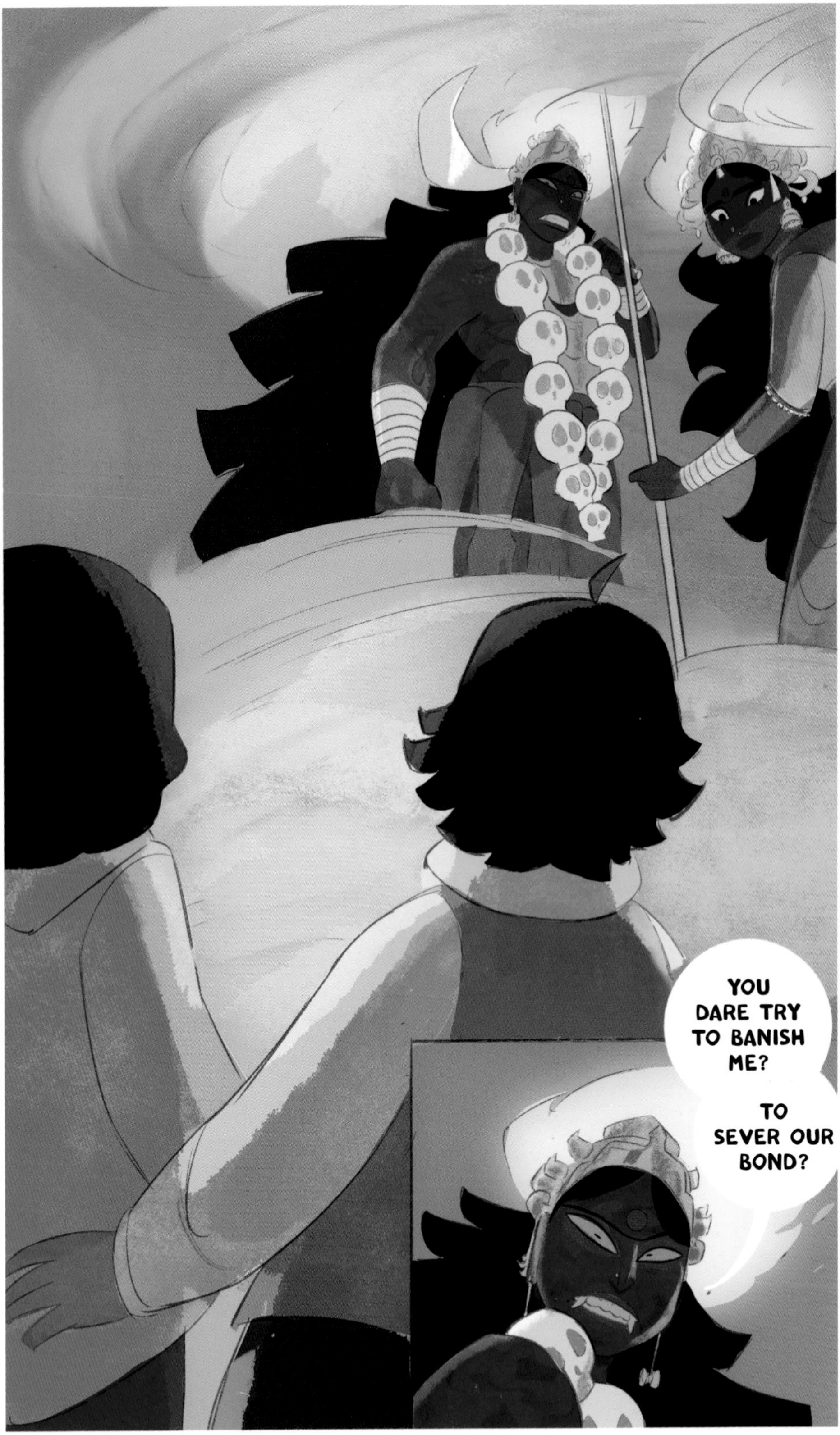
YOU DARE TRY TO BANISH ME?
TO SEVER OUR BOND?

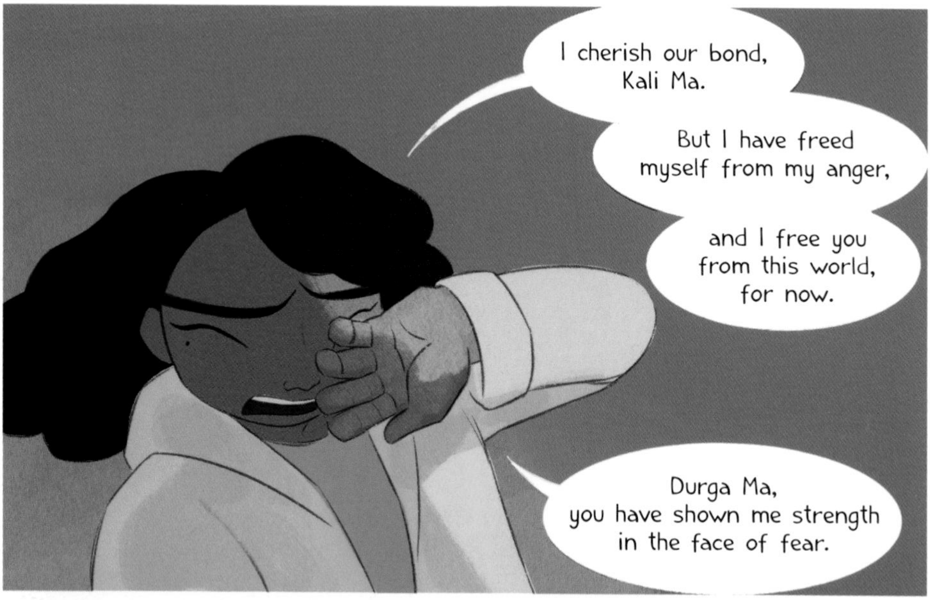
I cherish our bond,
Kali Ma.
But I have freed
myself from my anger,
and I free you
from this world,
for now.
Durga Ma,
you have shown me strength
in the face of fear.

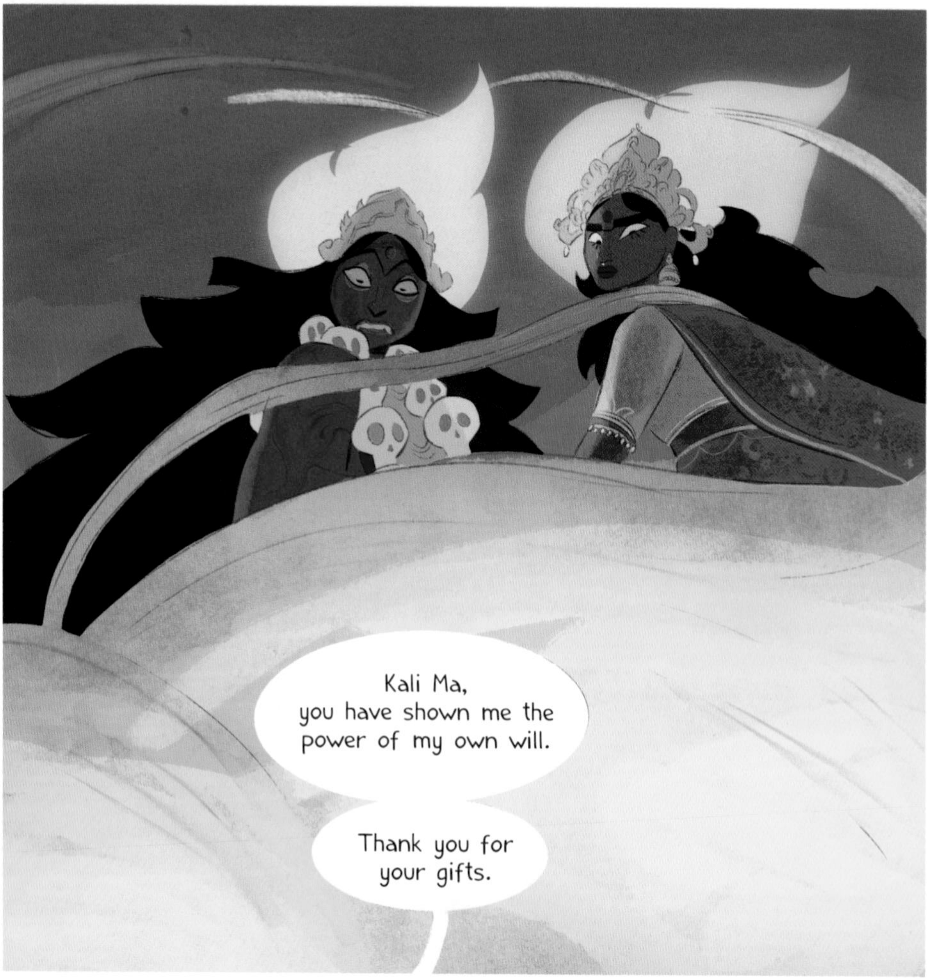
Kali Ma,
you have shown me the
power of my own will.
Thank you for
your gifts.

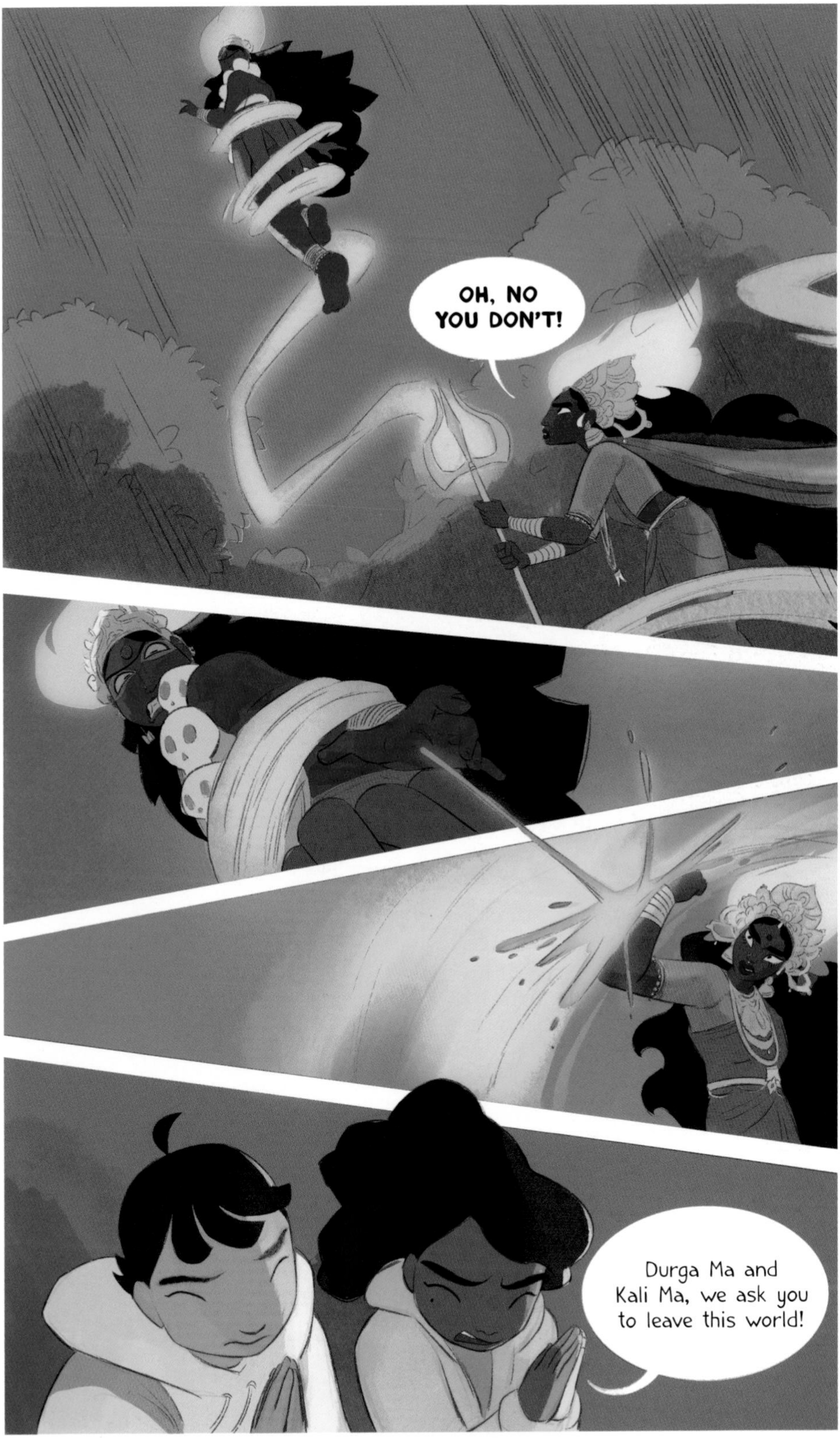
OH, NO YOU DON'T!
Durga Ma and Kali Ma, we ask you to leave this world!

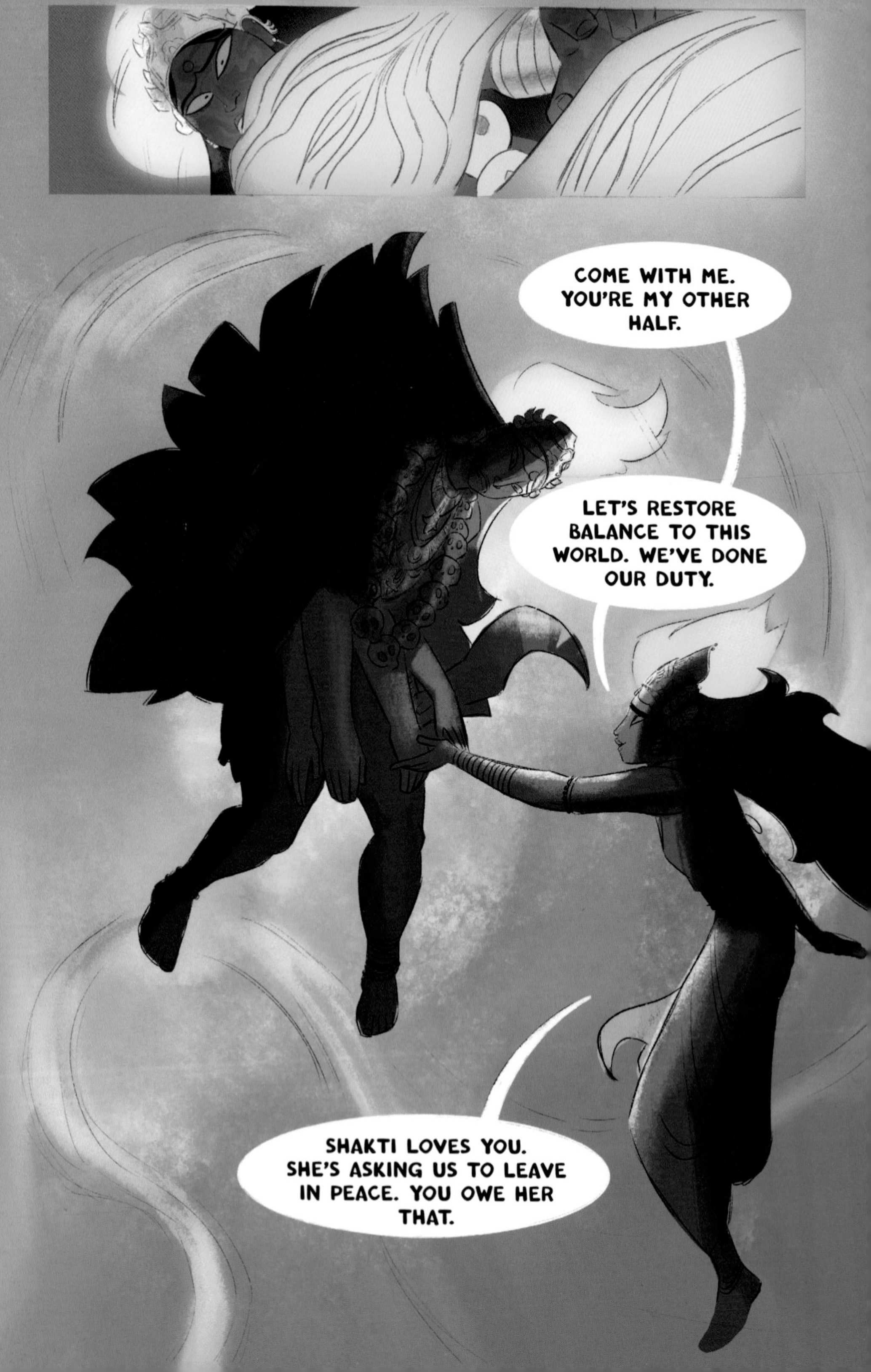
COME WITH ME. YOU'RE MY OTHER HALF.
LET'S RESTORE BALANCE TO THIS WORLD. WE'VE DONE OUR DUTY.
SHAKTI LOVES YOU. SHE'S ASKING US TO LEAVE IN PEACE. YOU OWE HER THAT.

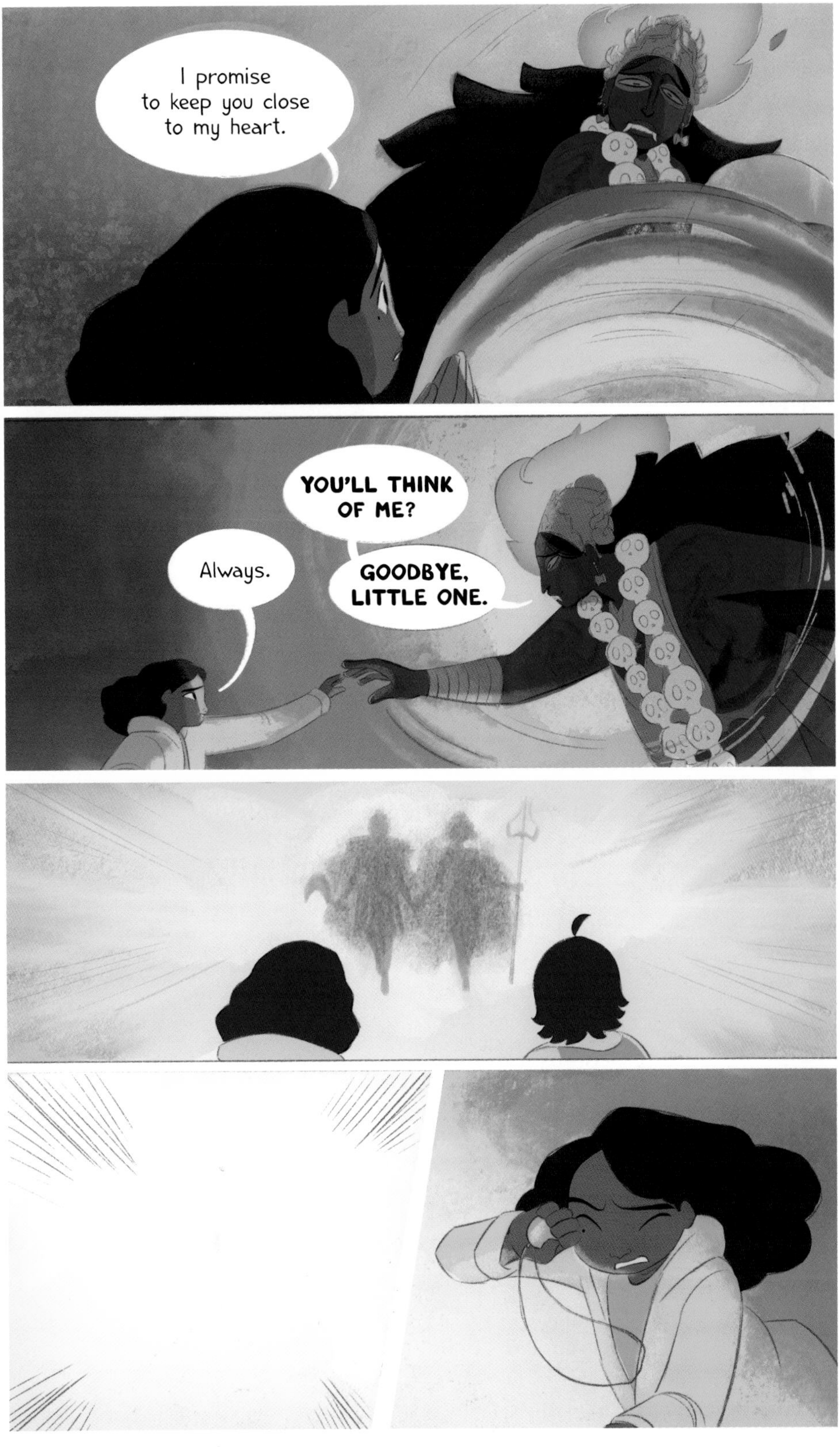
I promise to keep you close to my heart.
YOU'LL THINK OF ME?
Always.
GOODBYE, LITTLE ONE.

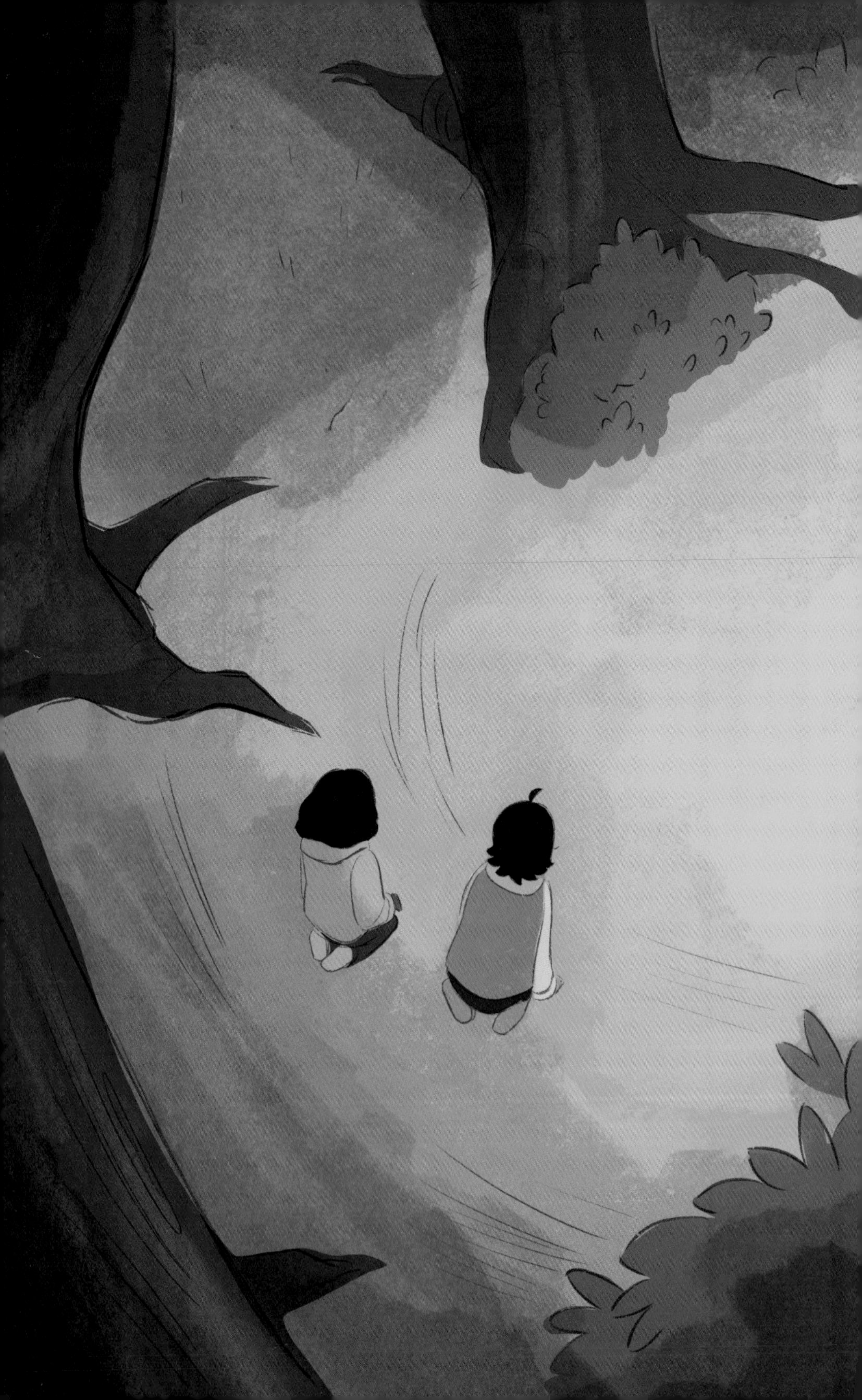

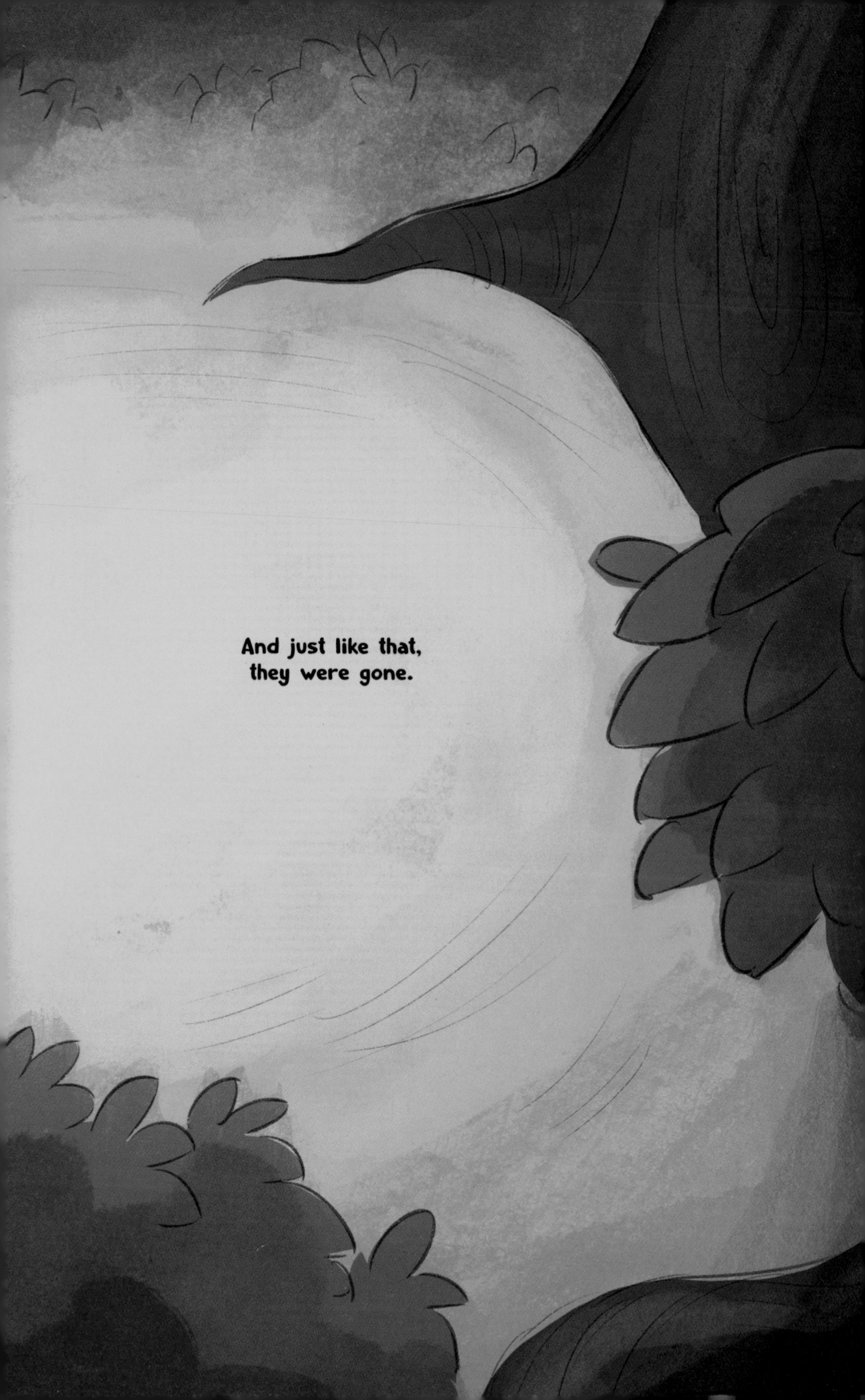
And just like that, they were gone.

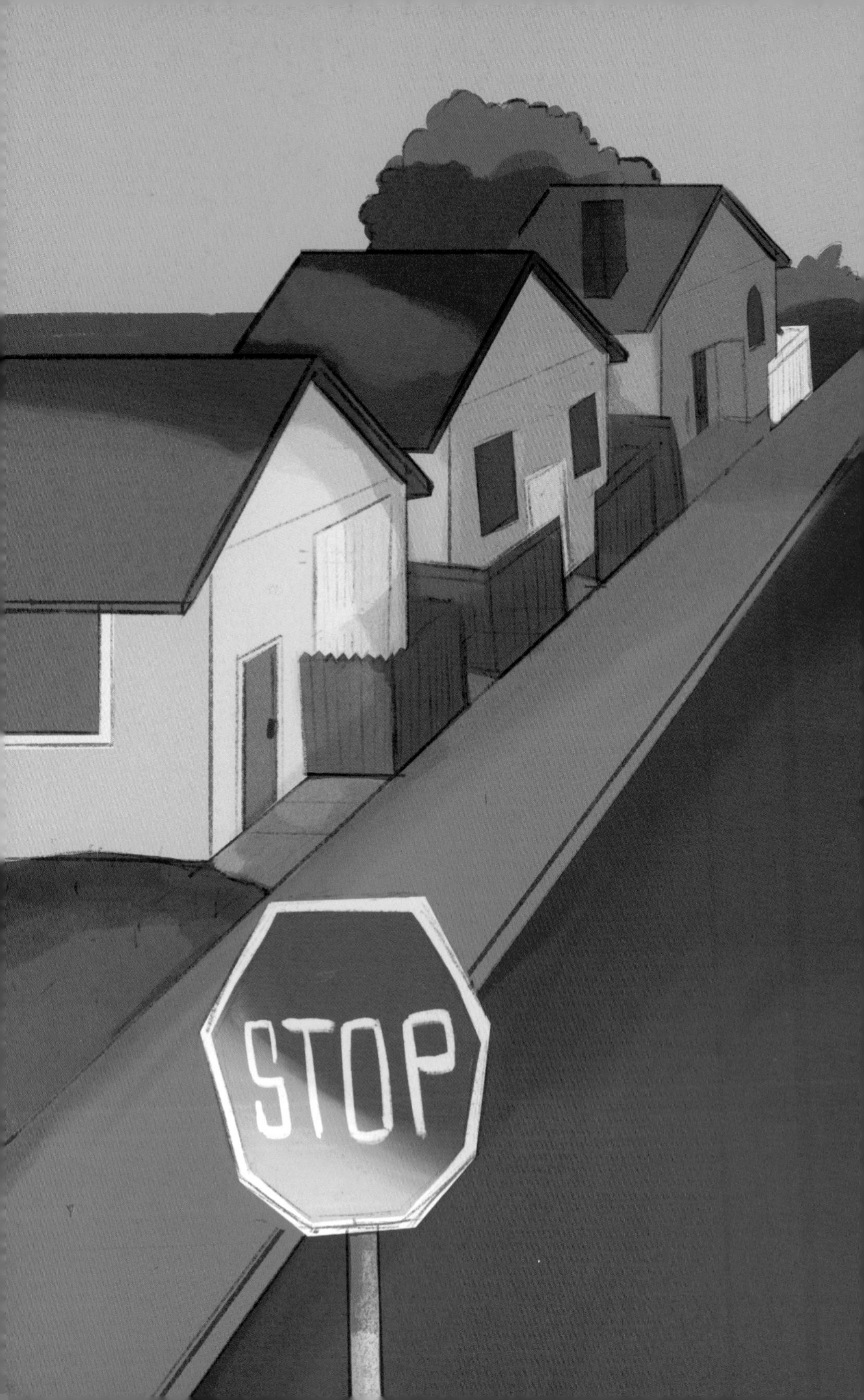
STOP

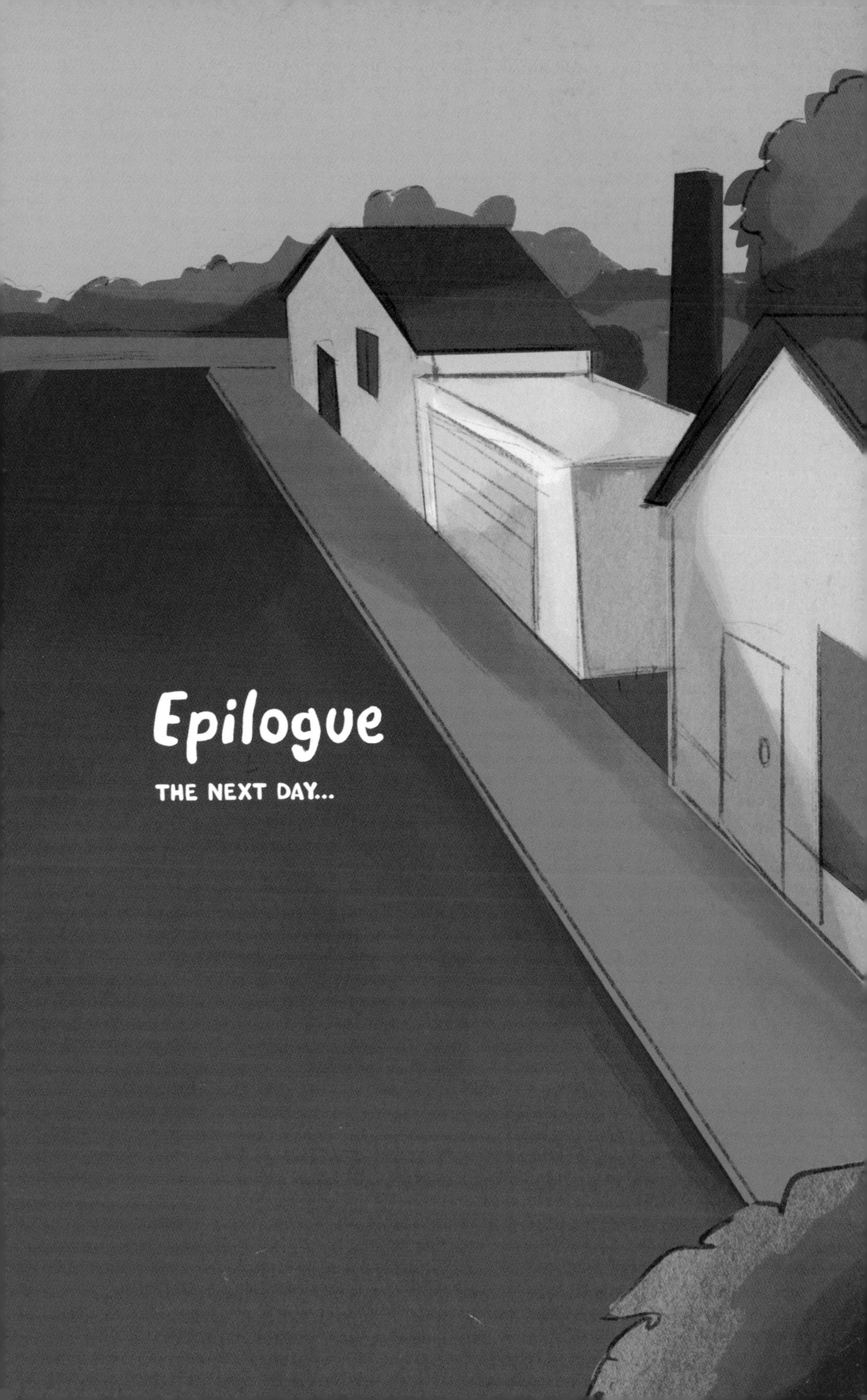
Epilogue
THE NEXT DAY...

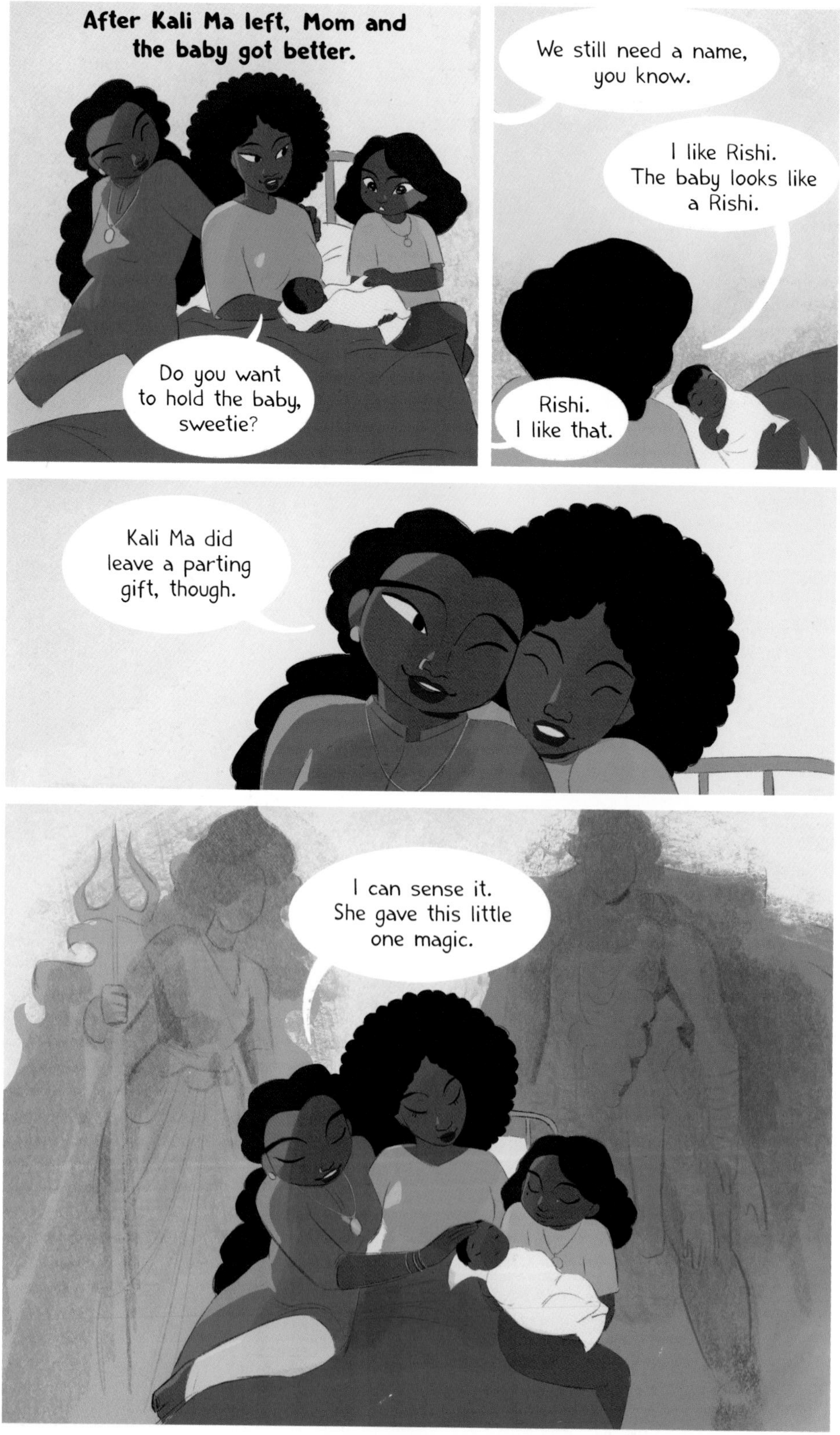
After Kali Ma left, Mom and the baby got better.
Do you want to hold the baby, sweetie?
We still need a name, you know.
I like Rishi. The baby looks like a Rishi.
Rishi. I like that.
Kali Ma did leave a parting gift, though.
I can sense it. She gave this little one magic.

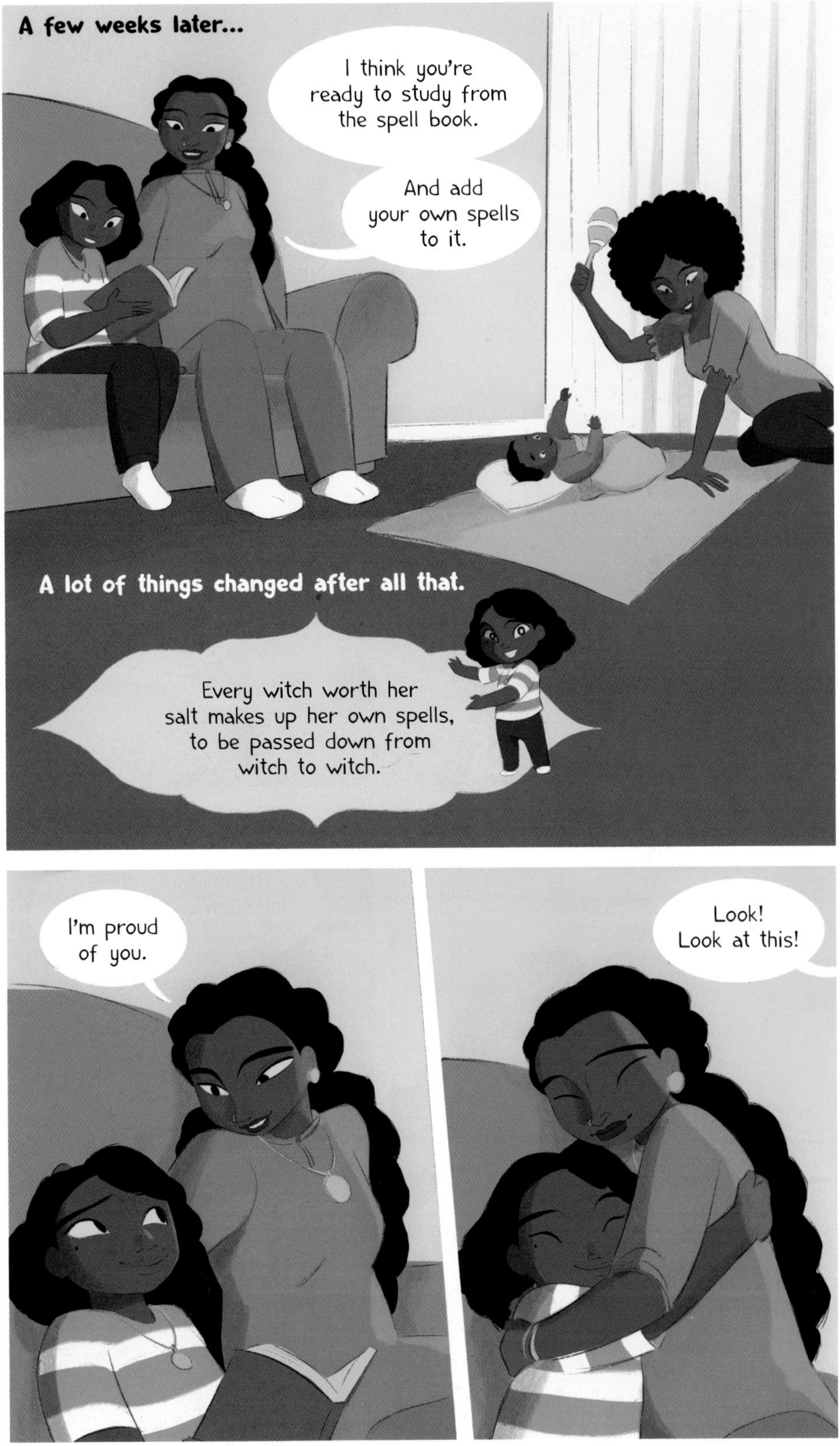
A few weeks later...
I think you're ready to study from the spell book.
And add your own spells to it.
A lot of things changed after all that.
Every witch worth her salt makes up her own spells, to be passed down from witch to witch.
I'm proud of you.
Look! Look at this!

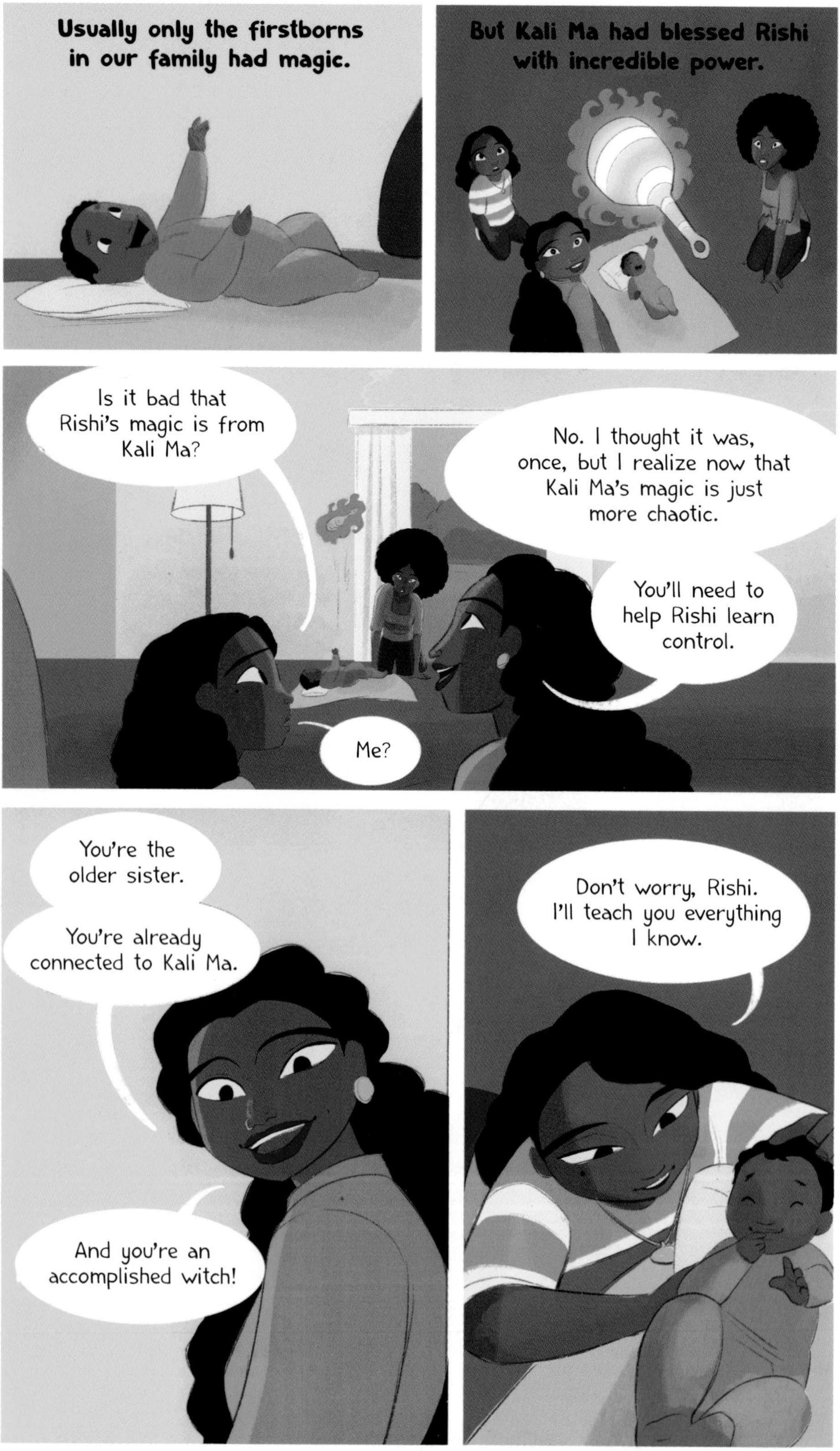

Usually only the firstborns in our family had magic.
But Kali Ma had blessed Rishi with incredible power.
Is it bad that Rishi's magic is from Kali Ma?
No. I thought it was, once, but I realize now that Kali Ma's magic is just more chaotic.
You'll need to help Rishi learn control.
Me?
You're the older sister.
You're already connected to Kali Ma.
And you're an accomplished witch!
Don't worry, Rishi. I'll teach you everything I know.

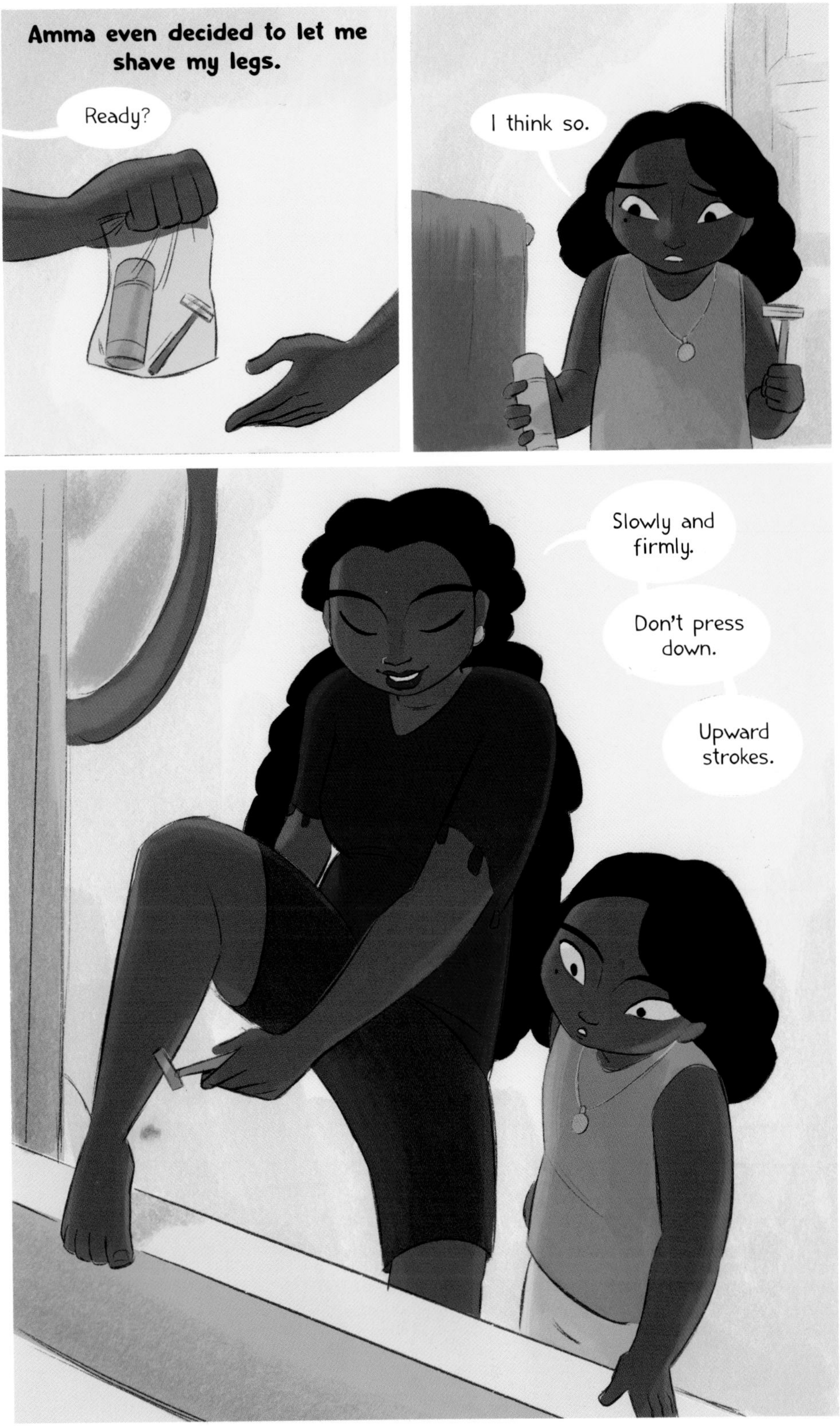
Amma even decided to let me shave my legs.
Ready?
I think so.
Slowly and firmly.
Don't press down.
Upward strokes.

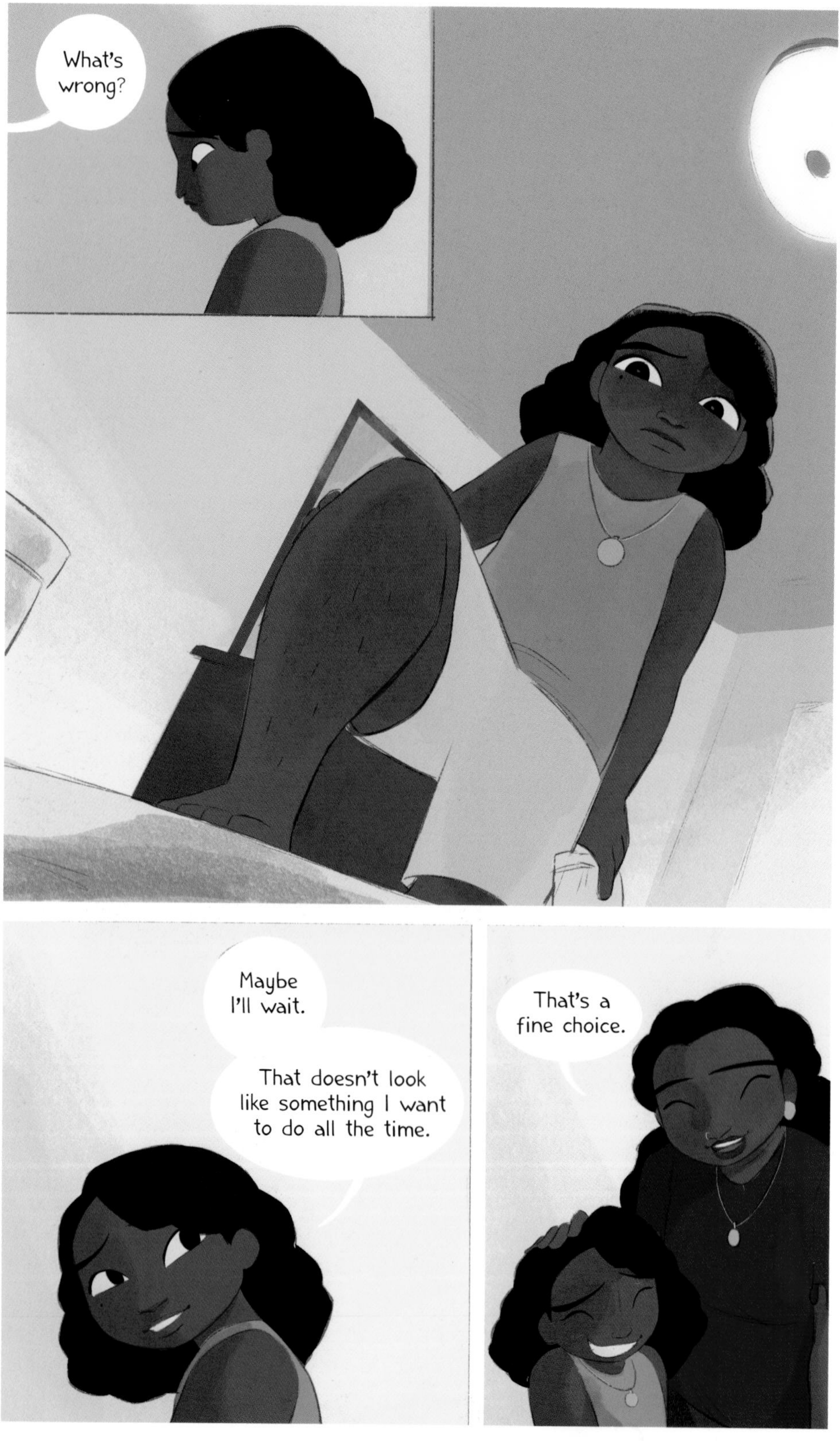
What's wrong?
Maybe I'll wait.
That doesn't look like something I want to do all the time.
That's a fine choice.

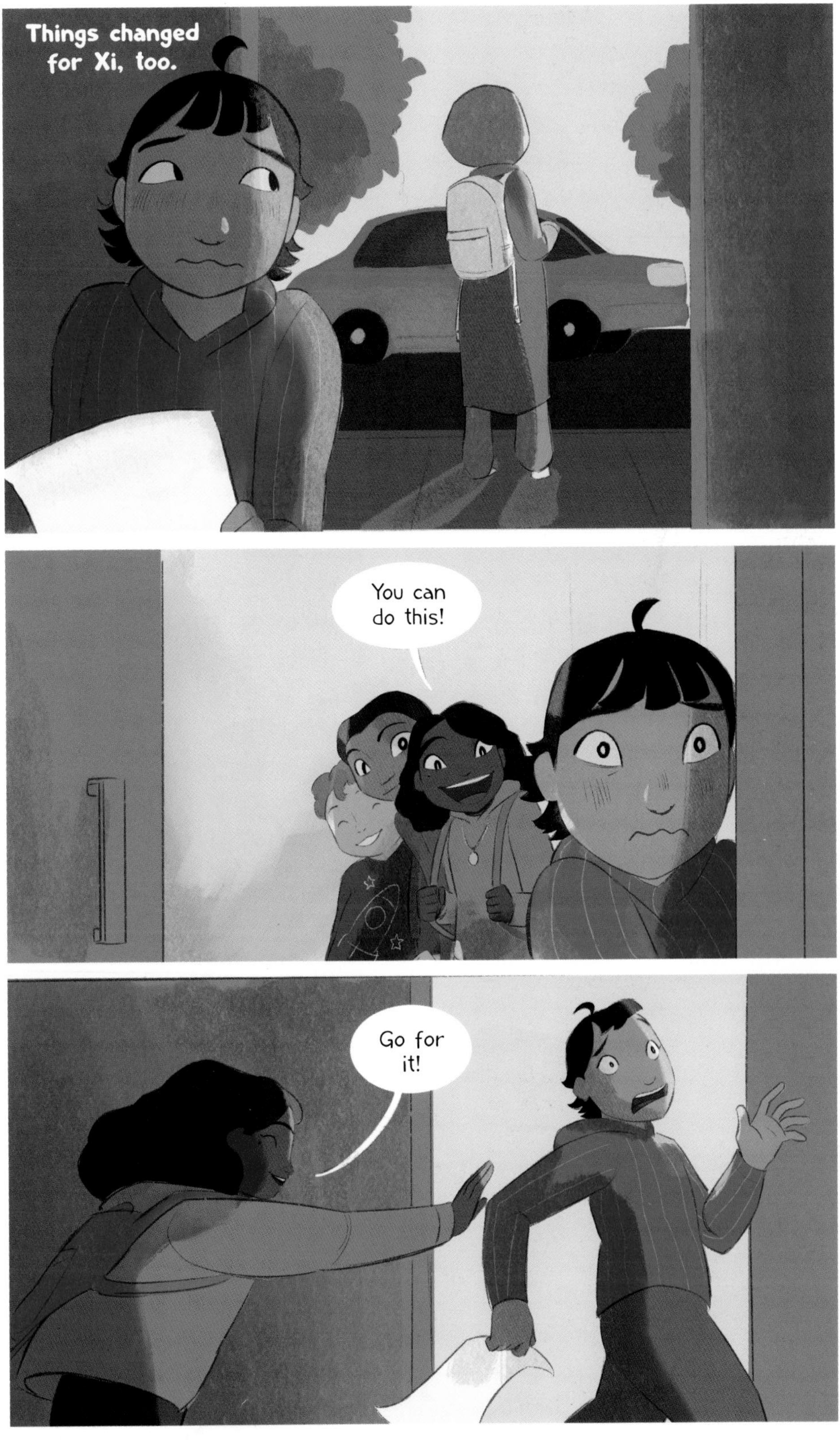
Things changed for Xi, too.
You can do this!
Go for it!

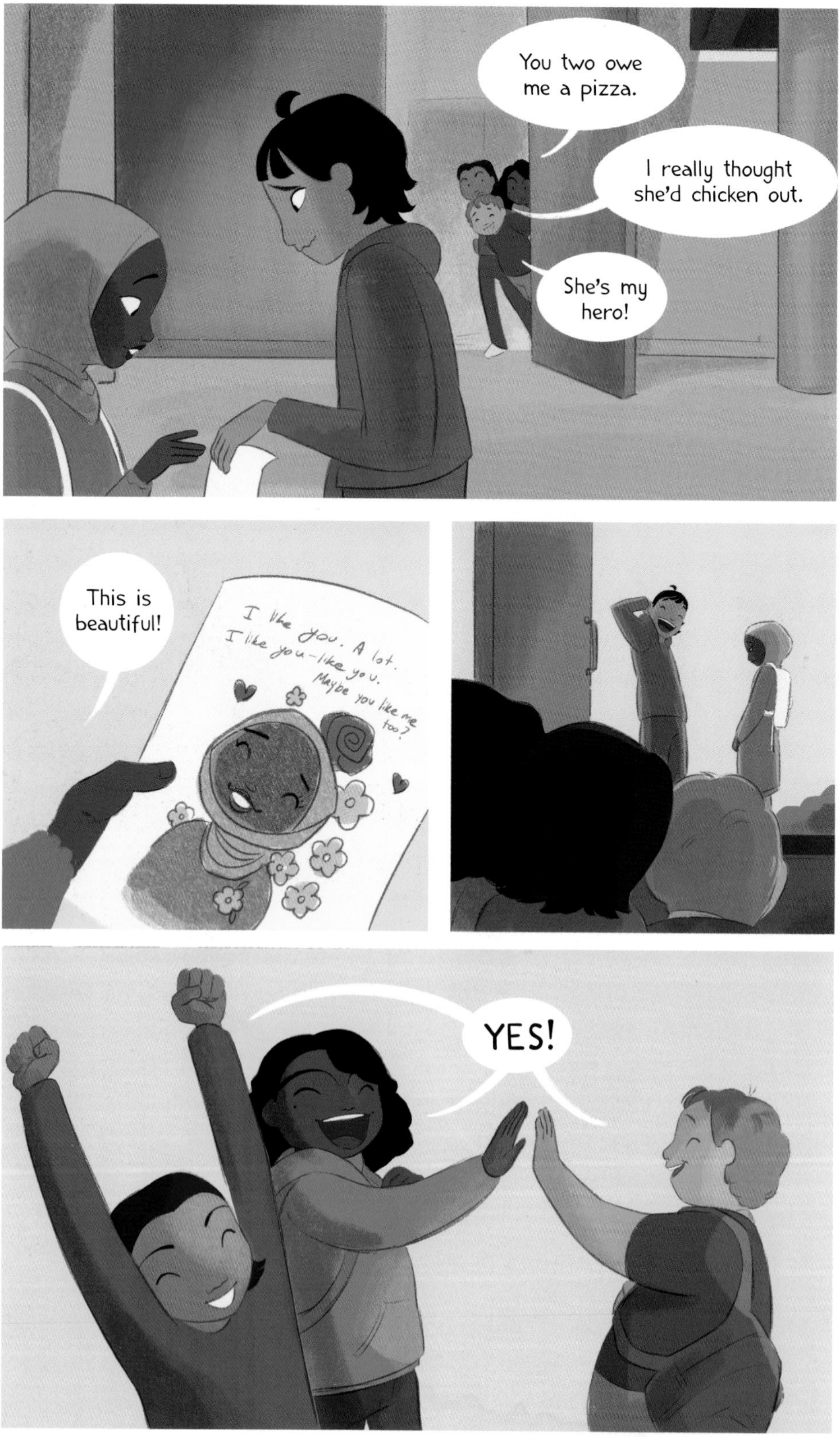
You two owe me a pizza.
I really thought she'd chicken out.
She's my hero!
This is beautiful!
I like you. A lot. I like you-like you. Maybe you like me too?
YES!

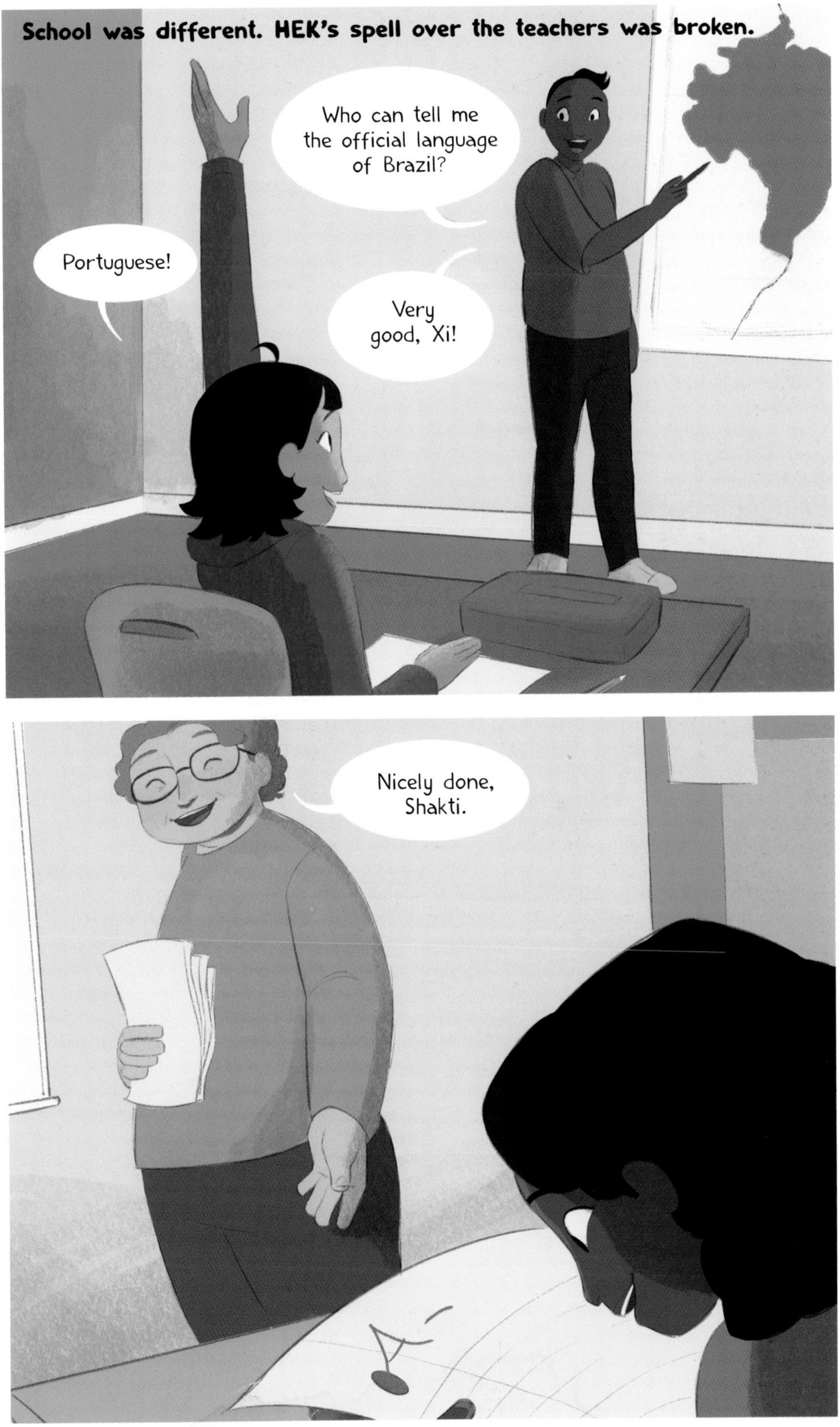
School was different. HEK's spell over the teachers was broken.
Who can tell me the official language of Brazil?
Portuguese!
Very good, Xi!
Nicely done, Shakti.

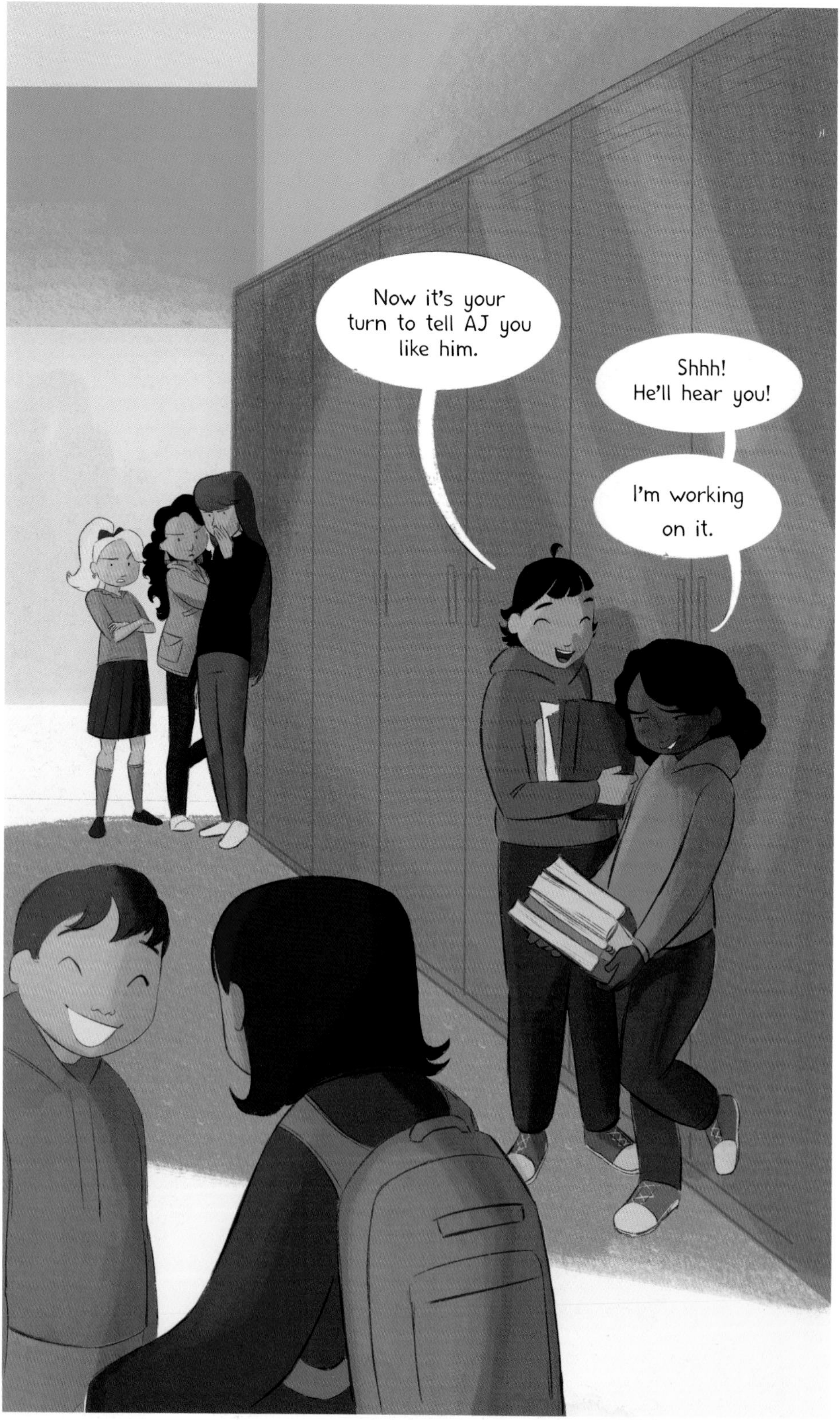
Now it's your turn to tell AJ you like him.
Shhh! He'll hear you!
I'm working on it.

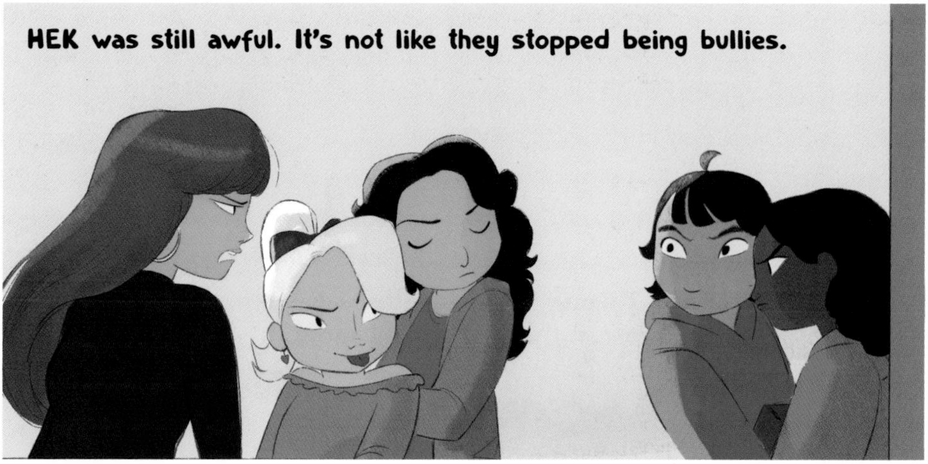
HEK was still awful. It's not like they stopped being bullies.

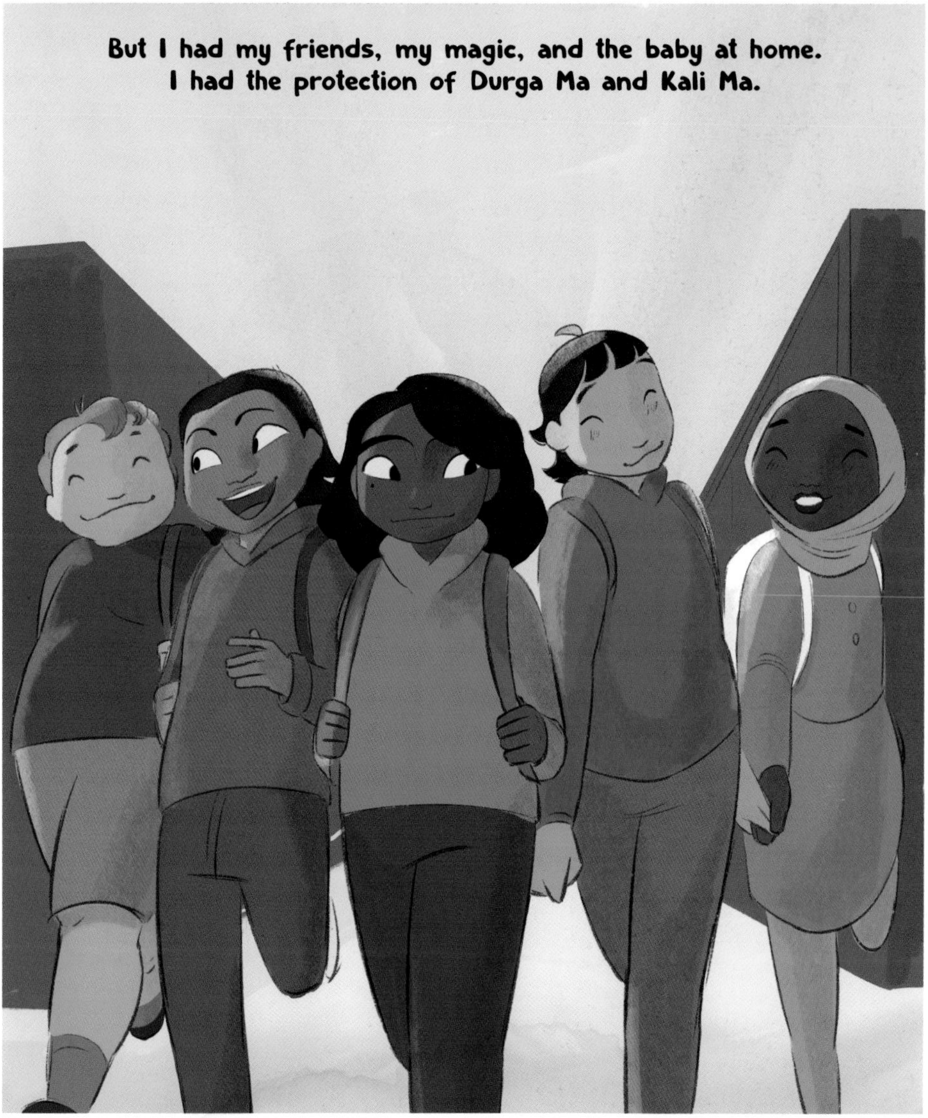
But I had my friends, my magic, and the baby at home.
I had the protection of Durga Ma and Kali Ma.

And I knew that no matter what life
threw my way, I could handle it.

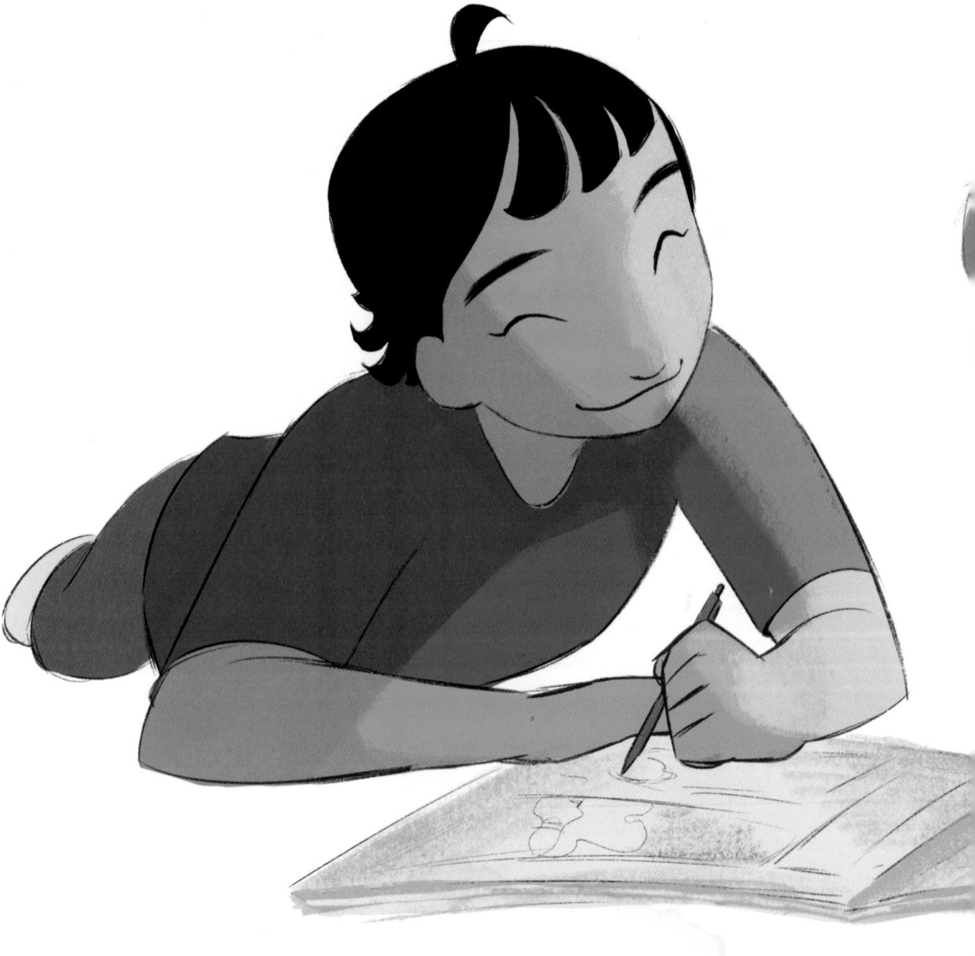

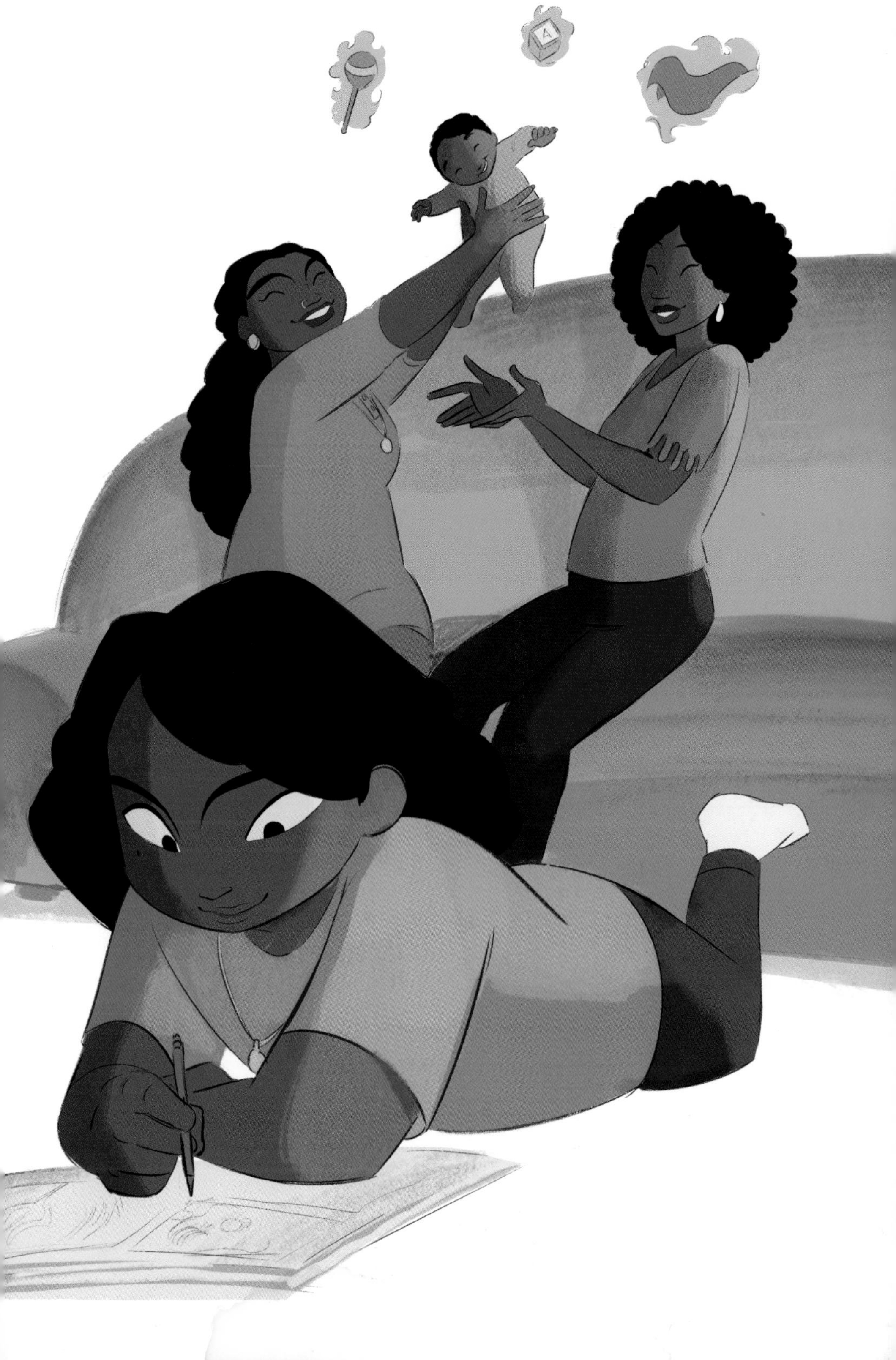

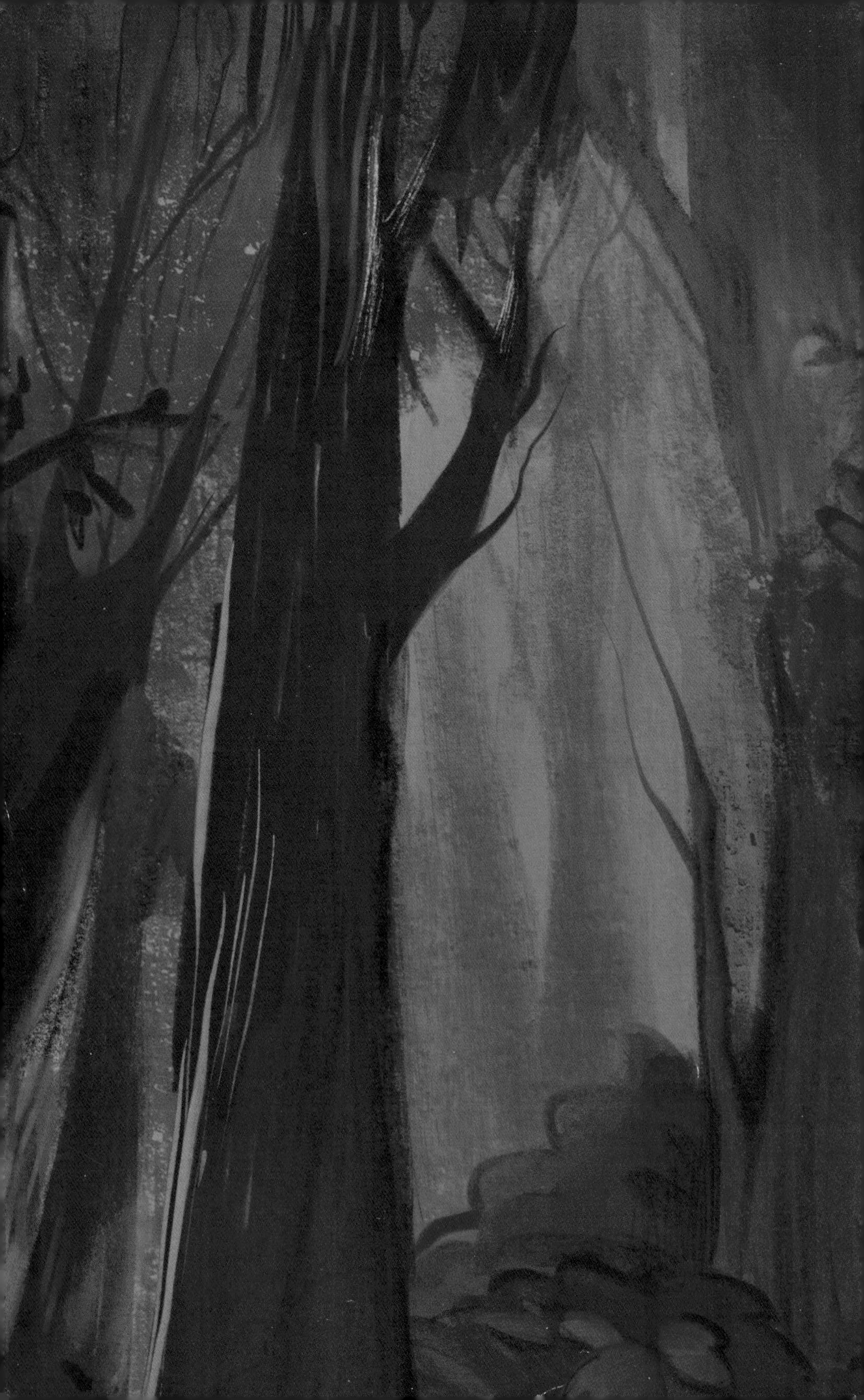

# LAND ACKNOWLEDGMENT

When I wrote this book, I resided on the traditional lands of many diverse First Nations, Inuit, and Métis peoples, in the Tkaronto territory that is governed by the Dish with One Spoon wampum belt covenant, including the Mississaugas of the New Credit First Nation, the Anishinaabe, the Haudenosaunee, and the Wendat peoples. They are the original caretakers and continue to care for the lands on which they have lived since time immemorial.

Please read and support Indigenous authors, such as Kateri Akiwenzie-Damm, Kenzie Allen, Cherie Dimaline, Louise Erdrich, Brandon Hobson, Randy Lundy, Tommy Orange, and Tommy Pico, among others. I also urge all of us to learn more about the histories and contemporary realities of the peoples of the lands in which we live and work. It is important to learn about the traditional Indigenous stewards of these lands. We need to ensure that land acknowledgments such as this one are not just empty gestures but are supported by meaningful actions toward justice and peace for Indigenous peoples, and toward forging healthy relationships between the land and the peoples who call it home.

Thank you to Kateri Akiwenzie-Damm and Randy Lundy for their advice and guidance in writing this land acknowledgment.

## ACKNOWLEDGMENTS

Thank you to my editor, Megan Ilnitzki, and the whole team at HarperAlley—Caitlin Lonning, Alexandra Rakaczki, Elaine Lopez-Levine, Maddy Price, Andrew Arnold, Vaishali Nayak, and Abby Dommert—for putting your magic behind this little book. Thank you also to Clarissa Wong for believing in this story. Thank you to Nabi H. Ali for bringing Shakti to life. Thank you to my agents, Erin Harris and John Cusick, for believing in me.

Thank you to my professors for everything you've taught me: Amelia Montes, Tim Schaffert, Joy Castro, Mark Winegardner, Elizabeth Stuckey-French, Skip Horack, and Barry Faulk.

Thank you to my writing group, SLCK, for all your feedback and unconditional support—Karen Tucker, Colleen Mayo, and Laurel Lathrop.

A special thank-you to Nika for the energy and spirit you gave to this story.

Thank you to my friends for the joy you bring to my life, especially Sam, for your consistent love.

Thank you to my family—Amma, Appa, Linda, Jeff, and Courtenay. Thank you also to my aunties, uncles, and cousins, especially Ishy, Athish, and Rishana, for keeping me grounded. Thank you to my brother, Varun, for bringing magic into my world.

Thank you to the blurbers who kindly took time out of their busy schedules to spend time with Shakti.

Thank you to Geoff, my partner in life and in writing, for everything.

—SJ Sindu